More critical praise for Daniel C

"In Carlos Lope[...] the throes of globalization [...] g Special Period. Fun and wit, Chavarría turns this basic story of survival into an erotic, fast-paced thriller. Times are hard, but who said they had to be dull?" —*Village Voice*

"This spritely translation marks the US debut of Chavarría, a classics-trained Uruguayan writer of novels, stories, literary journalism, and screenplays whose academic specialty—no surprise—is the origins and evolution of prostitution ... Set-ups, double-crosses, disguises, and shifts in gender clack and flutter like palm fronds, and readers who persevere through the most bawdy and stomach-churning passages of this mad, breezy romp will emerge battered and scorched and asking for more." —*Miami Herald*

"Continuing its excellence in publishing crime literature and following the success of the Edgar-nominated *Outcast* by José Latour, Akashic Books presents a delightful encore in their line of Cuban noir ... Chavarría, a professor of Latin, Greek, and Classical Literature makes a wonderful English-language debut with *Adios Muchachos*. If you have never visited Cuba and wish to do so—accompanied by a beautiful escort—this is your chance."
—Andrew McAleer, *Rex Stout Journal*

"Out of the mystery wrapped in an enigma that, over the last forty years, has been Cuba for the US, comes a voice so cheerful, a face so laughing, and a mind so deviously optimistic that we can only hope this is but the beginning of a flood of Cuba's indomitable novelists, playwrights, storytellers. Welcome, Daniel Chavarría."
—Donald Westlake, author of *Trust Me on This*

"Place *Adios Muchachos* alongside the work of John D. MacDonald, Carl Hiassen, and a good deal of Elmore Leonard, and it'll fit right in with those masters of incongruously sunny, quirky capers." —*PopMatters*

"... just about the perfect book to pack for a summer weekend at the beach." —*Ink19*

"Daniel Chavarría has long been recognized as one of Latin America's finest writers. Now he again proves why with *Adios Muchachos*, a comic mystery peopled by a delightfully mad band of miscreants, all of them led by a woman you will not soon forget—Alicia, the loveliest bicycle whore in all Havana."
—William Heffernan, author of *Beulah Hill*

DANIEL CHAVARRÍA was born in Uruguay in 1933. His novels, short stories, literary journalism, and screenplays have reached audiences across Latin America, Europe, and Asia. He has worked as a translator of literature into Spanish, and has taught Latin, Greek, and Classical Literature. Chavarría has won numerous literary awards around the world, including a 1992 Dashiell Hammett Award and a 2001 Edgar Award for *Adios Muchachos* (Akashic Books/Serpent's Tail), his comic suspense novel about a bicycle hooker in Havana.

THE **EYE** OF CYBELE

A NOVEL BY **DANIEL** CHAVARRÍA
TRANSLATION BY CARLOS LOPEZ

This is a work of fiction. All names, characters, places, and incidents are the product of the author's imagination. Any resemblance to real events or persons, living or dead, is entirely coincidental.

Published by Akashic Books & Serpent's Tail
Original English translation published in hardcover by Akashic Books
©2002, 2005 Daniel Chavarría
Translation ©2002, 2005 Carlos Lopez

Cover paintings by Jennifer Harris
Design by Melissa Farris

ISBN (USA & Canada): 1-888451-67-X
ISBN (UK & Commonwealth, Europe): 1-852428-85-6
Library of Congress Control Number: 2004106242
First paperback printing

Printed in Canada

Published in the United States by:
Akashic Books
PO Box 1456
New York, NY 10009
Akashic7@aol.com
www.akashicbooks.com

Published in the United Kingdom by:
Serpent's Tail
4 Blackstock Mews
London N4 2BT
www.serpentstail.com

AUTHOR'S NOTE

IN THE YEAR 430 B.C., a priest of Cybele was thrown into the Barathrum canyon for the crime of initiating the women of Athens in the mysteries of the Great Mother of the Gods. Aside from the rather stark reference I found in a classical handbook[1], this is a completely anonymous incident in the history of Athens. The desire to picture it in my mind is probably one of the motivations behind this novel. Some time later I found further encouragement in an inscription of the Roman period engraved by a slave on a slab in the mines of Laurium in the following terms:

> I, Xanthus the Lycian, slave of Gaius Orbius, have founded a temple to Mên Tyrannos, by order of the God himself. No one shall enter without being purified.[2]

Mên Tyrannos was a lunar deity of Phrygia. The pretentiousness of this slave suggested the first outlines of my main character. Thus, the priest of Cybele and Xanthus the Lycian found their way into the novel, although with different destinies.

The first people who read through the manuscript suggested I add notes to serve as a guide to the reader. There were those who felt that the frequent interweaving of historical characters and events with fictitious ones made it difficult to extricate the one from the other. And there were even some who accused me of manipulating the historical characters to make them suit my literary ends.

I, of course, refused to turn the novel into a didactically annotated primer. But those opinions did disquiet me somewhat, so I decided to add a glossary containing an alphabetical list of everything that is historical. Anything that does not appear in this list is the progeny of my own fiction. This is a guide for the reader.

The glossary explains all the mythological references and many of the terms of classical Greece that do not appear in your usual desktop dictionary. I've also included some terms, such as "democracy" and "apocalyptical," as they were used in the age of Pericles, sometimes quite differently from contemporary usage. But the reader will not have to struggle through footnotes and italics. Let each read and understand as he or she will, without constraints.

Since a number of outstanding historical personalities are also protagonists in the story, I have left out some of their biographical data to keep from giving away the suspense. On Pericles, Aspasia, Alcibiades, Socrates, and Nicias, I've given only the date of birth (not the date of death), profession, place of origin, and an invitation to discover their historicity in the pages of the novel. The punctilious reader will rush to his reference books; the benevolent will trust that these five and all my historical characters are faithful to Herodotus, Thucydides, Plato, Xenophon, and the post-classical historians.

Coming back to the glossary now, this is a gift to those very special readers of historical novels who use literature as a source of information. To the rest, may I remind you that a novel should explain itself from within, if it's worth its ink. And if it isn't, why explain anything?

January 2002

[1] *A Manual of Greek Antiquities*, Gardner & Jevons, London, 1898.

[2] *Associations Religieuses Chez les Grecs*, Foucart, Paris, 1873.

PART I

SUMMER
OF THE
ARCHON CRATES

1

A YOUNG SLAVE could be bought for two hundred drachmas. A well-trained Molossian hound cost five hundred.

Well-trained meant that he would always bite on the buttocks and deliver his captive alive and free of fractures.

The Assembly had issued an ordinance providing that anyone who kept a loose Molossian at a distance of less than one stadium from public places would be fined fifteen drachmas. On the streets of Athens, the guards had orders to confiscate all wandering Molossians, no matter who the negligent owner might be.

Molossians were lazy and rather boring dogs. They didn't even bark, although they yawned a lot when they woke up. They even yawned while they were walking around. And sudden confrontations with those impressive jaws spread wide and gaping down to the uvula had already caused too many fits and near-strokes in the City. Yes, fines had to be severe.

Even wolves shied away from Molossians, these beasts of a

single bite. If they chanced to miss their initial attack on the victim's jugular, they would latch onto the muzzle, the chest, or the stomach, and once their jaws locked, they would howl through the nose and tear at the flesh matter-of-factly until the piece came off.

In their rugged home country back in Molossia, they were known to lock onto large game and let themselves be dragged over cliffs or drowned in mountain rivers rather than let go of their victim. The shepherds knew where to find them, days later, floating in the lower course of the Arachthus, corpses with unflinching jaws.

They were bigger than wolves, and stronger. The hind molars, which they used only to kill, never to chew, could lock together so tightly that the dogs had to slide their jaws side-ways, like oxen chewing cud, to get them apart. And they could nip off a man's wrist with a single chomp.

Molossians could be seen wandering over their snow-covered mountains, alone or in pairs, but they were always loyal to the scattered pack. As soon as one of them bit onto a victim, the pack would hear the howling and move in, yawning all the way, to get a piece of the feast or the fight. That was why the local wolves, even when traveling in packs, gave lone Molossians a wide berth.

In Athens they were trained to catch runaway slaves. They learned to fast until they caught their victim and then to give up those juicy buttocks in exchange for pig's or goat's liver and heart, which the kennel master hurried to throw them as soon as their job was done. They then proceeded to devour their prize while the prisoner was being put in irons.

But never, since they had begun to serve the City, had the Molossians had to fast as long as during that month of Scirophorion, when the order went out to hunt down the beggar of the Goddess.

2

TRUNCHEON AND LYSIS liked to make love in the
afternoon, before the clients began to come in, but that
night Lysis got home at the crack of dawn and slipped into
Truncheon's room with her ointments and perfumes, and, ugh,
she should never have agreed to go with her flute to Timarcus's
house, and Truncheon undressing her, and Lysis with her hand
on her hips, oh, if Truncheon only knew what a rotten scrape
she had been through, but who could ever imagine that the
Acarnanian ambassador's mouth would smell so putrid, and
Truncheon listening and stroking her all the while, because
from a distance the Acarnanian looked attractive, but when you
got within range of his drunken emanations, gagh, and Lysis,
still on her feet, anointing her underarms with minted mastic
oil, letting Truncheon unfasten her bracelets and the brooch at
the back of her neck, and the Acarnanian had first offered two
hundred drachmas for the night, and Truncheon caressing her
waist and taking off the lavender-scented peplus, and then he

had gone up to two hundred and fifty, and Truncheon all over her neck, and then to three hundred, but Lysis had begun to play and dance to keep him away while she prayed for the arrival of dawn, and the younger Acarnanian would not keep still, and every time Lysis danced by the couch he would caress her buttocks, and she complained to Timarcus that if they went on kneading her she would take her flute and leave, and the ambassador offering three hundred drachmas, very drunk, and Truncheon, on her knees to take off one of her anklets, listening and nibbling at the most perfect hams in Athens, and Lysis would have taken him for a fortune if he had not smelled like a corpse, phew, her mouth tasted like a latrine just from imagining one of his kisses, and she kept saying yes, to be patient, that as soon as she finished they would be together, but she was going to disappear at first light, and the other slob just would not leave her ass alone and had pinched her, just let Truncheon look at the mark, and then Lysis had whacked him across the forehead with a silver chalice, and the uproar and the row, and Euclid, the fighter, perhaps Truncheon remembered him, had defended her until Otep got there with the dog, and she, feeling protected, had made them wash her feet, dress her, and put her sandals on, and she had left without being paid, ah, but Timarcus would have to pay double for getting her mixed up with vile-smelling heathens, as if she were common whorehouse fare, and Truncheon lowering the flame to the point where it made wrinkles invisible and accented Lysis's nacreous pinkish hues, and the Acarnanians fuming, and Timarcus screaming, Euclid protecting, and finally Otep and that monster dog to the rescue, oh, how Truncheon suffered when Lysis had engagements that took her out of the house, the horror of another crisis of her sickness with no one to help her, in that City, where banquets broke up in fights over women, but she

18

had to be coddled, she was as fickle as the Aegean in the autumn, and to keep her, Truncheon tolerated her whims, escapades, infidelities, and slights, but with each passing day, the web of love became stronger and the mesh of care and affection brought her closer, and surely Truncheon couldn't guess whom Lysis had run into on the Street of the Stonecutters, why Alcibiades, Clinias's son, who had cantered past her on his white stallion without so much as a glance, yes, another snub, and he had violets in his hair, a woman riding behind him and a train of admirers trailing along, and Lysis was suddenly seized by the notion to seduce him and offer his humiliation up to Aphrodite Pandemos, didn't Truncheon think the Goddess herself had inspired that thought? and that very instant Lysis took an oath, body and soul, to offer him as a victim, and Truncheon shuddered at the news but never dared say a word for fear of angering her or chilling her ardors that night that she had come of her own volition, and all the while listening and caressing, after months of living together, Truncheon had never feared any rival, but Alcibiades was a notorious favorite of Eros, wiser in the wiles of love than an old courtesan, and all the City knew that he had been tyrannizing lovers ever since he was a child, Lysis could never humiliate him before Aphrodite, Truncheon knew that all too well, there wasn't a woman in the City who could seduce him, and Lysis would wind up the victim, oh, rash, stubborn, unthinking child, how to make her understand that she was too green for that master rogue, and Truncheon would also come out the loser, for Alcibiades was eighteen and Truncheon was thirty-five, and Lysis naked in the bed, cupping her breasts, closing her eyes and begging to be caressed, Alcibiades, with his blond curls, was the most beautiful youth in the City, while Truncheon had to use wigs and perform miracles to keep the crow's feet from showing, and Lysis

19

on her stomach now, her bent arm framing her perfect profile, oh, rounded legs, oh, taut and graceful tendons, Alcibiades was of an illustrious Athenian family, a godson of Pericles, while Truncheon was not even Athenian, caressing that torso that might tomorrow belong to Alcibiades, and in three years, when he came into his inheritance from Clinias and Deinomache, Alcibiades would be much richer than Truncheon, and he was bold and graceful, a Panathenian champion, a favorite of Pallas, the son of a hero, a formidable enemy, and Lysis was determined to find out about his life and to have Otep follow him around, and as soon as she was certain that he had been invited to a feast, she would show up in full make-up, with her finest jewels, but Truncheon, senses overwhelmed by the smell of Lysis's lush blossoming sex, was no longer listening, oh, may the Gods make that sweet child respond again to those tender kisses, and thinking about Alcibiades, and Truncheon thinking about Aphrodite, Sweet-Rump of the Temple of Solon, the only one who could compare to the callipygian splendor of this beautiful doll, this morsel, this delight that now turned on her back, loving, legs apart, breasts erect, gasping for love, oh, yes, Truncheon would fight for her with every trick and artifice, would buy whatever service was required, whether filter or dagger, would risk everything to keep her, Alcibiades would never have her, and now Truncheon adjusted the short saffron wig and the Amorgos linen she wore to flatten her generous breasts when making love to Lysis of Miletus.

3

FROM ASPASIA IN ATHENS
TO EURYDICE IN SARDES

Twelfth day of Boedromion

PERHAPS THE GODS have accepted your offerings, because, unbelievably, Cleis has gotten better.

We have an old law here that says that when epilepsy strikes a house, it is the duty of those who live there to submit the sufferer to rites and purifications. I find the law repugnant, but it is illegal to ignore it in the home of Pericles. As soon as she had her first seizures, I found out from a venerable seer that the patient did not have to be present for the rituals. A cloth bearing the humors of a crisis would do for the purification, and that is what we did, with spittle from Cleis's mouth. Later, a physician of the Brotherhood of Halon ordered a diet that I just could not force on her: from the sea, she could take only mullets, urchins, and anchovies; from land, venison, suckling pig, and mutton; and of fowl, only doves, wild turkey, or cock. He forbade full baths, crossing one foot over the other, dressing in black, and touching goatskins. I just try to imagine what epileptics might do in Libya, where everything—beds, blankets, capes, and sandals—is made of goatskin.

The Halon Brothers also asked me to be mindful of her screams: If they sounded like a bleating goat, it would mean the illness came from the Mother of the Gods, but if they sounded like neighs, it came from Poseidon; and to check her stools, which, if they were big, might be the work of Enodia, or of Nomian Apollo if they came in pellets. If she foamed at the mouth while kicking, it was Ares who had descended on her. And for any of these things, she was to be purified with blood and objects that were later to be buried or thrown into the sea.

I would not believe a word of it. If the Gods are involved, we should make sacrifices, libations, take pure offerings to their temples and implore their favor, instead of running around hiding the cathartic instruments. What kind of piety is that? Can the human body be sullied by the touch of the Gods?

I, for one, decided to consult a young Asclepiad, who arrived from Larissa at the time and who said there was no such sacred disease. He said that epilepsy appeared when the brain became flooded with phlegmatic humors. He explained that humans, like beasts, have a double brain. When the struggle between the blood of the veins and the cerebral mucus is even, everything works out normally, but very strong heating or cooling can alter the balance and cause the "sacred" illness.

Unless the flow is very abundant and takes place in winter, however, it will not kill you. He said that the main cause was sun stroke, because heat softened the brain and drained the humors.

And according to whether the brain was too dry, too moist, too hot, or too cold, the body would suffer different diseases. Madness and delirium were caused by moisture, which can move anything. When the brain was dislocated, sight, hearing, and the other senses failed and the body moved of its own accord, contracting or stretching, like Cleis with her three fingers.

For treatment, he said she should avoid the sun on her head and have hellebore with her meals to dry up the humors. At the Temple of Asclepius, they told me that she would live without any great danger and that the disease would slowly give way as she became an old woman, somewhere approaching thirty.

Thanks to the Asclepiads, I was no longer terrified of the physical damage, but I feared greatly for her mind every time I heard her insist that the outstretched arm and three fingers were proof that the Three-Headed Goddess was claiming her body to carry her off into the underworld.

When I became enraged with impotence at so much senseless superstition, Pericles would say that I should then be enraged with most of the Greek population, for they too believe in such things. Cleis was no crazier than the Athenian government, which pays diviners and sends nuncios to Delphi to consult Apollo on miracles and prophecies before making any important State decisions. But I would hear none of it. As if the Immortals had no loftier concern for their leisure.

The thirteenth
Now, to your questions.

Yes, Hippodamus did return from Thurii, and when he found out that you were alive and well, he asked if you still had that saucy smile that made him tingle. I might ask the same, by the way.

No, Zosigenes's daughter did not take lessons from me. He made the proposition, but I turned it down. And he did not come to Pericles's house; he came to see me at the country house where I was staying with my nine girls.

Yes, all those you mention, except Gorgias of Leontini, did, at one time or another, attend my lectures. But you left out Herodotus of Halicarnassos, Damon, Ictinus, Philolaus of Croton, Pericles himself, Phidias, Euripides.

However, my public practice at the time came to be considered an insult to good manners and I had to quit. I also cut down the number of girls I took on as pupils.

When Pericles married me and installed me in his house in the City, I took only Cleis with me, and four others, which, by the way, gave enemy tongues much to wag about.

24 *The fifteenth*

I did not write to you yesterday because Pericles was preparing a speech he had to make to the Five Hundred and he needed me.

I was telling you about the school I used to have. Aside from dancing and music, which were taught by Timocles, the son of our Glaucus, I did everything else. I accepted only girls who were quite familiar with Homer and played well. I taught them lyrics and rhetoric; I taught them to think like Thales and Pythagoras, and to hate the gymnasium. I intended to teach the daughters of subjugated Ionia to subjugate the Athenians with their paideia.

Now Cleis, she was nine at the time, and I never really expected her to philosophize, but in her own way, I know she understood. And she was brilliant at music from the very start. When Damon returned from his ostracism, Pericles gave a party and Cleis accompanied an Anacreontic song for him. I almost burst with pride when I heard him say that my child had the divine gift and that, if he were not such an old man, he would take her on himself.

When you wrote me that she played well, I expected to hear the simpler monodies of the ancient Ionian chants, but she surprised us with rich embellishments and arpeggios. And her playing on the flute simply amazed us all. Callikrates said that she played with the indecent grace of the satyrs. Now I know it must have been easy for you to teach her; she simply embraces anything she loves in a single wave of inspiration, with little thought or practice.

The seventeenth

How can I tell her? I've been looking for the right words since yesterday. All morning I've been sitting here, the papyrus scraped clean, my quill poised, trying to find words that would not hurt, but since I cannot find them, let me just get rid of this thing that is beginning to burn me.

Cleis is no longer living with me.

One night she ran away again and they caught her close to the border with Megara. They brought her to me the following evening, just as I was about to go mad with uncertainty. She had disguised herself as a leprous pilgrim covering his sores with a long cloak and hood. But she was found out and taken for a runaway slave, which she said that she was and that she belonged to Aspasia of Miletus.

She told me that Aphrodite the Vulgar had visited her in a dream and given her very clear indications that she was to enter her service. She welcomed the vision in ecstasy, for she hoped that this might free her from her terror of Hecate, and she decided to begin immediately.

To keep from disgracing me and from compromising Pericles, if the City ever found out that his wife's niece had become a prostitute, she had tried to cross the border into Megara and from there into Corinth, where no one knew her, to offer herself in the Temple of Aphrodite. And she warned me that sooner or later she would fulfill the Goddess' order.

Now, what would you have done in that dilemma? I could only think of two ways out, the one more deplorable than the other: locking her up or letting her go. Ultimately, I came up with a third alternative, one that might keep us from going mad, she from confinement and me from remorse. After talking it over with Pericles, I convinced her that she should practice in Athens.

You must realize that her choice of a career does not bother me at all. But what Aspasia of Miletus believes is one thing, and what the wife of Pericles can do publicly is quite another. I suggested that she change her appearance so that she might remain in the City without being recognized.

She has matured so much recently that even old friends of ours pass by her in the Ceramicus without recognizing her under her courtesan's make-up and clothing. Now she is called Lysis. And with her sepia-tinted hair and her painted eyes and mouth, even I might pass her by. She cried with gratitude and praised Pericles's understanding. That's the way he is. If I'm in trouble, he pays no mind to the risks he runs for me. Could there ever be a greater love?

Once the decision was made, I sent her to Truncheon, an Ionian with a fate similar to ours, who has been established as an elegant courtesan in the City for years. She is also a high-ranking member of a society that practices the mysteries of Aphrodite the Vulgar. I know that her real name is Eulalia and that she comes from an excellent family in Ephesus. Her considerable beauty is complemented by the distinction of her breeding, which has won her lovers among politicians, generals, and artists. Hippodamus himself admires and respects her; and Sophocles, years ago, dedicated an ode to her. There's an old story in the City about a Cypriot who went mad with love for her and, in a desperate effort to win her favors, gave her a necklace that is famous in all of Athens. It was precisely because of that necklace that I had dealings with her some two years ago. Never have I been so attracted to a piece of jewelry. It is a braid of golden threads holding red chalcedony scarabs with gray jaspers of a matte luster and crowned by the biggest, most beautiful onyx Athens has ever seen, with Apollo and his lyre carved in it. On the other gems, the artist engraved the Nine Muses. Phidias, who used to frequent the banquets at Truncheon's when he lived in Athens, attributed it to Theodoros of Samos, so old was the engraving work. I offered her a fortune for it, and she refused. Others have offered her much more, but to no avail. It seems she's made some sort of sacred oath about not letting anyone else wear it, because she won't even lend it to Lysis, with whom she is passionately in love.

So for the last eight months our child has been living with this woman called Truncheon, who is instructing her in the arts of Aphrodite.

The nineteenth

Cleis is making fortunes with her flute. When it pleases her, she sleeps with men. And by the Two Goddesses, she fleeces them. Truncheon is connected with the City's best people. Her home is frequented exclusively by the eupatridae, or by those with enough money to get by without ancestors. Her banquet table is always laid out and ready for her guests to eat their fill and pay for it. Truncheon almost never practices now, but she's always there to animate her feasts with her brilliance. Her wine is fit for the Gods, though the prices she charges are ungodly. She is wise in her logos and graced by the Muses, but she can also cut loose like any clod in the agora. This delights them as well. Cleis is better off with her, among rich and illustrious men, than she would be in Corinth, and she's free of Hecate.

I've only seen her twice this summer. The last time was at the Synoecia, celebrated here to honor Theseus. She arrived at dusk with the Libyan slave and the huge Laconian hound that accompany her on her evening escapades. She was dressed in catonace, her bare feet filthy, and she came in the back door with a basket of grapes on her head. She's very careful not to give those who accuse me of being a bawd the slightest pretext.

I was amazed by the off-handed way she told me about the darker sides of her profession, without ever stopping to think that I might object. She thrills in the perverse pleasure of fleecing her admirers, and it's a holy pleasure, for the gold she moves does honor to Pandemos. Truncheon has taught her that if she has mercy on her victims when she's in the flower of youth, life will be merciless to her in the autumn of her decline. And Cleis has learned well, for she is sacking her own teacher. Truncheon pays for her most extravagant whims.

The twentieth

I feel better today. It's done me a lot of good to write to you. If what Melanthius, the goat-herder, says is true, that the Gods push similar to similar, you, too, should be glad about the metamorphosis Cleis has experienced.

In her most recent crises, she has not heard the three underground knocks. She says that Aphrodite makes them inaudible so she won't be terrified of death. In any case, her head is no longer full of terrors and forebodings. On that visit, she stayed with me until very late. She told me about her days and nights: her feasting, escapades, passions, rages, jealousies, mischiefs. The name Lysis appears day after day on the Ceramicus wall where the City's wealthy write their gallantries and offers to the most popular hetaerae, and she can have her pick. She's moderate in her spending, even a bit stingy.

So there you have it. Our young Ionian aristocrat is today a very fashionable prostitute. This is what she learned from her aunt. Is this the destiny the Gods had set aside for her?

Are you angry with me?

Ah, you should have seen her! She was triumphant! She painted and fixed herself up in different ways so I could see what she looked like at the banquets. I also taught her some elegant hairdos. All of the beauty that was hidden behind her childish features has burst into bloom. She's the image of my brother, but with your straight nose and earthy lips. From Alcinoë she got her shoulders and her straight black hair. But the most glorious of all are her terse, rounded buttocks, which, as she told me, quiver of their own, like yours, when they are seized with pleasure. From me she got her light eyes and the art of cold-blooded seduction. I hoped she would practice it on some rich and noble Athenian. She has charms enough and all the opportunities she could ask for. She might even have aspired to a legal marriage in the City, but for now, I've got to be content with her being a courtesan.

That night, she asked for her old transverse flute and played it for me. In her contacts with flutists from Asia, she's learned the Phrygian mode marvelously. Anyone might say that she was raised among Corybantes in a forest of Celaenae.

The twenty-second

Yesterday, when I was writing to you about her flute, she showed up again in her disguise. She read your scrolls avidly, and we talked about you. I told her of your misgivings about letting her go and she asked me to remind you how much she had insisted, ever since she was eight, upon coming to live with me. She said she would have preferred running away or dying rather than living with Orontas, that the hard feelings she once had were just jealousy and anger at the way you submitted to him, that her present ministry to Aphrodite had taught her how sinuous and unexpected the paths of love can be, and that she exonerates and forgives you. But she won't write, as you asked. She's tried, but she cannot.

Later she gave me a bit of news that has unsettled me: She's determined to ensnare a young eupatrid and humiliate him before Aphrodite. The victim is to be Alcibiades, the son of Clinias.

Have I ever mentioned the two orphans? Perhaps not, because the very thought of Alcibiades makes me angry.

He is two years older than Cleis and is supposed to begin his epheby soon. Athens has proclaimed him her most beautiful youth. His father was descended from Ajax, and he's related to Pericles by his mother's Alcmeonid line. In three years, when he comes into his father's estate, he's going to be one of Athens' richest young men. Furthermore, he's ambitious, intelligent as none other his age I've known, ingenious, learned, and valiant; but I swear to you by Panionian Poseidon that, as a lover for our Cleis, I prefer Truncheon.

When his father died, Alcibiades and his brother, Clinias, came to live with us. As the orphans' next of kin, Pericles and Ariphron became their guardians and trustees. Alcibiades was six then and Clinias four, the same age as Xanthippus and Paralus, Pericles's sons, who also lived with us.

Pericles says that Alcibiades has a temperament as strong as that of Themistocles. Just as I made plans for Cleis, he made them for his cousin's son. He tried to guide him, to address his gifts toward lofty goals, but, by Hecate, the child turned out to be a hydra.

When Cleis began to socialize with our friends, I no longer had anything to do with him. His relations with Pericles and myself were extremely hostile; he would spend the day out and come in without a word, bar himself in his room, and have his tutor take him his meals.

As Cleis tells it, she saw him only once, when she was playing the flute in the women's court. He had approached to listen, and she stopped playing. Alcibiades's beauty left her breathless. He took her by the chin, turned her head, and said that if she kept on blowing up her cheeks like Marsyas to play the vile instrument of the satyrs, she would soon be covered with wrinkles; that her lips would become hardened with the rubbing and lose efficiency in kissing, their primary function; that slave music dulled the senses and was not to the liking of Pallas Athena. She should take up the lyre.

Never again did she see him in the house, but she knew of his presence there.

Cleis had had a little dog buried behind the house and had placed an engraved stone there which one can still read: "Wayfarer, here lies Mirrhyne, daughter of Mone, Athenian. She was a loving and silent friend and accomplice. Dedicate a kind thought to her as you go by."

Days later, the stone appeared upside down. Alcibiades had written on it in charcoal: "Here lies Aspasia, daughter of Axiochus, Miletian. Fear not, wayfarer, she no longer bites." Cleis confessed that the incident had made her admire and wish to see him again. But Alcibiades left our house shortly after. He was already sneaking out nights, and we could find no tutor to rein him in. At about the time of his meeting with Cleis, he had spent a week leading street brawls in Piraeus, where his

31

band had profaned a sacred effigy. Pericles had to face charges of negligent guardianship in the Assembly. He came in raging one afternoon, bringing with him a Thracian slave he employed as a foreman in one of his quarries. The slave was to guard Alcibiades; he was to sleep in the boy's room and watch him day and night. The Thracian was a big, strong man, used to breaking wayward slaves, and Pericles authorized him to beat Alcibiades if he disobeyed. The young man, with his effeminate calm, said that the slave, if he dared lay a hand on him, could consider himself a dead man. Pericles, who had foreseen this reaction, signaled the slave, who immediately gave Alcibiades a sample beating.

Alcibiades spent the next few days walking around tamely with his head down. We were thankful he had finally met his master. But one morning, when he was anointing himself for a wrestling match, he saw the Thracian dozing against a tree. He silently picked up the oak pestle used to tamp down the wrestling court and sneaked up on him from behind. They say the first blow split his temple open. The Thracian died without knowing what hit him. When they brought him to me, he had no face. Xanthippus saw Alcibiades run a javelin through the back of his neck, just to make sure.

He never returned to the house after that. All Athens condemned the crime as something unworthy of a man capable of speech. But the young aristocrat, firstborn of a hero, suffered no punishment.

Pederasts were already courting him, and when he left the house, he gave himself to one democrates and then to others, whom he charged dearly for their passions.

In the evenings, he's either partying or getting involved in street fights. And since he has not yet come into his estate, he uses the wiles of whores on men. He milked his present lover for three thousand drachmas to buy the chariots and teams of Thessalian horses he used to win the great Panathenian Games, and he makes him spend fortunes on luxuries for himself and his friends. As the recognized dictator of youthful fashion, he has dared to wear cloaks in colors no Athenian would be seen in. He shows up in the agora dressed in pink or purple, with ribbons braided into his hair. As a sign of extreme elegance—which every fop and pansy immediately imitated—he has taken to dragging the corner of his cloak, and the City is much amazed that he can walk without stepping on it.

Everywhere he goes, he is followed by a Phoenician slave, whom he calls Phanes because of his repulsively bald, egg-shaped head. Alcibiades says he bought him to walk down the streets clearing the way and jokes that the man is so ugly that pedestrians immediately step aside when they see him. But he was probably more interested in the slave's skills as a knife fighter, which had gained him fame as a bouncer in a gambling den in Piraeus. Phanes is the perfect accomplice for his iniquities and serves him with the loyalty of a guard dog. A short time ago, he was suspected of being involved in a robbery and two murders, but Alcibiades used some of his influence and nothing further was said of the matter.

He recently gave us six of the forty Panathenian amphorae that were his prize for winning the chariot race. Then he showed up at the house humbly and was even pleasant to me. He made his peace with Pericles and begged him to talk to Hipponicus, father of Hipparete, whom he intends to marry. My husband was pleased with both his initiative and his taste, and has asked Hipponicus for the girl in marriage.

So this is the victim Cleis has chosen. She's determined to seduce him, erase Hipparete from his mind, humiliate him before the whole City, and consecrate him as an offering to

Aphrodite the Vulgar. It was useless to try to talk her out of it. She's much too sure of the bloom of her thighs and the magic of her flute.

I've taken the trouble to write you all this about Alcibiades so you'll know the abyss for which our child is headed. Tomorrow at dawn, I'm going to pray to the Twelve Gods for her.

Remember to use no other courier than Philarcus, who has been carrying scrolls for Pericles for twenty years. I'm not so much troubled by your husband's spies now as I am by my husband's enemies. They would give a great deal to know our secrets. Be happy.

DELIVERED INTO FRIENDLY HANDS ON THE
TWENTY-FOURTH OF BOEDROMION DURING
THE ARCHONSHIP OF CRATES

4

LYSIS FOUND OUT that Anytus was giving a banquet to celebrate Alcibiades's equestrian victory in the Great Panathenian Games. She supposed he would also be inviting his nephew Euclid, the wrestler.

That morning, Otep, Lysis's Libyan slave, found Euclid wrestling in a local ring and gave him a note from his mistress. Lysis was offering to play her flute wherever Euclid chose, out of gratitude for the beating he gave the Arcarnanians.

Euclid took the bait, but not all the way. He would invite her to the feast in the home of his uncle Anytus, who would pay her handsomely for her music and dancing, but he would consider himself repaid only if after the symposium was over she would receive him in her bed.

Lysis had her Libyan slave return with an amendment to Euclid's counteroffer: She would lie with him for two clepsydrae, but not all night.

The Libyan came back bearing Euclid's consent, with the

proviso that the clepsydrae were to be large ones.

She calculated that at that time of the year two large clep-sydrae would amount to about a quarter of the night, so she agreed. Otep was to run to tell him and, on the way, stop off at the wall and have her proposal-reader send her the latest.

The Libyan went to the agora first. It was the busiest time of the day in the market, but he found Euclid where he had left him, waiting for confirmation of the deal, and finally got back to Truncheon's house around midday. Euclid had agreed, and the wall-reader sent a note where he had copied a message left by a rich lamp-maker who, in a tangle of boorish gallantries, was offering Lysis of Miletus fifty drachmas.

She was really not in the mood for a lamp-maker, not even for four times that figure. She would not go to the wall. She wanted to feel quite rested for the next day. That night she did not accept any invitations and never even stepped out to chat with Truncheon's guests.

It was long past midday when Lysis arrived at Anytus's house escorted by Otep and the dog Laelaps, which was wearing a red collar the same hue as her sash. Under her white linen peplus, one could just make out her curves, without quite seeing the texture of her flesh.

She was wearing Persian buskins perched upon thick, purple-tinted cork soles. But Otep carried a pair of sandals for her in his knapsack. After dancing barefoot, it was pure torture for her to force her feet back into those impressive boots, which were only meant to support her grand entry at feasts, anyway. Her sepia hair, held with a purple band in a high, up-swept tourniquet over her head, cascaded like a mist over her brow and shoulders. She had done her lips in a pale shade of rose with alkanet root. And for jewelry, she wore a choker with a star-shaped pendant made of minute pearls, a ring with an emerald scarab, and on her ankle, the chain Truncheon had given her, with the clasp made in the likeness of a pair of mating doves.

The door servant went in to get Euclid, who came all the way to the entrance to receive her. He looked happy and relieved, as if he had not been altogether convinced that she would keep her promise.

Lysis had intentionally arrived late. She wanted to make sure that she entered the andron when all the guests were assembled, especially Alcibiades, but when she was approaching the house, she began to wonder why she could not hear the chatter or the music that usually accompanied the first tables at banquets.

Euclid told her right at the door that the guests were in the courtyard. Alcibiades, the guest of honor, had not shown up yet.

Anytus was a widower. He was living with his mother, and at times with a niece who resided in his country house at Myrrhinus.

When she entered, Lysis saw several men strolling around the peristyle. None looked her way. She could not remember ever having entered any place so unnoticed. Could it be that she had fallen in with uncouth, spiritless people? The atmosphere was certainly not festive. The first one she recognized was Hermippus, an ass with whom Truncheon had had words during the last Lenaea. Mnesilochus was there, too, a rotten writer of comedies who had hated her ever since she turned down a proposal he posted on the Ceramicus wall. Off in a corner she saw a young eunuch, a good flutist. With him were a buffoon and a lyrist.

Anytus was strolling arm in arm with a youth. Euclid remarked, ever so drolly, that when the doorkeeper had announced a flutist accompanied by a fearsome dog, many thought it was finally Alcibiades, whose latest amusement was scaring the whole City with a Locrian mastiff and going around with a Megarian flutist on his arm. When the others saw Lysis come in so elegantly attired (probably the reason no one recognized her), they must have supposed that she was the one with Alcibiades and therefore ignored her entrance in deference to Anytus. Lysis, of course, knew that Anytus was Alcibiades's lover; didn't she?

So, Alcibiades was going around with a flutist?

Euclid had heard it from Hermippus, who, claiming to be very worried about Alcibiades's behavior and Anytus's humiliation, had circulated the news among the guests. Euclid, too, was asking himself if Alcibiades would dare show up with the Megarian in Anytus's very home.

Lysis looked at Anytus out of the corner of her eye. He was a bald, somewhat lymphatic man, but good looking. He went on talking to Lysis quietly and kept turning constantly to look toward the entrance.

Suddenly, a loud knocking was heard coming from the door. Laelaps started to bark, and Otep, who had been squatting by the door slave, chatting, had to yank on the dog's leash several times to get him to shut up.

Alcibiades came in with his arm around a beautiful young lady with very disheveled hair, looking like someone just in from a binge. He had Aristarchus with him, just a bit under his wine, the same Aristarchus who had beaten Euclid in the Panathenian wrestling. Alcibiades, crowned with flowers, his arms encircled with wreaths, stormed in protesting. How could they receive him without an o-va-vation? So, Anytus had not come out in person; the only welcome he got was the b-b-barking of a Laconian monster? Whose was the beast, anyway?

Someone pointed to Lysis, and he looked at her carefully but coldly, without any sign of admiration.

Euclid said that there was a rumor circulating in the City that Alcibiades, who days earlier had been terrorizing Megara with his drinking buddies, had kidnaped her from a whorehouse. But Lysis could tell at a glance that it was just the idle chatter of some ignorant barber. The girl might be Megarian, but she did not look like a common whore, and she was certainly not a slave.

Alcibiades kept up his parody. Oh, how frightened he was of the dog! He had to have something to drink. When was the feast going to begin?

Anytus suggested that they pass into the andron. When he assigned the couches, he sent Aristarchus to one end with Hermippus and kept Alcibiades next to him. But Alcibiades went over with Aristarchus and sent Hermippus over to Anytus.

Lysis noticed that their host was smiling, as he would at some prank Alcibiades played. Oh, that child, what could you do with him, and pretending not to be hurting from the slight. Well, well, well, let each sit where he pleased.

Three slaves came in with basins and towels and began to wash the guests' feet.

Lysis made herself comfortable on a huge chair outside the oval formed by the couches. She refused to stand by Euclid, like the Megarian was doing with Alcibiades, who suffered her to kiss his neck and caress his myrtle-crowned head.

Ever since Lysis had begun to go to banquets in Athens, she had noticed that participating adolescents who had not done their epheby would sit quietly and respectfully outside the oval. But Alcibiades, his elbow propped up on the cushions, acted as if he had spent half his life in banquets. He immediately chose one of the best places. Aristarchus took the other end, which meant that he had to turn his back on the center of activities whenever he reached for some food.

When the slaves had washed all the guests, Anytus ordered the first tables brought in. Three handsome young slaves and the boy cupbearer brought out the plates and bowls of food and placed them on the tables flanking the couches. Anytus surprised the guests with his new silver service. No one in Athens, except Callias, used anything but earthenware.

Amid applause and ovations, the guests waited for the host to take the first morsel. Anytus, sitting up straight on his couch, said that everything his distinguished guests saw around them no longer belonged to him but to the honored champion, that no one was more entitled than he to order the beginning of the banquet, that although the ingrate had refused to share his couch and had chosen to lie with a fellow Panathenian champion, Anytus forgave him and reiterated that he was the master of the feast, the food, the drink, the service, the slaves, and other things not so readily visible, and Alcibiades, sitting up on his couch, calling for a slave girl to put his sandals on, began to strut around the center of the oval, and, yes, yes, he knew he was master of everything there, as he was of the winning horses Anytus had given him, and as master of the banquet, the first thing he ordered was that no one was to touch the food, because he had just received an inspiration from a God, and clap, clap, let's see, let's see, have the slaves clear the table and put the food back on the trays, get along, quickly, this is the master of the banquet who is ordering you, and master of the slaves, too, hadn't the excellent guests heard Anytus say that? so let's move, let's see those slaves hurry up there, and the guests, by Zeus, stared at one another in alarm, would that madman take the food practically out of their mouths? and they looked at Anytus, imploring, what could their host be waiting for before setting things straight? but Anytus just shrugged behind a non-committal smile, and the slaves, somewhat fearful by now, dumped the food back onto the trays, but would he really leave them all hungry? and Alcibiades, yes, yes, that's it, this dish over here, that tray over there, yes, put Aristarchus's sandals on, and would Sisymbrion, the Megarian flutist, pick up the silver service and put it into a large basket, but Sisymbrion refused in fear, she would not do that, and Alcibiades, reminding her that the service was his, too, wasn't that so, Anytus, dear? did Sisymbrion understand? hadn't the magnificent Anytus said that everything in sight belonged to Alcibiades? and amid the silence the only sounds heard were his voice and the little noises the slaves made in their work, while twenty pairs of eyes darted from one to another inquisitively and not even the buffoon could think of anything humorous, one simply does not play with food, Hermippus mumbled, but Anytus silenced him with a single glance, and there went the Copaic eels garnished with chard, and the veal, the oysters, and the spiced brains that no one was able to taste, and the eunuch and the lyrist, staring out from a corner, looked no happier that the guests, good-bye the delicious buns of pure white flour and the hare stewed in fragrant syrup, and Alcibiades was the only one tasting, hmm, a colabus, licking his fingers, hmmm, by Hermes, God of the marketplace! his other guests were going to be ecstatic, and Anytus was to congratulate the cook for those exquisite colabi, not only for the qu-qu-quail and onion stuffing, but for shaping them in the perfect likeness of lyre keys, hmmm, tasting another, delicious, like the music of Apollo, and so then, was everything gathered up? were Sisymbrion and Aristarchus ready? good health, then, and might the guests duly enjoy the second tables, and as for himself, to prove the truth of Anytus's words when he declared him master of the banquet, and, of

41

course, master of himself and of his inspirations, he was going to dine with others, but no one was to worry, because he was going to leave them, for their enjoyment, the buf-fa-foon, and clap, clap, let's go, pick up the trays, quickly, quickly, those slaves, see to it you don't trip and, yes, you in the corner, the lyrist and the eunuch, follow along with Alcibiades, and Sisymbrion was so frightened carrying the basket of silver, and Aristarchus looked embarrassed for his complicity in this irreverence, and Anytus, whose smile had already frozen into a travesty of a satirical mask, seeing that Alcibiades was leaving, that it was no joke, that he was leaving the court holding Sisymbrion around the waist and muttering things in her ear, and she, bursting out laughing and bending over into the basket and leaning on a column signaling Alcibiades to stop, because if he kept on with his joking, she was going to pee, and Lysis, excited at the daring of a youth just slightly older than she and capable of such a show of strength before men twice his age, could she really seduce him? could she humiliate him before Aphrodite Pandemos? he hadn't taken note of her this time either, how insufferable and how beautiful, in all Athens there was no other victim more sumptuous for Aphrodite the Vulgar, she'd give anything to follow him and see the outcome of this cruel prank, why not? no, that would be suicide, she could never break him that way, better to wait for another occasion, this was obviously not going to be an easy morsel to chew, Lysis would have to use all her arts, be patient, wait for the victim to step into the trap of his own accord, and now Hermippus and Mnesilochus were complaining out loud, this was an outrage, how could Anytus tolerate this? and Anytus could only ratify that Alcibiades was, in fact, master of everything he took and of Anytus himself, of his will and his senses, which were worthless save to spoil him more and more, and Alcibiades had been generous enough in leaving them something for the second tables, a huge tear in his eye, by Zeus! he loved him so, so much, he would give him everything, yes, Anytus would suffer for months just to give Alcibiades a moment's pleasure, but, pausing to hold back a sob and dry a tear with the corner of his himation, as soon as he got over his infatuation with the Megarian, he would return, like he had before, and then there were different voices and Laelaps's barking, and Anytus looking at the door again, his face lit up in a genuine smile at seeing Alcibiades come back into the house followed by the others and going directly over to Lysis, would it please her to come with them to the banquet Alcibiades was gi-giving himself in better company? and Euclid jumping off the couch in his bare feet, by Zeus! that was just about enough, Alcibiades might be master of the banquet but Lysis had come with him, she was his guest and he wanted her for himself, it had all been agreed since the day before, and Alcibiades, staring at her in exaggerated disbelief and pointing to Euclid, could she really have come with such an ugly thing? wouldn't she prefer the company of young people far more beautiful and better than Euclid, a losing wrestler? Alcibiades could assure her that she would have a much better time spending the evening with his gay and witty comrades, who were this very evening giving him the first of the farewell feasts programmed for the beginning of his epheby, and what was Marsyas's beautiful follower's name? Lysis? so! from Miletus? Alcibiades didn't know how he could live in the City and not know of the existence of such a beautiful Ionian, and in any case, what did Lysis pref-f-fer? and she, who had already come to a decision while he was stammering, took hold of his arm and said that she would pref-f-fer going with him, and Alcibiades, delighted at the little Miletian's mocking his stammer, took her by the waist, how beautifully she imitated him,

muttering behind closed eyes, and he could already see her in
his bed, imagine her, but Euclid was furious, protesting, vocif-
erating that, no, never, he would never tolerate such abuse, he
had not come here to be the butt of Alcibiades's pranks or to let
him take his flutist, whom he had brought himself, and he was
certainly not like Anytus to be humiliated by Alcibiades, and
Aristarchus's fist crashing in from above and smashing the tip
of his nose into his upper lip, and Alcibiades stepping back, oh,
how frightening, and taking advantage of his effeminate parody
of fear, embracing Lysis around the buttocks and begging her to
protect him and sinking his wreathed head into her breasts, by
Heracles, he was so afraid, and smelling her, and Lysis holding
on to him, following his lead, caressing the nape of his neck,
and the second blow laid Euclid out, and Alcibiades, oh, such
brutes, and Anytus crying in silence and Mnesilochus leading
the choir of protesters, and the others, yes, it was an outrage, an
insult, but Alcibiades reminded them of what Anytus had said,
he was doing nothing but taking what was his, and Hermippus,
beside himself, that Lysis did not belong to Alcibiades, but to
the other one, and Lysis interrupting him with her shrill voice,
screaming that, yes, Hermippus was right, she did not belong to
Alcibiades nor would she, but neither did she belong to Euclid,
nor even to herself, for she belonged body and soul to
Aphrodite, so the argument had nothing to do with her, she was
as free as a bird to choose her direction and, paraphrasing one
of Euripides's verses, her direction "would never be that of the
vanquished," and Mnesilochus protesting over the insolence of
the foreigner treating them all like a pack of palaestra bums,
come, come, who else had been vanquished? and Lysis, parry-
ing, you, you scribbler, you poetaster, who hasn't ever put
enough spirit into his comedies to deserve a prize at the
Lenaea, and Alcibiades clutching at his ribs and breathing

deeply to go on laughing, Lysis was so right and so sharp, and Sisymbrion trying to win back some ground, fighting for a piece of Alcibiades's arm, but he had eyes only for Lysis now, and shoving the Megarian away roughly, very well, let Lysis go on picking out the palaestra bums at the feast, this could get interesting, and Lysis mocking, crying out how Anytus had been dethroned by Sisymbrion, who that very night would be defeated by—but Alcibiades covered her mouth with a kiss and dragged her away with him, and Euclid, face bloody, himation stained, whore, ingrate, welsher, and charging at Aristarchus again, and Hermippus and Mnesilochus holding him back and he shaking them off, jumping, knocking over an amphora of Lesbian wine with one terrible kick, and let me go, by Heracles! the treacherous bitch, and others moving in to hold Euclid, and tearing off a piece of his himation, and Alcibiades mad with joy, this was his kind of p-p-party, and Aristarchus trying to pry himself free of Sisymbrion the Megarian, who was demanding the money promised by Alcibiades, she was tired of promise after promise without seeing a single obol in the three days she had been following him around from party to party, dancing for him, sleeping with him, watching over his drunken stupors, and crying out and scratching her face, liar, cheat, cad, and Alcibiades in the court, holding Lysis and turning to ask why the Megarian could not just d-d-die, phew, and stop annoying him with her demands for money, she could consider herself paid with the s-s-silver service, yes, yes, she could keep it, and Sisymbrion, looking around quite frightened now, saw Anytus sobbing on a couch, his shoulders heaving, his head buried in a cloak.

45

5

UNMIXED WINE. That was the only thing that would help. Maybe Alipius the Marathonian would give her a little wineskin on credit.

No credit. In fact, he threatened to have her beaten if she ever got drunk and pissed in his tavern again. But the tavern-keeper's wife called her around to the pantry and gave her a packet of gray hair and two rags with some of her brother-in-law's sweat. She wanted Hypothesis to prepare a philtre to make him impotent. The pig had fallen in love with one of the pornai at the Lantern whorehouse, and now he was neglecting his shop and starving his wife and children. Hypothesis of Athens got six cotyles of Attic wine in advance, with the condition that she go piss them someplace else.

Before the tavern woman could finish filling up her skin, a terrible noise came in from the kitchen. The Marathonian, enraged with a little Armenian slave who had spilled a jug of wine, was pounding and kicking him in a corner. As the beating and screaming increased, relatives and customers poured into the kitchen to see what was going on. Crazed from the beating, the Armenian grabbed a stake and gave Alipius a two-handed swat across the ear. While the tavern-keeper stumbled around trying to regain his senses, one of his sons charged the slave to try to get the stake away from him. Just then the Marathonian, senses recovered and doubly enraged, took hold of the first thing he could lay his hands on, a pan in which they had been frying some fish, and threw it at the Armenian's naked chest, with everything in it.

The son got some of it on his shoulder and immediately let go of the slave, who streaked out of the tavern, a screaming comet with a tail of smoke.

On the street he bit one of the tavern-keeper's neighbors and lashed out at everyone who tried to stop him. As his torture and fear increased, he became dangerous. He slammed his head into a stone wall several times and then, dripping blood, threw himself into a puddle by the Fountain of the Nereids, at the feet of a metragyrtes who nodded by a pedestal begging alms in the name of the Great Mother Cybele. Filthy red hair fell across the pot that the beggar held between his knees.

Awakened by the noise, the metragyrtes saw the Armenian fall on his knees and start beating his head against the marble relief of the fountain. The onlookers, impressed with his screaming and fierce determination to die, didn't even try to interfere. The tavern-keeper and his sons arrived with ropes and cautiously tried to surround him, while the others who had joined the hunt counseled, "Don't get too close! Hit him with a club first!"

Hypothesis got there with the tavern woman, just behind the Marathonian, who was desperately trying to make sure the slave did not take refuge in the neighboring Temple of Stormy

Zeus. He knew that his inhuman treatment of the slave was offensive to the Gods and that the priest could admit the slave to the altar, declare him inviolable, and even intercede for the City to force the owner to sell him to the highest bidder. If that happened, he probably would not get much more than fifty drachmas for the Armenian. Even if he had paid two hundred for him three months earlier, no one would be much interested in a slave with a record of attacking his master and attempting suicide.

Then Hypothesis witnessed a miracle that would be the talk of Piraeus for quite some time.

The metragyrtes with the long red mane and the motley attire rose to his feet, tinkling the bells that hung from his tunic. He, too, began to scream in his own language and jumped onto the Armenian, who was still beating his head and sprinkling blood. The metragyrtes flipped the Armenian on his back and planted a knee on his chest, ignoring the blood. The burned slave screeched his homicidal panic, spat out his tears, twisted his hips, and kicked his feet in the puddle.

When the metragyrtes finally had the Armenian's arms pinned to the ground, he brought his face closer and closer to the slave's until their noses practically touched. The tavernkeeper and his son were only too pleased with the help and stayed out of it.

The foreigner's words could be heard a stadium away from the Fountain of the Nereids. Their force overpowered the Armenian's screams, the street vendors' cries, and even the clang of the anvils lined up along the wharves. Then, in horrible, guttural, just-arrived, hardly understandable, impudent Greek, he ordered, "No pain! You no pain! You nothing pain!"

While he shouted, he looked hard into the Armenian's eyes. The slave quit twisting; his howling began to die down and he stared at the beggar with curiosity.

Seeing this, the tavern-keeper and his sons moved in to hobble the slave, but the metragyrtes halted them cold with a terrible look.

When the Armenian had completely stopped screeching and kicking, the beggar released his hands and squatted down next to him.

"You happy, you good, you many much good now; you laugh, ha, ha, you laugh big and fat," he repeated, as the curious onlookers silently circled them in.

The slave, who had been desperately trying to crack his head open a few seconds before, forgot about his burns, paid no attention to his pursuers, his pain, his fury, and began, before the astonished witnesses, to nod silently, then to smile, and finally to mumble that no pain now, that, yes, he was happy, much fatly happy, as he broke out into earnest laughter.

In the meanwhile, Hypothesis, who was enthralled with the events and dying to see the outcome, suddenly began to notice that she, too, was feeling better.

The metragyrtes aimed his gaze at the tavern-keeper and his sons, and again the savage thundering voice: "No touch slave! Happy! You as well much fatly happy, much good, eh?" And pointing to the others in the group: "And you happiness, and you, ha, ha, and you, too."

When he laughed imperatively in the face of a local clod, the man let loose a strident guffaw and with him everyone else, and the metragyrtes became the master of laughter.

The newcomers who kept swelling the crowd of onlookers saw him raise his arms with great dramatics, and actually lead the choir of laughter, much like an exarchon leading a dithyramb. With the one hand, he brought the choir to a hush; with the other, he pointed to a soloist, whom he prodded into a crescendo of guffaws until the man began to turn purple, his veins bursting, his eyes wide with madness. Hypothesis pissed. The tavern woman had tears streaming down her face, like she did when she went to the comedies at the Lenaea.

Suddenly, the beggar ordered a halt. In the startled silence, he snatched the rope from the tavern-keeper and brought his huge lavender eyes to within a palm of his face.

The tavern-keeper retreated, but the beggar held him by the corner of his chiton and, with a wave of the hand, silenced the murmurs of the crowd behind him.

"You hurt now," he ordered the tavern-keeper, driving a finger into his stomach. "You oil here; oil burn now inside. Oh, oh, how many much pain oil in fat belly yours!"

The tavern-keeper's grimace turned into uneven gasping. He grabbed his stomach and began stumbling backward toward the fountain with an unbelieving stare fixed on the metragyrtes, his shoulders arched, his chest sunken, and his face shriveled.

Then the beggar cried, "You fire belly! Many much fire burn! Much bad!"

The tavern-keeper let out a croak and fell on all fours in the very puddle where the slave had been. No one interfered. Some twenty awed faces watched the miracle. Hypothesis had never seen such powerful magic, either. The tavern-keeper was twisting facedown in the puddle, his throat an endless scream, while the beggar of Cybele swept the growing crowd with his eyes, the curious trying to get closer to the center.

The new arrivals, who could not see, were asking what was happening. Then they heard him thunder again, "No hurt! Pain no more!"

Those who were in the inner circle actually saw the tavern-keeper stop his screaming, exhale with relief, and smile. From the ground, oblivious to what had happened, he directed an inquisitive glance at his terrified sons who could not take their eyes off his horribly blistered stomach, like the Armenian's. The metragyrtes then had them both rise, silencing everyone with a swirl of his red mane, as he turned to the tavern-keeper.

"You no never stick bam-bam slave of you," he ordered, staring into his eyes. "If you bam-bam and flame, you die. You understand?"

The Marathonian wrinkled his forehead like one trying to understand and, without taking his eyes from the metragyrtes, nodded, nodded and kept on nodding without a word.

The beggar took the slave by the hand, delivered him to his master, and ordered them to go. Behind them went the wife and sons. The tavern-keeper and the Armenian strolled hand in hand, like two children on a walk.

The beggar then passed his alms pot among the onlookers, jingling his bells and chanting prayers in the Phrygian tongue. When the pot was full of obols for the Temple of the Great Mother, he pointed toward the sea.

"People many all go there."

Most of them started to move away. They walked with their heads down, without a backward glance.

When Hypothesis was almost at Themistocles's wharf, exactly opposite to where she wanted to go, she realized that she had not felt her migraine for quite a while. This was the first time in two years.

A miracle?

She turned and hurried as fast as her wineskins and packs of herbs would let her, up the long incline leading to the Fountain of the Nereids. But the metragyrtes was no longer there. No one could tell her which direction he had taken. What bad luck! He could have cured her forever.

She came back the next day, but to no avail. Nor the following. After waiting for him three days in Piraeus, she started looking for him in the City. Someone said they had seen him in Phalerum, and there she went, in vain. Then she heard that he was begging in Scyron, but when she got there he was gone. She gave up all hope of ever being cured and returned to wine, her only solace.

She had tried everything. Hellebore, laserwart, male snake scales with shredded cheese, leeches on her temples, facial massages at daybreak with the urine of a lactating donkey. She saw the City physician, went to the Temple of Asclepius, saw the Halon brothers, tried cauteries, bleeding, suction, and spells. But the only thing that worked against her migraine was to drink wine until she dropped. That was the only way to get some sleep.

At the age of thirty-two, just ten years after her first victory at the callipygian dances, she was already a hag. Of the three slaves she had been left with, one was dead and the others were as useless as she. They hardly made enough to eat in those rat-hole whorehouses. All that remained of the former Queen Sweet-Rump of Athens, the one who was crowned in the Temple of Solon, the beauty for whom libertines squandered fortunes, were ruins and memories.

The Thessalian who had been her doorkeeper in the golden days had taught Hypothesis cosmetics and a great deal of witchcraft. Now, in a drunken stupor to dull the migraine, she scoured the harbor whorehouses or went to Scyron to sell the brothel scum some of her chants, spells, love potions, philters, dyes, white lead, hexes, amulets, miraculous herbs, rouges, all of her own making.

But Hypothesis would not submit to that destiny. Aphrodite the Vulgar, who had twice given her the crown of victory as her favorite dancer, would remember her some day. Hadn't she had always served her with reverent devotion? Year after year, despite disease, old age, and increasing poverty, she had always had faith that Aphrodite would change her life. She simply could not believe that Aphrodite would let her die a peddler in the very streets that had witnessed her glory.

The Goddess had recently seemed to confirm her hopes. If Hypothesis was interpreting the dream brought on by the spotted mushrooms correctly, her luck would change very soon.

For some time now, she had been talking to the whorehouse girls, asking them ridiculous questions. She explained that she had clients who were looking for special women.

"She's crazy," was the usual remark.

But Hypothesis knew what she was looking for and was convinced she had already found it. Let those women think what they may. Hypothesis had just found out about a Miletian with a magnificent quivering rump, like hers in the good old days. If she could convince the Miletian woman, she would take her under her wing. No, she would not charge for her lessons, but she would make her swear, yes, she would make her take a solemn oath before an image of Aphrodite, that as soon as she was crowned Callipygous Queen and became the pet of Athens' rich, she would repay her efforts with three fifteen-year-old slave girls. That would be enough to get Hypothesis through the rest of her days.

53

She still cherished that hope. If it came true, she would live out her days, as long as the Moera decreed, but numb-drunk from dawn to dusk. And none of that Attic wine for two drachmas a cask. Phooey! From now on she would drink only Chios, Lesbos, Thasos, Rhodes, and she would mix it with snow in the summer and warm it in winter, heh, heh. No one would ever see her pissing all over herself and getting filthy in the streets again.

No, everything was not lost.

She counted the moons yet to go before the first of Boedromion. That was the day, the only day, when she could cut the spotted mushrooms.

6

AFTER SHE AWOKE, Lysis spent some time stroking his silken hair. Alcibiades was awake, but pretended not to be. He wanted to bring his plan into sharper focus in his mind. Missing the opportunity to make off with Aristarchus's pack was out of the question. Those fourteen Laconian hounds were famous in all Athens. The day before, when he was bragging that Lysis would give him anything, even Truncheon's necklace, if he asked her, Aristarchus had broken out laughing and told him not to be presumptuous: Truncheon would sooner part with her life than with her necklace. Didn't Alcibiades know that Callias had offered her a talent for it and she had turned him down? Truncheon had sworn not to lend it.

Alcibiades just shrugged and let it go, but he immediately began to connive a way to get his hands on those dogs. Aristarchus, for his part, was mad over Anemos, Alcibiades's white stallion. Yes, those could be the stakes. And if he played things right, in addition to the dogs, he might even get his Thessalian stable. There were two splendid colts there.

Aristarchus insisted that Truncheon would not let Lysis have the necklace. Alcibiades knew that, but who was to say that Lysis, crazed with love for him, would not steal it?

Except for Socrates, Alcibiades had never gone wrong with his lovers. He had always known exactly how far he could make them go to prove their love. Yes! That bet would cost Aristarchus his stable and his pack. He deserved it for being so ignorant. That was that.

He felt Lysis kissing his eyes.

She was terrified now and quite sorry she had sworn to seduce him and humiliate him before the City. The only desire she felt now was to cherish him. But she had to keep her oath to the Goddess.

Could it be true what they said about the herb woman's wine? She might try it, later on.

Suddenly she realized that her oath did not oblige her to vanquish Alcibiades immediately. It was actually impossible in such a short time. Pandemos must understand that her victim was leaving the day after to be interned and that the only thing Lysis could do for now was to be charming, to please him so that when his epheby was over he would return to her. And then ...

That thought comforted her. Of course! The promise to the Goddess was open-ended.

She recalled the two nights she had spent with him. Just a few hours earlier, when they were making love in the chariot or flying through the air as Aristarchus pushed the swing, she had thought that for the first time in her life it felt good to be subjected to a man, to be ready to do anything to please him. How strange! What could be happening to her that she even tolerated the close presence of a third person without complaining?

Could that be what Truncheon felt for her? It was something new, and very sweet. Until that moment in her life, she had never loved, just been loved. A few hours earlier, when it was still very dark and the three of them were quite drunk, Alcibiades had asked Lysis to cut his hair.

He sat her behind him on his horse, and together with Aristarchus, they rode out to a bend in the river. There, while Alcibiades floated on his back, the current spreading his tresses out into a golden fan, she cut his hair.

Alcibiades asked the river God to carry his offering down to wave-kissed Salamis. In improvised hexameters, he begged the numen of his ancestor Ajax to bless the weapons he would soon be wielding as an ephebus.

In two days, Alcibiades and Aristarchus would enter Oenoe fortress for four months of training. For two years, Lysis would not be able to see him except from afar during torch races or on parade days.

What would become of her? How would she ever suffer other men to get into her bed? She would, of course; it was her duty to the Goddess, so she would. But it would never be the same again.

When Alcibiades awoke, she tried to speak to him, but he signaled her to keep quiet. His head was twisted onto his shoulder as if he were trying to hear something going on very far away. When he finally spoke to her, he said that he had been trying to trap a dream, a strange and beautiful dream in which he and Aristarchus were vying for Lysis, pulling her by the arms. But she brought them together, made them embrace and kiss each other, and then asked them to treat her to simultaneous caresses. All three wound up lying on a mound of soft grass, loving each other in exquisite rotation.

Didn't Lysis understand that, to seal the friendship born between her and Alcibiades, the Goddess was asking them to use the blood that welled in Aristarchus, another Panathenian champion, another favorite of Athena, as a sacramental bond?

It was a proposal.

To please him, she would have agreed immediately, but it was dangerous to give in with no resistance at all.

Lysis stared into his eyes a moment and decided.

She would, then, accept going trio for just this one time, but only if Alcibiades swore before an image of the Goddess that he would love no other woman for the duration of his epheby— and that after that he would accept Lysis as his favorite friend.

Alcibiades's counterblow did not take long.

"Do you intend to be my future concubine?"

"I want you to come into my arms when you are bored with Hipparete."

He laughed at her being so well-informed.

As far as Hipparete was concerned, Alcibiades had already asked for her, but she would be merely the mother of ten or twelve of his children; if it wasn't Hipparete, it would be any other of the aristocrats available in the City who was healthy and rich enough. Breeding aristocrats wasn't difficult. Choosing a concubine, now that was a task. This was a choice that had to be favored by the immortal Gods. He felt he still had to mature before making such a choice. The house of a good lover was a man's real home, the place for the best things in the life of an Athenian like himself, friend of philosophers and artists, future host of distinguished foreigners, rhetors, musicians, sophists, for whom he would give banquets and feasts to taste ideas, wine, women, or, why not? boys, delicacies for men in their later years, the salt of life that was not shared with one's wife and children. Alcibiades's concubine would be his hostess

57

and lover, his shield from woes, his ewer of pleasures, the confidant of his dreams and hopes, his military and political counselor: She would have to be constant and not turn into a hydra when he stayed away a few days; nor could she slam the door and insult him when he came in at dawn, drunk, flanked by a pair of courtesans and surrounded by his rowdy friends. And if he should fall in love with some beautiful boy, like Zeus himself fell in love with Ganymede or Poseidon with Pelops, she would have to show the boy hospitality and affection, as she would a son. And she should be ready to give up anything, if he asked, money, jewels, everything she had, for him to give to a new lover, man or woman, as the fancy struck him. And his concubine had to be as beautiful as Helen, as faithful as Penelope, and a friend of the Muses. Where could he find such a woman?

Lysis stood on the bed and propped her hands up on her hips: Did he need a lamp to see what he had before him?

Alcibiades forced himself to hold back a laugh.

Fine, he agreed that Lysis was beautiful and in tight with the Muses, but how could he be certain that she was not lacking in the virtues, for him irreplaceable, of Penelope?

And she, challenging, "Put me to the test."

Alcibiades got to his feet, took her by the waist, bent her to rub himself with her nipples, and turned her around to nuzzle her neck. Then he cradled his rigor in her callipygous valley and whispered that he would fulfill his oath to Pandemos, but not before she, Lysis, made him a present of Truncheon's n-n-necklace.

7

SOCRATES, SOPHRONISCUS'S SON, was the only Athenian whom Alcibiades ever admired. Whenever Alcibiades heard Socrates talking, his heart would leap like a Corybantes. The others, sophists and rhetors alike, or orators like Pericles, did not move him at all. But Socrates bound him with his voice like an Orpheus; he made him lose his self-control; he made him furious with the thought of having his mind enslaved, or ecstatic with ideas that seemed born of his, Alcibiades's, own soul.

Only before Socrates did Alcibiades ever feel ashamed.

He was the only one he ever obeyed in his life.

Socrates was rather squat, his eyes much too far out of their sockets and his nose a bit too flat. He went around the City barefoot, and he waddled like a duck.

Alcibiades used to compare him to the statuettes of Silenus. He was certainly every bit as ugly, but, by Zeus, his words were a kind of music that bent the will, a mermaid's song that went from the ear straight to the soul.

When Alcibiades was at that beautiful age when boys begin to think about shaving, he was seized with the thought that Socrates desired him and decided to make him his lover. That way he could listen to him all he pleased and not have to share his wisdom with anyone.

One day, Alcibiades sent his hand-servant away and remained alone with Socrates under the sycamores of the Lyceum.

But the philosopher philosophized.

He did not speak of love. He did not succumb to Alcibiades's elaborate seduction, nor did he succumb later, their naked bodies as one on the palaestra, when Alcibiades challenged him to anoint for a match. Nor did he show the slightest interest the night they spent together in Alcibiades's quarters.

When the slaves were gone and the light turned off, they waited a while in silence, listening to each other's breathing.

"Are you asleep, Socrates?"

"No."

Alcibiades was ashamed at what he was going to say, and mortified at being ashamed.

"Do you know what I th-th-think?"

"No."

"I think you're the only one worthy of being my lover and you can't b-b-bring yourself to tell me."

Socrates remained silent.

Alcibiades lunged again.

"...and that it would be foolish for me not to give myself to you or to refuse you whatever you might demand of my fortune and influence."

Silence.

"...and that the important thing for a young man like me is to improve myself."

Alcibiades waited. Socrates would have to say something. "And?"

"And I'm certain that no one could help me improve myself any better than you."

"Ah, my dear Alcibiades! If you have seen in me some virtue that may help you improve, then you may not be such a frivolous young man. If you should see in me a beauty greater than your own perfect figure, and if seeing it you should want to exchange it for yours, you would certainly be the winner in gaining truth in exchange for falsehood, gold for bronze."

"But I'm not bronze, Socrates. I'm the t-t-touchstone for your golden soul. What is your decision?"

"I think we should decide together. From now on, you and I."

On hearing this, Alcibiades rushed out of his bed and into Socrates's. He covered his mouth with his hand to keep him from saying anything else. He was certain he had wounded him, and he laid down beside the philosopher snuggling against him under his tattered robes. He began to embrace him and kiss his face, calling him a wonderful man, a divine man.

But Socrates had no use for his beauty.

When the dawn finally broke, Alcibiades got up completely intact, as if he had slept with his father, Clinias.

He had not been able to get to Socrates. Alcibiades, however, had long ago suffered the bite of his philosophical speeches, more overpowering than a viper's venom when they were sown in the soul of a young man with natural gifts.

61

8

SHE HAD MADE HER DECISION the moment she
got through the wall. If Truncheon refused her the necklace, she would leave for the Cape, climb to the Temple of
Athena, and throw herself into the waters of the Saronic Sea.
What good was life without Alcibiades?

When they got to Truncheon's, she sent Otep around to the
back door with the dog and tapped her secret signal to the
doorkeeper. The Syrian told her that his mistress was entertaining clients and that one of them had come with the hope of
hearing her play the flute. Lysis told him she was feeling poorly
and would await Truncheon in her rooms. Once in the chamber, she took off her diadem and let her hair loose.

Ah, the smells of her godmother. She regarded the attributes
of her novitiate: the sea urchin, the cuttlefish, the imposing
gold phallus, the pink mother-of-pearl clitoris inlaid atop the
bivalve seashell. The statuette of the Mother Goddess that
Truncheon worshiped at dawn stared down at her from her

niche; atop a chest, surrounded by doves and sparrows, lay Pandemos, her legs spread apart on her bed of myrtle.

She no longer belonged to the room, or to Truncheon, or to this world. In a few moments, she would be joining Aphrodite among her waves; she would leap like Sappho from the Leucadian crag. The dying, reddish light that filtered in reminded her that she would not be seeing the dawn. She approached Pandemos, raised her palms, and stared directly at her. She waited for her tears to run and for her voice to respond. Oh! Why had Cypris, the wave-born, forsaken her? Why had she let her fall in love? Did she prefer him?

Behind her back, Truncheon heard her pleas.

She grew pale.

She could imagine her tears. She guessed everything. Lysis had lost, and so had she, Eulalia of Ephesus, the unvanquished.

She was surprised by her self-control. She didn't even break down when Lysis cried on the necklace of her misfortunes, which she wore high on her breast.

In a frenzy of babbling and delirium, Lysis let herself fall and embraced Truncheon around the knees. Alcibiades, fever, beaten, impossible to master him, her temples were burning, she could die at the thought of losing him, her beloved, her master, her owner, how could she live without him? unique, delicious, and he loved her, promised to keep her by him, but, oh, oh, words, "help me, oh wayward progeny of thought," Alcibiades wanted proof of her great love, Penelope, touchstone, evidence, sacrifice, ready to swear before the Goddess, to pact with her, ah, how difficult to speak, "oh, hateful day, hateful light my eyes are not to see, I shall die this very night, cold and forsaken," and Truncheon trembled, tried to seal her lips to keep her from babbling, to have out with it once and for all.

"Alcibiades asked me for your necklace, the one with the Muses."

While Lysis beat her forehead on the floor and yanked her hair, Truncheon took off her necklace and unflinchingly, without a word or grimace, knelt down and placed it around Lysis's neck.

"It's yours," she said, and returned to her wine.

She had been expecting such a blow, and she was ready.

Lysis was worth a hundred necklaces like that one; let Clinias's son keep it. But whether or not he would take the girl away from her was yet to be seen.

No more sadness.

She checked her make-up, arranged her hair, and returned to her guests with self-imposed grace.

Let the cupbearer serve her all the rounds she had missed, and may her honored guests please excuse her absence.

She proposed the subject for the gossip of the second tables. How could Hipponicus have accepted that fairy Alcibiades to be Hipparete's husband?

9

HIGH ON MOUNT CITHAERON, in the shade of an old cedar grove, there was a log temple devoted to the Great Mother of the Gods. The effigy was a rustic black wood stump, without face or members and hardly carved at all.

The beggar had been displeased with it back then, when he had entered the territory. It was the most disgraceful metroon he had found in all his journey from Asia. It was abandoned, smelly, a pen for wild animals. There was no offering to be seen anywhere, not even the remains of one.

He had spent two nights there, at the Goddess' feet. Before going on to Athens, he had washed the logs with water from the nearby stream and made a trellis to keep the wild animals out and the birds from shitting all over everything. He hung pine boughs on the walls and rubbed the effigy of the Goddess with lavender and marjoram.

When he bid her good-bye, she made no sign of response.

"How then, ingrate? Don't you recognize Atys of Pamphylia, your beggar?"

Then he realized that the image was blind and could hardly be expected to recognize him.

In his Phrygian language, he promised to return and give her eyes. He would return with chants and dances. He would return.

Lying at her feet, his promise delivered, he asked now if the flight of the owl the Goddess had shown him in a mountain pass in Thessaly really meant what he thought it did. Was it really in Athens that Cybele wanted him? Oh, why was she so misleading? In so many years of service, why had she never spoken to him in words?

After several days in Athens, the metragyrtes returned defeated to the metroon on the border. The journey to the City of the Owl had been completely useless. In vain had he tried to beg for Cybele. The Cybele they worshipped here was an impostor they called Rhea and stood painted between two lions; the legitimate one, the Phrygian Mother of the Gods, was so relegated that you had to get the approval of the Archons or of the priests of Athena to build a temple or even an insignificant altar.

And not a trace of the Eye of the Child.

Now, back on Cithaeron, in his discouragement, he reproached the Goddess. He cried at her feet, before her featureless image, and censured her for not rewarding his devotion with clear messages. Why had she sent him where they despised her instead of letting him return to Asia?

He spent a long time lying on the floor staring at the ceiling, without the will power to take a drink of water, find food, or build a fire against the beasts in the night.

There she was, still climbing and telling herself she had to grab Tyche, the furtive Goddess of Fortune, by her tresses.

As she penetrated deeper into the gorge where the density of the forest turned midday into dusk, the pounding in her temples forced her to sit on a rock. The migraine was a stake nailed between her eyebrows. The steeper the Cithaeron became, the stronger the pounding. And she still had a five-stadia climb before her. But Hypothesis could not miss the chance that only a new moon could give her.

She had promised herself not to have a drink until she had reached the spotted mushrooms, but she took her wineskin out of her haversack and had two long gulps with her eyes closed. Then she went on climbing.

Further on, she picked some salvia leaves and chewed them. She recalled how nimbly she used to climb ten years earlier, laughing at the gasping and complaining of the old Thessalian who was making her way up with the aid of a cane. Hypothesis did not need a cane, she was still strong. If it were not for her migraine, she would have more than enough strength to climb the Cithaeron and return to the City in a single day—not like now, when she would have to spend the night in the whore-houses of Acharnae.

Courage! Keep moving! The night of the new moon in Boedromion was the only time of the year when the sylvan deities performed the miracle of the mushrooms.

Suddenly, a sharp throb left her breathless and forced her to stop. She gasped and waited for the aching to subside, then she started climbing again, determined not to let the pain get in the way of her urgent task. To give herself courage, she kept imagining how the mushrooms she would harvest that day were going to have Talthybia's sweet-assed beauty, whoever she might be, wiggling her rump with a fervor never seen in Athens.

What a fox that Talthybia was! Hypothesis had only been able to get her to say that it was a Miletian with a quivery ass whom she used to find having her make-up done in the court-yard when she delivered her vegetables, and that the girl used to like to provoke her so she could laugh at her swearing and her quaint expressions. But Talthybia had refused to give her the address until she had her man back, even if he did have a gimp eye. In any case, Hypothesis had made her swear before Pandemos that, if her magic got the gimp to leave the other woman, Talthybia would not only give her the name of the Miletian, but would herself take her the spotted mushroom potion.

"Does he still mount you?" Hypothesis had asked.

"Just when he's run out of money and comes to the veg-etable stand to pick up a few obols."

"What if you refuse?"

"He beats me up and doesn't mount me."

Hypothesis promised to bless her vagina with a purple bell-flower philter. Just a single visit and the gimp would be caught. After that, he would be riding her all the time.

There could be no doubt about the dream. This was the first time she had appeared to him and spoken in words. Her voice was sweet and young, despite her appearance. The Goddess was ordering him to return to Athens to found her new church.

In the new church, Cybele would be water, because she who had given life to so many Gods, she, the mother-soul, the first-born whose black tits had even suckled powerful Zeus, she had to be water. The reasoning was logical, evident, phainomenon, as the Greeks said, because without water there could be no life; he remained motionless, even though his parched tongue felt rough on his palate. The slightest movement might dissipate the sediments of that apocalyptical dream.

He felt hungry.

How long had he slept? Two, three days? The sun had to be high because light was still filtering in; he closed his eyes again to avoid distraction. Lying face-up on the log floor of the metroon, he invoked the key image of his dream, the part where Cybele appeared to him with white hair, bent, held up by her grandchildren Dionysus and Aphrodite Pandemos, who were helping her walk and on whom she looked with gratitude. They were her favorites, her two pariahs, who, like her, had been run out of Olympus.

That was the first time the metragyrtes heard the voice of the Great Mother of the Gods. She told him that the three of them were one God, a single, indivisible God. The Cybele of Mount Dindymon would again be worshiped throughout the Ecumene. Then, before his closed eyes, the three embraced and fused into a trefoil of green fire.

Wasn't it clear that the Gods were ordering him to found their new church? If not, why had they shown him the apocalypse?

Yes, Atys of Pamphylia would become the First Priest of the New Church. But what was the Greekish word for First Priest? The Prostate? Protosacerdos? Hieraticos archon?

The High Priest of Cybele was called the Archigallus in Sardes. In Athens, on the other hand, Zeus's High Priest was called the Buzyges; the Eleusinian High Priest was the Hierophant; Apollo's was called the Primate; in Libya, the High Priest of Ammon was known as the Serene; and the High Priest of Mithra, in Persia, was simply The Highest.

The Highest Priest of the Church of the Trefoil? The High Priest of the Trefoil?

He tried titles in Phrygian, Lydian, Carian, but he realized that if the New Church was to be founded in Athens, he would have to have a Greekish title.

What if he called himself the Archigallus of the Church of the Three Gods?

No, no, no! Until such time as he was illuminated by new visions, he would simply be the High Priest of the Church of Cybele, Dionysus, and Aphrodite Pandemos. But that was much too long. And why not the Pappas, as the head of the Panionian congregation was known? Pappas meant "little father" Greekly. It was like the title of the one who led the faithful by the hand. No! That was just another title without weight or substance.

If the three Gods were one, why not call them the Sum?

Yes! That's it! He would call it the Church of the Sum, a short name and easy to remember. And he would be the High Priest of the Sum—or better yet, the Summoner of the Sum.

Excellent! A new title for the primate of a new religion. A sharp and catchy title and, to judge from its perfect sound, inspired by the Gods themselves.

But he kept his eyes closed. He had to go through the dream in minute detail to get every warning, every hint. Before wakefulness swept away the last of his visions, he had to unravel a multitude of clues that would help him define the objectives of his church.

It was useless. The sounds of the forest made themselves heard and wiped away the last embers of the dream.

Very well. The first thing he had to do, then, was to work out the liturgy. How would the conversion of the faithful be?

By communion, of course.

Should he retain the bloody rites and castrations of the worship of Cybele?

No, it was clear that the Goddess wanted no blood. If she had wanted blood, she would not have put so much stress on the water. Well, maybe a little bit of symbolic blood, something like the cement of communion, might be acceptable. But the main thing would be water, the essence of Cybele.

For Dionysus it would be done with wine.

And what about Aphrodite's third?

Burning myrtle?

What about that part in the dream where the virgins were all desiring him? That might indicate—

Of course. The dream was clearly and phainomenically ordering that communion with Aphrodite be performed through ritual coitus. That was it! Just like in the Temple of Ishtar, in Babylon, like in Dam. The novices would commune with the Goddess through the priest. Until he had an assistant, he would have to administer all the first communions of his church personally.

What about male converts? Shouldn't men be admitted to the Sum?

Then, like in Paphos and Babylon, there would have to be priestesses to administer communion to men.

While he was imagining the ritual, he again felt the erection and the religious enthousiasmos. But he did not want to open his eyes yet.

What had he gotten clear? Which would be his duties? What immediate measures must the founder take?

He told himself that he should never again let himself be seen in the motley robe of the metragyrtes.

How would the Summoner of the Sum dress from now on?

Fresh bellflowers have a very strong, sweet smell. All three trees were in bloom. She calculated that five of the big ones would be enough. She picked only five. Her Thessalian teacher had insisted that the Gods of the forest got angry when herbalists cut more than was necessary.

She tied them with fennel twigs and placed them in her bag very carefully to keep them from being crushed.

Then she sat on the trunk of a fallen cedar and reached for her wineskin again. She took three long swigs; thanks to Dionysus, her migraine was hardly bothering her at all.

That night she would sleep in Acharnae, and by noon the following day she would be back in Athens. The first thing to do was to prepare the mushroom potion and give it to Talthybia mixed with Thasian wine, which was so sweet it would mask the bitter taste of the powders.

She took off her sandals by the banks of the stream and waded in up to her knees. The cool water felt good and she stopped a few minutes in midstream. Yes, on the way back, she would take a swim in the pool that was a short way downstream.

From the other bank she could see the Temple of Cybele among the trees. It was a dark place. Her Thessalian doormaid had discovered that there were spotted mushrooms growing under the log floor, the very same mushrooms that Thessalian witches called storm mushrooms.

Atys would have to give up his colorful robe. No more flaps and bells. He was no longer a metragyrtes. From that moment on he would be known as the Summoner of the Sum. His robes would be green like the color of life. Or should he dress in white, which was the color of light? Wasn't light the most beautiful of all things and, as such, an attribute worthy of the Gods? He could also dress in black, to honor Cybele's eternal mourning. But no. His was to be a church of light.

So that was the second decision inspired by the Gods: the Summoner of the Sum would henceforth dress in green or in white.

And why not blue, like the ether, or red, like blood?

Perhaps the best thing to do was not to choose a single color, but several, that way he could use different colors for different occasions. All except saffron.

Yes. That was it. Decided.

Paraballs—or was it parables?—were certainly going to be a problem. How annoying! He never quite knew how to say things in Greek. So why not officiate in Phrygian or Lydian and let the followers translate? But that could not be. He had been ordered to found his new church in Athens and the Summoner of the Sum had to preach and officiate in Greek. And that's exactly what he would do. They, or rather the Sum, would inspire him to speak clearly in the Greek language. Or was it linguage?

Whom would he choose as his followers?

Everyone. The Sum would admit men and women, rich and poor, of all nations. Hadn't Cybele ordered him in her first appearance to travel throughout the known Ecumene and found temples in all the nations of mankind? And in her second appearance, had she not phainomenically shown him the circular horizon of all the inhabited world?

So, once they had taken communion, all the faithful would be equal in the church of Atys, whether they came from the mountains, the deserts, or the sea.

Could seawater be used as well for communion, on the side of Cybele's third?

Yes, phainomenon. As long as it was water, it would not matter if it came from a river, the sea, a lake, or—

How about rain water?

But certainly rain water comes from above, doesn't it?

Then he began thinking about the catechesis of the doctrine and the conversion of the faithful. Of course, one of his attributes as Summoner of the Sum would be to choose priestesses. This way he would—

But would he be the only one to choose priestesses?

He had to plan ahead; when his church became truly ecumenical it would be impossible for him to perform all the communions personally.

But that was a problem for the future. Right now, he had to solve the question of his first priestesses. Should the Summoner of the Sum be the one to choose them? Or should he wait for the Gods to choose them and let him know through some apocalyptical sign?

Which would be the ideal communion? Water and wine for Cybele and Dionysus. That was clear enough. But for Aphrodite's third, the Summoner would not admit just any ordinary, improvised coitus. No. If it was to be sacred, it had to follow a ritual. Now, where would he place the women? On an altar? On a bed of sacred herbs? Would the future priestesses go on top? Would they go on the bottom? Should he lie them on their backs or put them on all fours?

Yes, designing the liturgy was definitely very important.

Then, with the torrent of communion positions rushing through his mind, the Summoner of the Sum could think of nothing else.

As soon as she arrived, she dropped her pack of bellflowers and her sack. What if it were all in vain? Again she felt fear. The girl might be repelled by her ugliness and demand to see how the potion was brewed. But Hypothesis would never reveal her secret. She could not without violating her oath to the Thessalian.

Her long walk since the break of dawn had made her hungry. She thought about eating but changed her mind. First she would harvest her mushrooms; then she would cool her feet in the stream. That would be a good place to eat.

She came closer to examine the logs that held up the floor, waiting a while to let her eyes get accustomed to the dark. She had to get down on her knees to search the ground for the mushrooms with the red spots. By Pandemos, getting the mushrooms she required would be no trouble at all. There were so many! Before leaving she would have to do something to show her appreciation to the Mother of the Gods.

Following strictly in the order established by the ritual, she first sang a chant to Dionysus so that the vegetable nature would be propitious and her philters effective. When the chant was through, she lay down to be better able to get her left arm in through the logs. She cut the mushrooms with her left thumb and middle finger, the way the Thessalian had taught her, to ensure the power of the potion. It was no trouble at all; there were several right near the outer wall.

75

Ready. Now her devotion to Cybele and the trip home. She picked a few fresh pine boughs and with the point of her hair-pin pricked some blood from her finger. A drop of blood on the bough to symbolize the castration of Cybele's lover, converted into a pine tree.

With the bough between her hands, she started up the nine cedar logs that served as a stairway into the rustic metroon.

He first heard her footsteps among the dry leaves on the forest floor and remembered that the door to the temple was open. The Boeotians had told him that there were bears and wolves on Cithaeron. But he had nothing to worry about. No creature of the forest would dare attack the Summoner of the Sum, the chosen of the Gods themselves.

As the steps drew near, he realized that they definitely

belonged to a two-legged animal. He had lived too many years in the forests to miss that. And with his eyes still firmly closed, he knew they were the footsteps of a woman.

This was not the first time. He could tell when there was a woman around by a kind of warning tickle he felt somewhere in his chest. The voice immediately confirmed his decision; it was hoarse, but definitely female. And it made him very happy to recognize in the chant a litany he had heard many years before. The invocation reminded him of the time he had seen a band of women on the foothills of Parnassus doing honor to Dionysus. He had not heard it since his first visit to Greece, when he crossed Thessaly on the way to Dodona on his quest for the Eye of the Mother Child.

The woman who was approaching, whomever she might be, was certainly sent by Dionysus—and by Aphrodite, as well, as is any woman who intrudes into a man's solitude. He got excited again. It was the first movement he had made in his several days of apocalyptical lethargy.

That very moment, bursting with the desire to administer the first communion of the Church of the Sum, he understood why the Great Mother of the Gods had not let him castrate himself that time on Mount Dindymon. The very thought of it made him dizzy: testicles held high, ready to be sliced off by the sacred blade, and suddenly, an invisible hand, powerful, too powerful to be human, snatched the blade from his hand and cast it into the waters of the Hermus. The Great Mother had not wanted Atys to be a eunuch like all the other metragyrtes.

And this particular erection, was it marked by the three Gods of the Sum? Had they already agreed?

If so, this woman, who was about to enter the temple chanting in the Thessalian mode, might just be an ancient knot in the fabric woven by the Gods. Could she be a maenad?

He would know very soon. The test would be to lie very still, doing nothing to attract her. If she was sent by the Gods, he told himself as she climbed the log steps into the temple, they would fit together like iron and the Heraclean stone.

When she had the bough securely on the altar, she prayed fervently. May the Great Mother of the Gods give her the sweet-assed beauty with the trepidating orgasm Pandemos demanded! And she began to walk backward, chanting praise while facing the effigy.

Suddenly, to one side, she saw a shape she had not noticed when she came in. She stopped and recognized the figure of a man lying there in the dark.

Her first impulse was to run. She took another step backward. The shape remained motionless. Was it really a man? She stepped a little closer. Was he asleep? Could he be dead?

Her eyes, much more accustomed to the dark now, made out a large man. Of his head, the only thing she could see was his long hair. And he seemed to have a beard.

She approached cautiously. When she was right beside him, she bent over a little for a closer look and felt a peal of pain in her temples. She recognized the metragyrtes she had been looking for all over the City and the wharves. She was seized by the fear that he might be dead. She knelt. He opened his eyes.

"Who you are?"

"Hypothesis," she babbled.

He closed his eyes again and smiled. It was all coming together now. She was sent by the Gods. Her very name, that which goes beneath, made this much clear. What doubt could there be that he had been sent his first priestess? She would be the hypothesis, the female pillar of the Sum. It also meant that

77

in the ritual coitus she would go under him. She had been sent with that name to clear up his first liturgical dilemma.

"What you here do?"

She? There? Ah, well, she wanted to offer a bloody pine bough up to the Goddess Mother.

It occurred to her to invent a dream in which he had summoned her to Cithaeron to cure her of her headaches.

"You find now acorn and never no pain more."

As she walked away in search of her remedy, he dwelt on the wisdom of the Sum, which wove in every detail.

At the foot of an old oak, she found a big, fresh acorn and returned to the metroon. He had gotten to his feet; he seemed to be naked.

"Give acorn," he said.

As she approached, yes, he definitely was naked. He took the acorn and, raising it high, turned to the effigy and said a prayer in some barbarian language.

When he turned toward her again, Hypothesis saw that he had an impeccable erection. She shuddered.

He placed the acorn on her head.

"Hold," he ordered. She raised a hand to hold the acorn.

"Two hands," he ordered again.

She obeyed.

"Go in back me," he said, walking off toward the entrance.

From the very moment the acorn touched her head, she felt relief, the same relief she got when she had her fill of wine. The throbbing was still there, but it didn't torture her.

They walked off into the forest single file. He approached the stream without looking back at her and stopped in a clearing where the trees let in some sunlight. She could see his features quite clearly here. He was thinner than he had seemed in Piraeus, and he was beautiful.

She held the acorn securely on her head. He took her by the shoulders and placed her with her back toward the stream. Then he pressed on her temples and brought his eyes very close to hers. He mumbled in his own language for quite some time. And when he began to repeat in Greek, "You no pain," she felt as if the pain were draining into those eyes and all her being was sinking into a pool of water, thick like oil, that was anointing her with forgetfulness.

"You no pain," he repeated. But it was no longer necessary; her migraine was gone.

"You no pain," he insisted as he undressed her. She just stood there, not daring to smile.

When he finally had her naked, he ordered, "You acorn back."

She looked at him, uncomprehending.

"Acorn throw back, no look."

She threw it into the river without a glance.

"Head you no hurt, leg no hurt, nothing no hurt," he said, as he placed her hands on his phallus.

She held onto it like one holds a coveted treasure.

"You beautiful." She smiled. Then suddenly ashamed of her missing teeth, she let loose with one hand to cover her mouth. He brought her hand back to his phallus, never taking his stare off her.

"You yes tooths, you beautiful tooths, you tooths like snow, like cloud."

She did, indeed, feel her teeth in her mouth.

He put a finger into her mouth.

"Bite this dactyls mine." She could not bring herself to use her new teeth for fear of hurting him, so she wound up sucking his finger tips.

"You derma smooth, derma fifteen-year girl," he told her, caressing her deeply scarred buttocks.

He made her beautiful. He had to seek strongly within him-self to feel that he was squeezing a sweet-assed girl. The powers the Gods had given their Summoner of the Sum included the ability to improve the appearance of all the faithful who took the sacrament. Now he had bestowed powerful attractions on his first priestess, the hypothesis of all future converts.

She stooped to kiss him.

"No," he said. "First water of Cybele."

He baptized her in the waterfall.

He taught her the sacred ablutions and made her repeat a prayer to the Great Mother of the Gods in the Phrygian tongue.

She felt on wings: fifteen years, no pain, yes, teeth, and unexpectedly embracing a sumptuous phallus. Not in all her term as Callipygous Queen, not even when she stuffed purple bellflowers into herself, had she ever been so wet.

He helped her out and kissed her on the mouth.

"You wine drink?" he asked in surprise.

"Yes," Hypothesis said, "I brought a little wineskin for the journey."

Evident, very truth, very phainomenon, Gods foresee every-thing, beloved theoi send wine also for communion with Dionysus.

They made short work of the wine and the dried fish. Their joy increased.

"You now much happy inside feel?" She felt euphoros, extremely happy, like never before!

He too felt euphoros. He understood that the Holy Euphoria was descended on them. It was the feeling of ineffa-ble joy that the Sum confers on the chosen to encourage them in their sacramental obligations. Without a moment's delay, trembling with desire, Atys of Pamphylia prepared the Triple Bed of the Sum. On the soil covered with the sacred Cybelian pine needles, singing all the while, he spread the ivy of Dionysus and Aphrodite's myrtle.

There they lay and officiated.

Hypothesis of Athens received the full three thirds of the First Ordaining Communion of the New Church.

"First what?"

"You First Priestess now," he explained, eyes wide, eyebrows arched.

She, a First Priestess? Well!

Hypothesis of Athens broke out laughing with her cloud-colored teeth.

"Yes, you First Priestess," he repeated very seriously. "I teaching and you priesting when New Church have temple in Athens."

She smiled again.

Coming from that beautiful demigod, that powerful benefactor who had errupted into the evening tide of her life, she would happily accept slavery. So why not a priesthood, in whatever church he said?

Eyes brimming with tears, Hypothesis promised herself that the New Church would have a beautiful temple in the City. As priestess, she would see to it that her primate would not have to beg alms to build it.

Yes, he would have his temple soon: She had already cut the mushrooms.

10

ON A CERTAIN OCCASION, Socrates's personal daemon told him to learn his mother's art to be wiser with every passing day and to make men better.

By the dog! How could a man become wiser by learning the trades of women? What could be the sense in learning to be a midwife? For a long time Socrates searched in vain for an answer to the enigma.

The answer came to him one day as he was leaving the marketplace. He stopped at the foot of the Temple of Hephaestus to listen to a Pythagorean who was standing amid a group of onlookers drawing lines on the ground to demonstrate a theorem.

As soon as the demonstration was completed, Socrates set out on his way again, followed by one of his father's slaves.

When they were just about to begin the ascent of Wineskin Knoll, the slave confessed that he never understood anything the geometricians said.

Socrates had exactly the opposite conviction: The boy knew what the Pythagorean was demonstrating, but he thought he did not. Just the converse of what the false wise men thought about themselves.

There were different kinds of ignorance.

That very instant he saw a flash of lightning in the broad daylight.

He stopped. He began to chew his lip and took a few steps with his hands on his hips. The slave stopped too and waited for him, very much intrigued.

"Put your load down, Mysian," he said quite suddenly, crouching with his robe between his knees to smooth out the ground on the only flat spot on the hill. "Find a stick and come here," he ordered without raising his eyes.

The Mysian, overjoyed with his unexpected rest, quickly found a dry osier stick that Socrates broke down to a convenient size. He then made a point on it with his teeth.

"Draw a perfectly straight line here, one about the length of your foot," Socrates said, giving him the stick.

The slave stamped his footprint on the ground, stooped, drew the line, and wiped out the rest.

Socrates nodded approval and asked him to draw another line, parallel to the first but two feet long. When the slave was through, Socrates asked him the following question:

"How many times will the small line fit into the long one?"

"Twice," the slave said, smiling at the serious tone Socrates had used to ask such a foolish question.

"Very well, Mysian," Socrates said. "Now, draw three one-foot lines on the small one to make a square. Have you understood?"

"Yes, I've understood, O, son of Sophroniscus," the slave said, and stooped to comply.

Several passersby and neighboring vendors, who had noticed the slave measuring his feet on the ground and Socrates looking on from a crouch, stopped for a closer look.

A shoemaker carrying a string of sandals over his shoulder asked mockingly, "Have you gone Pythagorean on us, excellent Socrates?"

"No, Orestes," it occurred to him to answer, "I've become a midwife, like my mother."

A few of the onlookers laughed.

"So, who's going to give birth? That there Mysian?"

"Sure," Talthybia, the vegetable vendor, said. "He's going to give birth to two fleas out of his asshole."

They went on like that, with their gross jibes and jokes, but Socrates was dead serious. He knew he had just begun his first delivery of natural knowledge: not knowledge learned, but knowledge instilled by the Immortal Gods in the souls of men.

When the slave finished the square, Socrates had him stand up and placed him with his back toward the drawings.

"Take your time and think. If you answer my question correctly, I will give you half an obol; if you get it wrong, I'll have my father send you to bed without dinner."

"If you keep threatening him, he may have an abortion," Talthybia commented.

Even Socrates had to laugh.

"Pay attention," he finally said, and the onlookers listened to the question as if everything depended on it. "Imagine a second square constructed on the line that is twice the size of the small one. Would that square be twice as large as the first?"

The slave raised his head toward the Acropolis and closed his eyes as if he were invoking the resident divinities.

Socrates arched his eyebrows and pressed his index finger to his lips to keep the crowd from giving away the answer. Many were looking at the figures or making their own drawings in the air. Others were whispering answers in each other's ears.

"It would be more than twice as large," the Mysian said.

"How much larger?" Socrates pressed.

"Four times," the slave answered fearfully.

Several applauded. Socrates smiled and immediately gave him a full obol, which the Mysian put in his mouth.

"What if the squares had been made using my feet, which are larger than yours?"

"It would still fit four times," the Green-grocer said.

"And what if they had been made with the feet of Peleid Achilles?"

"Four times!" the voices chanted.

"May we say, then," Socrates asked, "that whenever a line is twice the length of another, the square constructed on it will be four times larger than the other?"

"Yes!" slaves and freemen chanted merrily.

"Now then," Socrates said, "I ask you all, did I put any knowledge into the mind of this Mysian or in your minds that was not already there?"

"No," answered a broom vendor, "but your questions made us think."

"And have you heard me give any answers?"

"Truly, we have not."

"May we say, then, that I merely helped this slave extract knowledge that was already in him?"

"So it was, by Heracles!"

"So, then, may we further say that from this day on I am a midwife of souls, just as my mother Phaenarete is a midwife of bellies?"

The people of Athens laughed. What will he think of next, this son of Sophroniscus the sculptor?

1 1

RUMOR AND UNCERTAINTY had seized the City. Enthralled by his warlock's eyes, screaming for communion with Dionysus or Sabazius or with Cybele—no one really knew—the women reenacted the fierce Carnivals of Thessaly, going to the extreme, unheard of in Attica, of sacrificing, tooth and nail, Polybius's bull out in the Athmonia district, and gorging themselves on the blood that flowed from its neck while the animal was still bellowing. To increase their enthousiasmos, they sacked the wine stocks of Marathon and ate three goats (two nannies and one billy) belonging to Philodemus of Probalinthus and, something never before seen, not even in the fierce Boeotian carnivals, they had communion by the mediation of the fat mosquitoes of Tricorythos, where, under the beggar's spell, they licked the squashed blood off each other's bodies.

"Impiety against Athena in the middle of the Scirophorian festival," exclaimed the Great Priestess.

King Archon was asked to get to the bottom of the events,

punish those who were guilty of sacrilege, and purify the territory.

The investigations carried out by his officials revealed that on the first day of the festivities, a group of Scirophoriants with veiled faces and covered heads had gone to the little altar to Georgian Athena on Mount Pentelikon. And that the rich horse merchant Polybius, Agathon's son, who at that moment was involved in refereeing a quail fight, approached the road's edge together with the others to get a closer look at the faceless women. Three witnesses could swear that Polybius never returned to the betting. They saw him going toward his grove accompanied by a stranger. Soon, his wife was asking him where he was going with their stud bull; he answered that he was going to service a cow. When he failed to return by dawn of the next day, his family and friends went out to look for him. They found him asleep under an oak on Mount Pentelikon. He could remember nothing that had happened the day before. When the animal turned up completely mauled, he denied he had led him out of the pen.

The investigation also revealed that at dawn of the same day, after his masters had left for their ceremonies in the City, Procles, slave of Demetrius in Marathon, allowed a metragyrtes and the said group of Scirophoriants to load a mule with five full skins of wine. And that the said slave Procles, who for twenty years had been an honest husbander, was crying and could not understand why he had been so foolish. He could not remember the events nor the people who arrived at his master's farm, but said people had been seen by Eusebius, the coal merchant, a neighbor who, having recognized Demetrius's mule, clearly saw the said metragyrtes and described him as a tall, thin man with long red hair.

Further investigation revealed that it was none other than the beggar of Cybele, who had been seen for several days in

Piraeus with his colored robes and later wandering about Mount Cithaeron.

The King's Court decreed that the wizard, spellbinder of freemen and slaves and, almost certainly, the instigator of the seven faceless women, was guilty of theft and rustling and of a horrendous impiety against Athena by desecrating the Scirophorian festivities, pretending to honor her with hymns and white parasols as a pretext for celebrating barbarous rites in the forest.

It further decreed that the pestiferous metragyrtes, whose very presence contaminated the territory with death, should be hunted down with Molossian dogs. And so he was hunted for many days during the month of Scirophorion, until two woodsmen on the border, duly sworn-in freemen, testified that they had seen him coming down the far side of Cithaeron, quite a way into Boeotian territory and about three stadia from Attica.

88

The impious offender gone, the priests of Athena were mollified. The territory was pure again.

So? You have reason to be satisfied, oh, Atys of Pamphylia? Were your days in Attica not fruitful? The effigy in the metroon had her eyes, as promised. You had performed seven perfect communions with the three sacred fluids. And you even had the perfect mystic cement of hot blood! Certainly the Gods themselves inspired that communion in the swamps, with human blood, so pleasant to Dionysus Omestes, the blood that the seven novices of the Sum licked off each other's flesh.

They were perfect communions.

Yes, you were satisfied, oh, Summoner of the Sum.

The day before, while all Athens was hunting you with dogs, a voice had ordered you to return to that gorge where the Great Mother of the Gods had appeared to you in dreams. It was the Holy Triad, instilled already in your soul, that was calling you.

Had the time come for you to be ordained?

Undoubtedly. There could be no better place for such a lofty investiture than that gorge, where the night winds sang their hymns. You were obediently on your way. Upon arriving you would lay yourself on the same slab, in the cave by the ravine. You would sleep watching the tossing vultures. Then, as soon as you felt your soul heavy with grace and your thoughts whetted by astute guides, you would return to found your New Church. How wise the Sum was! They were calling you to your first sanctuary, not only to anoint you but to make time for the Athenians to calm down and forget the metragyrtes. You too wanted to forget him.

Your Protopriestess had promised to get you new clothes. You asked her for a white robe, a green one, a red one like the one you used in Paphos, and a blue one to be able to officiate in single, but alternating, colors.

And you were going, oh, Summoner of the Sum, through the fields of Boeotia, toward the wind Boreas, heading for the gorge.

Gorge?

Just a gorge?

No. Such a sacred place, where the doors to the sacred dreams had been opened for you, had to be remembered with higher sounding words. You would decree that in prayers and hymns to the Sum it should be referred to by a more beautiful name, by an onoma kallion. The Portals of the Dream? Yes, a very beautiful onoma. And in Greekish: hai Pylai ton Hypnon? Oh, Gods, how beautiful that would sound when you said it in your bass voice during the rituals! And you walked many stadia. Farsangs you walked listening to hai Pylai ton Hypnon, reverberating with an echo of drums.

89

And why did it sound so fine to you now, the Greek, when a few months back you hated to have to speak it? Why, huh? Might the Gods have instilled it in you to fulfill your pastoral needs? The Portals of the Dream. Many times you had repeated your discovery during your trips; you had repeated it in Lydian, Phrygian, Pamphylian, Carian, Mysian, Scythian, Persian, Egyptian, Babylonian, but in no language of the inhabited Earth did it sound as full as hai Pylai ton Hypnon, popoPOM. Right there you decided that each time the rhythmic name of the Portals of the Dream was mentioned during the religious services, a copper kettle drum would beat: popoPOM. Or better still: poPOpom popoPOM.

So you were happy then, oh, Summoner of the Sum?

You had eaten nothing for the last three days. Your pouch was as empty as your stomach. But you were satisfied. You were nourished by the power of three Gods fused into one. There would be no King Archon or Scythians or Molossians to stand in the way of your return, fully ordained and ready to found the ecumenical church of the Sum. You were happy, poPOpom popoPOM.

1 2

ANEMOS DID NOT HAVE a single spot on his
white coat. Anytus had paid an exorbitant price for him
just to fulfill one of Alcibiades's whims. And against that single
stallion, Aristarchus was betting every last animal in his
Thessalian stables.

"The I-I-Ionian will take the necklace to the banquet,"
Alcibiades insisted.

Aristarchus challenged him to raise the stakes if he was so
sure.

And what would Aristarchus bet against twenty amphorae
of holy oil?

"Two of my Laconian dogs."

"Not en-n-nough."

"Three dogs, then."

"Not enough."

"The whole Laconian pack, by Artemis!"

Aristarchus was certain that Alcibiades would never see

the Ionian again. The business with the necklace was pure braggadocio.

It was midday when they got to Euphrosyne's house. Aristarchus's father was giving a banquet for the ephebi at his concubine's place.

Alcibiades gave his horse to the groom and ordered him to wash the mud off his legs.

"No one can say you're not honest," mocked Aristarchus. "I see you're getting ready to lose cleanly."

Alcibiades paid no attention. He looked into the silver mirror Phanes carried for him to check the rouge on his lips and cheeks, as well as his ribbons, of which he had used a great many to hide the shearing he had gotten in the river.

A few moments later, on fifteen couches, the ephebi and other guests awaited in the andron for the first tables to be ordered in.

Just then a hoarse barking from the street made Aristarchus shudder. That was Lysis's monster. He noticed a smile crossing Alcibiades's face. Good-bye, Thessalian stables! Good-bye, Aristarchus's Laconian pack!

A slave announced that Lysis of Miletus was at the door calling for the son of Clinias.

Make way for the most b-b-beautiful flutist in Athens!

But the slave returned, saying that she was waiting for him in the courtyard.

Aristarchus got his breath back. As Alcibiades had his sandals put on and then walked out of the room dragging the corner of his pink himation, Aristarchus speculated. Maybe the Ionian had not gotten the necklace. Could she be afraid that Alcibiades would mistreat her in public for having failed? Had she come to propose an extension? To apologize? Or did the little fox intend to participate anyway in the banquet and festivities that invariably followed the beautiful Cliniad like the tail on a shooting star?

But no. Alcibiades returned with Lysis, holding her around the waist. She approached, her gait proud, her countenance serene, accompanied by whispers of praise as they entered the oval and sat on a couch.

Aristarchus ignored the woman, but stared askance at Alcibiades and, arching his eyebrows: "Well?"

"The Gods have taken your side," Alcibiades began, while a slave took off his sandals, but he was interrupted by the entry of the first tables. The applause was an explosion.

Alcibiades had the place of honor, on the couch of honor. Aristarchus had his back to the center of the oval, but as winner of the wager, he showered the girl with praise: Please take a seat. What did the beautiful lady need? What were the symposium queen's orders?

Oh, what a wonderful day he was going to have tomorrow trotting the white stallion in front of Anytus's house! Did the Ionian know she had gotten him the finest stallion in Athens and twenty amphorae?

She made herself comfortable on her side, next to Alcibiades. Aristarchus could see her delectable pink flesh. The succulent legs he would be playing with that night! Oh, yes! Night of the androgynae.

Alcibiades seemed to have absorbed the blow with a great deal of sophrosyne. How noble! His friendship with Socrates had certainly taught him something. Undoubtedly a good loser, this Cliniad. Well, well, well! The day was certainly getting better.

There were another eleven ephebi present, and all of them

were hanging on Alcibiades's every word. They envied him the Ionian.

Two elegant hetaerae awaited outside the oval. They knew Lysis and would spread her success. There were certainly very few in Athens who could claim having lain between two perfectly sober aristocrats at the very beginning of a banquet. And there she was, so proud of Alcibiades and of belonging to that world where anyone could boast of great wealth, fine dogs, teams of horses, victorious ancestors, and trophies of the Panathenian, Olympic, Pythian, Isthmian, and Nemean Games.

When she had proven that she did fit in, that she knew how to behave like the good and the beautiful, because she was their equal, she yielded to the Delphic commandment to avoid excess, and midway through the first tables she rose to caress Alcibiades and serve him delicate morsels bitten off with her own mouth.

94

After the libations and the singing of the paean, the musicians and acrobats were called in. Alcibiades nominated himself symposiarch and was accepted, despite the presence of much older and more prestigious participants. Once in character, he ordered the slaves to put very little water in the wine and ordered two full-chalice, single-draft rounds.

As a member of the oval, Lysis also had to gulp down the twin cotyle rounds. But before the symposiants could plunge into the joys of the second tables, Alcibiades, absolute center of the banquet now, delivered a perfect prose encomium, following the fashion imposed by the sophists at the time; dedicated it to the ever-faithful Lysis of Miletus, who had given him excellent proof of her love; and, turning on Aristarchus with a deprecating smile, proceeded to extract, from among the folds of his robe, Truncheon's necklace.

He jumped to the floor barefoot and began to strut among the couches, imitating the airs of a courtesan. They applauded. Everyone wanted a closer look at the necklace the whole City coveted. The name of Eulalia of Ephesus was heard in the andron, and the older guests recalled the distichs of a resentful lover who had accused her of being the Cyclopean truncheon lurking behind mermaid songs. Aristarchus's father wanted Euphrosyne to wear the necklace, but Alcibiades refused. He wanted to be the only one in the City about whom it might later be said that he had worn Truncheon's necklace on his chest. Let all recall and tell of his feat.

The buffoon who arrived with the acrobats crowned Alcibiades with a wreath of myrtle, and Philocles, victor in the Dionysiae, improvised a comic epinicium to the illustrious champion in the battles of Aphrodite, oh, son of Clinias, whose arts won him the necklace that was inaccessible to Callias's talents.

In his advanced state of drunkenness, Aristarchus moaned and another ephebus tried to console him. What good were the horses and the dogs during the two years of their epheby? Away in their quarters, no one could enjoy them. And Alcibiades joined in, magnanimous, telling him everything that he had belonged to both, and kissing him and caressing his hair, and assuring him. The horses would remain at his father's estate, and the dogs, and he could use them as if they were his. And Aristarchus, sobbing, so why, then, why the lie about the Gods being on his side?

"They were on your side at the Panath-th-thenian wrestling matches," Alcibiades interrupted, wiping his tears with the corner of his himation, "but they abandoned you in the wager. That's what I was going to tell you."

And he stuttered another round and another encomium for his beloved Aristarchus, who was already drooling out of the corners of his mouth and practically dragging his eyelids. And Alcibiades insisting, let's have greater praise for Aristarchus's father and for their lovely hostess, of course. And then he prayed to Ares to favor him in the defense of his country, invoked the heroes of Marathon and Salamis, and drank a toast to his father, who fell heroically at Coronea.

Once the speeches were over, the hostess asked to hear the Miletian, whose flute was famous in all Athens.

Lysis sat on a great chair, barefoot, her ankles crossed on the seat.

Alcibiades let her hair down.

She tilted her head when she played. She rocked her shoulders, knit her brow, arched her eyebrows, and breathed in, smiling, while her face interpreted the melodies or marked the beat of the rhythms. Sometimes she would bend slightly at the waist, and her hair, as it billowed, perfumed the room with lavender.

Alcibiades loosened the brooch that held her peplus, which opened down to the waist. She listened to herself, her eyes turned upward, and her pink breasts could not be indifferent to the music.

Desire reigned in the andron. The absolute silence of the listeners was her greatest ovation.

Alcibiades began to withdraw; the symposiants, bewitched by the music and the nude, never saw him enter the atrium, where he signaled to Phanes. Quickly! Egghead was to bring him ink, a quill, and p-p-papyrus.

When Lysis recovered from her music amid applause and ovations, she noticed that Alcibiades was not wearing the necklace. He assured her that it was in a safe place. The drunken guests played cottabos and then blind-man's bluff. In payment of a forfeit, Lysis had to dance with one of the contracted girls. They were to represent an act of love between women, in Phrygian rhythm accompanied by flute and timbrel.

This would be a fine occasion to test the magic wine the Green-grocer had taken her. She had already given it to several of Truncheon's pornai slaves and nothing had happened to them. She stepped out by herself with the pretext that before dancing she wanted to make a brief devotional to Aphrodite at the altar in the courtyard. She asked Otep for the lekythos she had instructed him to store in his knapsack and drank it down to the last drop, just the way Talthybia had told her.

She had hardly gotten back to the andron when she began to feel bubbles in her blood and a sweet tickling sensation creeping up her legs.

Upon seeing the nude girl, she felt desire. They danced, brushed against each other, and finally, without touching the girl or herself, Lysis felt an irresistible trepidation in her legs. By Cypris, how her ass was quivering. Never had she experienced anything like it; transfixed with lust, she leaned her forehead and both hands against a wall and had the most incredible orgasm, standing there, which tore from her a deep, prolonged sigh. Just then the staring symposiants saw Alcibiades jump from the couch, make his way barefoot to Lysis, and carry her away in his arms.

97

He took her to the room where Aristarchus was sleeping off his wine. He wanted to possess her immediately, no preludes, just elementary fire. Yes, he wanted her like a woman, but in the hippopornos position, right now, and she, from the moment she awoke from her orgasm, had begun to taste the ominous bitterness in her mouth that announced another seizure of her disease.

By the Two Goddesses, what was she to do now? Oh, let

Cypris prevent her lover from seeing her all twisted and drooling! She had to get away from him under any pretext. She had to leave immediately.

Then she asked him to turn around. Yes, they would do the hippopornos, but first a surprise, come now, Alcibiades was to turn around, quickly, so that he could feel an Ionian caress, Asiatic love, the secrets of the initiates in the mysteries of the Callipygous Goddess, but with preliminaries that the beneficiary was not allowed to see, so come, come, turn around, one, two, silence, and although Alcibiades was aching to discharge everything he had in him, he held back, yielding to the promise of new sensations.

The Miletian had unexpectedly become a coveted morsel. Having discovered her gift, he regretted the time he had wasted during the previous nights.

Why didn't she quiver that way with him? What was the secret of the trembling? Aristarchus would have to wait. He was not to have her that night, either. Perhaps never. He was lamenting having sent Phanes with that note. But why was Lysis taking so long?

Lysis was running to beat her malady. The muzzled monster followed close behind. Otep pushed ahead with a torch, making way down a shortcut over goat paths. There were a good seven stadia from Euphrosyne's house to the Ceramicus. Lysis felt easier now. If the crisis seized her along the way, Otep would know what to do. He had his instructions. And down on the plain, that old panic. After a long absence, she was again hearing Hecate's horrendous beating under the grass. Had Aphrodite forsaken her? Was she being punished for not having mastered Alcibiades? Could it be the potion?

When she got to Truncheon's door, her saliva was profuse

and bitter as gall. Otep went in first and found Evardis, who was serving at the banquet, while he, as always when his mistress was stricken with the disease from above, stood guard with the dog in the courtyard, at her door. If she should happen to make noises, he would sic the monster to a fit of thunderous barking. That would also get rid of any slaves who might be in the vicinity.

Evardis cleared a corner, spread a cloak on the floor, and went out for cloths and water.

When Lysis began to feel the pressure of her thumb on her index finger, she turned on her back, paralyzed by the three blows that kept growing louder and louder. Hecate was calling her again! Would she die? Would Cypris turn her over to the furious call of the underworld? The pain was already making her arm stiff, raising it. The brutal contraction continued unabated. And then with her eyes and muscles gone wild, all control of her sphincter lost, the three fingers up straight, arched on the points of her heels and elbows, her jaws locked, she lost consciousness.

When Lysis was finally able to open her mouth, Evardis dried her lips, which tasted like blood; she dried the urine from her legs and gave her water steeped in fennel. The girl drank with her eyes closed and fell asleep.

When she awoke, the sun was high. Truncheon was smoothing her hair and whispering her love. Lysis raised her heavy eyelids.

What time was it? Late, no doubt! Truncheon was already made up and wearing her necklace.

Lysis sat up with a start, her face tense. By Pandemos! Had it all been a dream, then?

No, it had not been a dream.

While Lysis was still at Euphrosyne's, a package containing the necklace had arrived at the house. The slave also delivered this note from Alcibiades to Truncheon.

Lysis read: "I have already enjoyed your necklace. There you have it. Tomorrow you'll have your lover."

1 3

EVERYTHING ABOUT YOU is hypothesis," Theopompus of Lampsacus had told her one day.

At first, she hated the name; it suggested something like hypothecation.

He laughed with his beautiful dark eyes and cradled her head in the crook of his arm.

"Don't we call the tripod that sustains an amphora a hypothesis, and the foundations of buildings, and the assumptions on which we build theorems?"

She nodded, not really understanding what any of that had to do with her.

"Don't we call that which sustains anything a hypothesis?"

She nodded again.

"And when you feed me and house me, aren't you sustaining my body?"

She smiled.

"And doesn't your belaureled ass sustain my soul?"

Touched by his flattery, that afternoon she eagerly took the face-down position, the way he liked it. She wanted to feel all his weight on her. And she no longer objected to the celebrated geometrician and poet's spreading among the friends of the night an Alcaic strophe that became so famous that it consecrated her nickname in the City forever.

Theopompus was beautiful. His words were caresses. Living with him was a boon and an education. But one day he left. He promised to return but never did. The only thing he ever left her was the name Hypothesis. He had even gotten her in trouble with the authorities when word got around that he was a spy for the Persians. It was only her callipygian beauty that saved her. Having been crowned shortly before that, she was very much coveted by the libertines of the City, among whom were many influential men who took it upon themselves to help her. Her triumph had been quite an event. No one had considered her among the favorites because it was a foregone conclusion that no Athenian could compete in those dance festivals so utterly monopolized by Orientals, Ionians, and Lesbians. Who could imagine that a howler like her would one day be among the most expensive hetaerae of the Ceramicus?

Having been left an orphan at a very early age, Hypothesis barely got along as a beggar child. No sooner had her breasts budded than she began to make nighttime forays to the Heroes' Graveyard. While her village slept, she would steal among the shadows of the Sacred Way, down very close to Dipylum, and there she would begin her howling. There were many Athenian free-women who dared not show themselves in the City and resorted to howling. In the black of the night, the howls attracted the clients, who for two obols fornicated blind, on their feet or on the grass between the tombs. The future Hypothesis survived that way for a few months, but one moonlit night she was recognized by a farmer who rushed back to the village with his tale. She was sentenced to loss of civil rights and banished forever from her deme.

When she was no longer compelled to howl among the shadows of the tombs, she hired herself out for a while to a whorehouse in Piraeus. There she learned the tricks and guiles she had never needed in the dark. And her adolescent bloom was glorious. An old Thessalian who sold cosmetics and love potions was so impressed with her rump that she told her she was wasting a treasure. She advised her to offer herself hippopornos. The sailors would pay anything to ride her.

So she did. She left the whorehouse and began to work the streets, where she tripled her income.

Her real success was yet to come, however, in the callipygous dances. Without any formal instruction, purely on the strength of her beautiful ass, she began to dance naked, quite without pretensions. But they soon began to applaud her, and someone always showed up who was willing to pay to see her dance.

"She has the gift," an old Miletian dancer said.

It was not long before she had acquired a certain reputation in Piraeus, although she was still quite far from being able to compete with the queens of the City. She still had to learn technique, develop cunning and fantasy. The Thessalian witch told her one night she should compete in the Haloan festival. Hypothesis supposed she would never be accepted. No streetwalker from Piraeus could hope to win in a festival where the glorious dancers of the Ceramicus were competing. But a sincere fervor and the desire to honor Aphrodite Sweet-Rump drove her to the Temple of Solon. When she came on, she forgot about the contest and danced inwardly, for the Goddess who had entered her body.

103

When she was told that she had been admitted, she indulged in a mute joy. That was the first time she had ever felt important. She, the howler-child, the one who had never had a teacher, she was going to dance for the Goddess among the chosen. Her joy became gratitude and, ultimately, an enthousiasmos that made her tremble with lust.

She won. The rich wanted to see her; they invited her to their banquets; and Hypothesis's rump won her the promised treasures.

She gave the Thessalian hag who had advised her to compete a hundred drachmas and put her to work as her doorkeeper. She took a house in the City and was generous and kind.

Three years later, she again entered the Haloan festival dances. In the meantime, after a very long search, her doorkeeper witch had finally found storm mushrooms up on Mount Cithaeron, the same kind that she used in Thessaly to make her secret powders. She prepared a wine with the powders and gave some to Hypothesis to drink just before going into the temple. When the first roll of the Phrygian beat broke the stillness, her body was no longer mortal, perishable flesh, but Pandemos's very own divine sinew and marrow.

No other hetaera had ever won the coveted honor twice. From that day on, despite her ignorance and uncouth manners, she became one of the hetaera queens. During almost four years, she lived amid abundance and honors. But meteoric and unexpected as her rise to the summit had been, her fall into oblivion was even faster.

Some time during her second reign, she thoroughly fleeced a mattress-maker. She had made him sell his five carder slaves, his tools, his shop, and even his house in the City. When she had finally left him without a single obol, she locked him out of her house and told him to forget about her.

Ruined and insane with jealousy, the mattress-maker beat her practically to death and took the iron prongs of a carding comb to that marvelous ass of her perdition, depriving the world of its glory forever. "Not for me, not for anyone!" he screamed vengefully.

"She went too far," the ladies of the trade commented.

The only things she was able to salvage from the wreck of her career as a professional were three household slaves, which she rented out to a whorehouse. Her callipygian splendor was ruined. Without those beautiful upper thighs, she lost her affluent clientele. She returned to the docks and went on practicing her trade on her back, but it took her a month of hard work to make what she used to get in a single night in her days of glory.

Soon, she was not even able to do that. New evils forced her to retire altogether. Ever since the beating, she had been suffering terrible migraines, and too much wine caused her to have extemporaneous lapses of urinary and sphincter control. To top it off, a bunch of drunken ruffians had brawled one night down in Piraeus and had somehow bashed her teeth out, those very teeth that would have done so much now for her physical appearance on the way to Truncheon's house. She no longer had the Summoner of the Sum with her to convince Lysis of Miletus. Oh! The ingrate had never returned, and he had completely ruined her, living in her house and eating and drinking with the seven women he had instructed in the mysteries of the New Church before leaving to ravage the countryside. To make him comfortable and pay for his whims, Hypothesis had evicted the mule-skinner she had taken on as a boarder, sold the last two slaves she had left, and, finally, mortgaged her house to be able to buy him the robes for his priesthood. He should have been back a month ago. He had induced her to spend without a care and promised to mend everything as soon as he got back.

He was going to persuade the flutist and put her in Hypothesis's hands. Oh, the sweet liar! Just like with Theopompus, the handsome and virtuous lover, when she was with Alcibiades she forgot her migraine and found the courage to face life like a beautiful adventure.

Her first payment on the mortgage was a day overdue. Pasion, the banker, had lent her three hundred drachmas, which she was to return with interest in four quarterly payments of ninety-five drachmas each. And all Hypothesis had were the six obols she had used to pay for the wine of her latest binge. It was four days since she had eaten or left her house or even had the desire to go on living. The only valuables she had left were the robes she had had made for the Summoner of the Sum. Anyone would give her forty drachmas for them, but she still nurtured the hope of seeing him return and did not dare sell them. Ah, but late that night she had come to a decision. Pasion had given her a three-day extension on her mortgage payment, after which he would foreclose on her house. Hopelessness had given her courage: she would go and see Lysis of Miletus. Yes! She would overcome her fear of scaring the girl with her awful appearance. In any case, her destiny was already mapped out by the Gods. Nothing she could do would change that. The only thing to do was to face it, whatever it may be, without delay. If she could get the Ionian to accept, she would ask her for an advance with which to pay the banker. If she failed, she would sell the Summoner's robes, buy wine and food, lock herself in her house, and have a solitary feast for her two remaining days. Before the dawn of the day of foreclosure, she would finish off the last barrel and go to spend the rest of her days, which she hoped would be few, together with the destitute whores who begged alms in the vicinity of Aphrodite's Temple. She no longer had the strength to walk from whorehouse to whorehouse. That miserable life was simply not worth the effort. Let the spool of her Moera run out once and for all. Let the end of the thread appear and be done with it.

Before the sun had risen, while she was still under the effects of the wine, she had thought this alternative out carefully; but now, with the sun high over the horizon, approaching Truncheon's house and seeing the look the doorkeeper gave her, she realized that she was seriously lacking in courage, youth, and teeth. She recalled that she had sent Talthybia with the mushroom wine for Lysis days ago and had received no reply. Again she was beset by the fear of rejection. Oh, the Summoner of the Sum had abandoned her!

1 4

LYSIS SLEPT ALL DAY AND ALL NIGHT and awoke a little before dawn on the next day. Her body was racked with pain, much more than on other occasions, especially her hands, which had been twisted back during the whole of the crisis.

Truncheon had not gone to the banquet that night to be by her side. When she heard her sob, she turned up the oil lamp, brought her closer, and began to stroke her hair and dry her eyes.

"The three fingers . . . the three blows, oh, Hecate again," Lysis sobbed.

Truncheon knew what was coming and was resigned. It would do no good to console her until she had cried out all her terror. Even when she was going through her most optimistic periods, hearing the three blows during a crisis and feeling the pain in her fingers plunged her into inconsolable anguish. There had been times when she had cried for a whole day. It was useless to try to calm her. Her confounded obsession would not let her see beyond her own terror. And so she went through her pitiful monologue once again and finally fell asleep toward the end of the afternoon.

She woke up the next day with the morning sun quite high. Some color had returned to her face, and her gaze was fixed. The pain in her hand had died down.

When Truncheon approached, she asked to see Alcibiades's note again.

Truncheon passed her the note and she read out loud, "I have already enjoyed your necklace. There you have it. Tomorrow you'll have your lover."

She hung her head. After Alcibiades had obtained and shown off Truncheon's necklace, he had mocked her, scorned her. It was all too clear. She was in Hecate's hands now. Aphrodite had abandoned her because she had not only failed to humiliate Alcibiades, but had been humiliated by him, and by now the whole City must know of it.

"It's not true," Truncheon said calmly.

"I wasn't able to beat Alcibiades." She shook again, on the brink of tears.

"Nonsense, Alcibiades is wounded." Lysis looked up at her from under her eyelids. "He's desperate to see you."

"I wish that were true," Lysis muttered.

"Have I ever lied to you?"

"You don't know," Lysis sobbed, and turned away.

Truncheon waited for the tide to ebb.

"Otep told me about the dance," she smiled. "And I also know that you left Alcibiades standing there in a rage of passion."

Lysis stopped her sobbing and turned to look into her eyes.

Truncheon kissed her tears away and waited for her question. "How did Otep know about that?"

109

"Alcibiades told me."

"Did you go to see him?"

"No," she said smiling. "He came here."

Lysis felt a pang of fear. Despite her weakness, she raised herself up on her elbow and color rushed into her cheeks. Could it be true? What did the fiend want? To make more fun of her? Oh, by the Two Goddesses, would nothing ever free her from his spell?

"You've wounded him," Truncheon continued. "He hasn't been able to get you out of his mind since the moment he saw you dance."

"What did he say?"

"That he loves you; that he's sorry about the note; that he had intended it as a joke, but that after seeing you dance, he realized that he had never wanted anyone more than you. And now he is willing to swear you an oath."

"Are you telling me the truth?" Lysis begged, desperation in her eyes. All the pain drained from her body and she sat up on the bed.

"He's wounded," Truncheon continued.

"So what did you tell him?"

"That you were not going to receive him; that you were exhausted. Then he demanded to peek into your room to make certain that there was no one with you."

"Ohhhhh! Then Aphrodite . . ."

". . . has not abandoned you," Truncheon completed. "Quite the contrary, to protect you from him, she inspired your dance and then showed you just how perverse he is."

Lysis thought that the Goddess had, in any case, inspired her to drink Talthybia's wine. She recalled the tingling in her legs, the veiled pink color that had invaded the other dancer's body, the exacerbation of smells, the music exploding in her vagina, the tautness of her thighs, Alcibiades's savage urgency after the dance.

"And the whole City is gossiping about how you left him standing there; his friends have told everyone. And they keep talking about your dance . . . never before seen . . . you're unique . . . you've humiliated him."

Lysis let Truncheon embrace her and stroke her hair.

Oh, that wine Talthybia had brought her! She would always have a barrel of that most blessed of wines with her.

And Truncheon going on about how Alcibiades was trapped, beset by jealousy and uncertainty; she had seen him with her own eyes; Lysis had fulfilled her promise to the Goddess; Alcibiades was certainly the victim, crushed; Lysis could use him as her doormat; she could force him to humiliate himself at the Ceramicus wall; he was in her hands.

And Lysis, with the help of Pandemos, would not go on wanting to be his concubine. Now she just wanted the Goddess to help her wipe him forever from her heart, and as soon as she felt out of danger, she would make him pay for the infamy of the note with unspeakable suffering.

Just then, Evardis came in announcing that a certain Hypothesis was asking for Lysis.

"What business can that piss-smeared witch possibly have with Lysis?" Truncheon exploded.

"She says she was sent by Talthybia, the vegetable vendor."

"Tell her to go away," Truncheon ordered.

"No!" Lysis screamed, jumping to her feet unaided. "Have her come into the courtyard."

15

SO THEN, A YOUNG SLAVE was worth about two hundred drachmas in Athens. Mysians, Lydians, Carians, and Phrygians cost a bit less, because they were so lazy. Armenians and Aethiopes were also cheap, but because they were a risky investment, prone to disobedience and escaping. Syrians, Italics, Egyptians, Thracians, and others rarely brought more than two hundred drachmas in Aegean markets, unless they had some special talent that meant profit for the owner and only if they were apt for hard work on farms or in the mines.

For a Scythian slave, however, the Athenian State paid eight hundred drachmas. If he was tall and a good archer, up to fifteen minae.

Their sinewy arms could pull a bow string back to the ear and hit a target at inhuman distances. Their eyes, long accustomed to boreal hazes, could see everything much more clearly and up close in the bright light of Attica. Scythians could put a whole quiver into the forehead of a decoy a plethrum and a half away.

There was one who thoroughly impressed Athens with his marksmanship. Cratinus, the author of comedies, gave him the name Pandarus in praise, and it stuck. He had reached the heights of fame on the plains of Marathon when the City was sacrificing five hundred goats to thank Artemis for their victory over the Persians. Before the amazed crowd, Pandarus perforated twelve goat bladders from a distance of three hundred feet.

The first two bull's-eyes produced comments of approval. They were followed by increasingly loud applause and foot stamping until each successive bull's-eye unleashed indecorous ovations that were practically irreverent, considering the occasion. And it came to pass that first the ephebi, then the hoplites that had formed for the parade, broke their syntax, left their flags and banners unattended, and crowded in to make sure they did not miss the final arrow. Amid an almost unearthly silence, broken only by the rustle of the cedars on Mount Pentelikon, Pandarus skewered his twelfth bladder. Pandemonium!

Children, eupatrids, hags, and everyone within reach wanted to see the Scythian up close and, forgetting all their composure, called out to him, favorite of Apollo, chosen one, divine far-seer, forgetting that Pandarus was not a freeman or an Olympic champion, and while the strategi and priests of Artemis appealed for religious respect, the Scythian defended himself brusquely from the admiring throng that was trying to carry him on their shoulders. He was not very much inclined to being handled.

Scythians had their own way of thinking. They had their rules and they were anything but gregarious. The only things that moved them were military victories and favorable incarnations. Some of them, when taken as slaves, committed suicide out of homesickness for their steppes. When the Athenians began to buy them to use them as guardians of the City, the Scythians accepted that. As they saw it, that was not slavery at all. Slavery was toiling in the mines, tilling the soil, or stirring another man's milk. In their own country, beyond the Borysthenes, they imposed serious hardships on their war prisoners. During the winter they had them take turns all day and night stirring their mare's milk to keep it from freezing. And to keep them from running away or getting dizzy from walking around the immense community cauldrons with their stirring sticks, they gouged their eyes out.

So then, what were the humiliations and torments the Scythians had to put up with in the City? None at all! Therefore, they were not slaves. Working as a guardian for a powerful State was an honorable job for a warrior.

Athens, City of light, home of philosophers, rhetors, and artists, needed to employ barbarian guardians who would not notice a man's wealth, lineage, or knowledge when the time came to smack somebody in the agora or use the rope to herd in and mark fugitives from the call of the Assembly.

Athenians used to make fun of the broken Greek the Scythians spoke, but they were proud to have those huge men with almond eyes for guardians of the City. They liked to show visiting foreigners how compact their muscles were and explained that a Scythian hand falling on street rowdies weighed twice as much as a Greek hand. It was logical; if water got hard in winter, anyone could understand that someone from icy lands would need to have compact muscles to protect them from the cutting cold.

Thus had Herodotus taught the City.

The other virtue the Scythians had was their proverbial

calm. They considered fuss and irritation to be womanly things. They kept order in the City with their eyes; unruly Athenians either got themselves under control or took the blow from their hyperborean hands.

When he read his works in Athens, Herodotus said that, in all his travels throughout the inhabited Earth, he had never seen any other warriors like them. They could fight effectively even in retreat and no one had ever seen a Scythian troop break up. When Darius the Great, King of Kings, invaded their plains, they lost their patience and ravaged the confines of the Persian empire for twenty-eight years. Men who knew what war was about insisted that if all the Scythian tribes got together, they could certainly overwhelm the entire Ecumene.

Their worst defect was that they were great drinkers.

During the Archonship of Eutidemus, the Athenians had executed two Scythians. In a drunken stupor, they had climbed up to pee off the stairs of the Painted Portico, and there they had wagered to see who could hit Solon's statue in the head.

It was a well-known fact that in their home in Scythia they loved to drink rye wine, which they sometimes mixed with fermented mare's milk. Anyone who needed proof could merely look at Cleomenes, the Spartan king who had so many dealings with the Scythian nomads with whom he had banded against Darius that he decided to beat them at drinking, deteriorating from Scythian drunk to ridiculous fool in no time.

Following the execution of the profaners, the Assembly was going to pass the death penalty for any Scythian who got drunk, but Pericles proposed that only "public" drunkenness be punished. An absolute prohibition would have led to rioting. He also proposed that, out behind the Areopagus hill, in back of the barracks, an area be fenced in for Scythians themselves to bring women and drink to the ground. The place was so far out of the way that no one could be bothered by their Scythian carousing. A short time later, Pericles gave them thirty lactating mares they could milk without having to blow on their vulvas through a reed to get them to lower their cold-shrunken udders.

Following the capture of Samos, he got the people of Athens to pass a law giving any Scythian over sixty-five his freedom and residence in Athens with the rights of a resident foreigner, as long as his name did not appear on the list of transgressors.

Of the thirty who had already retired during the Archonship of Crates, a few got into breeding and training Molossian hounds. Athenians knew that they were handy with the animals and bought them ready trained. It came as no surprise to anyone that these warlike people should get along so well with Ares's favorite animals. They became good friends at the border posts, mines, and jails of Attica. When they were sent out for runaway slaves, they hunted them down without any barking or fuss at all.

And during that summer in the Archonship of Crates, Scythians and Molossians raked every coast, forest, mountain, cave, and swamp, trying to find the beggar of the Goddess.

16

HYPOTHESIS HARDLY HAD to say anything at all. Lysis immediately believed her dream. So Aphrodite wanted her to become her Queen Sweet-Rump. There was no doubt that this woman, with her notorious crafts and her strong wine, would lead her to victory. Wasn't it a toothless, ragged hag who used to bring happiness to mortals in the old myths?

There were only twelve days to go before the Haloan festival.

Lysis could already feel the crown on her head. With her unexpected teacher, dancer, and witch, she would soon master all the secrets of the callipygous art. The next time Alcibiades saw one of her dances, he would fall flat on his face, submerged in abject humiliation. The conceited eupatrid would soon learn just whom he had come up against. The seducer would pay for the infamy of the note. Oh, sweet vengeance of a queen!

Truncheon was decidedly against it, but Lysis accepted taking her lessons at the hag's house and gave her the eighty-three drachmas she owed Passion the Trapezites for the first payment on her mortgage. She was very generous from the very beginning. How could she be otherwise with one sent by the Goddess? She gave her perfumes, a very expensive wig, new sandals, and two linen pepli of forgotten excellence.

Her instruction lasted eleven days. On the first, Hypothesis spoke very little; to hide her missing teeth, she spoke without moving her upper lip. It was hard to understand her. However, her first remarks and some of the steps she showed Lysis revealed good taste and great skill. When she danced there was something beautiful in her worn face, a nostalgic sensuality, something childlike, which she spoiled as soon as she attempted to speak with her stiff upper lip.

From the very first day at Truncheon's house, Lysis showered her with kindness and gratitude. Together they went before an effigy of Aphrodite Pandemos, where, without a moment's vacillation, Lysis swore to reward Hypothesis with three fifteen-year-old slaves if she were crowned in the Haloan dances. When Hypothesis was leaving to go home the first day, Lysis hung on her neck as if they had been old friends, and on all the following days, whenever they met or said good-bye, she would kiss her like a mother.

The only thing Lysis could not stand in her was that insufferable stiff lip. On the third day, piqued because she could not understand something Hypothesis was shouting, she had the music stop and began to answer with her mouth practically closed, her voice much too twangy and her eyes twisted into a grimace.

The jibe was so evident that even the flutist and the eunuch drummer began to laugh. Hypothesis, confused with shame, surprise, and fear of losing her pupil, could think of nothing better than to cover her face with her hands and break out crying.

At the sight of the old woman's distress, Lysis ran over to embrace her lovingly and began to kiss her face, saying, "There, there, now, let me see my witchy's little teethies now."

When she finally got Hypothesis to laugh, she took her hands from her face and forced her to show her toothless gums. Then she hugged her even more strongly and dismissed the musicians.

When Hypothesis calmed down completely, she told Lysis how she had lost her teeth and her callipygian beauty. Lysis wanted to see and made her take her clothes off. There was no doubt about it, when she was young and without the horrible laceration of her buttocks, that body must have been something quite extraordinary. There were no classes that afternoon. They remained naked under the hypaithron, talking. Lysis accepted Hypothesis's invitation to share an ewer of terrible Attic wine, but after a single draft, she dressed, took some money from her purse, and went to the door to send Otep for an amphora of Samos or Lesbos. When she returned to Hypothesis, she made her promise to give her all her lessons nude. Then she started combing the wig and making her up a bit. Hypothesis, her head light from the wine, said she was going to tell her a secret and asked her to play some Lydian airs on the flute very slowly. Then she began to dance.

Hypothesis no longer had any beauty to show off, nor did she have the agility of a young dancer. The first movements of those lacerated buttocks were frankly lamentable, but little by little, her silhouette, especially her face, took on a halo of bewitching lust. With every passing instant, the grotesque dance became more and more lubricious, and when it was over, Lysis felt like touching herself.

Hypothesis approached and with half-closed eyes and a hoarse voice began to reveal her secret: Before taking a single step, members and hips immobile, you had to get your lips dancing, then your tongue, and finally your dimples. That was where Lysis always had to seek her response to the first few beats of the music. The facial dance, if done with internal vibrations, would call down Pandemos, who once in possession, took care of the rest. That afternoon, the Goddess had outdone herself, to judge from Lysis's unexpected excitement. When she found herself privy to that secret weapon with which even a beaten old hag could revalidate her callipygian arts, Lysis knew she was really in favor with Pandemos. If not, why had she made her the beneficiary of such a lofty art? She took her teacher by the hand anxiously, dragged her to the bed, and, in an offering of gratitude to the Sweet-Rump Goddess, had herself kissed until she was spent.

Good wine and that unexpected twenty-year-old morsel instilled new life into Hypothesis. She was so proud to discover that her dancing could still rouse a young beauty. Would Cypris give her back her regal powers? But that night she was again lamenting her untimely fall from the summit.

In a show of sympathy, Lysis told her about her own misfortunes. She told her about her crises, about how she peed, sometimes even defecated, and she showed her how her jaw got stuck and her extremities became twisted. And what could be behind the three blows and the three stiff fingers, eh?

That was her greatest fear.

Hypothesis used to perform rites in the trivia and knew a little something about the mysteries of the underworld. Yes, Hecate was, in fact, after her, but she had nothing to worry about because so was Aphrodite. There was no doubt about that. And which of the two was more powerful?

No, Lysis had nothing to worry about. Besides, it was a known fact that the Goddess of the Three Heads never gave up those she had chosen and that was why she would, occasionally, reassure her through unequivocal signs. As long as Lysis was the favorite of Pandemos, all the Carrion-eater Goddess' efforts would be in vain.

Hypothesis was taking her seriously and frankly admitted that there was a threat from the underworld, something which Truncheon and Aspasia denied. She was thankful to Hypothesis for not trying to fool her and for recognizing the danger fearlessly. With Hypothesis's interpretation of her crises, plus the secret she had confided to her that afternoon, Lysis was able to sleep for the first time fully convinced that she would never have to do without the guidance of Aphrodite.

When Otep and the dog came back without Lysis, Truncheon was beside herself with anger. That was to be the beginning of a difficult period for them.

After the day of the facial dance, her lessons in the Cynosarges got even better. Naked, paying no mind to the remains of her once glorious rump, Hypothesis had nothing to hide now. She could speak out, holding back nothing, using her usual profanities and street talk. And her pupil was a sponge. She caught on to the subtleties instantly, and as soon as she mastered one step, she would improvise figurations on it. No one could have doubted that she had the gift. It was no wonder that Aphrodite had sent her that dream.

From the second day onward, Lysis had mastered the Lydian airs; before a week was up, her thighs and shoulders were as conversant with the Phrygian drums as a veteran's. Two days before the contest, Hypothesis gave her a draft of storm wine and checked the mobility of her face, her lascivious hands, and the undulating and spasmodic pelvis. Finally, with the mere guidance of a thought, her pupil's young perfect flesh trembled in a genuine orgasm. Hypothesis knew she had before her eyes the future Queen Sweet-Rump of Athens. No one could take that crown from her.

And yet, on the day of the contest, Hypothesis awoke fearful and depressed. The need to feign optimism required an effort that exacerbated her migraine, and to moderate her nerves, she had to drink ten cotyles of wine before breakfast.

When the eliminations began, thirty-six pairs of buttocks paraded without music before the effigy of Pandemos. Hypothesis had withdrawn to one of the corners. In her haversack she carried a skin of wine and a lekythos of crushed hemlock. Her life was in Cypris's hands. If she gave her pupil victory, Hypothesis would live in honor and happiness; if she denied it, Hypothesis would not leave Solon's Temple alive.

The judges, presided over by Euphemia Doright, chose twelve callipygians in the first elimination. Lysis of Miletus was one of them.

Uhf! Hypothesis tossed back another cotyle of wine and leaned against a column to let the beating of her heart slow down.

For the second round, a slow flute accompanied by triangle and castanets inspired the competitors to improvise the positions of statues or do individual imitations of lovemaking. Lysis found a sunbeam that filtered in through one of the temple skylights and caught it between her avid lips. Then, trembling, she ran it over her eyes and cheeks, down across her breasts, her belly button, over to her hips, and around to shine on her splendid buttocks, all to the beat of gracious representations of copulatory preludes.

She was the first to be named among the five finalists chosen.

In her corner, palms upturned, Hypothesis again prayed to the Goddess. She prayed for life like one who was condemned. Eyes brimming with tears, she recalled her years of devotion.

Didn't she deserve an honorable and peaceful old age? It was not in the Goddess' interest to let her die. If Lysis won, she would induce her to pay for luxurious sacrifices and statues.

Following Hypothesis's instructions, Lysis drank the Thessalian wine during the second intermission.

The big favorite that year was Daphne of Chios, a tall, blond twenty-year-old with the best shaped legs in the City and solid thighs and buttocks that she wielded with the art of an expert. Her closest rival in the temple was Mnemosyne the Cyrenian, a brunette whose body, viewed from the front, was the most perfect of all among the contestants and whose dancing rivaled Daphne's. But no one was discarding Mamahelpme or Helen the Lantern, the previous year's queen, who had a kind of evil beauty in her face and could stir up excitingly perverse enthousiasmos with her interpretation of the Phrygian beats.

Lysis of Miletus, despite having the most beautiful thighs and her very creative play with the sunbeam, was not considered among the contenders for the prize. Some of the courtesans who were up on all the local gossip had heard about her encounter with Alcibiades and were glad she had driven him wild, but the experts never thought of her as anything more than a talented amateur. Getting in among the finalists of the temple was victory enough for her. Even Truncheon had been tempted to take a bet with her at ten-to-one odds. But in the end, she turned it down; she could not imagine Lysis a serious contender against such stiff competition.

Only Hypothesis of Athens was betting on Lysis all she had, which was just her life. And the Moera had given her good odds, too: for her present misery and poverty, a life of serene leisure, moistened with the finest wines.

Halfway through the Lydian beat, Lysis began to feel the tingling again; shapes lost their contours, the colors of her sur-

123

roundings changed, and then, only then, as she had promised Hypothesis, before falling into the trance produced by the storm wine, she evoked that afternoon when Alcibiades had lain faceup on the padded deck of a chariot driven by Aristarchus over uneven terrain, and she, on her knees, riding him frontward, holding on to the side rails, flowing with every unpredictable swerve of the chariot, screaming and laughing with pleasure and surprise, discovering new and powerful sensations in her own body, and exploding, as the road rose to meet the forest, into the most all-embracing orgasm of her courtesan life. And now, in the temple, she felt the deep rumblings of the orgasm and held it back for the final chords; then, the contest forgotten, burning with desire, straddling Alcibiades, she danced for the Goddess that had taken her. When the Phrygian flutes broke in amid the screams and delirious drumming, her body was no longer hers, but an obedient instrument of Pandemos, all marrow and lustful sinew. And in the end, on her knees, hands high in the air, not touching any part of herself, holding on to invisible chariot rails, her back slightly arched in an impeccable callipygous position, the final quake erupted in her buttocks with an intensity never before seen in the Haloae. Her satisfied flesh rippled like the terse waters of a lake caressed by a breeze. All of her, from the back of her knees to her waist, was trembling, and all the greats of her guild, the servants of Aphrodite, knew: They knew that no one could make mortal flesh do that without the direct intervention of the Goddess.

Lysis of Miletus had proven to be one of the chosen.

Euphemia Doright had not seen anything like it since the times of Hypothesis of Athens. And long before the beats were ended, every eye in the Temple was fixed on Lysis's thighs. Finally, she threw her arms and breasts forward, and remained in a quadrapedal trance, smiling, kissing the imaginary face she held in her hands. She was the new Sweet-Rump Queen of Athens.

When Euphemia Doright proclaimed the verdict, Hypothesis cried on her quite empty wineskin. She noticed that her migraine was gone. This time, the wine was giving her a tingling sensation that moved all over her chest, hic, or was it her soul? Under her feet, the reverberating floor of the Temple of Solon applauded her victory. Hypothesis of Athens had just recovered the favor of the Goddess. Soon she would be solvent and respected in the City, and yet she cried, for the Summoner of the Sum had not returned. Why is it that mortals are always, hic, plagued by infinite desires?

PART II

SPRING

OF THE

ARCHON APSEUDES

17

XANTHUS THE LYCIAN did not have punishment marks to give him away. Except for the calluses on his hands and the close-cropped hair his master, The Bale, insisted on, Xanthus might very well pass for a freeman. And thanks to his upbringing in Ephesus and Samos, he spoke Greek as well as any of the locals.

He had decided to run away from Athens in mid-Scirophorion, before the end of the year.

On the approach to the Scythian outpost, he decided to take a detour along the side of the hill to circumvent a part of the trail that was rather badly overgrown with briars and burdock. It was there that the Gods saw fit to make him trip and thereby change the course of his life.

He stumbled down the side of the hill until he recovered his balance and, while climbing back up onto the trail, he saw, rolling through the grass and soft earth dug up by his fall, a violet-colored stone that came to rest at his very feet amid the stunted absinthe.

As he stooped down to pick up the stone, he noticed it had a black sun in the middle and immediately recalled the amethyst everyone had been talking about two months earlier.

He looked around to make sure he wasn't being watched.

Yes, it had to be the same one stolen from the Parthenon. He was certain. It was about the size and shape of a large hazelnut; the onyx or obsidian inlay in the middle gave it the appearance of an eye. Xanthus had never actually seen it, but people in the City talked of nothing else after the capture of that Macedonian accused of stealing the eye and working a hex against the City.

How had the amethyst wound up in the grass? How much could it be worth with that inlay, whatever it was? And what was it worth to him?

He just stood there, not moving from the spot. That night, the purser might decide that going to bed without dinner would teach him not to be late.

Maybe the best thing would be to sell it in Megara or Corinth. He could hide it in a safe place and then swallow it on the day he decided to run away.

But what if he gave it back? What if he gave it to Artemon, The Bale, as it was his duty to do? Wouldn't that get him in good with his master and make it easier to escape?

Stupid. He knew perfectly well that all he would get was some praise for his honesty, a pat on the head, or, at best, The Bale might buy him a new catonace and some rough sandals.

But what would Parthenos have to say?

Bah! Let her vent her rage on the criminal who tore her eye out in the first place, whoever he was. The best thing would be to give it to One Eye, sell it, and split the take.

If One Eye managed to sell the stone, a few days later he could make good his escape, conceived over his bronze-smith's forge and minutely planned during sleepless nights and on the long treks back to Artemon's farm. He could finally go through with the plan that had given him hope over the last two years.

He ran up the hill with the tireless abandon of a young boy. It was as if all the thorns had been taken from his heart. It was getting dark. He collapsed on the cool grass to recover his breath, no longer caring if he got his dinner or not. He heard the chatter of a flock of ducks flying to nest in the marshes of Salamis. They might even go on to Megara.

Hope stormed through his heart like the wind.

1 8

WHEN THE ONE CALLED CEBES was pointed out to Atys, he advanced on the group of young men joking around a barber's chair. He stopped just a few steps away and went into a routine of wild gestures. As soon as he had their attention, he raised his arm. In the palm of his hand, he held a hen's egg with a red triangle, a green clover, and the letter *gamma* in blue. He began to chant in the Phrygian tongue at the top of his voice.

The first reaction was mocking laughter, but there was something so overwhelming in that fine, powerful voice that the group soon quieted down.

Atys continued his chant as he walked in a circle, tracing a border for the onlookers crowding around him there in the Theban agora. Cebes, one of the young aristocrats in the group, was in the front row. As Atys circled before them, he looked into their eyes, noting that they were all soapstone; there wasn't a single piece of flint among them. All the better.

Suddenly he cut off his chanting, brought the egg on a level with his eyes, and with his free hand pointed to Cebes.

"See! Eggest point to you!"

The boy smiled in confusion, knitted his brow a bit, and looked at the markings on the egg. Then Atys stared from behind the egg, opening his eyes very wide. They held the mystery and innocence of the stars. It was impossible not to look into them. Atys took a step closer, then another and another. Cebes felt his jaw loosen. The world was violet. He smiled.

"Oh, heat!" said Atys, fanning himself with his free hand.

Cebes felt his face grow red and ran his tongue over his lips.

"Much great heat! You no fan? And you? And him? And that one?"

Cebes let out a breath of air and began fanning himself with his hand. The onlookers pressed in, making it hard to breathe in the middle of the group. The young men were beginning to sweat.

But suddenly it was cold and Cebes and all his friends began to shiver. When the cold went, Atys crushed the egg and peep, peep, peep, a chick was born. They all stared as the chick much fast grew, became old, and Cebes could see him, oh, oh, so very fatly and much flying high over the Temple of Zeus.

Who in Thebes had ever seen a cock flying high like an eagle?

Atys followed the cock with his finger as it flew over the rooftops of Thebes. Twenty spellbound heads witnessed the miracle. And another hundred cupped their eyes with their hands to scan the skies, but saw no cock.

Neither did they see the redheaded man scurrying around the corner, followed by a strong young man, Cebes.

More people came. There were arguments. The group became a crowd. One of the priests of Zeus was incensed. Then,

133

just as the authorities were about to take a hand in the matter to break up the disorder they blamed on the youths, Cebes came trotting around the corner on all fours, completely naked, barking, growling, avidly lapping up the fetid blood dripping from a basket of offal, and capturing the horrified attention of the people of Thebes.

Diodorus was poor, but he paid for the services with a new cloak, a small wineskin, and a broad pigskin hat. There had to be three gifts. The Sum had ordained that all sacred services be paid for in threes. At the gateway of dreams, Atys had been blessed with a vision of the sacred symbols: his New Church would worship the Triangle, the Clover, and the Gamma. This would honor the holy triad and ensure the success of his sacred quest. He must never forget that was why the Sum had called him to the Pylai ton Hipnon, poPOpom popoPOM.

134

With his hat well down over his forehead and his feet moving at a brisk pace, he left Thebes on his way south. When he buried his mottled tunic in Thessaly, he buried with it the Beggar of the Goddess forever. This was the Summoner of the Sum, returning to the borders of Attica after many months of absence. No one in Thebes could recognize him for the bewitcher in the agora.

Cebes had come upon Basilia, slave and concubine of Diodorus, when she was washing in the river. Then he had used her, and because the girl put up a fight, he beat her so savagely that she died two days later.

But the Summoner of the Sum arrived and justice was done: Cebes would lead a dog's life for a few days, just long enough to dishonor his family, and then die, poisoned by the filth he was eating.

19

THE PORNAI OF ONE of Truncheon's brothels, the one run by One Eye, would pay five obols for each phallus with the mandatory inscription: "I was consecrated to Aphrodite Pandemos by . . ." Then, before offering it at an altar of the Goddess, each devotee would complete the text with her own name and nation. One Eye kept two obols and gave three to Xanthus the Lycian.

Xanthus and One Eye were joined by a secret oath of allegiance unknown to everyone in Athens. They had sworn the oath before an altar of the Mother Goddess in Samos. Together they had fought to defend their adopted island and together they were put in the lot that Pericles gave to Artemon. But One Eye, thanks to his sad physical condition, got lucky. Artemon could not profitably rent him out to the mines and quarries, so he sold him to Porphyrius the Cybernetes.

One Eye himself had been behind the deal. When he found out that the Cybernetes had made a sizable bundle in a slave auction, he made him a proposition in exchange for his freedom. Armed with examples that only a man of the trade could know, he sold him the idea of investing in a bordello. He explained in detail how he worked in Samos and convinced his master that, with the right kind of management, whores could be as profitable as his piloting, but without the hardships and the danger of being shipwrecked.

Porphyrius bought him from The Bale, and in six months' time, the whorehouse business was, indeed, flourishing. As agreed, One Eye earned his freedom. Two years later, the Cybernetes went down off the coasts of Cyrene, losing his cargo and his vessel. To pay off his debts and stave off bankruptcy, he had to sell the bordello. Truncheon, the new owner, moved furnishings and women to a house in the outer Ceramicus and kept One Eye on to run the place.

136

Truncheon was preparing to receive Pyrilampes the Birdman, who had announced he would be coming with a group of friends, including some merchants from Corcyra who did not want to leave Athens without seeing one of its greatest attractions: the callipygous dance of Lysis of Miletus. Truncheon was going over her plans for the banquet, while Lysis, stretched out on a bed, had her toenails painted by one of her slaves.

When the doorkeeper announced that One Eye wished an interview with the mistress, Truncheon had him brought in. How odd! One Eye never came around at this time. Had someone stabbed another porne, she wondered, or mugged another client?

No, it was none of that. One Eye had come to suggest a . . . hum . . . confidential deal. He was suddenly silent and looked around at the slaves.

Truncheon had them all leave the room.

"Speak," she said, indicating with a gesture that he was not to worry about Lysis, and sat beside her.

One Eye took a small bag out of his robes and handed it to Truncheon.

"Ah," exclaimed Lysis, immediately recognizing the stolen amethyst with its obsidian inlay.

Truncheon put it away hurriedly and with a stern expression said:

"Speak. What do you want?"

"I'd like to sell it to you."

"How did you come by it?"

And he explained that Xanthus, a Lycian slave, his oath brother whom he knew from Samos, his comrade in arms ...

Lysis had taken the bag from Truncheon's hands and gazed avidly at the amethyst. Truncheon took it from her without a word, put it in the bag, and gave it back to One Eye.

She could no longer contain her wrath and her whispered tirade sounded much more menacing than if she had screamed.

One Eye never expected to be scolded or to see her transformed into one of the Eumenides, eyes wide, calling him an idiot, a madman, a defiler, how did he dare traffic in sacred objects, if anyone found out that he was helping that Xanthus thing sell the eye stolen from the Goddess, both would be put through the most horrible torments, they would be thrown into the Barathrum, and yet, the beautiful Lysis seemed interested as she caressed the stone, looked at it close up and at arms length, and even asked the price, and Truncheon went on, had Lysis gone mad? why did she want to know the price? the fruits of sacrilege had no price, and again at One Eye, that he was mad, an unbeliever, that, in all the time she had known him, this was the most stupid thing he had ever done, and now that she knew the outrages he was capable of, she would have to reconsider

137

keeping him in her employ, and that he should leave immediately, that the very sight of him hurt her eyes, that he should consider himself lucky that she didn't turn him in to the King's Court, and One Eye arguing that, if she bought it and returned it to the Goddess, she would reap the gratitude and benevolence of the City, and Truncheon, even angrier, did the vile One Eye think that she did not fear the Gods? did he think her capable of trafficking in sacred objects? of provoking the wrath of Athena?

"Leave!"

And she threw him out without another word.

Lysis was very impressed. As soon as Truncheon calmed down, she explained that, although One Eye ran a tight brothel and was one of those who served her best and pilfered the least, she would have had no qualms about turning him over to the Basileus, except for the secret she had learned about the amethyst. The only thing the City knew about the stone was that Elpinice, sister of Cimon, had donated it to Phidias for the pedestal of Parthenos. But Cimon had once confessed to Sophocles, and he to Truncheon in the intimacy of her bed, that the stone had come from a statue of Cybele, pillaged by one of his patrols during the Eurymedon campaign. And Truncheon, who was a devotee of Cybele, would do nothing to return the stone to Athena. Who knows, maybe it was the divine will that had guided the thieving hand to the Parthenon and now pulled the strings behind One Eye's conniving.

Lysis was deep in thought.

And then the arrival of the guests was announced and both women went out into the courtyard to welcome them with wreaths and crowns.

138

20

FROM ASPASIA IN ATHENS TO EURYDICE IN SARDES

The sixth of Munyxion

AFTER SO MANY MONTHS without a word from you, I find it difficult to pick up the thread of our concerns, which are none other than those that Cleis, Cleis, and always Cleis, so full of events, piles up for us.

So then, to the point and, with a heart heavier than that of the rhapsodist of Ithaca when he was forced to sing at the banquet of the pretenders, I must tell you that after driving her mad with love, Alcibiades demanded that Lysis give him Truncheon's famous necklace. I could have jumped to the moon when I found out!

Fortunately, the necklace is back with its owner and

Alcibiades has left the City to do his epheby. Encouraged by Truncheon, Lysis has sworn to take revenge.

By Zeus, I can't begin to tell you how happy that made me! And how thankful I was for Truncheon's wise decision.

But the whole thing has left me a little nervous. I fear Alcibiades, for I know full well what a cad he is and how well he has learned to hide his hatreds and designs. My only consolation is that it will be quite some time before he sees her again.

Indeed, months have gone by and there is still no sign of him. Perhaps Ares and his military service in the fortress of Enoe have chilled his ardors. And besides, he has done nothing but train for the Olympic Games for months.

The seventh

I was forced to interrupt my letter yesterday because I had to prepare for a public appearance with Pericles at a torch race in honor of Apollo and Artemis, to whom the Delphinian feasts were devoted yesterday. That was the day Theseus departed for Crete, so the Athenians have chosen the anniversary to reopen navigation in the Aegean. So, you see, my scrolls will leave for Asia on the first ship out.

Today I want to tell you about something Cleis did. I'm still not sure that I should be happy about this, but anyway, about six months ago, during the Haloae, Cleis was crowned Callipygian Queen of the City. It would seem she has indeed been favored by Pandemos. The City simply cannot cease commenting on, and even exaggerating, her victory. Callipygous queens here are usually very experienced dancers and well known in libertine circles. No one could imagine that a simple flute player, limited to improvising a few steps to show off her blessings, could take the crown in the very difficult dance of the sweet-rumped Goddess. Since then, she has become one of the most popular hetaerae in Athens. In a way, it makes me happy, but that wasn't the destiny I wanted for her.

You know, I've been wondering if, before she left your care, you had noticed her very undesirable proclivity for flaunting the Greek gnomai. Cybele, Dionysus, and Pandemos are her Gods. I've never seen her revere the Olympians. To Apollo's lyre, she preferred the flute which, by the way, she devoted to heretics, such as Xenophanes and Archilochus, disdaining Solon, Theognis, Callinus, and others. Once, after much insistence, I was able to convince her to accompany an Argive reciting an elegy by Tyrtaeus. I remember it was a very martial poem, one of those that extols remaining in the front lines and marching to battle with clenched teeth to ward off fear. But Cleis played rhythms so lacking in inspiration that they sounded more like flatulation than anything else. The visitor stopped, realizing she was making fun of him. But she said that Tyrtaeus withered the pneuma residing in her breast, the inspirer of her music, whom she could not disobey. And she would admit no jokes about it. One morning, one of my servants asked her how her pneuma was, and Cleis screamed, "Hungry!" and bit her arm so hard she drew blood.

I find in her the lightning irascibility of my brother Diotimus and his foolhardy disdain for danger. One night, her pneuma inspired her to sneak out of the house and walk through the City down to the Ceramicus, at a time when the streets are the province of ruffians. Another time, she jumped from a very high cliff into the Cephisus in a place bristling with outcroppings because her pneuma suddenly demanded that she experience the same vertigo Sappho felt on the Leucadian crag. By the Two Goddesses! I can almost relive the horror and shortness of breath when I remember her plummeting completely naked, arms outstretched, and hair fanning out like the tail of a peacock.

When she was still a child, she climbed to the top of a poplar to rescue a baby bear she had been bottle-feeding. When the branch broke, she fell about four arm spans and hit her head so hard she was knocked unconscious.

She has done other things I haven't mentioned, because I want to spare you and because I prefer they remain forgotten. Her pneuma, which sometimes inspired her with unfounded fears, has invariably been stronger than my persuasive arts and arguments.

Fortunately, when she grew to womanhood, her taste for fear shifted away from nocturnal escapades and acrobatics, but she caused me considerable suffering with her inconvenient behavior in public. Just before she fell ill, in the presence of a venerable member of the Areopagus and Herodotus of Halicarnassus, who was in the City and paying us a visit, she said that she agreed with Heraclitus that Homer deserved to be beaten for stultifying the Greeks. Then she made fun of Pindar and the grandiloquence of the choral lyricists, no exception made for our beloved Ibycus of Rhegium.

On another occasion, in our very own andron, attempting to please her, a respectable old magistrate said that a girl with her beauty and paideia deserved to marry the finest of Athenians, even if she were a foreigner. Well, she flew into a rage. She said she would accept no marriage because there was only one Pericles in Athens and he was the only one who allowed his wife to consort with the men of Athens, express political opinions, and dress as she pleased. What Athenian matron could, like me, ride through the City in a chariot wearing an Egyptian hairdo? What eupatrid virgin could go to the theater, even to comedies, escorted by philosophers and artists? Would the respectable magistrate allow his wife and daughters to do that? And she even said that rather than marry an

Athenian and become a second-class citizen locked in the gyneceum, she would prefer to live the free life of a hetaera.

Pericles himself had to take a hand in the matter to change the subject.

Despite the disappointments and anxieties she still causes me, I love her as desperately as I do my only son. When I think that the last blood of my line is running through her veins, I can only see in her defects the signs of a very high spirit.

And she loves me too, as her confidences prove. The last night she was home, she confessed that she is more and more pleased with the irreverent poetry of Archilochus of Pharos, the shield dumper; or with the drunken and mocking Alcaeus; or with Anacreon, when he invites men to forget their arsenals and sing with raised cups. If you could only see how her face lights up and exudes lasciviousness when she praises the very realistic Eros by Hipponax of Ephesus, or the ardors of Sappho while contemplating the swaying of Anactoria.

She has even confessed that when she was still living with us, the mere thought of the poem by Alceus, where a filly prances and twists on the grass, made her yearn for a rider and fondle herself or alternate with one of my maids.

It was to be expected, considering her lineage.

And so, last year, her pneuma ordered her to disregard my warnings and Truncheon's and give herself with religious devotion to the teachings of one Hypothesis. She spent long days on end with her in a filthy hole in the suburbs. This caused no end of arguments with Truncheon, who considers this Hypothesis a harpy. And although, as a member of the Aphrodisian guild, Truncheon approved of her participation in the contest, she was enraged by the fact that Lysis was training at that woman's house.

Things got worse after her victory, when relations between teacher and pupil became closer than ever. When she found herself favored by Aphrodite, Cleis became devoted to the maker of her victory. She was so grateful that she bought Hypothesis three young slaves with which the woman makes a comfortable living. Then she put her in charge of her brothels and brought her to live in her own house.

A month after the Haloae, Cleis received three thousand drachmas from an Argive banker who wanted her all to himself for ten days. With this windfall and the money that poured in afterward, she purchased three girls and rented a house in the Ceramicus, where she entertains with music, callipygian dancing, and open banquets just like Truncheon. Since then she has bought ten of the most beautiful slaves ever sold in Athens and opened two luxurious brothels. And it is Hypothesis who deals with the pupils, teaching them the arts of love, cosmetics, and callipygian seduction. Cleis just handles the accounts, with the zeal of a banker. And so, this all-embracing presence of Hypothesis in Cleis's life brought about a break with Truncheon. For almost two months, they neither spoke nor saw one another. But then Cleis began to miss her; she went to her house, implored forgiveness, and said she wanted to be her friend again. Fortunately, things are back the way they were. When Cleis has no attractive clients at her house, she hides at Truncheon's or goes to her banquets, if she asks her, and they frequently sleep together and exchange confidences. Truncheon finally understood that her terrible jealousy of Hypothesis was completely unjustified. And I'm happy about the way things turned out. Since I can't have her with me, my only consolation is that she is with this prudent woman who loves her dearly.

Ever since her adventure with Alcibiades, her malady has become less frequent. When the crises do come, she is no longer so terrified by the three thumps from under the earth or by the way she stretches three fingers. But she insists on attributing it to Hecate. By the Two Goddesses, how stubborn she is! She is convinced that they are a sign and refuses to accept the fact that her malady is the result of pituitary weakness.

But, well, she's back in the graces of Aphrodite, successful in the City, humiliating men, making fortunes. She is convinced that her success is proof of the fact that Cyprian Aphrodite is looking out for her. All I can do is make sacrifices to the Twelve Gods so that they won't forsake her. So be it.

The eleventh

Your final comments on Orontas betrayed boredom and fear. Might this not be the moment to get rid of him? Come to Athens. I beg you. Now is when you should be looking after your child. I would feel much more at ease knowing that you're with her. You could do for her what I can no longer do alone. You would be happy here. We would go to the theater; you would meet the most brilliant men in the Hellas. I'll give you a good house. Don't forget that we swore to die together, hand in hand. Pick a date and a place in Ionia or Pontus, and Pericles will send a fast ship to meet you.

Be happy.

145

DELIVERED INTO FRIENDLY HANDS ON THE TWELFTH OF MUNYXION ARCHON APSEUDES

21

THE LITTLE HORSE was skinny and not very spirited, but, to judge from his fetlocks, he could not be very old. In the evening, One Eye had shined him up with mastic oil and mixed a lot of salt in with his rye. In the morning, the animal was whinnying for water, but One Eye gave him none until they crossed the Cephisus, when the sun was two hand spans over the horizon. He let him swell with water and then gave him more salty rye to make sure he would not urinate too much before noon. That would make him look fatter.

When he finally got to Corydallus, it was midday. By the agnocast of his meeting place, One Eye whistled as agreed and from behind a bush appeared Xanthus, who had been hiding there since the wee hours. One Eye gave him the package containing the cape, the sandals, the blond wig, and the hat.

One Eye had two reasons for helping Xanthus so enthusiastically, which he told him. First, there was the old oath they had sworn before the Great Mother of the Gods; but he was also keenly interested in seeing with his own eye if Xanthus actually made it. If he was captured, the Gods forbid, One Eye would have to run away before Xanthus was tortured in the cells of the Porticus. Since it was impossible for a miserable slave to round up a horse, a wig, and everything else, they would torture him day and night until he revealed who his accomplice was.

One Eye would position himself in Eleusis until he saw the squad of border guards returning to town from the outpost after they were relieved at noon. If they caught Xanthus at the border crossing, they would bring him to the town jail in chains. One Eye already had a plan for that contingency: As soon as he saw that they had Xanthus, he would walk across the border at that very point. Days before, he had applied for a pass at the Pritaneus, as was required of all freemen and foreigners to prove their condition, as well as for a safe-conduct stating that he owed nothing to the Gods or to any man. He had gotten them with the pretext of fulfilling a promise to Zeus in Olympia.

Xanthus acquiesced. It was reasonable. Who could be certain that he would not talk under torture? Besides, One Eye had been a loyal brother. Despite the very severe punishment reserved for any freemen who swore an oath of allegiance with a slave, One Eye had never abandoned him. He had lived up to their secret pact to that very day.

Finally, they agreed that Xanthus would go on hiding a good while in Corydallus to give One Eye time enough to walk to Eleusis.

They had a parting drink and reiterated their oath, and Xanthus went off to get dressed. When he returned with a broad smile on his face, One Eye praised him heartily. He looked him over from all angles. The man positively looked like an affluent pilgrim! The long blond wig under the hat had changed him completely; it matched his blue eyes and freckles to a tee.

The last thing they did was square their accounts: One Eye gave him forty drachmas. After a farewell embrace, One Eye walked off in the direction of Eleusis.

Of the three hundred drachmas the Cybernetes had paid for the stone, One Eye had spent a hundred and twenty-five on the horse and the wig. With a few more deductions for miscellaneous expenses, there were forty drachmas left over of Xanthus's share. With what he had already saved up and his share of the stone, One Eye now had a grand total of six hundred and eighty-seven drachmas. He was finally in a position to go into business for himself.

When he got to Eleusis, he went right by the jail and found himself a good spot in some old ruins by the side of the road. The sun was already heating up the soil, which smelled of mint and elders. Lizards scurried among the argemone growing out of the cracks and crannies of the Temple of Ares, which was destroyed in the Persian wars. Yes, One Eye had awaited his opportunity patiently. He always said that the difficult part was to start moving, like getting a large stone to roll over a steep incline. This was especially true in a business where women were so expensive. Two weeks earlier, according to his best calculations, he would have had to go on scrimping and saving for another year to be able to get started. And then, out of the clear blue sky, Xanthus shows up with the stone, Tyche gives him her hair, and snap! One Eye had two hundred and forty-seven drachmas he had never counted on. Besides, just a few days earlier he had heard about a fellow whoremonger in the demos of Scyron who was selling a batch of three old whores for twelve hundred drachmas. One Eye was certain that, with seven hundred cash, his colleague would agree to take the rest in monthly installments, plus interest.

Suddenly, he heard a horse whinny and looked down the road. Four horsemen were rounding the elm grove by the jail. He strained his eyes.

Was that Xanthus?

It was! Yes, the one on the right.

When the party was just a few pletri away, he saw that Xanthus was carrying on a friendly conversation with a group of Boeotian merchants who were leading a string of very heavily loaded mules.

As he watched him go by, he got that same feeling he had had when they said good-bye, not really knowing whether it was joy or sadness. Xanthus gave him a look of gratitude and raised his eyebrows in a mute farewell. That was the last he would ever see of that freckled friend who had shared his same fate since Samos. He was happy he had given him his friendship and loyalty, and the tear he had held back in Corydallus was finally allowed to flow. May Zeus and Apollo, guardians of roads, and the Great Mother of the Gods guide the good Xanthus. The Boeotians drew up their animals by the trough of a nearby fountain, and One Eye came a little closer to get a better look. He heard when they bid Xanthus good-bye because they were going to stop over in Eleusis to make a libation to the Gods and reorganize their cargo.

Xanthus went on alone.

One Eye followed him for a good spell, up to the bridge on the outskirts of the town. Several times it was all he could do to keep from laughing at the townspeople blessing Xanthus and stretching out their upturned palms.

"Zeus be with you, oh pilgrim!"

"And with you, good man," replied Xanthus politely, wish-

ing them good fortune for their homes and health for their children. One of them came right up to the horse and raised his
small child for Xanthus to touch his head and take with him to
the Altar of Zeus, in Olympia, the fleeting prayer of a father of
Attica seeking protection for his child with the passing anonymous touch of a pilgrim on horseback.

Who could ever doubt that the Lycian was just one more of
the many who preceded the caravans of the month of
Scirophorion, or one of those sent ahead by the merchants to
stake out a good spot on the hills surrounding the Altis of the
competitions.

From the bridge he watched him spur his horse up the hill
toward the forest embracing the road to the border with
Megara.

He dried his tears with the back of his hand. But then
again, he had nothing to worry about. The Lycian looked perfectly credible. With his shiny horse, he would easily cover the
ten stadia he still had to go to the border. No one who met him
could possibly suspect that this rider, who was the very image of
a boreal pilgrim, was hiding the shaven head of a slave. He was
sure he would get through.

But since no mortal has the right to be certain of anything
and the designs of the Gods are impenetrable, he sought the
shade of the elm grove, took his wineskin and a pouch of olives
from his pack, and sat back to wait for noon.

Yes, he had no doubt that if he could patch up the three
crones, cover their faces with wax, fill in their wrinkles with glue
and isinglass, and have them look out of an upper window close
to the piers of Aristides, where love-starved sailors first made
landfall, he could get at least six drachmas a day from them,
which was enough to cover the installments on his debt, and
still have enough to pay some forty drachmas for the rent on a

house with a high window. The high window was an absolute necessity. His gorgons could only be seen from below and no more than once. Then, once he had already closed the deal with the client, using the usual hand signs, the rest would take place in a dark, perfumed room where there were no wrinkles, no mange, no teeth, no years. And with his profits, One Eye could make sizable savings and buy better women, which he would put in another house, and, oh, yes, they would see what old One Eye was capable of, and knocking back another drink of wine, he stretched out on the mound to look at the sun, already nearing the zenith, and gave himself up to the memories evoked by the parting of good Xanthus. Just seven years ago, they had both been brought back from Samos in chains; now Xanthus was about to regain his freedom, and he, One Eye, was going to reopen his brothel, with the advantage that now he would be operating in the most famous and prosperous city in all Hellas.

151

It was at this point that he saw, in the distance, coming over the crest of the hill, the relieved border-guard detail. Their bronze shields shimmered in the noonday sun. A passing rider had stirred up a cloud of dust, making it difficult to see very well at that distance. One Eye climbed on a section of a broken column and stared out anxiously. It didn't look as if they were bringing a prisoner in chains, at least not in front of them, as they usually did. He came up close to the edge of the road to get a side view of them when they turned onto the bridge. No, they weren't dragging anyone, either.

He stabbed a fist in the air out of pure satisfaction.

The good Xanthus had gotten away with it!

That had to be it. He was sure. With that wig and riding a horse, there was no risk. It was an escape protected by the Gods. Why else would they have ordained that the Lycian find the amethyst? That evening, in the Metroon of Mount Ardetto,

One Eye offered a prayer of thanksgiving to the Mother of the Gods.

An Eleusian drayman picked him up five stadia from the town. He made the rest of the trip to the demos of Scyron riding comfortably on a bale of wool. He got off there and made straight for the brothel where they were selling the three gorgons. If he found them serviceable, he would negotiate the deal. One Eye had not wanted to take all his money with him until he was certain that Xanthus had gotten out of Attica safely.

22

S INCE THE DAY of her victory at the Haloae, Lysis had served Aphrodite with a hundred and thirty-five men, according to the entries in her papyrus of offerings.

About a month after that victory, when she was still asking only two hundred drachmas for the night, she found out that Daphne of Chios, incensed at not having been elected queen in the contest at the temple, decided that she would be the most expensive callipygian in Athens and began to charge two and a half minae. Hypothesis convinced Lysis that such presumption against her royal primacy could not be tolerated and induced her to begin charging three hundred drachmas.

The truth is that there was scarcely a day when she did not have some rich man or other ready to pay her price or some sailor willing to squander his earnings to be able to brag about his night with the most expensive hetaera in Athens, the city with the most expensive hetaera services in all the known world.

But as soon as the news got to Daphne, she raised her price to three hundred and fifty drachmas and, one by one, Mnemosine the Cyrenaican, Cassandra, Helen the Lantern, and Mamahelpme followed suit, driving Lysis of Miletus to raise her price to four minae.

The irreverent rise in prices required the intervention of the Eranos, the Secret Society of Aphrodite the Vulgar. It was summarily forbidden for the hetaerae of Athens to charge more than three minae. The six luminaries of the Ceramicus, the only ones who could command such a fortune, entered into a solemn pact in the presence of Euphemia Doright the Immovable, hierosophist and rector of the guild.

In the Temple of Solon, before the effigy of Pandemos, Doright, assisted by another three dignitaries of the Eranos, heard the three oaths and the case was closed.

154

After her crowning and formal entry into the high priesthood of Pandemos, Lysis set herself the task of carrying a papyrus in which she entered, in minute detail, all of Aphrodite's monies, because they came through her and to her they must accrue.

As profits from her first one hundred men, considering the initial price fluctuation, Lysis entered a total of twenty-seven thousand and seven hundred drachmas. But after the pact in the temple, Lysis knew that she could count on an income of thirty thousand drachmas from every one hundred men and, according to her estimates, calculated on the basis of one hecatanthropy every four months, her bedroom income would amount to one hundred and twenty thousand drachmas per annum.

If she could add to this another ten talents a year, the estimated income from her dancing and the open banquet, Aphrodite could count on some one hundred and eighty thousand drachmas a year. That would be her personal contribution, her offering.

By the end of the sixth month of her reign, aside from the three pornai she had given Hypothesis as her part of the bargain, Lysis acquired another eleven, which she distributed in two brothels. A few days before the Plynteria, Lysis spent nine thousand drachmas on Mnesis and Chloe, two beautiful fifteen-year-olds whom Truncheon was instructing in the manners of the symposium and Hypothesis was instructing in the art of callipygous dancing, to add to the attractions of the banquets in her house.

Lysis calculated that, by the end of four or five years, she would, with her brothels and the new slaves she was constantly buying, have enough to build a temple to Pandemos greater than Solon's. It would be a grand temple, made with marble from the Pentelikon, and it would have more sacred prostitutes than the one in Corinth. And if it turned out to be true that in the isthmic Temple of Aphrodite and the surrounding parks there were a thousand hierodulae, Lysis's temple would have a thousand one hundred.

Everything went according to plan for almost seven months. After receiving her crown, Lysis spent three days and nights in the sacrarium. There, the ancient Euphemia celebrated the Apocalypse of the sacred objects, recited the cannon of the priestesses, and heard Lysis's oath.

No one but priestesses with Divine Approval, as Lysis had evidently possessed since Aphrodite consecrated her in the Haloae, could be admitted to the mysteries of Pandemos. Not even Truncheon, despite her high position in the Eranos, could be admitted.

And the capital oath of the new Sweet-Rump Queen of Athens had been to serve Aphrodite Pandemos with the perfection of her body without ever rendering a service free of charge.

Lysis of Miletus was diligently true to her oath, until one day, when some mocking spirit, or perhaps a deity from the underworld, put the nefarious whim in her heart.

How could she have forgotten her cardinal oath to Aphrodite?

It all happened because of her sudden desire to give herself to Menon of Himera, the musician.

He had scarcely arrived from Sicily when praise of his beauty had become the talk of the City. Some found him even more beautiful than Alcibiades.

Lysis wanted to meet him and arranged to have him as a guest at her house. Not only was he beautiful, but gallant and inspired, and with his enchanting lyre, he completely captivated Lysis through her ears. She enjoyed him for three days. Since he had no money, he gave her his lyre as payment, upon leaving, and she, inebriated with wine and music, said that it was worth a thousand drachmas. But she well knew that it was worth no more than a hundred. To her complete horror, she realized the following day that she had given herself to a man for pure pleasure, without charging! The lyre was no payment, but a swindle, a sin against Pandemos, a violation of the First Commandment.

23

OH MY, MY, MY, what a mess, if One Eye only knew,
ran away, and Artemon is furious, One Eye feigning
ignorance, escaped? who? how? and Sosias, one could never
guess, and One Eye, that it must have been the Paphlagonian,
and Sosias that it wasn't, so it was Meron the Lydian, no, the
Rock Eater? neither, and One Eye couldn't guess, just yesterday?
yes, at night, what do you mean, at night? yes, at night, Xanthus
the Lycian, and One Eye, the Lycian ran away? could it be possible? but how? when? where? and Sosias, no one suspected,
right? yesterday evening, and One Eye, in the evening? and
Sosias the Carian, yes, he walked off, as usual, after midnight,
to the ergasterium of Alcides, the bronze-smith, who had rented
him, and around noon, Artemon received a note in his house in
the City from Alcides asking what was wrong with the Lycian,
who hadn't gone to work, and the news of the escape got out
right away, and One Eye, lowering his voice and giving Sosias a
stab of complicity in the ribs, so, Xanthus pulled it off, and

Sosias, pulled it off? did One Eye call being strung up like a sheep's hide pulling it off? and One Eye, stru . . . ung up? and Sosias, wiping his tears with the back of his hand, barely able to mutter, Artemon had ordered him branded with a *phi* and the poor soul would have to wear the infamous mark on his forehead for the rest of his life, and One Eye, alarmed, couldn't believe it, by the Gods in Hades! so they caught him? but when? how? and Sosias, that during the night the dogs had flushed him out trying to crawl across the Megaran border, and One Eye, turning to stare at the heights of the Lycabettus and the bluish profile of the Pentelikon, feeling like a hoplyte cornered on the battlefield and about to dump his shield to be able to get away that much faster, analyzing the terrain with his single eye, making speedy calculations, it might be better to start his retreat right now, would he have time to return to the Ceramicus for his things and continue on to Megara before Xanthus revealed his complicity? and what if Xanthus had already talked? they would certainly be looking for him, could he make it to the Megaran border with his pass? and Sosias explaining that Artemon himself had given him more lashes than there are mosquitoes in the marshes of Tricorythos, and what if he talked to the Cybernetes and asked him to ship him out? and Sosias, that he was completely naked, what? how? why was he naked? yes, many hours lying in the bushes, and One Eye, but why naked? and Sosias, that was just the way he heard it, the Lycian had been robbed, but by the Great Mother, what time had it happened, and Sosias, just after midday, but hadn't Sosias said that it had been midnight? yes, that was when the patrol caught him trying to cross the border, but when he left Eleusis, some five stadia distant, two men, also naked, had jumped him and beat him half to death, beat Xanthus? and Sosias, yes, more than you have to beat a stubborn donkey to get him to go from Athens to Sparta, and One Eye, but what about the horse? and Sosias, what nonsense, where would the Lycian get a horse? and One Eye, ahem, yes, well, no, he hadn't meant to say that, and would Sosias go on about the robbery, what rotten luck, and in Eleusis they thought he had been the victim of some other runaway slaves lying in ambush near the border, or Orestes's gang, which was working near the region, and they had made a hole this big in his head and it wouldn't stop bleeding, what about the wi—? and Sosias, the what? no, nothing, and just then One Eye caught on to what had happened, oooph, thank Zeus, he wouldn't have to go anywhere so urgently, the thieves had taken the horse, the wig, and everything, they had left him naked, and, except for the assailants, no one could take him for the pilgrim who had ridden by hours earlier, and it was evident that Xanthus had not mentioned the horse and other things, or how he had gotten them, or that he had found and sold the stone, or One Eye's complicity, phew, by the Mother, what a scare, and Sosias, that he had been whipped before the other slaves and it looked like he was going to die there staked spread-eagle by the roadside, and that he would be there without food or water for some time, and Artemon had said that if he got out of there alive, he would spend the rest of his life crawling through mine tunnels and never seeing the light of the sun again, but in any case, One Eye would have to be very careful, hide for a few days, ask the Cybernetes for help? he would have to give up his brothel, Sosias had been sent by the Gods, now he wouldn't invest a single obol on women, and if Xanthus confessed in the next few days and he had to leave Attica, it would certainly be convenient to have as much money as possible, from now on he would carry the money with him, and who could have told him that a day that had started so propitiously could land him in a predicament ten times worse than

159

before Xanthus's escape attempt, how could he ever sleep? oh, how difficult life was, kicking a stone, he was so tired of fighting and fighting against this mute destiny that muddled everything, rage and fear shone in his eye, and on the way home he tried to convince himself that Xanthus had nothing to gain by mentioning the amethyst or the horse or the wig, how he regretted having to give up his gorgons, how uncertain his Moira had become, oh, what a slender thread sustained his destiny!

24

THE CITY WAS CELEBRATING the Plynteria. For her yearly bath, the statue of Athena Polias would be carried from her residence in the Erechtheion to the coast of the Saronic Sea. With the temple of the tutelary Goddess closed and the people without protection, all commerce ceased and no one dared practice a trade.

Lysis decided to follow the procession down to the shore and attend the bathing of the Goddess. As she emerged from her own bath, her mind laden with recollections of the previous day, waiting for Evardis to pat her body dry with fresh linen, suddenly, that acid saliva, popopon popopon, that cursed rapping, and oh, so violent, popopon, popopon, they came in groups of three. It had been so long since the last time she had heard it that she had harbored the hope that she was free of the Three-Headed Goddess, but now she felt with horror the drumming on the soles of her feet, she was swaying, losing her balance, holding on to Evardis, sitting on the bottom of her tub, dumbstruck, covering her ears, crying, and then the tremors and contortions, the shaking and arching, and Evardis scared out of her wits, asking Otep to help, not knowing what to do, she had never seen feces that color or such a frightening crisis, she looked like she would snap and there was fury in her face, and there were worms in her excrements, and when she awoke, oh, all because of a mad whim, lost, she was lost, forsaken by Aphrodite, again in the clutches of the Scavenger, and she was dirty again, yagh, those filthy worms, there was no telling her that it was quite common, that the worms would go away in a few days with an infusion of nettle and sulfur water, but when Lysis confessed that she had violated her supreme oath and given herself the day before, free of charge, to Menon of Himera, Hypothesis was also dumbfounded; was such a sin possible? And she howled in pain and sympathy and anger and fear and she pulled at her hair, why, oh, why such great irreverence?

162

Lysis let her head drop to one side and her groans shook her shoulders. That night she dreamed of Hecate, the three-headed bitch that howled at her so urgently. She awoke in tears. There was a weight on her chest. The ominous presage made her tremble. It was a bad crisis. She would have to spend several days in bed.

On the third day, she stopped crying, as if she had dried up. She spoke to no one. She spent her days sleeping, engulfed in her lunar pallor. When she was awake, she stared into the void with misty eyes. Truncheon found out and came to see her. She twisted her hands in impotence before her beloved child who would not answer. Lysis opened her mouth just once to complain about the nauseating smell emanating from her body. Only she could smell it. Could Truncheon see the worms dropping onto the floor from her bed? That was all she could think about. She could see them everywhere.

She vomited everything she drank, even water. She grew very thin.

Finally, following the advice of Euphemia Doright, Hypothesis convinced her to submit to rites of exorcism in the home of a witch from Mantinea, who had a shack on Mount Ardettus, behind her house. If it could be proved that it was all the work of a mocking spirit, of a perverse incubus, and not her own sin, then there was hope that the Goddess might forgive.

And five days after the Plynteria, Hypothesis and Otep accompanied her along a path through the elder grove around the back of the Cynosarges. Lysis walked with hesitating steps, her face in shadows. The sun was setting over the heights of Corydallus. Suddenly, Lysis screamed and broke out crying on Hypothesis's shoulder. Oh, again that hateful, that unmistakable acrid taste in her mouth, oh somber destiny, it was useless to invoke the Goddess, useless to see that woman from Mantinea, couldn't Hypothesis see that the Goddess was denying her mercy? She had never had two crises in just five days, oh, heavens, oh, light that was nevermore to be, good-bye cruelest Aphrodite, to whom she could not raise a temple, and she pulled her hair and tore her clothes.

And you, oh, Atys of Pamphylia, what would you wear tonight, at the end of your long journey? You were ever so anxious to shed your blind beggar's rags and dress the tunics of your supreme priesthood, to transmit to your followers the messages of the Gateway of Dreams, confirmed by the words of the trees of Thrace and the auguries of the birds in the fields of Boeotia that escorted your steps with great turns to the right. It was noon when you crossed the Cythaeron, and in the Metroon on the border you sharpened your Phrygian knife to a razor's edge, and after cutting off great locks of your red hair, you shaved

163

your head leaving it smooth as the boulders that churn the Hermus on its way down Mount Dindymon, and you buried the hair so that Athens would not know of the hateful metragyrtes' return, and as you descended the Cythaeron, a day owl took flight on your right, and when you walked with your eyes closed tapping your staff along the road to Acarnes, a coal merchant had sneezed looking into the east, and all the signs, oh, Summoner of the Sum, favored your return to the land of Athena, and with your rags faded by alien suns, no one in Attica would recognize you, and in Phyle, they had given you half an obol and some crusts, which you softened in the springs that feed the Cephisus, and when you got to the walls, you again dabbed your lavender eyes with white honey to make them bleary and clouded so you could look at the road without danger of them being recognized, and you got to the gates of Acarnania at dusk, when you could see the first fires of the Acropolis, and you went around the walls, and when you crossed the Eridanus, you asked the help of some washer women who covered their noses when you approached, and you still have a long way to go before you reach the Cynosarges.

What about your clothes? Hypothesis promised to have them ready. Would the Protopriestess of the Sum keep her promise? While you were in Athens, Hypothesis showed great fervor for the New Church, and she worshipped you; and when she looked at you, there were always melodies in her eyes, and she was so zealous in the preparations for the sylvan carnival, and she brought in the first converts, and she gave you a home and sold her things to get you money, and she provided a place for you to perform the first baptisms of the Sum, yes, she was a devout and diligent priestess, oh, the desire to get there and sleep in a bed beside the warm body of a woman, and wash your eyes and open them without fear, and to walk straight, come now, liven your step, for you still have ten stadia to go before reaching Hypothesis's house in Athens, and then, oh, sacred vision, look, right there before the eyes of your soul, there appears the little house in the Cynosarges and it grows and it has columns and there on the marble pediment you see engraved, enormous, in shimmering gold, the Gamma, the Holy Three, most sacred sign of the Sum, within the triangle and behind it the Clover, oh, good fortune, again they speak to you from above and they send you the desire for miracles such as these to remain in the memories of the faithful so that future generations may know that when you were returning from the Gateway of Dreams and the Dionysian forests of Thrace, the Three in the One had inspired you to choose that very place to build a temple, so that Hypothesis's first task would be to find a scribe, one who knew the Greek language, to take note, in beautiful words, of the events of the Sum, as the priests of Marduk do in Babylon and those of Ammon do in Libya, writing down holy events, and as soon as the Protopriestess fitted your new tunic and had a biretta made, for the Gods had also inspired you to use a biretta like the Archigallus of Sardes, and once the scribe had been found, before him, the faithful would bear witness to his revelations and miracles, and neither should you forget, oh, Summoner of the Sum, to ask for liturgical drums and bells and the copper atabal that would go popopon each time the Pylai ton Hypnon were mentioned in the sacred places.

And she dropped to her knees and began scratching and beating the ground with her fists, and called the scavenging bitch to come for her, to take her and be done with it, and she went on digging to make her way to Hades, and Hypothesis, seeing her throwing dirt in her face and digging her nails into her flesh, grabbed her by the waist from behind, lifting her with the strength of a man and resting her against the trunk of an alder, and there, she slapped her desperately two, three times, and Lysis groaning and Hypothesis taking a stick, shut up, you wretch, you'll do as I say, and started pushing her, and Lysis, tame now, trembling, staring in befuddlement at Otep, who was obeying Hypothesis's orders and hushing Laelaps's barking, and Lysis spitting out her tears, a tremor in her cheeks, swallowing the acrid saliva, and Hypothesis pushing her downhill, leading her by the arm through the trees, and when they were down, she made straight for the little pink house by the forest. They might still get there before the evil struck.

And when night fell, you lamented not having your red hair where you hid the three-edged knife, you were now feeling through the false bandages on your leg, prepared with rotting offal, a better defense the stink than the knife, by the Dindymenian Mother, oh, how you want to get there, and at another fountain the water bearers gave you a wide berth as you approached to drink, and in the bosque at the foot of Mount Ardetto, you looked for the spring next to the cave and you took off your clothes and you bathed in the clear waters, splashing, and you got rid of your rags and bandages, and you took from your pack the cape earned for your service to Diodorus the Theban, and as you spread it the falling leaves of lavender covered it and their perfume was so soft, and with it you came to Hypothesis of Athens, the Protopriestess of the Sum, because in your church, the priests and priestesses will smell of lavender, of Persian rose and violets, and the scribe must write this down in the statutes, and the floors of your church will be clean and shiny, as in the Temple of Ishtar, but without blood, without slaves, because slaves have no will, and those initiated in the mysteries of the Sum must be completely devoted, thus have the Gods ordained, oh, Summoner of the Sum, and your church will care for the faithful and will give them clothes and vestments, and it will accept all, men and women, Greeks and barbarians, rich and poor alike, and this you will dictate to the scribe, and you will say, and write also, brother scribe, that I forbid you to accept in the Church of the Sum either thieves or murderers, or hunters of freemen, or persons who are incomplete or very ugly, or those with goiter, leprosy, clouded eyes, or split testicles, or those who are lame, no? why not accept the lame if they be neither unclean nor smelly? so be it, write down that we will accept the lame, but no one who is crooked, or mangy, or mute, or blind, or perhaps we can accept the blind, no, no, write that down, or eunuchs, or wild men, or dummies with slanted eyes, and you will live like brothers, like adelphoi, to put it Greekly, that is, and write down too that the enemy of one brother is the enemy of all brothers, and that whoever injures or kills a brother will die by decree of the Sum, and the Sum will not call for justice or take cases to the courts, and whoever robs or abuses a brother will die by stone, water, rope, dagger, or the malignant drugs we know how to prepare in the Church of the Sum, and it shall be known that the Sum is powerful and knows how to do justice, oh, but see here, with so much thinking about the statutes, you left the trees behind and went right on, now you've got to turn back, the pink house should be right on the other side, there, at the bottom of the hill, yes, look at it, look at it there, oh, Summoner of the Sum.

Lysis walked rigidly. As she entered she began to rave, she said good-bye to Hypothesis, to her faithful Otep, xaire, good-bye, for I must go and you must bide, yes, another crisis like the last one and she would give in; she would, she wanted to die, to

have the three-headed Goddess come for her, and Hypothesis
whispering tender words to her beloved child, and her queen
would see that as soon as the crisis was past she would be made
well by the woman from Mantinea, and her thumb closed on
her index, and the rigidity increasing, and Lysis dropping to the
floor, and Hypothesis ordering Otep to bring a moist cloth, and
Lysis would have wanted to say good-bye to Aspasia, and her
beloved Truncheon, and Otep returning, distressed, suffering
at the sight of his mistress, he tries to leave the room but
Hypothesis wants him close by, and Hypothesis wipes Lysis's
face with the cloth to remove the dirt, and Lysis, popopom,
popopom, and the floor is shaking, an earthquake? popopom,
she covers her ears letting out a hoarse scream, she hears voices
and barking calling her from below, the white bitch of Hades is
coming for her, oh, horrible sound, Lysis shakes her head and
screams with all her might to drown out the barking and the
thumps, she screams and screams, and now Hypothesis has to
lower her head crying, and covering her ears, and this time, oh
horror, Hypothesis distinctly hears the three blows, ah, so then
it was true, it was no hallucination, but how come she,
Hypothesis of Athens, heard the blows, could it be that the
Triple Goddess intended to take her, too? and for the second
time, struck by terror, her eyes tightly closed, biting her lip,
Hypothesis again hears the fearful popopom, and Otep, touching her shoulder and saying he heard knocking, Otep too?
would the Libyan escort them into the kingdom of the underworld? even the dog had his ears pricked, was it him barking?
and Otep that the popopom was coming from outside, that
someone was knocking at the door, and Laelaps barking again
in reply, and he leaves the room followed by the Libyan, and
Lysis raising her arm, and stretching her three fingers, a scream
in her eyes, and Otep returns, that a tall, bald, blind man said

to say that three in one, three in one? had Otep said three in one? and Lysis stretching, her arm high, her three fingers stiff, had the Summoner of the Sum returned, providential and helping, to cure Lysis? had he come to free her of Hecate? to consecrate her to the Three Gods of Life? and she runs to the door and, oh, yes, it was he, unexpected consolation, bald, as Otep had said, but also beautiful without his red hair, oh joy, oh soul, oh life, and she takes his hand and kisses him and drags him into the room.

And on entering, three fingers? who is she? the one screaming? but that's the sacred symbol three, whoever that woman is, she's his business, notice how she twists on the floor and makes the sign, and how she arches her body like a willow, it's all clear, she is visited by the Three Gods, if not, why would she make the sign with three fingers, she was a messenger of the Sum, evident, diaphanes, see the contortions of the young and supple body that is no longer hers, and although she is unconscious, she is still making the sign, a miracle, a new apocalypse before your lucid eyes, the Three Gods of Life have descended into her body, and Hypothesis tells you that the girl heard three blows, popopom, from under the ground, popopom, of course, and you logicos, phainomenon, you immediately understand that those three blows are the divine code, the one created by the Gods to refer to the Gateway of Dreams, and they undoubtedly mean to tell you that you do not have to journey to the mountains of Thessaly because from now on they would communicate through this girl, and what did they have to say? look at her closely, observe her gestures, note every last detail because she must certainly bear important tidings, and that pinkish spittle? and look, now she's beginning to tremble and shake, of course, no mortal can withstand the power of possession by three Gods, but you, oh, Summoner, no matter how hard you look at

169

her, almost naked, her fine clothes torn, you can't discover a clear sign, and you're curious and you feel an overwhelming liking for the magical girl, and Hypothesis says she's her pupil, Callipygous Queen of Athens, a great fear, of Hecate, because of the popopom, the three blows she heard underground, beautiful girl, rich, very rich, jewels, slaves, open banquet at her house, Hypothesis teacher, she dancer and hetaera in Ceramicus, but, oh great misfortune, Lysis irreverent, Lysis perjured, punishment of Aphrodite, and that's why popopom, Hecate, the underworld, but Hypothesis exorcism, and you, yes, go on with the story, so a rich hetaera from the Ceramicus, and Hypothesis filled with hope on hearing your knocking, perhaps you cure her with the power of your eyes, and you, cure? cure not needed, girl no nothing sick, no nothing need cure, girl receiving message from Sum, message for him, and you explain and order Hypothesis to shut up once and for all, and the three digits, popopom, popopom, seecrit messoge, yes, seecrit messoge from the Sum, not in vain had the Gods crossed the destiny of Hypothesis with those of Lysis and the Summoner of the Sum, and that old Mantinea not nothing know, no devil, no mocking spirit, and popopom, not Hecate, not Hades, and Hypothesis embraces you and cries for joy, will you really cure her beloved child? and you repeating that not need cure, that beautiful messenger of Gods not sick, she communicating with Summoner of the Sum, but look, look, the Gods are withdrawing, she much calm, and very soon, when she again breath calm, no doubt Gods send message diaphanes, message for you, and you also looking, oh Protopriesta, but now the girl opens her eyes and stares directly at you, she points to you and calls you, and you approach, and you call for a lamp to see her face clearly and dwell on every word and gesture, and as you approach with the lamp to look into her sleepwalker's eyes, she, in a stupor, saying that your eyes are violet, like the eye stolen from the Goddess, and you, hearing this, do not know what to do, you cannot speak, you cannot act, you close your eyes, lower your bald head, and you finally understand, oh, you understand that you have finally come on the spoor of the Dindymenian Eye, the spoor you have been seeking throughout the Ecumene, and you remain on your knees by her side, your breast full of gratitude to the Three Gods, joy, a desire to sing, to dance, to jump, but, no, careful, your are no longer a wild coribant, the metragyrtes with the long hair is a thing of the past, the filth and the mottle are gone, now you are the Summoner of the Sum, and the Gods have ordained that you officiate in single-color linens to sustain your priestly dignity, and thus, oh, Atys of Pamphylia, now that you receive messages from on high, you look into your soul with all the power of your eyes and you order yourself to contain the pristine joy dancing in your heart, and you rise, full of dignity and poise, and you declare to the Protopriestess of the Sum that the Three in One have passed their message, a very logicos message, very phainomenon, and by the way, where are the promised tunics? and Hypothesis explains that they have been waiting for the Summoner of the Sum for months, that they are right there, in the chest with the chains, wrapped with violets and lavender that she renews every week, and you thinking that the beautiful hetaera of the Ceramicus must not know, nor Hypothesis, nor those in Athens, nor may any mortal in the Known World know of your quest for the Dindymenian Eye, therefore the very Gods must have instructed the girl, and if she could compare the color of the Dindymenian Eye to the color of your eyes, it must be because she has seen it, the Eye is in Athens, of course, very phainomenon, by this they mean that you will soon culminate your long quest, the Gods have sent you to found your church in Athens so that you can

rescue the Eye and be relieved of your commitment to the
Mother of the Gods, so that you can devote yourself completely
to your priesthood for the Sum and build its temples, oh apocalyptic conjugation of three destinies, oh unfathomable workings of the Three in One, and as soon as the messenger girl
recovers from the visit of the Gods, you will give her the baptism of the Sum and name her High Priestess, and the three fingers will become another emblem of the New Church, because
the Gods have manifestly willed it so by letting you know this
way, and to her ordainment you will add the title of Seer of the
Dindymenian Eye, how is that in Greek? no matter, you will
soon find out, and while the Protopriestess is fitting your new
yellow tunic, you explain to her as something very phainomenon that the message that came through the Sweet-Rump
Queen confirmed the first one you received in the Pylai ton
Hypnon, poPOpom popoPOM.

172

2 5

O N THE MORNING of the Plynteria, Truncheon
awoke with a fever and a pain in her kidneys. She was
terrified when they told her that Lysis had had a relapse, was on
the brink of death, and had surrendered to Hecate. She went to
see Lysis, but there was nothing to be done. In fact, the visit
worsened her own malady, and she spent the night screaming
from the pain in her kidneys.

Days later, still sick in bed, she received a papyrus from
Lysis announcing that she had freed herself once and for all of
her fear of Hecate and the disgust her disease caused her. The
Gods, thanks once again to the excellent Hypothesis, had
brought her a new benefactor who had revealed to her the
meaning of the three rigid fingers and the three underground
thumps. Now she welcomed her disease, she welcomed the
Three Gods who visited her body, and she thrice blessed the
miraculous doctor.

Amid her suffering, Truncheon wondered why Lysis had

not brought the good news in person, as she always did. Something strange must have happened to her. So there was an unexpected benefactor? Then why hadn't Lysis come to her sickbed to share her joy and her radiant youth?

Truncheon knew that she would feel better just by having Lysis near and taking her hand in hers, but the days passed and Lysis never came, never answered. Oh, troubling suspicions. How could she, knowing that she was sick, that she was passing stones? Why didn't she come? Why didn't she take her to that miraculous doctor? Had she forgotten how she used to visit her almost every day to talk over their adventures and misadventures, or to lie with her in her bed during the day, or to discuss the business of Aphrodite? Then Truncheon sent her a second note, one expressing her pain, but no answer. And since there was nothing on Earth that she did not know of life and love, and she knew her Lysis, she was certain that she had found in that man, whoever he might be, something more than a doctor. Then she wrote a third note, an angry one, which she sent with Lysistrata, her most trusted slave, whom she commanded to see her and find out what had happened, why the silence, who the doctor was that Hypothesis had brought her. Lysistrata was to try to get a glimpse of him and bring back all the details: his height, age, color, clothes, and manners.

But Lysistrata was not even allowed into the house because Hypothesis, that pissing harpy, had said that Lysis was not there and that the doctor had gone, and taking the note from the slave, she had not even allowed her into the kitchen to talk to the Paphlagonian and quench her thirst with a draft of wine, as she usually did, and Lysistrata swore she had heard Lysis's flute and, passing by the back door on her return journey, she had also heard, as if coming from the women's court, Lysis's tinkling laughter, and that morning, as Truncheon attempted to

174

get up to fulfill a promise for her recovery at the Temple of Asclepius, Lysistrata handed her a papyrus just brought by Hypothesis, but what a disappointment, no loving words from Lysis, no, nothing, not a word about the doctor, not a question about her kidney stone, just questions about One Eye, whether Truncheon knew where he was, whether she had finally thrown him out of the brothel, and that Lysis wanted him as an adviser to purchase some slaves, and Truncheon suspicious, not believing a word of those transactions she had not even heard about, Lysis makes no decisions about slaves without consulting her, something was wrong, perhaps terribly wrong, and damn that harpy, what had she gotten the girl into, that food-for-vultures who just a few months before had wandered the streets drunk, in rags, and pissing all over herself, by Zeus, Hypothesis would certainly have something to do with the business with One Eye, of course, who else would be instigating her, who else could have her enthralled and blind so that she could see only through the eyes of the witch? And she was probably giving her potions to keep her under control, and the so-called doctor must be just like her and they had bewitched the child, that was why Lysis had ignored her advice, she had never done that, and Hypothesis going around bragging about the new slaves that "her child" had bought her, and Truncheon promised herself that the first time Hypothesis dared to call Lysis "her child" in her presence she was going to remind her that Lysis could not be the child of a filthy whore, of a harbor hypoporne, and although she could not deny that the pissing harpy had been behind her victory in the Haloae, Truncheon would have preferred it if she had never been crowned if that crown meant falling into their clutches, oh, but, by the Two Gods, she was not going to put up with that old shit's, that whore's presumption, and as she stepped into the courtyard, there was Hypothesis, unrecognizable in her new wig, elegant hairdo, and fine yellow linen that Truncheon herself had given Lysis, and Hypothesis pretending that she was so busy with Lysis's new brothels, and that she had come only because of One Eye, and that Lysis had sent her with Otep and the animal so that they could accompany Mnesis and Chloe, whom she was going to train in callipygian dancing, and Truncheon, incisive, how was Lysis, and Hypothesis, how should she be? beautiful, radiant, cured of her terrors, because Hypothesis really did take care of her, and thanks to her friends and Gods she had done for Lysis, heh, heh, heh, what no one in Athens had been able to do and besides, she had. But Truncheon interrupting again, that she knew nothing of One Eye, and if she did know, she would not tell, and that Lysis had said nothing of Mnesis and Chloe in the note, so she would not turn them over, and Truncheon found it very strange that instead of asking about One Eye, Lysis had not asked about her health, and Hypothesis, oh, yes, her child had mentioned that Truncheon had a rotten kidney again and was passing boulders, were there many? and Truncheon, a whole lot, huge, and, if Hypothesis wanted, she could give her some so she could clog up her holes, front and back, and out, out of the house, you whore, and slap, slap, clapping her hands and out, you pissing, shitting hypoporne, and the door slave pulling on Hypothesis's arm and Laelaps barking and Hypothesis from the street, why don't you die, damn you, I hope you piss a rock so big it slits the sides of your twat, and may your next turd be a crag as big as the Acropolis, and Laelaps seconding the motion with a bark, and the people of Athens enjoying the show and Otep dragging the dog and Hypothesis cursing for another two plethra, and when she recovers her breath, she dismisses Otep and goes on looking for One Eye, for whom Lysis had written a second papyrus ordering him to report to her house before sunset or the Basileus Archon would know of his traffic in sacred objects, of his great impiety against Athens. And the Summoner of the Sum had advised, not threatened, One Eye, before Truncheon told them where he was and that it was best to bring him in on good terms, offer him money, a thousand drachmas, anything, and Hypothesis went into one of Parapet's brothels and gave the note to the cook, a friend of hers, who did not know how to read, a message for the brothel keeper, and Hypothesis had not gone far when a little slave reached her with a message from One Eye who had just arrived, and One Eye swearing that it was the truth, that by the Twelve Gods, he would never hide from Hypothesis, and she dragging him by the sleeve to the end of the alley, checking that no one was listening, whispering, where was the amethyst he had offered Truncheon? oh, by the Great Mother of the Gods! he had washed his hands, he had given it back to Xanthus the Lycian, yes, yes, and for fear of being blamed, he had hidden for a while where they couldn't find him, but then, as the Lycian said nothing despite the torture, and he had been condemned to the silver mines of Laurium, Laurium? really? oh yes, now he was chained to the lever of a mill, coughing all day, and, well, One Eye knew nothing of the stone, he had given it back to Xanthus the day he had been scolded, and Xanthus certainly must have taken it with him on his escape, but since it had not been mentioned, One Eye supposed that Xanthus got rid of it or the thieves had taken it, and Hypothesis remembering that the Summoner also wanted to know which slaves were closest to Xanthus, and One Eye, that undoubtedly Sosias the Carian, and Hypothesis, very well, but in any case, if One Eye heard anything about the stone or imagined where Xanthus had hidden it, Lysis of Miletus would pay one thousand drachmas for it, and that night One Eye, a thousand drachmas? what could

Lysis want with the amethyst? why should she give a thousand drachmas for a stone that wasn't worth five hundred? she could certainly not wear it, or risk being cast into the Barathrum for impiety, but what if Lysis had gone mad? that was horrible, an irresponsible mad woman knowing what she did, by the Great Mother, again in mortal danger, how could he sleep nights? damn the day, damn the stone, damn Xanthus the Lycian, and damn that crazy whore Lysis of Miletus!

26

A ND THE RAT squeaking in the sack and the
Summoner of the Sum walking faster up the hill, and
Sosias, practically running, with his short legs, and that the
Summoner should stop before the crest of the hill and peek over
carefully because they were already getting there and perhaps, on
that treeless hill and with the full moon, the archers might see
him from the wall, and that the best way to get to the shrine of
the Omestes was to go around the trees, over there, and Sosias
could not take his mind off the rat, and he could not understand
why, just seven days after his communion with the Three Gods,
he had to have communion again with Dionysus Omestes, the
Eater of Raw Flesh, and drink the blood, buagh, such a filthy
host, and all the time descending toward the coast, and he wanting the Summoner to explain why, and the Summoner that it
was very simple, that the Three Thirds of the Sum repeat communion when one invokes a different nature, another physis of
the same God, Sosias now understand? and when Aphrodite,

not being Pandemos, but Urania, or Cyprinia, or Astarte the Syrian, or when Dionysus, being Bacchus or Sabazius the Phrygian, or the bull, or the snake, or Omestes, eater of raw flesh, and for the God, being propishus, and Sosias, propitious, exactly, for the God be propitious necessary honor him with good host and Eater of Raw Flesh like hot red blood, not matter rat, bull, robbit, and Sosias, you say rabbit, and standing to hide his retching and pointing to a promontory on the coast, that's where the abandoned mine is, and at the end of the tunnel, the grotto of Dionysus Omestes, and Atys stooping to drink from a spring and refresh his body, and Sosias sitting on a rock, waiting, and what was that moving in the Summoner's pack? was it the rat? yes, the filthy rat was poking his nose through a hole and gnawing away to make his escape, and the moon shining on it, should he warn the Summoner? why should he? hadn't he said that in the New Church the faithful should follow the direct inspiration of the Gods? and the Summoner going to pick up the pack to move on, and Sosias, don't! better to wait right there, by the spring, they would be able to see nothing in the shrine until daylight filtered in, and the rat almost had its head out and fighting desperately, but Sosias pointing uphill, that the Summoner should notice the light by the palisade, and the damned rat with a paw out, and could the Summoner see that high point, that was one of the knolls, and glancing at the ground, there! uff, at last! and two months earlier, the strategi had ordered the ocean side of the mines fenced in, and the Summoner bending to pick up his pack, rat run off, damn bitch rat escape, and the Summoner beating himself on the head with both hands and his thighs, still cursing in Pamphylian, and Sosias asking if it were not the will of the Gods, and the Summoner that anyway bad, bad omane, and Sosias, omen, had Omestes been angered? had the Summoner checked that the rat

180

was impeccable? because they said that Omestes was extremely touchy about the victims on his altars, and they say that since the times of Themistocles, a fugitive Egyptian had taken refuge in the grotto of Omestes and spent thirty days without food, and when he was only skin and bones, about to die, he dragged himself to the mouth of the tunnel to raise his last prayer to the Sun and the guards caught him, and since he was no good for work, his master ordered him sacrificed right there to Dionysus Omestes, who liked human sacrifices, and they did, right there on the altar the Summoner would see in a little while, and the impious Athenians forgot that none of the Hellenic Gods accepted victims that had been exploited by men, and the Summoner not understanding that exploited thing, and Sosias, victims that had produced profit, what be profit? explain in Carian tongue! but the Second Faithful continued in Greek, after thirty years in Athens, he no longer recalled his language, and no Greek God accepted on his altar an ox that had been worked or a horse that had been ridden, or a draft ass, or a fighting cock or quail that had produced cream, and what being cream? and Sosias had forgotten cream in Carian, but cream was like obols or money, and you, cream? another useful word to remember, and you should, oh Atys of Pamphylia, use these days with the Second Faithful among Men to learn many other fat words, very much good Greek words, and so then, because a used slave produced much cream for his master, sacrificing him to Omestes was great offense, and you, hum, wondering if the Eater of Raw Flesh accept, for example, those Scythians who had been chasing you with hounds all over Attica, did the slaves in the City produce cream? and after the sacrifice of the Egyptian, Athens shook, houses fell, and even the opistodomus of the Temple of Pluto, and that is why the Assembly of Athenian men prohibited human sacrifice, except for criminals and the impious, who were hurled into the Barathrum, and you, hum, the Scythians produced peace and order, but that was not cream, and well, no talking more, time to prepare trap for catch different victim, and taking a pick from his pack, that Sosias should make a handle and dig a pit, deep like this, four cubits, and the Summoner sitting down to braid loops for the trap, and Sosias in his seventh day as a freeman, guiding the steps of the Summoner of the Sum over the Laurium uplands, could it be a dream? would he wake up again the slave of Artemon the Bale, no, this sweat was no dream, nor the pick biting into the earth, no, no dream, Lysis had bought him for three times the price and had sworn his freedom the next day before the Three Gods of the Sum, and then the baptism of Aphrodite in the arms of the beautiful Chloe, oh, those perfumed legs and breasts, all for him, and Chloe allowed herself to be mounted, the sweet little sister of the Sum, and he licking her, and she laughing for pleasure, and such a wonder could only have come to him by the express order of the Summoner of the Sum, because you could understand if it happened to the Libyan Otep, the First Faithful among Men, who even as a slave could inspire whims in immortal Goddesses, but not Sosias the Carian, a scrawny, ugly slave who only fornicated with goats, donkeys, sows, and now he was the Second Faithful of the Sum among Men, and having dug the hole, and covered it with the ropes and dry leaves, the ash staves cut, the lances sharpened, that Sosias should take a position there, and you on the other side, some thirty feet away, by the stream, and when you were sure that Sosias could not see you, you took out the turds and moistened them to keep them fresh and covered them again with fig leaves, and you wanted a drink of wine, but you couldn't drink the offering, and it was best that Sosias did not know everything that was in the pack, better to make a bundle and put it at the bottom of the pack, there you could put the earth of Artemis Phosphoros with its glowworm oil, the white tunic, the poisoned honey, and the horse hooves, but then you would crush the turds, no, it would be better to put everything Sosias should not see in a bundle on top, you could tell him it was food, and in the bottom you could put the wine, the hooks, the ropes, and let Sosias carry the pick, the saw, the candles, the flint, and the rest of the food in his own pack, and you smiled, oh, Summoner of the Sum, and you mended the rat's hole, for you also had needle and thread, a man who has been a soldier and a sailor learns to pack the essentials, and not in vain had you lived in the forest and learned the value of a needle amid the ice, but that night the trap failed and the warm blood demanded by Omestes was not there in the morning, and you called Sosias to start a fire and warm up some salted fish, and then look! a lizard a hand-span long, climbing up a trunk, and the Sum sent you the idea that to make communion with Dionysus you did not need the dough of warm blood, and you recalled that Sabazius accepted whatever the Asian miners could offer, scorpions, beetles, so without a doubt that lizard was sent by the Three in One, and with your Phrygian dagger, you took aim at its middle, the widest part of its green body, and thwap, you got it, but in the tail, and it was nailed there, and Sosias, ugh, imagining himself chewing the reptile, oh, no, the Gods would not accept a victim that was not impeccable, and the Summoner tying it up, putting it into the pack, what missing make it not peccable? missing leg? missing head, maybe? and Sosias, that Omestes would not accept victims with the slightest scar and this one had a knife hole in it, look at that disfigured tail, it was indecent to sacrifice defective, cold-blooded reptiles, and the Summoner angry, shut up, you reptile, not understanding, head of rock, that Supreme Priest always guided by Gods, not understanding that they guide eye and hand to tail puint,

183

and Sosias, you say point, but you, oh, Summoner of the Sum, knew full well that you did not aim at the tail, but a detail like that was not to be allowed to undermine your authority before the faithful, come fast, stop dumb talk, and Sosias, damn talk, and you, no damn, dumb, you dumb, stupid, and before entering the grotto they wove the sacrificial regalia, and Sosias, with his small hands, braided an ivy garland for the victim, and a tiny poplar crown, and you, who were weaving your own regalia for the sacrifice, seeing his child's hands and small feet, asked yourself of what possible use he could have been in the shafts of Laurium, surely not to wield a pick or hammer, perhaps to cart the minerals in baskets like the children who lived and died hunched over in the tunnels, or perhaps the Three Gods had long ago ordained that the Carian should be familiar with the mines to be able, one day, to guide you in the rescue of the Dindymenian Eye, and with your eyes nailed to the small feet, the idea came to you, the very bright idea of carving a foot even smaller than brother Sosias's, there was plenty of cork oak bark around, the Athenians would find out, and having finished their weaving, they crawled into the shrine, and Sosias could walk on all fours, but the Summoner had to crawl on his elbows all the way into a great cavern with a very high roof, and, amid the shadows of the shrine, they made a fire with the flint, lit a candle, placed crowns and garlands on their arms, and, palms turned upward, saluted the black oval stone that represented Omestes, and Sosias, recalling that during the six months that Artemon had sent him to Laurium for punishment, on a Plynteria holiday, they had taken him and other slaves with good behavior, closely guarded, to worship the God, and the tunnel, abandoned since the appearance of the new lode in Maronea, was outside the mine periphery, and it was the shrine of Dionysus Omestes, whom the miners worshipped like Sabazius the Profound and

devoted to him the ritual of chewing bloodless animals, ugh, and
the Summoner tying the lizard to a small stone, and once
secured with a knot on its back, he decked it with the garlands
and the crown, and ugh, cutting off some fingers to leave only
three on each hand, and the victim would not keep its head
down as the ritual required, and no matter how much the
Summoner insisted by pressing its head against the altar, the
stubborn lizard raised its head once again, and stretched and
puffed its neck horribly, and Sosias didn't dare argue that it was
not a propitious host, and with his stomach in convulsions and
the conviction that no holy aim, nor his love for the New
Church, nor his respect and gratitude for the Summoner of the
Sum, not even the promise of another baptism with Chloe could
make him get that thing down his throat, agh, raw, and you, oh,
Summoner of the Sum, with such an irreverent host, so hard-
headed, having exhausted your priestly patience, crushed its
head against the altar with a holy blow, inspired by Dionysus?
and ordered your acolyte to sprinkle it with salt and sacrificial
meal, and Sosias, seeing that the Summoner took his knife and
cut the lizard into three pieces, fearing that he might vomit the
dried fish on the altar, and the Summoner had already put the
head in his mouth and was chewing, and he offered the middle
with the legs to the God, and with a severe admonitory look, he
placed the tail in the mouth of the Second Faithful among Men,
and Sosias chewing, but without bringing his teeth together, he
could not, oh no, so salty and hard, waagh, and his stomach
heaving and turning him inside out, and you, oh Summoner,
ordering him to take that great club and go over to the corner,
there where the flagstone was, and you were going to dance for
Dionysus the dance of the he-goat, that Sosias should stay back
because you needed a great stage for your leaps and the sacred
mimetic dance you learned with the Thracians, and Sosias was

to beat out the rhythm with the club, yes, very hard, as if he were compacting the soil, beating much very hard on the white flag-stone, like this, popopom, the sacred rhythmos of the three beats, Second Faithful understand? hard and much steady, and you made a libation of three drops of wine on the altar, and you drank all the rest, and with it swallowed the rest of the lizard, and Sosias chewing without chewing, and popopom went the club on the flagstone, and popopom his stomach, and you, tak-ing from the pack one of the bells you had saved from your old motley, interspersing chimes with the sacred popopom and singing a Thracian psalmody and improvising reasons for Omestes to accept the humble offering the Gods had ordered you to nail on a trunk with crack aim, green like the grapevines in spring, but then the Second Faithful vomited the host in the corner, why the rejection? what sin have you committed, oh,

Summoner of the Sum, for your acolyte to vomit at such an untimely moment? Oh, let Omestes not be angry, that the lizard was only, how could he explain? a provisional sacrifice, a preparatory joke, that was it, a kind of stimulating advance, wasn't it allowed in the New Church for the High Priest to play pious jokes on its Thirds, and the truth was, for the idea had just recently taken root in your soul, that you intended to sacrifice his favorite victim, the strong, white host of warm blood that the Omestes had not tasted in Athens for many years, and the thing with the lizard was just a joke, and Sosias valiantly, popopom, despite the vomiting, popopom, and you dancing and the enthou-siasmos gives you strength to leap and stomp powerfully, and let the rhythmos resound, let the Second Faithful go on beating, beating on the flagstone with spirit, much fast now, in the Phrygian mode, popopom, popopom, popopom, and the high leaps and terrible shakes leave you breathless, and on your knees you drink Dionysus's wine, panting, and another drink, and another, that's it, communion, oh, well beloved of the Sum, did Scythians produce cream? popopom, but never mind, oh Summoner, for everything you do has been previously ordained, otherwise how could you be living in Athens, popopom, playing jokes on the immortal Gods, you, a fugitive slave, who were born shackled to a field of saffron, who but the Gods could have made you the favorite of the most expensive girls in Hellas? doctor of the jealous Lysis of Miletus, popopom, who went into a rage yesterday and threw your acolytes from your bed, popopom, to make way for herself, to give herself to you, and feed you mouth to mouth with chewed figs and honey and wine, popopom, avidly trying to sound your lavender eyes, and she calls you Supreme Priest, and Doctor of Souls, and Supreme Man, and Supreme Love, and, popopom, look at yourself, oh work of the Gods, look, oh founder of new churches, and you laugh between leaps, imagining how surprised Xanthus the Lycian is going to be when he finds himself free of his chains, and you leap like the fish in the river, because your eyes would do what Lysis of Miletus's money could not, and you see Omestes smiling too, pleased with your joke, awaiting the promised succulent host on his altar, and you shake and you sing out laughing in the grotto, for soon you will make the abusive Athens, the haughty Athens, tremble, eh? what? where's the popopom? why is the popopom stilled? where's the Second Faithful? and the flagstone? ahh, terrible sign, oh divine Omestes, what have you done with Sosias the Carian? and hearing the shouts from afar, you approached the corner, and you looked, there, a hole, and from the bottom of the hole a voice, a moaning, get me out, help, don't leave me, and you, you realized that he had slipped in, the Second Faithful had fallen through along with the flagstone, the flagstone on which he was beating popopom.

2 7

IN HIS BARBER SHOP on the Street of the Hoopers, Eulogos was given to inventing indelible nicknames. He was the first to detect that Pericles's head was just like an onion, and ever since then, he called him Eschinocephalus, a nickname later to be immortalized by the comic Cratinus in one of his plays. And long before anyone else had started in on Euripides with the fact that his mother was a green-grocer, Eulogos was already calling him radish, scallion, and purslane.

When they saw him coming into the agora at the time of the plethora, followed by the slave who carried his bench, everyone who wanted to enjoy the creations of his evil tongue would gather round.

The day of the ominous events in Laurium, Eulogos took on the whole City, which was now praising and blessing the departure of Golden Ass for Olympia, heading the Athenian athletes.

So they had forgiven the impious libertine? In a single afternoon they had forgotten that ever since he was a child he had done nothing but scandalize and humiliate the City, and Eulogos, strutting languidly, eyelids drooping, and the onlookers laughing, and just because Golden Ass had sworn some days earlier, his head high, hair decked with ribbons, before the Temple of Zeus, that he, the illustrious son of Clinias, would never be second to anyone, and standing on the chariot that had cost Anytus twelve minae, raising the reins in offering, swearing that he would bring at least one victory from Elis, and why should anyone believe his bragging? let's see now, impious, sacrilegious, rouge on his cheeks, an asshole broader than the mouth of an amphora, and the Thessalian quadriga, manes decked with ribbons as well.

And talking about horses, Eulogos recalled when Second in Everything had asked for the floor during the last session of the Assembly to advise the men of Athens to sacrifice horses to Poseidon. Did he think that everyone had a thousand slaves working in Laurium, as he did, to be able to afford equine sacrifices?

189

And there was so much laughter around his stand that a visitor asked who Second in Everything might be, and Eulogos, snipping away in the air, never letting go of his client's head, how then lives there an Athenian who does not know who the Pantadeuteros was? might the curious stranger be a foreigner? aha! where from? Abdera? By Pallas! Then it could be no other than the famous Protagoras, the sophist who exchanged his science for money, and giving the crowd time to laugh and comment, and sweeping the hair away with his bare foot, spitting, scratching his back with the scissors, well, well now, so the wise Protagoras did not know who the Pantadeuteros was?

Elbow jabs, winks, remarks.

But Protagoras, humm, smiling, stroking his chin, darting a suspicious glance, well no, actually, he did not think he knew.

And Eulogos, so you think you don't know? well, the Abderite was very much mistaken, and Eulogos, son of Isarcus, Athenian, was going to prove that Protagoras did have that knowledge, and Eulogos would help him give birth, he would pull it from his soul with the maieutics Socrates used to teach free of charge in that same square, and the excellent Protagoras should try to think who in Athens might be first in arms.

Murmurs, whispering.

And Protagoras, humm . . . Lamacus?

Correct! Applause for Protagoras of Abdera!

And who might be first in politics and choruses?

And Protagoras, by Zeus! that would certainly be his friend, Pericles of Xanthippus.

More applause.

And did the excellent Abderite know who the richest man in Athens was?

And the sophist, without a moment's hesitation, why, Callias, the one from Hipponicus, that was why they called him Callias the Rich, right?

Bravo! By the dog! had everyone present seen how much true knowledge Protagoras had hidden in his soul?

Clamorous laughter.

And Protagoras laughed too, watching Eulogos waddling like a duck and imitating Socrates's guttural and high-pitched voice to announce that he was now going to ask the Abderite the birth question, the one that would bring to light that perfect knowledge, that child of his soul, whose head was already visible.

Ready?

Good! Let the distinguished sophist deduce, then, who might be second to Lamacus in arms, to Onion Head in politics and choruses, and to Callias in riches. Who was the

Pantadeuteros, then, who was not even the most ridiculous or superstitious man in Athens, that honor having been lost to Artemon the Bale?

And as soon as he could quiet his own laughter, the sophist said that, well, of course, he realized that Second in Everything could only be Nicias of Niceratus, and amid the general merriment, Eulogos proudly snipping in the air, for the foreigner's correct answer confirmed the fairness of the nickname, and Protagoras, could he please explain who Artemon the Bale was, he didn't know him, and, at the mere mention of the character, there was much hand wringing and expectant silence.

So that was the day, snip, snip, snipping, that Eulogos explained to Protagoras of Abdera that Artemon the Engineer, or Artemon Periphoretos, or Artemon the Bale, was the target of the unanimous mockery of Athens thanks to his asinine maneuvers to avoid the unavoidable designs of the Gods; as it happened, once, when he was commanding his war engines during the siege of Samos, he had a bad dream about his death, snip, snip, snip, and the following day, he sent an emissary to Delphi to consult the oracle; Apollo answered him a few days later, "You will die like Aeschylus," and in all of Hellas, it was known that the great Athenian tragedian had died while on a walk in Sicily, crushed by a turtle dropped on his head by a passing eagle, and from that moment on, Artemon never again ventured to walk under an open sky and, to protect himself from an empyrean brick, he had a sedan chair made with an iron top, and from that chair, carried by four slaves, he proceeded to command the operation of his engines against the walls, until the day Onion Head entered victorious, leading his troops; and Eulogos, snip, snip, himself a veteran of the Samos campaign, had once cut the Engineer's hair in his shop, and during the whole time, he had a slave beside him covering his

191

head with a shield, and since then, the astonished City would watch him going everywhere in his armored litter, like a Persian satrap.

Eulogos was still lashing Artemon for his superstitions when, quite unexpectedly, the Pantadeuteros, that very same General Nicias of Niceratus, who rarely let himself be seen in the agora at this time of day, rode by heading a squad of armed horsemen making their way to the tholos of the Prytaneum, where they tied their lathered horses to the columns.

And the news got out immediately, casting a pall on everyone there. The market was deserted in no time. The smoke of sacrifices began to pour from the chimneys. The terrified City could not do enough to placate the ire of the Gods.

Something horrible had happened in the mines of Laurium.

192

Ever since his epheby, many years before, Nicias had distinguished himself in combat. But many asked themselves how such a superstitious young man could fight so valiantly. A man who could see discouraging omens from the Gods in the most trivial daily occurrence. What they did not know was that his daring and personal courage were also rooted in a divine presage.

Just after he was born, an oracle had foretold that weapons would not be his undoing. And the prophecy came true nineteen years later, when Nicias fought as a volunteer at Coronea under the command of Tolmides, together with another one thousand scions of illustrious families. In that defeat, Nicias was the only survivor of an advance party of sixty hoplites, massacred in a fatal ambush between two mountains.

Nicias was hit on the head with a club. He fell unconscious

into a crevice in the rocks and the body of a slain comrade covered him all that afternoon. Later, a detachment of allied riders found him, helped him gain the heights of Helicon, and from there escorted him during the three-day march back to his country.

The City praised him as one of the few who was not killed or taken prisoner by the Boeotians in Coronea. Days later, when he had recovered from his ordeal, he was out hunting with his faithful dogs, when suddenly, Leucos, his favorite, showed up wagging his tail and carrying a live quail in his strong jaws. How strange! A dog, without barking, single-handedly catching a quail that the hunter had not even seen? Humm, that must certainly be a message from the Gods.

When he reached out, his faithful Leucos attacked, biting him furiously about the jaw. The scars, which he hid under a dense beard, were with him for the rest of his life.

He had the dog killed right there, and the following day he immediately consulted the diviners. But he never got a clear answer. Euphrantides interpreted that Artemis was ordering him to devote himself to Athenian politics, and from that moment on, Nicias began to frequent the aristocratic political circles of the City.

The year after the disaster at Coronea, the City sent him to its outpost in Megara, and when the revolt broke out, he survived and managed to get back to Athens. He had given proof of amazing valor.

The oracle of his birth was again fulfilled.

In the years after that, his cold blood in combat was such that at the early age of thirty-five he was already a member of the College of Strategi. And yet, from the very moment he was given command of armies, his personal valor was tempered by great prudence, a quality his troops appreciated. They felt much safer with a general who undertook no action without convincing auguries.

The song of a bird, a twisted branch on the road, a single word, an unexpected breeze, would be enough to halt a march or postpone a battle.

Along with the regular seers all armies had with them, Nicias employed others, at his own expense, and kept them by his side in every battle. He needed permanent augural counseling to dispel the shadows of the immediate future.

He consulted all the diviners about his misfortune with the dog, but the interpretations were so dissimilar and so contradictory that he never accepted any of them.

One day, he found out that the Buzyges was sending an embassy to Dodona, and he dispatched a tablet for Zeus and Dione asking which diviner he should believe in the matter of the incident with his dog Leucos.

The millenary oak of the oracle answered that about the whitest of his dogs he should believe the blackest of his seers. The answer was a disappointment. Of all the seers of Athens, none was notoriously darker than the rest.

Nicias did not know what to do.

Months later, he was to understand that the answer was precise, but now it was still flying in the winds of future days; it had always been flying among the oaks of Dodona.

At a slave auction run by some Ephesian sailors in Piraeus, Nicias acquired a Syrian about forty years of age because no one would give the initial asking price of one hundred and eighty drachmas. He was skinny, misshapen, and of a sickly, olive drab complexion. Nicias found that he had only fifteen teeth in his mouth and, although his skin was not healthy, at least it was not pocked or marked by torture. Nicias had smoke blown in the slave's face to make him cough and, detecting no sign of lung disease, he ordered his economus to haggle the price down to a maximum of one hundred and thirty drachmas.

And that was what he paid for him. By renting him out at an obol a day in Laurium, Nicias could recuperate his investment in two years and fifty days; if the Syrian held out for four years, it was a wise purchase.

Nicias could not have known that four years later he would have given three hundred thousand drachmas to keep from losing that slave.

Before they bundled him off to Laurium, the Syrian managed to get the word around that he was good with numbers. Nicias had him tested and his economus found that the slave could indeed do mental calculations surprisingly fast. To Nicias's questions, the slave explained that he had learned arithmomancy with the astrologers of Babylon.

So Nicias decided to rent him for three obols a day to Lysicles, the sheep merchant, who needed an accountant for his tanneries and pens. Because of his complexion, the other slaves called him Melas.

A short time after he was with Lysicles, the Syrian had a high fever and became delirious. He woke up several times during the night gasping and mumbling that he had seen his master Nicias going down with his ship in a storm.

A slave foreman whose sleeping mat was right next to Melas's commented the case with the water bearer of the ergasterium, who also served in the home of Nicias, and Melas's dream reached Nicias almost immediately.

As soon as Nicias heard that his slave, Melas the black, had had a prophetic dream, he recalled the warning of Zeus and Dione and sent his secretary for the details.

At the time, Nicias was head of the Hellenotamiae and was to sail the following day for Naxos. He was to go with the other tax collectors to adjust the tribute of the Delian League. His emissary had also found out that the Syrian had delivered a number of correct presages. All the slaves in the shop and even the ergasteriarch listened to him and treated him with deference.

Nicias found some pretext to postpone his voyage. And that day, approaching the end of summer, an untimely storm broke loose. Two Athenian ships went down. One of them was the flagship that was to have carried Nicias.

The Syrian was given his reward. Nicias did not renew his contract with Lysicles and from that day forward employed Melas as the market slave of his farm, since he had such a good head for numbers. He had not wanted to consult him about Leucos until he was more certain of his augural abilities. But for many months, Melas made no predictions.

Nicias still preferred consulting old Lampon; Euphrantides, grandson of Euphrantides of Salamis; or the oniromancy of young Eutidemus, scion of a long line of seers.

But a day came when Nicias saw in Melas the diviner mentioned by the oak of Zeus in Dodona.

It happened just after assuming his fourth choregia. Dionysus had rewarded his munificence and devotion seven times. Although others, for reasons of age, had more victories, Nicias was the only undefeated choregus. His secretary was present at all the rehearsals; he demanded that his actors train their voices with Olympic discipline, and he received daily reports on the state of the chorus' dormitories and food. The play assigned to Nicias was Sophocles's *Telephos*. One of the finest actors in the group was a young slave by the name of Myrsus, for whom Nicias had paid nine hundred drachmas the year before. At home, Nicias employed him as a wine server and sometimes as a reader, with access to the gynaeceum.

A Lydian by birth, Myrsus had been raised among the Greeks of Asia. He recited and sang beautifully, and his sprightly figure evoked great admiration when he danced.

Nicias had lodged the cast of *Telephos* at a farm in Colonus so that Sophocles, who was living nearby, could more easily help in the production of his tetralogy. And during one of the recesses, Myrsus jumped a wall to pick some figs and fell into the corral where an ornery billy goat was kept. The animal rammed him, wounding him in the neck, but Myrsus got away by leaping over the wall that gave onto the Sacred Way, right in plain view of several of the choristers, Sophocles himself, and Melas the Syrian, who was returning with a mule train of provisions.

The accident produced much consternation. Myrsus had been doing six characters in the four works they were rehearsing. The fact that a he-goat, an animal sacred to Dionysus, had rammed Myrsus would seem to anyone to be a veto. Just a week before the festival, where could they find a substitute capable of acting with such grace? No actor out of training, no matter how good he may have been, could acquire in so short a time the power that Myrsus had developed in projecting his voice. That was the whole reason behind the six months of special food and endless rehearsals that Nicias had paid for. Taking him from the cast would be a disaster.

So, when the choregus was told about the incident, he consulted several seers and the verdict was unanimous: Dionysus repudiated Myrsus and did not want to be played by him.

But Melas, who was secretly in love with Myrsus, had a different opinion. According to his interpretation, the attack by the goat had pushed Myrsus onto the road, that is, off Nicias's property. Might it not be that the God wanted him freed?

Nicias found the interpretation reasonable, but the diviners of Athens reiterated that Dionysus had repudiated Myrsus.

Sophocles very privately begged Nicias to listen to the Syrian and leave the young boy in the play. But Nicias's fear of losing the contest kept him vacillating for a whole day, and, when there were only five days left before the inauguration, he did something he had always avoided: He made a decision on his own. Against the unanimous opinion of the famed diviners, he opted for Melas's interpretation. He was already convinced that the Syrian was the dark seer announced by Dodona. He ran the risk of keeping Myrsus on. If the play failed and his decision was known, they might even accuse him of impiety. It would be the beginning of the end for his political career.

But from the very moment the Great Theater of Dionysus reverberated to the powerful echoes Myrsus's mighty voice sent careening off the cliff of the Acropolis, his appearances on the scene were received with obvious pleasure, and his mimesis of the character of Dionysus, including some spells of dancing at the head of a semichorus of Menades, brought the members of the audience to their feet several times.

At the end of the performance, certain now of his triumph, Nicias had Myrsus brought to him, called for silence, and, standing by the throne of the High Priest of Dionysus, said that it would be a sacrilege to keep in slavery such a beautiful body and a voice all of Athens had celebrated for its decorum and excellence in imitating the son of Zeus and Semele. Amid the ovation, he placed his hand on Myrsus's head and proclaimed his freedom.

When the public finally consecrated the tetralogy of *Telephos* with victory, Nicias had no further doubt that Melas the Syrian was not only the blackest, but indeed the best diviner in Athens, sent as a present from the immortals to protect him as a reward for his devotion.

A few days after the festival, Nicias had Melas swear that he would never leave his house. He brought him before the effigy of the Great Mother of the Gods, which the Syrian worshipped and which was in the Metroon. There, he had Melas repeat three times that, as a diviner, augurer, and dream-reader, he would presage exclusively for Nicias of Niceratus. That very day, Nicias gave him his freedom and installed him in his home.

Shortly before the secret service of Athens discovered the Peloponnesian conspiracy to attack the mines in Laurium in case of war, Nicias was appointed commander of the garrisons of Cape Sunium, Anaphlystus, and Thoricus. His command also included the six hundred hoplites and forty horsemen who guarded the twenty thousand slaves working in the mines. Although he was Pericles's political enemy, Nicias supported his proposal to fence in forty stadia in the danger zone and build nine lookout towers the height of three men to be able to detect a surprise landing. Pericles also proposed detailing one Scythian to each lookout tower and, around the perimeter of the fence, Molossian hounds. Given the grave threat, the College of Strategi unanimously approved Pericles's plan.

Cape Sunium was a promontory joined to the hills of the mining region by a narrow, sandy isthmus. From the vantage point on the highest part of the Temple of Athena standing on the crest of the promontory, the guards could easily detect an enemy fleet in the Saronic Sea at a distance of one hundred stadia from the coast. In the Aegean, however, the coasts off Mount Laurium had a number of coves and inlets that were invisible from the Cape.

After a close study of the coast, Nicias decided that the most favorable points for a landing against Laurium would be Aurora Inlet or Epsilon, a sandy cove with a flat, even bottom, which he wanted specially watched. Acting on his orders, the lookout towers were raised to the height of four men and the fences to half that height.

Once the works were completed, Nicias devoted all his time to organizing the control of the perimeter. The Scythian archers were not to abandon their towers for any reason. And no one, citizen or foreigner, was to approach the perimeter fence at night. Anyone violating this order was to have the Molossian hounds set on them. The Scythians were to loose their arrows and sound their alarm conchs. The Athenian riders were to patrol the area night and day and take turns checking the Scythian guards every two hours by riding around the interior of the perimeter, sounding bells and listening for the countersigns.

When everything was ready, Nicias sent his report to the College of Strategi: The guards were efficient and punctual; the morale of the Athenians was high; the archers were cooperating with the vigilance scheme which he personally, Nicias of Niceratus, had designed, tested, and verified.

But the scheme designed by Niceratus's son did fail.

It failed one day, at dawn, during the spring of Apseudes.

When the works were completed, Nicias gave up his quarters in the fortress. He wanted no familiarity with the officers of the detachment. To avoid it, he had two bungalows built behind the lookout tower above Aurora Inlet. Hiero, his secretary, spread the word that the general was paying for that retreat to be the first to detect and engage the enemy. His many responsibilities demanded that he be alone to think things out with prudence.

Whenever he could, Nicias avoided his fellow citizens, no matter what their rank. He had learned from his father that familiarity erodes authority and breeds contempt, as the people say. Hiero and the economus took over all those functions that did not require his personal presence.

He lived alone in the bungalows, accompanied by Melas and a few domestic slaves. It was around that time that Melas had predicted that Nicias would become one of the most out-standing citizens in the service of Athens, more than Pericles and that, in time, his greatness would be acknowledged.

Would he perhaps be as great as Themistocles? Like Milciades? Melas could not define the precise limits of his greatness, but he did reiterate that his was a very lofty destiny.

The day of the events in Epsilon Cove, Nicias had started off before dawn to a sea shrine hidden on Cape Sunium, among the cliffs on its western shore. It was a grotto frequented by fisher-men of the Saronic to implore the benevolence of Poseidon and to leave their humble offerings of wreaths and garlands.

When Nicias took over the military command of the zone and found out about the shrine, unknown to most Athenians, he realized the extent of the neglect in which the City had left the powerful God of the sea. Melas confirmed his judgment.

Why had Athens, a naval power that pinned its hopes of annihilating Sparta and its Peloponnesian allies precisely on the sea, not given Poseidon the preferential treatment he deserved? Zeus, Athena, Dionysus, Apollo, Artemis, Aphrodite were venerated in the City with great festivals. Hecate, Demeter, Hephaestus were honored, even Chronos, an inoper-ative, dethroned God, and simple heroes such as Ajax and Theseus. It was inadmissible that a brother of Zeus should not appear on the religious calendar, except on the day he was defeated by Pallas Athena in their dispute over the possession of Attica, in a commemoration which was, furthermore, quite sad for the citizens.

Nicias continued to twist the thread of his disagreement with democracy. Was this how the Athenians, governed by Pericles, intended to become a far-reaching naval power, dom-inate the islands, found colonies in Sicily? No one in Attica had sacrificed a horse to Poseidon, for example, like the Argives did.

A horse?

Humm ... What if he ... ?

Yes! He would be the first Athenian to sacrifice a horse to the Shaker of the Earth. Why, this sudden inspiration might be the beginning of a greater, hegemonic power of Athens over all of Hellas. It was a known fact that, for a young colt, Heliconius would turn down suovetauriliae and hecatombs.

This time he did not think it over. He did not consult seers. He decided on the spot. But it was already woven into the destiny of the son of Niceratus that his first equine sacrifice, offered to the Girdler of the Lands, would be defiled that day by the unfortunate events at Epsilon Cove.

202

When the news got out that Nicias gave his exclusive attention not to the pristine high-born seers, but to an obscure Syrian, Eulogos was the first to comment that now the Pantadeuteros was presuming to be the Great King. As far as Eulogos knew, snip, snip, only barbarians kept personal magicians and seers, and with other tongues, which, under the guidance of the barber of the Street of Hoopers, were becoming increasingly sharp and caustic, he mentioned that it was as un-Greek as hiding from the light, as having oneself carried around in a sedan chair with curtains, and in the porticos and palaestrae the gossip multiplied, Nicias was a fool, hoodwinked by a fast-talking Syrian. But Melas gave proof upon proof of his gifts, and Nicias would not give him up.

He was quite wary of the gossip in the demos. But he did not have a single qualm about Melas. The wagging tongues could not know that he was backed by an admonition from Zeus and Dione.

However, to mitigate the ill humor of some of the aristo-crats and counteract the loss of prestige stemming from his retaining the Syrian, he conceived of a program and changed secretaries.

It was in those days that Hiero, a ruined logographer and irredeemable poetaster, but, nevertheless, an excellent hyp-ocrites on the stage of life, convinced him that his abilities would defend him from the voice of the demos.

To exonerate himself before the offended seers, Nicias had Hiero go almost every day on his behalf to consult them on nonexistent or real matters, on which it was a foregone conclu-sion that he would listen exclusively to his inspired freeman.

With regard to the incident with the dog Leucos, Melas gave a very direct and simple interpretation. Nicias was to beware of anything found by his dogs. If any one of them brought him anything, he would also be bringing his ruin. That was all.

Melas was afraid of dogs. Ever since he was a child, there was something in him that irritated them. Even friendly and playful dogs would bite him as soon as they smelled him. And so that no domestic tooth would ever intimidate him, Melas spoke with Nicias. He was particularly vehement in recalling that anything a slave had belonged to the master. The misfor-tune of the excellent son of Niceratus, already foretold, could also come through the dog of one of his slaves or servants. Intricate indeed were the workings of the Gods!

Like Oedipus, who never returned to Corinth to avoid his destiny of incestuous parricide, like Artemon Periphoretus, who ceased walking and hid his bald head from the eagles of Zeus, thus did the son of Niceratus sacrifice his Locrian, Maltese, and Laconian packs: Molossians, greyhounds, set-ters, rat catchers, totaling twenty-nine dogs. He sacrificed

203

them to Hecate and Ares. With tears in his eyes, he slit the throat of Tachistus, his formidable deer hound, and gave up hunting forever.

But to be absolutely certain that the evil events predicted by Melas could not possibly come to pass, Nicias dictated an edict decreeing that whosoever of his urban or rural slaves, rented to shops, quarries, or mines, should be caught in the act of feeding, sheltering, petting, or in any way participating in underhanded canine affairs that suggest ownership by the slave of the animal, and further, that any slave or servant who allowed or abetted passage or harboring of dogs in the houses or fields of the son of Niceratus, and further, that any slave who allowed himself to be accompanied or followed by dogs during his itinerant labors or jobs assigned by the master, in and out of the territory of Attica, would be flogged, beaten, and subjected to severe torments.

Thanks to Melas, the son of Niceratus was free of his obsession with Leucos. And Melas was free of Nicias's twenty-nine dogs.

In his lodge overlooking Aurora Inlet, Nicias was tasting greatness and ruminating presages. Whenever he had to spend some days at home, he took up quarters toward the back, in the women's courtyard. If company came, they were attended to by Hiero, on their feet. Depending on the quality of the visitor, Hiero would walk with him a bit around the peristyle of the first court lamenting that Nicias was completely caught up in an enormous amount of work for the State, that he never allowed himself a moment's rest, that he was beset by urgent matters even at the table, in his bath, to the point of neglecting his personal affairs to look after those of the people, and that the exhausted general could almost never go to bed before the rest of Athens was already deep in the land of dreams. Oh, by Asclepius the Healer, how delicate his health was! How wry his humor, how inadequate to receive beloved friends as they deserved! But, well, maybe next time.

Nicias swore by humbug and repeated sententious phrases that Hiero made him memorize, like that epiphoneme by Agamemnon, in *Iphigenia*, when he declares in Aulis: "Majesty presides over our life, but of the multitude, we are slaves."

The first equine sacrifice with which Attica honored Him of the Cerulean Hair was a white colt no more than three months old. Long before the rosy fingers of dawn reached over the Aegean, Nicias and Melas were riding their mules, followed by two slaves on foot leading the victim.

Nicias suffered a great disappointment as they were descending the last foothills of Laurium before the isthmus: A weasel crossed his path, just five steps in front of him, and was lost in the underbrush of the hills. The bad omen was certainly for him, the leader of the group. There was no doubt about it. It was a weasel; the smell was unmistakable. To avoid crossing the filthy animal's path, they backtracked two stadia uphill to find a different slope that would take them to the sea. They might get to the isthmus along the coast. But what if the weasel had been there, too?

Nicias was about to suspend the sacrifice and return to the bungalows when he saw Melas bending over to pick up a leaf from the road, examining it closely, biting it.

Wild laurel. Would Nicias like to taste it?

Melas had seen it fall from that tree, that one up there, and graze the shoulder of the son of Niceratus, and Nicias, taking it between his teeth, oh, yes, aromatic, biting, mountain laurel, breathing deeply, one of the Gods had pointed the leaf toward the chosen shortcut, there could be no error, so hurry up, downhill, quickly, for Poseidon only received victims before the chariot of the envious Sun raises its axles to spy on him; and prodding the mules and crossing into the isthmus, that way, trotting, to the right, ha, mule! and the slaves pulling the favorite victim of the Earth Girdler, the one that Nicias would propitiate for his tour of Samos, Thasos, Imbros, and the Cyclades; and faster, to the shadow at the foot of the promontory, and the slaves should light a fire before the altar, there was little time, and Nicias, crowned with algae and garlands on his neck and arms to honor Heliconius, and he had the colt decorated with a braid of reeds woven by his daughters, and the slaves tying its legs and pulling him deeper, and Nicias pouring libations into the winy sea of the Aurora Inlet, and they would drown the colt on its feet, but he was so strong and stubborn, he would not let them drag him to the sea, and the slaves panting, and the colt raising its head and jumping with its tied hind legs, but the water was not up to its flanks yet, and toooot, what was that, by the Twelve Gods, toooot, and Nicias stopping to hear better, to count, toooot, and the slaves, still wrestling with the colt, looking up to the heights of Laurium, toooot, and Nicias and Melas with the water up to their hips, toooot, how many blasts had they heard? five? So it was an alarm in Epsilon Cove, and Nicias asking himself what to do, by Zeus, by Poseidon, hurrying the slaves, no more delays, something was happening and Nicias had to get right back to assume supreme command, and he, too, pulling, and the colt whinnying and kicking and Melas pushing him clumsily by the side and turning him, and Nicias shouting, not that way, on its feet, couldn't they hear his orders? but the animal going over on its flank, trying to breathe, complaining between the bubbles, and Nicias stepping on its neck and shouting orders to grab him here, to release him there, not that way, you on the other side, brusquely, irreverently? what a sloppy sacrifice! and regaining his composure, rectifying, very sweet words full of religious respect so that Poseidon would receive that immaculate offering that the son of Nicer, toooot, of Niceratus, piously, toooot, and the colt trying to get up again and breaking the garland, toooot, with a single swipe, toooot, and getting up, and Nicias pushing him with his gaze toward Laurium and forgetting the prayer he had memorized, he should have suspended the ill-fated sacrifice back at the weasel, but too late, and the conch's toooot, danger in Epsilon Cove, it was no runaway slave, and Nicias tripping, damn colt, again stepping on its neck, and the colt twisting its leg, and splashing, toooot, and Nicias wanting to cover his ears, very badly done, this first equine sacrifice in the seas of Attica, would Heliconius accept it? would he understand his situation, the urgency of the moment? the animal ceasing its struggles and, at last, the prayer, for the Sovereign with the Cerulean Hair, a victim fed in the stables of the son of Niceratus, Epsilon attacked by an enemy landing? in that sanctuary purified by the waves, daughters and messengers of your will, the shrine rescued by Nicias for permanent pan-Attic veneration, and the son of, toooot, Niceratus, again forgetting the, toooot, prayer, and remembering that he had to submerge his garland and place it around his neck again as the Argive ritual demanded, and the slaves taking the body of the white colt from the sated waves and carrying it to the altar, and Nicias slitting its throat and letting its blood stain the waters of the grotto, and the slaves quartering it quickly, toooot, nailing the best pieces on tridents, toooot, and delivering them to the fire for the God to enjoy them, and Nicias quickly reciting the, toooot, last words and breaking for the beach, the waters dripping from his beard, and trotting as fast as the mule would go along the sands of the

isthmus, and reaching the fortress of Sunium, and watching
the approach of Antidotus, Diocles's son, a young man of good
family and breeding whose precocious merits earned him the
command of the outpost at the mines, with a group of horsemen, all serious, concerned, reporting the disappearance of the
guard at post five, the one at Epsilon, all very mysterious, could
it be the weasel? run away across the sea, Poseidon angry at
Nicias? by Pallas, what a day, announced by early presages, and
Antidotus, that the Scythian who had disappeared was called
Pandarus, Pandarus? Pandarus? that sounded familiar, and the
horsemen making their rounds had repeated the bells and no
sign of Pandarus, and in the lookout tower no Pandarus, no
dog, but they soon found the dead Molossian, draped over
some rocks, without blood or signs of violence, but no
Pandarus, and Antidotus worried because at dawn they had
also discovered the escape of Xanthus the Lycian, a slave condemned to a correction gallery, a repeat runaway, marked on the
forehead, slept chained to a treadmill, very close to Epsilon
Cove, and the chains turned up filed, and Nicias suddenly
recalled Pandarus, the Scythian who split goat bladders in
honor of . . . and what traces had they found? and Antidotus,
that the traces only made for greater concern, first the imprint
of a very small foot, a child's foot, which did not belong to
Xanthus or Pandarus, and Antidotus saw the bloody tracks on
a stone slab, and there were many, but all left feet, and then no
tracks, as if they had flown in, and, whose foot could it be? but
Antidotus had no idea, and the hair on Nicias's neck beginning
to stand on end and his skin stretching behind his ears, and the
horsemen discovered something mysterious, and Nicias, impatient now, by Hecate, would Antidotus never cease recounting
horrors? and Antidotus lowering his voice, something unheard
of, on a small stretch of sand there appeared hoof marks, how?

hoof marks in a place inaccessible to horses? Yes, by Pallas, but, oh, son of Niceratus, and Nicias going pale, mouth hanging open, the terrible thing is that the horse walked only on its hind legs, without ever using the front legs, and Nicias short of breath, perplexed, making efforts to appear calm, staring at Antidotus, verifying and making him repeat, on two legs? and Antidotus staring back, and that the great Nicias should check the tracks near Epsilon, and with so many mysteries, Antidotus, disconcerted, decided to consult the supreme commander, but the supreme commander not in bungalows, and Nicias, enough talk, move out, downhill, uphill, gasping to allay his fear, as in battle, and galloping across a small plain, together with Antidotus, and Melas behind, with the riders, Nicias needed him at his side, and all silently toward Epsilon Cove, dismounting, and Nicias asking if the escape alarm had been given to the other outposts, and if Antidotus had sent signals to Anaphlistos, and sea patrols, and Nicias looking at Melas, trying to divine what the diviner would divine, but Melas pensive, evasive, going around the fence, descending to the beach on Epsilon, a tiny cove between rocks, and there was the dead Molossian, and there the hoof marks, and over there the tiny cleft footprints, and further over the fence, and on the lookout tower new guards, straining at the horizon, and Nicias, coming closer to examine the tracks of the tiny, bloody foot, only half a palm from toe to heel, a tiny jumping foot that crossed the slab three times, tracing a path in boustrophedon, all like Antidotus said, a left foot, what was a four-year-old child doing there jumping on a single foot? a child demon, bleeding, anthropomorphous, boustrophedon? by Zeus, and the hooves, indeed, only the hind hooves, horror, coming out of the sea and returning, by Zeus, and by his brother Poseidon, the other powerful Cronid, Cerulean Hair, Batterer, Girdler, Heliconius, angry at

209

Nicias, insulted by the liturgical sloppiness of this morning? or was it the weasel? and glancing again at Melas, but the diviner just stood there, and Nicias needed action, great action, old remedy against fear, ordering search parties, several men and a dog, and Nicias also ready to search, but no dogs, trusted slaves instead, foremen, engineers, scribes, accountants, and Antidotus, search without dogs? and Nicias moving uphill, in the woods, by the stream, searching in all directions, and by noon twenty patrols were checking holes, trees, reefs, beaches, caves, and Xanthus could not have gone too far, such a strange escape, witchcraft? and Nicias back to the boustrophedon and hooves, but impossible to escape by sea there, however, check every nook and cranny, swim among the rocks, but Nicias ultimately convinced that escape there was impossible for mortals, complicity of infernal powers? winged horse? search outside the fences, opposite side, but impossible for escapees to reach there without being seen by other guards, and Nicias heading twelve men, and Melas with him, checking high parts by the sea, and suddenly shouting from below, two of his men, almost at sea level calling, and Nicias and Melas and others fanning out and going down, halfway down the hill, shouting in bad Greek, me here, me find Pandarus, and the others explaining, foreman slave dragging himself from abandoned gallery, and more shouting, Egyptian accent, Pandarus . . . three fingers . . . Pandarus dead . . . sacrificed, horrible, and Nicias, sacrificed how? and others, that the gallery was abandoned since the times of Mardonius and inside was a miners' shrine, and the slave shouting that sacrifice much big, Pandarus consecrated to Dionysus, Pandarus fingers cut off, sacrificed to Omestes, and Nicias crouching at the entrance to the tunnel, and watching rivulets of water descending, and the slave inside, silence now, again muffled shouting, and Nicias, what about the slave? why hadn't he come out at once? and the slave, that, yes, already coming out, mumbling in his language, like praying, and close up panting, now his dusty head, crawling on his elbows, saying that Pandarus with ivy crown like lamb, oooh, and groaning and muttering in fright, crown on head, he not lie, on elbows, and Nicias, that he should come out of there, and coming out, all dirty, horrible stench, no teeth, and ouch, hitting his head on an outcropping, and throwing, just two steps from Nicias, horror, by All the Infernal Gods, throwing two human fingers, blue, swollen, and the Egyptian going on that Pandarus, all of him, placed on altar stone, but right hand mutilated, fingers on floor, and slave think fingers not consecrated to Dionysus, that why he bring for optimum Nicias, for all see he not lie or crazy, and Nicias getting his bearings, waiting on one knee, afraid to rise, unable to tear his eyes from the Egyptian's terrible find, thumb and index finger, still together, forming a tumescent arch, and the slave saying that Pandarus right hand only three fingers, arm tied over head with fennel, very high, tied to wall, Pandarus look like saying hello lying down, and slave not find fingers on altar, he not offend Dionysus, true he not offend? great general want he take fingers back? he find them thrown away, want bring them show great Nicias general, son of Niceratus, see with own eyes, did good? and face drawn, crying, much afraid, he not want, by Ammon, offend Dionysus Omest.

211

Shut up!!!

Nicias had the slave rise. He was a tall man, very thin, with a pointed head, high cheekbones, and a nose turned so high that the nostrils appeared to penetrate straight into his head. Nicias was certain that he had seen that strange face before.

Just then, some riders appeared over the rise asking what was happening. Someone answered that The Dog had just found Pandarus's body. The dog? The dog whose find Nicias was to fear?

The find that would cause his ruin?

He directed a glance of terror at Melas.

Melas returned the glance vacantly.

The ridiculous nickname made him suspicious; a vague suspicion crept into his temples, becoming less vague and more frightening.

Nicias called for silence and faced his destiny.

"What is your name, slave?"

"I be call Toreb of Egypt, but in mines some call Cynocephalus, others call 'The Dog,' " and he laughed, as if apologizing for such an undignified nickname.

It was as if all the blood had suddenly drained from Nicias's face onto the ground. He approached the slave, turning his back on the group.

He swallowed hard. He closed his eyes, trying to ask something, but unable to make the words come out. He choked.

Finally, he gasped out the already unnecessary question.

"And who is your master, Toreb?"

"Not recall, oh, son of Niceratus? You be master this Egyptian dog, hee, hee, hee."

Strange indeed were the workings of the Gods!

28

AND THAT MUCH useless his visit to Laurium, that Xanthus not have Dindymenian Eye, and that not nothing know of whereabouts, and Summoner not never mistaken, he look much deep in bottom of Xanthus thinking, and Sosias ratifying with mute shakings of shaven head, and the Summoner much certain Xanthus speaking truth, Xanthus swear by Dionysus, and One Eye much lying to Hypothesis, One Eye lying faaat lie, diaphanes that One Eye never return amethyst stone to Xanthus, and Hypothesis commanding capture of One Eye, and seeing him leaving the brothel almost at dawn, and Otep setting the dog on him and brother Green-grocer showing him the point of his dagger, and Fire-eater cutting him off, but One Eye very calm, not necessary, what did they want of him? and Hypothesis forcing him to accompany them, through the walls, enter Lysis's house, and that the miserable felon should listen, you will pay, and at daylight, Lysis herself would turn him in to the Areopagus for going around two months earlier trying to

sell the eye stolen from the Goddess, and you will die in torment, and you will be thrown into the Barathrum if you do not
confess where the stone is, and One Eye denying, One Eye was
convinced that Hypothesis was bluffing and knew nothing for
certain, and insisting he had returned the stone to Xanthus
that very day, and Hypothesis, oh, the impiety, didn't you buy
him a horse with the money from the sale? can you deny, oh,
monocular monster, that you also bought him a wig and clothes
for his getaway? and One Eye dismayed and confused, horror,
only the Lycian could have told them, so he finally talked? and
not knowing what to say or what expression to use, looking
askance at Cross Eye and Fire-eater, what were those two plotting with Hypothesis and Lysis? but it was useless to weave new
lies, and facing the hostile stare of Hypothesis, listening to her
start again with her threats of torment, Barathrum, impiety,
trafficking in sacred objects, and, all at once, like a soldier at the
supreme moment in combat, possessed of a sudden resignation, determined to face whatever his destiny had in store for
him as lucidly as possible, yes! enough! would they all shut up,
and gesturing to them that they should listen, that, yes, it was
true, that he had not returned it to Xanthus, but if they were
patient and Lysis maintained her offer of two thousand drachmas, he could get it back, and Hypothesis, who did you sell it to?
give me his name, and the Summoner and Lysis hidden, listening from the next room, and One Eye, master of himself again,
proclaiming that he would not reveal the name, that he would
not violate his oath, that he preferred the bottom of the
Barathrum to the demons that pursued oath-breakers, and the
Summoner whispering to Lysis what they had to do, and
Laelaps barking in the courtyard, and Lysis, with a transparent
linen peplus, forehead serene, hair loose, arms blushing, green
eyes murderous, mouth humid and despising, threatening,

moving very slowly, what did a three-hundred-drachma-a-night callipygian want with the stone? and she, very softly, that she agreed, that he should seek out the buyer of the stone and tell him that he had until the following day at the hour of the full market, that he was to deliver the stone to the home of Hypothesis, where he would receive the two thousand drach-mas, and that Lysis was convinced that both he and his myste-rious buyer would understand, as soon as they thought about it a bit, that they would prefer Lysis's silence and money to the consequences of a trial for impiety, that he should go get the stone, and that he should remember the hour of the full market, and after midnight, One Eye leaving the City with the expiatory procession, and just when it looked like he was going to make it big, wham, another blow from destiny, and Porphyrius the Cybernetes furious when he found out, why hadn't he told him that Truncheon and Lysis of Miletus also knew about the stone, eh? and One Eye swearing that they knew about Xanthus but not about Porphyrius, that they were prepared to pay, and the Cybernetes would gladly have beaten him to death if he had still been his slave, and that One Eye was to forget about the stone and the two thousand drachmas, it was impossible, and who could ensure the Cybertnetes that they would not catch that damned Lycian again? what would they do when he confessed under torment? and Porphyrius frantic, stomping around his cabin, did One Eye realize the fix he had gotten him into? so it turns out that the finder was precisely a fugitive whom all the City was trying to find, and as soon as they caught him he would turn One Eye in, and what was One Eye going to do when they took him and put hoops and tourniquets around his head? what would he do when Nicias had thorns stuck up his ass? what could he do but confess his sale to Porphyrius? and that very night when all Phalerum was watching the departure of the flagship, with its garlanded bow, sailing replete with dignitaries and priests to expiate Omestes in Epsilon Cove, a small four-oared boat unfurled its worn sail to the Boreal wind, heading for an islet in the Saronic Sea.

One Eye went to the hideout supplied by Porphyrius. No one would find him in that deserted place. He could wait there safely until they ascertained whether or not the Lycian confessed, if they caught him again. As far as Lysis was concerned, she wouldn't dare tell anyone, because then she would have to explain why she had not spoken two months earlier, so the thing was to get lost, disappear. Once there was no danger, One Eye could return to Athens, and if bad came to worse, the Cybernetes could ship him off to Egypt. One Eye's capture would do him no good either.

216

At dawn, the Cybernetes sailed for Phalerum.

What a night!

His body was heavy, but his heart was light.

One Eye was lying in a hollow under a cubit of sand. He deserved it for lying to the master who had given him his freedom.

In the bundle of clothes he had taken from the body before burying it, he had found eight hundred and twelve drachmas. Porphyrius the Cybernetes had been certain that old One Eye would never leave Athens without the money he had saved at the brothel.

29

FROM ASPASIA IN ATHENS
TO EURYDICE IN SARDES

The tenth of Scirophorion

DESPITE NOT HAVING received any reply to my last scrolls, I am hurrying to write to advise you to suspend your preparations to travel to Athens for now, if you had indeed undertaken them. Several reasons induce me to beg you to wait.

Two days ago a Scythian archer was found sacrificed on an altar of Dionysus Omestes. Nicias's agents are trying to convince everyone that the Scythian's mutilated hand is witchcraft by King Perdiccas of Macedonia, and they are accusing the democrats of attracting great calamities with their policies. They are saying that the members of the Assembly allowed themselves to be persuaded by Pericles's oratory when he proposed raising the six-thousand-talent tribute the Chalcidicean city of Potidaea had been paying until then to fifteen thousand talents. Pericles was, in fact, trying to irritate the Potidaeans, to induce them to abandon the Delian League and to conspire against Athens. He realized many years ago that war with Sparta was inevitable, and it is clear to him that the destiny of Athens will be decided by that war. Sparta has no fleet capable of sustained actions in a region so far away from its own territory, and their allies in Corinth could not use theirs because we would easily block their exit through the Saronic Sea. That is why he has prepared things so that the hostilities will break out precisely in Chalcidice. It would be foolhardy for them to come all the way down from their gulf and go around the turbulent extreme of the Peloponnesus just to help Potidaea. It is a perfect plan that we have prepared with extreme care. But that idiot, Nicias, has the men of Athens cowed with this thing about the sacrifice of the Scythian. He alleged that the three fingers on the mutilated hand, together with the tracks of a tiny, bloody foot, and of some two-legged horses, are Macedonian witchcraft instigated by Perdiccas, supreme priest of the barbarian rites and ally of the powerful hippean demons of his Boreal realm, but Pericles has cut him off and found an excellent pretext for setting off actions in Chalcidice. He intends to convince the Assembly that those three fingers are nothing but a plot designed by the Potidaeans precisely to intimidate superstitious men like Nicias, because the mutilated hand is identical to the outline of Chalcidice according to the rendering of Hecataeus of Miletus, whom everyone in Athens knows. So, now it is Pericles who is blessing those three fingers and their appearance at that moment, because they will account for his indignation with the evil arts of the Potidaeans and support his demand that the Assembly approve dispatching the fleet against Chalcidice before the end of summer.

As soon as Pericles got wind of what the son of Niceratus was about, he went to the home of Lampon, the diviner, and drew him to his side. The very afternoon that the news of the crime arrived in the Prytaneum, he hastened to give public proof of his devotion by heading a sacrifice on the Altar of Piety and an expiatory ceremony together with the religious hierarchy and the eupatrids.

So, the imminence of war, which will undoubtedly lead to an invasion of our territory by the Peloponnesians, has induced me to advise you to postpone your trip.

And there are other reasons.

The ever-present slanderers, no longer satisfied with their defamation of me in public, now intend to bring me before the courts on an accusation of procuring and pandering.

The trial was to have been held weeks ago, but Pericles has managed to get successive stays to give himself time to prepare my defense. I had not mentioned it earlier so as not to worry you, and the fact is that, until a few days ago, we had not given the affair much thought, but some very determined witnesses against me have recently turned up and there is a real danger that they just might convince the heliasts. Something has suddenly happened that I never thought possible. I am within a hair's breadth of being condemned to exile from Attica. Pericles, however, is quite calm and says he will discredit the plot.

And as if that were not enough, if you should come and I were not here to look after you, I do not think you could count on Cleis either, given the state of her affairs.

I am convinced that her disease has gotten worse again. But it is not her beautiful body that is suffering now. This time the evil is affecting her mind. This is the only explanation for her actions. She has confessed terrible things to me.

Just two days ago, she came to visit, in disguise, to ask me to intercede with a certain maker of war engines who has served Pericles and with whom I became good friends during the siege of Samos. It was about the purchase of one Xanthus, a bronze-smith slave. She told me she wanted him to make pots, pans, and piping to enlarge her baths, now that she has several women in her house, and she insists that she will have no other bronze-smith because this one is the best in Athens. Artemon, Xanthus's master, has rented him out for a half-obol a day to the mines in Laurium as punishment for his recent attempt to escape to Megara. This is what is usually done with fugitives in Athens, since no one will buy them. But Cleis offered to pay whatever his owner asked, even if it were five hundred drachmas. I warned her that it sounded crazy to me. She insisted and I wound up sending a note to Artemon, but he replied that the slave had offended him when he was caught by spitting on a foreman. After having him flogged almost to death, Artemon decided not to sell him at any price, not even a thousand drachmas, so that his reward for the spitting would be to spend the rest of his days vomiting dust and rock on a treadmill in the silver mines.

When I gave Cleis his reply, she said she would give the man fifteen hundred drachmas. Can you believe it? For a fugitive and violent Lycian with the heart of a pirate?

So I asked her what secret she was hiding from me. I acted hurt and told her right out that if I could not know what was behind it all, I could not help her, and that if she were afraid that I could not keep a secret, she could hear my oath.

Then she embraced me and petted me and said that asking me to swear an oath would be like confessing that she no longer loved me. In fact, she confessed that she was hiding a secret that she would have preferred to reveal to me some time later, but to keep me from feeling so hurt, she would open her heart to me immediately.

So her disease no longer frightens her because she is quite certain that she is not unclean, but very holy. She began to tell me about the man who cured her, to describe without shame or limits the new sensations he has revealed to her, and to extol his powers, his divine virtues. She repeated the same things over and over again, ceaselessly, like one of those bronze vases that goes on ringing until you put your hand on it.

She did not even notice my tears or my mute disappointment. I listened to her in silence. What was there to gain by screaming my disgust?

Imagine the worst, an impious and dangerous madman whom the Athenians have pursued with dogs like a fugitive slave, without being one. Nor is he a perforator of walls, nor a pirate, nor a hunter of freemen, nor a desecrator of tombs, nor a parricide. And yet, he is worse than the scum of the City, of all Greek cities, because his ilk is of the turbid and hairy depths of Asia. He is a ruffian unworthy of the respect, the friendship, the intercourse, or even a look from a young Ionian aristocrat. Oh, by Zeus! How it pains me to mention him! How it repels, disgusts, and torments me to have to describe him in these words of mine!

The monster has named her high priestess of a new religion, in the service of which she, Cleis, the granddaughter of my father Axiochus, has become, oh! the pain! an acolyte, most devout protector, and servant of a beggar of Cybele.

Can you believe it?

Well, there you have the sad truth. She is completely at the beck and call of one of those metragyrtes that abound in Sardes, Susa, Babylon, the very ones that caused us so much fear and disgust when we were children, when we heard them begging with their Phrygian litanies, their hairless faces and feminine contortions. But this one must also be an impostor, because he is not a eunuch like the rest of his breed; quite the contrary, he has caused public disorders with women and nocturnal carousing in the woods, which the whole City has condemned as sacrilegious. His pestiferous presence has been forbidden throughout the entire territory, and the diviners proclaim that if he ever sets foot again in Athens, the incensed Goddess would immediately visit upon us all the misfortunes the Thebans had to suffer because of Oedipus.

And right now, when the City is peacefully sleeping with the conviction that he is outside its borders, it is Cleis, the one who came to Athens through my paideia—she should never have told me!—who is hiding him in her own home in the Ceramicus, receiving him in her bed, dressing him in embroidered tunics and purple bonnets, giving herself to him with love. She has assigned beautiful slaves to care for him, and it is because of him that she insists on buying the fugitive bronzesmith.

Imagine what my days are like with this misfortune compounded by the imminent danger of being exiled, never again to see Pericles or my only son.

Receive my tears and kisses and my prayer that you will join me in sacrifices and libations for the immortal Gods to protect me and rescue Cleis from so much madness and impiety. Be happy.

DELIVERED INTO FRIENDLY HANDS
ON THE TWELFTH OF SCIROPHORION,
ARCHON APSEUDES

30

LYSANIAS UNROLLED a hand-span of the first vol-ume, turned his back on the dawn, and read:

*FROM THE COLLEGE OF STRATEGI TO THE KING
ARCHON*
*Indictment for the crimes of impiety and willful homicide.
Pursuant to the unwritten laws of the lofty ether ... by word
of mouth and the memory of men ...*

Lysanias unrolled another span to skip over the remaining
ritual language and examined the terms of the accusation:

*I, Nicias of Niceratus, General and Commander of the
Garrisons . . . the shrine of Dionysus Omestes . . . and
because it occurred in the region under my command ...*

Lysanias spared himself the mandatory execrations and the

well-known details of the find. In the second scroll he went directly into the substantive procedural issue:

> ... and in compliance with psephisma kappa, approved by the Assembly of Athens during the third pritany of the Archonship of Menon, whose text is annexed for the chest of anacrisis, do hereby request that Nicias, son of Niceratus, in his capacity as Commander of Laurium ... and, by State commission, master of Pandarus the Scythian, slave of the City ... be appointed hegemon of the case and Substantiator of the Anacrisis ...

Lysanias passed the text of the invoked psephisma to his secretary, for it to be verified in the library, and ordered him to enter the petition signed by Lamacus, vice-president of the College of Strategi. The third scroll carried Pericles's well-known seal of the green owl:

> ... and until such time as Nicias of Niceratus is appointed hegemon of the case ... this College requests that the approval of Artemon the Engineer, son of Archias, be obtained so that upon the capture of his slave Xanthus the Lycian, fugitive from Laurium and accused of both crimes, said Xanthus be immediately interrogated under maximum torment ...

This was followed by the usual formulations and was signed:

> Pericles of Xanthippus
> Autocrat General
> Prostate of the Demos of Athens

Lysanias contained an attack of rage. Leaning on the base of a column, he took off one of the cothurni imposed upon him by his dignity of Archon King and began rubbing a bunion. He tossed a dried broad bean into his mouth, and as he chewed with the prognathous motions of a man well into his seventies, he repeated to himself that there was no respect for titles in the city of Pallas Athena. What right did Pericles have to add to his title of Autocrat General the infamy of Prostate of the Demos? That title had not been given to him by the City but by the rabble that followed him, and he had no right to stamp it on official documents. In other circumstances, Lysanias would have returned the scroll, declaring it inadmissible, but with only eight days to go in his archonship, he preferred avoiding the protests his rejection would cause in the City, given the magnitude and urgency of the case. It was irritating to have to accede to another trick put over by the Onion Head, who had taken advantage of the emergency in the polis to officialize his bastard dignity as prostate.

225

31

NICIAS ORDERED THE DOG to clear away the mound of sand. The slave knelt and began to blow the sand off the top of the mound. He was ordered not to move the fingers from the position in which they had been left; when they appeared, quite black already, rotten, swollen, as if acting on some unheard command, everyone present tore out of the depths of their throats a large gob and spit loudly to clean the soul of impurities, as one did at burials.

The old seer stared at the hand with a blank expression and stooped slightly to get a better look; Pericles caught Nicias's eyes, anxious as ever, full of reproach.

The examination over, Lampon made no gesture. He walked with his head inclined over to the High Priest and whispered something in his ear. The old priest, in his turn, whispered something to Nicias, who commanded The Dog to pick up the loose fingers and the hand and, after duly incinerating them, to bury the remains in the pit he himself had dug two stadia away, behind the hill.

As soon as the slave left, guarded by a hoplite, the High Priest of Dionysus and two acolytes approached Lampon and offered him an earthen bowl of water that had been blessed by dousing one of the torches from the Lenaeum in it. The seer dipped his fingers in the water and let a few drops fall into his open eyes to purify them of the horrendous sight. The bowls were passed around and all purified their eyes. Then the incense bearers made their rounds for everyone to inhale the incense burned on Dionysian embers. Thus, they purified their nostrils and all the bodily passages by which the miasmas might creep into their souls.

. . . and three priests of Dionysus having entered, they verified that the body of the Scythian with his throat cut was prone on the altar, his head toward the Aurora. It was crowned with ivy and decked with wreaths of black poplar. The right arm was raised, tied with fennel to an outcropping on the wall, and three fingers of the mutilated hand outstretched, the thumb and index having been found by Toreb the Cynocephalus, slave of Nicias of Niceratus, on the floor of the shrine.

After the inspection was concluded, the remains were cremated and buried in a pit, except for the right hand. All the slaves who touched the body were purified with lustral water by pouring it over their shaven heads; the gallery was widened and the defiled shrine was perfumed with aromatic incense and adorned with thyrsi, wreaths, and garlands; and on the altars specially built outside the gallery, they sacrificed three impeccable bulls and nine male goats from the herd of the Lenaeum, which burned intact down to embers.

Menon, High Priest of Dionysus, having inspected the shrine, declared that he found on the Altar of Omestes human flesh of the most execrable kind, of a slave benefited for years by the entire City, and evidence of it having been garnished with the salt and barley flour used in divine sacrifices, which proves that it had been offered as food for the God. And advised the August Assembly of Athens with horror and revulsion that the supreme impurity corrupts our soil and our air, blemishes our citizens, our plants, our waters, and our animals, and as long as the guilty are not executed or verifiably out of our territory, we shall be subject to the wrath of Zeus and Semele for having been the passive venue of such great impiety, and, for that reason, Menon ordered the citizens to make expiatory sacrifices, raise prayers, and proffer anathemas, that the guilty may be cursed in the name of Dionysus, Zeus, Hera, and Poseidon; Athena, Apollo, and Artemis; Hecate, Ares, and Demeter; Hephaestus and Aphrodite Urania; and that the above mentioned desecrators be declared enemies; and that their lands cease to bear fruit; and that their women bear not children but macrocephalic monsters; and that their cattle not reproduce; and that a plague fall on their wheat, vineyards, and olive groves; and that they forever reap the worst from war, commerce, or the law; and that they themselves may perish and their homes and their race; and may their sacrifices never be acceptable to Dionysus, Zeus, Hera, and Poseidon; Athena, Apollo, and Artemis; Hecate, Ares, and Demeter; Hephaestus and Aphrodite Urania, but all their offerings rejected.

MAY THE RITES ORDAINED
BY THE HIGH PRIEST BE FULFILLED.

… and Lampon, son of Critias, Venerable Seer, did declare that the mutilated hand is not the work of Boreal demons, for on reciting the prescribed incantations during their examination, he did not perceive in his body the confirmation, nor any mes-

228

sage from the Gods, nor has he had apocalyptic dreams or visions; and it his opinion that the events in the shrine of Dionysus are the underhanded wiles and desecrations of enemies, who avail themselves of carrion and filth to intimidate the men of Athens who sit in this August Ecclesia.

The High Priest of Dionysus and Lampon the Seer approved the third and final version of the report written by Pericles, including the amendments they had made to the first two drafts. Pursuant to their agreements, that was to be the official version of the ominous events that occurred in Epsilon Cove, for the general information of the citizens. The signatures of Menon, High Priest of Dionysus, Lampon the Venerable, the Eponymous Archon Apseudes, and Pericles, Autocrat General, appeared at the bottom. The following morning the prytanes would have it read to their heralds in an extraordinary session of the Ecclesia.

229

 Pericles went to bed at midnight. His secretary and three scribes spent the rest of the night making copies.

PART III

SPRING

OF THE

APSEUDES

AND

SUMMER

OF

PYTHODORUS

3 2

THE FOUR OF US were at our oars and the soldier,
Nicander, was at the helm . . . Yes, we were born in the
demos of Prasias, in the tribe of the Pandionids . . . All four; and
then, as we approached Epsilon, Eustachius the Cripple, that's
him over there, was the first to see him, and, look, look there, by
the cliffs, there was a man leaping into the air and running
naked among the rocks, and then we began to row toward . . .
No, excellent Nicias, it would have done no good to blow the
alarm against the wind, and the soldier at the prow shouting,
turn yourself in, slave, and we all supposed it was Xanthus the
Lycian, but none of us knew him . . . No, we could not signal,
either, because the cliffs jutting out into the sea blocked the way
. . . No, I'm certain, the Scythian could not have seen Xanthus,
and we could not see the lookout tower . . . Well, we supposed it
was him because we were told that he was tall and blond, and
seeing him naked . . . In that place, he had to be a fugitive, and
Nicander shouting at him to stop, and ordering us to steer for

the reefs, but he went on jumping like a goat, from rock to rock, and suddenly, and when we were just three stadia away, splash, he began to swim away, but we rowed hard and cut him off, and when we had him within bow range ... Nicander? I don't know, great Nicias, he wanted to take him alive and he was threatening to shoot and shouting, stop, ungodly wretch, but Xanthus, splash, splash, as if a hydra was on his tail, swimming and swimming, and Nicander, his bow taut, but still not shooting, and we, what are you waiting for? shoot, and he, that it was better to take him alive, that there was no way he could get out of there, that if we didn't get him, the Scythian would, and when we were about fifty feet away ... More slowly? It's only that the words just pour out, well, now, it was then that Nicander jumped in with his sword and Alcides followed with a dagger between his teeth to try to get behind him because the boat could come no closer to the reefs, and the Cripple stayed by his oar and we both began to spread the net to trap him as soon as he came in range, but then, Xanthus climbed on a rock, that was when we saw the branded *phi* marking him as a fugitive, and we shouted together, give up, infidel, you're trapped, criminal, and he kept looking down trying to find something under the water, and finally he dove in and Nicander and Alcides surrounded the spot, and him and me with the net ready, blocking his way out of the cove, and when we all thought we had him and were waiting for him to come up for air, he just stayed down there, and a long while went by with us expecting him to break for air, but he didn't, he didn't, and when we were practically sure that he had been down there longer than even Euphemus the Argonaut could have held out, Nicander ordered us to come about and approach the rock where he had jumped, and that took another ... Oh, no, son of Niceratus, Nicander got on the boat and was searching the bottom, everywhere, looking for the body, and he finally dove in, and in a minute he broke, saying that there was a hole in the rocky bottom ... Yes, by Zeus, I saw it myself, or rather, right down there that it was like a funnel on its side, that's it, it got narrower between the rock walls, and at the end we could see a hole ... Big enough for Xanthus? Well, most excellent Nicias, yes, he might fit, it was very narrow, but I think he fit, and since he knew what to expect, the criminal probably tried to wedge himself in there to die quickly and not have to face the torment later, and that was when Nicander took the gaff and said that he was going to get close to the hole to see if he could recover the body, and we kept warning him to be careful he didn't get himself trapped in there too, but he said he was only going to try to gaff the body, and he climbed on the same rock as the Lycian to get to the bottom fast and swim over to the funnel, and me asking Poseidon in my mind to let us find the defiler's body to be able to placate Dionysus, but the same thing happened again, and Nicander didn't turn up, he just stayed down there, and we were looking at each other not knowing what to do, and Eustachius started crying and said he heard something like a whinny under the water, and I didn't hear it, but I was very scared, because I'm not afraid of any mortal, but ... Oh, yes, I'll be brief, and the Cripple saying he was going to dive and the rest of us saying, are you crazy? wasn't that what we said? until we saw the big bubble come up, plop, and we all knew that the good Nicander had given up his soul, and we got the boat out of there, and then I thought I heard a whinny myself ... Oh, no, great general, I couldn't take an oath because everything was very confused and we were so scared ... Well, to the lookout tower to sound the alarm ... By Poseidon, that's the way it happened, and when we got back to the place with the archers and the soldiers, we saw that the water was bloody, and we were even more scared, but Antidotus scolded

235

us and said we were silly girls, unworthy Thetes, but he hadn't heard the whinnies ... Don't be angry, oh son of Niceratus, I'm coming to the end, and then the brave Antidotus dove right there and disappeared under the water, and he came right back up saying that there were some feet sticking out of the hole, and he got a rope and went back down to tie it to one of the feet, and then we started pulling and there was Nicander's body, we had just been talking to him on the boat a few minutes before ... The marks? Yes, we all saw perfectly that they were horse hooves ... They were stamped on his chest, on his ribs, on his back, and when we got him into the boat, we saw that there were nine marks, horrible, oh son of Niceratus ...

33

SOCRATES WAS TWENTY-SEVEN years old when his father died. When he was still married to his first wife, he went on working in the shop with the two slaves. They made busts of the Gods, statuettes of Hermes, icons of Apollo, God of Streets, symbols, amulets, amphorae, pots, depending on the season.

But one day his personal demon instilled in him the sacred mission of philosophizing to help improve his fellow men. He got divorced and turned the shop and the two slaves over to a sculptor friend. With his share of the meager profits, Socrates covered his expenses and frugally supported his mother, Phaenarete, who was almost blind and had given up her mid-wifing profession.

That spring, Phaenarete began to fear that her only son might die in the war, leaving her no grandsons to one day honor the grave of Sophroniscus, and her own.

Although hostilities had not yet broken out, everyone knew

that the sailing of the fleet for Chalcidice was imminent. The generals had decided by lots and had chosen, among others, Socrates's class. In a few months, weeks perhaps, he would be mustered, together with the ephebi of the archonship of Euthydemus, to take up arms against Potidaea.

To please his mother, Socrates agreed to take a sacrifice to Artemis Phosphoros, bringer of light and patron of midwives.

At midnight, Phaenarete took from the oven a fawn that the slave had kneaded with flower and barley. It was a thick, heavy cake, about two hand-spans long, one of those they make for pilgrims who bring offerings. Its stomach was stuffed with sesame taffy and its heart was a ball of almond nougat.

Phaenarete was devoted to Artemis Phosphoros, who worked many miracles with women in labor and nursing babies. Socrates made ready to go to the demos of Phlya in his mother's name, to say the prayers his mother could not because of her disability. Phosphoros would certainly recognize Socrates, for she had saved him from a fever soon after he was born. Now she would protect him as an adult at arms.

"Will you not ask me to say a prayer for the threatened City?"

"If you return well from the war, it is certain that the City is not going to suffer calamities," Phaenarete said, raising her eyebrows to underscore her conjecture.

On the Street of the Florists, Socrates picked out a wreath in the shape of a bow and bought a hemiobol of garlands for his arms.

As he left the City, he saw a great many people with crowns walking under the full moon toward the shrines on Hymettus and Pentelikon. No one had seen so many sacrifice bearers on the roads of Attica since the eve of the battle of Coronea.

He arrived in Phlya at first light. Mount Artemisium was some five stadia from the demos. At the highest point shone the head of the Goddess. Its sacred white glitter was the pride of the village. A couple of years earlier, the Great Priestess of Athena had tried to use the yellow soil of Phlya to polish the effigy on Cape Sunium. She wanted the intense brilliance of the maiden warrior to be the guiding light of Athens, visible from a great distance. But the people of Phlya refused. They contended that Phosphoros, bearer of light, was the attribute of Artemis and of no other deity. If not, why had the quarries of yellow soil, unique in all of Attica, been placed precisely in Phlya? Only Artemis Phosphoros was entitled to that cephalic splendor.

Dawn was beginning to reach into the nave of the temple. Socrates could hear the crackling of the great fire that was devouring the fawn. He could smell the smoke and aromas of other sacrifices at the foot of the marble effigy, and he prayed to Artemis, as if she really could be pleased with the meat and milk burned in her honor, or with the marzipan that Phaenarete was offering in exchange for the life of her son. Socrates now felt closer to his mother and to the fleeting, unknown shadows that were there making sacrifices along with him.

On the way home, it occurred to him that just as bees cared for their queen, because only through her could they be strong and safe, so, too, must the citizens of a polis care for their Gods. The old rites were still the sacred foundations without which there would be no City and no individual dignity.

The rays of dawn were already creeping over the Pentelikon and stabbing the shadows toward the south. At the headwaters of the Ilissus, Socrates rested by the gentle stream. He was perspiring. The sun was heating the nape of his neck. He decided to take the soft slope down to the City, following the course of the river along its banks.

After a short rest, he bathed in the stream. The morning chill was pleasant. Further down, where the river grew wider

239

and the quiet waters flowed through smooth rocks, he barely avoided stepping on the figure of a human being shaped from the clay of the banks. It was on its back, nailed to the ground by a stake running through its heart.

He imagined that it must be some sort of vengeful curse, for they were quite frequent in the country around Hymettus, but when he saw the letter *phi* on its forehead and the *xi* on his chest, he understood that the curse was intended for the fugitive, Xanthus.

He went on. In the thickets along the bend where the river turned toward the City walls, he found a wax figurine hanging by its feet from a tree. It was about a foot long and also had a *phi* on its forehead. Pins pierced its eyes, its stomach, and its heart.

Could Xanthus really be so criminal a heathen that the Athenians leveled such malevolent execrations at him? Might it all not be just one of Nicias's silly hyperboles? By the dog! What could a fugitive stand to gain by sacrificing Pandarus? In a frenzy to escape, any slave can become a ruthless killer, but he would kill to get to the border as soon as possible. It simply did not make sense to spend so much time on such an elaborate sacrifice.

The reports about the hoof tracks at low tide and the tiny bloody footprints on the rock had frightened many. There was talk of Macedonian spirits at the service of King Perdiccas. Others said that there were old sins to be atoned for. The Athenian demos was as restless as on the eve of war. And there was gossip of terrible omens. They said that on the night of the sacrilege, on two occasions there had been flames in the sky, dancing about the effigy of Athena Promachus; that mysterious gasps were heard echoing through the cellars of the Erechtheion; that the bull calf sacrificed to Dionysus in the Lenaeum had opened an eye after it was dead; and that to ratify the portents, the cow of a widow in Eleusis had given birth to a three-headed monstrosity.

Socrates sat down to think, his gaze fixed on some rosebays with scarlet buds. This business was not at all clear, and panic spread falsehood. And furthermore, how could one give any credit to reports when that superstitious fool Nicias was involved?

Might not the foul deeds at Epsilon be some sort of fraud, some kind of human witchcraft? What need could a metaphysical demon have had of files to free Xanthus? Or could it be, as Pericles would have us believe, the work of the Potidaeans to strike fear into the heart of Athens? It was not completely without logic, but it was difficult to admit that other Greeks would dare perpetrate such a great offense against a Greek God.

It had to be the work of a barbarian. No Greek, not even Theopompus of Lampsacus, an atheist and enemy of the City, would dare so much. It was common knowledge that from the Macedonian courts he was helping the Potidaeans with his arts, but such a musical and metrical soul as his would be repelled by those degrading mutilations.

Just then, two charcoal burners from the deme of Acharnae approached on their way back from the City with an ass loaded with bags of dried fish. After only the most cursory hello, they began to babble and trip over each others' words, telling Socrates that everyone in the City was talking about what had happened at dawn, when some sailors had seen the abominable Xanthus. With the mention of his name, both noisily tore phlegm from the depths of their chests, as if purging themselves of having witnessed the foulness of a birth.

And when they were about to trap him between some rocks in the coast, he disappeared into the sea, whinnying under the water, and then a soldier went in after him and came up a

241

corpse with hoof marks stamped all over his body. Horrible, wasn't it, oh pilgrim? And more spitting, and Socrates considering the possibility of inviting them to discuss the matter and to try to convince them that it was foolish and harmful for the City to be spreading such hoaxes. But what would he use for arguments? Could he get them to understand how senseless it was for the magicians who aided Xanthus to have used files?

He decided against it. They would never listen. How great the incongruence in the souls of those two rustics who insisted on fanning their fear of equine enemy demons. When he was on his way again, Socrates wondered what Xanthus could have been doing in those waters. Didn't he want to escape? Then why didn't he ride away on his two-legged horse?

He smiled. After hearing this latest folly about horses kicking under the sea, he was convinced that the City would believe the wildest fantasies. Thus did the learned Athens sometimes bray.

A little after the noon hour, he stopped to cool his feet in the bubbling waters of a spring dedicated to the nymphs. He lay down on the grass-carpeted slope, the crooks of his forearms under the back of his head, and thought it all over again. Yes, the events at Epsilon were the work of a mad but very astute barbarian.

3 4

WHEN THE RIDER brought the news, Nicias was
placing colored beans on a map of Attica to mark the
routes of the patrols that were out stopping everyone who
could not satisfactorily explain who he was and where he came
from. Xanthus the Lycian had to be hiding somewhere in the
territory.

By the time they got to the part about the death of Nicander
and how he had been kicked by a horse under the water, Nicias
had no more ears for the report and ordered Hiero to take note
of every detail.

Nicias left the cabin to hide his nervousness and walked
down to the shore to be alone, to breathe in deep gasps of air.
His hands were shaking. He was haunted by the submarine
whinnies and the hoofs stamped on Nicander's body. Could it
be the work of demons conjured by King Perdiccas? Or were
they obeying the God of the Cerulean Hair, who was thus taking his reprisals for the botched sacrifice of the colt?

He waded into the serene waters in a dark place and prayed in humble words, his palms turned downward, his voice quaking, for the powerful Heliconian to forgive him, for the imperfect sacrifice was the result of his surprise at hearing the alarm and the anguish of his soul, but he, Nicias, would atone for the insult with an offering worthy of his liquid majesty, yes, in a few days he would build an altar, a temple, a fountain, exactly, he would build a fountain, and just then the sky was all light, and a rumble of approbatory thunder came rolling over the waves, and Nicias noticed that both signs had come from his right, and he bent over in gratitude to kiss the Poseidonian waters and bless the crystal-clear sign with which the God had accepted his promised reparations, and now, with his spirit mustered anew, he returned to the cabin. There, the blackest of all seers told him that sometimes the mocking spirits of the night made mortals see things that were never there, and that maybe things were not exactly the way the oarsmen told them, perhaps there had been no whinny under the sea, but just the perception of terrified ears, and Nicias, well, fine, but how could he explain the hoof marks on Nicander's body? And Melas had to admit that he had no answer for that, but something, perhaps the slightest tickle in the bottom of his seer's soul, kept asking him again and again why Xanthus stood staring into the sea, as the oarsmen said, and Hiero, for his part, could not understand how this Xanthus could have gotten all the way around from the watchtower to the entrance to the shrine over wide open and patrolled territory. It was quite impossible for him to have reached the shrine, uphill and downhill, the Scythian on his back, without being seen, and Nicias listened intently, approving with pursed lips, so both Melas and Hiero were suggesting that the excellent Nicias keep the area discreetly under surveillance, and Nicias, fully his own master now, rode off for the mines at dawn and took a boat out to inspect the cliff walls, which dropped straight down into the water, to see if one of the many holes was big enough to hide a couple of archers, and despite the consternation in Athens about the corpse that had been kicked under the sea and the demands of some for courageous volunteers to dive among the underwater caves, Nicias kept calm, he decided not to sacrifice anyone, and just as he had thought, some six fathoms up, about half an arrow-shot from the place where Xanthus had disappeared under the water, he could see a small entrance that grew wider toward the inside, and they brought ladders, and after clearing away a thick layer of bird droppings, it was big enough to hide two men, even more.

Nicias had two Scythians posted in the cave with their bows and a boar net. They were given food and water for a week, for they were not to move from the cave and had to keep the area under strict vigilance, especially at night.

Nicias was full of newfound energies. He took care of all the details and gave the archers their orders personally. They were to take Xanthus alive, aim only for the arms and legs.

The following day, in urgent consultations with the new archons and the senior priests, he got the necessary authorization to build, at his own expense, a fountain to Poseidon, with seawater and fish. He first proposed building it on the road to Phalerum, where the effigy of the Polias was carried every year for its bath in the Plynteria, but then he decided to honor Poseidon at the base of the Acropolis. Immediately, a hundred and fifty of his one thousand slaves were taken from Laurium and sent to cut and carry marble at the Pentelikon.

Many citizens considered it untimely for Nicias to make that hurried display in honor of Poseidon, especially since it was Dionysus who had been offended.

But a few days later, even the detractors of General Nicias had to admit that great Poseidon was on their side now. On the third day, the Scythians saw Xanthus reappear at the same spot.

Shortly before dawn, a head poked out as far as the nose and turned slowly, scanning everything in sight. Then a neck and shoulders appeared. When he was sure that he could not be seen from the surrounding reefs and that there were no boats on the coast, he came all the way out and sat there on a rock just barely protruding from the water, hugging his knees and looking at the stars.

The archer who was standing guard in the cave woke up his comrade. A moment later they were both aiming at the fugitive, but they could not be certain that their aim would be true in the dim starlight. They waited until they could get a better shot at his limbs.

After sitting there a long while, the fugitive swam out to another rock, flatter and broader and a bit further away. It was hot. No one could see him from the watchtower, and if a boat should round the breakers, they could not see him there either.

When the full disk of the sun was shining on the Aegean, Xanthus stood up and prayed.

The first arrow entered through the back of his thigh. He screamed in pain and set out swimming, using only his arms. One of the Scythians blew the alarm conch while the other slid down the rope they had tied to one of the outcroppings and threw the boar net over the place where Xanthus had appeared, so that he could not get back in. As the fugitive tried a difficult roundabout, the duty boat that was tied by the watchtower showed up. The three soldiers aboard had their javelins trained on him.

When he saw them, Xanthus dove down between two rocks

and, like the previous time, stayed down very long. But just as everyone began to think he had made another miraculous escape, he came up coughing and gasping for air, suddenly realizing that he had not made it under the net. Xanthus never said a word or offered resistance; he just gave himself up to the soldiers, who hauled him aboard by the hair, beat him up, and carried him away, hog-tied and bleeding from his skewered thigh.

And again Nicias strolling along the shore of that sea that Poseidon had now made propitious for Athens, and Hiero came and told him that the fugitive was tame as a lamb and about his confession to the soldiers, a hideout, a cave, a tunnel under the water, and Nicias thinking, how right Melas had been! what great news! good, that Hiero should send a rider to the City, urgently, and bring Scyllias the Diver, Nicias wanted him to explore Epsilon that very night, and to see what the cave was like, he wanted a detailed report, Nicias would not begin interrogating Xanthus until he knew what the cave was like, and rubbing his hands together, well, well, things were different now, and Nicias, like the rest of the City, what with the whinnies and the horse hooves under the water, facing the wrath of Poseidon, equine demons, but it was Xanthus, like any other flesh-and-blood mortal, hiding in a cave, so, the two-legged horse tracks and the whinnies under the water and the hooves that murdered Nicander, as the good Melas had said, were all the fraudulent arts of Xanthus, so make haste, find Scyllias, and Hiero clapping his hands and shouting orders to the slaves, and returning to the guard house, that they should remove the arrow, cure the prisoner, feed him, he was not to be mistreated, thus had the Substantiator of the Anacrisis ordained, he wanted him in good shape for the interrogation in the morning, and Nicias galloping to the isthmus, followed by Melas, entering the

247

Sunium, and may Heliconius accept the humble seaweed wreath, a testimony of his gratitude for delivering Xanthus to him, and very soon the Cronid of the moist beard would have in Athens what he had nowhere else in all Hellas, dolphins to honor him at the foot of the Acropolis, dozens of slaves carrying skins of seawater, and on the ride back, satisfied with having gained for Athens the favor of such a powerful God, certain that future generations would recall him as they did Miltiades, Themistocles, as the forger of the alliance with the Wave Dasher, and old Onion Head, with all his oratory and intrigues, would soon know who Nicias, son of Niceratus, was, and when his secretary returned and reported, yes, Scyllias from before dawn until noon in the cave, and, as always, a great job, one of the best divers in all Hellas, a grandson of the great Scyllias, Hiero was there when he made his first dive with rope and bells, but then he went down barehanded because the tunnel was too narrow, what courage! he went right down into the tunnel, and when everyone was lamenting his death, he turned up in the shrine of Omestes, great excitement in all of Laurium, that was it, a huge cavern never visited by mortals before Xanthus and his accomplices, and Nicias, accomplices? yes, yes, Scyllias had found a hole in the roof of the cavern with a wickerwork grill of thick branches covered with stones and dirt so that it could not be seen from above, and from the floor of the shrine to the bottom of the cavern there was a tree trunk with steps carved in it, all very proper, and you could see that there had been two, maybe more, it was not Xanthus alone, and Nicias, might old Onion Head be right? could it be a Potidaean fraud? two grass beds, lots of fish bones, the fish would swim into the cavern and Xanthus and his accomplices could certainly survive by fishing inside the cave, and they channeled the fresh water that flowed in the shrine cave along a gutter into a crevass where they gathered it drop by drop and stored it in a hole in the rocks, and Scyllias also found a small natural opening in the rock wall facing the sea, and it let in the daylight so they could see in the cavern, and the ungodly wretches made fires, for there were ashes all around, and everything was clearing up nicely, but Nicias was haunted by the doubt that the kicks and the whinnies were a pure fraud by Xanthus and his accomplices, and if that were the case, it was not the work of equine demons conjured by King Perdiccas, and then Pericles was right, could Xanthus be a Potidaean agent? if that were true, Nicias would make a fool of himself, and then a slave announcing that Scyllias wanted to see the Substantiator of the Anacrisis personally, and Nicias received him in the cabin, but Scyllias, carrying a haversack, wanted to see him alone, and Nicias asked Hiero to leave them, the diver must have something very important to be so cautious, and Scyllias, his eyes darting around the cabin, unable to keep his hands still, confirmed everything the secretary had said, but there was something else, and taking a package from the haversack, Scyllias wanted Nicias to be the second to see his discovery, that morning, a discovery that Scyllias had not wanted to show Hiero or anyone, so there would be no panic in the City, more panic? yes, beside a pile of ashes, Scyllias had found that which he would now reveal before the eyes of the great Nicias, and Nicias looking among the fig leaves, five horse turds, and Scyllias very much afraid, holding them for Nicias to smell, they were still fresh, and Nicias smelling, indeed, and looking at Scyllias disconcerted, and the diver pointing to some horse hairs sticking to one of the turds, and handing one over to Nicias, and Nicias, yes, they were certainly horse hairs, but why the alarm? because in the region of the shrine, there were many guards who took their horses . . . and Scyllias interrupting and apologizing, perhaps

249

the great son of Niceratus had not understood, those turds were found where no horse had ever been, they were inside the cavern, and Nicias confused, asking how big the hole in the floor of the shrine was, and Scyllias, holding his arms apart, about this big, no more than a cubit and a half, but not even the tiniest of horses could get through that hole or through the tunnel into the sea, and Scyllias was convinced that they were the hellish turds of a demon horse, and Nicias smelling again, unexplainably fresh, smelly, stinking, in fact, and then swallowing hard and wiping his forehead, what to do? so then the hoof marks on Nicander's chest were no fraud, nor the whinnies heard by the oarsmen, and Nicias feeling the hairs on his neck begin to stand on end with the confirmation of his suspicions, yes, by Hecate, equine demons, Macedonian witchcraft, he had said so all along. With such evidence and the testimony of the diver Scyllias, what could Onion Head allege? What could the warmongering mob say now?

3 5

I T WAS THE TWENTY-FIFTH DAY of the mandatory
month in Olympia. The aspirants had been training every
day under the supervision of the Hellanodicae. Before the dawn
of the twenty-sixth day, the authorities of Elis had begun to
inscribe, on the leucoma built by the stadium at the foot of
Mount Cronios, the names of the candidates who had been
accepted for the Games.

Months earlier, when Athens learned that Alcibiades had
managed to get into the Olympic Altis, there were many who
insisted that his trip out there would be in vain, that he would
never be accepted for the Games. It was unheard of for a man of
only nineteen to be allowed to sign up for the chariot race:
much too young to rival grown men; too unknown to challenge
the illustrious of Hellas for the olive crown.

That day, on the fifth eve of the opening, Olympic tradition
forbade any further training. The chosen athletes devoted the

day to giving thanks and to formulating promises in exchange for victory. The inscription of names began at first light. To keep the anxious crowd from getting in the way, the immense board had been surrounded by a cordon of guards. At midmorning, when they were finally allowed access to the board, Sthenelus, the charioteer, approached to check the list of chariots, oh joy, by Zeus! there he was, Alcibiades, son of Clinias, Athenian, they had allowed him four chariots! And the boy leaped and ran to wake up the fortunate Alcibiades, who was asleep in his tent, and all of his retainers came, and there were tears and embraces and they drank. The theoroi of Athens also came. Calias embraced him. He was proud of the young man. He confessed that until the day before he had not believed he would be admitted; Timon the Areopagite supposed that with a great deal of luck, in view of how well he had trained, they might admit a single chariot; but Tolmides knew that six of the ten judges were so impressed with the performance of his Thessalian teams and the expertise of his aurigas that they were ready to admit the seven quadrigae he had brought. However, the stubborn opposition of the other judges, who objected to his short years, forced a compromise solution whereby he had been allowed to enter only four. In the annals of Olympia, he was the youngest man ever permitted to compete with quadrigae.

Of course, he had always said that he would have his way. Of the twenty-five Athenians chosen to demonstrate their abilities in Olympia, only eleven got past the encrisis. Xanthippus, Pericles's son, had been vetoed for the horse races; Diomedes, who wept disconsolately, had not been admitted for the juvenile fighting; and Alcides, Critias's son, was excluded from the race in arms.

With the limited admission of Athenian athletes, the unexpected admittance of Alcibiades raised the expectations of the whole group, but he, after the embracing and backslapping, refused to celebrate, thanked all for their good wishes, said good-bye to everyone, and withdrew alone to the far end of Altis. He was going to thank Zeus and formulate promises. That is what he said.

He needed to be alone. He climbed a way up the slopes of Mount Cronios, and when he could no longer hear the murmur of the gathering, he sat in the shade of some poplars. Rather than toasting and listening to praise, he wanted to evoke the faces of the skeptics and the arguments against his plan. The inventory of obstacles he had overcome raised his spirits. He told himself once again that the son of Clinias was not going to the Games to witness the victories of others.

It had all begun when Aristarchus complained about his beard while they were wrestling on the palaestra of the Museum. Alcibiades noted with pleasure that the boy's skin was, in fact, irritated, and he told himself that if his beard was already so rough, he would compete with his quadrigae in Olympia.

Minors were not allowed to race chariots; according to the laws of Elis, one was a man when the adolescent fuzz turned into a rough beard, like the one that had inflamed Aristarchus's skin.

The incident had occurred when he was eight months into his epheby, with another sixteen to go. After the basic course in Oenoe, the atheletes were transferred to Museum Hill. There, he had to suffer through very boring guard duties, or stand guard at other public buildings that could not be left unprotected, or remain on his feet in absolute silence and without moving a muscle amid the chatter of the Assembly. There was nothing more that anyone could teach him about archery,

hoplomachy, or rowing, and the torch races seemed childish to
him.

He was a man now. His beard was the proof. He calculated
that there were still fourteen months to go before the Olympic
Games. Why not? His Hellenic ancestry was impeccable; he
had, to his credit, a victory at the Panathenian Games, and
there was his magnificent adulthood, which he ratified running his hand over his chin. Phemius, that year's Cosmetes,
was an Alcmeonid, his mother's cousin, who had praised his
skill with the chariot at the Panathenian Games. He could recommend him to the College of Strategi; who knows, they
might exempt him from further service. That way he could
train during the ten months demanded by the authorities in
Elis. For the past Olympics, they had, in fact, exempted
Sosigenes of Lamptrae so that he could compete in the juvenile wrestling; so why should they not free Clinias's firstborn,
who had a finer ancestry and was a Panathenian champion?
Since he had made his peace with Pericles . . . and now that
Callias was going to be his brother-in-law . . .

Before making his final decision, he had a message delivered to Socrates begging him to please meet him at the
Academy in the evening of the Day of the Fallen. He had to
stand guard by his father's tomb, and all ephebi who were
orphans of national heroes were given the night free so that
they could celebrate the Epitaphy with their own.

On hearing the plan, Socrates said that, even if Athens did
exempt him from service, his age would make it very difficult for
him to be admitted to Olympia. The chariot race was the privilege of Hellas's finest, of powerful politicians, tyrants, princes,
and kings, who could not compete for lack of strength or youth
and so made a show of their wealth.

Alcibiades replied that that was exactly why he wanted to

compete with them, to make himself known from the Phasis River to the Columns of Heracles, to earn himself a name among the Hellenes at his very early age. And, by the way, he was second to none on a chariot; nor was his ancestry any less than that of the Spartan kings; nor was he lacking in wealth or friends who would lend him whatever he needed. Did Socrates doubt his skill, his ability to train aurigas and horses? Alcibiades was certain that if he were allowed to train in Olympia, and if they saw his total dedication from sunrise to sunset in the hippodrome, he would earn the right to be admitted by the Hellanodicae. After listening to him for a long time, Socrates had to admit that it was worth making a try. That was all Alcibiades needed. If Socrates, the finest brain in Athens, thought it was possible, the decision would be irrevocable.

Pericles also objected because of his scant years and lack of fame, but in the long run, he let himself be convinced. In a few days, Alcibiades got his exemption. The only commitment he had to fulfill was to participate in official parades and ceremonies.

His categorical victory at the Great Panathenian Games, where he personally drove one of his chariots with hallucinating daring, had won him supporters; as soon as it was known that he was aspiring to Olympia, the whole City got behind him. Callias gave eleven horses and six tents for him and his retinue; Hipponicus, his future father-in-law, gave him Sthenelus, the best auriga in Athens, and put all of his stables at his disposal; his relatives on the Alcmeonid side followed suit; Pericles gave him four of his best animals, including a filly out of a champion of Delphos and Nemea; Ariphron, his other tutor, offered him three mares that had won considerable praise at the Panathenian Games and the use of a farm on the Thriasian plain, an ideal place to train; the Cosmetes gave him a team of twelve mules to carry his provisions, which Aristarchus's father promised to pay for in full; Alcamenes and Agoracritus offered to make his statue, if he were victorious; Anytus bought him six chariots, bringing his total up to twelve; and Alexis of Cnidus, the banker, added four thousand drachmas for the journey and promised to pay for all the gold, silver, and ivory his statue required.

He began his training right in the middle of the dog days of Hecatombaion, in full view of everyone who traveled along the Sacred Way. He broke Pericles's filly himself and spent his days training the horses and driving the chariots right there with his aurigas. He ate and slept with them and would tolerate no conversation other than equestrian. He forbade visits, even from Aristarchus. From the moment they got to the farm, not a single member of the team, freeman or slave, was allowed to return to the City for even a minute. When news of his total devotion got out, the Cosmetes exempted him from the parades and public presentations. He repressed his own desires for recreation and company. But there was one night when he awoke from a dream of Lysis of Miletus and was a hair's breadth away from calling Phanes, saddling up, and riding off with him to the Ceramicus to kidnap her. He got control of himself, however. There would be a time for such a move.

He had Anytus buy him one of the most famous mares in Athens, one that would make his quadriga from the Panathenian Games almost unbeatable. And he had excellent replacements.

Against the opinion of some of the veterans, he decided not to organize preferential quadrigae. From the very beginning, his horses learned to work together in different combinations; if there should be a contingency, any one of his forty horses could be used in his quadrigae in Olympia. But he was even more determined to impress the judges who were observing the training with his intense personal dedication.

In the first days of spring, the commission of the Hellanodicae arrived to register the aspirants from Attica. Alcibiades was accepted without any trouble. He proved his Greek ancestry, he had an adult beard, and all estimates showed that, by the beginning of the competitions, he would have had no less than ten mandatory months of uninterrupted training.

In midspring, Alcibiades departed with eleven chariots, forty horses, and a retinue of aurigas and slaves. They traveled together with the other Athenian aspirants. A multitude accompanied the group, in wagons, on horseback, or on foot, out to the Megaran border. The delegation to Olympia also included relatives and friends of the athletes, pilgrims, devotees with promises to keep, and the theoroi, the official ambassadors of the City. There were almost three hundred people crossing enemy territory in Megara, Corinth, and Arcadia. But they were unarmed. The hated Athenians had nothing to fear: The truce of Zeus made them inviolable.

257

At Pericles's suggestion, the Assembly instructed the theoroi to denounce the intromission of Spartans and Corinthians in the affairs of Chalcidice and their plotting with Potidaea. This way the Greeks in Olympia could tell everyone that Athens was neither attacking the Peloponnesians nor threatening them with war, but was, once again, assuming the defense of its allies in the Delian League. Although political statements were forbidden in Olympia, Zeus did allow the Greek cities to erect bronze, stone, or white poplar stele in their sacred Altis to make promises, treaties, violations, and claims known throughout Hellas.

The trip took twenty-two days. Alcibiades rode taciturnly.
As the group arrived in the territory of Elis, a motley multitude
cluttered the roads. The absence of women, who were barred
from the Games and from the road, forced the men to wash and
hang the clothing by the river, feed their little ones, and look
after the very old, who were making the pilgrimage to keep
promises on the Olympic altars; it was they who prepared and
sold food by the side of the road; jongleurs, poets, and rhap-
sodists animated the march; lines of tradesmen filed by with
their mules laden with wares; Greek travelers brought
Hyperborean curiosities from the Tauric land; from Tartessus
came gaily colored birds of Hesperides; saddlebags full of giant
Paphlagonian nuts arrived from Sinope; Cyrenaicans lead
strings of camels and hawked ivory from Ethiopia, miraculous
unguents, monkeys, and perfumes; Cypriots brought linen
from Amorgos, and rolls of Persian tapestries; at the crossroads
and in the woods where many took their evening rest, there
were makeshift stages populated by Sicilian mimes, comedians
from Megara, acrobats, fire-eaters, seers; richly attired dynasts
rode their fine horses with costly trappings, setting up camps
with their beasts of burden, wagons and retinues of slaves,
bearers of amphorae and statues, or offerings loudly
announced by trumpeting heralds.

No Greek city could have accommodated such a multitude.
Olympia lodged them on the slopes of the neighboring hills.
There, during the warmest time of the year, a whole tent city
would appear around Altis, a medley without streets or taverns,
without women or hats, forbidden out of respect for Zeus.

During the ride, Alcibiades took no notice of the itinerant
attractions. He did not see the landscape, or feel the heat, or
suffer thirst. A single idea dominated his mind and his senses.

In Olympia, he devoted himself to the care of his horses, to the instruction of his aurigas, to the planning and replanning of his tactics for the contest, and to spying on his rivals. The endless days in the hippodrome laboring naked under the blazing sun turned his blond hair the color of silver, in stark contrast with his deeply tanned skin. Except for the arrival ceremonies, which the delegations held in the Temple of Zeus and later before his open altar, Alcibiades never left the hippodrome. When night fell, he would return to his tent and virtually collapse from exhaustion.

The days went by, and if he had been made to leave at that moment, he would have been able to recall very little of Olympia.

Finally, Alcibiades could sit back and enjoy the certainty that, when Zeus's eagle flew over the hippodrome, his chariots would match those of the most powerful men in all Hellas.

He had nothing to fear from any of his rivals. Those who were favoring Pleistoanax, son of the Spartan King Pausanias, knew nothing of races or chariots. None of those quadrigae could beat his; nor could those of his countryman Gylippus, son of Cleander. After watching the favorites train for almost a month, he dismissed them in a batch: Corinthians, Boeotians, and all the Ionians together could never stand up to his quadrigae. Some, like the Thessalians and Epirots, had better horses, but their training was clumsy; no one could get them to pull as a single beast. Hermocrates of Syracuse, great-grandson of the tyrant Anaxilas, a famous breeder whose teams had won several Olympic meets, was the only one who commanded his respect, but as a trainer, he was lacking in logos and metros. When the final days were running out, he was already bragging about the certainty of his victory. Alcibiades decided to take advantage of his reputation for fatuousness and devised a plan. He began spreading the word that the Sicilian's training was a joke and that his aurigas were chicken shit. Two days before the competition, he got Hermocrates to take the reins personally. When he spotted him, Alcibiades posted himself by the stone that marked the finish line, and every time Hermocrates went by, he would laugh, calling him a coward and a woman. Why was he so afraid of the finish marker? Did he think it was that old Sicilian, Scylla? Haa, ha, ha. The constant jibes provoked Hermocrates's arrogance to drive his team so recklessly that, on one of the laps, he hit the stone marker and flipped his chariot, hurting his best lead mare when there was no time to train another.

That one was as good as beaten. Barring any accidents on the day of the race, any one of the four quadrigae Alcibiades had been allowed to enter, now fully rested and at the height of their training, could beat the best of the Sicilian's six. No one could take his victory from him. Soon, all of Hellas would know who he was: Alcibiades, son of Clinias, Athenian.

He walked off for the center of Altis. For the first time since coming to Olympia, he actually felt like looking around. He visited dozens of temples: Poseidon, Hera, Ares, Aphrodite, Apollo and Artemis, Hephaestus and Athena; the Olympians all had their temples in Altis. The Horae and the Mother of the Gods, too. The heroes, Pelops, Achilles, Heracles, and Theseus. The sacred river Alpheus, whose waters mixed with the ashes of the sacrifices, was used to tamp down the terraces of the Altar of Zeus, which grew higher and higher with the passing centuries.

He walked among the piles of white poplar firewood engulfed by the smoke of two hundred pyres where, on that day, the athletes were burning their offerings for victory; there he was accosted by a young man from Ambracia to show him a picture of his brother, who two years earlier had shipped out for Athens intending to sell some Mollosian hounds and had never returned; further on, a couple of Cretans approached him with the same petition; then an old man from Stagira asked about his son.

He stopped a moment to look at a strongman from Arcadia, who took an egg in his hand and bet a sheep against a hare or a cock that no man there could pry his hand open or squeeze it to make him crush the egg. The place was littered with blind people and cripples who traveled for weeks to keep promises; there were dozens of cases of sunstroke among the gawkers who stood there watching the acrobats, rope walkers, and jugglers, forgetting to wet their heads and passing out in the noonday sun.

He visited other altars and the chamber of votive treasures offered by individuals or cities; he spent part of the afternoon searching among the hundreds of statues for just the right one to serve as a model for his own. He no longer had any doubts that his effigy would stand forever in the Altis of Olympia. He saw statues made of ebony, stone, marble, bronze, ivory, gold, and every conceivable combination, strewn about without any order in time. Standing by the side of a child discus-thrower who had been the winner in the past Games, one could find a three-hundred-year-old fighter or the auriga Iolaus, who raced Heracles's mares to victory. There were statues of formidable pancratiasts, of trim throwers, and of riders. Alcibiades stopped at the Prytaneum by the marble quadriga of Anaxander, the first Olympic chariot race champion, portrayed in prayer to Zeus. Then he saw Polycles, waving a ribbon with his right hand; the inscription said that his quadrigae had also been victorious at the Isthmian Games, as well as in Nemea and Pythium. Standing by him were two children, one holding on to a wheel and the other asking for the ribbon. He finally found one statue, practically hidden behind some hedges in the back of the stadium, with the same noble features and attitude that he wanted for his own. It was the likeness of Lichas, son of Arcesilaus, a Lacedaemonian who competed for Thebes. Lichas was portrayed as he personally tied the ribbon of victory on his auriga; the statue suggested so much motion that one of the horses, with its front legs outside the pedestal, looked ready to fly away. At the bottom was the name of Myron of Eleutherae, the same Myron who had made the statue of Alcibiades's father, Clinias. Another example of the sculptor's genius, scorned by Pericles. How old might Myron be by now? If on returning to Athens, Alcibiades should find the old man keen of vision and steady of hand, he would turn down Alcamenes and Agoracritus and pose for him. Decided!

Annoyed by the heat, Alcibiades sought solace in the Temple of Zeus; this time he looked around avidly and noticed details he had not perceived when he had first arrived. At the foot of the statue, he read an inscription: "I was made by Phidias, son of Charmides, Athenian."

On his first visit, Alcibiades had confined himself to praying for help; he had not wanted to let himself be carried away with admiration for the colossus. Looking at the huge statue, he invoked the universal God of Socrates, the prime mover, omnipotent, meter of justice, and through him he invoked the spirit of his father. Did he not deserve victory? He reminded Zeus that he was an orphan, that his ever-present desire had been to reach adulthood so that he could die with glory and thus honor his lineage and rejoin his father's soul. Alcibiades reminded Zeus of the farewell, moments before Clinias departed to meet his heroic death in Coronea; how, after donning his armor, his father had picked him up and kissed him tenderly on the cheeks. And he wept again. His eyes always filled with tears when he recalled that last image.

And just as he had not noticed the incidents or seen the landscape during the trip from Attica, he had seen nothing in the temple except the face of Olympic Zeus.

The statue was approximately the height of ten men, a mass of gold and ivory, much greater than Athena Parthenos. Alcibiades understood the sheer volume Phidias had gained by carving him on his throne. If Phidias had made him on his feet, half the Thunderer's torso would have protruded through the roof. With Zeus in a sitting position, one could better see his features and his head crowned with wild olive. One could also see, with a richness of detail lacking in Athena, the highest embellishments of Zeus's scepter, forged from every metal, and even the face of the Nike he held in his right hand reaching toward the ceiling.

How unfortunate that Phidias had had to abandon Athens.

Alcibiades began to examine the throne, where the chryselephantine mass alternated with ebony and precious inlays. He was entranced by the paintings and engravings that adorned the sides. At the foot of the colossus, four Victories danced on the front side; on the base, just before the solid gold sandals, he recognized the rape of the Theban children, and further down, Apollo and Artemis shooting their arrows into Niobe's children.

Seeing beside the grill that closed off access to the pedestal a beautiful boy binding a fillet on his head, Alcibiades recalled the rumors about the famous Pantarces of Elis, a victorious fighter in the previous Olympic Games. Pantarces had been the last great love of Phidias, who had portrayed him in effigy next to Zeus.

And there were the paintings of Paenanus: Theseus and Pirithous; Hellas and Salamis; Heracles strangling the lion of Nemea; Ajax's rape of Cassandra; Penthesilea giving up her soul, held by Achilles; Oenomaus, praying to Warlike Zeus just before competing in his chariot against the pretenders of Hippodamia.

Suddenly, as if the soul of Oenomaus had inspired him, Alcibiades decided that he would not make his promise in that impersonal temple. Nor would he, as the others did, burn calves on the stadium altar; nor black rams for Pelops; nor suovetauriliae for Hera or Pallas Athena. Foolishness! His promise would be otherwise.

He set off for the smaller Temple of Warlike Zeus, at the far end of the hippodrome. His eyes were half closed, his face as motionless as those of the surrounding statues he no longer noticed. He walked fast, ignoring everyone. In his mind, he was defining the terms of the promise he would make once again to his father's soul. Like Oenomaus, his witness would be Warlike Zeus, whose terrible face was more fitting to the oath he was about to take in exchange for the Olympic olive wreath. It would be the oath of a good and beautiful Athenian who would rather die young than live without glory.

3 6

"GRINDING FINE ROCK" was the expression used among miners to refer to the worst torment known in Laurium.

Throughout the inhabited world, fugitives or slaves who attacked their masters were considered dangerous criminals. And since no one would buy them, in Athens their masters condemned them to the punishment wheel, where they ground fine rock.

Day and night, breathing in the ever-present cloud of lithargyric dust around the mills, they developed chronic diseases of the lungs and eyes.

The violent ones, those who sought release by bringing on their own death, got the whip, hot pepper in their wounds, thorns in the anus; even with the sores and fractures they inflicted on themselves, even with fevers, they were kept tied up days on end without water, torturing their comrades with their moaning, their throats scorched by the rock dust and the infinite thirst of Tantalus. Those who refused to push the wheel pegs were put in stocks that twisted their limbs or squeezed their necks or heads; they were changed from one to another torment every day so they could never get accustomed to any one of them. The overseers learned how to keep them alive. There was no respite from the torment. When one was completely exhausted or insensitive to pain, he was beaten or whipped to death as a lesson to the others.

Most of them simply gave in. They would slowly become less than animals, pushing the wheel in silence and meekly awaiting death.

After two months on the wheel, Xanthus was still holding out. Except for his weakness, a persistent cough and the irritation that kept his eyes bloodshot like a boar's, there was nothing really wrong with him. He had never fainted and he was still not delirious.

A Lydian slave whom he found chained to the same spoke told him about Sabazius, the God of miners in his country. He confessed that Sabazius came to him at night to give him courage: "Be joyful, for great will be your reward!" Just as flowers grow out of mud and manure, the life that was to begin with his death would bring him infinite consolations for his trials in this world; he would abide on a tall summit, surrounded by fertile valleys, amid love and beauty; there, the powerful, the good, and the beautiful of this world would be his slaves; for the great universal scales weighed each and every destiny in eternal oscillations like the white-crested waves that broke in terrible fury and returned to such perfect peace that you could see your face in their waters; and just as the great trees were engendered by tiny seeds, the pleasures of wine and love were followed by plagues and woes, for thus, in a perpetual accounting, did the scales find their perfect balance. But Sabazius also revealed to him that the most abominable sin was to quench, by your own hand, that life bestowed on you from above.

The day finally came when the Lydian began to rant. Xanthus could no longer understand his muttering. Soon after, the Lydian's knees bent and he fell at the foot of the wheel.

He died under the sticks of the overseers, but without a single moan. In his final moments, while they were twisting his limbs and breaking his bones in the presence of the other condemned slaves, his eyes stared serenely into the distance, almost smiling. His name was Belus.

Xanthus was no longer tortured by the dust in his throat and his lungs, which until then felt like they would burst from the coughing; he discovered the mysterious joy of suffering. The greater his thirst and pain, the more he became convinced of the wonders of his afterlife. He wished he would lose his mind very soon. He was certain that Belus, in his final days, had beatific visions. And how right he had been when he said that men achieved their purity like kneaded dough! The downtrodden and crushed, those who received no mercy in this life from the hand of destiny, would be the masters of the next. He welcomed the fine dust, his pig's eyes, the whip, and the stick. He thanked the Mother of the Gods and Sabazius deeply for frustrating his escape. The freedom sought in escape had been found in pain. Worthless the prosperity his talent as a bronzesmith would have earned him in Megara, worthless the glories of this world, for much richer by far was he now in the purity won on the punishment wheel.

The evening the Scythian showed up by the rock where he was chained nights and gave him the file, Xanthus was not even surprised that one of the guards should try to help him escape. He was undoubtedly acting under a psephisma of the Gods. And whatever the outcome, Xanthus would welcome it with joy.

267

Perhaps the Gods had ordained that he be caught trying to escape and put to death by the most terrible tortures. So be it. He did not fear the stocks nor the final beating. They were the keys to the prison of the flesh. He began to file, hoping for a speedy death.

What? . . . No, no, he could not . . . He only remembered that the Scythian had gone to fetch him and had taken him by way of his watchtower over to the shrine of Dionysus . . . but he never saw him again . . .

Well . . . when they got to the entrance to the tunnel, two men were waiting for him and one of them took his hand and began to talk to him . . . No. He could remember nothing. No, not the name, either . . . The face? Just a pair of very wide-open eyes . . . It was dark.

When he awoke in the cavern, he felt thirsty, and despite the darkness, he walked around the lagoon with perfect precision, straight to the hole where the fresh water collected, and drank deeply. Then he took some dry wood from the pile and revived the embers . . . Oh, that . . . He kept asking himself the same question; it was as if he had lived there a very long time, because from the very moment he awoke, he knew exactly where to find the tunnel that led to the sea, and how to harpoon the fish that ventured in, and how to find the knife in the darkness, and the salt, the hooks, and the flint . . . through the tunnel? You have much great care; you only come out nightly time . . . ?! Yes, you coming out only nightly. At first he thought he was at the portal to his new life, but when he ventured out into the sea, he saw the watchtowers and the palisades, and he decided to await what the Gods had in store for him . . . No, he came back only later, when he felt the need to see the stars, and the following day he explored out to the breakers, and then he went to a cleared pine wood, and since it was invisible from the palisades, he returned another night for torch wood … Yes, with the knife, to get it into the tunnel little by little … Yes, it was eight days then … Well, because he counted them, of course … After that? After that he went further uphill to try to see the palisades, and he found some watercress by a spring and gorged himself … No, the first time he tarried by a wild fig tree, that was why he was out after daybreak and the men in the boat saw him … The day he was wounded? Well, he used to wait for the sun to rise completely to offer up his prayers … No, he knew nothing about the sacrifice … Nothing about that.

And Nicias was beside himself, ordering that they ask him for the last time who was responsible for the sacrifice, what his name was, where he could be found, who had sent him, whether it was King Perdiccas of Macedonia, and Xanthus insisting that there was no king, no horse, that he knew nothing about any sacrifice, and Nicias, that he would have him tortured, and Xanthus, that he welcomed the soul-purifying torments, so fine, since the infidel was defiant and beginning to lie, the tourniquet, the ring on the head, pincers, twisting, and Xanthus, after two weeks of rest and good food in the cavern, feeling every bit of the tortures, crying, screaming, invoking Sabazius, Cybele, calling Belus the Lydian, fainting, but saying nothing of his accomplices on the second day of questioning, and on the third day, his fever very high, teeth broken, nails torn out, the arrow wound on his thigh beginning to exude pestilence, eyes turned up, smiling through bloody slaver, yes, he was well-ground wheat, the finest dough … farewell the prison of the flesh … and suddenly, raising the head that hung defeated on his chest, opening his eyes wide, no, brother, no, and facing his interrogator, focusing his eyes again, no, he did not have Athena's eye, One Eye lied, no, brothers, he was not going to take the amethyst to Megara ...

And Nicias, excited, was the infidel mixed up in the theft of the eye as well? The Gods were finally helping him in that anacrisis, and exchanging glances with Hiero, see how the accused confessed what no one had asked him, revelation of the sacrilege at the Parthenon was in his hands, too, and Xanthus, brothers, I would swear by the sacred sign of the three fingers, and Nicias, that was it! the three mutilated fingers must be a secret sign in Perdiccas's Boreal rituals, and Xanthus his main agent, an enemy of Athens, by the Twelve Gods, he would show those fools who mocked him in the Assembly, he would show Pericles, he would show Lampon, who denied the Macedonian witchcraft of the mutilated hand, fine, fine, go on, who was this One Eye with the horse and the wig? and you not never outside nightly, in the fair Samos, flowers bloomed from beaten bronze, the good dough had broken bones, such was the eternal bread, toothless, eyeless, popoPOM went the anvil in Samos ... By Zeus, the fiend was delirious again. Puagh, that leg stank. Have the cilice taken off him, and the bone crusher, and give him water, we cannot have him die yet, and from now on have scribes copy down everything he says, even if it makes no sense, everything, everything, and find that One Eye person who is somewhere with Athena's stolen eye.

37

FROM ONE TO THE OTHER

The ninth of Hecatombaion

I HAVE JUST LEARNED of certain statements extracted from someone in whom you showed extraordinary interest no more than a month ago. For two weeks now, I have been consumed by the suspicion that when you asked me to find him, you were not thinking of your baths. His confessions of today confirm my suspicions, and I see a new and terrible menace to you and to myself. Someone recognized you when you came in and accused me. I have hurried to write to warn you not to come here for any reason in the next few days. I am in great danger, and so too is the man I love and admire. If you still feel any gratitude for him, as you have said, and you have not ceased to love me, meet me tomorrow at dawn at Eulalia's house. This time it shall be I who turns up in disguise. I beg you not to fail me. We must speak as soon as possible. When you have read this note, tear it up and give it back to the slave. Be happy.

3 8

IF HE COULD GET an intelligible confession out of Xanthus, it might confirm that the theft of the eye and the mutilated hand were both the witchcraft of the Macedonian warlock. Nicias could prove that he was right in denouncing Pericles before the Assembly for bungling the City's affairs in Chalcidice.

The territory would be purified if he could catch and throw those brothers Xanthus kept talking about into the Barathrum; they were undoubtedly his accomplices. And how wonderful it would be if that One Eye still had the eye with him. The whole City would praise Nicias. What a great double move against Onion Head.

As soon as the torturers were able to divine a description of One Eye from Xanthus's babblings, the King Archon ordered an intense search of the City and the ports.

Someone had seen him leaving Truncheon's brothel one afternoon two weeks ago, but he had never returned. However, once the citizens found out that he was wanted in connection with the Epsilon sacrilege, several persons showed up at the Royal Portico to report that One Eye had last been seen in the expiatory pageant, heading for Phalerum. In Phalerum, a fisherman who had just returned from Munychia recalled that he had seen him in the port with Porphyrius the Cybernetes.

Brought before Nicias and having taken the mandatory oaths, Porphyrius testified that One Eye had come to him for help, to ship out for Delos. One Eye told him that he had made a little money and wanted to buy women to open up his own establishment in the City.

In the second interrogation of the brothel slaves, after the usual torture required by law before receiving testimony from slaves, none of them could recall that One Eye had any plans to travel or to buy women.

Truncheon ratified the testimonies of her slaves and servants.

In consultation with Hiero and Melas, the son of Niceratus came to the conclusion that One Eye had left the territory. That being the case, the City was relieved of his polluting presence, but he would have to give up the hope he had cherished of recovering the stolen amethyst, which had undoubtedly been taken to Macedonia, where at that very moment King Perdiccas was probably conjuring some evil against Athens.

By midafternoon, the City had very little hope of capturing the infidel.

We'll make him talk, and Xanthus, a mere mockery of a human being, babbling when he was conscious, staring into the distance, but Nicias ordering that they take down his every word, and in case he spoke too fast, two tachygraphers from the Assembly, brought to the cells of the Royal Portico, transcribing alternate fragments amid incessant finger-snapping by Hiero,

and the official interrogator repeating time and again what
Nicias and the Archon King suggested, ever hoping that in
another delirium like the day before, they might get further
clues and Xanthus might reveal who had stolen Athena's eye,
and Xanthus, in silence, staring at the interrogator in surprise,
and Nicias explaining that his mind was slipping, that the previous session had been the same, but insisting on repeating the
questions to get at least some nonsense out of him, and
Xanthus, suddenly, that the purest dough was made with much
beating and twisting, and that death was good, and free of his
carnal prison, he could leave for the valleys, and Nicias signaling to let him rant, flowery valleys of Samos, home, woman, in
the next life he would have a woman, that was the first thing,
the brothers would help him, and the interrogator, very good,
very good, tell us who the brothers are, and Xanthus, the brothers? and the official, who are the brothers? and Xanthus, eyes
closed, the brothers would not want him with the letter *phi*,
they were afraid to walk with him, but they would return and
Xanthus would leave with them. Did the brothers steal Athena's
eye? Was it One Eye? Who, who? And Xanthus, yes, no, who?
and seeing that they were losing him, quick, water, bread
dipped in wine, carry on, what was the meaning of the three
fingers? and Xanthus, oh, yes, the three fingers, and Nicias,
well, speak of the three fingers, and Xanthus, hee, hee, hee, and
Nicias ordering them to insist on that, and Xanthus barely able
to lift his arm, touching his forehead, you now letter *phi*, you
much fat danger not come with us, and the Archon bewildered,
why was he speaking like a barbarian? and Nicias, that he had
no idea, that it was the same in the previous session, and you
always here and not come up in daily, you wait you brothers,
and water, more water, and Nicias, careful, too much water and
he passes out, and Xanthus, like the horse, yes, like the horse,

274

and everyone so nice, and Nicias signaling for silence, perhaps he would say what the horse was doing in the cavern, ask who was riding the horse, and Xanthus, that One Eye, One Eye was riding the horse? and he had given him lots of water to make him fat so no one would suspect, and Xanthus, that too much water made him heavy on the slopes to Megara, and touching his forehead again, where was the long blond hair of the Macedonian horseman? and Nicias, attention, a Macedonian, an agent of King Perdiccas? and Xanthus, yes, Perdiccas, where, when, who was this blond Macedonian horseman? did he steal Athena's eye? and Xanthus, Athenians thieves, murderers of Samos, damned owls, fainting, and Nicias, quick, wine on his lips, and Xanthus, that soon he would have better wine, the wine of eternity, the finest bread, and preaching with a raised index finger that Nicias of Niceratus and all the archons would be slaves, dogs, they would be in the next life, haaa, ha, ha, coughing, vomiting, gasping, murmur in the chest, and after a long rest, opening his eyes, the official asking him about the horse turds in the cavern, and Xanthus, oh, the horse turds, and had One Eye taken the amethyst to King Perdiccas of Macedonia? and Xanthus drooling, eyes lost, that Perdiccas of Macedonia and that turds very much secret thing, and Nicias, fidgeting, leaning forward to hear better, and I giving you only one task, you pour little fresh water in morning, then little fresh water in night, and Nicias, excited, water on the turds? Macedonian witchcraft? who had given him those instructions? and the interrogator, very well, continue, what about the water? and Xanthus, babbling, and the scribes stopping, looking at each other, wondering, and Xanthus, that all much big clearly, and the official, spurred by Nicias, pushing him, was One Eye the chief Macedonian agent? who ordered the turds to be watered? and Xanthus, that it was King Perdiccas of

Macedonia, and Nicias, exchanging glances with the Archon and the Areopagites, good, good, and who are Perdiccas's other men in Athens? and again prolonged silence, Xanthus, closing his eyes, coughing, and, of course, good bronze also has to be beaten, and the Archon, why did they not try to find out about the underwater kick marks on Nicander's body? and the official, where was Xanthus when the horse kicked the soldier who went in after him? and Xanthus, pom pom, and the official, who gave the horse the orders? and Xanthus, King Perdiccas of Macedonia, but how, how? and Xanthus, opening his eyes very wide and raising his eyebrows, yes, brother, yes, and shaking his head with eyes closed, you no fear, you no fear, you wait enemy by tunnel door, when enemy head come in, you not let out, you much careful not let out head, you hold hair and zup, not let out, drown enemy, drown good . . . And Nicias, personally, on his feet, excited, bringing his head close to the prisoner's, so Perdiccas himself was in the cavern in spirit? and you, pom chest, horse kicks on chest, and popoPOM, much hard strike, strike like overseers by wheel . . . And the Archon Pisander, did you sacrifice the Scythian? and Xanthus, the Scythian, and squirting blood between his broken teeth, the Scythian, and Pisander, did you? and Xanthus, it was you . . . Where was the Scythian? and Xanthus, oh, the Scythian, yes, the next life, the good death, fugitive from the prison of the body, and the official, but who sacrificed him? and Xanthus, King Perdiccas of Macedonia, and did One Eye participate, too? and Xanthus, One Eye, too, aha! so One Eye, too, and how much did Perdiccas pay One Eye? and Xanthus, that he paid in phalluses, and that One Eye was the horse accomplice, and the cape and the wig, and Nicias looking around him, did they see how right he was? and where had One Eye gone? and Xanthus, to Eleusis, babbling again, and the scribes immobile, unintelligible fragments . . . And then? to Megara, and the official signaling that he was about to pass out again, and lowering his voice, and everyone silent, and Xanthus, oh, yes, to Megara, but disguised as an Olympic pilgrim . . . Oh, oh, Nicias and the Archon looking at each other, so One Eye was heading for Macedonia by way of Megara and not by way of Delos as the Cybernetes had said? and with whom did he go to Megara, and Xanthus, with King Perdiccas of Macedonia.

He never regained consciousness again. When it was evident that he was dying, the Archon King ordered him thrown into the Barathrum, condemned for willful homicide and impiety.

Xanthus was carried on a litter, followed by dignitaries and a great multitude. He was unconscious, hardly able to breathe. Having celebrated the rites and pronounced the terrible anathemas, they threw him over the edge. He rebounded three times from the outcroppings on the cliff and disappeared into the entrails of the pit.

That very night, the Primates of Dionysus and Athena dreamed unequivocal messages and announced that both Gods had accepted the execution of Xanthus the Lycian in atonement.

It was confirmed that the death of the soldier Nicander was the work of an underwater equine demon, and that Xanthus, a confessed agent of Perdiccas of Macedonia, was the perpetrator, in connivance with One Eye, of the impious human sacrifice in the shrine of Dionysus, and that One Eye, thief of the eye or accomplice of the Macedonian executed months earlier, had escaped over the Megaran border disguised as an Olympic pilgrim and headed for the court of Perdiccas.

The Supreme Priest of Dionysus pronounced execrations for damage to his eyes, legs, liver, lungs, heart, and for a quick death with horrible suffering; the Buzyges of Zeus and the

277

Primate of Apollo performed impeccable sacrifices in their temples to make the paths of his escape pernicious and unpassable.

Personally, Nicias slept a lot easier. Parthenos should be thankful to him, and Poseidon, obviously, had nothing to do with the Macedonian villainies.

With One Eye out of the territory and Xanthus condemned, the City's guilt was considerably relieved. Having confirmed the magical maneuvers of Perdiccas, the clergy of the Twelve Gods could proceed with the celebration of the Panathenian exorcism against the Boreal demons and stem the menace discovered thanks to the zeal of the Substantiator of the Anacrisis, who, having fulfilled his mission, ordered the incontestable summary evidence contained in the tachygraphic version of the testimony of Xanthus the Lysian deposited in the arc of the King's Tribunal.

278

Gone were the uncertainty and the fear. In a few days, peace returned to the City of Pallas Athena.

Despite his personal success, Nicias was bitter. If he had only had Xanthus's confession a week earlier, he could have prevented the bellicose Pericles from getting the Assembly and the Senate to issue an irrevocable psephisma to send the fleet against Chalcidice that very summer, under the command of Archestrastus.

THE VICTORY OF ALCIBIADES, son of Clinias,
Athenian, moved Olympia. Ever since the quadriga race
had been introduced in the twenty-fifth Olympics, two and a
half centuries earlier, no famous Hellenic breeder, no munifi-
cent monarch, no one had ever had three chariots in the first
four places.

Alcibiades missed winning only the third place, and that
was because Sthenelus, his best auriga, who was in the lead,
flipped his chariot when he grazed the finish marker on one of
the laps.

There was no similar equestrian victory in all the annals of
Olympia.

During the elimination heats, Pausanias, King of Sparta,
suffered an effusion of bile. When he saw his son Pleistoanax's
best two quadrigae turn over in their respective runs, and the
other two lagging lamentably behind, he gave orders to strike
his tents and anticipate his thanksgiving to Olympian Zeus.

As Pausanias was leaving with his retinue, he was told that Alcibiades had gotten all four chariots into the finals, and his displeasure turned to apprehension. The certainty that Alcibiades was going to win an unprecedented triumph took root in his soul, and he did not want to be a witness. After all his splendid offerings in the Heraeum of Sparta, and later to Zeus and Pelops in Olympia, the victory of this young Athenian, whose admission was in violation of Olympic traditions, was an ominous portent for the imminent war with Athens. Pausanias's alarm increased when he found out that the victor was an Alcmeonid, a relative of Pericles.

Anaxilas II of Syracuse lost a gold talent when his nephew had him bet Alexis of Cnidus that Alcibiades would not win.

Euphranor the Corinthian denounced before the Hellanodicae that Alcibiades had cheated at the starting line, and Gylippus, son of Cleander, said that, in the classification heat in which he participated and was in the lead, Alcibiades had thrown sand in his eyes. A prince of Thessaly complained that when his chariot was trying to pass Alcibiades's, the Athenian auriga had whipped him in the face.

Callias the Rich, as president of the Athenian delegation, remained duly calm, together with the other theoroi, but near the end, he was impressed with the magnificent display put on by Alcibiades's three chariots, combining gaits and weaving to keep their rivals from passing, and when he saw that the formidable Hermocrates of Syracuse had a single chariot among the leaders, and only in third place at that, he lost his composure and joined in the wild cheering and jumping of his compatriots.

When Alcibiades personally took the reins from the injured Sthenelus and brought his chariot in first, the compact mass of spectators who had been watching the elimination heats from the hills since dawn shook the summit of Cronios with their cheers.

The Hellanodicae crowned the victor with a wild olive wreath, braided by the twenty virgins of Elis, the only women authorized to be at the Games. While the three chariots made their triumphal lap around the hippodrome, the Athenians wept in each others' arms and thanked Zeus for rewarding them with an unforgettable performance. Heraldic trumpets reverberated through the Altis of Olympia and acrobats, comedians, and drummers took over the hippodrome. In the evening, poets from all over Hellas composed epinicia, and there were encomia in praise of the dexterity and beauty of the Cliniad.

And yet, after the three laps, with a smiling face and reins held high, the new champion hardly participated in the official ceremonies presided over by the magistrates of Elis; during the outdoor banquet offered by Callias in the evening, he was taciturn.

As soon as the libations were over, Alcibiades claimed to be very tired and withdrew to his tent.

For several days he was so evasive that his behavior worried the theoroi and the seer Euphrantides. On the very eve of the competitions, when someone had reproached him for not participating in the collective offering made by the Athenians on the Altar of Zeus, he had answered tersely and cryptically that he already entered into a personal agreement with Warlike Zeus.

Also unexpected was the combined success of the Athenian athletes. After the initial setback of having only eleven competitors among the twenty-eight aspirants, those eleven won four crowns. Aside from the chariots, Athens surprisingly outclassed the competition in the race in arms, wrestling, and children's wrestling, which were the traditional monopoly of the Lacedaemonians. Besides, they won second places in the pentathalon, the javelin, the long race, and the short children's race. No one could have imagined that so few competitors would have performed such a feat.

On the fifteenth of Hecatombaion, the last day of the competitions, moments after Alcibiades's crushing victory, Callias sent out a courier with orders to ride at full speed. The bearer of the joyous message arrived on the eighteenth in Athens, causing an uproar. Callias had him say that the victors would make the return ride home, Olympian Zeus and Apollo God of Streets willing, in twelve days, to be back in the City on the eve of the Panathenian festivities and celebrate with their compatriots the birthday of the Goddess on the twenty-eighth, which was also the birthday of the glorious Alcibiades.

282

The whole City flooded the streets. The news of the Cliniad's victory flew from mouth to mouth. The very scant number of Athenians admitted, announced in Olympia on the sixth and made known in the City a week later, had been taken as a terrible omen. But someone recalled that on the ninth of Hecatombaion, three days after the Athenian team was posted on the Leucoma of Altis, Athens had thrown the infidel Xanthus into the Barathrum. So the unexpected Olympic victories must be clear proof that the Gods considered the City purified. If his offspring Dionysus and Athena had not been placated, Olympic Zeus would not have blessed the Athenians with the victory of Alcibiades, who outshone his predecessors of all centuries. This had to be a sign to the Hellenes of how much he favored the City, and at what a moment!

No one abstained from the praise. Pericles gave a memorable speech; Alcamenes and Agoracritus submitted sketches of statues to commemorate the feat of the three chariots. Euripides composed his finest epinicium; Pythodorus, the new Eponymous Archon, proposed to the Assembly that coins be minted with the effigy of the Cliniad; the many who once criticized the son of Clinias for his childish impieties and wantonness now praised his behavior as the logical mischief of a favorite of Zeus; and Eulogos, the barber on the Street of the Hoopers, abstained from calling him Golden Ass.

During the ride back, Alcibiades remained aloof, speaking only in monosyllables. He was inexplicably discourteous to the magistrates of Elis who escorted the Athenian party all the way to the river Alpheus. Instead of taking the direct route back to Attica, Alcibiades had insisted on the southern route, to visit Mount Typaeum, the place from which they hurled women who dared to violate the prohibition on watching the Olympic Games.

283

One of the officials of Elis rode up beside Alcibiades to talk to him about his country. There was a real threat that he might go into exquisite detail and spoil the whole trip. He began by praising the delicate taste of the honey of Elis, at which point Alcibiades shot back that he had already tasted it at the banquet and, to the dismay of the Athenians listening, found the Attic honey of Mount Hymettus superior.

To change the topic, one of the Hellanodicae mentioned that a great wonder of Elis was that no donkey could get a mare pregnant within its borders. Alcibiades very seriously promised that as soon as he got back to Athens he would send him one of his donkeys with a cubit-long cock to see what he could do. The people of Elis would soon see if he could not get a whole herd of mares pregnant, borders or no borders.

Callias, who was riding beside him, whispered a mild

rebuke. By Zeus! Had he forgotten the benevolence of the Hellanodicae in admitting him to the Games and then giving him his crown? And he begged him to mind the respect he owed his elders. But Alcibiades asked mockingly, not caring a bit if they heard him, whether all that magistrate's years could possibly cover up his ears, which were longer than those of any of his sterile compatriot donkeys.

By Pallas, what was wrong with the boy?

No one could possibly imagine. That boy, who was determined to draw the greatest possible profit from his Olympic victory, needed the long ride to design his new public image; that was his immediate concern. In a few weeks, the Greeks of all the known world would be repeating his name in admiration. But he had his eye on farther horizons.

Of course, the great fortune he would inherit when he was twenty-one would certainly be of some help in his career, as would his ancestors, Clinias, Ajax, Clisthenes, Megacles, Alcmeon . . . And despite his stuttering, or rather, thanks to it, when he decided to persuade the men of Athens, not even Pericles could outdo him in oratory. And in right knowledge, who was his match in all the City? Well, of course, Socrates. But he was the only one, and aside from philosophizing and living in his eupraxia, he had no ambitions.

Personal courage was also very important. Was there a man among the good and the beautiful of Athens who was absolutely fearless, as he was? The answer was obvious: not a single one. Those who were not terrified of the misfortunes of this world were completely taken up with those of the next; he was indifferent to both. As indifferent as he was to what the City thought of his actions. In the end, everything would turn out for the best. The important thing was to keep them busy talking about him, even if it was just to criticize. He smiled as he remembered how pusillanimous Callias and the other theoroi had been when he decided to get those old fools of Elis off his back. And he had gotten rid of his chatty compatriots, to boot. He was not at all ready to have them interrupt his train of thought.

Virtues he had plenty. Could anyone name a single Greek, past or present, who at such a short age had amassed so many? That, in addition to his physical beauty, which drew mortals to him like a lodestone. And yet, many Athenians achieved glory without these... There was the great Themistocles, for example, the bastard son of a whore of the Cynosarges. He had covered himself with glory by saving his invaded country at Salamis through his courage and intelligence. One could actually understand how a grateful City might, for many years, forget his rather sullied lineage. And what about Solon? Ah, that was a different case altogether: he had the gift of poetry and of law to persuade the simple souls of the many. That was why he had no need of military glory nor of Olympic victories. Yet Miltiades and Cimon, who did have both, and fame and fortune as well, could not philosophize at all and knew nothing of law. Let us see, now, how was it possible for an ass, a Cimon or a Nicias, archenemy of the Logos and despised by the Muses, to rise successfully in Athenian politics? Well, Nicias had shown great personal courage, but what about Cimon? What was his claim to glory? His campaigns in Thrace and Eurymedon? Bah! It was no merit at all to have won a couple of skirmishes against the Persians at a time when Athens already had a powerful fleet thanks to the genius of Themistocles. The ignorance and superstition of the many magnified Cimon's fame. Superstition? Yes, superstition, like when they treated him as a God for finding Theseus's bones.

He recalled having commented on the matter with Socrates. It was obvious that Cimon had somehow run across

285

the skeleton of a huge man and then concocted the hoax of rescuing Theseus's bones to give them proper burial in Athens, a
sharp move that had won him the gratitude of the demos and
the reputation of being a saint. But Socrates, who knew Cimon,
insisted that it was not a fraud, that Cimon really believed what
he had found to be Theseus's bones. But the fact remained that
the acme of his glory had been that fraudulent finding.

As Alcibiades mused on all those things, the riders were
rapidly crossing the plains of Nemea at a fast trot, not at all the
gait most conducive to planning with the moderation required
by right knowledge. Nevertheless, he started to review the old
myths. There must be some beloved hero of the Athenians
whose bones he could recover. He smiled at the thought. What
was it that one of Hippocrates of Cos's pupils had said? Intense
movement agitates the brain mucus and muddies the mind. He
was absolutely right! That was why the trotting inspired only
foolishness.

He gazed into the distance at the slopes of Mount
Tricranos. Would it be useful to find the skeleton of the lion
that Heracles had strangled somewhere around there?

By Pallas, his mucus was going completely wild!

He quit thinking and enjoyed the landscape.

By the time they got into Corinthian territory, he had cleared up
many of his doubts and decided to meditate with a more con-
centric logos and arrive at a decision before entering Attica.
Now that the favor of Olympic Zeus had turned him into a pan-
Hellenic celebrity, what steps should he take to pave the way for
a future career in Athenian politics? That was what he was
going to think about the rest of the way.

On the second day, having reviewed the careers of his most
important predecessors in power, there was one thing that stood

out over everything else: Despite all his virtues, he could not hope to win power in Athens without first becoming one of the Strategi, which he could not do before the age of thirty, and then only by having at least one feat of heroism on the battlefield.

That was no mere opinion; that was pure and unadulterated, filtered scientific knowledge.

Being a military hero was not difficult. There was going to be a war against Sparta and her allies. But would they let him fight? Officially, he still had three months to go to conclude his epheby, and the Strategi would complain . . . Complaints? Objections? None of that! He would impose his status as the son of a hero, an Olympic champion; he would make threats, anything, but he would be with the first contingent to land in Potidaea, or wherever the fleet went. And in that very war, none other, he would become a hero, dead or alive. That was that. Next item.

The trouble would start if he survived. He was so young, they would never admit him to political power. By Zeus, he had to do something to compensate for his lack of years.

He spent a whole day on that problem, asking himself questions and coming up with answers, following the method Socrates had taught him. Was it possible to rise to glory without fulfilling all the requirements demanded by the ignorance of the many? Yes, it was! Themistocles, that bastard spawned by a bitch, was the best example. And if Themistocles had made it despite his mother, he would make it despite his lack of years. After all, rising to power in Athens should be easier for the young son of a hero than for an adult son of a bitch.

He focused on the thorniest aspects of the problem. How, when, where, with what could he hope to make up for his youth? In the intervening days before reaching the City, would he not be able to come up with something, some feat, to bewitch the City? Well . . . there were other ways. As soon as Pericles and Ariphron gave him his fortune, he would become the most praised choregus in the Athenian demos. That was a straight and narrow path to power, but, uff, so many years, one after the other, in the service of fools.

The bulk of the Athenian party, which was riding with the teams of pack horses and mules laden with the equipment and tents, was lagging several days behind. The vanguard was made up of the Olympic champions, those theoroi whose health allowed them to keep up with the pace of the forced march, and others with horses capable of taking the mountain shortcuts. Callias had ordered those in the rear to look after the common cargo.

Well into enemy territory in Corinth, the onlookers crowding the roads, anxious to catch a glance of Alcibiades, testified to the fact that his pan-Hellenic fame was more powerful than their hatred of Athens. And Megara, despite being the victim of the psephisma and the arrogant blockade of the Saronic Sea, also turned out in throngs to gaze on the beautiful Cliniad, the newest legend of the Greeks. The lack of insults, the silent veneration, the raised hands pointing at him, the whispering by the roadside as he passed, and the swarm of fascinated children running beside him, all sang his victory.

There were still many stadia to go before reaching the borders of Attica, when they began to hear, intermittently, something like the eleleu of a colossal army. But when the son of Clinias, at the head of the Athenian party, finally appeared on the crest of the hill on the road to the border, a multitude of compatriots crossed over and plunged into thunderous ovations that were to follow him until dawn.

On the very border, they made him get on a chariot that was the twin of the one he had driven to victory, drawn by four black stallions with shiny coats and braided manes. On either side, they put up moving barricades made of purple cordons and carried in a trot by the comrades of his unfinished epheby.

Beyond Eleusis, as the throng on the Sacred Way thickened, a second, more compact cordon of Scythians surrounded the ephebi to protect the hero from the unbridled love of the people. As they passed, women fainted, old people dropped to their knees, everyone shouted, and there were whistles and tears and rattles and well-wishing oaths and bells and drums.

A stadium away from the Dipylum, the crowd blocked the way, forcing them to detour along a new road laid just days before. The riders followed it to a breach specially made in the City walls to celebrate the return of Alcibiades, who was the first to ride through, followed by the other Olympic champions and the multitude, always the friend of glory.

On the other side of the wall: the Buzyges of Zeus, all the Primates, Pericles himself atop a splendid stallion, the nine Archons, the Strategi, the Prytanes, Sophocles, Euripides, the virgin basket-bearers with their offerings, and the newly whitewashed City decked with ribbons and garlands. The clamor was endless.

289

Alcibiades, crowned with wild olive, thanked the multitude with a serious countenance and studied gestures. Since they had had him inaugurate the new door in the walls, he would inaugurate his new image of a composed adult, a favorite of Zeus.

And peering out of a high window in the inner Ceramicus, oh, by Zeus, such splendor: Lysis of Miletus, the most beautiful of all! She looked taller. He looked on at her until she was lost in the distance. It was the only thing that made the adult son of Clinias smile through those unforgettable festivities.

The time had come to take on the Ionian again.

PART IV

AUTUMN

OF

PYTHODORUS

AND

SPRING

OF

EUTHYNUS

40

THE FLEET and three thousand men under the command of Callias were blocking the two gulfs of the peninsula. Some eighty stadia from the camp of the besiegers, two hundred hoplites and a few archers were guarding the narrow, albeit swift river with sheer banks that descended from the heights of Spartolus by the entrance to Pallene, in Chalcidice. It was the only way the Macedonian horsemen could get to Potidaea.

The bulk of the troops were camped at the foot of the walls. Artemon the Bale, ever under his roof, was directing the construction of his polyorcetic engines. Pericles had insisted on forcing the actions before the onset of winter. The soldiers were already suffering under the Boreal winds.

What none of the Athenians lying sleepless in their siege tents could possibly know was that, together with Boreas, an enemy party was advancing on them. Three hundred Corinthian hoplites were working their way through the neighboring mountains, guided by a group of Thracian slingsmen. These were the men Aristeus of Corinth had brought from the isthmus three months earlier.

Their mission had been carefully planned, long in advance, for that new moon, the first of autumn.

The strategy was to clear the way for the horsemen the Macedonian king would be sending to aid the Potidaeans. The tactics were to wait until dawn and attack the Athenians guarding the river.

After a long flanking movement that would bring them all the way around to the vicinity of Olynthus, they were to hit the Athenians from behind, as if they had come from Potidaea.

The plan agreed upon by Perdiccas and the Corinthian general was simple: At the very moment the Macedonian cavalry got across the river, the besieged troops would storm out of the four doors of the citadel simultaneously. They were to take the enemies by surprise and massacre them in the narrow confines of the Calcidic Isthmus. King Perdiccas's allies would light a signal fire on the cliffs of the Sithonian coast when they were ready; the Potidaeans would light a confirmation fire on the highest point on the walls.

Shouts of alarm, hunting horns, and suddenly a doe in her winter coat, pursued and whining, had come into Alcibiades's tent, the snow making her coat even whiter. She nuzzled her head, then her whole body under his warm cape, hiding there timidly, pressing herself against Alcibiades, the snow falling on his chest, while outside, horns and trumpets blared, but under the cape, oh, the doe has shed her downy fur and her hide is sooo soft, come Alcibiades, up! silky, warm, and she turns her backside to him, and he kissing her soft blushing neck, all mint and marjoram.

To arms, Alcibiades! By Zeus, the enemy is upon us!

The son of Clinias, touching and recognizing the coveted buttocks, and Aristarchus buckling his greaves and hauberk, oh that rump, unique among all species, and the doe reaching back to install him in her from behind in her tremoring urgency, and another shake, and since neither the shaking nor the ever-nearer clamor of arms could waken Alcibiades, still cuddled and panting softly, Aristarchus lost all patience and whacked him on the shoulder with his bronze helmet, and after a sudden scream, Aristarchus received a fist in the chest, couldn't Alcibiades hear the trumpeters sounding the alarm? by Zeus, wake up, great danger, Potidaeans everywhere, attacking by surprise.

Only then did Alcibiades realize where he was. As he emerged from the tent, he saw the Corinthians in the starlight.

"By the dog, son of Clinias, hurry! Can't you see we're under attack?" Socrates yelled, rushing out of his tent fully armed.

Shouts of combat and drums drowned out all else. The Corinthians were breaking through, downhill. The Athenians were retreating toward the trees, fighting in disarray.

Then the enemy vanguard appeared behind them. The Athenians were backed up to the river. Their only hope was to hold out in the forest a stadium away from the camp. The surprise had been complete, and the Athenians sustained many casualties in the first few minutes. About twenty of them were strewn around the camp, some naked, others half-armed, wearing a single greave, or without a hauberk.

The enemy was trying to cut off their retreat to the forest, and the fighting was getting wild. Alcibiades donned his armor in a second, but he had still not found his place in the fray when he stopped a sling stone with his right hand.

The pain knocked the sword out of his hand, and he saw that two Corinthians were emerging from a thicket and rushing at him from behind. There was no room for the lance, and a throw with his left would probably just be deflected by their Chalcidian swords. He tossed it aside. Using his wounded right hand to aid his left, he gripped his shield firmly, staving off slashing swords and backing toward the trees. Then his foot caught on some roots and he fell on his back. Just when they were about to chop off one of his feet, the only part of his body not protected by the great shield, Aristarchus appeared, challenging the Corinthians, but a Thracian caught him from behind, cleaving his head down to his nose with his long curved sword. When the attacker turned on Alcibiades, Socrates, from behind, sank his xiphos into him up to the hilt. The Thracian fell, in spasms, on top of Alcibiades, while Glaucus, son of Phrynicus, skewered one of the Corinthians by surprise and forced the other to retreat.

296

The pain in his hand was almost unbearable, but Alcibiades picked up his sword and Aristarchus's lance and helped Socrates drag the body out of the way.

Alcibiades wept, embracing his dead lover, who was lying on his stomach. He stroked his bloodied hair, blotched with brains.

As he turned, urged by the others, a sickly pallor altered his features. Socrates feared he would faint and took him by the arm to help him rise, but Alcibiades shook him off and, once on his feet, darted a reproachful glance at him. When he opened his mouth, Socrates expected some irreverence, but Alcibiades let out a terrible roar and stood there staring at the ground, lips outstretched, teeth bared in a horrible grimace.

From the opposite bank of the river came the roar of galloping horses, accompanied by shouts and frantic neighing.

Then the ranks of the formidable Macedonian cavalry appeared in a great dark blur, amid the clamor of swords striking bronze shields. The air was stale with the smell of the dung and urine of frightened horses.

Suddenly the pandemonium was broken by the blare of trumpets. They were sounding retreat! Outflanked and outnumbered by the terrible enemy, the Athenians were running wildly to take refuge in the forest.

Socrates and Glaucus called to him as they hurried away, but when he saw some hoplites of his own class dropping their shields to facilitate their flight, Alcibiades shouted after them:

"Fairies! Athenian queers! Are you running like whores, eh? Run for your lives, girls! And if you get to Athens alive, tell them how the son of Clinias died with honor, like the heroes of Marathon and Salamis!"

And raising high Aristarchus's lance, he charged the front rank of riders in mid-stream, shieldless. He was prepared to die in his first battle and fulfill his promise to his beloved father. Now he would be like him, a hero, paying off his bargain for the Olympic victory. May Warlike Zeus take his life. They would be even.

He charged with berserk determination, invoking Ares.

"Eleleeeeeeeu!"

Socrates was fifty steps into flight when he heard the war cry and halted. He saw Alcibiades charging to his death alone, and sinking his sword point into a fallen tree, hand propped on the hilt, eyes glued on his bare feet, he composed his thoughts.

Would it be nobler in such circumstances to be swayed by those impulses that adorn the lives and deaths of men, or to follow good sense to a life without encumbrances? How could he find the wisdom of truth in such a crisis?

He did not know what to do. The only thing he did know

was that he would spend the rest of his life in torment from his own recriminations.

By the dog! He would follow Alcibiades! Far nobler the folly of courage than the good sense of cowardice.

The son of the artisan Sophronicus chose death beside the son of Clinias like the good and the beautiful.

He rushed to his side.

Alcibiades had just lanced the lead rider when Socrates reached him. Other fleeing hoplites, whose legs had grown heavy with the Cliniad's invectives, joined Socrates. The first to arrive was Eucles, son of Therpander, then Menon, son of Lysias, and soon many more.

When Perdiccas's cavalry saw a full lojos of a hundred men in combat syntax, they turned tail in the middle of the river. They would have to attempt a crossing somewhere else. That narrow ford, with the water up to their horses' withers, was impossible. The only way out was a steep and muddy bank where they would be picked off one by one.

The Athenians struck up their combat paean. Their bronze shields reverberated. When one was certain of victory, that war hymn stirred the flesh and instilled more courage than the black wine of Chios garnished with sea onions.

The Corinthians had fanned out just a moment before to hunt down the fleeing Athenians, but when the cavalry withdrew, they hurried to regroup. Having sung their paean and played their trumpets, the Corinthians marched forward in the heavy pace of Peloponnesian hoplites. Protected by their tall shields, they advanced in a sideways step, like profiles sculpted on steles. Over the top, just eyes and the plumes of their helmets. War cries echoed to the beat of swords on bronze greaves, and they screeched like diving goshawks.

Alcibiades, just out of his epheby, marched on the left;

Socrates marched on the right, where only the best may fight. But before forming, Socrates changed places with Eucles, who was avid for honor, to be able to protect the brave novice.

When they engaged, Socrates took up a position behind Alcibiades, where he could keep an eye on him and jump to his side at the first sign of danger. But Alcibiades moved like a veteran. He invariably took positions that allowed him to move to the right to ward off attacks on his unshielded flank, and by the dog! he fought well, displaying a ferocity that Socrates had never suspected in his pupil. His eyes looked like they would pop out of their sockets. With every blow he would laugh, and his laughter terrified the enemy. Socrates saw him kick and even bite the cheek of a Corinthian who fell on him, dying.

But another one, whose sword arm Alcibiades had hacked off, managed to dig his xiphos down to the bone the whole length of the Athenian's thigh. Alcibiades passed out and fell to the ground smiling, relieved.

He lay on his back and was soon surrounded by the enemy, who had the edge on that flank.

When Socrates tried to rescue him, he was met by a solid wall of Corinthians. He wavered a moment, then leapt to the charge, hacking a clearing around himself. He caught the wounded Alcibiades by the heel and dragged him out of the fray, but he soon had to drop him to fight off a hail of swords from another wave of enemy soldiers.

Other young men of Alcibiades's class came to the rescue, and together they were able to keep the enemy off their comrade. Then Socrates hoisted Alcibiades onto his shoulders and carried him to the other side of the forest, some two stadia away. Glaucus and another hoplite covered his flanks when they had to pass by fighting troops.

Soon they were pleased to hear Athenian trumpets. The day

299

before, the enemy party coming over the mountains had been detected by an explorer who alerted the strategi commanding the siege. After midnight, two hundred hoplites had been dispatched from Potidaea. They made a forced march along the coast of the Thermaic Gulf and arrived just in time to tip the scales. The Corinthian vanguard was surrounded.

The Macedonian horsemen contemplated the massacre impotently. Cries of derision accompanied them in the Boreal wind.

41

ALTHOUGH SHE WAS BIG, and blond women could be very attractive, the Amazon had always been but just one more whore in the brothel. That is, until one night, when the Owl saw three Cypriot sailors fall over dead drunk while the Amazon tossed back pitchers three grown men could not handle. That gave him the best business inspiration of his life.

After a great deal of haggling, he bought her for seven hundred drachmas.

He took her down to Piraeus and set up shop challenging all the big drinkers. The wager was that anyone who could not hold his own against the Amazon had to pay for all the wine and ten drachmas for the Owl. Sometimes she would take on three at a time, and the Owl would pocket thirty drachmas in one fell swoop.

She was happy as a lark with her new profession. She never had the experience of tripping over her own tongue or stumbling. The worst that ever happened was that she would become a bit giddy and her face would light up. Then she would sing and be very accommodating. One time, after downing more than twenty pitchers, she got so tender that she gave herself to a Delian sailor absolutely free. When the Owl found out, he got his calfskin lash and left her buttocks like a bunch of peonies.

To work a bigger crowd and bring the money in faster, the Owl invented a spectacular challenge. He would take a rope of braided wool, about ten paces long, and stretch it out on the tavern floor. After each ration of wine, the competitors had to skip along the rope on one foot from one end to the other and back. Anyone who missed a skip automatically lost. After the fifth pitcher, almost everyone either missed a skip or fell.

The Amazon became famous. Groups of clients would often collect money to sponsor one of the local wine guzzlers who was ready to play the ass just to quench his thirst; other times, groups of foreign sailors would raise a bet for one of their best to drink for home and country.

For the first few months, the Owl was raking it in. When the Amazon became famous, he should have sold her for two thousand drachmas. But he was shortsighted. He never imagined that as soon as the word got around Attica, there would be no one to take her on.

And that was exactly what happened. In a year's time, the show had gone stale; everyone knew that the Amazon was invincible, and the challengers grew fewer and fewer.

During the Panathenian Games of the Archonship of Crates, the Owl had a bad run; to make things worse, two of his slaves ran away to Megara during one of his binges. He was left without an obol, his only property being the Amazon.

Finally, after cheating Scolotus out of a mare, he dyed the Amazon's hair red, dressed her in a green peplus with one tit hanging out, like Queen Penthesilea, and had her ride along the roads of the coarse Boeotia of the hippian Thessaly, from tavern to tavern, until they reached Chalcidice and the mountainous Thrace, a land of serious drinkers.

The undefeated Amazon got as far as the Tauric Chersonese. The first month they made a fortune and lived a life of ease.

Toward the end of autumn, the Amazon went up against one of Spartocus's soldiers, strong as a mule and twice the size of the Owl. The challenge was to drink on their feet, with no support, in the middle of two circles, about three cubits across, drawn on the floor. A multitude stood around them in the presence of Spartocus himself, who bet one hundred gold darics on his man. The first to touch the circumference was the loser.

The Amazon had whipped down nineteen pitchers without the slightest sign of drunkenness. It was a very black wine from Thasos, unmixed. The Taurian was drooling and his knees were beginning to bend. And then, the twentieth pitcher on her lips, the Amazon keeled over. Dead.

Two months later, in the heart of winter, the Owl lost his last obol in Olbia, betting on the cock fights and knuckle bones.

When he found out that his compatriots were laying siege to Potidaea, he set out on foot. Maybe the Strategi would lodge him in the camp. Maybe in the spring they would take him back to the City with the fleet. If not, he would at least run into people he knew, perhaps veterans of Samos, who would not let him die.

And again the unbridled horseplay in the shelter, and Eulogos holding his hand over the fire, would Lefty never shut up? every time Eulogos heard him talk such nonsense he felt a little colder, brrr, and pulling up his sheepskin over his shoulders, and Lefty insisting that it was all Pericles's fault for starting the war too

soon, and Eulogos, nonsense, the war had to be, and it was better right here and now, the one to blame for their being there,
cold and far from home, was Callias, by Hermes, after all, hadn't
he been in time to intercept Aristeus high in the Thermaicus
Sinus when he found out that he had left Corinth with his
troops? ah, but the great general did nothing but sail from one
side to the other, as Eulogos rowed in the air in all directions,
and of course, Callias first had to inspect Chalcidice and verify
that everything was in its place, that Mount Pallene was still
there, that Potidaea was still on the isthmus, and instead of
pursuing Aristeus, Callias, blah, blah, blah, conferring first with
Archestratus, and blah, blah, blah, with the one from Pydna,
and blah, blah, with the ones from Therma, and sailing to the
north and then to the south and back to the middle, and the
oarsmen were looking tall on the benches from the calluses
growing on their asses, and with Perdiccas of Macedonia, blah,
blah, as well, trying to put him off with diplomacy, what was the
good of talking to a flea-bitten, cheating wizard who was going
to send his cavalry against the camp anyway? since when did an
Athenian general believe the words and libations of a barbarian
like Perdiccas? and in the battle in the river, if it hadn't been for
Golden . . . for the son of Clinias, that favorite of the Gods,
maybe none of them would have made it to winter, and then
two hoplites on guard poking into the shelter, that Eulogos
should accompany them, on the orders of Cratinus, the lojagos,
who wanted to see him in his tent, and Eulogos, asking if he
had to take his scissors with him, could the chief want a hair-
cut, silly, long hair and a beard were better in the cold, and on
the way, that it was not that, that he had to identify a man with
one arm who said he lived on the Street of the Hoopers, and
when he got there, well, well, if it wasn't the Owl, he was so
skinny, and embraces, and some backslapping, a tear, faltering

voice, the Owl all emotional about being with his own after such a long time, and Eulogos identifying, of course, that was his neighbor and friend, he and Eulogos were fighting in the same detachment when he lost his arm, and the owl on his forehead was proof that he had been a prisoner in Samos, uhum, so he was to be given a soldier's ration, and Eulogos was to lodge him in his tent until they talked to Callias, and on the way back, the Owl going through his tragedy, the Amazon was no longer his, and now, returning to his country, his children, his funeral services, and Eulogos, that he should cheer up and not feel that way, and after a bowl of fish soup and a few drinks of Thasian wine, listening to the stories, seeing his compatriots telling anecdotes, smiling for the first time in two months, watching the dice game, running into friends, embracing his mother's cousin and others from his deme, and there was another owl, Alcinous, who shared his suffering in the prisons of Samos, and everyone bringing him up to date, Alcibiades a hero, Alcibiades Olympic champion, how much honor for Athens, and in the afternoon, tossing the knuckles for a comrade, the Owl always had a steady hand, and the winner gave him five hemiobols, and after all, with a little bit of luck, life was fine, and in the shelter, late in the afternoon, when the cold was getting bitter, Eulogos snapping his double-edged tongue, and didn't the Owl know about the Pantadeuteros's fountain, yes, to Poseidon, right near the Acropolis, first with seawater and dolphins, but they all died, one morning they were all floating on their backs, and Eulogos aping a dolphin's snout, opening his mouth and extending his nose with his index finger, and then more seawater and changing it every two days, and again dolphins, and more dead dolphins, and Eulogos with his eyes turned upward, could the Owl guess how Nicias had solved the problem? why, by bringing in fresh water from the Triton fountain and replacing the real dolphins with four bronze ones he had commissioned, and everyone laughing and hollering, and Lefty, maybe Nicias was right, and Eulogos, the Pantadeuteros right? about what, by Zeus? and Lefty, about the three fingers, about Perdiccas's curse, because the truth was that nothing was going very right in that war, and everyone arguing, yes, no, maybe Pericles, maybe Lampon, and the sacrifice of the Scythian, three fingers, and the Owl asking, what Scythian? which three fingers? when? aha, aha, in the final days of Apseudes, and counting on his fingers, of course, he had left Athens on the third month of Apseudes, at the end of summer, a long time before then, and did the Owl know nothing about the sacrilege? oh, yes, a terrible sacrilege in Laurium, Pandarus, a Scythian, had been sacrificed to Omestes, and Xanthus in the Barathrum, and One Eye in Macedonia, and Nicias, Substantiator of the Anacrisis, discovering the theft of the amethyst, and the Owl, suddenly afraid, on his feet, stolen amethyst? Athena's in the birth of Pandora? exactly, and a Macedonian executed, an agent for Perdiccas, yes, yes, in the fall of Apseudes, a Scythian, the thief was a Macedonian, skull crushed, without being able to get a confession from him.

And the stone?

Harder to find than Persephone.

Night was falling over the besieged city. The silhouettes of the Potidaean watchtowers high atop the walls stood out against the gray sky. At the base, the charred remains of two assault towers, the failed progeny of Artemon the Bale. Four bow-shots away, the vanguard of the besieging army, the allies of hunger, waited behind stone parapets protected by sloping wickerwork roofs. And beside both seas, the black line of Athenian tents.

The Owl picked his way among the frosted-over mud puddles. The low clouds sat on the purple foliage of the cedars. It was almost dark. A single stripe of golden light peeked over the western horizon.

The Owl recognized Socrates coming down a hill barefoot in the snow, his chin resting on his chest. Someone had told him that Socrates had spent the whole afternoon like that, pacing the isthmus from one coast to the other. One of the hoplites had bet an Ionian mercenary two obols that Socrates would go on that way until dark. And barefoot, brrr, by Hermes, as if it were summer! He was staring at the ground, his eyes wide open. The Owl used to see him near the Lyceum or the Academy, walking around the same way.

"He's crazy," he thought, as Socrates passed by once again, and went back to his own business.

He, too, had a lot of thinking to do. That was why he had left the tent. The theft of the amethyst had given him an idea.

Could it be possible? The idea had just popped into his head. Had some God moved over to his side again?

Everything seemed to indicate that he was the only one who knew the identity of the real thief of the amethyst. And everyone in the City saying, some Macedonian, One Eye, or that Xanthus. What a terrible mistake Lysanias and Nicias had made! And the defiler was still alive, unpunished, and contaminating the City.

Everything fit. It couldn't be otherwise.

By Pallas, how fortunate to be in the right place at the right time!

And he started counting his take. How much would the son of Niceratus pay? If the City ever found out about his failure as Substantiator of the Anacrisis.

But what if he got angry and took revenge?

Bah! The Owl was a freeman, an Athenian citizen, and he

had nothing to lose. What could Nicias accuse him of? Wasn't he turning in the real culprit and helping purify the City?

No, nothing could go wrong; he could get five hundred drachmas out of the Pantadeuteros. Maybe more!

4 2

ALTHOUGH THE LAWS of Athens provided that a person could inherit at the age of eighteen, an heir could be made to wait the full term until he was twenty-five, if it was the express will of the testator.

It was the will of Clinias that his firstborn should wait until he was twenty-one before inheriting, as if he had detected in his five-year-old son a proclivity for squandering. So when Alcibiades returned from Olympia, he found his tutors adamant; Zeus's olive wreath was to no avail.

Pericles and Ariphron refused once again to advance him any of the money from his estate until he was of age.

But a year later, when he returned wounded from the battlefield, despite the fact that he still had forty-eight days to go before his twenty-first birthday, the weight of his glory was so great that they agreed to petition the good graces of the Archon King, who ordered that he be advanced two talents and allowed to occupy the paternal mansion in the City and the farm on the banks of the Cephisus.

When Alcibiades arrived aboard the Trireme flagship and was helped ashore by General Callias, the port was once again wild with veneration. His feat in Potidaea made him the peer of the legendary heroes of Athens. A month later, with Alcibiades still limping from the wound in his thigh, twelve banquets had been given in his honor. When he finally had some of his money advanced to him along with the use of his houses, he announced that he was going to pay back the feasts, the first to be financed out of his own funds.

For many days after his arrival, the people of the City stared at him in adoration wherever he went.

"Thank you, oh son of Clinias!" they shouted from windows and porticos as he went by. To get through the crowds, he gave Phanes a stout club which the Phoenician twirled to make way for him. Alcibiades had given him his manumission on his spring leave, and Egghead was more attached to him than ever.

Alcibiades discovered that the more dolled up and feminine Phanes looked, the more fearsome his ugliness and the more effective his protection against adoring crowds. He had him wear beautiful pastel sandals and robes, knowing full well that it irritated the City, and enjoying the fact that no one dared say a word about it.

On his return from Olympia, Alcibiades had tried to create a new personality for himself; he strove to project an image of good sense and sobriety, one that would make him eligible for the government of the City. But he was disappointed when, after the initial euphoria, the people's interest began to wane. He needed to be on the lips of the many every day.

In time, he decided to change his image. That was it! Goodbye common sense, by Hermes! He would give them something to talk about; he would do what no one had ever done in the City, confound the demos, that mindless slave of folly and the lash. He would assault the City with his incomprehensible behavior; he, the favorite of Zeus and Ares, would soon be the Autocrat General, precisely because he could do what no one else dared. Living, like Nicias, in permanent fear of the adverse votes and opinions of the mob would never earn him respect.

When he returned from Potidaea, limp and all, he turned up in the agora again all made up and with pretty ribbons in his hair. Would anyone dare call a hero of Potidaea effeminate? The very same people who had been incensed and critical of his attire now shook their heads, smiling. Oh, that boy! and the way he dressed, with trinkets and ribbons and colors only a whore would wear, oh, well, that's the way he is, what can you do? heroes have their quirks, you know.

As an Olympic champion he had the enviable right to dine, for the rest of his life, at the table in the Prytaneum and partake of that holy food blessed by the tutelary fire of the City, together with the City's greatest soldiers, athletes, laurel-wreathed poets, and illustrious visitors. But after attending a couple of lunches, he said that he preferred his own food at home, prepared by his nurse and tasted by the Egghead, instead of those Sicilian stews prepared by Demodocus in the Prytaneum. But even this sacrilegious offense against the venerable home of the City was considered just another bit of mischief by the son of Clinias. No one would raise his voice against a favorite of the Gods.

When he learned of Socrates's return, a month after his own, he gave up his plan to pay back banquets and decided to honor his teacher and savior, though he kept that last part to himself.

He sent out thirty invitations for a fifteen-couch banquet. Twelve of his recent hosts showed up, all of them of the well-born, the good, and the beautiful. Also present were Sophocles and Euripides, who sang his feats in verse; there was Pericles himself; Hippodamus of Miletus; Myron, the ancient sculptor who was working on his Olympic statue; Protagoras of Abdera, the well-known sophist and friend of Pericles, who drafted the constitution of Thurii; Polus of Acragas, disciple of Gorgias, who had just arrived with a Leontinian embassy; and other distinguished foreign visitors, all honored guests of the City. Everyone was surprised to find that Alcibiades had not invited anyone his own age and quite amazed to see no one sharing his couch. When someone finally asked, he answered that he was reserving that place for the only man in Athens he admired. Everyone tried to overlook his discourteous remark, but Ariphon, Pericles's brother, commented that there were among the symposiasts illustrious scions of Athens with every right to be admired by a young man. Did his esteemed cousin intend to add to his victory with the chariots supreme pan-Hellenic laurels for rudeness?

312

But Alcibiades, the rising political star who had left his childish perversity behind, confessed that the merits of the glorious men meeting in that oval were so ponderous that their combined weight might well sink one of the Cyclades, that what he meant by admiration was total recognition of absolute superiority of mind and soul. Of course, he could enjoy the ecstasy of the fine works of the artists meeting there, all of them among the greatest in all Hellas; he could applaud the speeches of the no less famous speakers and rhetors; or he could nourish his mind with the thoughts of the philosophers who were honoring his home that afternoon. But with all the respect he owed them, he felt inferior to none. On the other hand, the man for whom that place was reserved ...

The slaves were already about their business, taking away the finger bowls and sweeping up for the second tables, when

Socrates appeared at the door and waddled in, smiling, somewhat embarrassed by the great gathering.

"But there he is, at last," Alcibiades exclaimed pointing toward the door, "there you have our guest of honor, the son of Sophroniscus, a boor who shows up halfway through the banquet, but whom we will forgive because he must surely have been delayed improving some fellow citizen he had run into at the palaestra of Taureas or on the way from the Academy."

Amid the laughter and sounding applause, the astonished Socrates allowed himself to be led by Phanes to Alcibiades's couch, where the young man welcomed him with an embrace. While the slaves washed his feet, crowned him, and decked his arms with garlands, Alcibiades continued his praise.

"Because this ugly body, which bears more resemblance to a satyr of the Phrygian forests than to a Greek, is stronger than any I have ever encountered," and he sat up on the couch to lay a friendly arm on his shoulders, "for he was the only man of all the Greeks and barbarians present at Potidaea who, throughout the winter, walked barefoot through the snow with no other garment than this dirty and wrinkled cloak you see here." And after another pause for the laughter to reverberate around the oval, Alcibiades continued, "And he is the only man who can drink without getting drunk, and believe me, oh, my friends, that in this body of iron dwells a golden soul, and when he speaks, I have no eyes but his eyes and no thoughts but those of that fat, lumpy head," and he stamped a kiss on the bald pate, bringing out of the guests another round of laughter. "How can I but admire him, when beyond all that, in the battle for which I was decorated, this Socrates you see here twice saved me from death; twice a thousand times may he be blessed; and you, my worthy guests, take not offense: It is only before this frog-eyed, flat-nosed satyr that I feel this infinite inferiority I call admiration."

313

The faithful Chaerephon, moved by such praise for his master, set off a storm of applause that thundered through the villa; all rudeness forgotten, they sang the paean.

Following the libation that marked the beginning of the feast of wines, just before the slaves brought in the second tables, Pericles, as was his custom, bid the gathering farewell with a few words in honor of his friend, the honored son of Sophroniscus. And to his kinsman Alcibiades, he reminded that at daybreak he was to stand before the Assembly, in the Pnyx, where he would be presented to the demos among the new ecclesiastes, and advised him not to banquet too long or drink too much.

Alcibiades thanked him for his solicitude, but remarked that the advice was more befitting Pericles's sixty-three years than his own twenty.

"At my age one can still share evenings with Dionysus and mornings with Ap-p-p-ollo."

Pericles shrugged his shoulders and raised his eyebrows, but withdrew without a word. Callicrates and Ariphron followed suit.

His departure was the signal for commentaries and speculation. Pericles had remained silent on his couch. Someone suggested that his bad mood might be due to the coming trial against Aspasia, scheduled for after the Synoecia, whose defense he was preparing.

When the food was brought in, Alcibiades nominated himself symposiarch. There were protests, but Anytus argued that it would not be fair to deny him that right at his first banquet, especially since at the most recent banquets his deportment had been plausibly sober.

As soon as he was accepted, Alcibiades ordered the Hesiodic mixture of three parts water for one part wine, as pre-

scribed by the most conservative symposiac nomos. To everyone's surprise, he announced that in his reign as sovereign of
the wine, there would be no mandatory rounds; each man
would be master of his chalice.

The unexpected magnanimity raised the first ovation of the
second tables.

Sophocles immediately commented that for fear of the
symposiarchal tyranny of the Cliniad, he had come prepared.
From the folds of his robe he brought out a large amethyst he
had hanging on his chest as an antidote to the wine. Callias,
however, didn't trust amethysts; he had some excellent spells,
like the one created by Abaris the Hyperborean or the spell of
Zalmoxis. A long, disorderly debate ensued, with the majority
defending the powers of the amethyst, which, when brought
into contact with the body, prevented drunkenness; Pyrilampes
wore it on his stomach and Polus on his throat as the wine
flowed by, while Chaerephon preferred rubbing it on his
tongue, and Euripides on his temples.

315

The debate on the powers of the amethyst inevitably led to
the issue of the theft of Athena's eye and the efforts of Nicias
and the Basileus to capture the one-eyed profaner.

Hippodamus related a dream of his compatriot Aspasia,
according to which the stone had never left the City.

"That's what I think," said Ictinus the architect, cautiously
trying to fan the flames of criticism against Nicias.

Could one take the confessions of a slave, delirious from
torture, seriously enough to affirm that One Eye had left with
the stone?

"So why don't we," interjected Protagoras of Abdera, tongue
in cheek, "ascertain the whereabouts of the amethyst, using the
infallible obstetrics of truth that Socrates teaches in Athens?"

"A very g-g-good idea!"

"Yes, by Zeus!" added Polus the Sicilian. "Let's have him make us give birth to the truth."

"Do not laugh," cautioned the faithful Chaerephon disapprovingly. "Socrates's obstetric art was created to investigate truth, love, the justice of the law; it should be used to give birth to the innate truths of the soul. Using it to find a material object would be mockery."

Protagoras came right back at him:

"Well, then, I must have been mistaken, oh, Chaerephon, for I was led to believe that the maieutic technique might also be used to bring forth enlightened opinions on things of everyday concern."

"And so it might, oh, illustrious visitor," Socrates interceded, picking up the gauntlet, "provided that you accept that an enlightened opinion can, nevertheless, be wrong."

"Could you, then, oh, son of Sophroniscus, guide us to an enlightened opinion about the hiding place of the amethyst of Athena?"

Socrates was about to make fun of that misguided purpose, but decided to play the game. Perhaps later he might provoke Protagoras and bring about a loftier dialogue, one of those that make men better.

"If you promise me that you will not forget that I only know that I know nothing," he said, "and that no opinion is certain wisdom, but at best precarious knowledge, I would say, oh, wisest Protagoras, that, in fact, my obstetric art is such that it can produce enlightened opinions on anything that is knowable."

"I've heard so much about your maieutic technique, oh, excellent Socrates, that I thought you capable of leading us not only to the knowable but to some other things as well," Protagoras answered.

Laughter everywhere.

Alcibiades, fearing that the two philosophers might cross swords in a serious debate and turn his feast into a philosophical discourse, decided to make use of his double privilege as host and symposiarch. He cut them off, calling for silence. When the last of the laughter stopped, he announced that Dionysus had just inspired him with a new game:

"Let us assume that Asp-p-pasia's dream is true," he proposed. "Then the stone has not left the City, am I correct? Very well. Any symposiast who has an enlightened opinion should tell us where the stone might be."

Having noticed that, somewhere in the rear, Sophocles had just stolen a kiss from a young pitcher bearer, he announced that the slave child, whose beauty was comparable to that of Charmides, son of Glaucon, would be the prize for the most enlightened opinion. He had been a present from Critias, son of Callaeschrus, there present, and he was worth at least two thousand drachmas.

"And I'll throw in two Persian peacocks worth five hundred," chimed in Pyrilampes the Birdman, who as a good friend of Pericles thought he detected a way to steer the joshing against Nicias.

When the applause died down, Euripides asked how they would know who the winner was.

"Let us choose a jury from among those who do not have enlightened opinions," proposed Pyrilampes.

"Well said, oh, son of Antiphon," Euphrantides the Seer exclaimed, volunteering with a hand in the air.

Polus of Acragas did likewise, as did Hipponicus, Alcibiades's future father-in-law.

Encouraged by what promised to be a night to tell their grandchildren about, some of the symposiasts sat up crosslegged on their couches so as to miss nothing.

Alcibiades thought, quite happy with himself, that
Protagoras, piqued by all the praise laid on Socrates, had decided
to try and drag him into a debate. But the Cliniad had taken
care of that. He had heard Protagoras on two occasions, and he
was very much afraid that, in a superficial skirmish, he might
very well carry the day.

The first to present his case was Chaerephon. It was his con-
tention that there was no proof that One Eye had left the City
and he could not at all rely on the statements of a scoundrel like
Xanthus, much less so when they had been extracted by Nicias
of Niceratus; he was convinced that One Eye had not left, but
was hiding somewhere in the City and had the stone with him.
Pyrilampes thought that the Macedonian sacrificed by Lysanias
had given the stone to Melas, Nicias's freeman and seer, head of
the paid agents of King Perdiccas of Macedonia. Amid the
laughing and clapping, Apollodorus of Phalerum took the floor.
He was well acquainted with the Cybernetes, a cad and a
scoundrel, because they were from the same deme. Curiously
enough, his father was an honest man, but the Cybernetes had
squandered a fortune. His family went hungry while he spent his
time in brothels and gambling warrens; he had mortgaged his
home, lost his last ship, and had become a complete wreck.
Then, just about the time the City was terror striken by the sacrilege at Epsilon, he suddenly turned up with money, bought
back the mortgage, and told everyone that he had won a fortune
in an afternoon of knuckle-bones against some sailors from
Rhodes. The fact, however, was that no one at the port of
Phalerum had ever heard about that game or seen the Rhodians,
and it was probably One Eye who had given him the stone,
which he sold to Perdiccas's agents or someone wanting to put a
hex on the City. Unfortunately, Apollodorus had no idea who

might have the stone; he could only affirm that it had been in the hands of Porphyrius the Cybernetes. Then it was Sophocles's turn. Very well, it was his opinion that the stone was with Orestes the Floor-smasher, because everyone knew that when Xanthus the Lycian attempted to get away across the border, he had been captured by members of his gang; the slave must certainly have had the stone with him to sell it in Megara. The opinion expressed by the didaskalos elicited praise, and the jury said that so far it was the most enlightened one. Critias, the son of Callaeschrus, thought that Pericles and Aspasia had the stone. When he was beginning to present his arguments with the joyful encouragement of the symposiasts, Polus of Acragas, who was a friend of the slandered couple and a guest of the City through their good offices, said that the time had come to give up his position in that jury to avoid being an accomplice in such blasphemy, but Pyrilampes, Hippodamus, Ictinus, and other well-known friends of Pericles gently explained that in Athens it was quite in good taste to make fun publicly of any personality, no matter how high his position, and that the worst thing that could happen to an Athenian politician was to take offense at burlesque slander, especially from the comic playwrights, against which the only known effective antidote was a witty reply full of what was known in Hellas as Attic salt. Any citizen that lacked it would find it impossible to succeed in politics. Well, now, Polus was familiar with the corrosive humor of Attic comedy, but since this was his first visit to the City, by Hera, he could never imagine that there could be such pointed joking at a symposium, and in his present state of embarrassment for having behaved like a clod, he apologized to Critias, and listened to him while he substantiated his claim that Pericles, and none other, had ordered the theft of the stone by the very guards of the Parthenon, just to have a necklace made for Aspasia, whom he obeyed like a puppy.

319

Despite the laughing and the praise for Critias's view, the judges still thought that Sophocles had expressed the most enlightened opinion. When it was Callias's turn, he began by recalling that One Eye ran a brothel for Eulalia of Ephesus, better known as Truncheon, and as he saw it, that Ionian hetaera was a member of the Persian secret service, a case very similar to that of Thargelia of Miletus, who fifty years earlier had seduced fourteen Greek commanders to facilitate Xerxes's advance on Greece. And just as the famous Thargelia came to live in the palaces of Larissa and marry none other than the king of Thessaly, Truncheon the spy, who was the lover of conspicuous personalities, some of them present that evening, maintained relations with loquacious representatives of the Athenian government and had been ordered to organize the theft of Athena's eye, for which she used her one-eyed pimp, who certainly must have gotten the stone out of the Parthenon by stuffing it in his empty eye socket.

320

The laughing and chatter seemed to go on and on, and Callias had to cut off his summary. Since no one else was raising a hand to express an enlightened opinion, the judges were about to hand down their decision, but Protagoras interrupted them, claiming that if Socrates's maieutic technique, which had merited so much praise, had inspired that diversion, it would only be fair for the son of Sophroniscus to share with them a sample of the enlightened opinions he claimed to have about all knowable things.

Alcibiades, again fearing a serious turn in the conversation, tried to intervene. He adduced that the barrel of poison was completely empty and, since Socrates was the guest of honor, he should be exempted from making a closing speech.

But Socrates did have an enlightened opinion on the whereabouts of the stone.

The others respectfully quieted down.

"Of all the opinions here expressed," he began, "the one that has most stirred my interest was that of Apollodorus of Phalerum, who was kind enough to inform us about Porphyrius the Pilot."

Socrates crossed one knee over the other and scratched his foot. The soles of his feet were gray, rough, and callused, more like hooves than human feet.

"But unfortunately," he continued, "our esteemed Phalerian has confessed that he has no answer to offer us. I believe he is wrong, for a very enlightened opinion certainly may be inferred from his words."

"And could your obstetric art help me give birth to all that enlightenment?" laughed Apollodorus, still basking in his glory.

"By the dog! You will give birth, if you accept my services."

"So be it, but quickly," said the Phalerian, rubbing his stomach, "for a single word from you and I'm already feeling cramps."

Socrates stared at him, nodding, as if talking to himself, and after a long pause, during which he appeared to be searching for just the right words, he asked:

"Judging from what you've said, this Porphyrius seems to be less expert at his trade than at carousing and hunting freemen; is that it?"

"Yes, I can vouch for that, oh, son of Sophronicus," answered the Phalerian. "He's an impious scoundrel known to everyone around the docks."

Other adjectives were murmured in the oval to illustrate the character's demerits: cad, brawler, cheat.

"I thought I heard you say, oh, excellent Apollodorus, that besides buying back his mortgage, he now hangs around the port buying drinks for the crowd and getting drunk."

"That's it, exactly."

"And you think he owes his prosperity to the sale of the stone?"

"That's what I think, yes."

"And how would you explain the fact that he has come into so much money from the sale of a stone worth no more than three hundred drachmas at the jewelers market?"

"It has occurred to me, as it has to many in the City, that the wizard Perdiccas would pay a very high price for the stone if he could use it for evil against the City."

The conversation was getting serious, and the murmurs had died away in the andron.

"And do you also believe, as someone has said, that Perdiccas would choose as his agent in the City a slave like Xanthus, one with no freedom of motion and who could not even enter the Parthenon without his master?"

"Well, yes, that does seem absurd."

"And wouldn't you consider that there might be others interested in the stone, people without evil intentions?"

"No, I can't imagine anything but evil bringing such a high price."

"Let's examine this point. Don't you believe that someone might derive much greater benefit from acquiring the stone so as to return it to the City?"

"I don't think I follow you."

Socrates's technique was beginning to produce effects; pensive faces stared at him, and some of the guests were propped up on their couches. Alcibiades was leaning forward, obviously interested in what Socrates was saying.

"Don't you believe that anyone who returned the stone to the Temple of Parthenos would be rendering the City a very important service?"

"Without a doubt, a very important service, but one without a reward; otherwise the Cybernetes himself would have returned the stone."

"And might it not be that someone with a great deal of money might be ready to pay a very high price for the privilege of gaining the Goddess' graces by returning her eye?"

"Well, yes, that might be true."

Several symposiasts nodded silently, as if they were breaking through the fog.

"Would you by chance know who it was who took on the mortgage for the Cybernetes's house?"

"Everyone in Phalerum knows that; it was Pasion, the banker."

Socrates remained pensive, as if he were trying to remember something.

"By the way," Apollodorus asked Hipponicus, "didn't Pasion get to Athens as one of your slaves?"

"No," corrected Hipponicus. "He arrived with Cimon, and then I bought him and later sold him to Eudorus the banker, who used him as clerk and accountant, and found him so faithful and astute that he gave him his freedom and placed him at the helm of his bank."

"And could you tell us what his country and family are?"

"Yes, I can," Hipponicus explained. "He is a Lydian, brought up on Colophon; when he made his fortune, he married an aristocrat from Mitylene, who has given him children and grandchildren in Athens."

"Isn't he," Protagoras asked, "a very skinny one, slightly hunched, who sets up shop by the Bouleuterion?"

"That's the one," cried Pyrilampes, then addressing Hipponicus, "and they say that in riches he rivals your son Callias."

"Very well," Socrates continued, taking the reins again, "and could you tell us, oh, Apollodorus, what is it that Pasion would want most of all in this City, where the law protects him and respects his fortune and family?"

Apollodorus took a few draughts as he pondered his answer and then tossed his head back. There was a great silence, broken only by the bustling of the pitcher slaves and the clinking of amphorae and chalices.

"I couldn't say, oh, Socrates," the Phalerian answered. "Perhaps he covets an isoteleia."

"Perfect," cried Socrates. "And what could be more natural for a man of his position, a wealthy banker forced to pay such high taxes? But, if Pasion were a metic of infinite ambition, what other desires might he have?"

The Phalerian stared at the ceiling, bit his lip, scratched his cheek.

"He might want to be an Olympic champion," he said with an obliging smile directed at Alcibiades, "or a hero of Athens..."

Socrates let the laughter and commentaries go by and returned to the fray.

"Let's see what you have told us so far, excellent Apollodorus. If Pasion were the right age, could he really hope for a chariot victory in Olympia?"

"No, of course not, no matter how much money he had."

"Could he own land in Attica or marry his sons to Athenian women?"

"Not with our laws, he couldn't!"

"And do our laws not provide for a foreigner like Pasion, a resident in the City, to be able to acquire full citizen's rights?"

"Why, yes, in fact, there are exceptions."

"And would you, oh Phalerian, explain for the benefit of our distinguished foreign guests exactly what those exceptions are?"

"Yes, of course," said Apollodorus, turning to the Theban Pythagorean sitting before him. "Citizenship may be bestowed on a foreigner who has rendered high services to the nation or to the Gods the City worships."

A few of those present were already smiling approvingly at Socrates's obstetric maneuvers.

"Feel yourself," interrupted the son of Clinias. "Feel yourself between your legs."

Apollodorus turned to Alcibiades, smiling but bewildered.

"Can't you feel your son p-p-oking his head out?"

This time even Socrates let out a laugh.

After the fun, everyone made ready to witness the imminent birth of an opinion which, indeed, promised to be very enlightened, as praise for Socrates traveled from couch to couch.

"And do you not believe, oh, Apollodorus, that a very wealthy metic, like Pasion, might covet the honors and privileges of full citizenship, or at least a significant enhancement of those he already has?"

"Yes, every rich foreigner has dreamed of that."

"And don't you think that by returning the stone he would be rendering us a great service?"

"Indeed, he would. By returning the stone he would be freeing the City of the danger of reprisals from the offended Goddess."

"And don't you think that recognition might be worth to him much more than the seven hundred or even a thousand drachmas he might have paid the Cybernetes?"

"Waah, waah," bawled Alcibiades.

"Catch him, Apollodorus, lest he fall," cried another.

"Bring in the hot water, slaves!"

"Let me cut his umbilical cord."

Before the uproar could get out of hand, Alcibiades, standing on his couch, called for silence to hear the verdict of the three judges, who unanimously voted for Socrates, for his very enlightened opinion.

Just then, Alcibiades clapped his hands and a neigh was heard at the door. In rode Egghead on a donkey, carrying two great saddlebags. From one of them protruded the unmistakable multicolored tails of two Persian peacocks, the present from Pyrilampes the Birdman; when they uncovered the second, there was the nude body of the beautiful slave boy.

Alcibiades personally crowned his master with a laurel and himself with violets. By now the noise was uncontrollable, so he called in the buffoon, the musicians, and the dancers.

The feast lasted until midnight. Alcibiades and Socrates were still talking at the break of dawn; then they climbed the Pnyx to attend the session of the Ecclesia.

At the hour of the plethora, everyone in the agora was celebrating the events at Alcibiades's first banquet.

Everyone except Pasion the banker.

43

T HE REPLACEMENT contingent arrived in Potidaea in the spring to begin the second year of the war. But the fleet returned to Athens carrying only the sick and wounded.

The following month, just before the eve of the feast of Cronus, there was a multitude camped out by the docks in Piraeus. Most of them were farmers who had arrived from their demes on mules and carts to await the fleet's second arrival.

Thirty ships arrived with the first one thousand hoplites. When the flagship Trireme rounded Cape Sunium, the entire multitude crowded into the docks. Some lit bonfires, roasted meat, and fought for the best shaded areas in which to receive their relatives with a thanksgiving dinner before returning to their homes.

When the docking maneuver finally concluded amid cheers and chants, the first to come ashore was the retiring general, Archestratus.

The last was the Owl, whom no one was expecting.

He came ashore without gear or weapons. He walked barefoot, wearing a frayed cloak and a bandage on his head.

After taking a careful look around, he disappeared into the City.

When he got to the agora, he approached a scribe who was dozing on the stairs leading up to the Royal Portico and whispered something into his ear. The man nodded and got his quill ready. For three drachmas, he had agreed to take an oath and write a message. The Owl had won the three drachmas gambling in Potidaea; it was everything he had in the world.

When he finished dictating, the scribe read out the message in a whisper:

> *TO NICIAS, SON OF NICERATUS*
>
> *The thief of Athena's eye was not Xanthus the Lycian, nor the man with one eye, nor the Macedonian executed by Lysanias. He is unpunished and living in the City, passing by you in the streets, polluting everyone. If you swear to give me a reward of a thousand drachmas, payable when the desecrator confesses, I will lead you to him.*
>
> *Hang a white ribbon from the window that opens to the south to let me know that you are expecting me. You have three days. If by the time of the Feasts of Theseus there is no ribbon, you will never hear from me again. I shall take my secret to Pericles, son of Xanthippus.*

Humm, that was just fine. The Owl turned over the three drachmas, and both walked over to the statue of Hermes, where the scribe swore an oath of silence and the Owl swore to give him another forty drachmas when Nicias paid up.

As he walked away in the direction of the Street of the Stonecutters, the Owl promised himself that as soon as he had the money he would buy himself a cloak and sandals. He would rent a room and begin a new life. He had nothing to fear, not even from the Scythian.

But what if Nicias refused to pay?

Foolishness, by Zeus! With what he knew, Pericles would have enough on Nicias to charge him with impiety in his substantiation of the anacrisis. Old Onion Head would like nothing better, now that Nicias had inveighed against Aspasia. Would a prude like Nicias refuse to pay, knowing full well that the very next day Pericles would send an army of detractors out into the streets, the agora, and the barbershops of Athens to accuse him of fraud?

Not a chance. Nicias would pay. He might haggle a bit, but he would definitely pay.

4 4

330
♉

THE SON OF CLINIAS, protagonist of two unforgettable feats, was again the talk of the City. His signature
appeared at the foot of an entreaty in verse promising a colossal amount for the favors of Lysis, the Sweet-Rump Queen of
Athens. That morning he had surprised the Assembly with a
daring and successful face-off with Pericles, and on their ride
along the narrow alleys of the Ceramicus, Polus of Acragas
admired the efficiency with which Phanes made way for them
through the swarm of onlookers spellbound by Alcibiades, and
the children elbowing their way in to be closer to Anemos, the
snow-white stallion, and the green-grocers and sausage vendors on the Street of the Drinking Trough sighing before their
hero and crying out, you ugly beast, die soon, queer, and
Alcibiades, thanking them proudly, and a fisherman, wishing
he couldn't get it up when he tried to stick it to Lysis of Miletus,
and he, laughing and holding up a stiff phallic forearm, and
Polus, commenting that it was also the custom in Sicily to

express good wishes in the form of apotropous insults, but only during victory parades on returning home from war or on certain festivities, and that the fact that it was done so freely in Athens explained the mordacity and grossness of Attic comedy, and, as they rounded the slope of Sisyphus, the oncoming crowd was so big that even the invincible ugliness of Egghead was hard put to keep them away, and the noise and the throng interrupted the riders' conversation, and as Polus admired the way Phanes tunneled through the crowd with his persuasive club, Alcibiades's thoughts went back to Lysis, to how dearly he had had to pay for his stunt with Truncheon's necklace, but how was he to imagine that his infatuation for the Sweet-Rump Ionian was to become a vital compulsion, born the past summer, when he began to send her messages, distiches, epithalamiums, elegies, entreaties, and the Ionian reminding him in her single reply that she had offered him up to Pandemos and that every time a servant of the Goddess turned a victim down it was accepted as a further oblation, but he went on insisting, visiting her first of all when he returned from Olympia, offering to pay, but she refusing, that her prices were not for adolescents, and when he became the hero of Potidaea, renewed and redoubled wooing, and now that he had an advance on his inheritance, he was willing to pay the incredible fee of three minae, and he, insisting on sending her presents, pleas for indulgence for his old transgression, for company during his lonely convalescence, poor little he, limping, had the Queen no mercy? and she, explaining that the statutes of her guild precluded any victim offered to the Goddess from ever enjoying the favors of the one who sacrificed him, unless he paid three times her fee, which in her case would make nine hundred drachmas, so why could not the son of Clinias content himself with watching her dance for five hundred and then cool his ardors with a less royal

331

and less expensive sweet-rump more in line with his youthful budget? and Alcibiades, suffering her mockery in silence, submitting to her only because he was convinced that as soon as they spent a night together he would again seduce her, and of one thing he was sure, that in the days of the necklace thing she had really fallen in love with him and that all this hatred and vengeance was because of that sarcastic note he wished he had never written, and that was why, as soon as Pericles and Ariphon gave him the advance of twelve thousand drachmas, he rushed over to Truncheon's for a night of banqueting with callipygian dances and the option of the evening with the Sweet-Rump Queen, but Truncheon asked for time to consult Lysis again, and when a few days went by without an answer, he insisted and Truncheon asked for more time to repeat the offer to Lysis who, now, as an official of the eranos had to devote time to the duties of her new position in the guild in connection with the mysteries of Pandemos, besides the growing avalanche of lovers and clients who came to her from every corner of Hellas, and two days later, she confirmed her acceptance, but with the proviso that he post a written offer very visibly on the Ceramicus wall declaring under his full name that he, Alcibiades Cliniad, mortally in love, was offering Lysis of Miletus nine hundred drachmas for a night, and, furthermore, that he had to be ready to pay two hundred drachmas for each guest he invited to the banquet, which would be at Truncheon's house, and another five hundred if he wanted to see her callipygous dance, and the blow was almost too much for him, especially since he was going to propose that she become his concubine, for her to be more famous and coveted than Aspasia of Miletus when she was in her prime, and for her name to shine throughout Hellas in the light of his military and Olympic victories, and his political glory as well, for he intended to storm the political summits of the City and had no intention of waiting until he was thirty to have himself named general, as the law demanded, none of that, by that time he would already be the Autocrat General of Athens, but fine, if she refused all that for the mere pleasure of humiliating him and taking revenge for the necklace incident, he would make himself ready, as he had for Olympia, and he would engage the enemy, and after the public humiliation on the Ceramicus wall, which was on everyone's lips since the day before, he would have to find a way, before that evening, of regaining lost ground, of making her fall in love again as she had three years ago, and when he did, he would make her a victim of the child Eros, he would ruin her life and beauty, everything, he knew how to bide his time, he had known ever since he was a child, like that time he pretended to submit to the Thracian slave until the moment was ripe to split his head open, but now he had to organize his forces with syntax, leave his left flank weak to let her penetrate, let her dance confident of his meekness and of the meekness of Polus of Acragas, his only guest, who was dying to meet the most beautiful and expensive hetaera in all of Hellas, and as he approached Truncheon's house, he reminded himself that he had to keep his alpha stance, his spear protruding from under his shield, but no aggression, during the banquet he had surrendered to Lysis's already mature beauty to carry through the first skirmish in that battle, that war of attrition, and when she saw him abandoning his shield on the battlefield in flight, when she was convinced of his weakness and enraptured submission, then he would pick up his shield and give her a taste of his spearhead, of his swords and daggers, he would charge with blade and mace, and that haughty Ionian rump would come to understand just how much logos, how much hoplomachy, she had challenged.

333

* * *

Porphyrion the Cybernetes had bet his last six drachmas on a speckled cock, which lost an eye in the first encounter and wound up hugging the rail and shirking combat without even a single mortal wound. The cock was a fairy!

Porphyrion left the yard cursing. He went around all the tables, poked into the rooms where they were shooting dice and arm wrestling, but he didn't manage to hit anyone for a loan.

An hour later, when night was falling and he was entering the City via the Ceramicus, Porphyrion heard cries and saw Alcibiades alighting from his famous white stallion and giving the reins to Egghead. He was accompanied by a foreigner riding a mare that, to judge by its bearing, might very well be one of Callias's. A door opened before them and they were welcomed by none other than Eulalia of Ephesus herself. Behind her he could see the Libyan, the one who accompanied Lysis of Miletus wherever she went, struggling to restrain two Laconian hounds. He was recalling the rumor he heard in the gambling place, about how the Ionian had bewitched the son of Clinias, when he had to make way for Egghead, who was leading the horses around to the back of the house. By Hermes, if he could only get his hands on just half of what the white stallion was worth, he could buy himself a small ship, mortgage it to Pasion for a loan, and sail for Egypt, where they were expecting a bumper papyrus crop that year. And if he got in early, he could make a killing, quadruple his investment back in Athens, and buy back his mortgage.

All the way back to Phalerum, the only thing he could think of was how lucky that Alcibiades was, spending the night with Lysis, and he wondered how many drachmas per plate the banquet cost at Truncheon's. They said that her new women were stupendous, and when the Great Bear was pointing toward the west, he decided that in the next few days, by the roll of the dice or the point of his dagger, he had to round up five hundred drachmas and get away for a while, leave Athens, where his luck had run out. He was certain that everything would be different as soon as he had a change of climate; maybe he could do a little piracy around the islands, or catch young black girls in Cyrene and sell them in Chios. But the important thing was to get away.

What if he went back to the banker for another loan? Should he threaten to turn him in for buying the stone?

No! That was impossible! He was as guilty as Pasion. Otherwise the banker would never have bought the thing. It might even cost him his life, nothing doing, Pasion would never give in, and yet, it might work, it was just a question of presenting the deal right, and he imagined himself approaching Pasion's table and telling him that he was tired of living, that he could no longer put up with his poverty, and that he had decided to kill himself, but before doing so, he would have to leave a note confessing that Pasion had bought the eye, that is, unless Pasion decided to help him with a five-hundred-drachma loan, otherwise, their souls would have to settle accounts in the other world, if his made it to the Barathrum, where Pasion's would certainly be.

Poppycock! The man would never give in; as soon as he felt threatened, he would pay assassins to tickle his ribs. In the final analysis, there was no hard evidence against the banker, and, aside from a somewhat uncomfortable interrogation, he had nothing to fear. He could say that it was pure fiction invented by Porphyrion in revenge for his refusal of any further loans, so once he was forewarned, all he had to do was hide the stone and deny everything, he was safe, and he was a man with a great many friends and people who owed him favors in Athens. No, no, trying to pressure Pasion would be foolhardy. As he entered Phalerum and passed by the house that was no longer his, he told himself that instead of planning nonsense he might best go down to Catharsis's tavern and see if he could get a little something out of the old bitch, even if it was just a skin of wine and a place to sleep.

He was wounded, oh, yes, when a man's face showed such lust and supplication at the same time, it meant he was a puppet in the hands of Aphrodite, and he hadn't even seen her new arts; the Lydian beat was just beginning, oh, by Pandemos, the initiative was so completely hers that she was finding it hard to understand how she could possibly have lost the skirmish over the necklace, and actually, if she had put her sharpest thinking on raising temples to the Goddess and not on shackling herself to the love of the one man, she would be victorious from very first combat, and what vision would she evoke that night to finish off Alcibiades when the drum of orgasms started its beat? would she recall the moment of lovemaking in the air? or perhaps the first baptism of Aphrodite? or when she had administered that ultraluxurious baptism to brother Fire-eater following the instructions of the Summoner, singing with her beautiful voice and her invented words? No, she had evoked the baptism of Fire-eater too many times and it was beginning to lose effect, and you, closing beautiful ophthalmoi, you putting much great thinking on memories, and that day Truncheon herself commenting on the wall idea, and telling her that Alcibiades was already her victim, that he was already bowing his head, nine hundred drachmas for a single night, plus five hundred for the dance, plus two hundred for his banquet guest, that little joke with the message was going to cost

336

him fifteen minae, but Lysis refusing, the cad would never
sleep with her again, he could save his nine hundred drachmas, his humiliation was enough for her, but, no, that not
good, you making error, that holy cream for First Temple of the
Sum, and she honestly confessing her fears, afraid of another
confrontation with the man who had once mastered her, you
not talk foolishness without logos, you not never forget you
High Priestess of the Sum, why I teach you mysteries of
Babylonian Ishtar? you look inside, you look much inside and
cad surely to lose, cad pay, three times cad son of Clinias pay,
and when first Phrygian flute play, you look much inside, and
she, submerged in violet memories from that day, he was there,
blue bonnet, pink robe, administering a triple baptism to
Nino, the Exact Masseuse, and Chloe and Mnesis in her room,
and just by looking at them, not even letting them touch themselves, he brought them to that sacred desperation, and
Alcibiades was astonished, the imposing display all along the
oval gave him second thoughts, like a soldier watching the
advance of an enemy with superior arms and position, and
now the Phrygian drums were making those buttocks move
faster and faster, and Polus swallowing hard, running his
tongue over his lips, smiling with restless hands, and
Truncheon savoring her wine with maternal pride, oh, her
child, the favorite of Pandemos, and Laelaps drooling at one
end of the oval and asking himself with doggish thoughts
what it was that gawking Phanes was doing crouching in that
ridiculous position and stirring up a storm under his robe, and
Otep holding down his erection with the same hand he held
onto Cratus, the new dog, that infallible guardian of the sym-
posian dances, trained to leap for the first hand that disturbed
his mistress' dance with caresses, and the musicians in full
enthousiasmos, accomplices in the vibrations of those immor-

337

tal thighs as they talked to the drums and sanctified the flutes, and Chloe and Nino rubbing nipples ever so softly, just the tips, and Lysis languishing with desire for the Cyprian caresses of Mnesis, and he sitting there, all voice and scintillating eyes, singing, where, how, and with what, and guessing and announcing what each of them would feel, and what each one felt all four felt, and when the first Phrygian beat came, popoPOM, you remember always much good orgasm, and before the bed of Alcibiades, Lysis closed her eyes and remembered straddling the firm dark thighs of Mnesis, and now you riding, walk, yes, like that, very slow walk, one side to the other, back and forth, and around, much around, and now you trotting, and sister Mnesis letting herself be rubbed, and twisting and gasping, and now you galloping popoPOM, and now run, faster run, and when Mnesis begin murmur in Lydian tongue with eyes turned up, stop, you no more not move, and ordering Mnesis to let all desire in her stomach flood over her skin, run down her back, her neck, and Nino and Chloe watching and in pain from desire, but the Summoner had forbidden them to touch themselves, and he ordered Chloe to focus all her desire in her lips, and she wetting and biting them, and he centered Nino's desire in her hands, but desire must follow trail up along belly button, and now climbing to soft fat base of breasts, and she moaning, ohhhh, and desire passing arms and going to pretty your hands, and then Chloe kiss and lick and suck fingers of Nino, and you now touch Lysis with hands, with hands magnetized from tingling lips, and Nino's fingers caressing Lysis's body, all the secret points illustrated in the teachings of Ishtar where the words of the Summoner provoked eruptions of pleasure that reverberated in the dance as the drums and flutes went wild in the final beat, and Lysis, her back to Alcibiades, on the threshold of her trembling orgasm, watching as the Summoner opens the front of his pink linen robe, fists on his hips, revealing the solid and impeccable rectitude of his manhood, and she sees Nino's nervous hands hurrying to pay him tribute, and Chloe's thick lips, and the vision unleashes the first callipygian tremors, and he taking Chloe, lifting her by the waist like a doll, penetrating her in a single, long, slow stroke, and at the end, the child trembles with culminating spasms, and then Nino, and then Mnesis, and they all fall from his hands like squeezed fruit, and you now, now, High Priestess, come to me, and on the urgent bed, she rides him, oh iron, oh flint, and he ordering her to hold back and singing the sweetest airs of Asia for her to dance on him, shoulders and hips, and seeing them in their final rigors, the others beginning their mutual touching again, and then, hearing his dithyrams to life, to the seed, hearing him announce his orgasm, praising it in brutal untranslatable poetry, his desire for Lysis melting his bones, his bones now foam riding ocean waves, and he went out to her, reaching out, arriving with his boiling river, with his thick white wine flowing toward her, descending to the High Priestess like the Dindymenian waters of the Meander flow down to the vaginal bay of Miletus, and then the final spasms, sparks racing from his eyes, his improvised chants never ceasing, and the drums quickening the pace of the dance, and Alcibiades, seeing her twisting in a tremor much more impressive than that time at Euphrosine's, feeling the trepidation in his temples and in the floor and the walls, getting ready to descend from his couch and starting at Cratus's savage bark as he blocked his way, and Lysis awaking, too, feline, a blush blanketing her body, sighing deliquescent, allowing a tingle to rush from her marrow and embrace her, and fade away with the last vibrations of the music, and then, turning on her stomach, coyly crossing her ankles, gathering her hair, framing her profile with her raised arms, radiating from the floor the peace of tranquil waters, and Alcibiades and Polus, immobilized on their couches by the authoritarian growls, seeing Lysis being carried away by Otep, followed by her slave attendants, almost naked, prancing on tiptoes, escorting her to her perfumed bath, and Lysis satisfied once again that her ephemeral callipygian tremors were turning into money to buy ageless marble for the Sum.

Ugh, it was hotter in Catharsis's dump than in Libya, and what with the rats and Galatea's screeches, would they never end, sleep was impossible, he needed five hundred drachmas, what could he do? he might try a fraud, or stealing a ship, or holdups, perhaps rustling, or an ambush against somebody like Alcibiades, at that very moment the son of Clinias was probably drinking cool wine, lording over Lysis's rump, eating figs from her lips, his every wish attended by Truncheon's beautiful slaves, surrounded by the splendor of silver chalices, jewels, necklaces, jewels? hmmmmm, hadn't One Eye said something about Truncheon scolding him for having the amethyst, and then rising from the floor, hearing some drunk pissing every-where but in the pot? and Codrus, the damned ruffian, had been beating her for half a clepsydra, why didn't he just kill the screaming whore? and Porphyrion putting on his robe, he needed air, a breeze to ventilate that idea, and walking along the deserted docks, there was nothing to lose by checking, and on the way to the City, dagger in hand, with his lousy luck, he might just run into the Floor-smasher's gang, and looking at the night sky, he could make it before dawn without hurrying, and when Arcturus sank into the humid night and the fingers of dawn reached over the horizon, there were no voices or music coming from the house, rotten luck, they had all gone to bed. Now he would have to postpone his talk with Truncheon until midday. Practically dawn for whores.

And since he had so much time, the best thing would be to find a piece of papyrus.

There was no other body as desirable, the night was well worth nine hundred drachmas, and that monster guarding her dance, panting at the end of the oval, made her nudity even more brutal, and that moment during the dance, certainly rehearsed, when she stood before those jaws offering her thighs to his submissive licking, and spinning, breasts vibrating, waist quivering, holding out her hands to be licked, and shrugging her shoulders with a searing pout on her lips, Polus of Acragas was unable to hold back a sigh, and Alcibiades, chafing as he rode away, had drawn a blank, now he would have to find some young, tender bottom, a shame he had given that slave boy to Socrates, that cunning bitch, after tempting him with burning looks throughout the dance, after accepting a kiss on a bitten pear, after talking to him, she thought she was so smart, after sharing his couch during the banquet, and when Polus went off with the Syrian slave, Lysis refusing, and he, very big mistake, reminding her of when she wanted to be his concubine, and she mocking, laughing, did Truncheon hear such folly? where had Alcibiades gotten the idea that she ever wanted to be his concubine? another laugh from her perfect teeth, magnetic clear eyes, graceful neck, how beautiful she was, how skilled in repartee, what an admirable pupil for Truncheon's wisdom, and then both of them making fun of him, well, that was fine, let them enjoy their momentary victory, the son of Clinias knew how to wait, that was the most important thing a politician had to learn, and since she would never share his bed willingly, she

341

would have to be kidnapped, Phanes would do the job when the time came, but first he had to decide where to take her and keep her until she was thoroughly pierced by the divine arrows of Eros, one day the insolent ninny would learn that there was a price to pay for making the firstborn of Clinias and Deinomache humble his name on the Ceramicus wall.

After the days of her kidney crisis, Truncheon's jealousy over Hypothesis ebbed. She was determined to save her relationship with Lysis, and she resolved to see her as an adult who no longer needed her guidance. Indeed, Lysis was now her superior in the order of Pandemos! Folly it would have been to demand anything but sporadic and passive gratitude on her bed and the filial loyalty she had always shown her. That was the most she could charge her for her initiation and loving sponsorship, and seeing her so devoted to building a temple with the fruit of her trade, it would have been a sacrilege to protest simply because she no longer gave her so many evenings in her bedroom.

She remembered that she had not had her in her arms since that day a year ago when she had come to her house to watch the returning Olympians from the window, and now, reclining on her bed, fanning her profile, she recalled that what had happened a few hours earlier in that room was absolutely without precedent in their relationship. Shattering. Lysis had taken the initiative and started the fires; then, for the first time, it was Lysis who commanded the actions with unknown caresses. It was as if she were showing off her new repertory. She must have grown a great deal in Aphrodite's favor for the Goddess to have made her so expert.

After the morning ritual of the phalluses and her prayers to the Mother of the Gods, Truncheon left Lysis in the semidarkness and ordered a slave to fan her while she slept.

When she went into the yard, the sun had passed the zenith. The doorkeeper gave her a small dirty scroll written in an ugly scrawl:

Last night I dreamed that Athena was rebuking me for not telling the whole truth to the Substantiator of the Anacrisis when he questioned me about the doings of One Eye. I never told him that you and Lysis of Miletus had known that he had the eye stolen from the Goddess. Now I live in fear of her divine anger. I wish to get away to pay for my sins in foreign lands. I shall buy a boat and sail away to Egypt to seek the protection of Osiris. Do you have any idea who could lend me five hundred drachmas? Or would you recommend that I atone by confessing everything I know? I also seem to remember that One Eye was selling the stone for you, for a commission. If you should like to chat, I will be waiting until midafternoon in the tavern of the Cyclops, not far from your home. In the event that something should happen to me, there is a sealed copy of this note with the papyrus containing my will.

Truncheon sent the slave away and woke Lysis without her usual caresses.

Lysis noticed that she was beside herself, cursing the Cybernetes, One Eye, damn them, profaners, liars all of them.

What? But what was going on? and Lysis rubbing her eyes as Truncheon ran the curtains letting in the faint light from the courtyard, and knitting her brow, and reading the papyrus, and Truncheon realizing that she was not furious but smiling and arching her eyebrows, and Truncheon protesting, so she thought the dirty stab in the back was all a joke? she knew she should have turned that damned One Eye in, did Lysis understand how right she had been, how well-founded her fears? ah, but that rat Porphyrion would soon know who he had come up against, Truncheon was not a citizen, but she had much more influence than he did, and that very morning she would send a message to her friend Pythodorus, and to the Areopagus, and to that Court of . . . and Lysis rising naked from the bed and embracing her, and no, Truncheon would not send messages and would not talk to anyone, and that if she still loved her child, she would set her anger aside, Lysis would pay the five hundred drachmas, she had a better plan to do away with the rat without danger, and Truncheon was to swear immediately, on the effigy of Pandemos, that she would leave everything in her hands and never mention it again.

45

THE ASSEMBLY was simply no place for a man like him.
Aside from formal attendance when he was summoned,
pursuant to his duty as a citizen, he really had nothing to do
with that menagerie, the realm of fancy words and trickery
enshrined by the Eschinocephalus and those other songbirds
of democracy. But that morning Nicias was elated as he climbed
the slope of the Pnyx. About twenty of his senior partisans
escorted him, followed by a multitude of hangers-on and
freemen servants, and his optimism so filled him that for the
first time in many years he failed to take his ball of wax with
him.

And the son of Niceratus had reason enough to be happy.
That afternoon, the Tribunal would hear old Onion Head's
defense of the Milesian bitch. The heliasts were expected to
condemn her to banishment for life. A reliable official source
had just informed him that the sentence was a foregone conclusion. Yes, at least by a majority of three votes.

Hadn't he said that he would do it, that it was just a question of time? Well, there it was, another brilliant implementation of his formula, another link in the chain of successes he had begun a year earlier with the execution of Xanthus the Lycian.

It was obvious that the Girdler of the Lands was favoring the City. Slowly but surely, and with increasing frequency, as the Archonship of Pythodorus elapsed, he was praised in the Ecclesia, and in the next-to-last ordinary session of the past year, several demes of the Saronic had spontaneously organized to send a delegate to the Assembly to present a motion of gratitude to Nicias, for they attributed the unprecedented catch in the gulf that season to his great piety toward the Wave Dasher.

And in the fourteen days since the new year, there were additional reasons for him to be happy. Public opinion, which Pericles had whipped up to support the war, was beginning to grow critical of the lengthy siege. Potidaea had not fallen in the summer, as he had promised, and the situation had not improved in the three months of the recent spring. The expedition led by Archestratus faltered from the very beginning; the assault engines designed by Artemon the Bale failed miserably; and Pericles's initiative to block their water sources and reduce the Potidaeans by thirst also went nowhere. As the besiegers soon discovered, the city's defenders had, with immense foresight, implemented the arts of Theopompus of Lampsacus to dig wells within their walls, so they had no need for outside sources. With their graineries and stables well stocked, thanks to the aid of King Perdiccas, Potidaea could hold out.

The war that Pericles insisted on taking to the Chalcidian theater, to force on the Spartans a naval deployment for which they were not prepared, did not succeed in distracting a single hoplite or a single oar. Instead, two thousand Corinthians, who had taken the overland route under the command of Aristeus, arrived in Potidaea before the fleets commanded by Archestratus and Callias. And during the coming winter, four thousand Athenian hoplites would be freezing in their inaction before the Boreal walls of Potidaea at a time when there was talk of an imminent invasion of Attica from the Peloponnesians. The way things were going, the siege could last a great many more months.

Thus, the very people who once laughed at Nicias's qualms were now saying that he had been right to oppose Pericles's strategy. With this turnabout in the opinion of the many, and with confirmed indications of a decline in old Onion Head's reputation, Nicias launched his attack against Aspasia, following a secretly and meticulously prepared plan.

His intuition in setting up a permanent watch on Pericles's home from a nearby house rented in the name of one of his own men had been a stroke of genius. As luck would have it, on two different occasions his spies detected a young hetaera of the Ceramicus entering the house by the back door, once disguised as a florist and another time as a fish monger. On both occasions, she had arrived after dusk and left before dawn. What else could it be but the procuring and pandering of Aspasia, who introduced women of her own ilk for the unholy purposes of the Onion?

And as if things were not bad enough for Pericles, the Spartans had dug up their old complaint against the Alcmeonidae about the murder of the supplicants in the Acropolis and were demanding the purification of Athens as a prerequisite to any peace negotiations. Hiero then explained to Nicias the convenience of exploiting the complaint, and together they orchestrated a campaign to spread the rumor that the City could be victorious in the coming war only if it ordered the ostracism of the Alcmeonid Pericles.

Things were going well for Nicias. His most recent victories had made him the undisputed hegemon of the aristocratic party, and in the last few months, slander from the enemy ranks had waned considerably. Furthermore, as a clear harbinger of the new times to come, the unpredictable Alcibiades had made his debut two days earlier in the Assembly, inveighing against Onion Head.

He had probably realized that Pericles was already a political corpse, a corpse that would fall with a crash that very afternoon when the tribunal passed a sentence banishing the unholy Milesian courtesan, for, despite all her preposterous philosophy and rhetorics, that was all she was.

Both Nicias and his closest advisors interpreted Alcibiades's attack against Pericles as a signal to the opposition party, informing Nicias and his people: "Here I am; take me as one of your own; I'm a talented young man who can face Eschinocephalus."

When they arived, Nicias and his highest-ranking supporters moved toward their seats in the proedra. Just a moment earlier, the heralds had announced the presence of the six thousand ecclesiastes required to make a quorum for extraordinary Assemblies, and the procedures for the purification of the premises had already begun. Amid the religious silence, as the Epistates of the Prytaneum raised his palms up to the Altar of the Twelve Gods and the officials sprinkled the perimeter with the blood of a suckling pig, the group headed by Nicias and Lysanias advanced respectfully, but not without making unseemly squeaks on the sand of the Pnyx.

They moved toward the right wing, already occupied by a hundred followers and free servants who were reserving seats for their higher-ranking members behind the proedra and facing the back of the seat to which the son of Niceratus, as a strategus, was righfully entitled.

Once in their seats, as the blazing fire crackled and the sacrificial victim burned, Nicias directed his gaze toward the plains of the Cephisus, whose waters flowed peacefully after their fall from Parnes and Pentelikon.

When the sacrifice was over and the required invocations were said, as they read the long probuleuma of the Council of Five Hundred dealing with the alternatives facing them in the Potidaean war, the officials of the Prytaneum distributed wreaths of myrtle to the Assembly members.

Nicias gazed out at the hills of Acharnae and began to rehearse the speech intended for Alcibiades. He would have quite enough time as the official read slowly from the podium of the proedra and the litany was repeated by a herald with a thunderous voice.

Two days Hiero and Nicias had worked on the speech in the cabin in Aurora. On many walks along the lonely Isthmus of Sunium, Nicias had memorized every word and rehearsed every pause, every inflection, every gesture and expression recommended by Hiero.

He had to speak that day. His secretary had convinced him of the need to win over the son of Clinias in public, so that the news would fly through the countryside like wildfire. The insinuation the boy had made two days earlier was not to be disdained; the great Nicias had to have all the citizens, down to the humblest fisherman in Attica, see Pericles's most brilliant relative cross over to the aristocrats. Did the son of Niceratus not understand that that would singe the beard off his face? What would the many think? How would they interpret the move by that promising young man, that favorite of Zeus and Ares, to abandon the party headed by the Onion and the populist line laid down by his great-grandfather Clisthenes?

Did the lofty strategus not see what would happen? From

the dumbest woodcutter down to the last dunce in the deme of Acharnae, all would lose confidence in the Head and his much tooted democracy. How could he command trust from anyone when his own family disowned him? That was what the son of Niceratus must not forget: the important thing was not to recruit the son of Clinias, but to get him to defect from Pericles.

It was obvious. Fully convinced, Nicias gave orders that he was not to be disturbed and left for the lodge in Aurora to memorize his speech.

Although he had learned it perfectly, down to the last comma, he ignored the speakers and went on rehearsing. He stared at the shining bald pate of Euthynus, the new eponymous archon sitting among the Prytanes, and spent a long time repeating the most important fragments. On several occasions, however, he was distracted by certain screeching voices. He regretted not having brought wax. How could he have forgotten that the asses would interrupt his train of thought?

By midmorning, Nicias had not listened to a single speech. The men of Athens were giving their opinions on the number of ships and hoplites that had to remain stationed in Chalcidice; his people had instructions to speak according to the guidelines laid down by Hiero and support the positions presented by Pythodorus and Lysanias. He would vote as they did; it didn't matter at all what had been said. He was not going to utter a single syllable in the debates until he had spouted his speech and freed himself of the bloated feeling caused by the butterflies under his sternum. He would have preferred to don the myrtle crown immediately and get it over with among the first speakers, but Hiero had advised waiting; if the son of Clinias took the floor and attacked Pericles, Nicias's speech would fit right in and might even be interpreted as a sample of his spontaneous eloquence.

Alcibiades was seated at the other end of the proedra. Despite his recent membership in the Assembly, his Olympic victory had earned him a place in the front rows among the one hundred reserved for the guests of the Prytaneum. And there he was, sitting between Euripides and Philocles, the tragic victor in the latest Dionysian Festivals.

Of all the seats for the College of Strategi, Pericles's was the only one ostensibly empty. His views on the continuation of the war in Chalcidice were known to all and would be defended by the spokesmen of democracy. His unheard-of absence was due to the defense he was preparing, which was to be delivered that afternoon at Aspasia's trial. Could that be why Alcibiades had not donned the wreath to be recognized? Maybe he was reserving his attack for when the Head was present. How expertly he had faced Pericles two days earlier! Incredible for someone so young! Yes, he had to be brought over. Because of his stuttering, no one had ever augured well for him as an orator. But it was the other way around; he had turned his supposed limitation into a weapon that he used admirably to make his pauses (some of them deliberate, Hiero had said) and underscore the key elements in his speeches.

In the distance, Nicias saw some oxen pulling a cart on Pyrilampes's farm, but he was assailed again by the image of Alcibiades bringing the Assembly to red heat by mocking Pericles's defenders, and then that unforgetable parry and thrust when the Head decided to speak, and relying on his lineage and his blah, blah, blah, and the Head saying how, when he was young like Alcibiades, he, too, had abused that passion for truth and that stubborn insistence on calling things by their names, and Alcibiades regretting that he had not known his relative then, when he had some self-respect, and instead of the oxen, Nicias again had the vision of the Assembly gone wild,

shaken by the loudest and most unanimous guffaws he had ever
heard in all the years since he first visited the baths, and Nicias,
too, lost control and laughed, for the first time in public, at
Pericles's embarrassment, the impotent laughingstock could
not understand that attack, on the eve of the trial against his
bitch, an attack from his godson, the one he had raised, and just
then a tap on his shoulder and Agathon the Ephetae passing
him a note from Hiero telling him to don the wreath, what?
why? hadn't they agreed to . . . ? and looking up at the guests, he
noticed that Alcibiades had already asked for the floor, and
Nicias immediately crowning himself with the myrtle, and now
really listening to what was going on, and, yes, Alcibiades was
going to speak about . . . but now he was interrupting one of
Pericles's detractors, asking to make a clarification on the point,
and the absolute silence confirming everyone's interest in what
he was about to say, surely he would continue fanning the
flames against his kinsman, but what was that? he was defending Pericles, what side was he on then? and Nicias turning to
look at Hiero, standing in one of the lateral aisles, and
Alcibiades stuttering hyperbolic praise for the creator of Great
Athens, for the uncorruptible son of Xanthippus, an honest life,
courageous, formidable intelligence at the service of Athens,
had they made up? had the son of Clinias let himself be bribed?
what was Nicias to do with his speech now? and Pericles the
b-b-brilliant visionary, with his grain policy in the Pontus and
in the Tauric Chersonese, and his criticism the other day of his
d-d-difficulties with the supplies could not cloud the genius of
Pericles, who a year earlier had foreseen the patrols of the
Persian fleet to impede shipments from Egypt, and the blocking
of transportation from Ssss-sicily through Corinthian interfer-
ence, and the road he had opened, with his long negotiated
alliance with Spartocus, to the Tauric wheat, everything attested

to his wisdom and foresight, and the war in Potidaea was a necessary evil because it was the only way to ensure stability in the region of the Boreas, where did such a young man get all that poise, by Zeus, all that eloquence? what did he intend to gain from his senseless changes of opinion? Nicias had been right in the beginning, when he rejected Hiero's suggestion, how could he, the son of Niceratus, deliver a speech so full of praise for that fairy? and Hiero insisting for days that it was a good occasion, that he was a hero, son of a hero, Olympic champion, the time was perfect, and Nicias, but those colored robes and ribbons in his hair, and nine hundred drachmas for a whore's ass, who could understand that volatile libertine? and Alcibiades, a newcomer to the Assembly, speaking like a veteran strategus and saying what the fleet should do and how the islands should be controlled, but, by Zeus! who did he think he was? and now proclaiming Pericles's wisdom in increasing the contributions of Athens's allies, and that the fleet alone, with armed landings, was enough to keep the League members in line, and that if Athens hoped to be the naval power that Themistocles envisioned, it had to be along the road chosen by Pericles and not by building f-f-fountains with bronze fish for the God of the sea, and Nicias overwhelmed by the booing of the ecclesiastes, what could all that mean, by the Twelve Gods? and looking straight forward, his eyes glued to the honeysuckle hanging from the Prytaneum table, regretting not having brought his wax, he was disarmed without it, terrible negligence, he would have to listen, could he keep still? would his face reflect the impact of the attacks? and Pythodorus interrupting Alcibiades to remind him that the man who had built the pious offering to Poseidon was the same man who had earned for Athens the favor of the Gods, and the son of Clinias should know that the august Assembly of Athens was not the Lenaeum nor the ovals of his disorderly banquets, notorious sources of evil gossip, and instead of so much censure for the son of Niceratus, he should thank him for the good sense with which he had placated the Immortals by substantiating the anacrisis of Xanthus the Lycian, for without that, Zeus would not have given him his victories in Olympia, and Alcibiades responding that his victories were not due to Nicias's intervention but to his personal pledges to Warlike Zeus, about which no one had any knowledge, and which he reiterated right there before the Twelve Gods, and a long pause for applause and ovations.

The session was suspended due to the imminent fall of night. It could not resume for two days; it was forbidden by the Feasts of Theseus.

Nicias withdrew, walking very tall and surrounded by hundreds of cheering supporters. Along the way he received several expressions of gratitudes, but he reached home depressed. He refused to have any dinner and spent a long while shut up in his study.

Never in his long career had he ever seen anything like what had happened that day on the Pnyx. In the final speeches, some had referred to the Pantadeuteros. They had wounded his dignity! Horrible! Thousands of idiots laughing at Eulogos's jokes about the fountain, and what was worse, they would return to their demes to spread malevolent doubts about his purification of the City.

Alcibiades had completely overturned months worth of careful work. What was left now of the admiration and respect the City had for him? Oh, the ungrateful many! It was all he could do to control his rage against Hiero, who had misled him about Alcibiades. But he did not want to take Hiero to task until he had just the right words, so he sent him off to find out what was going on at Aspasia's trial and then shut himself in.

The first thing he had to do was cool down; then he had to think and make a decision. Why had everyone laughed so much at the Pantadeuteros thing that miserable barber had spawned? Never again would he go to an Assembly meeting without his wax. How could he preserve his reputation for coolheadedness without plugging up his ears? Had his face revealed what he was feeling back there before all those mocking thetes? What a blow to his public image!

Then it occured to him that as soon as Aspasia's sentence was confirmed, he would begin to see things in a different light and slowly but surely the balms of time would heal his wounded dignity.

At the last light of dusk, he took a soothing hot bath, and later, when he was about to ask Melas about the immediate future, after the fall of Pericles, Hiero showed up.

Hiero appeared pale and somber, and Nicias knew there was nothing to be said. All he could do was stare at him.

The whole City was commenting . . . that was all they talked about . . . Pericles had gotten her off . . . absolved. Theatrical defense . . . righteous indignation . . . fainting spells . . . bitter tears . . . and what with the court so impressed . . .

Nicias ceased to listen. He let his gaze wander over the diffuse shadows of the peristile on the walls. For the first time in his life he considered giving up public affairs. He no longer needed Melas to forecast anything. After the day's events, what for? And he waved him away.

Nicias went off to the gynaeceum, which he had not visited in several days, and lay down on his matrimonial bed. He asked his wife to get him an infusion of silphium with a few drops of hellebore and refused to discuss the marriage of his eldest daughter, who had been spoken for by Crates's family for their firstborn, Melampus.

But there was more bad news in store for the son of Niceratus that day.

A slave came to tell him that Hiero had something urgent to report. Nicias got up, wondering if there might have been some mistake in the reports about Aspasia's trial, and walked over to the men's courtyard.

Hiero's message had nothing to do with the trial.

The door slave had received an anonymous message two days earlier. Having been ordered not to disturb his master during those days, he had told no one and put it away in the message chest, which the economus had not checked until that very moment because he had spent those days at the farm.

Nicias read:

> TO NICIAS, SON OF NICERATUS ... *thief of Athena's eye not Xanthus ... polluting all ... one thousand drachmas ... my secret to Pericles ...*

And without a moment's consideration, he gave the order to hang the white ribbon of acceptance from the highest window in his house.

He desperately needed to see and hear the man who had written the note; he had to make sure it was not some delinquent trying to capitalize on the events at the Assembly. What if it were some raving lunatic?

There would be time enough to decide about the thousand drachmas.

He read the note several times over.

This unknown informant had to be very certain of what he was saying if he demanded payment only after the thief had confessed. And if he had no proof, he would certainly not risk the reprisals Nicias could easily arrange for him.

Did he really know something? Could it be another one of Pericles's tricks?

Hiero was of the opinion that the man should be given his say. If he really knew something, he could not be allowed to take his information to Pericles.

Then Hiero added a touch of terror for which Nicias had no need at all; did the worthy son of Niceratus not think that Alcibiades, or Eulogos, or both, might be mixed up in this? Could they possibly have some of the details of what the unknown informant claimed he knew? How, then, would they have risked browbeating Nicias about the Xanthus affair?

Perhaps what they really hoped to gain with their defamation was to force Nicias to defend himself and then crush him with the secret information.

He was racked with doubt, wavering like a storm tide on the Euripus. Would there never be any lasting certainty about anything in this world?

4 6

ALEXIS OF CNIDUS was still in his twenties when he set up his stand in Piraeus to deal in maritime insurance.

He lent money to ship owners at high interest, which he collected in the form a percentage of the sale value of the imported merchandise after a charge on the whole ship and cargo; out of his first one hundred ventures, he had lost only three ships and suffered the default of one deserter who decided to turn pirate.

He had become a very popular man during the archonships of Euthymenes and Antiochides by providing soft conditions to foster the grain policy implemented by Pericles. As soon as he heard about the contractual libations and sacrifices made by the Athenians and Taurians, Alexis began to promote an intense wheat import trade using every kind of vessel available.

The City was also very beholden to him for the rather important loan he had made Alcibiades for his expedition to

Olympia, and later, for the statue, with no collateral other than his word. But beyond all this, his greatest popular acclaim was due to the huge amount of money he had bet on the Athenian quadrigae.

The City considered it the justice of Zeus that an Ionian immigrant should win almost three talents on the chariots of the son of Clinias.

What no one in Athens knew was that Alexis of Cnidus had not risked a single obol on Pericles or on Alcibiades. Both risks had been very secretly covered by his colleague, Pasion the Colophonian.

When Pericles returned with his fleet from the expedition to Pontus, Pasion immediately saw that there was good business to be done with the region of the Boreas, but he could not openly support Pericles because his own political connections were with Pericles's bitterest enemies.

Ever since then, he had been a silent partner behind Alexis's deals. The young Cnidian's obvious good luck had a lot to do with his choice, but so did the fact that Alexis was quite happy to support Pericles without risking an obol.

Alexis opened subsidiaries in the Athenian colonies at Sinope and Amisus, branching out from insurance to develop his own shipping concern. The capital and the risks went on the account of the Colophonian. Alexis got ten percent of the profits for serving as the front man.

Pasion, for his part, was a long-time partner of Nicias of Niceratus in the usury business. Like all foreigners, he was not allowed to own real estate on Attic soil, so the mortgages he took as collateral on his loans included Nicias as beneficiary through the mediation of another Athenian, whose only job was to keep quiet and make sure the City never found out for whom he was fronting. The name of the son of Niceratus did not appear on any document, but he got one eighth of Pasion's income on interests and ten percent of the value of properties acquired on foreclosures.

In the last few years, Nicias's usury earnings were beginning to rival his income from the one thousand slaves he had rented out to mines and quarries. In exchange, in the constant litigation and the frequent intimidations that went with the business, Pasion got the very hefty political and legal protection Nicias could muster through his connections.

When Alexis of Cnidus decided to support the Cliniad's Olympic undertaking, once again Pasion was behind the scene, secretly pulling the strings. Days before the departure for Olympia, Alexis received a visit from his powerful colleague, who proposed that he accompany the Athenian delegation and take bets against Alcibiades. He explained that if the Hellanodicae allowed Alcibiades to race his chariots, it would be easy to find many people in Altis who would be willing to give three-to-one, and even five-to-one odds against that unknown young man who was venturing to take on the best and finest in Hellas.

Of course, ever since Pasion had seen him race his own quadrigae in the Great Panathenian Games, he was convinced that this young man would some day be an Olympic champion. And if he had ever had the slightest doubt, Alcibiades's almost fanatical training did away with it. During the days of preparation for the Athenian expedition, Pasion often saw Alcibiades in his dreams, wearing the olive crown.

Alexis was no man's fool. He knew that Pasion had a devotion to young men. Perhaps the beautiful Alcibiades had inspired in him some unspeakable love?

So, without a second thought, the Cnidian accepted the

offer. As a Greek, he had always wanted to travel to Olympia, and Pasion was giving him the same deal he had in the business in the region of the Boreas. Since Alcibiades was related to Pericles, Pasion could not show his face in this deal either. Alexis had nothing to lose: If Alcibiades won, the profits would be well worth any inconvenience he might suffer, and there was also the prestige he would earn in the City if things turned out right.

That afternoon, on the eve of the Feasts of Theseus, while the City anxiously awaited the decision of the judges in the trial against Aspasia, Alcibiades, on returning from the Pnyx, received a note from the hands of Egghead:

> *FROM ALEXIS OF CNIDUS*
> *TO THE EXCELLENT SON OF CLINIAS*
> *It is urgent that I see you. Can it be today? One of my slaves*
> *will be waiting for your reply. Be happy.*

Had Alexis imagined that Alcibiades was already in possession of his estate? Did he intend to collect so soon? Impossible! Alexis was not so foolish as to ruin the esteem in which Alcibiades held him by trying to collect.

It had to be something else.

The Egghead should t-t-tell him to come, to get to his house immediately.

Alexis had no intention of collecting.

On the contrary. As his first point, he reminded Alcibiades that on the morrow the City would be celebrating the Feast of Coexistence between Athenians and foreigners; in honor of Theseus, who instituted them, Alexis had come to inform him that his debt for twelve thousand drachmas had been canceled.

"You intend to cancel a debt for two talents?" Alcibiades was on guard.

"And in the second place, oh, son of Clinias, know you that it was not I who lent you that money . . ."

"By Zeus, you intrigue me, good Alexis!"

"Nor did I bet on your chariots in Olympia."

"Well, now!" The thing was getting interesting. Could it be Anytus again? Maybe Hipponicus. Or Callias? Or perhaps Pericles?

"So, then, who was this anonymous benef-f-factor?"

Alexis smiled and prolonged the pause.

"It was a colleague of mine."

"Zorus the Syrian?"

"No."

"Belus, the one from the Temple of Heracles?"

"No."

"The son of Phil-l-l-larchus?"

"None of them, oh, excellent Alcibiades; it is useless for you to go on trying, you would never guess."

". . . ?"

"It is someone in whose name I come and who begs you to give ear to another advantageous offer. It is Pasion the Colophonian."

Alcibiades recalled Socrates's entertaining reasoning leading to Pasion as the guilty party holding the amethyst of Athena. Could the Colophonian be so foolish as to have taken offense? Would he be reminding him of the loans and the bets in order to demand rectification of the things said that night?

What a strange man! Alcibiades remembered him standing next to his stand, but he had never spoken to him.

"And w-w-what is this offer?"

"This I do not know, oh, son of Clinias," said Alexis, a little embarrassed with his assigned role of message bearer; "I am not privileged to know all my colleague's secrets. My only task here is to bring you the message."

They met the following morning in a house that Alexis had rented in the City. They talked privately.

The Trapezites spoke in a very low voice, darting continuous glances toward the door, where one of his slaves made certain no one approached.

He began by confessing his admiration: Panathenian auriga; certain to win in Olympia; how he had celebrated his crowning; and then Potidaea; hero, race of heroes, Clinias, Clisthenes, Ajax; and now a brilliant politician; outstanding addresses before the Assembly; the most brilliant of the youngest...

What was the Colophonian trying to get at with all this beating around the bush? And why had he kept silent about the loans and the bets in Olympia? Very strange!

Pasion was convinced, oh, yes, he had no doubt that Alcibiades would be Pericles's successor, and he would be honored to place his experience and fortune at the service of that noble destiny. Pericles was already declining, and there was no one in the following age group in the demos or in the opposition, and Nicias was a fool, as the son of Clinias had said the day before, it was the talk of the City, and one of Pasion's eyes closed halfway as he talked, and he was constantly rubbing his thumb and index finger like spinners did, and so, what happened was that a few days earlier, someone had come to sell a stone, a sacred gem stolen from a temple, someone who had found it in the tall grass by the Areopagus, and Alcibiades, the am...! and Pasion nodding and hurrying on with his story, holding up a hand to ward off the interruption, and Alcibiades

363

. . . m-me . . . ! struggling with his mouth and eyes, and Pasion
was going to give it to him, and Alcibiades . . . th-thyst of
Athena?! and in a single spasm, he was on his feet, turning to
look at Pasion with stupor, censure, disconcert, fear, wanting
to laugh, babbling in confusion, pointing at Pasion in disbelief, blinking rapidly, scratching his head, pacing around the
room with his hands on his hips, turning to stare fixedly at
Pasion, and finally letting out a loud laugh and dropping into
a throne, pounding his knee and recalling the admirable,
divine, wise Socrates, who even in games got to the essence of
things, and Pasion, after a moment of terror, also laughed
spasmodically, one eye closing, and then they stared at each
other, face to face, nodding, as if everything had already been
said and understood, and the following day, Pasion was planning to return the amethyst directly to the Parthenon, but he
had a dream in which Alcibiades, crowned with the olive
branches of his victories, asked to be allowed to return the eye
of the Goddess, and in exchange, Pasion was to have his support and friendship, and very soon the Colophonian and his
sons would receive great benefits from his hands, and then
Pasion remembered that the twenty-eighth of Hecatombaion,
the Goddess' anniversary, was also the birthday of the son of
Clinias, and he decided that he had to heed the message in his
dream.

Alcibiades played the game. He liked that Colophonian, despite
his terrific ugliness. He was an old and money-wise gamester
who was betting on him, first in the chariot races and now in
the much riskier race for power. This flattered him and made
him take an instant liking to him.

 Pasion brought the amethyst out from under his robes.
When Alcibiades had it in his hands, he was amazed that he felt

neither fear nor guilt. What evil could stem from all that? None! On the contrary, the City would be grateful to him. In any case, he faked a tremor of devotion and kissed the stone.

The banker observed him with reverence.

Alcibiades told himself that it was well worth his while to have a rogue with so much logos, and so much money, on his side.

"And who was it that f-f-found the stone?"

"I cannot say," the banker answered. "I have taken an oath."

He admired the lie as well; the scoundrel was passing himself off as a believer.

The question was useless anyway. After Socrates's reasoning, who else could it be but the Cybernetes?

There was danger here. Porphyrius must never know about this. He had no doubts about the banker. He had given proof of admirable patience. After risking a fortune on him in Olympia, he had waited a full year to tell him.

Had he bought the stone thinking of Alcibiades?

No! Absurd! He had certainly bought it thinking of himself, or perhaps of one of his sons, to distinguish himself through some outstanding service to the City. Socrates was right: The Colophonian aspired to greater rights or citizenship. But Socrates had made him abort the stone. When the Colophonian heard about the conclusion Apollodorus had given birth to, he had been forced to change his plans. He could not claim to have found the stone. That was obvious. If he did, many would begin to believe that the story circulating in the City now was much more than a simple joke. It would become evident that Socrates had hit upon the truth. Pasion would be exposed to an accusation of sacrilegious commerce.

Exactly. And to avoid losing his investment, he was going to bet it all on Alcibiades again. A high-flying game. And very logical. After his success in Olympia and Potidaea, plus his two addresses before the Assembly, wasn't he a reasonable bet for a banker with the soul of a gambler?

Nevertheless, Pasion insisted that no one should know about the Olympic bet nor about their future friendship.

It was also hard to understand why he used Alexis, paying him a part of his profits, to remain behind the scenes. Any other foreigner would have swaggered around the City, bragging about his courage in betting or his devotion for equestrian sports, just like Alexis. How strange that he should prefer to keep silent . . . No matter. This was an ideal partner for ambitious undertakings. Did he have the Cybernetes muzzled with some threat? Be that as it may, it was simply stupid to run the risk of having a ruffian like that stumble onto the truth some day.

That was why . . .

Yes! That would meet with a speedy solution!

366

That very afternoon, Alcibiades ordered Phanes to abandon his plans to kidnap Lysis of Miletus for the time being. He locked himself away with him in one of the rooms. They had a long conversation in very subdued tones.

When the conversation was over, the Egghead sharpened his Persian dagger. Then he put on a rustic tunic, pulled a hood over his head, and set his mule on a course for Phalerum.

47

CLEONICE LAID A burning knee against him. Nicias drew his thigh away. His troubles took turns keeping him awake. When he was not thinking about the humiliation in the Pnyx, it was the two hateful obligations he had for the day: attending the ceremony at the Theseium and receiving that owl character who had sent the anonymous letter.

He sat on the edge of the bed, picked up his bassinet, and proceeded to pee as the drumming of the rain on the roof tiles grew stronger. The stream of piss striking the copper vessel played counterpoint to the rain and slowly entered into a ralentando until it harmonized with the patter on the roof.

The great hourglass by the little altar to Athena was running out, announcing the arrival of dawn.

He lit a torch and left the room for the cool air of the jasmine and honeysuckle tapestried court, walking naked along the paved edge of the colonnade, wet with the overflow from the full water vessels.

When he turned to the wall to light the great torches, the eunuch showed up, all obsequious, with his chiming voice.

Did the master need anything?

The slave women labored among the tremoring shadows of the kitchen.

Two of the gutters that collected the runoff from the roof surrounding the hypaithron were cracked; some of the water never made it to the great vessels, but formed puddles on the floor.

"Bring me linens and sandals," he ordered the boy, and began showering under the cool stream gushing into the hypaithron.

Confounded ceremony! There had to be some way of getting out of it!

Looking up into the sky, he saw black clouds scurrying along a gray, menacing background. A waft of dung and lavender reached him from the Eridanus pastures. The shadows of the peristyle wavered across the whitewashed wall.

The plump, hairless eunuch returned at a trot, placed the sandals on the floor, and waited by a column, linens draped over his arm to dry his master.

Nicias enjoyed the rain a long while. The eight hydrias were almost full.

He raised his arms to the eaves around the hypaithron to deflect one of the wooden spouts and let the full force of the stream fall directly on his head. The holy water sent by Zeus inspired him to consult Melas about the message.

As the boy dried him, his thoughts went back to the tribute to Theseus.

How could he get out of it?

Impossible! After Aspasia's acquittal, it would be interpreted as cowardice. Impassive and proud, as on the battlefield, he would see it through. When the party of celebrants stopped to praise Micon's latest travesties, Nicias would stand by the remains of Theseus and pray for inspiration in this predicament.

When the boy finished drying him, he returned to his bed, where his wife was still sleeping. He put on his robe and walked over to the kitchen; his two pieces of bread were waiting for him, one with oil and garlic and the other dipped in wine. He ate nothing. He had just a sip of warm sage tea and went over to the andronitis; all his men, slaves and freemen, were already up and waiting for him.

The rain had stopped and the sky was clearing. Two slaves carried pitchers of water from the hydrias in the court to the men's bathroom. Street vendors were already coming out in force and the neighbors grinding the grain for the noon meal thudded their mortars almost in unison with the chink of chisels. There were many sculptors in this section of the City.

Hiero and Melas were talking with the economus in his office. As soon as they saw Nicias, they all stood and wished him health and joy on the Feasts of Theseus.

As he did every thirtieth and fifteenth of each month, Nicias began to pace around the court with the economus to hear the report on events at his farm and the bimonthly balance of accounts. One thousand one hundred and twelve slaves rented to the mines, three dead, seventeen sick, the income from Laurium for the fortnight was twenty-eight minae, minus five hundred and twenty drachmas for the dead slaves and two hundred and four obols for the sick, that came to twenty-six minae and twenty drachmas, and from the quarries, so much, and from the farm, and the wool, and the milk, the chickens, eggs, purchase of sheep, loaves of bread . . .

Nicias was no longer listening. He could not get the anonymous message out of his mind. The sender wanted no less than one thousand of the two thousand seven hundred and twenty drachmas he had earned in Laurium in the past two weeks.

But what hurt the son of Niceratus most was the insolence of demanding an oath on his own altar, as if his word were not his bond, like some ruffian without honor. He called Hiero and ordered him to receive the man, show him the purse with the money, allow him to count it if he liked. Nicias would not see the scoundrel; let Hiero take care of everything, the oath as well.

He ordered the economus to make ready his black horse. He sent Hiero on his way, called Melas, and continued pacing around the columns slowly, hands clasped behind his back, staring at the tips of his sandals.

Melas kept in front of him, twisting his body until he was walking almost sideways. It was crucial to see his face, and there was little light in the hypaithron at that time of day. When one is a professional diviner, the first thing one has to divine is what the client wants to hear.

Nicias wanted him to be on the lookout for the slightest omen. What should he do about delivering the money demanded in the message? Should he pay? Should he believe the man? Should he take the oath?

While Nicias was busy at the shrine of Theseus, Melas was to rally all his powers and have an answer ready by noon.

To avoid having to cross the agora with hundreds of indiscreet eyes watching and waspish tongues wagging, Nicias decided not to take the Street of the Tripods. Escorted by Hiero and two lackeys who made way for him, he headed for the Theseium by the route that led around the back of the Temple of Hephaestus, following the twisting path that meandered between the Pnyx and the Areopagus. It was the trail used by herdsmen, laborers, and washer women on their way to the fountain of the Museum with their bundles on their heads.

Things were not going well. Nicias imagined that all his countrymen, at whom he dared not look, were smiling at his failure in the trial against Aspasia. Had she been sentenced, he would have ridden victorious and arrived at that asinine ceremony along the Street of the Tripods, letting everyone get a good look at him and even stopping a while in the agora.

But the fact was that the trial fiasco was not what was bothering him; it was just one more lost battle, like any other in the life of a general. What really disturbed him was that, because of this failure, he could no longer keep Onion Head from continuing to magnify the significance of the Synoecia to the detriment of the traditional Theseian festival of autumn. What he had done to those festivals was infamous! Over the last few years, without the citizens even suspecting what was going on, Pericles had gradually stripped the Theseia of all their solemnity, turning them into mere contests of equestrian and athletic skill, with torch races and other games for the young. In the meantime, he had been imbuing the Synoecia with a religious atmosphere they had never had, and all this just to transform them, like the Coexistence Festivities, into a reverent framework for the political activism and prominence of his gang of foreign supporters.

That morning, Micon, that servile snake, would unveil his paintings before the Priest of Theseus and the other Primates, Archons, and strategi in ungodly connivance with the Milesian bitch, Hippodamus, Ictinus, Callicrates, Polygnotus, and all his accomplices in their ostentatious marble and philosophy, under the protective shadow of the national hero.

Everyone knew that Micon had intentionally delayed the conclusion of his paintings to prevent the remodeled shrine from being opened during the past Theseia, delaying it until now to suit the Head's plans.

And there they were. On the three broad steps of the shrine, still closed off, stood a throng of personalities and foreigners. There was the proud bitch, victorious, showing off her Ionian hairdo, receiving the praise of the chorus, the object of admiration and envy, standing by the Great Priestess of Athena, and moments later, Pericles, blah, blah, inaugurating, blabbing, and the multitude crowding in from the agora, listening to him invoke the protection of the hero for all the inhabitants of Attica, both Athenians and foreigners, and then, sacrilege, infamy, the bitch herself, the unworthy hetaera, the false teacher of rhetoric, just a few steps away from the sacred bones of Theseus, singing praise for Toxaris, the doctor hero for whose services the City expressed its gratitude by sacrificing white victims at his shrine, and for Scyllias of Scyone, the diver of Salamis, and the great artists, architects, masters of music, of rhetoric, philosophers. What a disgrace! Would no one ever stop her? Was it possible that not a single voice from among the many would make itself heard? And Aspasia now mentioning the irreverent Anaxagoras of Clazomenae, the Head's teacher, who doubted the existence of the Gods, and she even dared mention the proscribed Phidias, thief, liar, fugitive? Would he have to put up with that?

When the doors opened, the official party got its first glimpse of Theseus, a striking resemblance to Alcibiades, on one of the walls, commanding the battle between the Athenians and the Amazons. On the opposite wall were Centaurs and Lapiths; to the side, Theseus and Amphitrite in their underwater meeting. The affront so galled the son of Niceratus that he was simply unable to see anything, not even the outraged faces of his friends, who could do nothing but exchange furious glances. Impossible to vent their indignation in a shrine! Not even the headstrong Lysanias dared make a move. They all knew that it would only suit the Head's designs; they never imagined that she, she! who until the day before had been charged with procuring and pornosboskia, would presume to take the floor and go so far as to mention the names of the proscribed Anaxagoras and Phidias. Pythodorus's face was so completely drained of blood that he seemed about to pass out.

Nicias concentrated all his efforts on keeping a straight face.

On the way home he shook silently, letting out his pent-up wrath. He was impervious to the heat and never heard the clamor of the noonday cicadas. What a blow this must be to the ghost of Cimon!

The anonymous message writer was named Habron. He had shown up just after Nicias left for the tribute to Theseus. The altogether unsavory individual was missing an arm and carried on his forehead the owl that the Samians branded on their Athenian prisoners. Hiero showed him the purse with the one thousand drachmas and offered to take the oath, but the rogue insisted that it be the son of Niceratus. He was to swear before his own altar to Hestia, invoke the Gods that Habron would name, and swear by his daughters, his soul, and his sword. Habron said he would return at midday, and if Nicias refused, he would go directly to Pericles.

And as soon as the Owl left, Melas saw in the mirror of his visions a great ear. They had to listen to the man. The successive green flashes of flame in the fire of "the well-wrought Altar of Zeus of the Court" ratified the vision. He was convinced that there was no other way; it was preferable to put up with the humiliation of the oath the beggar demanded than to run the risk of having the man actually know something and go to Pericles with the information.

When the man returned, Nicias locked himself away with him in the andron. He swore with his hands and lips, with his palms raised to the fire of Hestia, repeating everything the Owl recited. He reiterated that he, Nicias, son of Niceratus, agreed to pay one thousand drachmas to Habron, son of Eratosthenes, if the information on the theft of the Goddess' eye was proven correct; if Nicias reneged on the payment, may Hera make his two daughters barren and take them both without leaving descendants to honor his tomb, may Hecate forever mortify his contemptible soul, may Ares break his sword in battle, may Pallas Athena make him the great loser in Athenian politics, may Apollo turn all courts against him and shoot pestilent darts at his cattle, may Zeus help his slaves run away and send him terrible epidemics, may Hermes ruin his business and send thieves against him, and may Zeus, Hera, Apollo, Pallas, Ares, Hermes, and Hecate end his life with a long, vile-smelling, painful death if he did not fulfill his promise to Habron, son of Eratosthenes.

The Owl was satisfied. He stood there before Nicias watching Melas and Hiero enter the room, then the three of them sitting, inquisition, severe eyes fixed on him, doubting that thousand-drachma truths could be hidden behind those tattered rags, and Nicias, with an air of indignation, hand on his chin, well, out with it, and then the Owl going on about the Amazon, seven hundred drachmas, huge chryselephantine whore, very blond and white and fat, great drinker, sponge, bets in Phalerum, Piraeus, Scyron, a fortune in six months, two shows a day, unbeaten, bad streak in gambling, two slaves fled to Megara, no money, only the Amazon, and around the time of the theft from the Goddess, Owl making many plans, need for fancy clothes

for Amazon, new campaign around the taverns of the surrounding demes where she was unknown, and an Athenian soldier on guard at the Areopagus suggested visiting the Scythian
barracks, good bets, and although as slaves of the State they
were obol-less, many had valuable possessions, and others who
attended were retired, and some with money from training
Molossian hounds, and then he took her around the back,
where whores were allowed, and the Amazon beat five
Scythians the first time out, and the Owl won twenty drachmas
despite the wheat wine, and the second time was even better, a
gold fibula and an engraved copper chalice he sold for thirty
drachmas, and the Amazon attributed her resistance to a spell
learned among the witches of Thrace, and she always put her
hair up with a wooden tibia clasped with a fibula, and there was
a small amethyst set in the tibia, and before drinking the first
pitcher, the Amazon took off the brooch, let her hair down,
closed her eyes, and mumbled something holding one hand
over her mouth while with the other she rubbed the amethyst
over her temples and stomach, and during the third visit to the
barracks, a Scythian named Scolotus found the Owl and offered
him a Persian dagger with a silver handle inlaid with two emer-
alds in exchange for the spell, the dagger was a war trophy
picked up in Samos and worth eighty drachmas, but the Owl
refused, he had already tried the spell and gotten so drunk he
almost died, and if it failed with the Scythian, there would be
trouble, and winding up along some road with an arrow
through him simply wasn't worth eighty drachmas, but a few
days later, Scolotus insisted, and besides the dagger, he offered
a Molossian hound or an old mare, and the mare got him thinking, because if the spell didn't work, he could always ride away
on the mare, take his fat Amazon out of Attica, and it sounded
sweet to his ears, working the pilgrim's road to Olympia, or to

375

Delphi and Dodona, and they would take on all comers on the roads of Hellas, and after sleeping on it, he sought out Scolotus, took a look at the mare, and closed the deal, and he spent days learning the spell in the barbarian tongue, and the more he repeated it, the dumber it seemed to trade a mare and a dagger for a few words, and he decided to give himself time to get far enough away if the spell failed, so he told the Scythian that he had to get himself an amethyst, that was it, because the spell only worked for the person who had stolen it, and he figured that while the Scythian looked for some drunk or some porne to waylay, he would have enough time to get away from Attica with his Amazon, and the Scythian agreed, and they exchanged oaths in the Temple of Ares, and then they had to spend a whole afternoon together to get the Scythian, with his granite brain, to learn the Amazon's spell, and three days later, after buying her robes, rouge, an Amazon helmet, a quiver, and arrows, they left the City, a single tit for all to see, heading for the Boreas, and did the excellent son of Niceratus know when all that happened? Well, a few days before the sacrilegious theft against Athena in the Parthenon. Could anyone doubt that Scolotus was the thief, especially when the whole City knew that it was that very Scythian who had first seen and clubbed the Macedonian who was passed off as the culprit?

48

A ND WHEN brother Shipwreck returned from Delos and Fire-eater from Megara without having seen or heard anything of One Eye, Lysis broke out crying in disappointment and saying that he had probably gone off to Egypt, or even further, and you silenced your anger at the Gods of the Sum, who first revealed to Lysis the whereabouts of the Dindymenian Eye, and after you, going through so much trouble to get into Laurium, with turds, with astute horses' hooves, with poisoned honey, and then polishing your pate so that it would shine without Sosias seeing you, and so much sweating for what? so that after you talking with Xanthus and learning who having stone, Gods, puff! One Eye gone, spoor of Dindymenian Eye gone again? and when brother Fire-eater wanting to kidnap Nicias, and Lysis very much crazy wanting to steal ark of anacrisis, you order tongues no wag, forbid crying and gloom, and lie down to get signal from Gods, and not letting anyone talk, and five days ago Cybernetes scaring

Truncheon, threatening to tell Nicias that she seeing amethyst stone in hands of One Eye, and Lysis coming very happy to you, and you saying, you see, impatient woman, Gods foresee everything, and this time it was Lysis who speak with thoughts like knife that stab and cut and get to bone of truth, and telling you that if Cybernetes demanding money from Truncheon, that mean One Eye told him that he offer stone to Truncheon, and Lysis saying that very logicus, that if One Eye so trust Cybernetes to tell him secret, then very possible Cybernetes know hiding place of One Eye, and then you have Cybernetes watched, so when he alonely, brothers of the Sum take him and popopom on the head, and bring him on brother Green-grocer's cart, and then you look at him deep and ask in which where One Eye hiding, and then all brothers and sisters of Sum saying yes, very astute plan, and from that day, no person in brotherhood of Sum beating skinny, boneless ideas, and you appointed Kidnap Committee to follow Cybernetes with invisible steps, and first day Cybernetes gambling monies of Truncheon in dens of Phalerum, and another day passing, and another, and on fourth day of following, he always with people, by selfly never, and on fifth day, brothers in ambush and Sosias in tree watchfullest, finally seeing at dusk when Cybernetes going out by selfly, and Green-grocer with net and Fire-eater with club like you use to escape Damas, and Cybernetes walking by oak grove to docks, and Sosias whistling whistle of Sum, and then going home to tell you that when Cybernetes approaching, oh, long scream, and from other trees more far away, Sosias seeing man with hood, and with first stab Cybernetes great scream, but hood man cover mouth and stab many times, and Sosias counting, five, six, eight, oh, eleven stabs, and in struggle hood fall back and Sosias much diaphanes see Egghead, Alcibiades's freeman, who quickly stoop down, and Sosias thinking that to search and steal, and then fixing hood and looking all ways, and running through trees, and when approaching corpse, all brothers seeing three fingers cut off, much samely like Pandarus, and all seeing in three-finger hand much sacred signal of Sum, and Otep and Shipwreck and all five brothers swearing, saying that Sosias talking faithful, and Carian much certain stabber is Alcibiades's freeman, and now you turn, only you, oh, Summoner of the Sum, you five days much sharp thinking, thinking with apocalyptical sharpness until arrive at evil truth that Alcibiades have Cybernetes killed because he, too, ask vile money, like ask from Truncheon, and then diaphanestly clear that Cybernetes know that Alcibiades also know of stone, knowing that Alcibiades very knowing and much accomplice, or maybe same Alcibiades, yes, buying stone from One Eye, and again you see that your footsteps have been preordained, from that very first day in Pamphylia to this very last as you rise from the bed to call Lysis, and obeying what the Sum has inspired in you, carefully putting one word on the other, you order her to fall in love again with the beautiful Alcibiades, son of Clinias, but this time with double edge and great trap.

379

49

OF COURSE, with a second mutilated hand, the many are going to think that the murderers of Pandarus are still free, and that the wizard Perdiccas is indeed still hexing the City, so Phanes not only freed you forever of the evil tongue of Porphyrius the Cybernetes, he actually unleashed a new terror on the City, and the day when you miraculously find the eye, some will believe you out of fear and others out of ignorance, but all will want to believe, and they will bless you like a new Cimon, that is a certainty, it cannot fail, so on with it, forget about kidnapping Lysis for a while, because you have to move fast, and the fact is that Pasion's gift has brought things to a head, could it be true, as Socrates says, that Cimon really believed he had found Theseus's bones? Of course, the Athenians let themselves be impressed with his great personal glory, because he was his father's son, yes, but Cimon was a nobody when he was twenty, and all of Hellas already knows you, and the fact is that when Cimon won his battles in Thrace and Pamphylia, he was already thirty-five, whereas you, why, at twenty you were already dining at the Prytaneum, and the only thing Cimon had over you was that his father was Athens's greatest forefather, but in nothing else could he compare to you, and if one as ugly as Cimon, such a bad orator, never a winner in the choruses or in the races, got himself sanctified by the Athenians for his fraudulent rescue of Theseus's skeleton, what else could they do but sanctify you, a friend of the logos, a favorite of the Gods, for rescuing the true eye of Athena? And if the many believed in that pack of bones brought in by Cimon after pockmarking the whole of the lonely island of Scyros, all the more reason for believing in you when you find the stone before thousands of Athenian witnesses, so you have to devote all your nous to designing some very convincing scheme, and remember, you have only ten days, and you still have to find a reliable bronze-smith . . .

The sound of steps interrupted his train of thought.

Someone was walking on the dry leaves.

Ah, it was Phanes.

The purple circles under the Phoenician's eyes had grown even larger with his recent vigil. His bones showed through the sharp, yellowish contours of his face. When he smiled, like now, he seemed to be suffering.

Alcibiades, who had been walking nude along the banks of the Ilissus, stopped in his tracks, questioningly. Why had he returned so soon? Had they already discovered the body?

Yes, the day before, at dusk.

Were there many c-c-commentaries?

The agora was in an uproar, they talked of nothing else. Phanes had been listening to the different versions all morning; many were already convinced that One Eye was in the City, and since the body had been found in an oak grove, in a gully . . .

Fine, anything else?

Yes, Phanes had come because on returning home from the agora, he had seen Otep the Libyan delivering a note to the door slave, and then seeing who the sender was ...

He turned the roll over to Alcibiades, who received it with a grimace of intrigue.

Well, so it was ...

LYSIS OF MILETUS TO ALCIBIADES

It has been six days since I saw you again and I regret not having been nicer to you. Aphrodite would have me offer a tribute to your feats, at my house. There is nothing to pay. If you accept, set the date and let me know how many guests you will be having. Be happy.

Alcibiades let the papyrus drop on the grass, turned pensive, smiled, and suddenly dove between two rocks. When he came to the surface, he fixed his eyes, unseeing, on the greenish light that sparkled on the sacred olive tree. Again he saw her pink flesh, her thighs. So he would not have to kidnap her after all?

Fine. He would take care of her after the Panathenian Games. Right now, he had to devote all his efforts and attention to preparing a convincing scheme for the delivery of the stone.

He came out of the water and sat on a large rock. Close by a cicada was chirping. He sprawled naked on the rock and covered his eyes with his forearm.

The first thing to be decided was the part about his visions. Where, when, before whom? At the Ecclesia? Impossible. It would not be convened until after the Panathenians. In the agora? No, not there either. Too many people. The noise would drown out anything he said. In his own home? No, someone might suspect that it had been contrived. And if he invited people, there might be doubts. Right out in the street, then? Hardly. He had no intention of staging his drama for passersby. Far better to choose his witnesses. And suddenly he opened his eyes and sat upright on the rock. What if he choose the banquet offered by Lysis in his honor as the stage for his visions?

He sprang up full of energy, put on his chiton, returned home, and wrote a note:

FROM THE SON OF CLINIAS TO LYSIS OF MILETUS
You may honor me with a banquet for twenty couches. You will contract the finest musicians in Athens; there will be games and prizes; there will be acrobats and comedians. It will take place at your house, two days hence. I shall decide tomorrow who my guests shall be. Please send your reply with my messenger. Be happy.

And Phanes left with the papyrus.

383

50

RUMOR AGAIN REIGNED in the streets. The City was filled with hope at the confession that Nicias of Niceratus had just gotten out of the Scythian Scolotus.

Almost two years earlier, when the theft of the amethyst from the Parthenon was discovered, Scolotus had testified that from the entrance of the sacrarium of the opistodomus, where he was standing guard, he had seen a man from behind, who was getting too close to the base on the side that supports the Goddess' left leg. Although he could not see exactly what the man was doing, Scolotus saw him extend his hand toward the bas-relief representing the birth of Pandora. Since the man's actions seemed very suspicious, Scolotus walked toward the man who, on seeing him approach, took off in the opposite direction. When the Scythian noticed that the eye had been tampered with and the stone was missing, he gave pursuit. The righteous indignation in Scolotus's arguments, his ill-sustained reasons during the beating of the Macedonian: it was all a fraud, and so cunning that none of the supervisors of the temple guards ever suspected that they were being taken in. The uproar and the commotion started by Scolotus spoke for him. No one suspected, not even when, after the beating and the search, the amethyst was not found on the Macedonian. Neither was it found in his stools, which were checked during the days of interrogation and torture. When the investigation was completed, the Archon Lysanias arrived at the conclusion that, after the theft of the stone, the Macedonian had succeeded in giving it to an accomplice, who had hidden it or gotten away from the scene unnoticed.

But Nicias, son of Niceratus, had gotten to the bottom of things. With public opinion fully persuaded by the evidence, the impious Scythian was categorically convicted of the theft. Who could have imagined that a man of that rugged, rustic race, so praised for its obedience and honesty, would be capable of reenacting the wiles of a Sisyphus, or of an Odysseus Laertid?

385

His craftiness was so great that he took the eye from the Parthenon right under the very noses of at least thirty visitors. He had prepared everything down to the last detail. The amethyst was wedged into a hole in the marble. Athena's profile was looking down on the infant, Pandora. The stone was held in exclusively by the plaster eyelids. Scolotus confessed under torture that, when he approached with the pretext of inspecting the bas-relief, he was already carrying a small knife in his hand and, with a single stab, cracked the eyelids, took out the eye, and hid it in his clothing before starting his ruckus and sounding the alarm.

It was also public knowledge that, at the beginning of the torture, the Scythian withstood the most terrible torments without uttering a word. But his will was soon overcome and he confessed to a string of crimes. He admitted that he had perpetrated the sacrilege under orders from King Perdiccas, for whom he was an agent and who had promised to allow him to reside in Macedonia as one of the court guards. It was also perfectly substantiated that he, Scolotus, and none other, had facilitated the escape of Xanthus the Lycian and that, with his complicity and that of One Eye, they had consummated the human sacrifice in the sanctuary of Dionysus Omestes.

When he was asked the meaning of the mutilation, he said that he merely followed Macedonian orders without inquiring about the reasons. He denied having any accomplices other than Xanthus and One Eye. Unfortunately, when Evileye, the torturer contracted by Nicias, tightened the iron band around his head too far, the prisoner's skull caved in, killing him instantly.

As was required in interrogations for the crime of impiety, witnesses from the King's Tribunal had been called. But they were delayed, and given the premature death of the prisoner, the Substantiator of the Anacrisis himself, Hiero, who was serving as tachygrapher scribe, and the aforementioned Evileye, swore before the Altar of the Twelve Gods that their description of the proceedings was faithful to the recorded minutes.

Thanks to the son of Niceratus, the City was purified of the two impieties that had polluted it for months.

Nicias's peace of mind, however, was short-lived. On the afternoon of the same day, the news got out about the discovery of another body with the fingers cut off; when the people found out that the dead man was Porphyrius the Cybernetes, the terror of the citizens increased, and there were many who recalled that, whenever Evileye was called in to apply the torments, the prisoners invariably confessed to anything the Substantiator was trying to substantiate.

Everyone wanted Nicias to be right and for the City to be

really free of any threat, but what was the meaning of those mutilated fingers on the Cybernetes? It was only logical to assume that whoever had cut the fingers off Pandarus the Scythian was probably the same one who had mutilated Porphyrius in exactly the same way. Was it really true that One Eye had left the territory?

At dusk that day, which had begun so auspiciously with the confession of Scolotus, the brows of the citizens again darkened. The agora, the porticos, and the barbershops were soon deserted and once again the roofs of the City were plumed with the oily smoke of expiatory sacrifices.

51

FROM ASPASIA IN ATHENS
TO EURIDICE IN SARDES

The eighteenth of Hecatombaion

WE'VE WON. Just three days ago, Pericles won my acquittal. He was never more eloquent or more coura- geous. He spoke with power; he shed genuine tears; he gazed at me with such adoring love that, quite against all the forecasts and my own pessimism, he destroyed the plot. His indignation at the defamation was so convincing that it touched the Helliasts, who absolved me unanimously amid the cheers of our supporters.

After so many months of uncertainty and nightmares, I still wake up drenched in perspiration. I look around me, touch myself, smell, I get up on my elbows and shake my hair to assure myself that it is not a cruel dream. I no longer have to choose between exile and poison.

This verdict has given me back the light, my books, my loved ones. And you. And here I am, at first light, sitting in my courtyard, once again enjoying a waft of jasmine and the crow of the cocks.

To your reproaches for my year-long silence, to your fears for not having any news of us, I can only reply that for many weeks I lay waning for lack of sleep and nourishment, hoarding my strength to keep control of myself before my Pericles and to console myself every day with the conviction that all this cruelty heaped upon me by Athens was well worth the privilege of my twenty years here beside the most important man in all Hellas. Forgetfulness will be my balm; the wound is deep, but I must see it healed. May nothing ever again be said of this infamy.

The nineteenth

It is true, the triple champion is Alcibiades of Clinias. I did not know that his fame had gotten so far beyond the borders of Hellas. But the news that most likely has not gotten to Sardes is that, after his Olympic victories, he distinguished himself on the battle fields of Chalcidice. Of course, anointed with glory at the age of twenty and heir to the estate of Clinias, he is the most promising young man in the City.

He has never met with Cleis again. She is now at the pinnacle of her fame. The City boasts about having her; they say that in all the known world there is no hetaera like her. She is the newest attraction for rich visitors. The Athenians are so proud of her that they they claim to outdo Corinth in the worship of Aphrodite; hers is the first name they mention.

It would seem that my fears of a year ago were a bit exaggerated. That metragyrtes I loathed so much does not appear to have done her any harm. Truncheon insists that, for the first time in her life, Cleis is free of dread and that the new influence

389

has made her uncharacteristically serene and poised. Now I feel that through some dark dealing of that man's, I, too, am in his debt. In my very presence, one of the brightest personalities in Athens has praised the beauty and paideia of Lysis of Miletus. Poets write eulogies and hymns comparing her to Helen. Her open banquet and her callipygian dances have become the most expensive evening entertainment in the City, and she, the Tenth Muse, yields to the ardors of mortal men only when she is moved by the weight of their purses. For gold, as she confessed to me in a letter, is the only masculine virtue her new priestly dignity compels her to respect. And since she officiates with all her mind set on building temples, she gives herself to men with an enthousiasmos that precludes any concern for virile attractions, lineage, or logos. I, personally, do not see how it is possible, but the fact is that, with her new religion, she has learned to find joy in whomever she serves in her bed. Her explanation is that, since her bed is an altar to Aphrodite Pandemos, her caresses and orgasms there must be as genuine as the gold that buys them.

390

I swear to you by Pallas that all of the absurd and dark dealings behind her success often fill me with panic terror, but then I tell myself that I should not be concerned with things I know nothing of, because perhaps she has found the safest path to the goals she has set herself in life.

I have not actually seen her in months. She quit coming to my house to protect me. You know, someone saw through her disguise and accused me of procuring for Pericles. I never told you before now, but that was the first point in the writ accusing me of pornosboskia. Forgive me. I forgot myself; I refuse to talk about that.

Fortunately, no one has discovered that we are related. Since it was impossible for me to see her, I confided my secret to Hippodamus, who, despite his years, is still quite nocturnal. I asked him to mediate, and for all these long months, he has been my faithful courier and emissary. Ah, but I refuse to give up hope of seeing her, even if it is I who must don the disguise. In fact, I already did it, once.

About a year ago, when they discovered her visits to me, I hurried to send a note asking her not to come again, but the following day we met at Truncheon's. I wore a wig and all sorts of stuffings, and walked with the same limp as one of my cooks.

Oh, do you remember the Scythian archer sacrificed to Dionysus Omestes? Well, the culprit confessed his guilt; it was that fugitive slave that Cleis wanted me to buy for her. Well, you can just imagine; seeing her mixed up in such affairs, and with the company she was keeping, I feared the worst. But curiously enough, I suspect that I, too, received a great boon from that company. In fact, I am practically certain of it, because that time at Truncheon's, Cleis questioned me in great detail about the writ against me, about the witness who recognized her, and about two others bribed by Pericles's enemies. Then, just a few days before the trial, she told me, through Hippodamus, that those maligning tongues would henceforth be as quiet as Talthybius, Agamemnon's lookout.

And that was the way things worked out, to everyone's surprise, especially Pericles, who had seen them very recently spreading evil gossip about me.

The day before yesterday, when Hippodamus asked Cleis how much the ox weighed that had stilled the enemy tongues, she answered that the brothers of the New Church could persuade without spending an obol; the words of the High Priest, sharper and much weightier than a hundred gold oxen, were quite enough. From the few bits of information I have managed to piece together, I deduce that magic rather

391

than money was employed to my benefit. The witnesses were so uncertain and wavering during the trial that their testimony worked much more strongly for my defense than for the prosecution. Yes, I am convinced that there was no money involved.

The twenty-first

Since it was magic we were talking about when I cut off two days ago, let me tell you that the City is still racked by superstitious fears fanned by our enemies here and abroad.

Two hundred years ago, an armed group stormed and occupied the Acropolis in an attempt to make Cylon, a eupatrid and Olympic champion, tyrant of Athens. When there was no doubt about their failure, they took refuge in the temples, deprived of food and water. The Alcmeonidae, who at the time were in charge of the guard of the Acropolis, swore that their lives would be spared if they surrendered. When they did surrender, the Alcmeonidae had their throats cut. As the news spread and the Athenians found out about the horrendous violation of the oath, they voted to expel the Alcmeonidae and put a curse on their line forever as the only way to cleanse the territory. But a few decades later, the Alcmeonidae returned and recovered their former power. For a few months now, the ambassadors of the Peloponnesus have been demanding throughout Hellas that the first condition to be met prior to any truce or pact with Athens is that the City restore the curse and exile the Alcmeonidae. They have gone so far as to file a protest in Elis contesting Alcibiades's victories. This offensive has served the purposes of Pericles's enemies in stirring up the superstitious fear of the many. But he has turned the tables on the Spartans, demanding that they must first purify themselves, for their present dynasts are heirs to another, much more recent violation, the one committed in Taenarum, when they massacred a group of rebel helots who had claimed sanctuary in the Temple of Poseidon.

Albeit without oaths or sacrifices and libations, our internal enemies have made an open alliance with the Spartan campaign against Pericles. Nicias is behind the intrigues; the day before my trial, he had his henchmen write on the City walls: "Death to the unclean Alcmeonidae, defenders of procuresses."

Are you beginning to get an idea of how great Pericles's eloquence had to be to win my absolution? He admitted, however, that the change of temper in the witnesses was decisive in swaying the opinion of the judges.

As regards to his personal war with Nicias, when he arrived last night, he was euphoric. He had just found out about the discovery of another body with a mutilated hand. The event has unleashed a new terror in the City, and people are openly questioning Nicias's hoax in connection with the mutilation of the Scythian archer.

These are, then, the wars that occupy the Greeks of here and there: age-old prejudices and severed fingers their weapons. I often wonder if the light will ever penetrate the specter-ridden souls of mortal men.

The twenty-third

Yesterday, when I was making ready to seal these scrolls and send them off with a slave, Hippodamus brought Polus of Acragas, a young sophist and a disciple of Gorgias of Leontini, who has become a friend to us.

Hippodamus forced the visit on me because he wanted to surprise me with news about Cleis, so I had to postpone sending the scroll to be able to tell you all about it.

The twenty-fourth

I was interrupted yesterday, but today I refuse to see anyone.

Cleis and Alcibiades are at it again.

A few days ago she danced for him, but she charged him a fortune and then locked him out of her room. But guess what? Yesterday she held one of the most splendid banquets Athens has seen this year. For Alcibiades, and completely free.

Hippodamus told me that Polus was one of the guests and had given him a detailed description of the affair, which he would probably repeat for me if I asked him.

However, when Hippodamus led up to the topic, Polus seemed to avoid it. I explained my interest in finding out something, at least, about the hetaera Lysis of Miletus. According to the writ accusing me before the tribunal of procuring, it was precisely this famous compatriot of mine whom I had used to gratify Pericles in our own home. When the young Sicilian began to hide behind the limits imposed upon him by the fact that I was a woman, I accused him of treating me like an ignorant matron and threatened to withdraw my friendship. Pericles, who had joined us during dinner, encouraged him to have out with it, for I would interpret the most ribald or immoral details as a tribute to my open-mindedness and paideia.

Polus apologized and explained that there was nothing really immoral, just some very unrestrained libidinousness, and that if it was my will, he would tell all, as if he were among men. I will transcribe his words as far as I can remember:

Lysis kept out of sight until Alcibiades arrived. He was accompanied by Timon of Cyrene, Anaximenes of Colophon, and myself. The rest, some fourteen, who had also been invited by the guest of honor and were awaiting his arrival in the courtyard, were unable to hold back gasps and exclamations when she made her entry escorted by three callipygians and a dozen ravishing slaves carrying garlands and wreaths for the guests. They were all wearing transparent pepli and walked like Goddesses. One of Alcibiades's intimates feigned an attack and dropped dead on the floor amid the laughter of the others. Almost all of them were young eupatrids, comrades of Alcibiades in his outrages and epheby. Of his older friends, there were only Critias and Pyrilampes the Birdman. I found it strange that Socrates and his many admirers were absent; according to my information, they are the Cliniad's favorite company these days.

While her companions took care of the others, Lysis came to us alone and crowned Alcibiades with myrtle, ivy, and pine. She gave us garlands of poplar and violets. Her jet-black hair tumbled over her shoulders, and all she was wearing was some alkanet on her lips and a rose-colored peplus, the only one that was not completely transparent and therefore the most enticing. Perched atop her Persian cork-platform sandals, she was almost as tall as the son of Clinias.

Her nearness moved me as much as it had a few days earlier, when she danced for Alcibiades. So great is my turmoil that over a whole week I have found myself time and time again thinking about that dance. Her nude body is of an almost sinful perfection. And she knows it. Behind her wet lips and the rare smile of her eyes, she seems to be saying, "Don't you feel sorry for yourself, you sad soul, going through your whole life without a taste of me?" and with the pitiful certainty that I could not in a whole year of my sophistics earn enough for a single week in her bedroom, I have felt primitive, ignorant, even cowardly. I have accused myself of going around preaching that there are only uncertain truths and never daring to make of my

395

life a summation of glorious moments. Could there possibly be a more absolute truth than a night in the arms of Lysis? That woman could destroy any philosopher! Even Socrates would be lost if she directed a loving glance at him. If Protagoras of Abdera could one day be master of those thighs, they would become the measure of all things, insofar as they are, or insofar as they are not.

After crowning Alcibiades, Lysis went on to Timon and Anaximenes. Me, she called by my name and treated like an old friend. As she crowned me, she laid a hand on my chest, and I stole a fleeting touch of her forearm. Timon and Anaximenes got so flustered that they began to shower her with silly praise, just as I had done the first time. In her presence, they lose all the wit they brandish when they have control of themselves.

Alcibiades was more sober and natural. After letting himself be crowned without a word, he followed Lysis, who had taken him by the hand.

As they passed along the peristyle to the andron, acrobats and actors greeted the Cliniad with leaps and cheers of welcome. No less than five women followed. I calculated that, counting the callipygians, slaves, and women of the Muses, there were quite enough for everyone to get his share.

Twenty-one couches were ready in the broad andron, luxuriously faced with marble up to a height of three cubits. Lysis took her place together with Alcibiades on the eleventh; the rest of us had our choice.

Around the oval, there were two long tables covered with tureens, trays, richly engraved chalices, and baskets of bread. Somewhere between two large hydrias and several amphorae stood the cupbearer, an old eunuch, aided by four adolescent female slaves with nude torsos and budding breasts. Outside the oval there were several large chairs prepared for the arrival of personalities who needed no invitation, for the magnificence of the banquet was known to the entire City.

The twenty-fifth

Yesterday I had to interrupt Polus because one of my back teeth began to hurt. Let me tell you that this mouth of mine, which you so praised, has already lost twenty teeth, but I still have nine healthy, white front teeth with no gaps visible. Today at dawn, I had the torturous tooth pulled, and now that the pain has lessened, I can try to finish my letter.

Polus the Sicilian, whom I considered rather circumspect and insipid, turned out to be of surprising spirit and quite entertaining. His story kept me fascinated until very late, and he told it in such interesting detail that I shall only be able to give you the most prominent events, that is, if I expect to get this scroll on its way to you tomorrow.

Alcibiades, as always, appointed himself symposiarch of the feast, but this time he ordered a very tame mixture, spaced the rounds, and used his authority to prevent premature drunkenness. So halfway through the second tables, the wine was still bright and the feast was orderly. After the acrobats, when the company was calling for the callipygians and the moment seemed ripe for putting a bit more life into the party, Alcibiades ordered the actors to come on before the dancers.

They announced the rescue of Danae, a famous scene from Aeschylus's *Diktyoulkoi*. Suddenly, Alcibiades got up from the couch, whispered something in Cleis's ear, and walked off barefoot to where the chorus was getting ready. Then, when the satyrs entered escorting the lascivious Silenus, Alcibiades was among them, his stomach and buttocks immense, leaping provocatively into the air. Lysis broke out laughing at the enormous phallus he had chosen, the glans crowned with violets.

He moved it with his knees, keeping the rhythm, as if he had spent his whole life dancing in satyrical choruses. Polus says he was very funny and original in his improvisation of obscenities, that he beat the phallus on the couches, and when Danae was praying to the Gods to save her from the lecherous Silenus, Alcibiades stripped a beautiful pitcher bearer and acted out an abduction and fornication that provoked a round of applause. When the parodos ended and the satyrs were singing anapests to the marriage of Danae and Silenus, Alcibiades removed the stuffing and the phallus and returned to the couch.

Cleis, who was laughing with pleasure, and until then leaning on the other end of the couch, reached out for him to join her on her side. While a slave washed his feet, Cleis caressed his hair. Then they kissed and she cuddled up between his arms with her back on his chest. They watched the whole next scene that way and the second recital by the chorus, followed by the part when Danae and Perseus's son get away from the satyrs in the chest they used as a boat and are rescued by the cliffs of Seriphos. Some fishermen feel an enormous weight in their nets and believe they have made a great catch. Then the king's brother comes and cries out that he has had a vision in which there is something sacred hidden in the fish's stomach.

At this point, Alcibiades lept like a man possessed toward the actors, opened the chest, pulled out the boy playing Danae, and felt all around inside. Suddenly he remained quite still, kneeling beside the chest as if he had just awakened from a dream.

When he was told what he had done, he apologized to the actors and promised compensation for the interruption. Later, when he had calmed down, he explained that some time before he had been watching one of his slaves carrying a sea bass and had a vision in which his ancestor Ajax had appeared telling him to look for a miracle in the stomach of the fish. When he awoke, he had his knife in the fish's stomach. He went right off to consult Euphrantides and other seers, but none of them were able to divine the meaning. The venerable Lampon recommended that he do nothing and wait until the Gods gave him an explicit sign. And at that moment in the play, when he heard that there was something divine in the fish, Alcibiades suddenly saw a a great light shining from the chest . . .

He could not remember . . .

Having reiterated his apologies to the company, he again assumed his authority as symposiarch, had the slaves double the amount of wine in the mixture, ordered several full-chalice rounds, and relinquished the reins of the feast. The stage was set for pandemonium.

Several of the young men began to rival one another for the favors of the women. They fumbled around the couches after them, their robes stained with wine, while the women made fun of them hiding behind the great chairs surrounding the oval. Finally, they took the drunkest off to their rooms.

Alcibiades remarked to Polus that if Lysis had charged for the banquet, the dances, her own included, the acrobats and actors, and for having twenty men spend the night at her house, all of it would have cost well over three thousand drachmas.

Polus, who by this time was quite drunk, was put up in a luxurious room by a callipyge whom he was not able to enjoy that night, but who treated him to her expert arts the following morning. Although he never got to see the end of the party, he did find out that, after Cleis's dance, they had had to call in the dogs to contain the wild passions.

I could give you more details, but I really want to tell you what happened after that and get the scroll on its way.

Cleis and Alcibiades have not been apart for a single instant

399

since that night. They have been partying for three days and parading along the streets together. The whole City is commenting that Alcibiades has gone crazy with love. Personally, I wish I could believe that. But the fact is, he has been behaving like a madman these last few days.

The morning after the banquet, he showed up on his finest stallion, Cleis on the croup, no less than at the home of Hipponicus, his future father-in-law, who was just arriving from the market.

They say that Alcibiades pounced on him, calling him an impious thief, and, after knocking him down with a single blow, attacked the market slave who was following Hipponicus carrying a basket with a striped mullet. Alcibiades then pulled out his knife and started gutting the fish. It took everything Phanes and Cleis's Libyan could do, with the help of a few others, to subdue him. When he came to and they told him what he had done, he broke out crying, stripped before Hipponicus, and turned his back to be whipped like a slave to atone for the offense.

Today, I was told that Hipponicus simply walked away in confusion, forgiving him that very night. Alcibiades said that he was blinded by the same shining he had seen on the day of the banquet, again issuing from the stomach of a fish. And since he has proven himself to be a favorite of the Gods, both in combat and in Olympia, everyone thinks it must be a God trying to communicate with him, for the benefit of Athens.

What they all ignore, however, is that none of it is true. In the note I received from Truncheon today, she says that it was Cleis who demanded that he slap Hipponicus in public, as proof of his love, because now he wants her to be his concubine and she refuses. According to Truncheon, there is nothing to fear from Alcibiades this time. She insists that Cleis is faking everything and that all her fervors are inspired by her physician. (That is what she calls the man who cured her of her fears.) She is completely devoted to him and obeys him in everything. And I must admit that this doctor's arts, whatever they may be, were the only effective and lasting treatment. He convinced her that her illness does not make her unclean, but sacred. We do have to thank the doctor for this, and for returning her to health and freeing her of that humiliating Eros for Alcibiades. I only wish I will have the opportunity to pay him my debt of gratitude. In any case, let the will be done of that God who is the beginning and the end of all things. Be happy.

DELIVERED INTO FRIENDLY HANDS ON
THE TWENTY-FIFTH OF HECATOMBAION
ARCHON EUTHYNUS

PART V

THE SUMMER
OF
EUTHYNUS

5 2

SOCRATES WAS QUITE LATE arriving at the banquet
hosted by Critias, son of Callaeschrus, and, as chance
would have it, made his entrance together with Alcibiades and
Lysis.

Alcibiades's recent bizarre antics, that incredible smack he
gave his future father-in-law, and his association with Lysis of
Miletus, who had been his constant companion since their re-
encounter, were the hottest gossip in the City, competing for
the attention of the many with the mutilation, three days ago,
of the Cybernetes, and Scolotus's confession.

Amid the festive atmosphere of the second tables, the
appearance of the unannounced and uninvited Callipygous
Queen was received with great applause, while her companions
entered almost unnoticed. But the son of Clinias cooled down
the general enthusiasm by announcing that the Gods had given
Lysis of Miletus not only the perfection of her Olympian rump,
but also the beauty of her soul, and that if she had condescended

to share the banquet, it was not as the Sweet-Rump flutist, but as a friend of the logos and the Muses, who was attracted by the high-minded discourse, which must have already begun, to judge from the quality of the company.

As guest of honor, the Cliniad took his place on the central couch, together with Lysis.

Socrates shared a couch with Chaerephon, who was saving him a place. He apologized for being late and declared that he was very hungry.

"You deserve to go hungry," scolded Critias, who immediately signaled to a slave, gesturing toward the tables loaded with smoking tureens and bread baskets placed before the new arrivals.

Hippodamus had been appointed symposiarch and had ordered light wine widely spaced, but with the arrival of his beautiful compatriot, he commanded a full-chalice, bottoms-up round.

Critias, in a gesture of special deference to the only woman with a place in the oval, asked Lysis to dictate the topic of the lofty colloquium to which they aspired, or, if she preferred, a symposium game of her liking.

"Nothing would please me more than to give birth, assisted by Socrates, of course," she said, smiling timidly at the philosopher.

Socrates laughed loud and heartily, infecting the rest of the company in the andron.

And in note that read brother Palaemon, Lysis say that Alcibiades much know about Eye, and that much certainly have Eye in home, but Lysis not seeing and not asking and Alcibiades not saying, and if Lysis guess with great heart of chosen Great Priestess, and if Alcibiades hide Eye, that very better, yes, quick, now you Sosias and brother Green-grocer watch house of Critias and whistle for Otep, that way Otep going to door with note for Lysis, and you, oh brother Sybarite, now you write words I say for her.

"Tell us, then, what you dreamed," Socrates suggested.

"I dreamed I was seeing Passion/Pasion the Banker in my room..."

Several of the guests laughed.

"...and that instead of paying me with money, he gave me a beautiful amethyst."

"By the dog!" objected Socrates, raising his arms for mercy. "Don't ask me, beautiful Milesian, to go back to the game of guessing where the stone is. To judge from what the son of Clinias has said of you, I thought you were sincerely interested in finding some deep truth within you."

"And so I am, oh, son of Sophroniscus, with all my heart."

Socrates twisted his head in disbelief and stared at her askance.

"Some weeks ago," she continued, "my friend Hippodamus, here present, told me about your conversation at Alcibiades's house and the amusing conclusion you helped Chaerephon deliver."

"Yes, indeed," Socrates said, chewing and smiling as he wiped his fingers on a crust of bread, "and I very much regretted the evil gossip that circulated around the City about that honest foreigner."

"And yet, I'm certain that Pasion has the stone."

Even the slaves who were sweeping away the remains of the first tables froze where they were, brooms in the air, mouths open.

Could Lysis be serious? Everyone studied her face for sign of a joke. Some exchanged conspiratorial smiles; some glared at her. All had been thrown off balance.

Did the Ionian courtesan intend to ridicule them?

Alcibiades said nothing. He merely shrugged, arched his eyebrows, stripped the meat from a quail drumstick, and threw the bone on the floor, outside the oval.

With a gesture of resignation, as if lamenting he had ever had the idea, Critias encouraged her to speak.

"Very well, tell us your story."

"Three times I had the same dream," she said, with such a grave countenance that the last remaining smiles disappeared from the oval. "Ever since I was a child, whenever a dream repeated itself, it invariably came true. I feel so certain; I feel this in my heart to be so true that I implore you, oh, excellent Socrates: make me give birth to a certain truth to dispel my doubts; help me see what it is I must do to serve the City and Pallas Athena."

Several voices were raised to ask Socrates to undertake the delivery. Maybe it was true; maybe the Milesian did receive genuine visions from the Gods; maybe her soul did hold the secret that Nicias had been unable to tear from Scolotus. Why not? Let Socrates proceed!

"I accept," Socrates capitulated, raising his arms for silence, "but on the condition that the Milesian shall make me a promise."

"Whatever your condition, I accept," she declared.

Socrates gave her a cunning smile.

"You are bold, oh, beautiful Milesian. Have you no fear that I will demand something harmful to you, or at least annoying?"

Lysis shook her head in silence and, before the baffled congregation, left Alcibiades's couch barefoot to approach Socrates. She stood before him, respectful and composed.

"What is the worst you might ask of me?" she asked, her eyes upturned as if thinking out loud. "That I become your slave? I would kill myself, of course, if I had to be another's, but as your slave I would be the richer, for as some slaves occasionally steal wine, cheese, or figs, I would steal from you every day, drop by drop, all of your wisdom; I would steal from you knowledge of myself and the art of true philosophy which, as you teach, is the only perfect joy."

"You would not have to steal that from me," said Socrates, caressing her hair.

"Oh, yes, by your side I would learn that wisdom is not born of wealth, but that riches are the fruit of virtue; I would understand that the spirit is deceitfully sated by the pleasures of the body, which are ephemeral and invariably turn to pain; if I were yours, I would nourish my spirit in the contemplation of your perfect soul."

"And in what way would I benefit?" Socrates asked.

Lysis reached up to the two brooches that fastened her peplus and suddenly stood naked before him.

Amid the general ovation and commentaries, she walked slowly in a circle before Socrates, one hand on her hip and her head held high, as if saying, "Would you ask for more than this?"

"Would you pay me with pleasures that you yourself admit lead to nothing but pain?" Socrates asked, feigning outrage at such ungratefulness.

"Oh, no, beloved master," she said, approaching Socrates's couch and placing her perfumed nipples within reach of his hands. "I would be but a jewel in your house, a nude, living statue, greater than any of the works of art of Myron or Polygnotus. And I would be very useful, for by your abstention, you would, each day, be exercising the mastery of soul over body."

The ensuing laughter was perhaps the loudest and most prolonged of any banquet held that year in Athens. The uproar lasted long enough for Lysis to pick up her peplus with coquet-tish ease and bend over to bestow a kiss on Socrates, who turned his cheek away in a lightning maneuver and took it on the lips.

On her way back to Alcibiades, she passed by Polus of Acragas, the Sicilian sophist, who could still see her as naked as she was the moment before. Even under the tightly spun linen, her creamy flesh was alive and summoning. "Uncloakable!" the Sicilian thought. "Once you have seen that flesh, no fabric can ever hide its allure." And again he hated the destiny that drove him through life without any hope of ever tasting such a woman.

The grace with which she had taunted Socrates absolved her of all malice. No one imagined that her conservative rhetoric might lead to such a bold closing irony. And since Socrates was rather pleased with the honor implied, it was not at all difficult to convince him to assist with his obstetric art. Her proof of wit and paideia made her worthy of that deference.

They would work, then, at giving birth to truth, but it would be only a game, as it had been that day at the banquet hosted by the Cliniad.

And Alcibiades asked himself how that twenty-year-old courtesan had come to know so much of the doctrines of Socrates. By Pallas! the Milesian was a treasure chest of bewitching charms. Where had she ever learned to improvise encomiums in prose with such eloquence?

And Lysis wondered how much longer she would have to deprive herself of his lavender ecstasy and his invented words?

. . . and you write there, oh brother scribe, that I say first she put much untrue love on Alcibiades, and always with him, daily, nightly, and no never ask nothing straight about amethyst, and do everything with twisted soul so Alcibiades tongue dance with drunk words, and second, if caressing wine and perjury love not bring words, if knife of Lysis not cut out thoughts of Alcibiades, then wait for birthday and hide in feasting wine of Alcibiades much canny sleeping philtres sister Hypothesis of Athens make . . .

". . . so I must ask you how many years you have been in Athens."

"Half of my life, oh, Socrates," answered Lysis.

"And would you say, oh, beautiful Milesian, that you are quite familiar with our customs?"

"Much can be learned in half a lifetime in the service of the men of Athens."

Again laughter rewarded her reply, but Socrates was deeply pensive, as if the game had somehow become something worthy of his full attention.

"And which, then, would you say, is the most coveted prize to be aspired to by a foreigner in Athens?"

"Equality of rights, without a doubt."

"And would you say that Pasion the Trapezites, despite his wealth and friendship with the illustrious men of Athens, would also covet that status?"

"Yes, I would."

"And judging from what you know of our laws and customs, do you believe that the great service of returning the Eye of Athena to the City might immediately earn the banker citizen's rights?"

"I do not."

"But you do believe that the City would be grateful to him?"

"Without a doubt, for it would be a great service."

"Very good reasons, oh, beautiful one," said Socrates, taking a full chalice from the hands of a slave.

"Let us suppose, now, that the delivery of the sacred amethyst should take place during a ceremony of great devotion by the citizens to the Goddess. Let us further suppose that it takes place under circumstances that might be considered miraculous, as if Pallas herself had directed the banker's actions, and suddenly, within sight of everyone, the stone appeared in his hands. Do you follow me?"

"Perfectly, oh, Socrates."

At that moment, Alcibiades saw what was coming. He felt anxious, but his love for the son of Sophroniscus soared to even greater heights. Surely this was the most formidable mind in Athens.

"On seeing Pasion with the stone in his hands, as if fallen from the heavens, would not the many of the City believe that the banker was a favorite of Athena?"

"We would all believe, oh, Socrates, if we were present," said Lysis.

The company was enthralled by the dialogue. Some nodded in silent approval, as if they were, in fact, witnessing the birth of a great truth. Even the slaves kept their eyes fixed on Lysis and Socrates as they absentmindedly cracked nuts and replenished the figs and honey of the second tables.

"So, then, do you, who have lived half your life in Athens and learned so much serving Aphrodite with the most illustrious men of Athens, believe that the good and the beautiful, the friends of the logos and good philosophy, would also see in the banker a favorite of the Goddess?"

"Indeed, oh, son of Sophroniscus, I do believe that most of those of whom you speak would see it so."

"And the priests, archons, generals, areopagites, and

judges, would they also see in this foreigner, Pasion, a favorite of Athena?"

"So would they all," Lysis nodded.

"Well, now, if most of the citizens, including the most illustrious in the politics and government of Athens, have seen him work a miracle for the benefit of the City, and agree that Pasion is a favorite of the Goddess, would those be circumstances weighty enough to merit conferring citizen's rights upon him?"

"As you describe it, I believe that they would, in fact, give him that boon."

. . . and later, when Alcibiades very sleeping, she order Otep and dogs watch door so no drunk watching love with Alcibiades, and when no one looking, she call Otep to break great chest under Alcibiades's bed, and tell her also, oh, brother Sybarite, that both run to hide with sister Green-grocer before Alcibiades awake, and write that this her last task in rescue Dindymenian Eye, and if Eye not in chest, then third, Congregation of the Sum kidnap Alcibiades and take him with much gag and tight in water cart to Piraeus, and hide in ship of brother Shipwreck and then, fourth, sail into blackest sea, where no one not hear, and there Summoner of the Sum look deeply inside Alcibiades to find hiding of Eye, but hold, well you know, oh, Atys, that Alcibiades not sleep with power of eyes, and much diaphanes you see that Alcibiades not suck other's strength, Alcibiades spray his own much great strength through his eyes, you much know that Alcibiades not sponge, but flint, so, fine, fifth, if you not able sleep Alcibiades, you hook point your Phrygian knife under eyelid and you say, give me Dindymenian Eye or I take your beautiful eye, yes, you do that, oh, yes, this new sacred inspiration from Gods of Sum, but you quiet, not tell brother Sybarite this now . . .

* * *

"And which would be, in your opinion, the occasion chosen by Pasion to perpetrate his fraud?"

"As you have said, oh, Socrates, the charlatan would choose a moment of great devotion to Pallas Athena."

"Let us see if you are truly familiar with our customs; which do you think would be that moment of greatest civic devotion?"

"It would be, I believe, the bathing of the effigy in the sea, during the Plynteria, or the march of the parasols, during the Scirophoriae." Then, opening wide her eyes and knitting her brow, as if she had just seen the light, she added pensively, "And ... of course, during the inagural procession of the Panathenian Games."

"There you have the answer you have given yourself: Pasion will pretend that the stone appeared in his hands during the Panathenian procession on the twenty-eighth of Hecatombaion."

A solid wave of applause was the reward for the ingenious conclusion of the dialogue.

"You can go right off and file an accusation with the Basileus," said Pyrilampes.

"That way you can sleep in peace," added Hippodamus, smiling, as he ordered another round to celebrate the successful delivery.

Lysis ran over all her deductions and things started falling into place. Alcibiades had the Cybernetes killed and then began to fake visions.

She had first begun to suspect that Alcibiades not only knew something, as the Summoner thought, but actually had the stone, when she saw him slap Hipponicus. That farce, put on very intentionally by Alcibiades to satisfy one of her whims, had looked so real. His face was the face of a man possessed, just like the other night when he attacked the chest carrying Danae and Perseus, believing it to be a fish. Later, in successive seizures on the streets, she saw his eyes go white and his face stiffen with those very realistic convulsions he had had when he attacked Hipponicus.

Therefore, if it was fake with Hipponicus, all his seizures were fakes.

But what for? Why go through so much trouble? Why was he tearing fish apart? And that story about Ajax? And the shining that blinded him?

The only possible answer was that Alcibiades was leaving himself open to the ridicule of the many because he wanted the City to think him a visionary.

She also recalled that during that first attack at her house, after the callipygous dance and the wine of the re-encounter, Alcibiades had offered to make her his permanent concubine. When she refused, he promised fidelity, respect; he said he would make another Aspasia of her, and as soon as he had all the power of Athens in his hands, he would, as Pericles had, make her his lawful wife. He said that very soon, even before he was the required age, he would be head of Pericles's party.

"Why should they take orders from such a young man who has not even been named a general?" she asked.

"Because I am a f-f-favorite of Zeus, as I proved in Olympia, and of Ares, as I proved in Potidaea, and I shall soon prove that I am a favorite of Pallas Athena."

"But you already proved that three years ago," reminded Lysis.

He stared at her for a moment.

"Why, yes, yes, of course," nodding as if he had suddenly remembered. "I had forgotten that I was also a Panathenian champion."

So, if Alcibiades was already a favorite of Athena's, what further need for proof?

That slip was definitely a clue; he was plotting something having to do with Athena. On the day before Critias's banquet, she got the final clue that made her certain that Alcibiades had the amethyst.

During a stroll in the countryside along the banks of the Ilissus, after they had slept off the evening's wine under the shade of a sycamore, Alcibiades awoke, still very dizzy, and told her that Cimon, the son of Miltiades, had come to him in a dream to announce that, just as he had served his country by recovering the bones of the hero Theseus, Alcibiades was also destined to recover something very sacred.

That was it! She finally understood his game! To stand out in Athenian politics and be second to none, as he had sworn before the Altar of Zeus, Alcibiades had to become the undisputed favorite of the patron Goddess of Athens. Not just another favorite among the many champions of the Games in her honor, but the one favorite, the great righter of a wrong, like Cimon, anointed with divine benevolence. That would certainly be a shortcut to glory.

Then, finally, Socrates had helped her give birth. The game using the banker as scapegoat had unearthed the scheme the son of Clinias planned to use to perpetrate his hoax.

The Socratic conclusion was reinforced by the fact that the date on which the Panathenian Games were to be inagurated was also Alcibiades's birthday.

Without a doubt in her mind, Lysis informed her brothers of the Sum that on the twenty-eighth of Hecatombaion, Alcibiades would stage his sham, whatever it might be.

53

AGATHYRSUS THE SCYTHIAN had given proof of his skill and courage before the walls of Samos. From that moment on he was one of Pericles's favorites. He was given his freedom and named commander of the Scythian detachment. At the age of seventy, he could still drink with the best of his men. The City treated him with the respect due a distinguished foreigner. At the time of the theft of the Eye, Agathyrsus was convinced, as was all Athens, that the thief was the Macedonian executed by order of Lysanias, but he did not quite understand the uproar made by Scolotus, which was not at all in keeping with the style and traditions of the Scythians.

Scolotus was a serious man, a good drinker, and quiet. Even when drunk, he was not much given to talking. When Agathyrsus learned of the ruckus and his girlish shouting in the Acropolis, he merely made some derogatory comment and forgot about the whole thing. In any case, the boy did his duty and Athens was grateful for his zeal.

However, after Nicias forced him to confess his guilt, Agathyrsus began to put two and two together and got to wondering.

Why should Scolotus take such a great risk to steal the amethyst? Scythians did not steal money or jewels. They might, of course, steal a weapon, or a horse, or a chalice for their wine, or anything worthy of a warrior, but what Scythian head could possibly contemplate the theft of an amethyst? Scythians never wore rings or necklaces. If they hung anything at all on their bodies, it would be amulets or things sacred to a warrior. Jewels were something for the long-haired Persians or the effeminate Greeks of Asia.

And it was simply impossible for Scolotus to have been conspiring with Potidaeans or Macedonians. No, it was all some infamy of Nicias's to mortify Pericles.

The incongruence led him to call in two Scythians who had been on duty in the Parthenon on the day of the theft for questioning about the events. He heard their stories separately, and both confirmed that the guard closest to the statue was not Scolotus, who was by the opistodomus, but Targitaus, who was watching the Boreal entrance.

Both witnesses agreed that it was unwise of Scolotus to begin his chase after the Macedonian by shouting from within the temple; the only thing that he did was scare the thief and force him to throw the stone away or pass it to an accomplice.

Had Targitaus joined the mob chasing the Macedonian?

No. Neither recalled having seen Targitaus anywhere near Scolotus, whose actions were quite foolish. Why had he tarried?

Why had he not apprehended the Macedonian as soon as he noticed his suspicious behavior?

When he found out that Scolotus had captured the Macedonian quite some distance from the Parthenon,

Agathyrsus realized what had happened. Of course, he needed to get the Macedonian as far away as possible to be able to start his ruckus and get everyone out of the temple grounds. When they saw him give chase calling for help to catch the thief, no one remained inside. The real thief then had a free hand. By the Unnameable One! The amethyst was for Targitaus, who was dishonored by his inability to hold his own in drinking bouts with the rest of the men. Targitaus, who had never been able to stay on his feet after fifteen skulls; but for that, he would have been the most brilliant young man in his detachment, for Targitaus was a prince by birth, unbeatable with the bow, and the strongest weight lifter. But Scythian traditions considered a man who could not master his wine to be incapable of mastering horses or women. Any man who fell off his saddle or tolerated tears deserved no respect, no honor, and could never be a chief of his tribe.

419

No Scythian would steal a gem to sell it, much less to have it on his body, but any one of them would have stolen anything to free himself of the infamous weakness that kept Targitaus from participating in the rounds of drink with the men. The last time he had been allowed to try, he had collapsed vomiting at Agathyrsus's feet after only eleven skulls.

Scolotus, on the other hand, could hold more than twenty. He could drink with Agathyrsus himself. It was obvious that he had helped his oath-brother steal the amethyst. Faithful to his warrior creed, he had died without a word. He took all the blame and let them crush his skull to keep from sullying the memory of his brother by their oath before the Unnameable One. Now that was a real man. He deserved a fitting reincarnation.

Pericles, protector of the Scythians, would be happy to learn that the confession torn out of Scolotus was just another of Nicias's deceptions, in collusion with Hiero and Evileye. But

Agathyrsus would be even happier the day it was shown that the son of Niceratus was a liar and a cheat, for no Scythian archer had ever been, nor ever could be, a spy for Perdiccas of Macedonia, or anyone's agent.

5 4

UPON COMING INTO his inheritance, Alcibiades
had the panoply hall converted into a sanctuary of Eros
and Aphrodite. When his father had been alive, he had used a
desk, where he attended business matters and met with his
economus to discuss the affairs of the farm. Alcibiades left the
arsenal as it was, but replaced the desk and chairs with a great
bed. The arrangement was fine, as the hall was right next to the
andron. He said that the bed was also a battlefield and there
could be no better place for it than under those glory-laden
ancestral weapons.

Two days before the Panathenian Games, after the callipygian dance, lust and wine invaded the andron.

Alone with Lysis in the arsenal, sometime around midnight, he drank a chalice of pure Rhodes wine from her lips, kiss
by kiss, together with the narcotic the brothers of the Sum had
put in it the night before.

Alcibiades lost that battle; he never even engaged the enemy.

As soon as he was out, Lysis called in Otep to break into the chest, but it was all in vain, for there were only rings, seals, papyri, documents. Then they broke into the smaller chest. Otep destroyed the catch and the ring, but nothing: coins, emblem seals, miniatures, gold amulets.

And she could have sworn that the Dindymenian Eye was there!

Alcibiades was fast asleep, snoring; there was plenty of time, but she had to act with sharp soul and much great calm. The first thing was to get Otep out to guard the door again. If she needed him, she would call.

Of the forty amphorae Alcibiades had won three years earlier in the Panathenian Games, he still had seven completely full of the oil of the Goddess. The economus kept them covered with linen and sealed with flour paste to keep the slaves from stealing the oil of the sacred olive groves, which was in great demand to cure diseases and heal wounds.

Lysis tore open the linens without a thought and began to poke around the bottom with the shaft of an arrow. No amethyst; the seven anphorae contained only oil.

And it was so warm!

She called the Libyan in again, leaving the dogs on guard at the chamber curtain.

How strange that Alcibiades did not have a sturdy door with a crossbar to protect the many valuables he had in the room.

The latch on the cupboard was very strong, and Otep had given it everything he had without being able to break it. Suddenly, Alcibiades grunted and shook in his bed. Lysis turned and stared, not moving a muscle, but he just mumbled something unintelligible and sank back into deep slumber.

Fortunately, the music of flute and drums again filled the

andron, and Otep was able to get back to work without too much concern about the noise. He put all his weight on the bar and tore off one of the hinges. Laelaps heard the clatter and started barking nervously, but Otep quieted him down with a low whistle.

As soon as she had access to the bale, Lysis sent Otep back out to his position at the door.

Inside, Lysis found clothing and another chest, unlocked and full of silver talents. There were several lecythi with unguents and perfumes, but one, with a delightful aroma of jasmine, had an extremely long neck sealed with wax. And there was something inside that rattled. She immediately broke the seal and emptied the perfume into a basin, but the thing inside would not come out. She could not get to it, for the neck was longer than her finger.

Without a second thought, she smashed it against the floor, but it was only a piece of amber. They had probably put it in there when it was melted. Such a disappointment.

Then she went through the bale bit by bit; she tore open cushions, broke into two wooden boxes, and explored every single thing that might contain an amethyst. She was certain that Alcibiades had it in that room, where no slave or servant was allowed to enter without his permission.

She broke, tore, scratched, poked, and sorted through everything that could hide the Dindymenian Eye, but all in vain.

Complete failure. Nine days with their nights away from the Summoner of the Sum, and all for nothing. The only thing left to do was to wait a day and a half. If Alcibiades did return the Eye to the Parthenon, there would be time enough for the brothers to conjure up some new rescue plan. The Summoner had said once that, with just such an emergency in mind, the

Gods had inspired him to learn how the Icaridae of Mount Ida made their wings. If bad came to worse, he would fashion his wings, enter the Parthenon himself, rescue the Dindymenian Eye, and fly through the air out to the plains.

The Gods had ordained that Lysis was not to be the finder of the Eye. Were they reserving the holy exploit for the Summoner of the Sum, who had spent so many years searching for it throughout the known world?

55

SUDDENLY, TWO SHADOWS left the farm building
by the back door, and when they were about ten paces
from the poplar where I was hiding, I recognized Phanes,
Alcibiades's servant . . .

No, I wasn't able to see the other's face, but it had to be a
slave because he was doing all the carrying, and he walked
behind Phanes, yes, exactly, and I said to myself, now, what are
you going to do, Green-grocer? And although I had no orders to
follow anyone, nor to abandon my place watching the farm-
house, from which I could hear music and the sound of feasting, the Sum inspired me with the thought that those two were
on some secret mission for Alcibiades, and I was completely
convinced when I saw them put on hoods as they crossed the
Sacred Way. Oh, no, because instead of going along the road,
they walked through the thorns and brambles, and when they
got to the bridge, they didn't use it, they waded across with the
water up to their waists. What? Oh, yes, excellent brother, they

did all they could to conceal themselves. Me? Well, about eighty
paces behind. Well, I may be cross-eyed, but I can see like a cat
in the dark, and all along I was telling myself how much
sophrosyne the brothers of the Sum had brought me, for I was
no longer a troublemaking gambler, a scourge to my loving
green-wife, for now, under the guidance of the Gods of the ...
What? Later? Oh, fine, whatever you say, oh, good Summoner,
so then Phanes stopped by a holly tree, took a dagger from
under his cloak, and cut off a rod about five cubits long to make
a walking staff, and without ever using the road, set off for the
Dipylum. No, they entered the City through the hole they made
in the wall for Alcibiades on his triumphal return from
Olympia. That's it, and from there they turned south heading
between the Areopagus and the Pnyx and coming to the
Propylaea. And my heart kept telling me that so much secrecy
had to be for something very evil. Yes, oh, Summoner, and then
they rounded the Acropolis about halfway up until they came to
the incline and continued toward a small cedar wood, where
they disappeared, but then I saw the slave again, the one who
had left his pack behind, and he was waiting in hiding by an
ash, at the entrance to the path that leads to the fountain of
Poseidon. Yes, the one that Nicias had paved, and he was sort of
watching to make sure no one saw what the other one was
doing inside, and then Phanes returned with the pack. Oh, yes,
you can be sure that he had something in it. Well, because when
they set out again ... No, the slave carried it over his shoulder
and it was swinging across his waist. Yes, and then they
returned along the thickets on the slope and followed the same
path to the Cephisus, and there to my great surprise, they did
not wade across the river, but followed the banks for about five
stadia and then doubled back toward the City, and that's when
I understood that they were headed for the Barathrum. I no

426

longer had any doubts that they did not want to be seen. Otherwise, why the long roundabout with so much conceal-ment? Fear? No, not at all, which proves that the Three-in-One was guiding me, isn't that true, oh, Summoner? Yes, yes, of course, and I crawled among the shadows and saw them stop at the entrance to the elm grove flanking the sunset side of the Barathrum, and there Phanes took the pack... Yes, the slave had carried it all the way, but now Phanes... Well, maybe about forty paces, and despite the silence I could hear nothing, but I did see how Phanes went off to the edge of the cliff and the slave stayed behind, watching among the elms and blocking my way. How long? Well, the time it takes to walk two stadia. Oh, no, impos-sible, I would have had to get to the edge of the cliff and they would have seen me. Well, I can't remember now, but when they returned to the farm, the slave was not carrying anything. Yes, yes, I swear, whatever they had in the pack is now at the bottom of the Barathrum. What? In the deepest part? Hmmmm, that no one can tell, venerable brother. No, no mortal has ever returned from the Barathrum. You? Aren't you afraid, oh, Summoner of the Sum? By Hecate! Take care! Remember that the Barathrum is infested with snakes and evil spirits and a myriad of criminal souls.

427

5 6

AFTER BREAKING INTO practically everything
Alcibiades had in the weapons room, Lysis could hardly
return to the Ceramicus. What would the doctor say when he
found out about her failure? Would he be happy to have her
back?

According to the plan, she was to hide at the Green-grocer's
after the holy rescue and he would see her there. Perhaps that
very night she would again hear his love songs with invented
words!

A tingle, somewhat stronger than at other times, almost an
itching, rose up from her thighs.

Alcibiades was snoring lightly.

She went out into the courtyard accompanied by Otep and
the two dogs, avoiding the casual glances of the last survivors of
the evening's entertainment, now conversing in the andron.

Otep told the door slave that his mistress was going out for
a walk because the efforts required by her callipygous dance and

all the wine had made her a bit sick and she needed to get some fresh air out in the clear night.

They strolled calmly, trying to give the impression that they were going to the river, but as soon as they were behind the nearest grove, they headed straight for the Academy.

It was still dark, but Otep recommended not lighting a torch. With the night so dark, a torch might attract the attention of Orestes's gang, who, people were saying, had recently come down from the mountains. The night before, a group of travelers who ran into them had returned to Corydallus completely naked. Otep led the way, a dagger in his left hand, a sling and two stones tied across his chest, and Cratus's leash in his right. Lysis had to keep tugging at Laelaps's leash to slow him down, for the great brute was practically dragging her along the dark path.

When they arrived, the Green-grocer's wife was waiting, very nervous, as she had been since she was informed of her part in the plan. The Summoner of the Sum? In her house? No, she knew nothing about that, and she had even talked to him that afternoon in the Ceramicus, but he never said he was going to her house to meet the sister Great Priestess.

The house was small and dingy.

As Lysis looked around and started imagining herself stuffed away in that rathole for days on end, running the risk that the Summoner might forget about her, she forgot her orders, put aside all fears of Alcibiades's reprisals, and ordered Otep, in her most commanding voice, to take her back to the Ceramicus.

No, without disguises; just the way they were.

But...

Quickly, now, and have Talthybia come along, because the Three-in-One had just inspired her to return to her home. No, no fear at all. An adequate hideout would turn up for her and for Otep, who also had to hide from the ire of the Cliniad. They would set up a watch, and as soon as Alcibiades came anywhere near, they would hide in a chest or in some empty cistern.

As she went into the Summoner's room, she noticed that he was sleeping with the Cyrenian, a fifteen-year-old Syrian callipygian, and with Nino, the masseuse with the perfect hands. Well now, this was too much. Lysis lost all control. Out with the sluts! And the Summoner! Instead of yearning for his Great Priestess and waiting anxiously for her at the Green-grocer's, the Summoner of the Sum was sleeping in the arms of the new girls. She would have all three of them sent to a third-rate whorehouse.

And he, insisting that his duties as the Baptist had much great prioritiness in the Church of the Sum, and Cyrenian sister and Syrian sister merely receiving baptism of the Sum, and later he going to Green-grocer's . . .

And Nino? What was Nino doing in his bed? How many times was he going to baptize her?

And now the Summoner was growing angry. She could not dictate new laws for the Sum. Had she forgotten the statutes? A Great Priestess could not tell the Summoner to doing this and not doing that, because Summoner of the Sum always obeying priestliest vocation, brother Sybarite much great clear reading out to congregation, and she must going fast now from dangerous house, must hiding from fat anger of Alcibiades in house of Green-grocer, and Lysis, that she would not: this was her home and here she would stay; she was not afraid of Alcibiades, for the Gods had inspired her as well, and she strutted proudly out of the room, ordering Evardis to prepare her a hot bath. She was going to get a good night's rest to be ready to reopen her banquet hall the next evening, whether the Summoner of the Sum liked it or not.

Just then brother Green-grocer arrived, very excited, and whispered something to the Summoner, who led him to a far room.

Lysis repressed her fury, but she refused to talk to anyone, not even Hypothesis, who tried in vain to calm her down.

When Lysis went to her bath, Evardis was stoking the fire under the tub.

Lysis tested the water with the tip of her toe and complained that it was only lukewarm, that she had ordered a hot bath, and that Evardis should go out to the kitchen for some more hot water. Evardis brought two more pitchers of boiling water. When Lysis found the temperature just right, she complained that the marble bottom of the tub was too hot and ordered Evardis to bring the oak platform she used in those cases.

431

Otep and the Missian brought two thick poles to keep the broad plank off the hot bottom. Lysis lay prone, with her hair up in a knot, her head so that the water just touched the tip of her chin. With soft, rhythmic undulations of her body, she swirled the water up from her toes, around her buttocks, across her waist, and up to the base of her neck.

Neither of the slaves looked; that was the first thing they had learned years ago when they entered the service of Truncheon: never look, and above all, never see.

Lysis turned on her back, languishing in the soothing warmth. When she felt her pores open and her skin tingling, she rang her bell.

Evardis entered with two jars of oil and some soda and began to mix them into a yellowish paste. When the soap was ready, Lysis emerged from the tub and stood there for Evardis to do her back while she did her breasts and underarms herself. As Evardis began to scrub her, she twisted her head, turned up her eyes, and began to bite her lips. Finally, she gave a careless shrug and giggled.

"Have Otep come in," she ordered.

Evardis looked at her in surprise and left without a word. She returned smiling and expectant, leading Otep, who never took his eyes off the floor.

"Scrub my back."

Otep looked for some clue from Evardis, who simply handed him the xystron with more than a bit of teasing in her smile. But with the look of reproach she got from her mistress, she averted her eyes submissively and started to leave.

"Where do you think you're going?" Lysis said authoritatively. "And you, get on with it; I said do my back."

The Libyan began to rub, but kept his left hand behind his back.

"You're doing it all wrong," Lysis barked. "Evardis, show him how it's done."

The slave took the xystron in her right hand. With her left she streched the skin between her index finger and thumb and scrubbed with her right as she moved along her mistress' body.

Otep stood petrified. When he started to scrub, Lysis climbed on the marble stool next to the tub and spoke to him at his own height.

"Take off your clothes so you won't get them wet."

For the first time, the Libyan dared steal a look at her face, which was turned away.

Was the mistress drunk?

Lysis went on rubbing one of her breasts and turned just enough to enjoy his confusion.

As he undressed, she could hardly keep from laughing. The

slave looked as if he were about to cry. She wondered how old he was. Thirty? Lysis looked straight at him with admiring approval. My, my, a powerful specimen . . . and beautiful! She was quite satisfied. His skin was terse, free of whip scars or brands, his muscles well defined, arms strong, legs straight, a bit thin, but all in perfect harmony, and such a beautiful face. She wondered what he had been in his native land.

When he finally got his clothes off, Otep began to scrub at the height of her shoulders. He scrubbed the same spot for some time, until Lysis pointed to her waist.

"Scrub here, now."

Otep went on rubbing up and down, but she wanted it from side to side. He had to bring himself around a little, enough to see the profile of her body. Lysis complained that Evardis had not put enough smegma on her, and when the girl was about to add some more, she stopped her.

"Let him do it."

This time Evardis blushed and passed the jar to Otep, her eyes nailed to the tub.

Lysis made a gesture of disapproval and told the girl to go for some cold water.

As Otep spread the smegma along her waist, she turned to confront him with the blush of her erect nipples.

"Put some on here," she pointed.

As the big black fellow gently ran his hands over those full, quivering breasts that slithered out of his soapy hands, a wave of heat crept all over his body, making him feel that his ears were melting, and his mouth filled with saliva.

Trapped between his shame and his desire, he would have liked to close his eyes, but dared not. His mistress might think it disobedient. Oh, merciful Ammon, she was going to notice what was happening to him.

When Evardis came in and saw Otep kneading Lysis's breasts with both hands, she tried to look at her mistress for some explanation, but could not tear her eyes away from that great, proud, black phallus.

Lysis turned, placing her elbows on Otep's shoulders, and told him to scrub her back. The Libyan had to contort his body to get his hands around to her back without touching her with the tip of his inflamed member.

At that very moment, Lysis smiled triumphantly at Evardis, her elbows still resting on Otep's shoulders.

"Go," she said, "I'll call you if I need you."

Alone with the terrified Otep, she imprisoned his phallus between her thighs, bringing out a sigh of death, or glory, from the depths of the African's soul. She ordered him to lie on the floor. Oh, sweet Ammon, what if the Summoner finds out?

Lysis straddled him, her back to his face. A brief callipygian gallop was all the poor man could take before he erupted, groaning and filling his chest with a deep breath. Lysis received him with professional timing and smiled as Otep recalled the burning earth of Egypt swelling with the first waters of the flooding Nile.

"That was fine, Otep," she said, retaking her authoritarian tone. "I just wanted to see what kind of man was responsible for my safety. Call Evardis and tell her to come rinse me. Go!"

5 7

YES, AFTER MIDNIGHT, but alone, five brothers and
nobody more, shhhh, womans not need to know, no
brother say nothing, and after, when Summoner come back, he
tell womans and others, and Sosias twisting and biting the tip
of his cloak because the night before he had dreamed that a
great serpent had attacked the Summoner, and you have fear,
oh, second faithful? you forget statutes of Sum? and only
Palaemon the Sybarite is calm, and the Summoner reveals that
he, too, received an apocalyptical sign, and you think priestly
dream not better than Sosiasian nightmare? and you afraid,
too? but Otep keeps silent, hoping to hear the dream, and you?
and the Green-grocer, well, not really what you call fear, but he
reminds the Summoner of the huge serpents, the dragons, that
the bottom of the Barathrum is full of screeching souls, and if
he trips on the descent, and the Summoner, bah, a wave of the
hand, he goes down side of Barathrum more easy than down
steps of Great Theater, and not afraid because Three-in-One

going down with him and not leave Dindymenian Eye for play-
thing of Barathrian scum, and when scoundrel demons see
Summoner come, they see he great sovereign and chastiser
priest and no more screech, no more yell and mock, and when
Summoner light three fires of Sum in bottom, demons flee,
dragons swallow fire, and bite tongue, and serpents hiding, but
after midnight, when the Summoner had inched about four
cubits down the rope, following the vertical wall of the cliff, his
back to the abyss, Sosias again started trembling and weeping,
and the Summoner stopping and coming back up furious, and
taking Sosias by the hair, speaking right into his face, and you
not no more afraid now, no shake, no weep, and his voice was
hard, like the darkness flooding the bottomless pit, and he
turned to Otep, Green-grocer, Shipwreck, here nobody afraid,
Summoner go down, Summoner come up, and no nothing danger or monster attack protected of the Three Gods, and now you
laugh, very happy, now, ha, ha, ha, because Summoner going
down to search Athenian inferno, and all sigh and smile
relieved, and now when I go rescue, each tell all about miracles
of Summoner of the Sum, and they watch him begin to climb
down again, and they admire him, and when they have to lean
over too far to see him in the blackness, he lets go of the rope
and waves them away, and the brothers wait among the elms,
and Sosias recalling when he saw him from a distance, walking
through the water toward the Scythian's watchtower, his
shaven head shining like Artemis Phosphoros, and he was very
tall, Sosias thought it was a spirit coming out of the sea, but
then he realized that it was the Summoner, and if he changed
that way, it was because the Gods guided him, and Sosias was
no longer afraid, well, he was a little afraid when he saw the
Molossian rushing him, but the Summoner calmly pointed his
staff at the hound, and instead of attacking, a miracle, he began

licking the point of the staff, and went on licking up the staff, and wound up licking the Summoner's hand, and then he stayed with them, at his feet, and then came Pandarus the Scythian, and the Summoner touched his head with his staff and put his hands on his shoulders, miraculous power, and ever since then, Sosias the Carian believed, and when fear returned, the Summoner said, no never fear, and Sosias was not even afraid of a hairy lion licking his jowls, and the Summoner once told Green-grocer that the next time he beat his wife his hands would swell, and with his hands swollen, numb, enormous, bursting, he had gone to the Summoner for help, and the Summoner relieved the swelling by blowing on them, and from that day on he and his wife were devoted to the Sum, and Otep withdrawn, talking to himself, shaking his head, and Sosias, what was wrong with the Libyan? and Otep asking Palaemon if he thought it was right for the Summoner and Lysis to go off to Asia to return the Eye, without a guard, and confessing that he could never again be away from sister Lysis of Miletus, and that he wanted to be her slave again, and live by her, and die for her, and protect her from dangers and enemies, and that just by being near her his soul swelled, but he could never bring himself to ask the Summoner to let him follow her to Asia, together with Cratus and Laelaps, and that if he had to be far from her, he would kill himself, and he begged Palaemon the Sybarite that, oh, the third faithful ask the Summoner to let him go as a guard, and he had no peace until the Sybarite remarked that the idea was reasonable and that it was certain that the great love that Otep had for the Great Priestess was inspired by the Sum, so that he would take good care of her, and Sosias and Shipwreck crossing smiling glances, and commenting that, yes, the Summoner would understand, and Otep, that if he could no longer see her, he would tear out his eyes, because even with-

437

out eyes, he would always be seeing her, facing him, right there, on the threshold of his purest thoughts, and Palaemon asking if he did not intend to see her a little from behind, and all of them laughing, Otep as well, quieted by the brother Sybarite's promise, and cuckoo, cuckoo, cuckoo, ohh, the Summoner was calling them, and on approaching the cliff, the great light tells them that the three holy fires had been lit by the Summoner, and the long rope is very heavy, and all three pull, and when they had pulled up some thirty fathoms, they see something tied to the end, it looks like the pack, and Shipwreck, who has been counting the fathoms, calculates that the Summoner must have cut off about one third of the rope, meaning that the bottom of the Barathrum was less than fifty fathoms down, and the pulling grew easier, and when they still had about ten fathoms to go, they hear something metallic in the pack when it hit the side of the cliff, and when they open the pack, they find the pick, the flint, and the other things the Summoner had taken with him, but there is also a bronze fish about three palms long, and Sosias taking the fish and studying it, and Shipwreck and Otep discovering some writing on its stomach, and Palaemon, turning his back on the pit to see in the light of the three holy fires, and reading, "NN offered me to Poseidon," and Shipwreck, NN? and Palaemon, that it had to be Nicias of Niceratus, and all agree that it had to be one of the bronze fish Nicias had had made for Poseidon's fountain, and Palaemon shaking it and hearing it rattle, but the noise was too high-pitched, it did not seem to be the Eye, but what did the fish mean? why throw it into the Barathrum? and Shipwreck, that when the City was talking about the slap Alcibiades had given Hipponicus, everyone said that he had torn apart a fish that had just been bought in the agora, and Otep, yes, yes, and at Lysis's he had mistaken a chest for another fish, and Palaemon, that the Summoner would decide, or the Three Gods would send him a sign, enough, that the brothers should send the rope back down again, and all waiting by the edge, anxious, pensive, could it be that the Cliniad had had another fishy vision? some new dream that had made him send Phanes to the fountain and then to the Barathrum? and why had Alcibiades picked on NN's fish? and again, cuckoo, cuckoo, and they see the Summoner climbing, then resting on a ledge, and climbing again along the knots, pushing against the rocky face of the cliff, and when he gets to the top, his face is brooding, says nothing, and on the way back, Sosias finally dares ask him about the inferno at the bottom of the Barathrum, and the Summoner, riding his mule, withdrawn, taciturn, that there was no inferno there, there being paradise like King of Kings have in Celaenae, and in very bottom of Barathrum gushes fountain, and he not see dragons, no terrible serpents, and very diaphanes that, seeing Summoner of the Sum, bandit demons and scoundrel souls run with fear, and nobody attack him or bother, and just some white bones, and Athenian inferno little thing, real inferno in Pamphylian saffron field where Summoner live in chains when child.

439

5 8

WHEN NICIAS made Hiero his secretary, one of the first tasks he gave him was to create for him a suitable epithet. There was Solon the Lawgiver, Miltiades the Great, Aristides the Just, Pericles the Incorruptible ...

The excellent son of Niceratus had to have some exalting appellation with his own name. How would he like to be known for his unvarying self-control, his serenity of soul? Could there be a finer quality than ataraxia, an ancient virtue, sanctified by the gnomai of the Greeks? Someday he would be known as Nicias the Ataraktos, more imperturbable than a coral snake in the middle of a thunder storm.

Nicias liked that. He would be the Imperturbable, in the face of fortune or misfortune; the Imperturbable, in peace and in war.

In the five years that Hiero had spent in Nicias's employ, the new epithet was far from having taken root, but the City was already talking about the dignity of his silence in the meetings of the men.

He almost never opened his mouth in public. In matters of his personal interest or in the interest of his party, Hiero saw to it that his supporters did the bickering. The Greeks always admired the suasive virtue of the spoken word, but by that very same token, they equally glorified those who could withstand its attacks with dignity, those who knew how to hold their peace until the moment came to crush the enemy's eloquence.

Such a man was Cimon. He spoke little, did much, and was master of his reactions in danger or adversity.

Hiero, a cousin to Cleonice, Nicias's wife, was a failed actor and a horrible speech-writer, but he turned out to be an inspired secretary. When he discovered this vocation for ataraxia in the son of Niceratus, he decided to fashion a public personality for him along that line. Nicias was an imposing man, a master of silence and scarce gestures, he had an immense fortune, and had never known the meaning of fear in battle. Ah, but for the high-stakes game he wanted to play, he needed more hide.

Hide? He needed hide? What on Earth?

"Hide," repeated Hiero, slapping his own face demonstratively, "tough hide on your face, like Onion Head's."

Had the excellent son of Niceratus not noticed that Pericles never blushed or blanched in public, that he never revealed the turmoil of his soul? No! He only revealed what he wanted people to believe, depending on the occasion. Pericles also had the shield of his oratory, a shield with a very tough hide that was impenetrable to enemy attacks. Nicias, on the other hand, would lose control when his dignity was insulted in public; he would get befuddled, and since he was no orator, all he could do, like most soldiers, was mumble absurdities. Was this or was this not true?

But that had never happened in the Assembly.

Not yet, no, but if he assumed the active role incumbent on his position as head of his party, he would be the target of permanent attacks and the butt of endless ridicule. Nicias would be easy prey for any orator with wit or guts enough to exasperate him in the Assembly.

It was true; his difficulty in speaking before an audience was undoubtedly a handicap in public life. He used pat phrases, repeated himself, mumbled, forgot what he was going to say, and invariably got mixed up in long paragraphs. A fatal defect in that land where gilded rhetoric was the sovereign of the many.

But with his known courage, his wealth, and the favor of the Gods, he could aspire to the apex of Athenian politics. The first thing he had to do was never open his mouth in Assemblies without first having memorized his speech. Second, never listen to attacks against his character or his actions.

"But that's impossible," objected Nicias.

"No, it's not," insisted Hiero, "and my method is nothing new; they say it was first used by Lycurgus."

And what was this method?

Plugging up his ears with soft wax.

But what if someone was impertinent or insulted him while his ears were plugged?

All the better; he could retaliate on some other occasion, with learned words.

"They would accuse me of cowardice," protested the son of Niceratus.

But Hiero managed to convince him that, with all the personal courage he had displayed on the battlefield, no one in the City could possibly think him a coward.

The results were unsurpassable.

Nicias let his hair grow around the temples to hide the plugs and to allow him to put them on or take them off in public without anyone noticing. Thus, in time, he became the undisputed master of the wax plug.

At the time when he was appointed to substantiate the anacrisis against the blasphemers of Epsilon Cove, many of the demos were already commenting on his proverbial ability to abstain from the quarreling in the Assemblies; others applauded his rare, but always well-founded interventions, some of them full of civic courage; and many others praised his imperturbable temper.

It was the twenty-seventh day of Hecatombaion and the market was overflowing.

Nicias, Carcinus, and Proteas were walking along together down the Street of the Tripods under the expectant watchfulness of the many.

Early that morning, the heralds had circulated an urgent summons signed by Pericles. The meeting was to take place that very morning in the Strategeion at the time of the full market. All the members of the College had been notified.

During their walk, the three generals exchanged discreet conjectures.

It had to be something very important to merit such an urgent summons.

And just one day before the Panathenian Games!

Perhaps it had to do with the siege of Potidaea? Could it have to do with the rumors about a Theban attack against Plataea?

Yes, that sounded reasonable.

Or maybe it was some secret report the Onion Head wanted to clear with the College before presenting it to the Assembly.

That might also be true, but Carcinus wondered if it might not have something to do with the panic let loose in the City by the Cybernetes affair.

Hummmm, hardly. Why should he summon the College of Generals for that?

Yes, but the Onion was tricky, unpredictable . . .

What if he were planning some attack against Nicias?

Against him? In the presence of all the colleagues?

Nicias shrugged and made no further comments.

They were approaching the agora: white heat, short shadows, thyme, the acid smell of cheese, sandals full of sand.

The son of Niceratus raised his chin and proceeded to the Stoa of the Hermae.

The din was so great that it drowned out the smells.

Carcinus might not be so far off the mark. Nicias had been informed about the commentaries circulating in the City.

Salted meat, brooms, marjoram, savory, amphorae from Samos.

When news of how the Cybernetes had been mutilated got around, the ungrateful Athenian demos began to doubt the confession of Scolotus the Scythian. They were blaming him and Evileye. Onion Head's rumor mill was spreading the word that Pallas Athena had run out of patience and would consider the festive dances, the Games, and the offering of a new peplus in her honor an insult. The Goddess would have nothing to do with the Athenians on that woeful anniversary in that City open to sacrilege and impunity.

Ugh! rotting offal, dried fish, flies, prestidigitation, armpits, eels, barbers with umbrellas, smack, a mosquito in midday . . .

The Cybernetes case had come in very handy to support the rumor that the killers of Epsilon were loose in the City; the profaners would be present at the festivities with which the Athenians commemorated the crowning of the Goddess in the very territory they were sullying with their mere presence.

Nicias's enemies were saying that, whether or not they were accomplices of the confessed culprit Scolotus, the criminals who had mutilated Porphyrius the Cybernetes had cut off his fingers in exactly the same way as they had seen in the sacrifice of the Scythian.

Banks, Greeks from Asia, Sicily, changing darics for drachmas, quails, acrobats, blind men, cripples, snip, snip, snip, beggars, fire-eaters, vinegar, green dung dropping from under a horse's tail, the smell of burnt meat coming from the Altar of the Twelve Gods.

They were almost there.

On the steps of the Temple of Hephaestus, they were joined by Phormio, the son of Euclid; a group of generals were waiting at the entrance to the Strategeion. Nicias saw Archestratus, Eucrates, and Cleopompus . . . but where was the Head?

The noisy throng grew respectfully silent as the four generals went by, then resumed their infernal chatter, stirring the Scythian's confessions with the fingers of the Cybernetes.

Further up, Eulogus, who had set up his stand next to the Tholos of the Prytaneum, snip, snip, snip, suddenly immobilized his scissors atop a huge head of curly hair. He watched the four generals go by. At this time? On the eve of the Panathenian Games? He whispered something to his clients. Generalized laughter.

Athens the defamer; Athens the fickle!

Many of the many were even daring to say that the City was not purified at all and that the execution of innocent men had infected her even more.

The generals approached the Strategeion to greet their colleagues. The heat deafened the augurs.

Might it be cooler inside? They decided to await the Autocrat General in the Hall of the Triad.

But the heat of Hecatombaion scorched the flesh.

The generals sweated, they complained, and they fanned themselves with the corners of their cloaks.

Some drank water; others asked the ushers to bring barley orgeat.

Nicias was unperturbed by the heat. Nothing perturbed him. Now fully in his role as Nicias Ataraktos, he neither fanned himself nor drank anything.

The convergence of eight generals in the Strategeion at the time of the full market sufficed to unleash a wave of conjecture.

The arrival of Pericles, followed by Agathyrsus and another Scythian, turned the wave into a tide. By noon, the whole City knew that the College of Generals was meeting at its headquarters, behind the Assembly's back, to deal with something about the confession that Evileye had torn out of Scolotus. Otherwise, why were the Scythians there?

The only general that was absent was Callias, who had to leave for Chalcidice to take over command of the siege of Potidaea.

In the Hall of the Triad, there were two parallel rows of five thrones each facing one another. The eleventh throne closed off one end, and there was a table at the other for the officers who attended the meetings of the College. The center was a spacious rectangle.

Pericles comes in alone, greets no one, and walks directly to his throne at the head of the rectangle. The aide approaches, followed by two ushers carrying the tray of offerings. Pericles whispers instructions to them.

As soon as the generals see that the sacrifices are not taken to the Altar of Ares but to Athena Promachos, they realize that the meeting has nothing to do with the war. Besides, Ares, besmirched with death, and Apollo, who wounds from afar, receive only libations in the ritual of the Strategeion.

The official diviner was particularly hasty that day examining the entrails of the sacrificed kid and approving the color of the first three fires.

None of the Gods opposed the session.

By virtue of his autocratic prerogatives, Pericles orders the deliberations to be held behind closed doors with no other witnesses than a battery of three tachygraphers. He wants his words recorded exactly so they can be conveyed to the table of the Prytanes during the first Assembly in Metageitnion.

The extreme precautions raise the uneasiness of the College.

As soon as the Hall is cleared of the uninvited, Pericles begins:

447

"Athenian Generals, as you well know, since the times of Solon, each citizen has had the legal right, and not only the right, but the duty, to execute, by whatever means is most convenient, whomever he might discover attempting to subvert the constitution of Athens. Just as our forefathers were obliged to exile Miltiades, Aristides, Themistocles, and even Cimon and other heroes from the territory of Attica for making vain promises that incited the demos to take foolish steps against the enemy, I appeal today to those same laws to accuse, before this august College, one of the generals here present."

All gazes converge on Nicias, who is occupying the seat furthest from Pericles on the left.

"I am doing so without the slightest fear of mistake in the gravity of the crime..."

Pericles spoke these words in a rising tone, using one of his well-known anticadences.

"... and without the anguish of having to attack a hero of Athens, as were Miltiades, Aristides, Themistocles, and Cimon."

Pericles notices how Nicias turns to one side and searches for something among his robes.

Seven heads are facing him directly.

Thirteen eyes are moving in anxious expectation.

"I, Pericles, son of Xanthippus, Autocrat General of Athens, in fulfillment of the psephisma of Praxiergus ..."

He shakes his head to stress his words. There is wrath in his demeanor. After a long pause, a deep breath, Pericles walks across the auditorium, looking around selectively. Nicias is intentionally excluded.

Is Pericles controlling his righteous indignation?

Is he taking his time to see the effects that mentioning the harsh decree of Praxiergus has on the generals?

In the deep silence, the only sound that can be heard is the scratching of quills on papyrus coming from the tachygraphers' table.

Pericles notices Nicias's immutable profile out of the corner of his eye. He gets the impression that his chin is a little too high. He wonders if this time, too, he is going to be able to remain silent and imperturbable.

Cleopompus opens his cavernous mouth; Archestratus chews on the corner of his robe. On the other side, Hagnon, the oldest of the generals, stares at Pericles with his only eye. Carcinus scratches a disgusting rash he has on his knee.

"... issued during the archonship of Ancestorides, which makes it mandatory for generals in active service to report in this hall any and all legal actions against any of the members before filing the corresponding writ with the tribunals of the City ..."

When he was rehearsing the speech before Aspasia, she suggested that, once he had created the necessary tension with just the right gestures and the tremor in his voice, the accusation itself should be pronounced with even serenity. But at that moment, to deprive Nicias of the protection of his profile, Pericles stands squarely in front of him, just two paces away from his face so that he will have to look at his eyes.

Then, in an unexpectedly formal tone, he continues:

"I accuse you, oh, son of Niceratus, of bribing citizens, of impiety, and of violating the democratic constitution of Athens."

Pericles returns to the head of the rectangle, his hands behind his back.

Everyone looks at Nicias, who keeps his eyes fixed on the Altar of Athena. He looks very pale, but his face is admirably composed.

"I accuse Nicias of bribing Philodorus, son of Clearchus, and Licophron, son of Eumenes . . ."

Now it is Pericles who turns his profile, with Nicias staring straight at him.

The colleagues in the opposite row look in vain at that serene face for any sign of the blow. He must have felt it. The accusation was terrible. And yet, his color has not changed and he has not even batted an eyelash. How lamentable, this war among colleagues, Hagnon ponders. In vain he tries to read some expression on Nicias's face. How has he taken it? The only one who seems to be happy about the situation is Ares, whose altar he has before him. To the old general's weak eyes, the statue seems to have changed its aggressive grimace to a twisted smile.

"... so that they would spread through the City vile slander against my legitimate wife and then present before the tribunal

449

of the King a written accusation in which they swear that they saw a very well-known courtesan entering my home."

Nicias's only response is to straighten the pleats of his himation and to pick up one leg, the knee between his clenched hands.

Archestratus hates Nicias, but cannot help admiring that virile composure. The man is beautiful: tall, slim, straight nose, jet-black hair, large eyes, terse skin, powerful beard.

"... and when the time comes, I will substantiate my accusation of bribery with the fact that the witnesses at the trial were incapable of maintaining their perjury. When they were directed to swear before the effigies of the Twelve Gods that they were both certain they had seen the courtesan, both backed down; they realized the magnitude of the infamy and preferred to keep silent. So it was the will of fate that the perjury ultimately benefited the person I was defending, my wife. On that day, the Gods did not choose to favor Nicias of Niceratus."

Toward the end of his speech, the Autocrat General again resorts to his deep confirmatory nodding and his fencing with his index finger.

Hagnon feels that the formidable son of Zeus and Hera is staring at him with sarcasm, as if the figures of Discord, Terror, and Flight are dancing on his helmet.

"... and they shall favor him even less one day soon, when it will be I who summon those very same witnesses before the very same Gods and command them to swear that they did not take a bribe ..."

Nicias remains calm.

Onion Head would see just who the son of Niceratus was.

A man who had always faced death in battle fearlessly would certainly never fear a pack of lies.

Pericles regains control of his voice and takes a deep breath. He twists his blond moustache and narrrows his deep-blue eyes.

"I accuse Nicias of Niceratus of inciting civic panic; I accuse him of exploiting that panic to spread unfounded rumors; I accuse him of hampering the timely sailing of the fleet against Potidaea..."

Nicias fixes his gaze on Athena Promachos; the time has not yet come to plug up.

". . . and I accuse him of instilling that panic in the Assemblies of last summer, thereby delaying operations against Chalcidice until autumn; I accuse him of following the dictates of his hatred against me to the detriment of the best interests of the City..."

By Pallas! What could the Onion be up to? Philodorus and Licophron could not possibly have lied. They swore to having seen the bitch entering his house. Were they capable of perjury before the Gods? Had they sold out to the Head? How dare he say that he...

"... I accuse him of insisting that Perdiccas of Macedonia is casting evil spells on us and of sacrilegious disregard for the conclusive dictates of the High Priest of Dionysus, and I accuse him of having Hiero, his secretary, spread insults about me and rumors that Lampon, our most venerable seer, is senile and incapable; I accuse him, as well, of conjuring sacred terrors to be able to pass himself off as the savior of the imperiled country."

Hagnon stares at the aggressive, deadly, perverse, bronze son of Zeus and Hera, who is now smiling with contempt.

Nicias scratches an ear, his gaze still fixed on the Virgin Warrior.

"I accuse him, indeed, of harboring that intention when he forced Xanthus the Lycian, a miserable slave whose only crime was to try to escape, to confess to complicity in the theft of the Eye with which Athena comtemplates the birth of Pandora; I accuse him of using inhumane torments, unworthy of men endowed with speech, to drive Xanthus to delirium and madness to extract from him a confession that would inflame spirits against anyone who denounced his scheme; I accuse him of doubly defrauding the City, first with an unjustified terror, and then with an impious and deceitful purification of the territory through the capture and homicide of an innocent man."

Nicias scratches his other ear. He begins to feel that his anger may get the best of him. He tells himself that he has to maintain his composure no matter what. What if the Head challenges him? Impossible! The psephisma of Praxiergus authorizes him to present his scheme, but not to challenge him before the College of Generals.

He would give no hint of his anger. His ataraxia would be the best response.

To keep from thinking about Pericles, Nicias begins to recite *The Iliad* in his mind, song theta, and Pericles going on that Nicias had not given conclusive proof that Xanthus the Lycian had had, or had even seen, the stolen amethyst, and therefore it was false that the City had been purified, and Nicias lifting his chin even further, again master of his soul and his face, composing his image, and Hector, not having found his excellent wife inside, stopped in the threshold and spoke to the slaves, and Pericles that it was fraud, the confession was a sham, Nicias had made Xanthus say what he wanted him to say, and One Eye had taken the stone out of the territory, and Hector, there, slaves, tell me the truth, where has Andromache of the white arms gone? and Nicias had dared to allege that because of certain visions, the origin of which he refused to reveal, he was absolutely certain that the guilty pimp was in

Macedonia, and in this City, you did not have to be a seer to know that Nicias saw through the eyes of Melas, his private seer, and that because of that obscure and unknown Syrian, he disregarded Athens's most prestigious masters of the divine art, sons and grandsons of illustrious seers, but the irreverent audacity of Nicias in attributing the Olympic victories of the son of Clinias and of the other Athenian champions to the indulgence of the Gods, thanks to his personal zeal, when, in fact, the truth was quite the contrary, and the Gods were angry because he had allowed the pollution of the City to continue, as in the Thebes of the Cadmeans, and when Hector of the flashing helm came to the Scaean gate, there came running to meet him his bounteous wife Andromache, daughter of great-hearted Eetion, and as the eminent Athenian generals might recall, when the Archon Lysanias ordered the execution of the suspect, Nicias gave his full support to what turned out to be a crime, for as Scolotus's confession later revealed, the Macedonian was an innocent victim, and Pericles, his hand on his chest, lamenting the crime against that honest, devout pilgrim, like so many who came from far horizons to fulfill promises to Athena or revere her, a man for whom at this very moment a widow and orphans might be mourning, and Andromache, ah, my husband, this prowess of thine will be thy doom, neither hast thou any pity for thine infant child nor for hapless me that soon shall be thy widow? and the generals should consider if Athens might not one day have to pay for that crime, and then Hector, the man-slayer, said that Nicias had tortured a miserable fugitive slave and driven him out of his mind to make him confess his services to Perdiccas of Macedonia, his complicity in the murder of the Scythian, and the theft of the amethyst, and that the distinguished generals should say if it was not evident that Nicias was trying to put the blame for all the crimes

on that one slave to be able to appear before the City as its savior and purifier, and everyone knew that Evileye could make
anyone confess anything his employer wanted, and that was
why he had been removed as official torturer from the cells of
the Royal Portico, and with an insolence without precedent in
Athens, Nicias presumed to have everyone believe that it was
his dedication and proficiency that had revealed to the City the
head of the Macedonian spy ring, who turned out to be
Scolotus, another slave, the property of the City, the thief himself, promoter of Xanthus's escape, co-murderer of Pandarus,
and having said this, the clearsighted Hector donned his horse-
hair-plumed helmet, and the beloved wife returned home, but
fortunately, the intrigues of Nicias, son of Niceratus, had not
driven all the logos and the sophrosyne out of the City of Pallas
Athena, and albeit belatedly, the Assembly did approve the sailing of the fleet, and after the war began, the Athenians had not
yet suffered any of the calamities that, according to Nicias,
Perdiccas's witchcraft would visit upon them, and now that
another cadaver had turned up with two mutilated fingers,
what did the son of Niceratus have to say about that? Were the
mutilators of the Cybernetes agents in the employ of the king
of Macedonia? Not at all, nor did Paris tarry long in his lofty
house, but did put on his glorius armour, light with bronze, and
hastened through the City, trusting in his fleetness of foot.

Pericles wants Nicias to speak so that he can ridicule him,
but the Imperturbable keeps absolute silence and never moves
a muscle in his face.

"And so that you may fully understand just how great were
the fraud and the spite against our plans to teach the rebellious
Potidaeans an exemplary lesson, I will reveal a secret that has
been guarded until this day for reasons you will later understand."

Pericles brushes a fly from his forehead, walks to the hydria by the wall, fills a bowl, and drinks it in a single draught.

"When Callias and Archestratus were accused of delaying combat last summer," he continues, drying his moustache with the back of his hand, "they were under express orders from me to enter into a pact with Perdiccas of Macedonia, who a month before the sailing of the fleet had sent me his personal ambassador. Through our emissaries, we exchanged oaths, and as all of you know, I was, for these and other secret maneuvers, empowered by the Athenian demos when I was named its Autocrat General."

Pericles again scans the anxious faces. Incredible! Nicias is the only one there who shows no surprise at the revelation of that evidence.

"Perdiccas is at this moment our ally," he continues, "although he pretends to be allied with Potidaea. One of the conditions of our agreement was that I should not reveal it to the Assembly of the Athenians until the beginning of summer, and this I will do during my tribe's next Pritany. Nicias ignores that this very same Perdiccas he would use to scare us, and who, he would have us believe, has filled the City with his spies and sorcerers, is the one who has been supplying us with food, hides, horses, guides, and wise advice for the capture of Potidaea, as I shall very soon report in detail to the Athenian demos. Here with us is Archestratus, whom I shall release from his oath of secrecy, so that he may confirm my statements, if you so desire."

Archestratus nods several times.

All the generals turn to Nicias, expecting some sort of reply, but he remains pensive, pointing at Pericles with his chin. In vain the supporters of Pericles look for any sign of irritation, indignation, shame, insecurity, anything. Nothing, he never even blinks.

By Zeus! What can that man be made of? His serenity is winning him many supporters; it places him above the affairs and things of men.

"It was a great lie, then, that Perdiccas had agents in our City; a lie that his agents stole the Eye of Athena; a lie that they were responsible for the crime at Epsilon; a lie that Xanthus and One Eye had anything to do with the theft of the Eye. And it was a lie that the Scythian Scolotus ever laid hands on the Eye of Athena."

At this point, Pericles stretches his arm high in the air, his index finger waving, and walks directly toward the front. The generals watch him in alarm, and see him pull vigorously, with one hand, at the heavy door and signal for two Scythians to come into the meeting.

Although they are unarmed, they walk with the metallic clatter of soldiers. Agathyrsus has high cheekbones and narrow eyes. He walks with the open-legged swagger of command and strokes a great white moustache that reaches down to his chin. The other is a tall, young redhead, like many of the men of the plains beyond Thrace. He is barefoot, without bow or dagger, but preserves his pharetra and scabbard, which he wears on one side of his wide leather belt. On the other side, he carries a horn for his water supply, and several bear's teeth and cheap bronze amulets dangle from his neck.

Pericles calls Agathyrsus to his side and sits down.

"Will you now ratify, oh, Agathyrsus, before the generals of Athens, the same oath you gave me on the altars?"

"I swearing by the Unnameable and by Oitosyros and Thamimasadas, if I not saying to excellent generals thought I thinking, if not saying beliefs I believing, if I saying only my convenience, may my body perish with terbull pain and soul of me return in body of filthy spider."

Having heard Agathyrsus's oath, the generals make ready to hear his testimony.

By midafternoon, the entire City knew what had happened in the Strategeion. They knew that the generals had voted, by a majority of one, to authorize Pericles to arraign Nicias before the competent tribunals. Once the case was referred to the civilian tribunals, pursuant to the psephisma of Praxiergus and for the satisfaction of the citizens, Pericles had the heralds read out to all the City a summary of his accusation and of the proof brought in by the Scythians.

Everyone was informed that the profanation had not been the work of Scolotus, but of Targitaus. When the indignant Athenians asked where the profaner was, they were informed that Targitaus was, in fact, Pandarus, the archer sacrificed in Epsilon, and the one who stole the amethyst to gain honors with his assimilation of wine.

457

Everyone realized that he had not been the victim of Perdiccas's agents but, very deservedly, of an avenging hand guided by the wrath of Athena.

Nicias was the last to know.

When Hiero gave him the report, he remained silent a while, his eyes closed. Then he sent for Melas and spoke with him in private. The seer was to go to Delphi; along the roads of Boeotia, he was to sharpen all his gifts, notice all signs, make special note of his dreams and visions, study the flight of migrating birds and the entrails of his sacrifices. Melas was to make certain that Phoebus Apollo gave a clear reply. That was why he was sending an expert seer like himself. Nicias wanted no more mistakes. Apollo was to answer one simple question: Should the son of Niceratus persist or retire forever from Athenian politics?

At dusk, Nicias went to the Lenaeum and sacrificed the most handsome billy goat on his farm to Dionysus. At dawn, he was seen climbing to the Acropolis with two white calves for Athena, who inflames the people and prevails in battle.

59

CLING CLANG, CLING CLANG, hammer and chisel, cling clang, and brother Fire-eater cutting ably away, and cling clang, and the Summoner and Lysis and the Protopriestess, and the brothers present, eyes glued to the stomach of the bronze fish, and when the crack is big enough to wedge a chisel in, and Fire-eater grunting, and the Summoner, enough good, hole fat, give me, and shaking the fish, but no amethyst, only a little bronze ball on the ground, and Fire-eater, that it must be off a rivet, and the Summoner, already knowing that all fat trouble in Barathrum, and not understanding why Phanes so much work throw fish of Nicias in pit nightly with such hiding, and Lysis, sweet as ever, calm again, asking herself why the slave with Phanes was carrying a load to the fount, and suddenly, an idea, yes, Lysis wanted to know how many bronze fish Nicias had put in his fountain, and Sosias that there were four, and Otep, and Shipwreck, and the Paphlagonian, all agreed, yes, four, one in front of Poseidon, one on each side, and one behind, and Lysis, very good, now quickly, Otep lightfoot, the fastest of the brothers, was to go to the fountain and check to see how many were left, and the Summoner, why that? why count fish in fountain? and Lysis insisting, by Poseidon, brother Green-grocer had said that the slave accompanying Phanes was carrying a load from the house to the fountain as well as from the fountain to the Barathrum, and the second load went into the pit, but what about the first? what was in that pack? and the Summoner pensive, nodding, beginning to understand, yes, possible Phanes change fish, whetted thought of astute Lysis, Lysis being right possiblest truth, and she interrupting, she was feeling a message from the Gods, an order, they were saying something, please, could the Summoner help her understand? only them, he should go to her room with her for a consultation, and on Otep's return, the

Summoner and Lysis were still in consultation with the Gods and took a while longer, and she showed up radiant, and he wore his bonnet for great occasions and his green tunic, and the dawn was breaking, and Otep saying that there were still four fish in the fountain, and the Summoner saying that the Gods had told the Great Priestess the same, so then logicos that Phanes take fish of Nicias NN and throw in Barathrum and put different fish in fountain, and he and Great Priestess already finish consultation, and now, much quickly, prepare to go to fountain, tomorrow before dawn, before many people bypassing, and Sosias, you say passersby, and Hypothesis stabbing him in the chest with an elbow, how dare the confounded Carian interrupt the Summoner's holy inspiration, and the other brothers growling, and the Summoner explaining that in the rescue of the Eye only Lysis giving orders, Lysis favorite of Three-in-One, and only her know ways of Eye, she smelling better than even Summoner, she hound with holy nose, and all obeying now words of Lysis that God whisper in her ear, words of Sum like ripe figs dropping on Lysis soul, and that Lysis go tomorrow to fountain of NN, and that he, in name of Cybele, Dionysus, and Aphrodite Pandemos, all Three-in-One, naming her captain of attack on fountain, but Otep wary, what if Alcibiades's men show up? what if daggerman Phanes attacks escortless sister Lysis? but Lysis, that the First Faithful should abandon his fears, no one would see her face, the Gods had inspired her plan, and Lysis ordering that the one to go to the rescue of the Eye would be the Protopriestess Hypothesis of Athens, but dressed in rags, and also Sosias the Second Faithful among the men, and also Fire-eater the Twentieth Faithful, and she would use the day to make a perfect disguise, and Fire-eater was to take the fish recovered from the Barathrum, they had cut it open for nothing, and he should hammer it shut so the gash could not be seen, and he should then engrave a drawing and a message she would tell him later, and in the meantime, Hypothesis and Evardis should find Lysis a black penthimon somewhere in the City, so that no one would recognize her shape, and the Paphlagonian was to weave a basket of tender olive twigs, like the ones used by young widows to hide their faces when they pray to Athena in processions to the Acropolis.

461

6 0

LOOK, OVER THERE, the black seagulls are back again, calling you. See how they soar against the Pamphylian sunset, and you open your arms and take off screeching a hoarse greeting. You fly over the slave barracks where your mother is chanting the lament of the harvest slaves, and you climb and climb, and the seagulls come to welcome you and fly with you, and they fly around you making lovely pirouettes, and the saffron field is far behind, and you are no longer that starved and dirty little bundle of human flesh chained to a tree, nor a captured fugitive with ankle chains that barely let you inch your way over the fields, hoe in hand, from sunrise to sunset, no! look at yourself now, the Summoner of the Sum flying with his red mane flowing in the breeze, your white tunic billowing, and you soar very high and bank steeply, folding your wings and letting yourself plummet like a brilliant shooting star heading for the foamy waves, and the thrill overwhelms you, and you screech again...

"Eh? What?"

Nino and Chloe heard you screaming?

No. There was nothing wrong; you were not calling anyone. You were in consultation with the Gods.

Oh, irony! The sisters' concern dispels your visions.

Then you order Nino, the Exact Masseuse, to call for Palaemon. You need the services of a scribe. Yes, hurry up.

Was it possible that the Gods had finally decided that you could fly? Might it be true?

And while the Sybarite is on his way, think. Think Phrygianly. Rein in your fleet thoughts like an able auriga. Clearly now, is it not evident that the Gods are announcing something wonderful? Perhaps the reward for recovering the Eye is to make you an aerial priest? Could it be that their intention is for Atys of Pamphylia to be the highest priest in all the known world, so that his New Church can be the brightest and truest? Is this why they kept you from dying in the saffron fields and tinted your eyes lavender? When Palaemon comes, you must tell him about that time before the Doors of Syria, the doors that kept you from escaping to Cilicia, how you caught a bat and studied its wings, how you made your own out of wicker and linen stolen from your master, the pirate, and ask him why you did not kill yourself, why you survived your fall on the reefs at the foot of the cliffs without a single scratch, and let him say whether or not that was clear proof that the hand of the Gods was protecting you. Yes, all that must go into the Book of Miracles, and that the crash did not kill your determination, and that you went to Crete to learn to fly with the sons of Icarus, and he is to write that you left because they only flew downward, gliding from the summit of Mount Ida, with their tricky science of inflated skins. But you, oh, Atys of Pamphylia, were destined to fly up among the Gods, and let the Sybarite say

463

if it is not perfectly diaphanes that they were secretly training you to supervise the many temples of the Sum, destined since those times to become the most popular and ecumenical of all churches.

6 1

MORE THAN A HUNDRED old men have already arrived at the agora by the first light of dawn, occupying the steps leading up to the King's Tribunal, while others reserved seats on stands by the Temple of Hephaestus.

Some Prytaneum slaves are placing wooden benches by the Painted Portico and adorning the Altar of Piety with garlands and wreaths. Lysis, her face completely hidden inside her basket, is instructing Hypothesis and Fire-eater about the riot they are to start, and when the agora authorities come to take them away, Sosias is to offer them the gold stater and tell them that she is a relative, a poor mad woman, and Lysis is already moving toward the fountain, walking across the agora, and Hypothesis, making believe she just ran into Fire-eater, and, come here, you rat, this is how I wanted to catch you, before the Temple of Hephaestus, protector of blacksmiths, to see if he can protect you from my staff, and wham, the staff across the shoulders, and jumping on him, ruffian, thief, will you dare deny here before the temple that you have been owing me three drachmas for about a year, and Fire-eater struggling with her, why doesn't the old sorceress die, the slanderer, how dare she tell such lies and malign an honest blacksmith on a holy day, and his patron Hephaestus knew very well that he owed the poisonous old witch nothing, and she, shut up, you old pederast, fornicator of mangy donkeys, and he taking her by the hair, and she biting his arm, and both of them rolling in the dirt, and Sosias trying to separate them, and Lysis, with everyone enjoying the fracas, moving along the cobblestone path to the fountain, and the few stragglers still near the fountain move quickly to the agora to see what the commotion is all about, and Lysis trying fruitlessly to reach one of the fish from the edge, and then wading in, and Fire-eater screaming, ouch, let go of me, you old Gorgon, you're getting fleas on me, ouch, help, call the agora authorities, call the Scythians, she's pissing on me! the stench is killing me, and two Scythians and an agoranomos coming from the tent by the Altar of the Twelve Gods, and Lysis with the water up to her knees and her penthimon rolled up around her thighs, shaking the third fish, but no rattle, could it be that the Gods had sent her a false inspiration? and back at the agora, let go, piss-ass, you dog-eater, and she, what about you, bugger of unburied corpses, go on, hit me some more, and the agoranomos beating them both with his staff, and the Scythians grabbing them, and Fire-eater letting go of Hypothesis and feeling himself pulled from behind, and the Scythian twisting the tunic, and watch out, damn you, don't tear it, and the Scythian pushing him and making him tiptoe, and Hypothesis on his other arm, practically flying, and the agoranomos ordering that the disturbers of the peace be locked away in the Prytaneum dungeon, and Sosias asking if the excellent agoranomos would be so kind as to tell him how much the fine would be, and Lysis shaking the fourth fish, and listening, oh, joy, the rattle was music to her ears, a holy and wished-for sound, there was no doubt now, and feeling fresh strength welling up inside her, an incredible effervescence in her blood, her eyes sharper than ever, oh miracle, and the sun, which was just beginning to peek over Pentelikon, suddenly shifting to Dindymenian Asia, and the newborn day takes on a lavender tint, and she hardly has time to sigh when the vision disappears, and she immediately understands the unequivocal sign from the Three-in-One, message received, the Gods were confirming the rescue, and without even looking inside the fish, Lysis knows that she has the Dindymenian Eye, a thousand blessings on the Gods of the Sum, and the agoranomos staring at the golden stater in Sosias's hand, and understanding that putting people in the dungeons was bad luck for the City on the holiest day of the Panathenian Festivals, and since the blacksmith was an honest man and the other a poor mad woman, they could go their way, but the hag was not to show herself in the agora for the rest of the day, not even at noon, when the procession of the Goddess set out, and Sosias promising, and Lysis letting down her penthimon to cover her heels, and her widow's basket on her head, now crossing the agora, now approaching the onlookers, now seeing Fire-eater leaving the Prytaneum and heading for the Street of the Tripods, and Hypothesis not much later, with the Carian, taking opposite directions, and Lysis taking a fourth direction and smiling, for the bronze fish in the fountain were also heading in different directions, and thanks to Lysis of Miletus, the fountain once again has the same fish placed there by Nicias of Niceratus.

467

6 2

FROM ASPASIA IN ATHENS
TO EURYDICE IN SARDES

The thirtieth of Hecatombaion

WHEN THEY TOLD ME that the ship was not sailing until dawn tomorrow, I ran to pick up the scrolls
so that I could send the latest bit of gossip in the City.
Something very important and unexpected has happened, and
I hope my quill is fast enough to get it all down.

Very early yesterday morning, Cleis showed up at the
house, wrapped in a penthimon and her head hidden in the
kálathos of a widow. She said she was in a very big hurry; she
had just come by for a parting kiss, for she was leaving the City
immediately. She left so soon I had no time to feel sad. We
spoke in whispers, in my room, and we never even sat down.

Dumbfounded by all the surprises, I just listened.

There were private reasons that obliged her to leave immediately to fulfill a secret mission from her new Gods. Then she kissed me, put on her basket, and left. It was terrible to see her go. I thought I had certainly lost her forever, and I was surprised that I felt no anxiety. Maybe I am going through the same sort of process dogs experience when they wean their grown pups; the truth is, there is a certain strength about her that outweighs all my desire to protect her. I have begun to love her in a different way. Seeing her so strong has freed me of the horrible fear of seeing her fail, or die, because of my neglect. I feel that even my questions are of no use to her, and I realize how needless were my concerns for her health, her libertine life, and her doctor. This, and no other, was the destiny assigned to her by the Gods.

I, of course, had no idea what the reason might have been for her hasty departure, but that afternoon, something happened that gave me a rather good hint.

But first I must tell you about Alcibiades, as always, in the center of things in Athens.

Pericles was rather pleased with Alcibiades's recent antics; he was certain that they were some sort of play-acting aimed at breaking up the campaign against the Alcmeonidae. Immediately after the first inscriptions of "Death to the impure Alcmeonidae, defenders of procuresses," came the riddles. From the moment Alcibiades made his docile declaration of love for Cleis on the Ceramicus wall, Nicias's men began to write on the walls of the City: "Who is the impure Alcmeonid, victorious before Zeus, Ares, and Athena, but a groveling loser before Aphrodite Sweet-Rump?" And, "Who are the two impure Alcmeonidae in love with a brace of Milesian whores?"

On the very wall of the Ceramicus appeared tongue twisters

469

and obscenities alluding to the cringing verses with which Alcibiades petitioned Cleis. Rumor has it that a certain writer of comedies, whom both offended at a banquet, is the author of the invectives. Since Alcibiades made no reaction, Pericles was certain that his visions were just a trick, groundwork for his reply to the provocations. Now it would seem that he was not too far off the mark, to judge from what happened yesterday during the inaugural procession for the Panathenian Festivals.

When the devotees were beginning to climb the hill to the Acropolis, carrying the new peplus and singing hymns to the Goddess, Alcibiades, who as hero, Olympic and Panathenian champion, was in the front ranks behind the Arrephorian Virgins, began to spin around in the middle of the procession like a man possessed. People say they saw him run away shouting that the Goddess was staring at him with the Eye stolen from the Parthenon and that he felt a salty taste in his mouth, something like seawater. And that he shouted, "What do you want of me? Speak, I beg of you, oh flashing-eyed Athene." And all this with his palms and eyes turned up toward the Citadel, as if he were talking to the effigy of Promachus.

Pericles was close by. He says he saw him veer to the side, spinning and falling back, as if some invisible force were dragging him by the cloak. Thus did he leave the slope in the direction of a small clearing where Nicias had a fountain made for Poseidon. The procession had to stop, and everyone saw him wade into the water up to his knees. There was a clamor, of course, but not even the High Priestess of Athena, taken by surprise like everyone else, thought to stop him. Pericles says that they silenced the hymns to the Goddess, everyone was expecting a miracle; Alcibiades seemed to be possessed by one of the deities. From the middle of the fountain, he turned, looking toward the Acropolis, and continued screaming, "What do you want of me, oh child of Zeus that beareth the Aegis! Why do you stare at me with a single eye?"

Finally, he stooped in the water, took one of the bronze dolphins from the bottom and began to turn it in his hands and study it closely, as if expecting to hear something from inside. Then he did the same with the second dolphin, and then with the remaining two, after which, they say he looked like he had been struck by lightning, deathly pale. Ultimately, he threw one of the fish into the trees and ran off dripping water, pushing everyone aside, and losing himself among the crowds in the agora.

When Nicias of Niceratus and others, paralyzed by the magnitude of the sacrilege, came to their senses, they ran to return the dolphin to the water. Its stomach had been cut open and someone had engraved a phallus and an inscription: "For Alcibiades, son of Clinias."

471

That very afternoon, Alcibiades, now in full control of himself, swore he remembered nothing of what had happened and claimed that he felt horrified and crushed by the events. His friends say he was possessed by an evil spirit. But what the City does not know is that from the hill leading up to the Acropolis, he ran all the way to the Ceramicus. Accompanied by a few slaves, he crossed the agora and made his way to Cleis's house, which was empty, except for the doorman and a slave. Then he stabbed a dog to death, entered the house, and proceeded to break into every chest and bale, accompanying his slaves through every room and even searching the well. Not having found Cleis, he tried to learn her whereabouts from the slave, who was able to tell him nothing. The poor thing is still unconscious, agonizing, disfigured by the beating.

Then he went to Truncheon's. By this time he was a little more collected, but he threatened to kill her if she did not let him search her house thoroughly. She even had to open her pantries and chests, any place where Cleis might be hiding.

When he left, Truncheon sent a slave to me to implore Cleis, just in case she was with me, to keep out of Alcibiades's way, for he would certainly kill her.

Pericles and I immediately supposed what it was that might have happened. It fills me with pride to see the way she got back at him for her humiliation with the necklace incident.

Alcibiades's behavior and his disruption of such a solemn procession have again provided fuel for those who fan the flames of hatred against the Alcmeonidae and are demanding, together with the Peloponnesians, that they be ostracized to purify the City. Many insist that Alcibiades's offence against Poseidon will lead to disasters at sea.

Since the official seers have not come to any unanimous conclusion, there will be a delegation leaving tomorrow for Delphi to consult Apollo about the measures the City must take.

But we, friends of the logos, know that the first victories in Chalcidice will allay the fears of the many and the wave of superstition will wane. Once again, Pericles will have had his way. Be happy.

DELIVERED IN ATHENS ON THE THIRTIETH OF HECATOMBAION ARCHON EUTHYNUS

FROM

SPRING

OF

APPOLLODORUS

TO

SUMMER

OF

EPAMEINON

63

A S HE CRAWLED OUT of the cave, he was overcome by a dizzy spell. The trees of the swamp began to spin. He waited, panting on all fours, until the dry heaves allowed him stand up. He started walking like a drunk, stiff, teetering. After so many days in the shadows, the strident dawn forced him to shade his eyes. At the foot of a walnut tree, he cut off a branch and trimmed it with his knife. Without a staff he would never be able to climb Mount Dindymon.

When the first fevers had subsided, he took refuge in the cave to try to regain some of his strength for the ascent, but the fevers came back, and the vomiting. The dry fish was impossible to hold down, and the crackers and bag of wild berries were all in vain.

The fever left him exhausted, he even vomited the water he drank. For ten days his stomach could hold nothing, but when he emerged from his last delirium, he realized that, if he kept on postponing the ascent, he would never make it to the summit of Dindymon. He would die without returning the Eye.

As he recovered his breath, he put all his weight on the staff and started down the slope to the swamps. The water was halfway up his leg, and the mud clung and sucked at his ankles. He fell on his knees in the water, holding onto the staff for his life. There was still half a farsang to go, all uphill.

When he finally reached the reeds on the bank, he tripped and fell flat. It was no use trying to get up. He lay there on his side, resting his cheek on the creamy coolness of the putrid mud. Before passing out, he checked the muddy mound of hair on the back of his head. Yes, the bag was still there in the braided knot.

Before the plague in Athens, he had never been sick, except for whips, the sticks of the slave drivers in the saffron fields, or the long fasts during his pilgrimages.

He was not afraid of death. Indeed, he had often wished for it. But it had never been so close. He could discern voices he had already heard, but now they were coming from the other side of the moon.

The sun was high over the east when the flapping wings of a flock of cranes woke him. He propped his elbows on the muddy bank, then got to his knees and crawled toward the dry earth. With the help of his staff, he struggled to his feet and started up the side of the hill.

Several halts later, he had made it up the first slope. There, almost at the very summit, he could see the Great Temple of the Mother of the Gods, the shining cupolas given by Croesus, and the silver pine tree offered by the princes of Phrygia.

As he approached the rocks at the mouth of the Cave of the Shepherds, a bat winged a frantic escape, fluttering over his head. Everything was the same on Dindymon, as if he had never left its foothills. And it was terrible that nothing had changed. He wanted to cry. He was no longer the adolescent who climbed up from the widow's shack to perform his devotions in the temple. Was he a traveler as old as the world? No! He was an insect. His life was as brief as a mayfly's. He could feel the eternal landscape mocking him. A smoldering rancor, dull as the beating of a bat's wings.

He looked into the bottom of the ravine. Yes, there was the green clearing into which he had jumped with the cupola made of the linen he had stolen from the mansion of the Archigallus. How sad, the sacramental perfume of the pine trees, the choir of the trembling waters, and the occasional glitter of the sunflowers by the pilgrims' pavilion.

How different he had imagined his return! For years he had seen himself rushing uphill like the wind; as he reached the second summit, all the faithful of the region, the metragyrtes coming from the barracks of Celaenae, the Gallus of the temple, and the Archigallus of Sardes would all be waiting, singing praise for the Child Mother.

He would reverently place the Eye on a silver tray and preside over the Restitution Entourage to the accompaniment of Phrygian flutes, pan pipes, and tambourines. More recently, he had dreamed that he was flying, diving down among the entire congregation of priests waiting on the esplanade of the Great Temple. Not at all like the snail he was, ignored by the world, crawling with his last ounce of strength.

The autumnal meanders of the Hermus were far behind; here the young river leapt in foamy cascades. And Atys cried. His tears eroded gullies down his muddy cheeks. When he got to the first fall, he collapsed on his stomach, drank his fill, and then vomited everything under the shade of a tired old willow. A sudden chill shook his body and clouded his vision. He dragged himself to the soft bed of needles under the pines. He lay there hugging his knees, trembling, until the intense cold left him and his teeth stopped chattering. The fever was coming back. There were shadows in the sky, and he could see the far mountains quivering. If he got any weaker, he might never be able to get on his feet. He might even die from the next fever spell. And it was all so near. It was no use looking inside himself; his eyes had lost their power. Might that be the announcement of his death? Perhaps the Three-in-One had only given him enough strength to rescue the Eye. He tried to get up, clinging to a young pine, and fell down again. He still had two stadia to go before he got to the Cave of the Child, all uphill. At last he got to his feet, stumbled, ran to keep from falling, bumped into a pine, and fell back on his elbows, the fever burning his eyes, the mountain blue, the trees undulating like the bottom of a lake, and again the beautiful face of Lysis of Miletus spoke to him without words, we are but a breath and a shadow, ánemos kaì skiá, and her face begins to stretch, becomes a thread, and the Scythian takes the dagger in the throat, and again the screech of the seagull on the cliffs, and Atys soars from Mount Cithaeron, and the wind lifts him over the cypresses, and since he cannot fly, he holds onto a treetop that bends, bends, and breaks, dropping him on the providential branch of a beech, and as he was losing consciousness, he had a vision of the Pythia on the tripod. Why, why hadn't they come to Dindymon? Whatever had the brothers of the Sum been doing among the winds of Epirus, in arid Libya, or in plague-ridden Egypt? Could it have been he who had gotten everyone sick by feeding them that rat after convincing them that it was venison? Hypothesis smiles at him with her teeth of clouds, and Sosias the Carian crying on the summit of Cithaeron, no, don't jump, no one can fly with just their arms, the Summoner of the Sum is going to be killed, and he telling him to shut up, and looking at him and at Nino, the Exact Masseuse, and then Palaemon and Shipwreck and Otep, and Lysis raising the three fingers of the Sum and swearing that if he died she would take the Dindymenian Eye back to the Great Mother, and look! look! his feet are rising from the ground, and everyone contemplating in ecstasy, and he telling them that he was already up a hand span, two, three, five, and flying over their heads, and they obediently looking up, and Nino's legs fail her, and Sosias has his hair on end, and that day the brothers knew what veneration was, a cold tickle akin to horror, like a nearby lightning strike that twists one's features, and when all were following his ascent into the heavens, he scurried off to the edge of the cliff, spread his arms, and dove off to fly, but again the vertigo, the slapping of the branches, and the slapping of the boat off Cape Malea, trying to save Nino, the poor child swept away by the waves, and her scream lingers and grows and becomes one with the moan of time, and brother Shipwreck at the tiller, fighting the summer storm, the terrified eyes of Palaemon, Lysis crying, and since the Eye had been rescued, why was the Sum forcing them away from the straight path back to Mount Dindymon? why demand that the Eye of Cybele be recognized by Apollo, Zeus, Ammon, and Osiris? and clutching the root of a Dindymenian pine, face sunken in the needles, he again saw the beautiful, serene face of Palaemon the Sybarite, interpreting the vision, and the Pythia, sitting on a smoking slab in the Temple of Apollo, examining the Eye, and the message was very clear, before going to Asia, they had to go to Delphi, and everything got complicated, first toward the Great Bear, then to the south ... and now, just a hundred paces from the Child Goddess, the Sum was denying him the strength he had had to squander on the pilgrimage.

479

Someone coming ...

He somehow managed to raise his head. It was Lysis of

Miletus, walking down the hill in graceful strides. She came up next to him and kneeled, smiling, but the caress he intended for her sank into the pine needles. Damned delirium! The whole damned place, just a few steps from the Child Mother, might be delirium. Why did the trees undulate and the mountains sing in the distance? What did they want from him, those voices in forgotten tongues that swarmed in his ears? Was there ever a redhaired metragyrtes in Athens? Had a woman named Lysis of Miletus ever existed? And digging his nails into a tree to get on his feet, he could feel the pulse of the warm sap under the bark. On his feet, he again saw the face of terror of Sosias the Carian, that time when he had scared him with the whinny, and Lysis must have existed, yes, she had existed, and she had died in his arms, eyes deep set, face swollen, festering, her breath horrid and gasping, yes, he had done that to her, and Atys got angry, why did the Sum hound him with the worst of his memories? and he raised a threatening fist to heaven, and Lysis gasping for life, her face purple from the sores, yellowish pools of plague that could not stand the touch of a piece of linen, and the house without water, and trying to soothe her in the fountain of Dipylon, precious cool water in the wretched summer, dragging her, helped by Palaemon, Fire-eater, Sosias, Hypothesis, only to find the fountain beset by others of the dying, pushing with indecent desperation, driven by the thirst, one on top of the other, and the brothers making way toward the coveted water, and he, Atys of Pamphylia, had known before any Athenian the feeling of a furnace in his head, swollen gums, the burning of split lips, bleeding tongue and throat, and his eyes were powerless against the disease sent by the Gods, and the sneezing, and that murderous cough that pushed the rot toward the heart, and waagh, the cholera vomit, the apocatharsis, and one avid drink and another and another, and the thirst that will not yield, all the water in the world is not enough, and the plague descends to the stomach and your life drains away in diarrhea, and the pain twists your guts, and when you cough, you have rusted files in your chest, daggers in your stomach, hot coals in your festering sphincter, and you moan like a child, crying in vain, oh, brothers, give to me gift of good death, you, Fire-eater, Gods command you kill me hard in head, but the Gods spared him, and Otep, the second follower of the Sum to be stricken, delirious, forgetting the Greek language, eyes rotten, without will or memory, and the third one was Lysis, lying there by the fountain, and beside her another victim tearing off pieces of his body with his crazed hands, and brother Green-grocer, still alive, recognizing no one, there, beside the others, face full of holes, his lungs rumbling with the purr of death, and then his wife began with the fevers and the swelling eyes, and she carried her husband on her shoulders, but when she appeared to be heading for the fountain, she hurled his body into a funeral pyre and then threw herself on the flames, no respect at all for the soul being cremated or for the family contemplating the sacred rites, and suffering Athens had lost all semblance of civilization, no one cared for the rites for the dead, and despite the protests of the priests, the pyres in the besieged City burned men and women, children and old people, the dead and the dying, and those who inherited goods and monies from the victims were getting drunk, look at them, all over the streets, no respect for anything, desperately trying to spend as much as possible before the plague got them, and people shamelessly fornicating in the porticos, under trees, by the wall, men with children, women with women, and how strange that there are no birds on the unburied bodies, by day or by night, and even the vultures avoided them, and Atys admitted that it was a disease sent by the Gods, and Palaemon nodded, saying that even

481

the dogs, those curious creatures that smell everything, avoided contact with people, and again his lavender eyes turned to the slopes of Dindymon, he looked up, angry with the Sum, why was the Triple God bringing those memories of the plague on him? were they a threat? was it mockery again just a few steps from the Sacred Grotto? May the scoundrel God die! and obscene gestures with his hands, excretory noises for the ungrateful Sum that failed to care for its Summoner, and the rage gave him strength, and he stood up, leaning on a trunk and taking a step, and another, and he checked the braid where the Holy Stone was hidden, and his eyes were burning, tongue swelling, tottering, eyes fixed on the summit half an arrowshot away, then faster, tripping on the last trunks, running, fists clenched, biting his tongue, no sensation in his legs, he no longer feared that his heart might burst inside his chest or that the fever might melt his brain, and up, and up, tearing open the braid, feeling the Earth spin and the trees throb, and when he finally reached the entrance to the grotto, he exploded, screaming with his last breath in the Phrygian tongue, "KRISKA MAMA OLA, KRISKA! I am here, oh Great Mother, I am here!" and he fell on the ground and crawled into the grotto on his elbows, KRISKA MAMA OLA, and the stones in the grotto quivering and the mountains howling and the gulls of Pamphylia screeching loudly, and he, inspired by Lysis's flute, and again he heard all the voices of his life, like at the Pylai ton Hipnon, popopom popopom, and dragging himself to the effigy carved in the hard rock, he kissed the bare feet and the bare legs, and clutching the incipient breasts of the child, he got to his feet, and the darkness would not let him see her features, but he could feel, his fingers were exploring the missing eye, and he drew nearer to kiss the empty socket and lick the salt of her mourning, and Atys cried too, and the mute popopom

482

increasing in his ears, and the overall song of the world rising around him, and bit by bit the effigy took shape, and finally, when Atys could see the face, he slowly raised his hand, bringing the Eye toward the empty socket, and he heard Phrygian flutes and bells, and felt his blood pounding, and suddenly he heard the unmistakable silence that precedes the divine word, the trees and the wind hush, and just when he was about to place the Eye, the Child Goddess threw her head back and disappeared from his sight.

Atys tumbled against the moss-covered wall.

"What happened to the Child Mother?" he screamed in the Phrygian, his face twisted with evil, demanding.

And a masculine voice, deep and metallic, answered in Greek: "OUPOTE EGENETO TOIAUTE THEA. *That Goddess never existed.*"

"But she was there!" screamed Atys. "She had a single eye." 483

"PSEUDEIS! *You lie!*"

Atys lowered his head as if he had, in fact, been caught lying. He knit his brow, blinked, shook his head, clearing away the vapors of a long dream. He was confused. Fifteen, twenty years had gone by. The God was right. The only effigy that had been plundered was that of the Great Mother of the Gods in the Major Temple. And he suddenly realized that he had never seen the Goddess with a missing eye. When he had first gotten to Dindymon, they had already replaced the stolen eyes with two new ones made of ivory and diamonds, a gift of the satrap. Then why had he been convinced that there was a child with a single eye in that grotto?

He felt ashamed. Could it be that some mocking God had put that in his head?

"OUPOTE EGENETO PAIDEIOS METER. *There never was a Child Mother.*"

"Now I hear Three-in-One," declared Atys in Greek.

High up in a hollow in the roof of the grotto, there appeared a heavenly light. Atys squinted and shaded his eyes with his hand.

"You are wrong," the voice from above informed him. "I am not your Three-in-One."

"Yes," Atys replied, suddenly angry, "you that very fat voice, wooo, who talk Greekly in Athens, you Sum, ox voice, you not fool, you Cybele, Dionysus, Aphrodite."

"Yes," thundered the voice in the grotto, "I am Cybele, Dionysus, and Aphrodite, for I am All Gods, the Alpha and the Omega, I am who I am, the Total God, the One God, the Monos Theos, as you shall henceforth know me."

"I not call you nothing, never more obey!" screamed Atys, striking the wall where the effigy should have been. "Why you fooling me? For your fault, of deceiver, I pursue Eye with so many much death, and I walk on lonely ice like bear, and drink sand in deserts, eat rats, eat owl vomit in mountains, and now you say I lie! Was it not you," he shouted, swallowing his tear, "was it not you who putting false Child Mother in my head? Why, oh, worst God, so cheating?"

"Short is your vision still," said the ox voice, soothingly. "Keep the Eye until you find your destiny. Be joyful and break forth into song that I have chosen you and that I am now confirming you as my High Priest."

Atys stood frozen with his fist in the air; he shook his head, looked around in surprise, and pointed an index finger at his chest.

Him? Truth? Confirmed again as Summoner? So then the One God was not angry about his role in the Church of the Sum? Nor about his doings as a beggar of the Goddess? Nor about the ladies?

"O glorious great!" he exclaimed, standing on his feet without support and raising his palms. "I salute you, oh, very one MONOS THEOS! Forgive words of pain, oh, beloved God, giver to me of Dindymenian Eye, for I to seeing more strongly."

"OUK OPSEI ALL'OFTHESEI. *Through that eye you shall not see, but be seen,*" the God said. "It is with your own eyes that you shall one day decipher the enigma."

"And why you not make for me miracle of gulls and I fly in your temples?"

"Your paths fly not in the ether, but lie in the swamps of your soul," said the Monos Theos. "Only by crawling like a vile insect will you find the path to me. But if it is your will to fly, so be it; I shall allow you to fly within yourself. You shall have breezes and winds within, and colorful landscapes, and you shall have falls and suffer blows as strong as my hatred. But in a coming century, with the dung of your existence, you shall fertilize the New Flower, which will exude the perfume of the millennia. And this is the mission I give you. Go now and compose new truths, without denying the old."

Atys rose, his eyes full of tears. As he left the grotto, he felt strength flowing again in his legs. The trees watched silently as he descended the hill toward the place where the sun was setting, very far in the distance, over Aegean waters.

"Noooo!" echoed the admonitory voice from the grotto, the voice of God. "Journey into the rising sun, for there they are expecting you."

485

6 4

FROM ASPASIA IN ATHENS
TO ANAXAGORAS IN LAMPSACUS

Twelfth of Elaphebolion

ON THE NIGHT of your escape, Pericles told me that he would fight for your return, so that one day you will be able to enjoy the high honors Athens owes you. But he asked me, if he should die before then, to send you, as proof of his love and admiration, the rolls of Oedipus, written in the hand of the Didaskalos, as well as the scepter with the seal of the owl that belonged to his father, Xanthippus.

On the eve of the third enemy invasion, I am hurrying to fulfill his last desire. Pericles succumbed to the plague ten days ago.

You were on his mind until the very last moment. Not long

ago, in the presence of Hippodamus, Ictinus, and two honorable generals who visited him despite their fear of the plague, he maintained that because you were the first to bring Ionian philosophy to this City, where no one knew how to think, you deserved to be a lifetime guest at the Prytaneum, that they should have crowned you with Olympic laurels for your victory over superstition, praised you for teaching that the sun and the moon were not Gods, and raised your effigies in the streets for teaching us that our intelligence can perceive what our senses cannot. He recalled that memorable day when you made us see air and humidity by compressing a wineskin inside a clepsydra.

Another day, he made Sophocles and Philolaus of Crotona laugh by imitating your inflections and gestures; he used the same words we all heard you speak when you told us that the very same piece of bread that fed us, and that makes the hair and the nails and the flesh grow, must necessarily have in it the essences of hair, nails, and flesh, invisible to the senses, but clearly discernible to the nous; he imitated you perfectly in the way you squinted your eyes and ceaselessly scratched your elbow as you spoke; he knew your works by heart, and the poem on Heraclitus; and in reciting the idea that the black is in the white and the white in the black, he exaggerated, as you did, the etas and the omegas in the Ionian fashion.

He died convinced that the spirit is the purest and most subtle of all essences and that there are no predetermined destinies, nor Gods, that meddle in human affairs.

On one of his last days, he went into a long delirious speech in which he lectured on strategy; suddenly, he surprised us all by improvising an apologia of you, as if he were defending you before the heliasts. "Do you not understand, oh, men of Athens," he explained, "that the teachings of Anaxagoras of Clazomene have brought innumerable benefits to this ungrate-

487

ful City that today condemns and expels him? Who was it who conceived of this great Athens you have today? It was Anaxagoras, undoubtedly. And he gave you the Parthenon and the Propylaea. Who, if not he, gave you Euripides and Sophocles, who have made the Athenian stage great with the loftiest poetry? Blind you are if you cannot see that all that is beautiful and true amongst us came into the City following his footsteps, like a shadow."

Pericles died on the side of truth and of mortals, an enemy of false Gods, destinies, and superstitions. He died faithful to your nous, and with festering lips and the slightest waft of a voice, he quoted, among his last lucid words, the verse that your doctrine inspired in Euripides: "Our intelligence is the only divinity that guides us."

He bade me farewell with beautiful words that are today my company and my support. Among his most cherished loved ones, he mentioned Damon, Sophocles, Hippodamus, and Phidias. But you were his favorite. You were never absent from our home. When we had get-togethers in the andron with our closest friends, he always set aside the couch where you used to lie. And on the threshold of his parting, Pericles asked me to ensure that you could live comfortably and with decorum, wherever you might be. And this I will do, as soon as you let me know what you require. Need I remind you that I, too, consider you a faithful friend?

The thirteenth

Blind superstition again reigns in the City. The Athenians are convinced that they are victims of the rage of Dionysus and Athena because of certain offenses committed not long ago in their temples. So great is their fear that they have all agreed to keep silent. They are convinced that their silence will show that

488

they accept the punishment. To make things worse, for some time now the enemies of Pericles have been denouncing him as the cause of the calamities. They accuse him through his Alcmeonid lineage, which is infecting the territory with its ancestral guilt.

Now that Athens is without him, it has fallen into the hands of the faint-hearted and the demagogues, headed by Nicias of Niceratus. For years, Pericles had been calculating the steps that had to be taken to ensure that this inevitable war might favor Athens. He left nothing to chance. He knew they would invade us and mow down our fields. His clear foresight told him that the cattle had to be sent to the island of Euboea and that the peasant population had to be protected within the City walls. He was prepared for adversity and confident of victory. The day that Athens ruled over all of Hellas without constraints would be the day that his dream and yours would come true: to install in Athens the reign of philosophy, beauty, and greater justice among men.

489

The first time we looked over our walls and saw the Spartans chopping down the olive groves and burning the fields, thousands of irate refugees demanded to go out and fight the enemy to defend their property. But Pericles persuaded them that this war would be won on the seas, that their homes, their fields, their olive groves, and their crops were nothing compared to the wealth that victory would bring. He persuaded them time and again. During the first year, he remained in command. His detractors fanned the flames of ignorant calumny and claimed that the plague proved them right, but he remained serene. Not even when he was torn by the pain of burying his two eldest sons did he fail to do his duty. Never did he vacillate or give up for a single moment. There you would find him quieting the demos with his oratory and his persuasion. He would be out on the streets, in the Collegium, in the Tholos, or on the Pnyx, night and day, looking after public affairs, planning the counterattacks of the fleet, actually serving as captain of that fleet last summer against Epidaurus. And with his courage and dedication, he was able to overcome the first waves of malevolence raised by his enemies.

But the plague was to break the back of his determination. It was the most pestilent and murderous disease in the memory of men. No doctors ever found a remedy. They were among the first to die. Those opposed to Pericles convinced the many that the plague was not only a punishment for the recent offenses against Dionysus and Athena, but also, and very especially, the purifying expiation for the crime of the Alcmeonidae. Since all their seers, prayers, promises, and sacrifices were to no avail, they demanded that Pericles resign. And again he faced them in the Assembly. He tried to prove to them that the plague could not be the fault of the Alcmeonidae, for it had risen in Ethiopia and then invaded Egypt, Libya, and other territories of the Great King, as everyone knew. He reminded them that the plague had broken out in Piraeus, proving that it had come by sea. But he was not successful and was deposed two months before contracting the disease. I buried him myself, and the City paid him no tribute.

You cannot imagine, oh, beloved teacher, what the plague has done to Athens. I would be happy to lose my memory forever just to forget the terror that hounds me without quarter for my young Pericles. Even the invading troops fled from the infection, during the second month of the siege.

When we were able to go out into the fields and visit out farm, Pericles cried beside the stump of the first olive tree planted by his father, after the Persians.

When the army of Xerxes burned and chopped down all of

Attica, Pericles was sixteen years old, and he had to wait until he was fifty to see the fruit of those groves that the Peloponnesian axes are cutting down today. They have left neither a single vineyard nor fig tree. They burned down the pines and cedars on the hills of Laurium; if the war continues, soon there will not even be firewood for the furnaces in the mines, and your pupil Socrates will no longer be able to teach in the shade of the sycamores by the Ilissus.

"When we are victorious," Pericles announced at the outbreak of the war, "no one will ever again cut down the trees of Athens."

Now, after two years of war and victory no nearer than on the first day, I no longer know what to think. The destiny of Pericles reminds me of Oedipus. Like Oedipus he was good and noble; like Oedipus he saw the paths leading to the well-being of the citizens and guided Athens along those paths. But now I realize that when he was proclaiming the School of Hellas, the home of the Dike, the incarnation of the exact measure, his policies were already stirring up the revolt in Samos. Today I ask myself if the genius of Sophocles, that great diviner, might not have created his Antigone as a warning to our beloved statesman. Is it not true that the Athenian fleet was violating unwritten laws? Is there anyone who does not know that Athens violated the oath it swore in Delos? And like Oedipus, when Pericles thought that he was working for the loftiest destinies of the City, he was, in fact, forging its ruin.

So here I am, alone. Besides Pericles, I lost Cleis, the young flutist you so praised, and every minute of every day, I am reminded that, come the spring, we will again be invaded and thousands of peasants will crowd into the City. And I tell myself: yes, the existence of the nous is necessary; it is the intelligence that orders the world, as Anaxagoras taught us; it has, undoubtedly, decreed the flow of the hours, the germination of seeds, and that the fly be the nourishment of the spider and the deer of the wolf. But what creator of order is this that first gives us speech, science, and poetry, then drives us to devour one another, and forgets to give us the logos and the harmony it lavishes on the ether, where the inert stars make their way, accommodate and respect their mutual fields?

To console me in my loneliness, imminent old age is freeing me of fears and appetites. Now I know that a large part of my life was made up of postures before a mirror and a vain make-up of the spirit. What is left to me in my emptiness after the death of Pericles? I have our son, whom I refuse to cling to, for he is being stalked by the plague; at any moment he will take up arms in this war which is to last for many years. And the most precious thing, oh, my wise friend: I have, as you do, that unquenchable desire to know. I have the enigma of this spider weaving its web in a corner of the yard, under the Altar of Hermes. I have instructed the slaves not to touch it, and I spend long hours watching it. Who taught it to make that octagonal web, with regular nodes and lines, with equal distances that no human weaver could possibly duplicate, not even with rulers and compasses?

How do I differ from that mute and ephemeral toiler? How much are my thoughts and words worth, driven by the winds of the centuries, in comparison with the geometrical poetry of that web? Poetry! Yes, I have that, too. This is the true divining art, the supreme art, imbued with divinity. Its presaging essence persuades me more and more in these terrible times that, whatever Gods, intelligence, or nous order the universe, they are very much aware of men, do meddle in human affairs, and do hold the tiller of our destinies.

So you see, dear teacher, Pericles died faithful to your teachings while I begin to abjure. But I love you as ever.

ATHENS FIFTEENTH OF ELAPHEBOLION
ARCHON APOLLODORUS

65

NO OTHER GOD ever existed except the Monos Theos, the Alpha and the Omega, the Beginning and the End of all things. Palaemon the Sybarite was the first to see the Alpha in the thumb crossed over the index finger and the Omega in Lysis's other three fingers.

At daybreak of the previous day, when Atys was descending Mount Lebanon, there appeared a break in the clouds that were hugging the tops of the trees. That was the signal. Would the Monos let him know when he arrived in the Promised Land? He spoke to some shepherds who were gathering their flocks, and he discovered that that nation of coarse men already knew and worshipped the One God. He was told that all men, both rich and poor, in all the lands south of there worshipped Him without images.

Atys of Pamphylia, again a priest, understood what the God had prophesied on Mount Dindymon. "There they are expecting you," he had said.

As dusk approached, he happened onto a fast-moving river where some camel drivers were watering their animals. He approached to ask them who they were, where they were coming from, what good place was their destination, and what the name of the river was, and the name of the snowy peak visible in the east.

They were the snows of Hermon, eternally looking upon Damascus, where they, merchants from Byblos, were heading with a load of papyrus, myrrh of Sidon, and healing herbs from Mount Carmel. Toward daybreak, the Arabian desert; toward dusk, prosperous, seafaring Tyre. Those were the waters of the River Jordan, which was born laughing on the slopes of Lebanon and ended its journey crying tears of salt into a dead sea.

Atys thanked them in Phoenician, and they offered him barley bread and soup with onions and cured mutton. Later they drank the tea of good dreams, perfumed, warm. And while the men discussed business in Damascus, caravans to Damascus, Atys fell asleep lying on his back at the foot of a willow.

Damascus, Damascus . . .

He awoke with a start as he was telling the brothers of his flight through the skies of Boeotia, Thessaly, and out to war-torn Potidaea.

When he stood to get a drink in the river, his ears were filled with a dull murmur. As he raised his eyes, his head began to spin. He clutched his head, fearful of the fevers, but it was cool.

All the others were asleep. The river shone brightly in the moonlight. Recently he had been having starts and visions on nights with a full moon.

He lay on the shallow bank and drank water from his cupped palms. Then, as he was refreshing his forehead and cheeks, he again heard the familiar ox voice telling him in

Greek: "NIΨONANOMHMAMHMONANOΨIN. *Wash your sins, not only your face.*"

The God was repeating the palindrome!

He was very scared. Sins? Him? Damascus?

He went back to the willow and lay on his back by his haversack. That inscription they had found one day on the way to Dodona, the one that could be read equally from front to back or back to front, could that have been a message for him from the Alpha and the Omega?

All the water he drank could not wash away the bitter taste of his newly acquired knowledge. He turned on his side, with his back toward the blue moon that was swelling on its sides. Its shimmering light between the branches made him dizzy. Lately, the God had been announcing Himself by tricking him with the colors and shapes of the world.

He closed his eyes.

The Monos had ordered him to wash away his sins. What could He mean? Was He recriminating him for Cyprus? Was it the thing with Ecbatana? Or was it the affair with the Scythian in Laurium? It was perfectly clear that those things were not sins. And if the Monos was Ishtar, Cybele, and Dionysus, and All Gods, then he should make good the promises they had made him. Sins? Him? Atys of Pamphylia? For following the dictates of a divine will?

Atys had always obeyed.

Except in Damascus!

And there it was again after so many years, the image of the girl in the Temple of Astarte, hateful memory, a childish face, giving herself to you, and you perform the ritual deflowering on the Bed of Brides under the cupola of the temple, and you pay her at the foot of the effigy with a purse of coins, and the girl of Damascus, raising her palms, offering her virginity, reciting the canon of marriageable girls who pray to Astarte, on that her first night of ritual prostitution, learning the arts and secrets of love that would make her future husband happy, and you, inebriated with the sacred harp and poppy wine, and the girl following you naked, while you use your cloak to cover the jars of wine you had just stolen from the sacrarium, and then you lie with her in the Forest of Rites, sighs in the night, laughter, the panting of the novice, wine so rich and seasoned, and the girl is all fire and wanting to learn everything during that night, and suddenly you are attacked by a nauseating hyena that bites you on the chest and you, horrified, defend yourself on your back, and you dig with your powerful fingers and hard nails, oh, how could you? and once free of the filthy creature, you retreat on your elbows, and you awake trembling, and you hear her groaning, and the moon reveals a white bundle, a naked woman, a bloody face, an empty eye, and the young virgin groans unconscious, and you approach on your knees, and transfixed with terror you see the eye, an unmoving eye, alone, accusing, looking at you, staring at you from the dead leaves, and it is no use seeking the aid of the Gods, none of them sent you, and you run to get away from the temple, and you hide, and you attack a passerby with a club and steal his cloak, and in your new guise, you cross the walls and leave Damascus forever, and suddenly, in your ears, woooo, what? how? what was the bovine voice of the Monos saying now?

"NIPSON, NIPSON, EN TO HIERO POTAMO. *Cleanse yourself, cleanse yourself, in the sacred river!*" thundered the God.

The voice would accept no reply.

You move on your knees, turning your head, looking askance, like a dog fearing a lashing.

And by the river's edge, your ears hum, and a furious bird flaps its wings within your chest.

As you reach out, the God pushes you toward the river, and the freshness of the water frees you of hummings and tremors. You let yourself sink to the bottom, and you would sleep forever in the cleansing waters.

But again the voice thunders:

"KEKATHARSAI."

When you emerge, purified of all your sins, you take off the cloak, toss it on the bank, and dive in again. But the Monos, having consummated the miracle of baptismal purification, is no longer with you.

The moon is again white and palid. Your ears no longer roar, and the banks of the Jordan are still.

You float on your back with the still waters of the bend. And peaceful, too, are the waters of your soul.

Such is the magnanimity of the One God.

"You have been purified," He said to you Greekly at the bottom of the river.

He has freed you of all your impurities. Even those you no longer remember! Now, for the first time, you are a clean priest. All that had gone before was but a dream. A trial.

Good! Now, oh, Atys of Pamphylia, Supreme Priest of the Monos Theos by His express mandate, having arrived in the Promised Land, you will found the New Church.

The Church of the New Flower?

Which will be your first task in the lands of the Jordan? Shall you reveal that you have come to strengthen and guide the faith of these people in the Monos? That you have come to lead them all as their Supreme Priest?

No!

Your sharp traveler's science, or perhaps an inspiration from the God, counsels you to keep the sacred mandate secret. The God has already made you an expert at founding churches.

It is not wise to arrive where you are known to no one and announce that you are the Supreme Priest.

Many were the lessons you learned in Athens. Also in Delphi. You had to go all the way to the oracle to know yourself and avoid excesses. But then, adding what you learned on your own along the paths of life, you also know that, after you know yourself, you cannot reveal yourself as you are without first ascertaining, in each case, the essence of your fellow man.

And what might these fellow men in the Promised Land be like?

The shepherds you ran into on the foothills of Mount Lebanon spoke a language very similar to the Syrian. You could understand them well enough, but you were lacking the words with which to sound their souls. And before you can speak to them of God with full priestly authority, you will have to spend some days among them.

499

The best thing will be to move among them little by little. Never again will you act in haste. You shall set yourself as your first task in the Promised Land to make yourself known without any great ado and learn the language of these people so that you can express yourself as perfectly as you do Phrygianly, Greekly, or Lydianly.

You feel cold.

You emerge from the holy river with light steps.

You look at it with gratitude.

You stoop to caress its redeeming waters, letting it flow between your fingers. May the God keep you always close to its cathartic waters.

On your feet now, you look at the moon and add your nudity to the river landscape.

How truthful the holy bovine voice has been! Way back on Mount Dindymon He told you that you would find your way crawling among the impurities of your soul. And now He reminds you of your sin in Damascus. Was that your only one? Better to wash them all away in these holy waters and get it over with. You are purified. KEKATHARSAI, the voice had said clearly.

Clearly? With so many dizzy spells and mute noises you felt inside and out?

No! No! It would be impiety to doubt now. Out! Out of your head impious doubt!

KEKATHARSAI, the Monos had said, without a doubt.

Could this catharsis mean that the God has already consecrated you for the supreme priesthood?

Oh, how great the logos with which He has woven the threads of your destiny!

For a long time you did not understand the messages. When you were delirious with fever just a few steps from the grotto, you reproached the God for delaying you, misleading you, driving you away from Dindymon. But three months later, fully recovered, when you were crossing the paradises of Phrygian Celaenae, you understood that the long pilgrimage through Delphi, Dodona, Libya, Egypt, and the return to Athens was your teaching and your apocalypsis. Oh, those conceptuous Greek words! How could one say apocalypsis in the language of these rustic people?

How clear everything was!

First he called you to Delphi so that you might learn to know yourself, that supreme science that cannot be ignored by a founder of churches.

That fateful afternoon, when you leapt to a certain death, convinced that the Gods would allow you to fly, it was diaphanest that you did not know yourself. The bruises all over your body were the first lesson. But several months went by before you understood that, in the lesson learned from hard branches and coarse bark, the Monos was giving you the gift of a great fat fruit, the nectar of logos, the juice of moderation.

Before revealing Himself in all His Holy Oneness, the God wanted to teach you a lesson, so that you would never again venture into flying foolishness unworthy of a Supreme Priest. Or any other excess. That was why first came the bruises, and then He made you insist on knowing what was written on those two steles exhibited in the áditon of the temple. And when Lysis read "nothing in excess" and "know yourself," you never imagined that those four Greek words, MEDEN AGAN and GNOTHI SAUTON, contained messages from the Monos to you. None of that sounded to you like science with whetted edge and sharp point. The GNOTHI SAUTON thing provoked in you mocking insolence. What was all that about telling a person to know himself, as if mortals were cold stone without feelings? Did it mean to imply that men did not know their own fears, smells, hungers, and pleasures?

Palaemon the Sybarite did explain to you that the gnomai of Greek wise men might sometimes be disconcerting but were, nevertheless, a certain science, mellowed by the centuries. He told you the story of a king who for failing to know himself wound up a blind beggar roaming the roads of Greece. Palaemon explained that, indeed, anyone who did not know himself would always live his life like a blind man. But you insisted that it was impossible to be alive and not know yourself, and you made fun of that science, and you said that the Apollic lyre needed tuning. "Apollonian!" corrected Lysis, not even bothering to control her laughter. How many beautiful words you had learned with Lysis!

You never again thought about the Delphic gnome until that night, when you were hunting with traps and meditating

501

at the edge of a forest in Pisidia. In the delirium of your fevers, you again heard the voice of the Monos Theos telling you, "GNOTHI SAUTON, O PEPTOMENE LARE. *Know yourself, oh, fallen seagull!*" And then you knew that the God had called you to Delphi to confront you with your sin of excess, born of your ignorance of yourself. Can anyone who really knows himself assume the virtues of a seagull?

Conversely, you discovered the reason behind the trip to Egypt and the absurd venture back to Athens before being able to return the Eye to Mount Dindymon long before that.

In the beginning, you kept asking yourself what you could possibly be doing in the City, a year after your flight, despite knowing full well that the only thing to be expected there was prison, torture, and the infamous Barathrum. And who could deny that it was divine cruelty to send you that storm and keep you adrift along the coasts of Libya and the wastelands of Egypt? But everything had been planned by the God so that He could come to Lysis that afternoon during the mysteries of Osiris. She had insisted in the certainty of her interpretation of the message: As the Great Priestess of the Sum, she declared herself penetrated by the God and instructed to tell the brothers that, before presenting themselves to the Child Mother with the rescued Eye, they must return to the City to implore the permission of Athena Parthenos.

Much later, someone interpreted that perhaps the Sum had sent Lysis, Shipwreck, and Otep to die where the surviving brothers could honor their tombs.

But the real intention of the Gods remained a mystery to you until that afternoon when you, Palaemon, and Hypothesis buried Lysis and Truncheon, who was also admitted to the common grave of the brothers.

With the last handful of earth, incensed with the merciless

God who had taken your Great Priestess, you insulted him in Phrygian in full view of the whole City, you tore off your wig and disguise, revealing your red hair, and you walked away, crying out loud before the dying eyes of the waves of Athenians that cluttered the streets and squares. And no one, not a single person, even gave you a second glance. Your hermeneutic brother, Palaemon, who followed you everywhere with suicidal loyalty, told you the details of what you did and then gave you the correct interpretation of the miracle.

When you awoke from your long sleep by the banks of the Eridanus, Palaemon was there beside you. As soon as you were able to listen, the Sybarite gave you his hermeneutic conclusions. At first you had a moment of horrified rejection, but then you began to understand the brother's reasoning.

Wasn't it you, Atys of Pamphylia, who was first afflicted by the plague in all your congregation? Isn't it evident that everything was planned so that you, and no one but you, would land during your escape to try to find food in that cadaver-infested town on the coast of Egypt? The dried venison you brought from aboard was surely contaminated with the plague.

And he urged you to recall that you had been struck by the first fevers on the high seas, during the return crossing to Athens. And who but you brought the plague to Athens? The Gods had chosen you as their instrument of justice. They sent you to punish the City for the abuses of the Athenian fleet in Chalcidice, for the looting of the islands, for what they did in Sybaris, Pontus, and the Tauric land.

Palaemon insisted vehemently. Couldn't you see it clearly? Had you ever found, in all your long travels throught the Ecumene, any city, nay, a single mortal, who did not hate the abusive Athens and wish upon it the worst kind of extermination?

And there was Palaemon again. How clearly his image

503

came to you, counting off on his fingers the reasons for hating Athens, for she was hated not only by her Persian enemies and the Greeks of the Peloponnesus, but by her own allies, since they were unwilling allies whose wealth was plundered by Athens with the pretext of protecting them from the barbarians. She was hated by the Greeks of Ionia, Thrace, and Sicily. You must know, oh, Summoner of the Sum, of the perfidy of Pericles when he promised to rebuild Sybaris. What was the outcome of that promise? Yes, the founding of Thurii, a colony without a single Sybarite, but overflowing with Athenian officials with full rights and powers. And what about the promise to his allies in the League, when he brazenly took their treasure? He had taken it from the island of Delos to Athens, again with the pretext of protecting it from an eventual enemy attack. And do you know what he did with it? He gave it to the Athenian demos. He began to pay the bouleutaí, the heliasts, and every last ragtag in Athens. Unheard of! He paid them to vote in the Assembly, to judge in the courts, and for whatever nonsense occurred to him; thus did the idle of Athens live at the expense of its allies in the League. If any one of them protested, they were threatened with the fleet, with an invasion of hoplites, with destruction of their walls. The squandering became so lavish that it defied belief; they built the Propylaea, the Parthenon, temples by the dozen; they paid for the grandeur of the Great Dionysian and Great Panathenian festivals; and the village that was Athens before the Persians flourished into a city of marble and chryselephantine colossi.

The wise Palaemon was right. The Gods, outraged by all that fraud, had done justice in Hellas, and they had sent you with that murderous plague.

So there had been nothing sterile in that year of wandering which began and finished in Athens.

How understandable, how transparent the intentions of the Monos seemed to you now.

Atys found it impossible to sleep any longer. He spent the rest of that night by the redeeming banks, touching himself, smelling himself, becoming familiar with his new catharsis.

At first light, he sang a prayer of gratitude to the One God. The camel drivers were preparing their departure when they saw him standing by the river, naked, palms and head turned toward the heavens, and singing in that beautiful voice. They understood that he was a man of God. Before leaving, they offered him dates and wine. Atys walked with them a while amid the pleasant greens of that valley. When they reached the first clearing, he blessed them in Syrian, and they listened to him with grave demeanors. Atys stood and watched them filing away on the road to Damascus. The rhythmic swaying of the last she-camel raised in him the desire for a woman with generous thighs.

The blush on the eternal snows of Hermon was announcing the advent of the sun. Atys returned to the bend in the river and sang further praise for Jordan's waters, for the gentle meander that shaped the soft banks, and for the trees. He felt crystalline, with a perfumed soul, capable of purifying people and things.

He generously blessed the inhabitants of the region, the animals and the crops, the mass of local insects; there was even a blessing for the stones and the fleeting breeze.

In his New Church, that place would be known as the Exonerating Meander, because there the God had seen fit to free him of a great weight he had been carrying for years, like an incubus, without knowing it.

He breathed with satisfaction.

He rubbed his palms.

Good. Now he would have to find a wise man of that region, another Palaemon, to translate his Greek, Phrygian, and Lydian inspirations into the language of the land.

When the sun was a span over the horizon of Arabia, Atys set his course for the west. He came to a place called Cedes, where he asked about the matters of God, never revealing his high priesthood. He entered, leading a blind pilgrim. There he cured an old man of the pains in his bones and a new mother of her melancholy. Many gathered to beg relief. He looked upon all of them and gave them the gift of hope. On the third day, the beggars accompanied him to Hazor, a place further to the south. The people of Hazor were awaiting him. He ministered to the crippled and diseased; he cured bodies and souls. He looked on them and they forgot their afflictions. They praised him and gave him crusts of bread; they were his guides to the neighboring towns. He put love and meekness in his voice and gestures to soften the impression of his imperfect speech. Everyone understood him, just like in Greece.

Before leaving he would teach them to make the Alpha and the Omega with their fingers. Whoever came to them with that sign would be his emissary. His farewell was a song of blessing, improvised in their own language, and looking deeply into their souls, he sent them back to their homes with a bounty of consolation.

On the twentieth day, he again left the Jordan behind. He came to Samaria, fragrant with laurels. There he found again the tree with the red bark that the Phrygians used to cure swamp fever. Ever since that old metragyrtes had taught him to prepare the infusion, he was cured of his fevers, and he recovered all the power of his eyes.

Again in the service of the God, he consoled the wretched.

When he left the towns, there was always a multitude to bid him farewell; everywhere, he was preceeded by praise and fame.

In Samaria, they saw him rise three spans from the ground and remain there a long time speaking to the people. His fame spread throughout those lands.

Each day he asked himself if the time had come to found his New Church or if he should wait for some explicit sign from the Monos.

From Samaria he went to Sichem, where he was sent for by a merchant of Ramá who was suffering from a toothache. Atys looked at him and told him that he would feel no pain; as he sang, he tore out the sick tooth. Another man he cured of a pain in the head. The son of a blacksmith of Magdala, who was possessed and screamed impurities and threw excrement at passersby, he freed of his chains and sent home sane and gentle. And as he came to new towns, the cripple, the blind, the invalid, and those who harbored demons in their bodies were already waiting at their doors, a multitude of miseries.

Many wanted to accompany him over the countryside, but he wanted no followers.

In Bethlehem, he arbitrated in the quarrels of shepherds, and he passed judgements that everyone accepted. Then he decided to return to the river Jordan, and as he approached a town on the way to Jericho, he heard the outcries of an angry multitude. Coming nearer he saw about a hundred people, arranged in a semicircle around two trees and stoning a man and a woman tied to the trunks. In the center, an old priest with a black hat was shaking his staff and proffering execrations while the others took stones from a pile they had gathered. They threw them with curses at the noseless, faceless couple. Burning with righteous pleasure, men, women, children, and old people, exploding eyes, breaking teeth. The two heads hung and swung with each impact, dripping on the torn bodies.

"The will of God be done," shouted the old priest commanding the stoning, overjoyed with rage.

Atys wanted to know, but no one had time for anything but the stones and the victims. A blind man seconding his insults by frantically beating with his staff on a rock mumbled that they were stoning an adulteress and her lover, who were caught together by the husband down by the river.

Atys withdrew toward the Jordan without a backward glance. He knew that his eyes were powerless against that lascivious rage unbound.

Coming down the slope toward the river, Atys again felt the desire for a woman, the need for caresses, for tender words whispered in his ears, and unexpected tears welled in his lavender eyes. His thoughts went back to Athens, where one could relish the joy of love, where no unfortunate woman was stoned for adultery, where love was worshipped and no one was ashamed of the naked bodies that the young exhibited on the palaestrae and that the artists immortalized in statues.

By the waters of the Jordan, he saw a slender washerwoman walking away with her basket on her head.

Is she married? Does she have vengeful brothers?

No! Stay away!

If the Highest Priest of the New Church cannot abstain from virgins and married women, those people will not heed his ministry.

Ah, but how can he abstain? He already knows himself. Castration? That was the only way.

But can you be chaste if you are castrated?

As he bent over to take a drink by a stone that split the cool rushing waters, his dagger fell out of his clothes onto the rocky river bottom.

Oh!

An admonition from the God?

Could this sign be a confirmation that he is to castrate himself? That he must do for the One God what he never did for Cybele by the Hermus?

Yes! That much seems clear. The Monos needed him in His service in that austere land. Without a second thought, he took the dagger and scanned the banks.

"There," he said, spying a large flat rock just under the waters. That would be the altar of his sacrifice.

He walked along the river bank toward the rock and landed on it with a single leap.

He took the whetstone from his haversack and began to sharpen the dagger.

Should he make one quick slice? From the bottom up, like they did on Mount Dindymon?

No! For the New Church, a new ritual. He would do it slowly and with solemnity. First a small cut of offering, on the bottom side. Then a prayer and a presentation of the sacrifice. Yes, that was it. Then a second and a third cut along the sides, accompanied by chants of praise for the One God. And lastly, the complete castration. As a ceremonial innovation, he would throw his testicles over his shoulder without noting where they fell. This would mean that he had forever abandoned the passions of the flesh. Gone would be lust, enthraller of the spirit.

When the edge was sharp enough, he put away his things and took a soft cloth.

Again he studied the river bank. No one would see him. He raised his tunic and tied it at his waist. He spread his legs, flexing them just a bit. The water flowed over his ankles. He placed

509

his feet farther apart, took the dagger in his right hand, and lifted his testicles with his left. The bottom cut produced the first drops of blood that dripped to be purified in the sacred waters. This was his second communion with the Jordan. He then sang the first hymn to the New Church. The God now had his blood turned into a river, for centuries to come. For the second cut, he pulled the testicles to one side and rested the razor-sharp edge on the other, but suddenly, his thumb, his index finger, and then his whole hand, went lax and he could not hold onto the dagger, which dropped into the water on the rock.

The same thing that happened twenty years earlier, in the Hermus!

The Monos wants no eunuchs, either.

But what can he do? How can one have testicles and live among those coarse, intolerant people?

What if he swore chastity to the Monos?

Total chastity?

Impossible.

What if he swore not to touch another's woman? Could he do that?

Perhaps, if he confined himself to widows and virgins.

Virgins with stone-crazed fathers and brothers?

No! That would not be wise.

He would stick to widows.

Widows and courtesans? In the big cities, there were many and beautiful.

Would it be proper for the Supreme Priest of the Monos Theos to fornicate with courtesans?

It would be unseemly. He would have to sneak about to do it and that would damage his prestige among the faithful.

Decided! Just widows.

Perhaps he should take a wife?

510

But just one?

No, a Supreme Priest cannot become the father of a family.

With his palms raised, Atys of Pamphylia swore to the Monos Theos not to take another's wife, or virgins, or courtesans; he would not take them by the power of his eyes or by his personal charm, even if they gave themselves to him.

The God was satisfied with his oath, for there was no sign of reproach.

Some time later, as he trod the sands on the way to Jericho, he was approached by a man riding a mule and leading a pack donkey behind him. Dismounting, and going through the required greetings, he introduced himself as a servant of Gideon of Jerusalem, a dyer of fabrics, explaining that he had been sent out days ago to find him, and Gideon promised him clothing and money if he could cure his wife, who had gone mute and did nothing but cry, and Atys, what is the woman like? is she young? but the slave has never seen her, the dyer bought her in Galilee, and since they were married a month ago, he has kept her very well locked away in his house, no male servant nor any of the slaves of the shop have ever seen her, and they entered Jerusalem shortly after noon, and many recognized him by his height and the red hair tied atop his head, and the beggars and water bearers spread the word, and soon the whole City knew that the red-haired worker of wonders had arrived riding a donkey belonging to Gideon the dyer, a Nazarene drayman swore that in his land the stranger floated above the ground, but that was nothing, because in Bethania he had flown, and a Magdalene had actually seen him with his own eyes walking on the waters of the Sea of Galilee, and in Capernaum he had become a fish, and in Arimathaea a seagull, and someone said that he had turned water into wine for some shepherds in Bethlehem, and another said that in Gaza he had

511

brought rain, and everywhere he had cured mange, dropsy, pee-
ing sickness, and why had he come to the house of Gideon? and
they were welcomed in the stable by the master himself, an old
man with warts and rat's eyes, and, yes, the girl had cost him
one hundred dinars, and he had hardly touched her a couple of
times, because on the first night she had gone mute ...

Hmmmm ... on the first night? How had Gideon touched
her? How? With his hands? This way or that way?

And the dyer evasive, but Atys must know everything to
apply the adequate medicines or spells, and the old man dispatching the servant girls and recounting his nights in a whisper, and Atys, his thinking sharp, searching for the pit in the
olive.

Exactly when did the girl go mute? Before or after?

And Gideon, well, actually, he could not do it ...

How not do it?

And Gideon that, no, because at her crying he had gone
soft ...

And the next day? And the next?

And Gideon, no, impossible, and even less possible when
she was mute and crying, well, you see, Gideon was no longer
twenty years old ...

And Atys looking and studying the old man, yes, it sufficed
to take one look at the black wart on his nose, the size of a small
ripe olive, to make any woman go dumb, and he was probably
stingy and cranky, and Atys had his diagnosis, yes, this was certainly the same disease as in the case of Ecbatana's crying.

And what was the old man waiting for? Atys had to see the
girl at once.

And Gideon searching in his clothes for the key he wore on
a chain around his neck, yes, would Atys please wait while he
went for Rachel?

No, no, not possible in the yard. Silence and crying be cured only in patient's bedroom, and upon entering, very young woman, red cheeks, eyes surprised, swollen from crying, but curious, inspecting Atys, assessing with caution not bereft of interest, and Atys:

"I cure," he announced, "and you," addressing the man, "there, silent waiting. Mute woman who cry, you have pain here?" he asked, pointing to her head.

She shook her head, lowered her eyes, and blushed.

"You walk for me," he ordered the woman.

She looked at the old man and cringed, expectantly.

Atys reached out to her and she took two steps toward him.

Atys bent slightly and touched her temple.

"Hurt here?"

Another shake of the head.

"Tongue hurt? Throat hurt?"

No!

"Raise head and open eyes big."

She obeyed.

He looked at her a long while, speaking softly so the old man could not hear.

A hint of a smile flashed in the depths of her dark eyes.

"You much happy, like fishes plop, plop, jumping, greeting the sun."

She smiled then, her lips thick as ripe figs in Paphlagonia, sweet, shiny, ahhh . . .

"What your name?"

She raised her eyebrows, for she was mute.

"Not mattering, you talk later, and I knowing that behind cool teeth your name Rachel."

The old man made a sound.

Atys waved a hand. Shush!

"You lend for me two your hands," he ordered Rachel.

She extended her hands, and he turned her palms downward. He looked at her steadily and, with the tips of his fingers, applied the caress of the pollen, which he had learned from the Great Porne of Cyprus in the Temple of Paphos. He awaited the results.

Yes, an imperceptible tremor ran over her lips. Atys knew that the girl's eyes were now seeing a lavender world, and her ears would obey his command.

The old man grunted.

"You no noise," he shouted, as he raised the girl's dress.

His fingers, trained in Cyprus and Babylon, touched her forearm, the inside of her elbow, gliding ever so softly over the taught, blushing skin very close to her underarm. He brought his eyes closer and made his gaze sharper.

Her mouth opened; her eyelids lowered.

Unmistakeable! This woman wanted a man.

"Your eye here," he said, picking a red carnation from a pot. "Look, carnation turning white."

The old man coughed.

Then turning toward him:

"You looking here," he ordered, "you never seeing green carnation?"

The old man looked concerned, he knitted his brow, ran his hand over his bald head, but when Atys stooped before him and looked hard over the lavender flower, Gideon, his mouth open, jaw dropping, head tilting, smile meek, saw the carnation turn red, now jasmine, oh, look, now five jasmines, and a white dove taking flight and lighting on Rachel's shoulder, and fluttering around the ceiling, and escaping through the skylight, flying under the midday sun toward the medicinal Arabia to find the thistle of the desert, very good tongue-tie-loosing medicine, and Gideon could no longer hold his head up or keep his eyes open, invaded by a relentless sleepiness that barely left him time to obey the order to take off his clothes and collapse, asleep, on the bridal bed.

And Atys calling for food, and Rachel bringing pitchers of wine, dry figs, sesame buns, and without a word from Atys, she runs the bar across the door, and turning busy and smiling, and Atys giving her wine from his cup, and she drinking with gentle composure, but fire in her eyes, and skin so much very red, epithymia, to say it Greekly, now diaphanes that desire whipping her flesh, the cure advances, step by step the canon of Astarte would be fulfilled, and Atys certain that that very afternoon the beautiful dyer's wife will recover her speech, and turning his back on her, and asking her to untie his hair, and she seeing the huge amethyst fall at her feet, and he, that that stone not stone, that stone holy Eye, miraculous Eye that cure her disease, and following what was undoubtedly a new inspiration put in his soul by the Monos, he submerges the stone in wine, offering her a drink, and she taking the cup with both hands over his, and he, you look, Eye touch wine and wine get warm and go to head, and she, oh, yes, and after another taste, oh, yes, a miracle, and he, Eye touch again and taste like honey, and touch carnation and smell like nard, touch and violets, touch and jasmine, and she laughing soundless, laughing with eyes and hands, and Atys running the stone over her hair, rubbing it on her tattered, dirty clothes, and beautiful Rachel should smell in her body the lavender of Carmel, and she wetting her lips, looking on him with desire, and he taking her hand, she squeezing strongly, and he pulling her toward the bed, but she shaking her head, knitting brow and pointing to old man, sleeping on his back, and Atys, no, you look and smell, and

515

passing the Eye over the old man, and from the rancid skin, the fragrance of lilies invades Rachel, your old man smell good, no? and rubbing his pate, the stains and scabs disappear, and Eye touch head, Eye touch nose, Eye touch eye, Eye touch hair, touch jaw, touch ear, and Rachel sees a handsome face, red hair and beard of the softest texture, and the clouded, colorless eyes are now a splenderous lavender, and touch arm, and touch leg, and touch chest, and limbs of muscular beauty appear, and his legs grow thicker, and now the magical stone has straightened his bunyons, and now it frees him of spots, dandruff, scales, and gone are the warts, and the skin grows terse, and Rachel watching as the greenish, bloodless herring, the terror of her nights, swells into a thick, straight, firm phallus crowned with a great, shining acorn, and she moves toward the bed, and she cannot see Atys, but she moves closer, rubbing against him, squeezing her breasts, stroking her arms, taking off her clothes, crushing her fingers with her legs, panting wildly, and he sitting on the bed by the old man, pulsing with his fingers and his voice every string in that abandoned lyre, giving her the tickles of Ishtar, the touches of Aphrodite, the pinches of Astarte, and she caressing herself avidly, and he enthralled by the fig before him trickling nectar on his lips, and he bites it, sucks it, tastes it, and drinks of the shimmering honey . . . extract with a kiss the slumbering words? and further down the two gamboling kids, and waking her up, and she surprised, with that powerful present in her hands, moaning her first sound, her nasal gratitude, would Atys accept priestess in his New Church? and suddenly a horrifying peal of thunder shaking the entrails of the Earth, and Atys raising his head, and she urging him on, caressing him, pulling him in, and brilliant sunlight streaming in through the skylight, and more thunder, horror, another warning from the God? could He be displeased with the cure? perhaps the God thought that Atys was violating his oath of the previous day, perhaps He thought he was doing that out of lust, but the God must remember that they had gone to fetch him in Jericho to cure the mute girl, could the Monos want her condemned to eternal silence? Ah, no, Atys would never abandon her, who else could cure her? why had the God taken him to that house? and embracing her more strongly, his lips imprisoning a warm, turgid breast, and why was the Monos like that, eh? always so tricky and mocking? why? why did the God do those things to him? why did He induce him to cure her and then, when she was about to speak . . . thunder in sunlight? and placing her hurriedly on the floor, and she opening her marvelously shaped legs, revealing the nervous sinews of her ankles, hugging him, biting him, how could he stop himself? didn't the God realize that he was a mortal? and she spreading impatiently, and another thunderbolt, and another, and he trying to hurry, could it be possible? did the God want him to leave now? and at that very moment: ELI, ELI! a murmur, a word, a scream, victory, oooh, she had spoken, then there was no adultery or sin, it was the blessing of God on that culminating embrace, and the word ELI meant "my God," and she shaking all over, what would baptism be like in the New Church? and she in her delirium, gasping laughter, sighing, and he completely certain now, diaphanes, those peals of thunder were God's approval, they could never be recrimination or threats, if the Monos had not already approved of her cure, would He have allowed His name to be the first word that issued from the mute girl's lips after her rescue from silence? no! it was all logicos, diaphanest, phainomenalest, the God was much satisfied, would He thunder again out of joy because Atys had not broken his oath? because the God well knew that none of that had been inspired by lust, but that it was a religious communion, Atys had given the

517

unfortunate Rachel back her voice, and he would give Gideon back an obliging wife, and at that very instant, the God inspired Atys to give Rachel the Dindymenian Eye, and he would look at her deeply before leaving, and to instruct her, he would make his gaze three-edged so that whenever she touched herself with desire, or when Gideon needed her, she would not see the old man but Atys of Pamphylia, and it would be like having him with her forever, and she would live without tears, and the old man would be pleased and would give her tunics, tunics? of different colors? and why not ask her to embroider gowns and bonnets for him? and Atys had understood, everything was clear, the thunder under a sunlit sky was the much-awaited signal from the Monos, He was announcing that he could found the New Church now, and if He had chosen that moment of his service to the mute girl, wasn't it evident that he had sanctified the act? and behold, during the treatment, she had asked him to make her fertile, which evidently meant that the God had ordained that his blood, already mixed with the waters of the holy river, was to be forever mixed with the blood of those people of the Promised Land, but what was most significant and diaphanes was that He had sent him to a dyer, which indicated that the time had come for him to look after his clothes, for the God most certainly wanted his Supreme Priest to have many tunics of different colors, and Atys pouring himself more wine, and the thunder was also to announce to Atys that the Dindymenian prophecy had come true, when God had told him that Atys would not see through that Eye, but be seen, OUK OPSEI ALL'OFTHESEI, Greekly said in the most beautiful of tongues, which was why the God had chosen it for His own, and she giving him more wine from her lips, and caressing him insatiably, and Atys wanting to know what threads she would use to embroider his caps and bonnets, and she, fully awake,

awake and pleased as never before in her brief but long life, and in exchange for that magic Eye, she would embroider for him using threads of gold and silver and of all the colors of the peacock and the rainbow, fifty tunics, a hundred multicolored caps, and he agreeing, as long as none of them were the color of saffron, and more kisses and caressing mischief, and he returning caresses of proven efficacy, and thinking that everything was diaphanest, now he had to inaugurate his priesthood, round up a congregation, decide on baptism, find a couple of competent scribes, would there be priestesses? raise money to build the temple, good, good, and she, relaxed now, wanting more and more, let it never stop, and indeed, the duty of any doctor is to carry through the cure of his patient, and that afternoon Atys of Pamphylia honored God another two times, confirming and reconfirming the cure of the mute girl.

Having concluded that first service, Atys declared the New Church founded.

519

"And you, now, One God," said Atys Greekly to the Monos, "guide the New Church with much astute acumen for the centuries to come."

NOTES

PERICLES DID, IN FACT, die during the plague of the year 429; Nicias, in 415, after the failure of the fleet he was commanding in a colonizing expedition; Alcibiades, in 402, in a satrapy of the Persian empire in whose service he was employed . . . against Athens. (He died valiantly, pierced by arrows. His remains were taken to the City by Letho, a Corinthian hetaera who was his last lover.)

Aspasia married Lysicles, a sheep merchant and a humble man, and she ended her days in peace, toward the end of the ninetieth Olympiad. Socrates was condemned to drink hemlock in the year 399 for corrupting the young and introducing new Gods in Athens, they said.

Lysis of Miletus and Atys of Pamphylia are still with us, alive and doing very well.

The Peloponnesian War began, according to Thucydides, during the Archonship of Pythodorus, in the spring of the year 431

B.C. In this novel, it takes place toward the end of summer, when the archon was Euthynus.

Aspasia was tried in 432, not in 431, as we have read here.

Alcibiades was a victor in the Olympic Games, but the exact date is unknown. I have taken the liberty of crowning him when he was still very young, a few months before his heroism in combat during the battle of Potidaea, where Socrates also played an outstanding role.

Except for these three licenses, events in the story adhere to the dates given by Thucydides.

The palindrome quoted in the last chapter is from the Christian era and includes the noun ANOMHMA. There is no record of it in the fifth century B.C., but I could not resist the temptation of including it, with the hope that it may still be useful to some of my readers.

D.Ch.
February 2002

GLOSSARY

ALPHABETICAL INDEX OF SUNDRY REFERENCES TO ANCIENT GREECE

All dates are Before Christ unless otherwise indicated.

Abaris the Hyperborean. Priest of Apollo who is said to have traveled the whole world without eating and carrying always with him the symbol of his divine mission: an arrow given to him by his God (Herodotus, IV, 36).

Academy. A former property of Academus, located close to the northeastern part of the City. It was in a grove of this suburb that Plato founded his school.

Achilles. Son of the Goddess Thetis and the hero Peleus. He was one of the foremost protagonists of *The Iliad*. Among his Homeric epithets were "Podartes," "he of the light feet," or "fleet-footed," according to some.

Acme. The culminating moment, the pinnacle.

Aeschylus. 525–456. He was the first of the three great Athenian tragedians. He sang to the glory of his country. He praised the justice enshrined by democracy in his times. He had the great honor of having fought at Salamis and Marathon, battles that helped free Greece from the Persian yoke. So great was his reverence for these achievements that in his own epitaph he made no mention of his poetic merits and said rather, "Passerby, here lies Aeschylus, son of Euphorion, Athenian. Was he brave? Ask the long-haired Persian and the trees of Marathon wood." He died near Gela, in Sicily, during a walk, but his compatriots preferred the version that he had been stricken by a turtle dropped by an eagle of Zeus. Could there be any better proof that he was one of the chosen?

Agamemnon. King of Argos; father of Electra, Iphigenia, and Orestes; husband of Clytemnestra; commander-in-chief of the pan-Hellenic expedition against Troy. In his *Iphigenia in Aulis*, Euripides retakes the sad destiny of the young girl sacrificed by her father to Artemis to implore favorable winds so that the fleet could set sail for the fields of Troy. In *Agamemnon*, Aeschylus tells of the return of the king after an absence of ten years. Clytemnestra, who never forgave him for sacrificing their daughter, had taken Aegisthus, Agamemnon's cousin, for a lover. In the opening monologue, Talthybius, the lookout, tells us that a "great ox" weighs heavily on his tongue. Scholars suppose that the "ox" is an allusion to a coin of the times. The "ox" was the price Clytemnestra paid for his silence. When the victorious Agamemnon arrived at the palace, he was immediately hacked to death in one of the baths.

Agora. Marketplace. When it is mentioned in connection with Athens, with no other qualifier, it refers to the market of the Ceramicus.

Agoranomos. Marketplace officials responsible for first-hand enforcement of public order; they collected the corresponding taxes and controlled people who were unruly or dishonest. Athens had ten.

Aguyeus. An epithet of Apollo. Cf. *Apollo.*

Ajax. Homeric hero born in Salamis. Alcibiades claimed descent from Ajax on his father's side. Sophocles wrote a tragedy with the same name.

Alcamenes. Sculptor, student, and rival of Phidias.

Alcaeus. Greek lyrical poet of the seventh century born in Mitylene, a city on the island of Lesbos. Inventor of the Alcaic verse.

Alcibiades. Born in Athens between 452 and 449.

Alcmeon, son of Amphiaraus. Mythical founder of the powerful line of the Alcmeonidae. It was said that after he murdered his mother he was condemned to wander the Earth without rest until he happened on a land that did not exist at the time of his crime. That land was Acarnania, which was formed during his wanderings by the deposits of the river Achelous.

Alcmeonidae. A family of Attica descended from Alcmeon.

All the Infernal Gods. Cf. *Infernal Gods.*

Altis. A grove in Olympia sacred to Zeus, as well as the adjoining plains where the Games were held.

Amazons. The Amazons, daughters of Ares and Hermione, originally dwelt by the banks of the Tanais but later moved to the region of Cappadocia, from which they extended their power and influence to Thrace and Phrygia. It was said that they founded cities such as Ephesus and Smyrna. Among the Amazons, males were devoted to domestic work. Their arms and legs were broken at birth so that they would not be capable of anything worthy. War and government were the affairs of women. Their luck ran out, however, because the ninth labor of Hercules was to get his hands on the Golden Girdle of Ares, worn by Hippolyta, one of the queens of the Amazons. The hapless Amazon, overwhelmed with love at the sight of the Greek's biceps, gave him the Girdle of Ares as proof of her love. Suddenly, there was a stir and the Amazons began to mount their horses in a hurry. Hercules immediately suspected foul play and did away with Hippolyta. War broke out and ended in the slaughter and dispersal of the Amazons. But, as if that were not bad enough, Antiope fell in love with Theseus, betrayed her sisters for his sake, and followed him to Athens. Antiope's sister Oreitia swore revenge and marched upon Athens with a great army. On her arrival she made sacrifices to Ares on a neighboring hill that became known as the Areopagus. This was the first foreign invasion ever suffered by Attica. For strategic and logistical reasons, the Amazons moved troops to the isthmus of Corinth and held intimidating maneuvers in the Peloponnesus. Her army was ultimately defeated and Oreitia retired with a handful of survivors to Megara, where she died of melancholy for having seen her sister fighting fiercely at the side of Theseus. Antiope's fidelity was to no avail, however, for Theseus signed an alliance with the king of Crete and agreed to marry his daughter Phaedra. Although Antiope was the mother of prince Hippolytus, she was a barbarian and could not become the legal wife of an Athenian. On the day of the wedding, she stormed the place armed to the teeth and ready to interrupt the ceremony and mow down all the guests, but Theseus and his people were able to take refuge in the palace and finally killed her in a brief and lusterless encounter. Those episodes are amply reflected in the metopes of the Parthenon, the reliefs on the shield of Athena, and the paintings in the Temple of Theseus. Some scholars affirm that Antiope was not a traitor, but that she was kidnapped first by Theseus, who later seduced her. Cf. *Penthesilea*.

Ammon. During earlier periods this Egyptian deity of Thebes was represented with the body of a man and the head of a ram. Later he was transformed into an anthropomorphic God to whom stud rams were sacrificed. According to Egyptian beliefs, the God Ammon would take the shape of the reigning monarch and so disguised would impregnate the queen. There are many representations of divine procreation in the paintings of the more ancient Egyptian temples. During the classical period in Greece, Ammon was also the main deity of the Libyans.

Amphitrite. Daughter of Nereus and wife of Poseidon. When Theseus arrived in Crete, King Minos coveted one of the Athenian virgins. To defend her,

Theseus declared that he was a son of Poseidon and that he would not allow such an outrage. Minos thought it was a sham and laughed. When had Poseidon ever stood in the way of his desire for a woman? Doubting that the upstart had such a high pedigree, Minos threw a ring into the sea and challenged Theseus to recover it. Theseus dove in without a second thought and was escorted by an entourage of dolphins to the palace of the Nereids. Queen Amphitrite welcomed him with honors and sent her Nereids to find the ring. (This was the episode that Micon painted on the walls of the Temple of Theseus in Athens.)

Anabasis. "Ascension," in Greek, but in military terms it also means the assault on a wall.

Anacreon. An Ionian lyric poet of the sixth century born in Teos. In the face of the Persian threat, the people of his home city emigrated in ships to Abdera, but in those days, tyrants were friends of the muses and Anacreon was summoned to Samos. For many years he lived in the court of Polycrates; legend has it that when the Persians finally put an end to the power of Samos, the tyrant Hipparchus of Athens sent a ship with fifty oarsmen to rescue the poet. A great many of his works were composed in Athens. He spent his life supported by his lyre and holding his wine glass on high. He was the most courtly and refined of the symposiac poets. His poetry does not dwell on war or hatred, or nostalgia for bygone splendors, for his is a sensual and gratifying present. Suggesting the erotic through thinly veiled images, he attained the highest development in archaic lyrical poetry. He had a lucid wine that he mixed with Hesiodic temperance. Athenian pottery represented him in its figures as composing music for beautiful dancers.

Anacreontic. A composition by or in the style of Anacreon.

Anacrisis. Judicial inquest, investigation, inquiry. In Athenian trials, the anacrisis was assigned a chest or coffer in which the evidence and the testimony linked to the trial were deposited.

Anactorie. A young woman loved by the poetess Sappho.

Anapest. A metrical foot used in Greek poetry made up by two short followed by one long. It was often used in the parabasis of the comedy, in comic dialogues, and in satire.

Anaxagoras of Clazomene, 500–428. Philosopher of the Ionian school; teacher of Socrates and Pericles.

Anaxander. First Olympic champion in the chariot races.

Anaxilas. A tyrant of Syracuse during the sixth century.

Ancestorides. Eponymous Archon of the year 470.

Androgynae. Mythological hermaphroditic beings. The etymology of the word means "man-woman." Plato advances a theory on them in "The Speech of Aristophanes" in *The Symposium* (Banquet, 189e).

Andromache, She of the Snow-White Arms. Wife of Hector, Hero of Troy.

Andron. A spacious salon located in the front of the Greek houses and used only by men. It was the natural setting for banquets.

Andronitis. The part of Greek manor houses (more or less half) that was used by the men. During the fifth century, this part of the house contained the bedrooms for freemen and slaves, an open atrium with columns, the andron, an arsenal, food and wine stores, the library, bath, latrine, and gate. No men, except very close relatives, could cross the threshold of the door connecting the andronitis with the gynaeceum. More modest homes lacked the atrium and columns, and had fewer rooms, but a clear distinction was always maintained between the andronitis and the gynaeceum. Cf. *Gynaeceum.*

Antiochides. Eponymous Archon of the year 435.

Anytus. A rich and passionate Athenian aristocrat. Plutarch has left us a rich store of gossip about his unbridled infatuation with the beautiful Cliniad (*Parallel Lives*, Alcibiades, V).

Aphrodite. The Aphrodite who resides in Olympus is Urania or Celestial. Of her affairs as Aphrodite Pandemos, the Vulgar, protector of prostitutes, the Olympians preferred not to hear. But whether she was in her heavenly home or all made up and spread-eagle in the local cat houses, her nature had nothing to do with lofty spirituality. Aphrodite invariably fostered tangible love. Celestial or vulgar, she always plied the same trade. By divine decree of Zeus, her adopted father, she married Hephaestus, the illustrious cripple, the laughingstock at the banquet of the Gods, the one whose only genius was his craft. But while Hephaestus had a twisted body, Aphrodite had a twisted soul and she was unfaithful to him with Ares. She was attracted to the latter's vigor in bed and the warlike firmness of his member. She was not concerned that the other Gods considered him a pain in the ass and a party pooper. One adulterous dawning, in the cloudy Thrace, the two lovers were seen by the Sun, a snitch who ran to rat them out in Aetna, where Hephaestus had his headquarters. The irate blacksmith forged an unbreakable net as sheer as a spider web and hid it among the folds of his matrimonial bed. When she returned, Aphrodite lied about where she had been, telling him she had come from Corinth. Hephaestus then told her he was leaving for his beloved island of Lemnos on personal business. Aphrodite begged off on the pretext that she was tired, and he, all compassionate and understanding, limped off in the company of Hermes. Aphrodite wasted no time in introducing Ares to her bedroom. The very next day, Hephaestus summoned all the Gods and exhibited the adulterers in their trap, naked except for the net. He begged Zeus to return the bride-price, but the Olympian patriarch returned nothing and even derided him, saying that only a hapless cripple would make his own discredit public. The judgment of Zeus was born out when Hephaestus forgave Aphrodite and withdrew his divorce suit. The grapevine in Olympus had it that Aphrodite's three children—Phobos, Deimos, and Hermione—were actually sired by Ares. In successive peccadilloes, Aphrodite had Hermaphroditus and Priapus, each more aberrant, the former by Hermes and the latter by Dionysus. As a special attribute, Aphrodite had a magical girdle that exacerbated men's desire. Other Goddesses coveted it, but she almost never agreed to lend it. Among mortals, Aphrodite loved Anchises, king of the Dardanians, but Zeus heard him boasting and punished him with a bolt of Olympian lightning that did not kill him but left him so weak that he was never really able to get his lovely attribute up again. From his short-lived affair with the Goddess, Aeneas, the heroic forefather of the Romans, was born. Aphrodite was known to the Romans as Venus, and from her Greco-Roman etymology, we have *aphrodisiacs* and *venereal diseases*. Cf. *Cypris, Pandemos*.

Apocalyptic. This word is used exclusively in its original meaning of revelation and should never be interpreted in the Christian sense of "terrifying."

Apollo. Son of Zeus and Leto; God of light, the arts, and divination. As Apollo Nomius he was also the protector of herds; as Agyieus he protected passersby; and when he was the greatest of archers, it was always a good idea to implore his aid in achieving good marksmanship. He had his little weaknesses and a feminine proclivity for the arts. Although he had a number of lovers and several children, he never felt the need for marriage. He frequented Helicon and Parnassus and took great pains to direct the choir of Muses, but he had a quick temper and punished insolence with pestilential arrows. The archers who were attacking Troy were taught a lesson for offending one of his priests, as were Marsyas and Pan for attempting to best him in music. Those who, like Niobe, offended his mother, Leto, fared no better, nor did the great serpent Python, which he ultimately destroyed. His vengeance took place at Delphi, at a fault in the terrain, which was later the location of the tripod where Pythia inhaled the prophetic emanations and answered the questions of the Greeks. His most frequent Homeric epithets were: "He who wounds from afar," "He of the silver bow," and "Like the night," when he stormed angrily from Olympus to settle accounts. Cf. *Delos, Delphi, Marsyas, Niobe, Pan, Pythia*.

Apollodorus of Phalerum. Friend and disciple of Socrates.

Apollodorus. Eponymous Archon for the year 430.

Apotropous. That which keeps evil away. Insulting loved ones and wishing them bad things was frequently done in ancient times to achieve the opposite effect.

Apseudes. Eponymous Archon for the year 433.

Arcesilaus. Father of Lichas, an Olympic Champion.

Archestratus. Athenian general who commanded the first incursion of the fleet against Chalcidice at the beginning of the Peloponnesian War.

Archigallus. High priest of the Phrygian worship of Cybele.

Archilochus of Pharos. Lyrical poet of the seventh century. Irreverent and inspired, he is credited with the invention of iambic verse.

Archon. There were nine Archons in Athens. The Archon King looked after judicial affairs. The Eponymous Archon, among other things, provided the name for the year of his archonship. The other Archons are of no interest in this novel.

Archonship. The year during which the Eponymous Archon held office. The Athenian year ran from the beginning of July to the end of June. Cf. *Months.*

Arcturus. A northern constellation. Along with "Arctic," it is derived from the root *arktos,* which meant "bear," in Greek.

Areopagite. A member of the Areopagus.

Areopagus. A hill outside of Athens that was originally the venue of a council of former archons, aged aristocrats who, as the Roman Senate, dominated the constitution and government of Athens. Solon, first, and subsequently the leaders of democracy—Clisthenes, Ephialtes, Pericles—eroded their powers until they became the Tribunal of the Areopagus, reduced to purely judicial functions. By the end of the fifth century, its only power was to try cases of homicide, as Aeschylus counseled the people of Athens in *The Eumenides.*

Ares. God of war. His most frequent epithets were: "Besmirched with Homicide" and "Horrific son of Zeus and Hera." His twin Discord, his son Terror, and Fugue were his accomplices and admirers. Hades also admired his work, but the rest of the Olympians considered him an unbearable jerk. Even his parents despised him. No one could ever understand what Aphrodite saw in him to be yearning for him all the time. In war he was never on anyone's side, but for war itself, which he helped bring about and prolong. Cf. *Aphrodite.*

Ariphron. Brother of Pericles; tutor of Alcibiades.

Aristeus of Corinth. A general who participated in the action at Potidaea.

Aristides. 530–468. Athenian general and politician. Despite the glory garnered at Marathon, he was not able to keep Themistocles from having him ostracized. On his return he fought heroically at Salamis and Plataea. When he was restored to power, he became one of the main founders of the Delian League. His probity in State affairs was such that he was called "The Just."

Arithmomancer. Diviner, cabalist.

Arithmomancy. Prophesy through numbers. Cabbalah.

Arrhephorian Virgins. Virgins who transported the vestments and accoutrements sacred to Athena in procession.

Artemis Phosphoros. Bearer of light and protector of midwives; worshiped by the demos of Phlya (Pausanias, *Description of Greece,* I, 31, 4).

Artemis. Daughter of Zeus and Leto. She was born on the island of Ortygia just moments before Apollo on Delos. It was a hard test for her mother. Arriving from the Cyclades with Python the serpent in hot pursuit, Leto had to go from island to island seeking a safe place to give birth. When she found out about the difficult circumstances attending her birth, Artemis chose for herself modesty and eternal virginity, conditions that she imposed on all of her numerous entourage. When Artemis found out that Zeus had seduced Callisto, she turned her into a bear; when Acteon dared to look upon Artemis as she was bathing, she turned him into a stag and had her dogs tear him apart. Artemis wore her hair short, used cothurni, dressed in the short tunic of a boy well above the knees, and was never seen without her bow and arrows. Although she was an avid huntress, she protected human and animal babies and attended births. Artemis was the Diana of the Romans. Cf. *Niobe*.

Artemon the Bale, or the Machinist, or Periphoretos. This character is only half real. Ephorus, a historian of the fourth century, left us an account of the circumstances that led to his nickname and described him as a military engineer in the war of Samos. His contemporary, Heraclides of Pontus, had him adducing reasons taken from Anacreon. (In our novel, Artemon is a composite of both sources and a bit of fiction, for we have made him an Athenian citizen instead of a resident foreigner from Clazomene, as he appears to have been.)

Asclepiad. A member of the medical brotherhood of Asclepius.

Asclepius. God of medicine, son of Apollo. He was known as Asclepius to the Romans. His temple in Athens was a veritable hospital attended by the Asclepiads.

Aspasia of Miletus, 470-? Philosopher, master of Rhetoric, feminist, supreme liberal, adviser and consort of Pericles.

Assembly. A body made up of all Athenian males over the age of eighteen and born of Athenian parents. Each member of the Assembly personally participated in the government of Athens through his direct vote. Assembly meetings usually consisted of about two thousand participants, but a quorum of six thousand was required when deciding issues of maximum importance. At the time when this novel takes place, the members of the Assembly usually met on Pnyx Hill, but they also got together in the Great Theater of Dionysus, the agora, or in Piraeus. They met no fewer than forty times a year.

Astarte. The Syrian Aphrodite; worshipped in Asia.

Ataraxia. Imperturbability.

Athena. "Zeus, King of the Gods, took to wife Metis, wisest among mortals and immortals. When she was to give birth to Athena, she of the owl's eyes, Zeus confused her heart with sly mellifluous words and suddenly swallowed her and imprisoned her in his own entrails. He was following the counsel of the Earth and the Starry Heavens to ensure that the honor of that birth would be exclusively his" (Hesiod, *Theogony*, 886–893). This scene was said to have taken place by the shores of Lake Triton in Libya. Seized with indigestion, Zeus began to scream and was beset by a terrible headache that was not to leave him until he received "from the arte of Hephaestus, a blow on the head with a bronze ax. Then, Athena sprang from his forehead giving a formidable cry that caused Uranus and Mother Earth to tremble" (Pindar, *Olympics*, VII, 35–40). *Metis* means "prudence, reflection, wisdom." What better mother for a Goddess of thought? But Athena has many facets. As a warrior she was capable of defeating Poseidon and even Ares on two occasions, but she prefered peace, order, and the rule of law. A precursor of science, she taught men numbers and made the owl her sacred animal. She fostered industry, particularly pottery, and is credited with numerous inventions, including the plow, the yoke, the bridle, chariots, boats. The olive tree she gave to the Athenians was a priceless gift and symbolic of her civilizing mission, but she was also a friend of the arts and invented the double flute made from deer bones, although she later repudiated it when she looked into a pond and saw her cheeks deformed from the effort of blowing it. Like Artemis, she preferred solitude and celibacy, though she was not as repressive toward Peeping Toms and rapists. When Hephaestus let himself be overwhelmed by his love for her, the Olympians greatly praised her controlled reaction. She understood that the poor Hephaestus had been fooled by Poseidon, who told him that he had it on the best authority that Athena would only give herself to the one who could overcome her with his passion. Although she was able to reject the assault, she could not prevent Hephaestus from ejaculating on her legs. The sheepskin she used to wipe off the semen fertilized the Earth, which gave birth to Erichthonius, a male serpent with a human head. Despite the revulsion she felt at the memory of the trembling, hairy cripple and his disgusting ejaculation, Athena behaved like a mother. She adopted the child and entrusted his upbringing to Aglaurus, daughter of King Cecrops of Athens. The anthropocephalic serpent crawled through the cellars of the Erechtheion, watched over the night in the Acropolis, helped the Goddess protect the City, and fed on a bowl of milk laid at the mouth of its cave by the priestesses. Three nymphs dressed in goatskins looked after Athena in Libya. The Aegis, the magical pelt made from the hide of Amalthea, the goat that nursed the infant Zeus, was always a part of her vestments. The Aegis was comprised of a serpent and from it hung the head of Medusa as a protective amulet that Athena herself had attached when Perseus cut it off. In Libya, Athena made friends with Pallas, a child whom she accidentally killed when they were playing at combat with spears. The Romans knew her as Minerva. Cf. *Artemis, Georgica, Parthenos, Polias, Poseidon, Promachos*.

Atlas. Son of the Titan Iapetus and the Nymph Clymene; brother of Prometheus, Epimetheus, and Menecius. He was the father of the Pleiades, Hyades, and

Hesperides. He had a great and civilized kingdom beyond the Pillars of Hercules, toward the end of sunset. He made the mistake of taking command of the revolt of the Titans against the Olympians. He expiated his transgression by bearing the weight of the heavens on his shoulders.

Aurora. Latin name of the Titan Eos, daughter of Hyperion and Theia. She was the wife of Astraeus who fathered the "violent-hearted winds: Zephyr, who lit the Heavens; Boreas, of the Rapid Race; Notus ... and the Morning Star" (Hesiod, *Theogony*, 378–381). According to Homer, in Canto 5 of *The Odyssey*, "Aurora arose from the bed, leaving the illustrious Tithonus, to bring the light to the Immortals." But as it turned out, this young man, son of Ilo, was not the only one to share the bed of the nymphomaniac Eos. "She took Clitus for his beauty to keep him with the Immortals" (Ibidem, XV, 250). And she also had Orion, Cephalous, and that very same Ganymede that Zeus later had. Ares also committed adultery with her. But her rather light morals might indicate that the half-light of dawn abetted secret loves, for when she showed up in Olympus born by Lampus and Phaeton, with her winged steeds, and announced the imminent arrival of her brother, the Sun, she immediately became Hemera (day) and later Hespera (evening). Then her behavior was beyond reproach. Her most frequent epithets were: "she of the golden throne" and "she of the rosy fingers."

Autocrat General. In times of great danger, the Assembly would confer special powers on one of the ten generals of the College of Strategi. It was only a temporary appointment, but after the war of Samos, Pericles held the position for long periods and on several occasions.

Axiochus. Father of Aspasia.

Barathrum. A deep dark abyss in Athens into which criminals were thrown.

Basileus. King. The Basileus Archon, or simply the Basileus, was the King Archon.

Beggar of the Goddess. Cf. *Metragyrtes.*

Bellicose. "Polemikos," in Greek. This was the name of an altar to Zeus in Olympia. It was said that this altar was used by Oenomaus to sacrifice a stud ram before the chariot races against the pretenders of Hippodamia (Pausanias, *Description of Greece*, V, 14, 6). Cf. *Oenomaus.*

Boedromion. Third month of the Athenian calendar. Cf. *Months.*

Boreas. The wind blowing from the north. More generally: the North.

Bosphorus. "Bosporos" was what the Greeks called the straits between the Propontis and the Pontus Euxinus (the modern Sea of Marmara and the Black Sea). Its etymology means "ox ford," in an allusion to the poor Io who was turned into a cow and pursued to the very shores of the Bosphorus by the gadfly turned loose on her by Hera.

Bouleuterion. Venue of the council of Five Hundred; hence, a council chamber.

Boustrophedon. Etymologically, it means "the turn of the ox." The term refers to the way of writing that alternates lines from right to left and left to right.

Buzyges. High Priest of Zeus in Athens.

Cacographer. A bad writer.

Cacus. In Greek, "the evil or malignant one." Son of Hephaestus and Medusa; a three-headed cad who belched flames. He terrorized the region of the Aventine, by the banks of the Tiber, until the day he stole from Hercules and felt the rigor of his club. It is said that all that was left of the three heads was a mass of jelly.

Cadmeans. A dynasty of Theban kings.

Callaeschrus. Father of Critias, a character in Plato's *Dialogues*.

Callias the Rich. Athenian general, son of Hipponicus. Ancient historiography does not allow us to be certain that the founder of the Peace of Callias, c. 462 (also a son of Hipponicus), was the brother-in-law of Alcibiades, who thirty years later commanded the expedition against Potidaea.

Callicrates. One of the architects of the Parthenon. He collaborated with Ictinus and Mnesicles. He drew up the plans for the Temple of Athena Nike, restored the accesses to the Acropolis to keep fugitive slaves out, and built the third of the Long Walls that joined Athens to the ports. He was a great friend of Pericles.

Callinus of Ephesus. Elegiac poet of the seventh century. Muse of epic poetry and of eloquence. Cf. *Tyrtaeus*.

Callipygian. From the Greek *kallípygos*, "having beautiful buttocks." Cf. *Sweet-Rump*.

Callirrhoe. At the beginning of *Axiochus*, one of the apocryphal *Dialogues* of Plato (generally attributed to an academic of the first century), Socrates said, "I had left to go to the Cinosarges and I was near the Ilissus when I heard a voice that called: Socrates, Socrates! I turned to see where it was coming from and I saw Clinias, the son of Axiochus, who was running in the direction of the fountain of Callirrhoe . . ." Since Socrates did not mention which way he left, it takes only a bit of imagination to alter the choreography of this scene and place the fountain in different places, as long as they are close to the Ilissus and the Cinosarges. Callirrhoe was also known as Enneacrunus, or *The Nine Pipes*, and its waters were used in prenuptial ceremonies.

Carcinus. One of the generals of the College of Strategi who participated in the beginning of the Peloponnesian War.

Cassandra. A Trojan princess.

Cathartic. Purifying.

Catonace. A rough, thick tunic usually worn by slaves.

Cattalos. A pastime of Sicilian origin that was very popular among the party-going young people of Athens. The idea was to shoot a stream of wine into wine glasses in a metal holder while calling out the name of a woman. If the stream produced a vibrant sound, it was interpreted to mean that his love was reciprocated.

Centaurs. Peaceful and obliging monsters, half man and half horse, who lived in the horse country of Magnesia. Chiron, the fairest of them all, was preceptor of Achilles. However, when Pirithous, king of the Lapiths, invited them to his wedding, the centaurs had a bit too much to drink and started a memorable melee at the instigation of Discord, twin sister of Ares and a well-known party-pooper. From that moment on, the Lapiths and the centaurs became mortal enemies. Cf. *Pirithous.*

Ceramicus. This was the name of two sections of Athens. The Outer Ceramicus, along the walls, was a popular center for prostitution. Toward the middle of the fifth century, the elegant and commercial Inner Ceramicus, which extended all the way to the agora, was already being used by a number of Athens's queens of the night.

Cerulean. The Sovereign of the Cerulean Hair. An epithet for Poseidon. Cf. *Poseidon.*

Charmides, Son of Glaucon. A beautiful Athenian boy, inspiration for one of Plato's *Dialogues.*

Charmides. Father of Phidias and Panainos.

Charybdis. The famous whirlpool in the straits of Mesina. Cf. *Scylla.*

Cherephon. A friend and pupil of Socrates. A character in Plato's *Gorgias* (447 b, etc.) and Xenophon's *Memorabilia* (2, 3, 1, etc.).

Chi. Third from last letter of the Greek alphabet.

Child. Cf. *Cybele*

Chiton. The chiton used in Athens reached down to the feet, but young people could and did wear it halfway up the leg or even above the knees by means of a belt they used to hold it up. It did not have any sleeves, left both arms bare, and was held together with brooches over the shoulders. The material covered only the left flank, and the right one remained open. Unfastening the brooch on the right shoulder would uncover the breast, and when the belt was loosened, nearly the whole body was bare. In winter, a chiton was sometimes worn under the himation. It was the usual garment worn by young people.

Choregia. During the annual dramatic contests, the Athenian State did not have to spend a single obol on the choruses and casts. From the very first day of rehearsals until the end of the last performance in the Great Theater, the choregus covered all expenses. Members were always very wealthy men and, by financing a Dionysian chorus, they were discharging one of the most prestigious obligations imposed upon them by their social class. It was believed that Dionysus himself inspired the final, consecratory acclamation by the spectators that determined the victorious tetralogy of each year. The triumphant poet, anointed favorite of the Gods, was entitled from that day on, until the day of his death, to dine in the Prytaneum at the expense of the State. But along with the poet, Athens also glorified the choregus whose personal fortune and zeal were responsible for feeding the cast, providing luxurious costumes, staging a magnificent production, and, in sum, ensuring that the Athenian demos never forgot the virtuous lessons implicit in all works inspired by Dionysus. Except for victory in battle, few things could be a greater asset to the career of an Athenian politician than the manifest favor of a God.

Choregus. The person who undertook the production expenses for staging the Greater Dionysian Festivals or Dionysia. Cf. *Choregia.*

Choreut (choreutés). A member of the dramatic chorus in the Greek theater.

Chorus. This is a term that sometimes leads to confusion. On the one hand, it alludes to the group of persons who danced and sang in a dramatic work; on the other hand, it alludes to the entire cast. But when Pericles and Nicias triumphed "in the choruses," it was not by dancing or reciting. Cf. *Choregia; Dionysia; Eponymous; Great Theater of Dionysus.*

Cimon. Son of Miltiades. 510—449. Athenian patriot.

City. The City is the Polis of Athens and refers to the urban settlement, as well as to the Athenian State and all its territory.

Cleandridas. Spartan general, father of Gyllipus.

Cleomenes. Spartan king reputed to be a drunkard.

Cleopompus. Athenian general.

Cliniad. Alcibiades and his brother.

Clinias. Father and younger brother of Alcibiades. Cf. *Coronea.*

Clisthenes. Social reformer of the sixth century. Founder of Athenian Democracy. He belonged to the line of the Alcmeonidae.

Colabus. A sweet fritter shaped in the form of a lyre.

College of Strategi. Its ten members were public servants of the demos of Athens, which was supposed to elect them in the Assembly. However, they were relatively autonomous in their management of the army and the fleet; they organized levies; they worked with civil justice to prosecute cases of desertion, contempt, and cowardice. In the area of foreign policy, they negotiated capitulations, armistices, and treaties pending the ratification of the citizens. It was the only organ of the Athenian government empowered to convene special sessions of the Assembly.

Coronea. A city in Boeotia and scene of a famous Athenian military defeat in the year 447. Clinias, father of Alcibiades, was killed in the battle.

Corybant. A priest of Cybele. These priests were made fun of among the Greeks for their jumping dances and wild gesticulation.

Corydallus. Hills to the west of Attica.

Cosmetes. A military officer who was in charge of the instruction of Athenian youths during their training as ephebi.

Cothurnus. A high, thick-soled shoe worn by Greek tragedians to appear taller on stage. It was also part of the attire of the Archon King.

Cotyle. A measure of volume, approximately 273 cc.

Council of Five Hundred. Cf. *Five Hundred.*

Crates. Eponymous Archon for the year 434.

Cratinus. Athenian writer of comedies of the fifth century.

Cream. Pronounced "hrema" in Greek. It was used to mean money, monetary gain, profit.

Critias. Son of Callaeschrus and well-known character in Plato's *Dialogues.*

Croesus. The last king of Lydia, 560–546. After bringing all of Asia Minor under his control, he was ultimately defeated by Cyrus the Great and his kingdom was incorporated into the Persian Empire.

Cronid. The sons of Cronus, such as Zeus and his brothers.

Cronus. God of the Hellenes, son of Uranus and Gaea, overthrown by Zeus. Since then he has resided in Hades. He is identified with the Roman Saturn.

Crotona. Cf. *Sybaris.*

Cubit. A unit of measurement equal to a foot and a half.

Cybele. The Goddess known as the Mother, the Child, the Mother-Child.

Cybernetes. Helmsman. *Kybernetiké* or cybernetics, the term the Greeks used to describe the art of guiding ships, is now used for the governance of other communications devices.

Cylon. A young Athenian aristocrat, winner of the race in the Olympic Games of 640. To his athletic glory he added the social victory of his marriage to the daughter of Theagenes, Tyrant of Megara. Counting on the support of his powerful father-in-law, he conspired with a group of eupatrids of his age group to overthrow the government of Athens. With the aid of the hoplites sent to him by Theagenes, he succeeded in capturing the Acropolis, where the events described in this novel subsequently took place (Chap. 46, "Day Twenty One"). Cf. *Megacles.*

Cynocephalus. "Dog Head."

Cypris. Born of the waves. Aphrodite was born of the ocean foam. Pink and naked, she rode the waves on a bivalve seashell. Pink because the engendering foam had been dyed with the blood that streamed from the genitals of Uranus, who had been emasculated by his son, Cronus. On that vehicle of genitalian conception, she arrived in the island of Cythera. But the Goddess of Love needed a more intimate venue, and she found it on Cyprus. In the perfumed city of Paphos, friend of shadows, she installed the venue of her irresistible worship. She then presided over amorous desire, the all-powerful force that drives mortals. Of her own choosing, Aphrodite became a Cypriot or Cypria or Cypriana or Cyprina, but she never forgot her origins in the sea. That is why she held sacred the sea urchin, the conch, and the starfish, and her priestesses dyed their hair sepia with the ink of cuttlefish and the fruits of the sea, which are considered aphrodisiacs. But in tending to her carnal affairs, Aphrodite traveled through the air. She was escorted by flocks of turtledoves and sparrows, birds that were well known for their licentiousness. (According to other, less reliable theologies, Aphrodite was the daughter of Zeus and Dione. Others make her the mother of the child Eros, who would have been fathered by Hermes or Ares.) Cf. *Aphrodite, Pandemos.*

Daemon. A divinity, spirit, or demon, but without the malignant connotation that the word carries in Christianity.

Damon. A famous musician; teacher of Pericles.

Danae. The mythical daughter of the king of Argos. From her affair with Zeus, Perseus was born. Cf. *Perseus.*

Darius the Great. King of Kings, 558–486. This high-sounding title was not empty vanity; this sovereign of the Persian Empire inherited the conquests of Cyrus and Cambyses, bringing under his power the kingdoms of Media, Babylon, Egypt, and Lydia. But Darius enlarged and organized the Empire. He also made himself king of the Greeks of Asia, and of the Carians, Mysians, Phrygians, Cappadocians, Paphlagonians, Cilicians, Pamphylians, Pisidians, as well as the Syrians and Palestinians, Cyrenaics, Libyans, Parthians, Caspians, and Armenians, and other kingdoms that were the new subjects of the Persian Empire. In 490 Darius sent against Greece the greatest army ever seen in the peninsula, and he was defeated at Marathon by the citizens of democratic Athens under the command of Miltiades, father of Cimon.

Day of the Fallen. Also known as the Epitaphia. Its etymology, literally "over the tombs," is a giveaway for the autumnal ceremonies held by Athenians with sacrifices, and probably speeches, dedicated to the fighting men who gave their lives for their country.

Decoy. A kind of dummy made of solid wood and used for archery target practice.

Deinomache. An Alcmeonid, mother of Alcibiades.

Delian League. The alliance, also known as the Confederation of Delos or Athenian Naval Alliance, founded by Aristides in the year 477 (three years after the victory over the Persians in Salamis) was a pan-Hellenic group headed by Athens and intended to create a great fleet to protect the common interest against the Persian danger. Sparta, cautious and jealous of the immense power Athens acquired at the helm of the Delian League, founded its own Peloponnesian Alliance. In 431 the two coalitions got involved in a conflict that went on for three decades: the Peloponnesian War. Cf. *Delos.*

Delos. When Leto became pregnant by Zeus, the jealous Hera sent the serpent Python with orders to pursue her over the face of the Earth and prevent her from having the baby. With the aid of the South Wind, however, Leto was able to give birth to Artemis on the island of Ortygia, and later to Apollo on the island of Delos, which had been a drifting island but since then was forever fixed in the middle of the Aegean. On that sacred island the heroic

Athenians, who had defeated the invading Persians at Marathon and Salamis, formed a league, a naval alliance against the Persian threat. And in the sanctuary of Apollo they swore a solemn oath to defend their allies. But alas, after a few years ...

Delphi. A city in Phocis, on the southwest approach to Mount Parnassus and occupying a magnificent place where Apollo had a temple. From the seventh to the fourth centuries, the aristocratic Delphic priests held considerable sway over the spiritual and political life of ancient Greece through the oracles of the Pythia. Cf. *Pythia.*

Delphinia or Delphic Feasts. Festivities and processions in honor of Artemis and Apollo.

Demeter. Daughter of Cronus and Rhea, sister of Hestia, Hera, Hades, Poseidon, and Zeus. She is the most important agrarian deity of the Greeks. In extramarital relations with Zeus, she had Iacchus and Kore. She had Pluto with one of the Titans. Her life was marked by the grief of losing Kore, carried away by Hades to his subterranean kingdom. After a long pilgrimage of mourning, a few threats, and a long hunger strike, Demeter was able to get Zeus to enter into a pact by which Kore, known as Persephone, would spend three months of the year as wife of Hades and queen of the underworld, and the rest of the year with her mother.

Some scholars have suggested that Demeter and Persephone represent the old grain—new grain identity or a duality in which Demeter would be the Earth and Persephone the seed. In any case, together they allude to the cyclical death and rebirth of the vegetable kingdom. Demeter grew sad when her daughter descended into the underworld and became joyous when she returned to the light. Other Gods also wept for the loss of a loved one in the agrarian worship of Astarte and Adonis (Syria), Cybele and Atis (Phrygia), Isis and Osiris (Egypt). In Greece, the greatest cultural expression of this myth occurred in the Eleusinian mysteries in which the candidates to initiation had to fast, participate in a torch parade, and, covered in sheepskins, wait in religious silence, listen to sacred revelations in gross languages, and drink barley water in a holy chalice. (Homeric Hymn to Demeter.) According to Clement of Alexandria, the Eleusinian ritual was represented like a sacred drama. Those who were initiated in these mysteries were known as Mystoe, from the same root as *mystic*. Nothing certain is known about the great revelation to which they were made privy at the end of the ceremonies, but the literature contains abundant allusions to the joy of the Mystoe in the certainty of a luminous human destiny and the immortality of the soul. Just as the seed lies in the soil until it is reborn in spring into a new life, the Eleusinian Mystics must have had the hope that man, beyond this Earth and beyond the tomb, could expect a better existence in an unknown world of light. Demeter and Persephone appear crowned with sprays and holding a grain stalk in their hands. The Romans knew them as Ceres and Proserpine. Cf. *Hades, Pelops, Persephone, Thesmophoria.*

Democracy. One way to understand the difference between democracy and oligarchy in the ancient world is to resort to numbers. Toward the end of the sixth century, the free, but poor, men of Athens had triumphed over the oligarchs and gained political power that they exercised through the right to a direct, one-man-one-vote participation in the Assembly. Thus, during the time of Pericles, the 280,000 inhabitants of Attica were ruled by 40,000 adult male citizens who were the offspring of Athenian fathers and mothers. They ruled over women, minors, foreigners, and slaves. Each citizen ruled over seven noncitizens. This was the essence of the slave democracy of Athens. In Sparta, however, twenty-eight aged oligarchs, the heads of the most ancient families, the owners of the lands in the valley of the Evrotas river, elected their kings and Ephors, decreed what the Assembly should approve by acclamation, and ruled over a population group fifty times greater than their own in which the many free, but poor, peasants, called helots, had no rights at all and lived worse than the slaves. This was the essence of the slave oligarchy of Sparta. This rather formalistic schematic of the ancient Greek societies glosses over the fact that the Athenian Assembly, which rarely had a quorum of more than six thousand, was manipulated by the political bosses, while the twenty-eight omnipotent elders of the Spartan *Gerusia* ruled in the interests of the fifty families who were the traditional masters of the lands and the power. The outstanding difference was that no Athenian demagogue could take overtly antipopular measures, while the Spartan Elders ensured that the interests of their class could never be legally challenged. Cf. *Assembly, Helots, Sparta.*

Democrates. An Athenian pederast, according to Plutarch (Alc. 3).

Demon. Cf. *Daemon.*

Demos. The name used for both the village and the people.

Diaphanes. Clear, evident, transparent.

Didaskalos. "Teacher," in Greek. This was the title reserved by the Athenian demos for the poets who were victorious in the Greater Dionysia. The Didaskalos *par excellence* during the last third of the fifth century was undoubtedly Sophocles, the most honored of all the tragedians.

Dike. The personification of Justice.

Diktyoulkoi. The literal translation of this word means "those who pull in the nets." It is the name of a satyr play by Aeschylus that closed a tetralogy on Perseus. The only fragments that have reached us are those alluded to in the novel.

Dindymenian Mother. The Great Mother or Great Mother of the Gods or the Mother Goddess, etc. She was a deity of Asia Minor and the center of her worship was in Phrygia. By the fifth century, however, she was worshipped throughout Hellas.

Dindymon. A mountain in Phrygia where the center of the worship of Cybele was established and where she had the greatest of her temples sponsored by the kings of ancient Lydia and later favored by the Persian conquerors.

Dione. A nymph, daughter of Uranus and Gaea. She was loved by Zeus and continued to be associated with him through the oracle at Dodona.

Dionysia. Athenian festivals in honor of Dionysus. The Greater Dionysia or Urban Dionysia were the occasion for dramatic competitions. The Lesser or Rural Dionysia, which took place in winter, did not have the solemnity of the Urban Festivals. In a more intimate and agrarian setting, the Athenians celebrated their ancient phallic rites and the mysteries of the yearly renewal of the vegetable kingdom.

Dionysus. God of vegetation, especially of wine. He is the Bacchus of the Romans. Dressed in the guise of a mortal man, Zeus had won the favors of Semele, daughter of Cadmus, king of Thebes. When the jealous Hera found out that Semele was pregnant, she adopted the figure of an old woman and warned the ardent young woman to be careful. What if her mysterious lover turned out to be a monster? She advised her to demand that the unknown lover present himself in his true form. Semele followed the advice, but after Zeus refused to comply, she barred him from her bed. Since that is what the stubborn girl wanted, the angry Zeus presented himself with his thunder and lightning. Semele was consumed like a blade of straw in the divine incandescence, but Hermes was able to save the fetus. (The myths do not explain how Hermes did it, but it is said that he sewed it to the inner thigh of Zeus, where it was incubated for another three months, long enough for the unique birth by his father.) When he became an adult, Dionysus wandered all over the known Ecumene and one day returned to his homeland in Boeotia, having become a universal deity. With the passage of time, Zeus was so pleased with the increasing Hellenization of his son's barbarous sect that he finally called him to Olympus and sat him at his right hand among the twelve Great Gods. Finding himself in such a good situation, Dionysus descended to Tartarus, bribed Persephone, and saved Semele, who ascended to Olympus with the name Thyone. Zeus assigned her a lifetime pension and residence, and Hera ultimately forgot her old quarrel.

Discord, Terror, and Flight. Maleficent deities represented on the helmet worn by Ares, God of war.

Distich. In Greek and Latin poetry, two verses in which the first is a hexameter and the second a pentameter. Together, they usually represent a single, complete idea.

Dithyramb. A choral hymn in honor of Dionysus.

Dodona. At this famous temple in Epirus, devoted to Zeus and Dione, the questions to be answered were written on lead tablets. The Gods were expected to answer as if they were policemen, doctors, lawyers, or market analysts.

540

Among the tablets that have survived, there is one by a certain Agis, who wanted to know what had happened to some mattresses and pillows that disappeared from his house. Lysanias wanted to know if the child Annyla was carrying was really his. An ancient capitalist wanted to know if his investment in a sheep farm was going to be profitable. There are also official queries about the success of military alliances, colonial expeditions, wars, treaties, etc. There is one in which the city-state of Corcyra asked to which Gods it had to make offerings and sacrifices in order to attain domestic harmony. Although there is no historical certainty, there is reason to believe that the oak or oaks sacred to Zeus would wave in the wind and murmur the reply. Just as in Delphi, the priests of the temple interpreted the divine words for the benefit of the visitors.

Drachma. The drachma contained six obols; one hundred drachmas made up a mina, and six thousand drachmas made up a talent.

Ecbatana. Capital of the kingdom of the Medes, incorporated in the sixth century into the Persian Empire. It is the modern Iranian city of Hamadan.

Ecclesia. The Greek name for the Assembly. It survives in modern English word forms, such as *ecclesiastical.* Cf. *Assembly.*

Ecclesiastes. A member of the Ecclesia or Assembly, an Assemblyman; used here in the plural.

Ecumene. The "inhabited lands," i.e., the world.

Eetion. Father of Andromache.

Elaphebolion. The third month of winter. Cf. *Months.*

Elea. A Greek city in southern Italy, center of an important school of philosophy with outstanding figures such as Parmenides and Xenon.

Elegy. A poetic form used in ancient Greece; elegiac poets. Cf. *Tyrtaeus.*

Eleleu. A war cry.

Eleusis. An Athenian demos where the mysteries in honor of Demeter and Persephone were celebrated. The information we have about the Eleusinian religion would seem to indicate that it was one of the earliest expressions of ancient mysticism. It acquired great importance in the spiritual life of Attica. Cf. *Demeter, Persephone.*

Empyrean. Of or pertaining to the heavens.

Encomium. A poetic genre; elegy.

Encrisis. Admission to the contests, after giving proof of aptitude.

Enodia. An epithet of Hecate, protector of roads.

Epameinon. Eponymous Archon of 429.

Ephebus. A youth, a young man of military age.

Epheby. Military service in Athens. The ephebi began their service at the age of eighteen and concluded at the age of twenty.

Ephetae. Judges of the criminal courts of Delphinium, Palladium, Prytaneum, and Phreatys, whose sentence was final.

541

Epilepsy. Etymologically from the Greek, *epi* (over, above) + *lep* (radical of the verb "to seize"). In modern European languages, it has come down to us in the form of the "high affliction," or the "affliction from above," clearly meaning that the condition was thought to have divine origins.

Epinicium. Etymologically from the Greek, *epi* (over, in respect of) + *nike* (victory). A composition intended to praise the winners in any competition.

Epistates. Director, head, president. On the day of his election, the Epistates of the Prytaneum presided over the Council of Five Hundred and the Assembly.

Epitaphia. Cf. *Day of the Fallen.*

Epithalamium. Etymologically from the Greek *epi* (over, in respect of) + *thalamos* (bridal chamber). A composition dedicated to a wedding.

Epithymia. "Passion," in Greek.

Eponymous. The Hellenic peoples, their "nation" spread out in hundreds of city-states on three continents, did not standardize their calendar until the fourth century, when they began to use the Olympiads as a reference. Before that, years in Athens were identified with the name of the Eponymous Archon, which simply means "the one with the name of the year," since all Archons and practically all officials held office for one year. However, since the Athenian year began six months after our year, when we say that Menon is the eponym for the year 487, we must bear in mind that he was in office from June 21, 487 to June 20, 486. Hence, the spring of Menon is the end of his term and the summer is the beginning. Cf. *Months.* Eponyms played important legal roles in connection with the family, having to do with tutorships, orphans, trusts, marriages, dowries, etc. Their most important function, however, was to preside over the Dionysia. The eponym for each year had to read the many works presented to compete in the dramatic festivals. Choosing the three finalists was his exclusive domain and, given the religious nature of the event, it would be malicious to suppose that he used "ghost readers" as contemporary officials do. When the reading was completed, the Archon would assign to each of the victorious poets a choregus and a chorus, i.e., a rich patron to pay all the expenses and a cast that would rehearse the four works of the tetralogy for months. In the week of the festival, during the three days of presentations, the six thousand spectators who crowded into the Great Theater of Dionysus watched a total of twelve works. The great political importance of a victory in the Greater Dionysia made the eponym, during the year of his Archonship, a magistrate with a great deal of personal power. Cf. *Chorus; Choregia; Dionysia; Great Theater of Dionysus.*

Eranos. Guild, sect, secret society.

Erechtheion. The temple dedicated to Erechtheus in the Acropolis of Athens.

Erechtheus. Mythical hero, founder of one of the great families of Attica.

Ergasteriarch. The owner of an ergasterium.

Ergasterium. A crafts shop where slaves generally worked.

Eridanus. A river in Attica. It entered the City through the Diomean Gate and exited through the Dipylon. The river known today as the Po, in northern Italy, was also called Eridanus.

Eros. The child Amour (the naughty and extremely cruel Cupid of the Romans), who pierced humans with his arrows that carried the amorous plague.

Esceas. The doors through the Trojan walls.

Eschinocephalus. "Having a head like a marine onion," one of the nicknames given to Pericles. Cf. *Onion Head.*

Eucrates. An Athenian general during the Peloponnesian War.

Eulogos. "The well spoken." (As an inveterate iconoclast and giver of nicknames, the barber in our story would better have been called Cacologos.)

Eumenides. Literally, it means "the benevolent ones"; another name used to placate the vengeful Erinyes (the Roman Furies). These three hags, Tisiphone, Megaera, and Alecto, who lived on Mount Erebus, were deities dating back much farther than the Gods of Olympus. They punished crimes against one's own blood, against elders, against hospitality, and against suppliants. They pursued their victims incessantly over any and all regions. Their hair was snakes on dog's heads; their bodies were black as coal; they had the wings of bats and the bloodshot eyes of wild boars.

Eupatrid. Literally, "sons of good fathers"; the well-born, the Athenian aristocracy.

Euphemus. One of the Argonauts; a great swimmer.

Euphoros. Happy, euphoric.

Euphrantides. The seer who was in vogue when Themistocles was high and dry awaiting the battle of Salamis. Following the tradition that the firstborn took the name of the grandfather, our character (fictitious) would be the grandchild of the real seer.

Eupolis. An ancient Greek writer of comedies.

Eupraxia. The Greek verb *prattein* means both to "act well" and to "feel well." This fortunate semantic duality allowed Socrates to proclaim that those who practiced in his eupraxia would simultaneously be "acting with virtue" and "feeling well." But according to Socrates, the most virtuous life is that of the person who "studies himself to find ways to be better, and they live very happily for being vividly conscious of their constant improvement" (Xenophon, *Memorabilia*, IV, 3).

Euripides. 480–406. Age-wise, the third of the three great Athenian tragedians. It is said that when Aeschylus was fighting the Persians, Sophocles was an ephebus directing the triumphal dance and Euripides was born on the very day of the victory at Salamis. He was separated from his two great predecessors by the broad river of sophism that came upon Athens during the years of his youth. The sophists taught people to think and especially to speak per-

543

suasively. They gave their students an implacable critical attitude that stopped neither at the traditional nor the sacred. They taught the youth that to climb to political heights they had to have a critical, agnostic, and relativistic vision of the world. They also generalized the custom of charging for their teaching. There were formidable and original thinkers among the sophists, such as Protagoras of Abdera and Gorgias of Leontini, but there were also cheats and frauds. The teachings of the sophists had far ranging consequences: They attacked tradition, renewed several fields of the ancient physics, and had an influence in morality, religion, and art. Euripides was the first great spokesman of the influence of sophism in the tragedy. His skeptical works—sometimes unstable and contradictory, but always artistically refined—rejected the givens of traditional drama. He provided a new vision of the world, one that denounced Olympus as the source of all injustice and barbarity and populated Attica with unprejudiced and reflexive mortals.

Euripus. The straits between Euboea and Boeotia, feared for its troubled waters.

Eurymedon. A river of Pamphylia (today southern Turkey) that empties into the Mediterranean. The Eurymedon was the scene of a victory won by the Athenians under the leadership of Cimon.

Euthydemus. An Athenian seer who inspired one of Plato's *Dialogues.*

Euthydemus. Eponymous Archon for 450, the year when Socrates, who was born in 470, concluded his training as an ephebus.

Euthymenes. Eponymous Archon for the year 437.

Exorkismos. Exorcism.

Five Hundred. The Council of Five Hundred. In Greek, the Boule. It was made up of the ten tribes of Attica, each one represented by fifty members, who were also members of the Assembly. With the exception of holidays and bad luck days, they met on a daily basis and were convened by the Prytanes. They met in the Bouleuterion, or in open spaces, where the members were separated from the public by a rope. When they were discussing secret affairs, however, no "strangers" were allowed to listen. They screened the initiatives that the Assembly was to hear. After this first level, the Five Hundred reexamined the issues and voted. However, except on very rare occasions authorized by the Assembly itself, all matters returned to the Assembly for the final and sovereign vote of "the many."

Foreigner. This refers to the foreign freemen living in Attica. They were obliged to pay a special tax and to fight in wars. They had no political rights and could neither marry Athenian women nor own real estate in the territory. For meritorious service to the City-State or to the Gods, they could win an exemption from taxation, and in very distinguished cases, they could even win Athenian citizenship. Cf. *Isoteleia.*

Games. The Panathenian Games or Panathenaea were annual athletic metes held in Attica and reserved exclusively for Athenian athletes. They were held during the festivities celebrated on the twenty-eighth of Hecatombaion in honor of Athena. Among the pan-Hellenic athletic contests, the most important were the Olympic Games, in Elis, devoted to Zeus. They were followed by the Isthmic Games, held by the Corinthians in honor of Poseidon; the Pythian Games of Delphi, instituted by Diomedes in honor of Apollo; the Nemean Games, in the region of the same name in Argolis, instituted by the hero Adrastus to mark the death of the child Opheltes. (Many of the Greek games were born as part of funeral rites that later took on a certain periodicity. A good example might be the games ordered by Achilles in *The Iliad* [Canto XXIII] to mark the death of Patroclus.) Cf. *Panathenaean Amphorae.*

Gamma. Third letter of the Greek alphabet. It is also the symbol for the number three.

Ganymede. The son of King Tros. He was the most beautiful of all boys. The Olympians chose him to be cupbearer for Zeus, who preferred having him in his bed and disguised himself as an eagle to kidnap him from Troy. The myth of Zeus and Ganymede acquired immense popularity in Greece and Rome, especially as a religious support for adults who wanted to have sexual relations with boys. Plato used it in *Phaedrus* to justify his love for his young pupils, although in his *Laws* he condemned sodomy as love *contra natura* (against nature).

Georgica. "Agricultural," in Greek. This is another of the epithets used for Athena who, among her other gifts to Attica, included the olive tree and the plow. Cf. *Athena.*

Geryon. The three-headed king of the Tartessians. He also had three torsos and six arms. He was the son of Callirrhoe and grandson of Ocean. His red cattle were so beautiful they were the envy of all. But as fate would have it, the tenth labor of Hercules was precisely to take the red cattle without paying. One day, as they were grazing on an island, Hercules took them and clubbed the dog Orthus and the herdsman Eurython. There is no consensus on the final combat, but it is believed that Hercules skewered all three of Geryon's bodies. It was also around that time that he erected his famous pillars, one on the tip of Europe and the other on the tip of Africa. But there is no consensus on whether he erected them on the way to or from Tartessus.

Gnome. In the strict sense, it means *intelligence,* but almost invariably with a more deontological than scientific connotation. In the plural, the gnomai represent traditional knowledge, expressed in the maxims and aphorisms of wise men. In archaic poetry, poets like Solon, Theognis, Callinus, Phocilides, etc., who sang the ancient knowledge of the Greeks in sententious language, were known as the gnomic poets.

Gnothi Sauton. The famous *know thyself* was engraved in a stele at the entrance to the Temple of Apollo at Delphi. Rather than introspective insight, the phrase is closer to "know your place," a call for acceptance of the limits of human nature. The meaning of this well-known maxim was completed by another, adjacent inscription that said: *meden agan* ("nothing in excess"). Read together, the two maxims would seem to indicate that any aspiration to the divine would be tantamount to insolence and punishable by the Gods; it was an admonition that became a leitmotif for the gnomic poets. Socrates, however, adopted *gnothi sauton* as the motto of his eupraxia, which considers introspective self-knowledge to be one of the greatest virtues of human endeavor and the root of ultimate happiness. Cf. *Eupraxia.*

God of Streets. An epithet of Apollo, as the protector of passersby. Cf. *Apollo.*

Gorgias of Leontini. 487–380? In his work, *On Non-Being or Nature,* this brilliant Sicilian nonagenarian attempted to prove three theses: "nothing exists"; "if something did exist, it would not be knowable"; "if it were knowable, it would not be transmissible." Unfortunately, his works and postulates have not reached us except in the form of fragments through Plato, Sextus Empiricus, and a controversial anonymous peripatetic. He traveled widely, but little is known of his itineraries. In 427, as ambassador of his homeland of Leontini, he visited Athens, where his eloquence was the object of admiration. As a master of rhetoric he represented the most essential aspects of the sophistic vocation toward the end of the fifth century: to train the future political leaders of Greece, to teach them the art of persuasion through oratory. The sophists were the targets of a great deal of criticism, particularly Gorgias and Protagoras, who charged money for their teaching.

Gorgons. Cf. *Medusa.*

Graphe. A denunciation.

Great Theater of Dionysus. With its seating galleries carved into the living rock of the southern slope of the Acropolis, the Great Theater could accommodate about six thousand spectators. Around the orchestra there were a few aisles of comfortable seats for official dignitaries and distinguished guests. The best spot in the house, however, was reserved for the marble throne of the High Priest of Dionysus. As in all Greek theaters of the time, productions were staged outdoors and went from daybreak to dusk. Despite the good acoustics provided by the reflected sound from the cliffs, only very powerful and well-trained voices could make themselves heard throughout the auditorium.

Gylippus. A Spartan general, son of Cleandridas. He gained fame in 415 as an ally of Syracuse against the Athenians who were attacking Sicily under the command of Nicias.

Gynaeceum. A part of the Greek manor, usually toward the rear, reserved for the women and children. In the fifth century, it included the kitchen, larders, the master bedroom, the quarters of the female slaves, the spinning room, bath, latrine, an open atrium with its colonnade, and sometimes a piece of land that could be accessed from the rear and comprised the coral, hen-house, kennels, etc. The only men admitted to the gynaeceum were the freemen of the family, very close relatives, and trusted slaves, especially the very old, effeminate, or eunuchs. Cf. *Andronitis.*

Hades. The God of the underworld whom the Romans called Pluto. By extension, the word *Hades* was also used to denote the entire underworld kingdom or the palace where the God lived with Persephone, who had Hecate as her lady in waiting. At the very bottom of the underworld of Hades is Tartarus, where Zeus sent those who really got on his nerves. Among the other locations in Hades are Erebus, the home of the Erinyes; the Asphodel Plains, set aside for those who had been neither good nor bad; and the Elysian Fields, happy land of perpetual daylight where the souls of the virtuous dwelt.

Hagnon. An Athenian general during the Peloponnesian War.

Halicarnassus. A Greek city in Caria, homeland of Herodotus and Dionysus; also famous for the Mausoleum (the monument to King Mausolus). Its modern name is Bodrum (in southeast Turkey).

Haloae. When the peasants finished their wine harvest, they would consecrate these festivals to Demeter and Dionysus with great feasting in the demos. Aside from being the occasion for the hermetic contest of the callipygian dances mentioned in the novel, the Haloae were also celebrated by the hetaerae with banquets to which they invited their lovers to participate in the licentious ritual they called the "minor mysteries of Demeter." Paul Lacroix, using the pseudonym Pierre Dufour, in his *History of Prostitution* (Seré, Paris, 1851, p. 128), quotes the *Letters of Alciphron* ("Megaera to Bacchis" and "Thaïs to Thessala") to illustrate the excitement that the Haloae stirred in the profession.

Halon. A hero of medicine linked to Asclepius and Chiron, and in whose guild it is said that Socrates held a position as priest.

Hecanthropy. Just as the hecatomboea is an offering of a hundred oxen to Zeus or Apollo, every one hundred clients that a prostitute offered up to Aphrodite constituted a hecanthropy.

Hecate. Protector of witches. She was the lady in waiting of Persephone in Hades and escorted her to the light for her annual rendezvous with her mother Demeter. She had three bodies and three dog's heads. (In the oldest version, the heads were of a lion, a dog, and a mare; or she had a hundred heads, as attested to by the Greek root "hecaton.") She lived in Erebus together with the Erinyes. Since she had the privileges that go with being one of the ancient Gods, Zeus did not object if Hecate granted or denied the wishes of a mortal. In an allusion to her triple nature, she was worshipped at the intersections of three roads where her rustic open altars stank of decomposing offerings. Hesiod considered Hecate, according to the pre-Hellenic tradition preserved in Boeotia, to be the Triple Goddess that ruled in Heaven, Earth, and the Tartarus. The Athenians, however, stressed her repressive and lethal nature, and by the fifth century, she was the object of necromantic rituals, homicidal execrations, and all sorts of things of the night that took place at the crossroads where she had her altars. Hecate was identified with the moon and with dogs, for their love of howling at the moon and eating carrion. Her sacred animals were black lambs, white dogs, and weasels. Among her more outstanding priestesses was the witch Medea.

Hecateus of Miletus. Historian and geographer of the sixth century; student of Anaximander and classmate of Anaximenes. He traveled a great deal and lived at the center of Ionian spiritual life. Although he does not mention him by name, it is pretty evident that Herodotus (IV, 36) makes fun of his writings, especially his schematic map in which the Earth is divided into four quadrants marked by perpendicular axes that go from north to south following a line from the Hister (lower Danube) to the Nile, and from west to east from the Mediterranean to the Black Sea. His speculative writings, in which he tried to stick to the eastern physics of Anaximander, and his maps of Greece and Aegea, inspired by travel narratives and by his own travels, were immensely useful until the end of the fifth century.

Hecatombaion. The first month of summer and the first month of the year in Attica. Cf. *Months.*

Hector. Son of Priam and Hecuba. The most outstanding of Trojan heroes, killed in combat by Achilles. According to some translators, the Greek epithets given to him by Homer are rendered "killer of men," "enlightened," "of the shimmering helmet."

Hegemon. Military commander, guide, leader. By extension, anyone who presides over or governs civilian activities.

Hegemony. Command, leadership, guidance.

Helen. Daughter of Zeus and Leda; sister of Castor and Polydeuces; unfaithful wife of Menelaus; kidnapped by Paris. It was over her, the most beautiful princess of the time, that Troy was burned.

Helenotamias. Tax collectors.

Heliasts. Judges.

Helicon. A mountain in Boeotia dedicated to the Muses.

Heliconius. This Homeric epithet was shared by Apollo (a Mount Helicon habitué) and Poseidon (master of Helice).

Hellanodicae. Officials who traveled throughout the Greek cities to register athletes who qualified for the Olympic Games. They also worked as judges in the Games.

Hellas. This was the word used by the Greeks for their nation ("Greece" is a Roman name that the Greeks never used). But Hellas is a much broader concept than the modern Greek state circumscribed to the Balkans. The Greeks of the peninsula were no more Hellenic than those who lived in the colonies in Africa, Asia, or Western Europe.

Hellebore. A plant used in treatments against madness.

Helots. The peasants of Sparta, who were turned into serfs by the local oligarchy. Cf. *Democracy, Sparta.*

Hemiobol. Half of one obol.

Hephaestus. Son of Zeus and Hera. Blacksmith and cripple. He was so grotesque and naïve that he was the butt of mockery in Olympus. Twice he was thrown from Olympus; the first time by his mother, who had just given birth to him. Her pride could not stand the humiliation of giving birth to a cripple, so she cast him into the sea where he was picked up by Eurynome and Thetis. In *The Iliad* (XVIII, 396), he himself reports on his underwater upbringing: "Nine years I lived with them crafting bronze pieces— brooches, round bracelets, rings, and necklaces—deep in a cave and surrounded by the immense, murmuring, and foamy current of the ocean." With practice he learned to make complex machines, mechanical helpers, and automaton beings. When Hera found out about his incomparable talents, she wanted him at her service. She had Zeus grant him residence in Olympus, she set him up in a modern smithy with all the necessary tools, she provided him with the volcanic forges of Mount Etna, and she gave him to wife Aphrodite, who mercilessly betrayed him with his own brothers. But in his inadmissible ridiculousness, Hephaestus forgave his wife's adultery and the cruelty of his mother. Once, when Zeus threatened to lay his invincible hands on Hera, Hephaestus intervened as moderator: "Suffer him, mother, and support all, though it pain you; may my eyes never see you, so beloved, beaten without me being able to come to your aid, for it is difficult to counter the Olympic one. On another occasion, when I tried to defend you, he took me by the foot and threw me through the divine threshold" (*The Iliad*: I, 586). And that was his second heave-ho. An entire day his fall lasted. At sunset he landed in Lemnos and broke both his legs. He became not only cripple, but an invalid as well. He walked using two golden statues to support his weight. In Athens, Hephaestus had his main temple in the agora. Among the Romans he was known as Vulcan. His best known Homeric epithets were: "illustrious craftsman," "blacksmith," "bronzesmith," "ingenious," "illustrious cripple in both feet." Cf. *Aphrodite, Athena.*

Hera. Daughter of Cronus and Rhea. Sister of Hestia, Demeter, Hades, Poseidon, and Zeus. Mother of Ares, Hephaestus, and Hebe. "The people of Samos believe that the Goddess was born on their island on the banks the river Imbrasus, under a willow that still grows in the sanctuary" (Pausanias, *Description of Greece*, VII, 4, 4). But the Stymphalians aver that she was brought up in their region, that her tutor was one Temenos, son of Pelasgus, whom she visited frequently when she returned in an irritable mood after a fight with her husband (Ibid, VIII, 22, 2). Together with Zeus, she ruled in the lofty ether where the rain-pregnant clouds gather. As first lady of

549

Olympus, she was the incarnation of the chaste and faithful Greek matron, who could also be irritable and nagging, and the storms that shook her marriage were reminiscent of the violence of celestial phenomena. Aside from presiding over births, her main activity seemed to be trying to keep Zeus from being unfaithful and chasing after rivals with their children or fetuses. But it was not at all easy to catch Zeus with his hand in the cookie jar or to follow the twisting trail of a God who was so able at disguise. She, herself, who at first rejected his advances, was ultimately fooled when he appeared to her as a lost cuckoo. When Hera offered the poor bird the warmth of her breast, she saw how he began to retransform into a God, but it was too late to stop him from scoring. Other times, in her attempts to foil her rivals, she would actually favor them, as in the case of the beautiful Ganymede. In response to Hera's jealous "intromission" in his affairs with the boy, and just to see her scream, Zeus immortalized him in the constellation of Aquarius (the Water Bearer) so that his cupbearer would be remembered for all eternity. As a wife, Hera alternated between the rage she felt at her husband's peccadilloes and her fear of getting him angry and feeling on her body the weight of his invincible hands. As a mother, she was no great bargain, either: She hated Ares for being such a brute, and she threw Hephaestus from Olympus into the sea because he was ugly and misshapen. As a daughter, we know that she was an accessory in the overthrow of her father Cronus. The Spartans were particularly devoted to Hera. Athenian women used to swear by her. Her most frequent Homeric epithets were: "venerated," "daring," "incorrigible," "the Goddess with calf's eyes," "she of the snow-white arms." In Rome she was known as Juno. Cf. *Bosphorus, Delos, Dionysus.*

Heraclean Stone. The name the Greeks gave to the magnet.

Heracles. The son of Zeus and Alcmene; he personified strength. Because he killed his wife Megaera, he had to do the famous twelve labors. He is the Hercules of the Romans. Cf. *Cacus, Geryon, Iolaus.*

Heraclitus of Ephesus, 540?–470? One of the great geniuses of antiquity. An Ionian, he was the first theoretician of primitive dialectics. He maintained that fire was the One, and that matter was eternally changing and was the result of the confrontation of opposites.

Heraeum. Temple of Hera.

Herkeios. An epithet of Zeus. It referred to the effigy the Greeks placed in the outer yard. Etymologically, it means "he of the enclosure," and in Homeric times the Greeks were already placing this effigy in the roofless front yard of rural houses so that, from their very first steps within the fence, visitors might feel that they enjoyed the hospitality of Zeus. Some translators have rendered it "protector of the grounds" (*The Odyssey*, XXII, 335).

Hermes. Son of Zeus and Maia. Messenger of Olympus. God of eloquence and another great musician; inventor of the seven-stringed lyre; protector of commerce and of thieves. As a child he was full of mischief. When he was just a baby, he stole a wonderful herd that Apollo had set out to graze in Pieria. To avoid leaving a telltale trail, Hermes made some shoes from bark, and with the cattle so shod, he absconded with them in the night. In vain did Apollo search from Macedonia to the end of the Peloponnesus; they had vanished into thin air. Realizing that he would never find them on his own, Apollo offered a reward to anyone who came forth with information leading to the recovery of the herd. Silenus and his troop of covetous satyrs, experts in sylvan highways and hideaways, set out to trail Hermes and finally came upon him in Arcadia, together with his mother. When Apollo denounced him before Zeus, the child thief declared that of the entire herd he had only sacrificed two heads and had eaten only a twelfth part of their meat, the share that was due him as the Twelfth God of Olympus. The rest he had duly burned in honor of the other eleven. This cute explanation, and his talent for playing an ingenious toy he had invented, ultimately won him the favor of Apollo. In his images he carries the caduceus, a laurel or olive rod with two wings on the upper end and two serpents intertwined along the lower part. He wore golden sandals with which he flew fleetly to do the errands of Zeus. In Rome he was known as Mercury.

Hermippus. Of this prolific poet of the Ancient Comedy, who wrote some forty works, nothing has reached us, but we do know that he was one of the most iconoclastic poets and that a full decade before Aristophanes and Eupolis, he had wielded the mighty mace of satire and mockery against the warlike policies of Pericles. Plutarch (Pericles, 32) reports that he swore out a complaint against Aspasia accusing her of atheism and pandering.

Hermocrates of Syracuse. Great-grandson of the tyrant Anaxilas. When an Athenian fleet carrying Alcibiades and Nicias sailed against Syracuse, Hermocrates turned out to be one of the most able defenders of Syracuse.

Hermon. To avoid giving away the end of the novel, we have excluded from this glossary the ultranoteworthy geographical locations to the south of this mountain.

Herodotus of Halicarnassus. The thirst for knowledge awakened in Ionia by the first firm steps in the development of western science drove him to become a world traveler. He visited Egypt, Phoenicia, Babylon, Scythia. He was involved in the convulsive cultural movement sponsored by Pericles that turned Athens into the center of the spiritual world of the Hellenes. Although he was ideologically on the side opposing the sophists, both in Athens and in Italy he met with and knew outstanding personalities, such as Protagoras of Abdera. But his archaic heart was closer to Sophocles, who was his great friend and believed, as he did, that destiny is not a blind force but the unavoidable will of divinity. Thus, oracles played an important role in the etiology of his narratives, which also abound in Gods who are hostile to mortals and in parenthetical statements in the epic fashion. The ancient critics accused him of "Homericism" (*homerikótatos*), and in his *Histories* it is evident that he had an irrepressible need to tell the story. Although his scientific observation of nature was a constant compromise with mythology, he was nevertheless aware of the fact that by using unverifiable traditions in his works he was introducing elements of uncertainty. Thus it was that he said (VII, 152): "My duty is to relate what is said, but I am by no means bound to believe it all; and this caveat is valid for all I write." Despite the myths, the hyperbole, and the epic spirit that is ever-present in his work, a rich river of history flows from its inner depths. The ancient Greeks already considered him a precursor, and Cicero called him the "Father of History."

Hesiodic. In his labors and day, Hesiod sang the hard life of the peasants of Boeotia in the later part of the eighth century. It was from that austere world, where all sorts of moderation was recommended for the management of rural poverty, that the term "Hesiodic" became a synonym for "moderate." Among the Greeks, who produced very strong wines, it was the custom to drink wine mixed with water. Drinking straight wine was indicative of people who were prone to vices, barbarians, or non-Hesiodic sots like the Scythians.

Hesperia. One of the names the Greeks used for Italy and the Romans used for Spain. It comes from *Hespera*, which in Greeks means "evening" and refers to the west. (In Latin it later became *vesper, vespertinus*.)

Hestia. Daughter of Cronus and Rhea; sister of Demeter, Hera, Hades, Poseidon, and Zeus. As Goddess of the hearth (the home fire), she was the protector of homes. Because she had taught the art of building, her altar always occupied a privileged position in Greek homes. Hestia's sacred fire was the object of constant attention. If it went out, the house and its dwellers would be left without protection. She was essentially a benign Goddess and never participated in the "palace intrigues" in Olympus. Because of a promise made to Zeus back in the times of the revolt against Cronus, she forever remained celibate. She was the Olympian version of the old maid. She, Artemis, and Athena were the only virgins in the family. The Romans called her Vesta.

Hetaerae. Courtesans. Free women who were elegant and often quite knowledgeable. As sexual workers they had absolutely nothing in common with the pornai, who were almost invariably bordello slaves.

Heureka. Pursuant to the dictates of Greek prosody and phonetics, this should be the spelling of the famous "Eureka!" attributed to Archimedes when a fit of scientific rapture drove him streaking bald-ass naked through the streets of Syracuse.

Hieraticus Archon. Sacred archon or holy leader.

Hiero. Secretary to Nicias. A frustrated actor and poet. Of the scams and swindles he staged to protect the public image of his master, we have the juicy testimony of Plutarch in his *Parallel Lives* (Nicias, V).

Hierodulae. Holy prostitutes who worked in a temple. Their earnings went to the Gods.

Hierophant. The title of the High Priest of Demeter in the Eleusinian mysteries. "He who speaks what is holy."

Hierosophist. An expert in holy matters.

Himation. An enormous rectangular, folded piece of material, white or brown, that covered the front of the body up to the pectorals and the back down to the calves. On the back side it covered the left arm and shoulder to the elbow. Men wore it with their right arm and shoulder completely bare. Women pinned the folds together to let the upper flap down to cover the bust. (In the novel, they are generally called *cloaks*.) The himation was the longest and warmest piece of clothing used at the time. In the fifth century, Athenian freemen alternated the himation with the chiton. The gentlemen of the times kept their left hand covered. There were a number of details in the drape of the pleats that denoted breeding and elegance. Baring the knees or inverting the cover of the flanks was the sign of a dullard (Aristophanes, *Clouds*, 1567). The use of sleeves was reserved for certain types of chiton or the rustic tunic used by slaves. Young men did not use the himation until Alcibiades set the fashion in Athens.

Hipparete. Daughter of Hipponicus, wife of Alcibiades.

Hippocrates of Cos. Little and much is known about this unique Ionian scientist. He is supposed to have been born sometime around 460 and his birthplace appears to be an island said to have been linked by family tradition to a corporation of doctors that claimed descent from the mythical Asclepius. Despite all that is dark and controversial in his theories, there is no doubt that his medical works make up the first known system elaborated on observation and expressed in general principles in the manner of the natural philosophers. The most significant aspect of his legacy was his conceptualization very early in history of a methodological approach to therapeutics, as opposed to the traditional case-by-case approach deeply intertwined with primitive magic. Having made such astounding progress in the scientific method, we would tend to be forgiving if his physiological explanation of epilepsy, as it appears in this novel, is so distant from the discoveries of modern medicine. The *Corpus Hippocraticum*, as it appears in the colossal Littré edition, fills seventy-three tomes, including fifty-eight works written in the Ionian dialect. A great deal has been argued and counterargued about the unity of the *Corpus* and about its exclusive authorship by Hippocrates. The studies of Hans Diller advance the plausible theory that the great mass of Hippocratic works was a working tool used by the school of Cos and amassed in its library throughout the sixth and fifth centuries.

Hippodamia. Cf. *Oenomaus.*

Hippodamus of Miletus. A compatriot and close friend of Aspasia. A famous archi-
    tect and the greatest urban planner of ancient Greece. He laid out streets in
    a gridiron pattern to replace the spontaneous conglomeration of twisting
    alleys. Some time around 446, he remodeled the port of Piraeus. About 443
    we find him laying out the famous quadrilateral in the Italian colony of
    Thurii, where Pericles had decided to carry out a pan-Hellenic experiment
    on the ruins of Sybaris.

Hipponax of Ephesus. A poet of the sixth century and, together with Archilochus,
    one of the creators of iambic poetry. He was extremely popular throughout
    antiquity, but only fragments of his works remain. Some are so raunchy that
    certain scholars believe that they might have been the inspiration behind
    Petronius's famous *Encolpius*, among others (*Satyricon*, c. 138).

Hipponicus. Father of Callias the Rich and Hipparete. Father-in-law of Alcibiades.

Hippopornos. Lewdness on horseback; a position of love-making that for the sake
    of good taste we have chosen not to describe here.

Hipporchema. Although there is no consensus among the experts, it is supposed
    to be a pantomime of military origins in honor of Apollo. It was performed
    with accompanying music and singing. The lyrics of the songs, which were
    written by poets, would also have had the same name.

Homer. Were the Homeric poems the work of a single bard? Are they a sponta-
    neous compilation of oral texts taken from different times and lands?
    Scholars have been asking these questions since the nineteenth century
    A.D., giving rise to a learned dispute known as the "Homeric Question." The
    outcome of the polemic has been to establish without a reasonable doubt
    that the structure we know today as *The Iliad* and *The Odyssey* are the work
    of a single author. Whether his name was Homer, or he was blind, or he was
    born in Ionia, or he lived in the ninth or eighth century, has yet to be
    proven. In any case, whoever the poetic genius might have been, he has
    earned himself a name: Homer.

Hoplite. A soldier of the heavy infantry armed with a helmet, cuirass, greaves,
    shield, sword, and lance.

Horae. According to Hesiod, their names are Eunomia, Dike, and Eirene, daugh-
    ters of Zeus and Themis. They guarded Heaven and Olympus, whose doors
    creaked when they opened (*The Iliad*, 5, 749).

Hospitalis. Nausicaä said it all in *The Odyssey* (VI, 207): "All strangers and poor
    people belong to Zeus." Mistreating supplicants, pilgrims, or beggars was a
    grievous offense against Zeus Hospitalis.

Howler. Literally a "she-wolf" in ancient Athens; the lowest class of street whore.

Hydra. Scholars of mythology are still debating whether it was a unique monster or
    some sort of gigantic sea serpent; neither have they come to any consensus on
    whether, when one of her heads was cut off, she grew back two heads or one.

Whatever the particular characteristics of her physiognomy, the most famous of all hydras would seem to be the one at Lerna, which was "nurtured by Hera, the Goddess with the snow-white arms, to satisfy her consuming hatred of Hercules the Strong, who destroyed it with his implacable bronze" (Hesiod, *Theogony*, 314–317). Her parents were the titan Typhon and Echidna, the notorious gynecocephalic serpent. The region of Lerna was terrorized by the hydra, who had her lair by a swamp which, according to Graves's *Greek Myths*, had become the tomb of many an unwary pilgrim. The hydra was supposed to have the body of a powerful dog and eight or nine serpents' heads, one of which was immortal. She was so poisonous that her mere spoor could kill.

Hydrias. Earthen vessels used to catch, store, or pour water.

Hypaithron. The rectangular opening in the roof of Greek homes. It created an atrium into which the inwardly sloping roof tiles channeled rain water and allowed the family to make the maximum use of the daylight. (With Greek words transliterated into English, the *h* is aspirated and the *y* is pronounced like the French *une*.)

Hypocrites. In its most ancient connotation, it refers to the interpreter of dreams or visions; later it meant a tragic or comic actor. Might this be further proof of the sacred origins of Greek Theater? In any case, in classical Greece it was never used with the connotation of "hypocrite" as the *septuaginta* did in translating the Bible (known as the *Septuagint*) into Greek.

Hypothesis. There was a young woman of Maronea named Hipparchia who lived in the fourth century and wrote a number of philosophical and poetic works, as well as a treatise on geometry. She became the lover of Crates the Cynic who, in his determination to open the way to a healthy return to nature's ways without the prejudices of civilizations, lived the life of a dog in the streets of Athens. (*Cynic*, *kynikos*, in Greek, means "doggish.") And since Hipparchia had no prejudice against fulfilling her connubial duties in public on the streets of Athens, she was given the nickname of Hypothesis, whose etymology refers to both her scientific calling as well as her cavalier attitude toward placing herself in the *hypo* (bottom) + *thesis* (position). It is she who lent her name to Hypothesis of Athens (Lacroix, Paul, *History of Prostitution*, Seré, Paris, 1851, p. 295).

Iacchus. The name used in the Eleusinian mysteries for Dionysus as civilizer of the human race. He was also called Bakjos (Sophocles, *Oedipus Rex*, 211), a precursor of the Roman Bacchus.

Iambographers. Writers of iambs.

Iambs. A foot in Greek and Latin metrics made up by one brief syllable and one long one. Its etymology seems to suggest the verb "to insult" (Aristotle, *Poetics*, 4.30). It was associated from a very early date with the crude and vulgar language of the fertility cults and became the favorite foot of the satiric poets.

555

THE EYE OF CYBELE

Ibycus of Rhegium. Very little is known about this Greek born in Rhegium (now Reggio di Calabria, Italy), except that during the sixth century, while residing in the court of Polycrates of Samos, he produced choral works of such pronounced erotic content that they earned him an article in the suda and a commentary by Cicero (Tusc. 4, 71) where he is described as "the poet of impassioned love."

Icon. "Image," in Greek.

Ictinus. The principal architect of the Parthenon.

Infernal Gods. The Gods who inhabited the Underworld: King Hades, his wife Persephone, Hecate, the Erinyes, the overthrown Cronus; and also Minos, Radamant, and Eacos, the three judges who made up the tribunal of dead souls. Although some of them inspired fear and were somewhat anachronic for the pantheon of the fifth century, they were not regarded pejoratively or malignantly. They were worthy and respectable Gods who came from the "lower" part of the Greek universe. Cf. *Eumenides, Hades, Orpheus.*

Iolaus. Son of Iphicles; nephew, charioteer, and shield-bearer of Hercules, whom he served during his travels to discharge the twelve Labors. He was an Olympic champion charioteer driving his uncle's mares.

Ionia. Greek communities from the peninsula began to settle on the Aegean coasts of Asia Minor from the end of the second millennium. They gave rise to a flourishing commercial society headed by Miletus, which later extended outward with its colonies, mainly toward the Black Sea. Between the fifth and the seventh centuries, Ionia gave the world personalities such as Thales, Anaximander, Anaximenes, Hecateus, and Hippodamus, all from Miletus; Heraclitus of Ephesus; Democritus and Protagoras of Abdera; Anaxagoras of Clazomene; Hippocrates of Cos; Herodotus of Halicarnassus; Xenophanes of Colophon; Pythagoras of Samos. The two from Abdera and the Samian were not of the Ionic race, but they were the progeny of the spiritual environment that Ionia radiated to the neighboring cities. If there is any one land in the west to be venerated as the cradle of modern science and philosophical thought, it is Ionia.

Iphigenia. Cf. *Agamemnon.*

Ishtar. A deity of Semitic origin and known as Astarte in Syria, Cyprus, and Asia Minor. This deity corresponded in part to the Greek Aphrodite. Young maidens were obliged by a primitive tradition to prostitute themselves with strangers before marriage in Ishtar's temples. The act, as such, and the money thereby earned, were an offering to the Great Mother of the Gods, whose name varied throughout the different regions of Asia.

Isoteleia. A kind of manumission decreed in favor of foreigners who had rendered distinguished services to the State or to the Gods. With the isoteleia, the person was exempted from all taxes and was left with no other obligations than those incumbent on citizens, but he was still prevented from participating in the political life of the City and could not own real estate in Attica or legally marry an Athenian woman, etc.

Isthmic. Cf. *Games.*

Ithaca. Homeland and kingdom of Odysseus. After the sacking of Troy, the hero wandered for ten years before he was able to return to Ithaca. The poet quoted by Aspasia was named Phemius (*The Odyssey*, XXII, 330).

Ixion. King of the Lapiths (and father of Pirithous) who, after receiving a great boon from Zeus, attempted to seduce Hera. He was considered one of history's great criminals.

Jason. A Thessalian hero, son of Aeson, king of Iolcos. As captain of the Argo, he sailed to Colchis with a hand-picked crew to recover the Golden Fleece. He returned with the Fleece and Princess Medea, a sorceress and priestess of Hecate whom he made his wife. (He would have been better advised to leave her in her barbaric land!)

Kappa. Tenth letter of the Greek alphabet.

King of Kings. Cf. *Darius.*

Laconia. Just as Attica was the territory of the City-State of Athens, Laconia, also known as Lacedaemon, was the region of Sparta. (Regarding the adjective "laconic," it was Plato in his *Protagoras* (343b) who first described the precise, stark language of the Spartans as *brachyología laconiké.*)

Ladas. An athlete of Achaia, winner of the Olympic race, and immortalized as "The Runner" by Myron of Eleutherae.

Laertid. An epithet used for Odysseus; son of Laertes.

Lamachus. One of the most outstanding Athenian generals during the Peloponnesian war.

Lampon. A famous soothsayer of Athens.

Lapiths. A people of Thessaly. Cf. *Centaurs, Pirithous.*

Laserpico. Silphium; a plant used as medicine and for seasoning food.

Laurium. Highlands in southeastern Attica, famous for their mines and precious metals.

Lecythus. A small flask with a long, narrow neck, used to keep oil or perfume.

Laelaps. One of the hounds of Artemis. In modern English rendered as Lailaps, "whirlwind." He lent his name to the huge animal that accompanied Lysis.

Lenaea. The Dionysian festivals of winter held on the occasion of the pressing of the grapes, which took place in the Lenaeum. They were the framework for the annual comedy contest where, as opposed to the solemn festivities of the Greater Dionysia, the rule was lewd apotropaic buffoonery, drunken ribaldry, and orgiastic processions reminiscent of the primitive fertility rites presided over by the phallic symbol.

Lenaeum. A Temple of Athena that housed a very ancient effigy of Dionysus, associated with a pristine cult, which was much cruder than the made-over Dionysus Eleutherios (the Liberator), who was officially acknowledged as the patron God of the tragic festivals. Cf. *Dionysus.*

Leno. A pimp. A manager of bordellos.

Lesbian. A person born in Lesbos. Cf. *Tribade.*

Leto. Cf. *Apollo, Artemis.*

Leucadian Cliff or Promontory. Cf. *Leucadian, Sappho.*

Leucadian. Referring to the crag or rock on the island of Leuca. In *The Odyssey* (XXIV, 11), it appears as a mythical place involved in the transit to the beyond, but in ancient poetics, almost certainly it acquired the meaning of a leap into the unknown, forgetfulness, or death. Its relationship with Sappho is first documented in the *New Comedy*, and it is Menander in his Leucadia (which we know through Strabo, 10,452) who tells us that Sappho was the first one to leap from the crag into the abyss. Note: Although our novel takes place about a century before the birth of Menander, we may be certain that the romanticized suicide of the greatest poetess of Hellas would have been an established tradition by the fifth century.

Leucoma. A white board on which people wrote public announcement of all kinds: public citations, names of the proscribed, magistrates, etc. In Olympia, it was used to post official announcements during the Games.

Lichas. Son of Arcesilaus; an Olympic champion whose statue still stood in the times of Pausanias, who included it in his *Description of Greece.*

Logicos, Logicon. Logical.

Logographer. A writer of political or judicial speeches. In the courts of Athens, each person had to defend his own cause. Pursuant to the method in fashion in the fifth century, litigants who were less eloquent would pay a logographer to write their appeal, which they would commit to memory and then spew out on the day of the hearing.

Logos. In this novel, it is used almost invariably to mean "rationality." But it was also used to mean: word, proposition, argument, proverb, discourse, promise, divine revelation, rumor, speech, conversation, etc., depending on the context.

Lojagos. A military rank vaguely comparable to a modern captain or a Roman centurion.

Lojos. A squadron or company. In Athens it included a hundred men.

Long Walls. The walls joining Athens with Piraeus, Munychia, and Phalerum. Cf. *Themistocles.*

Lucian of Samosata. A Greek writer of the second century A.D. He was outstanding in his mastery of the classical Attic language and was a valuable source on antiquity. A sarcastic critic of religion and its customs, in his later life he was offered an attractive position working for the Roman Empire in Egypt and did not hesitate to become a full-scale palinodist and join in eulogizing the Empire. ("Nihil sub sole novum.")

Lyceum. An epithet of Apollo, probably derived from *lykos*, which meant "wolf" in Greek. There are a number of interpretations of the origin of the term. (J. G.

Frazer, Commentaries on his translation of Pausanias's *Description of Greece*, I, 19,3); the most interesting one derives from a legend in Attica that Apollo had earned the lupine epithet because, on a certain occasion when the City was infested with wolves, he ordered a sacrifice that produced a smell that was fatal to the invaders. Thus the place outside the walls on the eastern side of the City ultimately became a public square around an altar consecrated to Apollo Lyceum (*Lykeios*). The tie-in with learning, later acquired by the word *lyceum* in many modern European languages, would probably refer to the fact that in later times it was the location of one of the most famous gymnasia of Athens. Together with the Academy it was one of Socrates's favorite places, and then, in the fourth century, the site of the covered walkway or Aristotelian Peripatos.

Lycurgus. Lawgiver of the Spartans, deeply enmeshed in legend. He would appear to have been a great traveler and a good political organizer. He lived in the ninth century.

Lydia. A kingdom of Asia Minor that flourished in the sixth century. The last of its kings was the fabulously rich Croesus who was defeated by Cyrus the Great, founder of the Persian Empire.

Lyrophorus. Lyrist.

Macedonia. During the times of Pericles, Macedonia was still a semibarbaric kingdom. Although they were not allowed to participate in the Olympic Games until the fourth century, the Macedonians were in great measure of Hellenic stock. Today, Macedonia is between Greece and Yugoslavia.

Maenads. Bacchantes. Celebrants of the Dionysian rites, who under the influence of wine and music, went into frenetic trances.

Maieutics. Maieutike, in Greek, means "obstetrics" or "midwifery" and refers to the method used by Socrates to help people "give birth" to truths they already had in their minds but could not remember. It is known today as the Socratic method, which consists of asking successive questions until the person being questioned gains the insight.

Marathon. The Persian Empire, divided into twenty-one satrapies and covering a territory from the subjected Egypt and the borders of Europe to the banks of the Indus. Darius was master of thousands of cities and commander of the most powerful army ever seen, invincible until it was defeated by a handful of Athenians and expelled from Greece in ignominious disarray. Left on the battlefield were 6,400 Persians and only 192 Athenians. Great was the rage of the King of Kings against Athens, but time and again he had to postpone destroying the City and enslaving its people because during those years he was obliged to put down rebellions in Egypt and quell the nomadic Scythians, who had invaded him. He died before he was able to get even. Xerxes inherited both his father's empire and his hatred for the Athenians. Mentioning the name of Athens was forbidden in his court. It was a thorn firmly lodged in the imperial throat. However, during the eight years following the insolence suffered at Marathon, one of Xerxes's aids had a standing order to whisper in his ear every day, "Sire, remember Athens." And when he finally had the time, he assembled an army much greater than the entire pan-Hellenic alliance would have been capable of mobilizing, and marched on . . . Cf. *Aeschylus, Darius, Salamis, Triassic Plains.*

Mardonius. Following the Persian defeat at Salamis, Xerxes returned to Asia and left his land troops under the command of his brother-in-law, General Mardonius, who set about sacking and pillaging the countryside. For the Athenians, the "times of Mardonius" meant great destruction of the City and the wasting and burning of their fields.

Marduk. The main Babylonian deity since the time of Hammurabi.

Maronea. A famous silver lode discovered in the mines of Attica during the fifth century. It was much richer than any of the previously known lodes. With the discovery, the Athenians reorganized the exploitation of the Laurium mines and at the initiative of Themistocles dedicated a great share of the output, which had hitherto been divided up among the citizens, to getting ready to defend the City against the Persians.

Marsyas. A satyr who lived in the forests of Phrygia. He was a master musician on the flute and the rustics of the region dared to say that his music was superior to Apollo's. The offended God challenged him to a musical duel. The jury of the Muses found in favor of Apollo, who skinned Marsyas for his insolence and hung up his hide in a cave in Celene. Cf. *Satyrs.*

Meden Agan. "Nothing in excess," in Greek. One of the most famous of the Delphic gnomai and still valid today.

Medusa. The only mortal among the Gorgons. She lived in Libya and was beautiful, but one night she was found in the arms of Poseidon in the act of profaning one of Athena's temples. As punishment she grew horse's teeth, a trembling snake's tongue that never fit in her mouth, bronze talons, and serpents for hair. Just setting eyes on her was enough to freeze the blood and turn humans into stone. When she was decapitated by Perseus, Athena picked up the head and fixed it to her aegis or breastplate to serve as an amulet. (Although her two sisters were immortals and never suffered such an atrocious fate, the Gorgons are always associated with petrifying ugliness.)

Megacles. Head of the Alcmeonid family and archon for the year 640. It was because of the role he played in the perjury and massacre of the people who had taken asylum in the Acropolis at the time of Cylon's conspiracy that two centuries later his descendant, Pericles, was accused of impiety.

Melanthius. A character in *The Odyssey.*

Menon. Eponymous Archon for the year 473.

Metageitnion. Second month of the Athenian calendar. Cf. *Months.*

Metragyrtes. A minor priest in the worship of Cybele. In Greek it meant "Beggar of the Mother." The metragyrtes would beg for the temples of the Great Mother Cybele. They were generally eunuchs and dressed in mottled rags with innumerable little bells and chimes. The guise of the metragyrtes was often used by thieves and grifters. Those who were already circulating through the Greek cities of the fifth century would give street performances of self-mutilation, trances, and dervishlike dances. It is no wonder they were looked upon with mistrust in Athens.

Metragyrte. One of the names given to Cybele.

Metretus. A measure of liquid volume equivalent to some forty liters.

Metroon. A Temple of Cybele (who was identified with Rhea in Athens). The name stems from *meter,* "mother."

Micon. Athenian painter and sculptor of the fifth century.

Miltiades. 540–489. Athenian general and victor over the Persians at Marathon. He was head of the Philaid clan and of the oligarchic party. Miltiades was an irreconcilable enemy of the Alcmeonidae. He was the father of Cimon.

Mimnermus of Colophon. Poet and musician of the late seventh century, he was the initiator of the erotic elegy.

Mina. In Athens it was about half a kilogram of silver. It was also a ten-drachma coin. Ten silver minas made one gold mina; sixty silver minas made one talent.

Mithra. The most important deity of the Persians. Master of the elements and judge of the dead. Mithra was the center of a religion whose mysteries spread throughout Hellenistic Greece and Rome.

Mitylene. Birthplace of Alceus, one of the greatest of the ancient lyrical poets; capital of the island of Lesbos.

Mnemosyne. Goddess of memory; daughter of Uranus; she was the mother of the nine Muses after an equal number of days and nights in the arms of the fecund Zeus.

Moira. Goddess that personified destiny. The word in Greek meant "portion," and so it was that a "portion" of inescapable and personal uncertainties were assigned to mortals at birth. She used to be likened to a ball of twine whose ends and turnings were unknowable, even when duly kept on a spindle. In other cases, Moira is adverse destiny and may represent death or bad luck.

Moirai. When used in the plural, it referred to three very ancient Goddesses, daughters of Nox (night) and Erebus. They had a number of formidable brothers (Fatality, Old Age, Death, Crime, Vengeance, Misery, Humiliation) and some others who were more amenable (the three Hesperides, Commiseration, Friendship, and Joy). The names of the Moirai were Clotho, Lachesis, and Atropos and not in vain did these names mean "weft," "hazard," and "irreversible," for their mission was to weave human destiny and ultimately cut the thread of life. In Rome they were known as the Parcae.

Months (of the Athenian calendar):

Hecatombaion: June 21 to July 20; *Metageitnion:* July 21 to August 20; *Boedromion:* August 21 to September 20; *Pyanepsion:* September 21 to October 20; *Maimakterion:* October 21 to November 20; *Poseideon:* November 21 to December 20; *Gamelion:* December 21 to January 20; *Anthesterion:* January 21 to February 20; *Elaphebolion:* February 21 to March 20; *Munyxion:* March 21 to April 20; *Thargelion:* April 21 to May 20; *Scirophorion:* May 21 to June 20.

In this simplified distribution of the Athenian months, the beginning of the year coincides with the summer solstice, but the first of Hecatombaion used to fall closer to June 24. Furthermore, the months were not uniformly thirty days long as we see them here; they actually alternated between thirty and twenty-nine, in compliance with the lunar cycles. But that would have given them a year with only 354 days; in order to be in line with the astronomical cycle of 365 days, five hours, forty-eight minutes, and forty-eight seconds we know today, every year they had to add eleven days and a fraction. To do this, every two or three years they would insert an additional winter month which they called Second Poseidon. Every sixteen years they incorporated the lost fractions by inserting a few days. But despite all the efforts of Meton and other outstanding observers of the heavens, the Ancient Greeks never developed a periodic formula with which to measure the year accurately down to the minutes and seconds. Cf. *Eponymous Mother Goddess.* Cybele or Rhea.

Mother or Great Mother or Mother of the Gods or Great Mother of the Gods or Mother Goddess, or Child Goddess or Child Mother or Dindymenian Mother. Cf. *Cybele.*

Munyxion. Tenth month of the Athenian calendar. Cf. *Months*

Muses. The Muses were nymphs of dubious paternity. In earlier times there were only three, whose names in the Boeotian dialect meant "practice," "memory," and "song." In some sources, they are considered daughters of Zeus and Mnemosyne, in others of Uranus and Gaea . . . and there are other genealogies. However, during the classical period there were nine Muses. In one of his elegies, Mimnermus told us that the three eldest were daughters of Uranus and the other six of Zeus (Pausanias, *Description of Greece,* IX, 29, 3). As wild mountain nymphs, they spent their time in frenetic songs and dances, but when Apollo taught them that nothing should be taken to extremes, their art took on an exquisite harmony. From that day on, they were habitués at Delphi and Olympus, where the moderate lyre of the master accompanied alternate songs at the banquet of the immortals (*The Iliad,* I, 601–604). By this time the Greeks had developed their arts and made of the Muses their zealous godmothers. Clio was the Muse of history, Euterpe of music, Thalia of comedy, Melponene of tragedy, Terpsichore of dance, Erato of elegies, Polyhymnia of lyrical poetry, Urania of astronomy, and Calliope of eloquence.

Museum. The Temple of the Muses. (Thence the modern museums, temples of art). The hill of the Museum was southwest of Athens, near the Ionian Gate.

Myron of Eleutherae. Athenian sculptor of the middle of the fifth century. To the manly dignity of Peloponnesian sculpture and the grace of the Ionic, Myron added movement. His Discobolus remains as an eternal model of the ancient genius. His contemporaries, however, were more fond of his Ladas the Runner and Athena and Marsyas.

Nemea. A city in Argolis that was indebted to Hercules for having strangled the lion who had become a scourge in the neighboring plains. It was also the venue of the Nemean Games.

Nemean. Cf. *Games.*

Nereids. Fifty nymphs, daughters of Doris and Nereus, granddaughters of Poseidon. They were gentle and beneficial helpers of Tethys, a Goddess of the sea.

Niceratus. Father of Nicias.

Nicias. 470–? An Athenian general. Enemy of Pericles.

Niobe. Daughter of Tantalus, sister of Pelops and Broteas. There are many versions of the Niobe story. Niobe, a priestess of the White Goddess, of Phrygian origin, behaved irreverently toward the Olympians. She married Amphion, king of Thebes, and bore him seven boys and seven girls. She was so proud of her children that she dared to look down on Leto for having born only Apollo, a music-playing pansy, and Artemis, a tomboy who spent her time chasing her dogs through the forests. When Apollo found out, he sought out Niobe's children, who were hunting on Mount Cithaeron and killed them one by one with his arrows. In the meanwhile, back at the palace, Artemis killed all the girls while they were weaving. Of all Niobe's children, the only survivors were Amyclas and Meliboea, who, after their mother's foolishness, ran to beg forgiveness from Leto with their prayers.

Nomius. An epithet given to Apollo as protector of pastors and herds. Cf. *Apollo.*

Nomos. As the general opinion on rule of conduct and tradition, it had the force of law.

Nous. The ability to think; intelligence. Anaxagoras of Clazomene, the teacher of Pericles, used nous to explain the conception of a universal intelligence that gave order to the primal chaos. Ironically, he was expelled from Athens for atheism.

Numen. Deity.

Obol. A sixth of a drachma. It was divided into two hemiobols.

Odontes. "Teeth" in Greek.

Odysseus. Cf. *Laertid.*

Oedipus. Son of Laius and Jocasta, king and queen of Thebes. The oracle of

Apollo at Delphi had prophesied that he would kill his father and be husband to his mother. When Oedipus was born, his father turned him over to one of the pastors to have him abandoned in the mountains. The pastor took pity on the child and gave him to a Corinthian who took Oedipus home to his own country, where the sovereigns, lacking a son, raised him as their own. When he was a grown man, he went to Delphi, where Apollo revealed to him that he would kill his father. In an attempt to avoid such a horrible destiny, Oedipus resolved never to return to Corinth and headed in the opposite direction, toward Thebes. Along the way he unwittingly killed Laius and later became king and husband of Queen Jocasta. The terrible impiety brought plagues and calamities to the territory of Thebes, and once again Apollo spoke from Delphi, saying that the sufferings of the city would continue until the murderer of King Laius was expelled. Sophocles recreated the myth in his *Oedipus Rex*, a perfect tragedy whose theme has been used in some of the most original plots in contemporary mystery writing. Here, Oedipus becomes the diligent inspector investigating his own case, and each additional clue raises suspicions pointing to him like in a nightmare. When he finally finds himself face to face with himself and realizes that he has committed parricide and incest most foul, he rips out his eyes and roams the byways of Greece accompanied by Antigone, his daughter and stepsister.

564

Oenomaus. King of Arcadia, famous breeder of horses; owner of the fastest chariot of his times, driven by the charioteer, Myrtilus, son of the God Hermes. An oracle had announced to him that he would die by the hand of his son-in-law. Other sources say that he was in love with his daughter, Hippodamia, whose suitors he forced to enter into a race against death. If Oenomaus won, he would personally skewer the loser. If he lost, he would accept death and the suitor could have Hippodamia. The number of dead suitors was so great that Oenomaus intended to build a temple with their skulls. But, alas, he was not able to build his temple. He was vanquished by Pelops with a golden chariot and winged horses, a gift from Poseidon.

Oitosyros. According to Herodotus (*Histories,* IV, 59), this was the name of one of the Scythian Gods, the counterpart to the Greek Apollo.

Olympic Games. Cf. Games.

Omestes. An epithet of Dionysus. Eater of raw flesh, thence butcher, ferocious. This epithet is a reminiscence of the barbarian Dionysus, whose orgiastic rites invaded Greece from the wilds of Thrace.

Onion Head. Or Head of a Sea Onion, or Head, Big-Head, Sea Onion, Big-Onion, Eschinocephalus, etc., all names used for Pericles.

Oniromant. An interpreter of dreams.

Onoma Kallion. "A very handsome man" in Greek.

Ophthalmoi. "Eyes" in Greek

Opistodomus. The back side of a home or building. In temples it used to be used as a sacristy or treasury.

Orchestra. The part of the Greek theater between the stage and the seats, where the chorus danced or went through its motions. (Despite the modern musical connotation of the term, its root is the same as the Greek verb, "to dance.")

Orestes the Floor-breaker. During the times of Pericles, there were in Athens thieves called *toihoryhoi* who would literally "break" into homes through the walls. They were able to act speedily and silently thanks to the soft adobe that was used to build most homes. The variant of tunneling under the target and breaking through the floor was time-consuming and was only practiced when the prize was worth it. In the latter third of the fifth century, a certain Orestes and his gang were terrorizing the City to the point that one of the characters in Aristophanes, who was angry with another, could think of nothing worse than to wish him a nocturnal encounter with Orestes, who would "clean him out." When the Floor-breaker was not busy perforating walls, he would complete his agenda by stealing clothes as a common street thief.

Orpheus. Son of the Muse Calliope and Oeagrus, a king of Thrace. Apollo gave him a lyre and the Muses taught him how to play with such mastery that wild beasts grew tame on hearing him playing; incapable of renouncing his music, the rocks and trees would follow him. In his descent into the Underworld, he charmed Charon, made Cerberus cry, and overcame the resistance of the Three Judges of the Dead. The very King of Hades was so entranced with his music that he allowed Orpheus to take his beloved Eurydice back with him into the light, although he later took her back painfully. The worship of Orpheus evolved into the Orphic mysteries in connection with Pythagorean philosophy and the development of mysticism in the west.

Orphic Mysteries. Cf. *Orphism.*

Orphism. Orpheus, the musician from Thrace, was also a seer and doctor; his lyre chased away demons, purified people and things. Who could be a better choice for a candidate for Dionysus, the national God of his homeland, to choose as his prophet and to reveal to him the secrets of a new religion? Although there are no canonical sources extant, the Orphic hymns and theogonies of different origins and times do provide an insight into the essentials. Ever present is the link between religion and philosophical speculation. Man must free his soul from the prison of his body, and not only one body but an unbearable succession of corporeal prisons into which he must reincarnate. But the soul does have an avenue of salvation through the Orphic mysteries, ceremonies in which Dionysus himself plays the role of liberator. Then the initiates are required to live a life characterized by abstinence from the flesh and other cathartic forms of self-denial that prepare the soul for the true life, which is in death itself, but with no further incarnations. Thereafter they may enjoy the eternal pleasure of a divine world whose gratifying splendor no mortal eye could ever withstand. The new characteristic of this religion was, above all, the dynamic vitality of Orphic death that so vividly contrasted with the misery of Hades, populated by Homer with crippled and confused shadows, or in the best of cases, bored souls forever lamenting the loss of their bodies. According to Herodotus (II,81), the doctrine owed a great debt to Pythagoras or to the Pythagoreans, who were thought to have brought back from Egypt ascetic models and rituals adopted by the Orpheans in Greece. It is much more probable, however, that when Pythagoras arrived in Italy he found Orphic communities of long standing which influenced the spirituality and sectarianism that characterized his school in Crotona (Rhode, Erwin, *Psyché*, Payot, Paris, 1928, p. 349 sq). If we are to believe Aristotle, the founder of the sect in Athens was Onomacritus, a poet in the court of Pisistratus, in the sixth century, "who set to verse the doctrines of Orpheus" (Philosophy, frag. 10. Ros.).

Osiris. God of agriculture; the most popular God among the Egyptians. He was the husband of Isis and father of Horus. His death and resurrection, celebrated with alternating mourning and jubilation, was the personification of the great annual change in the vegetable kingdom. Because of his relationship with grains and plants, his worship had analogies with those of Demeter and Dionysus. To a certain degree in Greece, but particularly in Rome, the worship of Osiris and Isis achieved widespread popularity.

Ostracism. Exile from Athens. The practice was established by Cleisthenes following the expulsion of the Pisistratids. Once a year, and only if the Ecclesia so decided, the *ostracophoria* was convened in a plenary session in which the Assembly members cast in the voting urns of their respective tribes, in the presence of the archons, an earthenware shard with the name of the citizen who, in the opinion of the individual voter, was a danger of becoming a tyrant or threatened to subvert the democratic institutions of Athens. If there was a turnout of six thousand votes, the person with the majority would be banished for ten years. If without the six thousand votes, no one could be ostracized, no matter how many votes he received. Among the more illustrious victims of this singular recourse were the Alcmeonid Megacles, Xanthippus (father of Pericles), Aristides, Themistocles, Cimon, Thucydides, and Alcibiades. Although ostracism was feared, it did not imply infamy, loss of rights, or the confiscation of property. The name derives from *ostrakon*, which means "seashell." In the early days, the "ballot" may have had the shape of a seashell, but toward the end of the fifth century, the Assembly members scribbled the name of the undesirable citizen on any old shard of pottery. Ostracism was abolished in the year 403.

Owl. The symbol of Athena and of her City, Athens.

Paean. A solemn hymn in honor of the Gods, especially to Apollo. It was also used as a lament, to implore salvation and benefits, or as a battle hymn before, during, or after combat. Paeans were also sung to express grief in funeral ceremonies, to express joy at feasts, or in gratitude for victories.

Paideia. A word derived from the root *pais, paidos,* "child." It originally referred to the instruction of children—grammar school, so to speak—but later, by extension, it came to mean "humanistic culture" or "knowledge of the liberal arts."

Painted Portico or *Pecile Portico.* A porch or portico in the agora of Athens adorned with numerous paintings. By the same tradition that the Platonists are identified with the Academy and the Aristotelians with the Lyceum—ever since Zeno of Citium began to teach in the *Stoa* early in the third century— the word began to be used by historians and philosophers as a synonym for the "Stoic School." The term *stoic,* then, means "those in the portico."

Palaestra. Etymologically, "place where one wrestles." An open place with sandy soil that was tamped down firmly before matches or practice bouts. It was generally enclosed with a colonnade. On three of its sides, in the shade of grapevines or the surrounding trees, bleachers were installed for onlookers. On the fourth side, there was a paved strip for exercising with weights and other gymnastic equipment. In the immediate vicinity, there were diverse halls where the clients could use the baths, get a rubdown, or have themselves anointed. However, most of these services were more often provided in the outdoors. After perspiring profusely by the fires, the gymnasts would give themselves to the ministrations of the palaestra slaves who lathered them up and then, strigil in hand, scraped them and rinsed them off with water. In fifth-century Athens, palaestrae were still rather rustic, and although they were the forerunners of the great Roman baths, they had not developed into anything so luxurious and sensual.

Pallas. From the Greek *pallax,* "youth." Cf. *Athena.*

Pan. A pastor God of very controversial origins. It is generally conceded that he was raised together with Zeus and suckled in Crete by the goat Amalthea. The most widely acknowledged genealogy has it that he was the son of Hermes and Dryope. As an adult, he took up residence in the forests of Arcadia where he was devoted to wine, naps, and nocturnal romps among the Maenads. He had the beard, horns, hooves, and tail of a goat, but his lack of masculine beauty never cramped his style as an accomplished seducer, for he had the gifts of music and prophecy. When seduction failed, he had a bag of tricks sufficient to get to any nymph who caught his eye. If anyone doubts this, just ask Echo, Eupheme, Pithys, Syrinx, or Selene herself. And about his defeat before the lyre of Apollo, the word is that King Midas, who was acting as referee, was partial in favor of Apollo. So far, Pan is the only God known to have died. Cf. *Selene.*

Panainos. A Famous painter, brother of Phidias.

Panathenaea. Cf. *Games.*

Panathenaean Amphorae. Champions of the Great Panathenaea received as a prize, among others, amphorae of oil from the sacred olive groves of Athena. Aside from the civil privilege implicit in the trophy that would for generations honor the descendents of the victorious young man, just having the sacred oil in the pantry ensured favor with the Goddess and was an excellent omen of family prosperity.

Pancratiasts. Athletes who practiced the pancratium, the most savage of Greek sports. Etymologically it means "all ways to fight," but, in fact, it was a kind of catch-as-catch-can sport in which the contestants could gouge eyes, dislocate limbs, or strangle the adversary. Biting or hitting with closed fists was not allowed. Go figure.

Pandarus. A Trojan military commander famous for his mastery with the bow that he received from Apollo himself (*The Iliad*, II, 824).

Pandemos. A epithet of Aphrodite. It means "belonging to all the people" and has been traditionally rendered into modern languages as "the Vulgar." But it was not intended to mean vulgar in the sense of grossness, as might be inferred from Aphrodite's protection of prostitutes. In the strict translation from Latin, *vulgar* means "of the people," as opposed to her other, aristocratic nature as Urania or Celestial, who resides in Olympus. Cf. *Aphrodite, Cypris.*

Pandionids. A tribe in Attica.

Pandora. One of the bas-reliefs in the pedestal that supported the colossal sandals of Athena Parthenos contained a representation of the birth of Pandora. According to the myth, Zeus was so angry about Prometheus's stealing fire from Olympus and giving it to the mortals that he ordered Hephaestus to fashion a woman of clay, the most beautiful ever created. He ordered the Four Winds to breath life into her and commanded all the Goddesses of Olympus to attend her birth to adorn her with immortal regalia. Zeus made her crazy, perverse, and a cheat. He sent her to Epimetheus, the thief's brother, with a box containing all the evils that still afflict humanity: old age, labor, disease, madness, vice, and passion.

Panionian Poseidon. Cf. *Panionian.*

Panionian. A temple consecrated to Poseidon Heliconius by unanimous decision of all the Ionian cities of Asia Minor. It was built in Mycale, on a promontory on the coast that gives onto the island of Samos. By extension, the word also refers to the deity.

Pantarces of Elis. A boy of great beauty; a champion in the Olympic juniors. He was the great love of Phidias, who sculpted him at the foot of Zeus. (Pausanias, *Description of Greece*, 1, 10, 6.)

Paralus. One of the two elder sons of Pericles.

Parapetasmata. Curtains made of heavy woolen fabric. They were used between rooms in place of doors, which were still scarce in interiors during the fifth century.

Paris. Son of Priam and Hecuba. Raptor and husband of Helen of Troy.

Parnassus. A mountain frequently visited by Apollo. He would go there to direct the choir of Muses, who lived there. Located between Phocis and Locris, it still exhibits imposing beauties to travelers who approach it from Delphi.

Parodos. "Sideways," in Greek. In the language of the stage, it was the aisle through which the chorus approached the orchestra; by extension, it was also the name given to the first piece the chorus executed while it was entering.

Parsangs. Persian measure of length, roughly equal to a modern league.

Parthenon. A great deal has already been said in books and encyclopedias about this temple consecrated to Athena, undoubtedly the most famous component of the monumental construction program undertaken by Pericles for his new Athens. Here we will only review some vital data. Phidias was put in charge of the project. Also participating in the work were Ictinus, the architect, and sculptors Agoracritus and Alcamenes. The building was built almost exclusively with Pentelik marble. It had eight frontal columns and seventeen lateral ones. It was fifty-two meters long by twenty-two meters wide. At the back was raised a statue of Athena Parthenos. Numerous colonnades subdivided the interior space into naves. There were rooms and sanctuaries richly adorned with offerings of gold and silver, as well as votive effigies. The colossal gold and ivory statue of Athena Polias measured fifteen meters from the base and was the personal work of Phidias. The standing Goddess was wearing a sleeveless tunic tied at the waist. On her breast and back, she wore her armor adorned with the head of the Gorgon. On her right forearm, held up by a little column, she carried a Nike, and she rested her left arm on her shield, around which was entwined the serpent Erichthon. The reliefs on the shield represented the head of Medusa and combats between Athenians and Amazons. The 160-meter frieze, the ninety-two metopes, and the two pediments contain reliefs depicting episodes from the mythical history of Athens, from the war with the Amazons, the Trojan War, the gigantomachy, and, as a modern note, a Panathenaean procession. The entire project, including the friezes, was finished around 432. Phidias, however, was forced to leave Athens a lot earlier; the enemies of Pericles had accused him of absconding with the gold and ivory of the Goddess.

Parthenos. "Virgin, maiden" in Greek. This is also the name given to the monumental gold and ivory statue that Phidias made for the Parthenon. Cf. *Polias.*

Pausanias of Cappadocia (or Lydia). In this book, we have frequently quoted this Greek historian and geographer of the second century A.D., the author of a

569

detailed *Description of Greece* (*Hellados Periegesis*). In his travels, some six centuries after the death of Pericles and despite the methodical sacking of everything Greek by the Romans, he still found many living traditions and languages, and he was able to detail many monuments and buildings of the Classical period. Thus, his work is of immense architectural importance.

Pausanias. The name of several kings of Sparta.

Peleid. Achilles, for being the son of Peleus.

Pelops. Son of King Tantalus, brother of Niobe and Broteas. His father, a personal friend of Zeus, was often invited to Olympus, where he was treated to nectar and ambrosia. To reciprocate all of these attentions, Tantalus decided to offer a banquet for the Olympians, but fearing that his larder would not be great enough for the immortal gourmands, he carved up his son Pelops and served him up craftily camouflaged. Did he do it to prove his dedication as a host to the Gods? Did he do it to test the omniscience of Zeus? Well, the jury is still out on that one. The fact is that not a single one of the Gods failed to notice what had been served to them, except for Demeter, who was so grief-stricken over the loss of Persephone that she absentmindedly chewed a few morsels from the shoulder. Zeus condemned Tantalus to the ruin of his kingdom and, after killing him with his own invincible hands, sent him to eternal torment along with the worst of criminals: Sisyphus, Ixion, Tityus, and the Danaïds. He then ordered Hermes to recover parts of Pelops's body and boil them again in a cauldron over which he pronounced a spell. When the boiling froth gave forth a living youth of Apollonian beauty, Poseidon was struck with love at first sight and took the boy to Olympus in his chariot drawn by golden horses, where he made him his cupbearer and concubine. Among the many mythical events surrounding the character of Pelops, one of the most outstanding is his chariot victory over Oenomaus to win the hand of Hippodamia. Ultimately, the place where most of his feats took place was immortalized: Peloponnesus, which means "the island of Pelops." Cf. *Tantalus.*

Penelope. A patient and virtuous spinner; wife of Odysseus.

Pentelikon. A mountain in Attica famous for its quarries of white marble.

Penthesilea. Queen of the Amazons, daughter of Ares and Otrere. After accidentally killing her sister Hippolyta, she had to flee from the persistent persecution of the Erinyes. During her exile in Troy, where King Priam purified her, the Greek invasion took place. Penthesilea was so outstanding in combat that on more than one occasion Achilles himself had to give up his ground. Some people say she went so far as to kill him, but that his mother Thetis pestered Zeus until he brought him back to life. The fact seems to be that in one of his lightning attacks, Achilles did manage to kill her. The moment when she lay dead in his arms inspired Panainos, the brother of Phidias, to paint the mural in the Temple of Zeus in Olympia. It is a known fact that the vision of that nude body, beautiful in its perfection, so inspired Achilles with necrophilic ardors that he immediately possessed her. Cf. *Amazons.*

Penthimon. A robe of mourning.

Peplus. An oblong piece of woolen cloth with no stitching. In the Classical period, it might have been made of linen and have had different lengths and thickness. Two fibulae on either side of the neck joined the back and front sides making a discreet neckline. Other brooches could be used on the front part to make something akin to sleeves. Sometimes they would stitch from the waist to the feet, or use a lower neckline, and a great variety of pleats, embroidery, and colors. But we must advise the reader that by the time of Pericles the peplus had already lost its strict archaic significance and was used to describe almost any feminine robe that generally followed the original model in its simplicity and loose pleats.

Perdiccas II of Macedonia. 450–413. Around the year 437, he was already openly conspiring against the influence of Athens in Chalcidice and promoting a local league. A few years later, he turned up as an ally of Athens, but the Athenians were secretly supporting the party of his brother Philip. Perdiccas gave them back some of their own medicine and began to instigate the revolt in Chalcidice that gave rise to the Potidaean war. When he revealed himself to be an open ally of Corinth and Sparta, he had already established secret agreements with Pericles. A short time later, when his cavalry was fighting on the side of Athens, he helped the Peloponnesians who were operating on the Acarnanian front. Things would seem to indicate that he was not a reliable ally.

Peribasia or Peribasoo. The "Spread-legged," a nickname for the first Athenian effigy of Aphrodite, consecrated by Theseus. Cf. *Temple of Solon.*

Pericles. 495–? Undoubtedly the most outstanding political leader in the history of Athens. A great orator, a democrat, and an intellectual.

Periphoretos. "Carried to and fro." Another nickname for Artemon the Bale.

Peristyle. The etymology is clear: "around the columns." Among the ancients it was the place, open or closed, around a colonnade. Now it is used for the gallery or colonnade surrounding a building.

Persephone or Kore. Daughter of Zeus and Demeter. The Homeric Hymn to Demeter tells of a time when Kore was in the fields gathering lilies, roses, violets, saffron, and hyacinths, but she also wanted some narcissus. As she moved further and further away to reach them, she got to a point where the Earth split open; out came her uncle Hades, who took her with him, wanting to make her queen of his gloomy domains. In her grief, Demeter searched for her all over the lands and seas of the world. Finally the Sun told her what had happened and she withdrew to Eleusis, where she went on a hunger strike and caused seeds to become sterile in the ground. Furthermore, she said that she would not return to Olympus until her

571

daughter was returned to her. Because of an agreement with his brother Hades, Zeus looked the other way, but he became very much alarmed when he saw that, no matter how much the plows worked the arid soil, nothing would grow. He realized that, if he could not come up with some accommodation for Demeter, all mortals would perish and the Gods would have to do without the necessary sacrifices. After a number of attempts, an agreement was reached that was acceptable to both parties: Kore, with her name of Persephone, would spend one third of the year with her infernal husband and two thirds with her mother. (In other versions, Persephone split her time fifty-fifty.) Cf. *Demeter, Hades, Hecate.*

Perseus. Acrisius, King of Argos, had not been able to engender male children. His wife Aganipe had only given him a daughter, Danae. Proetus, the king's twin brother, seduced his niece without too much resistance. At about that time, Acrisius learned through an oracle that he would never have male children and that he would die at the hands of his grandson. In nothing flat, Danae was locked up behind bronze doors, but to no avail. For Zeus, bronze doors did not a prison make, and he came to Danae in the guise of a golden rain that left her pregnant with Perseus. The child, following on the heels of his impetuous father, was born almost immediately. Acrisius never suspected that the child was the mischief of the king of Olympus and thought that his brother Proetus was up to his old tricks. Not daring to openly kill someone of his own blood, he had Danae and Perseus locked in a wooden crate and thrown into the sea to perish. Thus, mother and child washed up on the island of Seriphus, where Dictys, a brother of King Polydectes, fished them out of the sea with his nets. (This is the episode that inspired Sophocles's satirical drama *Dictiulcos.*)

Persian Empire. Cf. *Darius.*

Phaenarete. Mother of Socrates.

Phainomenos, Phainomene, Phainomenon. Masculine, feminine, and neuter of the medial passive present participle of the verb *Faino*: "he, she, or it that is manifested." The three forms may correspond to the modern concept of (that which is) *apparent.*

Phasis. The region irrigated by the River Phasis. This was the eastern limit of Greek colonization. Thus, it is often mentioned as one of the most remote corners of Hellas, together with its western extreme, which, not without a bit of megalomania, the Greeks placed at the Pillars of Hercules (Gibraltar). Cf. *Geryon.*

Phi. A consonant in the Greek alphabet with the sound of our "F." (The mark branded on Xanthus's forehead would have been his master's idea of punishment for his attempted "escape"; *fugue*, in Greek.)

Phidias. 500?–431. Athenian sculptor. His colossal Athena Polias has been commented upon in several eras, giving us a picture of her standing almost fifteen meters high, all gold and ivory, emanating that "noble naïveté and serene greatness" that Winckelmann admired so much in Greek sculpture. But of her artistic essence, all we have left are some statuettes of the Roman period, unfortunate copies, probably travesties. Of his master work, Zeus seated in Olympus, all we have are the details related by the boring Pausanias and the worn effigies imprinted on the coins of Elide. In order to imagine the beauty and truth of Phidias's work, we must trust in the testimony of the sober Quintillian, who was so impressed that he wrote that the art of Phidias added something new to the inherited religion. Any good encyclopedia contains abundant information of the profuse works of Phidias. (Our story adds some gossip on his ties with Pericles and the Parthenon affair.)

Philocles. The son of one of Aeschylus's sisters. He was the young poet who the tetralogy prevailed over (the Oedipus of Sophocles). Could he have been a young genius whose career was cut short by a premature death during the plague? Or was he the beneficiary of the brazen arbitrariness of Dionysus, supreme judge of the dramatic contest?

Philolaus of Crotona. Follower of Pythagoras, teacher of Simias and Cebes, whom Plato presented in his *Phaedo* as a student of Socrates. According to Demetrius of Magnesia (commented by Diogenes Laërtius, 8, 85), Philolaus was the first to publish the doctrines of Pythagoras in book form.

Phocis. A region of Greece between Boeotia and Thessaly. Mount Parnassus and the Delphic Temple of Apollo with its Oracle turned Phocis into a holy place for all the Hellenes. As mariners these were the first people (after Hercules, of course) to reach the ocean, and they founded cities as distant as Marseille and Lampsacus, in the Dardanelles.

Phormio. A general at the beginning of the Peloponnesian War.

Phoros. This was the tribute that Athens imposed on its allies in the Delian League. Cf. *Delos.*

Phosphoros. Cf. *Artemis Phosphoros.*

Phrygia. A region of Asia Minor. The ancient kingdom of the Phrygians, conquered by the Lydians, wound up being a satrapy of the great Persian Empire. It was the center of the worship of Cybele.

Physis. In Greek, "nature."

Pillars of Hercules. The present Straits of Gibraltar. Cf. *Geryon.*

Pindar of Cynoscephalae. 518–443? The greatest of the Greek choral poets. A Boeotian born in the vicinity of Thebes, from early childhood he was intimately tied to the Athenian aristocracy. He did a great deal of traveling and had prolonged sojourns in Athens, Aegina, Sicily, Corinth, and the African city of Cyrene. He composed epinicia and encomia for cities, tyrants, kings, and dynasties, including a number of victorious athletes, Megacles the Alcmeonid, and Xenophon of Corinth, who offered fifty sacred prostitutes

573

to the Temple of Aphrodite Pandemos. He also composed parthenia, hymns, gnomai, paeans, prosodia, hipporchemas, and, except for a few scenes more properly belonging to the Orphic-Pythagorean persuasion, he dedicated his religiosity to Zeus, "lord and provider of all things," and Apollo, protector of the aristocracy and resident of Delphi. He composed in a lofty style in which he used the epic language with a sprinkling of Aeolian and Boeotian words, and in the majority of his hymns, he used an obscure syntactical style that has for centuries plagued erudite poetry in different parts of the world. (It is not surprising that the iconoclastic Lysis of Miletus should hate him.) The great poet died, according to some, on the knees of his beloved Theoxenus of Tenedos when he was well into his eighties.

Pirithous. It is no wonder that he appears together with his well-loved Theseus among the Olympic paintings of Panainos. The great friendship began when Pirithous, king of the Lapiths, became jealous of the strength and courage that was so praised in Theseus and decided to test them against himself. Pirithous went down to Attica where Theseus had some cows grazing in Marathon. Theseus, who had a quick temper, set out after him and, just when Pirithous turned to offer combat, a miracle happened! The two men were so impressed with the nobility and demeanor of one another that they forgot about the cows and swore oaths of eternal friendship.

Plethora. "The time of the plethora" in Athens was midmorning when the agora was most crowded.

Plethrum. About a hundred feet.

Plistoanax, Plistonax. Son of Pausanias, King of Sparta. During the Peloponnesian War, he favored peace with Athens.

Plutos. He was the God of wealth. His parents, the Titan Lasius and Demeter, fell in love during the wedding of Cadmus and Harmonia. The nectar that flowed abundantly at the wedding went to their heads, and they wandered off and laid together on the moist soil of a plowed field. When Zeus saw them return disheveled and muddy, he imagined what they had been up to. Angered by the gall of the Titan, who dared to seduce his sister and ex, he slew him immediately with one of his lethal bolts. (This Plutos, son of Demeter, must not be confused with Pluto, another name for the underworldly Hades.)

Plynteria. A festivity celebrated on the twenty-fifth of Thargelion, when Athena's clothing and ornaments were washed. During the time when all her statues were undressed, they were kept totally cloaked from head to toe. Symbolically, Athena ceased in her functions as godmother and protector; thus all significant activity was forbidden during the wash time. The most important ceremony was the procession in which the ancient effigy kept in the Erechtheion was bathed in the seas of Attica.

Pneuma. In Greek, "air, breath, spirit."

Polias. An epithet of Athena, who was honored with the name in the Erechtheion
as protector of the City. Wilhelm Dörpfeld, an eminent Hellenic scholar of
the nineteenth century, determined that there were three sanctuaries in the
Acropolis of Athens where Athena Polias could be worshiped: the old
Schliemann Temple, burned down by the Persians and rebuilt in the times
of Cimon; one of the wings of the Erechtheion; and the Parthenon. The
unquestionable authority of Dr. Dörpfeld, earned pick-in-hand together
with Schliemann in the unforgettable excavations of Troy, Mycenae, and
Tiryns, led people to believe that in the times of Pericles all allusions to the
"Temple of Polias" without further specification referred to the Parthenon
and, therefore, to the chryselephantine statue by Phidias. But in 1897, Sir
James G. Frazer of Trinity College Cambridge broadsided Dörpfeld with one
of those jewels of nineteenth-century erudite sleuthing. The key is in an
appendix to the *Description of Greece*, which Frazer translated into English,
demolishing the pillars of a false conjectural edifice one after the other.
Dörpfeld had sold his opinions to most scholars on the basis of data from
Clement of Alexandria, Eustace of Constantinople, and an unknown scho-
liast of Aristophanes. Frazer refuted them with the *Inscriptiones Graecae*,
Homer, Aeschines, Philochorus, Strabo, Plutarch, Pausanias, Lucian of
Samosata, Philostratus, and Himerius. One outstanding argument wielded
by Sir James was a quote from Dionysus of Halicarnassus on a passage by
Philochorus, an Athenian historian who lived in the fourth or third century:
"A bitch who had entered the Temple of Polias went from there to the
Pandrosium, then up to the Altar of Zeus Herceus that is under the olive
tree, and there she laid down." Given the proximity to the Pandrosium, it
is evident that the Temple to Polias (without adjectives) was the
Erechtheion. That is why in this novel we take "Parthenos" to mean the
chrysel-ephantine statue made by Phidias, and "Polias" to mean the
ancient wooden effigy installed in one of the wings of the Erechtheion.
Thanks to Sir James, Dionysus, Philochorus, and a trespassing Athenian
bitch, all doubts have been dissipated.

Polis. As an urbanistic concept, it may be translated as "city," but politically it
comprised the city and the surrounding territory up to the borders of the
neighboring states. Thus, it is more accurately rendered "city-state."

Polus of Acragas. A Sicilian sophist, disciple of Gorgias of Leontini, whom he
accompanied on some of his travels. He was the author of a treatise on
rhetoric. Plato made him one of the characters in his *Gorgias*, in which he
came to the aid of his master, who was ensnared by the questioning of
Socrates.

Polycles. A champion athlete at the Olympic, Isthmic, Nemean, and Pythian
Games.

Polygnotus. A painter born on the island of Thasus. He was the most famous painter of the fifth century. One of his paintings depicting the Greeks after the fall of Troy was on exhibit at the Painted Portico. Of course, nothing is left of the paintings of the times, except some reproductions that potters included in their wares and the commentaries of Pausanias and Pliny the Elder, which allows us to get some idea of their thematic material and artistic qualities.

Polyhymnia. The Muse of lyrical poetry.

Pontus Euxinus. Etymologically, it meant "good to strangers," i.e., "hospitable." It is the modern Black Sea.

Porne. (Pl. *Pornai*) A bordello prostitute, generally a slave.

Pornosboskia. The profession of one who manages a bordello. It was a legal profession, but hardly respectable for the wife of an Autocrat General.

Poseidon. Having overthrown their father Cronus, the three usurping brothers—Zeus, Poseidon, and Hades—drew lots from a helmet to decide the hierarchies in the heavens, seas, and underworld. Poseidon felt very diminished in power and that made him a troublemaker. Not content with his submarine palace, with its prime position on the centrally located coasts of Euboea, he also aspired to properties here, there, and everywhere: He claimed Aegina from Zeus, Naxos from Dionysus, Corinth from Helios, Argolis from Hera, and in his tantrums he would whip up storms and floods or dry up springs and rivers. He disputed Athena's right to Trezene and challenged her to one-to-one combat over possession of Attica. Zeus, however, ordered an arbitration hearing among the Olympians and the Virgin Warrior won ... by one female vote. In his cerulean stables, Poseidon kept white steeds with bronze hooves and golden manes. Golden, too, was his chariot, escorted by sea monsters who stilled the storm waves with their passage. For his queen he first courted the Nereid Thetis, but he desisted when he learned that she would give birth to a son greater than his father, and he turned her over to one Peleus, of the mortal persuasion. He then moved on Amphitrite, who ran off into the mountains when she saw his mossy skin and knock-kneed legs. With her resistance later worn down, however, she bore him a son, Triton, and daughters Rhode and Benthesicyme. She was betrayed with nymphs, Goddesses, boys, and chimeras. The most frequent Homeric epithets for Poseidon were the "Earth Girdler," "Heliconius," "Earth Dasher," and "Sovereign of the Cerulean Hair." He was the Neptune of the Romans.

Potidaea. A city founded by Corinthian colonists in Chalcidice. In their conflict with Athens, they turned for help to their motherland, Corinth, which was a member of the Peloponnesian League.

Potidaeans. The people of Potidaea.

Prasias. A demos of Attica.

Praxiergus. Eponymous Archon for 470.

Pritany. A period of thirty-five to thirty-six days in which the prytanes presided over the Senate (or Council of Five Hundred). The year was divided into ten pritanies (for a total of three hundred and fifty days).

Probalintus. A demos of Attica.

Probuleuma. A decree issued by the Council of Five Hundred for ratification by the Assembly.

Prodicus. 470–? A native of the Ionian island of Ceos, he represented his country's interests in Athens. As a rhetor he studied the language, particularly the phenomena involved in synonyms. In philosophy he was the creator of the dieresis or "separation," which later became an important methodical instrument in the Platonic Academy. Certain commentators of antiquity have him as an atheist.

Proedra. A term used to describe the presidency or the front seats.

Promachos or Promaxos. "She who fights in the vanguard." An effigy of Athena. She was the one who defended the City in war. Phidias made her high atop the Acropolis. Cast in bronze and placed between the Propylaea and the Erechtheion, she stood twenty meters high (including the pedestal) to serve as a guide for mariners. Among the models that remain extant, there is the Lenormant, a muscular creature more at home in a circus than in a holy place, and the Varvakka, a face devoid of all expression on a bust perched on a mattress of snakes. The original by Phidias was almost certainly more convincing.

Propylaea. The monumental portals that welcomed visitors to the Acropolis from the moment they mounted the marble stairs on the upper part of the hill. Left unfinished around 436, about the time that opposition to Pericles began to develop, they were built almost exclusively by the architect Mnesicles. Constructed entirely of marble, they framed five spaces and had a Doric portico before each. Hence the name "Propylaea," which means "before the doors." The porticos had pediments and friezes with metopes and triglyphs. At one end there were paintings by Polygnotus and other artists, as well as votive tablets made of clay or marble and known as *pinakes*. It was the first time in history that the word *pinakothek* was used.

Prosodiae. Hymns to be sung during processions. From the Greek roots *pros* (idea of advancement) + *odos* (path). (This term must not be confused with the grammatical term "prosody," which comes from a different Greek root.)

Prostate. Etymologically, "in front of" (anything): the government, an agency; and in anatomy, well, you know…

Protagoras of Abdera. Another son of the radiating Ionian culture that reached his native Thrace; considered the founder of the sophist school. Like many of the early sophists, he was a man without a real country, something that Plato criticized. We suppose that he traveled widely, and we know that he visited Sicily and lived in Athens for long periods of time. Pericles commissioned him to draft the constitution of Thurii. In his famous relativistic proposition that "man is the measure of all things," he opposed the Eleatic school's postulate of an absolute, immutable essence accessible only through thought. In the treasure chest of quotations included by Diogenes Laërtius in his history of Greek philosophy, the following one is of important contemporary interest: "Of the Gods, it is not given to me to know whether they exist or not, nor what they are made of, for it is precluded by many things, such as their own invisibility and the brevity of human life." It's no wonder that he was chased out of Athens for impiety! Cf. *Sophists*.

Prote. "First," in Greek.

Proteas. An Athenian general who participated in the Peloponnesian War.

Prytaneum. A tholos-shaped building in the agora of Athens where the sacred fire was preserved. A number of dignitaries, guests, and honored pensioners took their meals there.

Psephisma. Decree.

Psi. Penultimate letter of the Greek alphabet.

Pyanepsion. Fourth month of the Athenian calendar. Cf. *Months*.

Pylai ton Hypnon. "Portals of Dreams," in Greek.

Pyrilampes the Birdman. According to Plato (*Charmides*, 153a), he was one of the most attractive adults of his times. If it was really true, then he could not have had a better name, for it means "brilliant as fire."

Pythagoras of Samos. 580–500? One of the most outstanding figures in the history of human thought. He founded a religious brotherhood in the Italian city of Crotona that lasted almost a century. He was, perhaps, the one who coined the word "philosophy," a way of life based on the love of knowledge. He created the science of mathematics, discovered the first laws of musical harmony, and made pivotal discoveries in geometry. In the mathematical ratio between the pitch of a sound and the length of the string, he found the starting point for his philosophy. Like the lyre, there are also bodies, souls, ideas that are in tune or out of tune, depending on their resonance with the universal scale. From his general work with sound, he derived a formula which revealed, for example, that good physical health depended on the adequate balance of cold and hot, wet and dry, and so on, and that a harmonious blend of opposites was crucial in everything, even the soul, which is a set of mathematical relations. And if the musical scale continues to exist despite the breaking of the lyre, so, too, the soul survives eternally after the death of the body. And this is how mathematics, so intimately linked to practical reality, went on to become another of the foundations of his mysticism, which tied him in with Orphism and made him a herald and inspiration of the Socratics, Stoics, and Neo-Platonists.

Pythia. The prophet of Apollo in Delphi. The use of the word "python" for a seer, as well as the "Pythian" epithet for Apollo, and the "Pythian Games," all derive from the name of the serpent (Python) killed by Apollo at Delphi. Strabo of Apamea (IX, 419) tells us that in the temple, beside the smoking crack leading into a cave, there was a tripod where the current Pythia would be placed to inhale the vapors of prophesy. Once she had spoken to Apollo, she would begin to reproduce the divine messages in the form of murmurs, stutters, grunts, exclamations, gibberish, and other incoherencies. Furthermore, according to Lucian of Samosata, she was also made to drink from the sacred fountain and chew laurel leaves. We must not forget that those vapors, emanating from the wounds inflicted by Apollo on the serpent Python, infected anyone who breathed them with the confusion into which the monster had fallen. The Apollonian message reproduced by Pythia came through in an exalted and not always understandable style. To get around that difficulty, the seer was aided by a group of *ad hoc* interpreters chosen from among the Delphic Priests, the only ones empowered to decipher the admonitory mumblings, and they, in turn, ciphered them into hexameters for the consumption of the pilgrims. At times when there was a run-on, up to three "Pythias" would rotate on the tripod. Plutarch mentioned that the Pythia of his times was a young peasant girl of impeccable reputation. Cf. *Apollo, Delos, Delphi.*

Pythian or *Pythic Games.* Cf. *Games.*

Pythodorus. Eponymous Archon for the year 432.

Python. Cf. *Apollo, Delos, Pythia.*

Revolt of Samos. Cf. *Samos*

Rhapsodist of Ithaca. Cf. *Ithaca.*

Rhea. Sister of Cronus, usurper of Uranus; mother and accomplice of Zeus, usurper of Cronus. Also mother of Hestia, Demeter, Hera, Hades, and Poseidon, to mention just a few. In the complex variants of her worship, depending on the time and place, she might be identified with the "titaness" Dione or Diana, or with the Triple Goddess, or with Pandora, or especially with Cybele. Her relationship with the worship of Dionysus leads one to believe that she must have had a Phrygian origin. In her most Hellenized variant, she is mother of the Cronids and grandmother of almost all of Olympus. But Zeus had some difficulties with her and kept her away.

Royal Portico. The unfortunate ambiguity of Pausanias in his use of the Greek preposition *hyper* (which can mean "behind" or "over") has led to a great many doubts about the location of this and other famous buildings in the Athenian agora. In any case, we do know this was the colonnade of the tribunal and the office where the Archon King worked. Cf. *Tribunal of the King.*

Rythmos. "Rhythm," in Greek.

Sabazius. A Phrygian deity identified with Dionysus who gained great popularity among slaves, peasants, and miners in Asia Minor. Toward the end of the fifth century, his worship began to penetrate into Athens, much to the chagrin of the establishment.

Salamis. An Athenian island in the Sea (or Gulf) of Saronicus. It was the site of the naval victory that consolidated the freedom of Greece vis-à-vis the threat from Persia. According to the most reliable data unearthed by scholars who have demystified the legend and toned down the hyperbolic pro-Attica enthusiasm of Herodotus, in that battle (summer of 480) the Greeks would have lost about forty ships, as opposed to two hundred lost by the enemy. This was enough to shift the balance in a war that would seem to have been heading for a Persian victory after the rout of the Greeks in northern and central Greece and the occupation of the Acropolis of Athens. The military genius of Themistocles had predicted that a reasonable Greek superiority on the seas would oblige the Persians to give up their conquests on land and return immediately to Asia. Any news of a second defeat in Athens would certainly have led to uprisings in a number of subject states, particularly the Ionian cities. After fighting to get the General Staff of the allies to adopt his strategy, Themistocles infiltrated an agent provocateur in the enemy fleet anchored by Phalerum to pass the disinformation that the Greeks were going to flee in their ships that very night to regroup in the Isthmus of Corinth. Xerxes took the bait hook, line, and sinker and ordered his fleet to engage the Greeks in the narrows of Salamis where the Persian fleet and ships, which were much larger than those of the Greeks, were cramped and unable to maneuver as they had on the high seas. This, of course, is precisely what the great Themistocles wanted. Cf. *Aeschylus, Darius, Marathon, Triassic Plains.*

Samos. An island in the Aegean belonging to the group of the Sporades. It was famous in antiquity for the quality of its wines, its glyptics, and its shipyards. It was also the homeland of Pythagoras. Samos was the scene of an uprising against Athens. Although it was a member of the Delian League, it enjoyed a certain autonomy and the right to have its own fleet. In the year 441, its oligarchic government had a falling out with Miletus because of the neighboring Priene. Miletus turned to the democratic government of Athens, and Pericles personally sailed with the fleet. Samos then turned to Pisuthnes, Satrap of Sardis and nephew of the Great King. The Athenians landed their hoplites and laid siege. In one of the cruel episodes of the War of Samos, the Athenian prisoners were branded with an owl on the forehead. Evil tongues, enemies of Pericles, began to spread the story that the whole thing was stirred up by Aspasia to get back at the enemies of her own country. In any case, it was the most open imperial retaliation that the "New Athens" had ever carried out against an ally. It was the intention of Pericles to get the others to take the hint. Given the horror of the confederates, Ion of Chios, the kind of rabble-rouser that never fails to appear, began to say that, while Agamemnon had taken ten years to subjugate Troy, Pericles had only taken ten months to quell the most powerful and haughtiest state in all of Ionia.

Sappho. Greece and Rome venerated this aristocrat of Lesbos. Catullus and
   Horace—the loftiest of poets—have drunk from her well. On the threshold
   between the seventh and sixth centuries, she lived for some time in exile in
   Sicily. Her mother and her daughter were named Cleis and her father,
   Scamandronimus. She devoted a lot of her poetry to her brother Charaxus,
   an air-headed wine merchant whose irresponsible escapades, such as getting himself "taken to the cleaners" by an Egyptian woman he purchased as
   a slave and then treated like a Goddess, never ceased to burden her. Her
   universal fraternal concern continues to impress us, as if we were listening
   to a neighbor. In her verse, we find a coexistence of the dramatic civil struggles of Lesbos, as well as her advice to a little blond girl to use garlands in
   her hair instead of purple ribbons. Her works highlight the simple monodic
   songs of Lesbos, accompanied on the lyre, but her contemporaries especially
   admired her epithalamia composed to be sung by choruses. The imitations
   by Catullus and Ovid testified to her unquestionable mastery of the subject
   of love. In the very mutilated fragments of her relics, there are poetic motifs
   that have been reiterated over the centuries: "The young woman shone like
   a golden apple on a high branch. The harvesters had forgotten her: but no,
   that was not it, they merely could not reach her." A young woman utters the
   lament: "Virginity, virginity, wherefore flee you from me?" And virginity
   replies, "Nevermore will I return to you, nevermore!" Her images of erotic
   desire, unprecedented in the written poetry of the world, still echo after
   twenty-six centuries in the song lyrics of our world. It is a well-known fact
   that she was the center of a group of young women who were closely linked
   to her, which was nothing out of the ordinary in the society of Lesbos. She
   herself told us of Andromeda and Gorgos, whom she considered her rivals
   as "captains" of other groups. (Andromeda had seduced a girl that Sappho
   loved.) There have been a number of opinions on her intimate relations
   with her students. Pierre Bayle, in his *Dictionary* (1695), considered her to
   be depraved, which contrasts with appraisals such as the one by Maximus of
   Tyre, which compared Sappho to Socrates. Seneca questioned whether
   "Sappho publica fuerit" (Sappho was a prostitute; Lesky, A., *Geschichte der
   Griechischen Literatur*, Bern, 1963).

Sardis. Ancient capital of the kingdom of Lydia and then of the satrapy of the
   same name in the Persian Empire.

Satrap. The governor of a province in the Persian Empire. The Greeks simplified
   the original pronunciation of shatrap, which in ancient Persian meant "official of the Shah."

Satyrs. Rustic demigods represented with long pointy ears, flat nose, small horns
   on the forehead, and the tail and hind legs of a goat. Cf. *Marsyas*.

Scirophoriae. Etymologically, "carrying of umbrellas." The Scirophoriae were
   solemn festivals in honor of Athena and were reserved exclusively for

581

women who paraded carrying white parasols. Infiltration by a man in disguise was considered a grievous offense to the Goddess.

Scirophoriants. Participants in the Scirophoriae.

Scirophorion. The last month of spring and the end of the year in Attica. It took its name from the Scirophoriae festivals. Cf. *Months.*

Scylla. The famous rocks near Sicily, feared by mariners in songs by poets of antiquity.

Scyllias. It was said that this Greek from Scione swam eighty-six stadia under the sea (sixteen kilometers) to get to the Greek fleet at Salamis. Even Herodotus, who despite being the father of history was not immune to believing some real whoppers, thought that this one was a bit too much (*Histories*, VIII, 8). This Scyllias might, pursuant to the traditions of the times, have had a grandson with the same name and profession living in Athens. It is the grandson who appears in this novel.

Selene. The moon. Daughter of the Titan Hiperion and of Theia. Sister of the Sun (Helios) and of the Dawn (Eos). A name variant of Helena, Helen, or Helle in the old worship of the Moon Goddess. She was all woman and footloose. Pan seduced her in disguise and had his way with her. Then, madly in love with Endimion, the beautiful son of Zeus, she bore him fifty children. Her worship is closely related to that of Artemis, Aphrodite, and Semele, mother of Dionysus, on whose orgies she shone her light during the mountain rites of the Maenads. Cf. *Pan.*

Semele. Daughter of Cadmus, king of Thebes, mother of Dionysus. Cf. *Dionysus.*

Shield dumper. A derogatory epithet. A soldier who threw his shield away to flee the battlefield.

Silenus. This character and his children, the satyrs, ever present in the comedies of Attica, would seem to have their origins in the mountains of northern Greece. They were called autochthonoi. According to some versions, Silenus was sired by Pan with a nymph.

Silphium. Cf. *Laserpico.*

Sisyphus. King of Corinth. Son of Aeolus, son-in-law of Apollo, and a great cad. His scams and thefts were innumerable, but his sentence in the underworld was for being a snitch. When Zeus carried off Aegina, her father Asopus, a powerful river God, was enraged and came down to the isthmus to find her. Sisyphus, who had seen the entire Zeus caper, promised to tell him everything if he (Asopus) would cause a spring to flow eternally in the Acropolis of Corinth. And so it was that Asopus did his part and Sisyphus rattled off all he had seen. Having been convicted of revealing divine secrets, he was sentenced to Tartarus, where he was to push a stone up a hill. Invariably, when he was a step from the summit, covered with sweat, muscles tense, amid a great cloud of dust and thinking he would succeed, the stone would roll back down the hill.

Skene. Originally the term meant "campaign tent" and later came to mean "scene." During early production of Greek drama, before the introduction of theater facilities, a tent was erected, abutting on the orchestra. This method allowed the actors to alternate with the appearances of the chorus, change their costumes, masks, characterization, etc. With the passage of time, the tent was put up on a stand and ultimately became a permanent facility made of wood or masonry where the actors faced the public in the great amphitheaters of the fifth century. The chorus, however, remained below, within the circle made by the orchestra.

Smegma. The ancient equivalent of our soap. The substance used to wash away oils.

Smintheus. One of the surnames of Apollo. According to some it refers to Sminthe, a city of Troas; others take it to mean "destroyer of rats"; and according to Doederlein, it means "lover of baths and of washing."

Socrates. 470–399? Athenian philosopher. *De eo in fabula narratur.*

Soldier's Ration. "Choenix," in Greek. A measure of volume for grains equal to about 1.094 liters. It was the forty-eighth part of a medimnus and was considered the normal ration of dry food for a man.

Solon, Temple of. One of the legends tells us that the first deity worshiped by the people of Athens was Pandemos, to whom Theseus erected a statue where she preached, open-legged, from the ground. Up until the latter part of the seventh century, holy prostitutes practiced their profession in the Temples of Aphrodite and exclusively with foreigners. The income belonged to the Goddess, who entrusted its administration to the clergy. The devotees would arrive crowned with myrtle and would deposit their purses at the foot of the altars. Solon, who was concerned with the public finances of Athens, organized a state-run bordello, sent out to the east for young girls, and put them to work. He brought in torrid Phoenicians, Lydians, Phrygians of erotic gyrations, Ethiopians, Egyptians, and fixed the price of enjoying their ministrations at one obol, all in the understanding that each act of love-making was a religious offering. With the income from his new undertaking, he had a temple built to The Vulgar right across the way so that the open-legged Aphrodite of Theseus would be honored both with the smoke of the sacrifices and the panting of the votive coitus. That was the Temple of Solon.

Solon. 640–558? The first poet of Attica. He composed elegies of gnomic inspiration, but at the service of social progress and justice. He was also one of the real, flesh and blood forefathers of the Athenians. He lived in an era convulsed by the development of the monetary economy. As a politician and legislator, he introduced legal and demographic reforms that virtually restructured the entire socio-economic foundation of Athens.

Sophists, Sophistics. Cf. *Euripides.*

Sophocles. 496–406. The Athenian tragedian with the greatest number of awards. In the records of the Greater Dionysia, he is credited with no less than eighteen wins, and it is a known fact that he was never left in third place. We know that he is credited with having written some 130 tragedies, of which seven are extant. He also wrote hymns, odes, paeans, elegies, comedies. He lived a long and happy life; he never lost his popularity among his contemporaries, who appreciated the charm of his personality. It is rather amazing that this life without travails could have been the fountainhead of such poetic depth capable of revealing the misery and loneliness of man. His works warn against the fragility of human illusions and against the violation of the eternal unwritten laws of the "lofty ether." He believed in prophesy, with the certainty that all ambiguity is cleared away when the divine will is done. His works speak out against sophism and for tradition, but he is not known to have had detractors, perhaps because his works, like that of no other poet of his time, conveyed the cathartic pleasure of the tragic. In his famous epigram, Hölderlin said of Sophocles, "Many have tried in vain to express the most joyous in joy: here I have finally found it expressed, in pain."

Sophroniscus. Father of Socrates.

Sophrosyne. Moderation; one of the gnomic virtues.

584

Sparta. Also known as Lacedaemon, it was the capital of Laconia, a narrow valley watered by the Evrotas. The sources that have transmitted its history to us are very uncertain. Since Sparta was the very incarnation of the political ideal of the oligarchy, many Laconophiles, including the Athenians Xeno, Plato, and Aristotle, manipulated the historical data. We know that the population was made up by slaves, helots, perioeci, and citizens. The helots would appear to be the original agricultural population who were left in conditions very similar to serfdom when the region was conquered and subjugated. The perioeci made up autonomous communities on the periphery, most of them artisans and tradesmen, without voice or vote in the political life of Sparta. The citizens were the governing military caste. They called themselves the "equals" and were the only owners of the land. Sparta had two rather decorative kings, a college of five Ephors, an Assembly of all the citizens, and the Senate, made up of twenty-eight elders. This Senate or Gerusia was the real government, with the greatest power and decision-making authority in all areas of public life. It is not surprising that the social model of Athenian democracy made the Spartans all more than a bit nervous. The oligarchic and military nature of Spartan society was quite evident in the education of the equals. Up to the age of eight, male children lived with their families. Then they were organized into platoons and turned over to an official educator (paidonomos) who gave them gymnastic and military training, and subjected them to educational privations, hardships, hunger, and cold. He taught them to steal to feed themselves, to put up with torture and all sorts of physical suffering with a smile on their lips. By way of spiritual development, they were taught to sing and accompany themselves only in patriotic and war songs and to speak with the strictest economy of words (laconism). By the age of eighteen, perfectly trained and practically illiterate, their education was complete. At twenty they graduated as Spartan soldiers and became part of a detachment (*loios*) in which they remained until the age of sixty. The members of these fraternities (*sissitias*) were joined forever by solemn oaths; from that moment on, in war or in peace, they slept under the same roof and spent all of their lives together. One of the normal practices of the juvenile detachments was the cryptia. The Spartan youth would spread out over the rural areas to raid the villages of the helots, where, according to some sources, they would kill the strongest. With these methods the State hoped to fulfill a double objective: keeping their troops on their toes and preventing uprisings. But despite such drastic methods, or, perhaps, precisely because of them, helot uprisings sometimes assumed formidable proportions, and the equals had to appeal to neighboring oligarchs for help. The Spartan castes developed one of the most powerful and famous militias in all of Hellas. Their social model had many admirers. Cf. *Delian League, Democracy.*

Spartocus. In 437, this Greek mercenary took over the kingdom of the Cimmerian Bosphorus and immediately set out to offer Pericles trade privileges in exchange for recognition as the new dynast (*Diodorus Siculus*, XII, 31, 36).

Stadium. A unit of length or distance; about 185 meters.

Stagira. A city in Macedonia (the modern Stavros); homeland of Aristotle.

Stoa. Cf. *Royal Portico.*

Strabo. A Greek geographer who lived during the lifetime of Jesus Christ.

Strategeion. The venue of the College of Strategi.

Strategus. General.

Suovetauriliae. A Latin term used to designate the joint sacrifice of a pig, a ship, and a cow (or bull), a practice also popular among the Greeks.

Sweet-Rump. An epithet used for Aphrodite. It is a loose version of the Greek word, *kallípygos*, "of the beautiful buttocks," and term that has sometimes found its way into the English language as *callipygous.* The Callipygian or Sweet-Rump Queen was crowned in Athens at the competitions during the Haloae or Haloan Festivals. Cf. *Aphrodite.*

Sybaris. The Sybarites were famous toward the end of the sixth century for being the pioneers of "la dolce vita" in the west. Their wealth, their luxury, and the eccentricity of their customs were proverbial in Hellas. Neighboring Crotona, on the other hand, was the venue of the austere sect of the Pythagoreans, of the brilliant school of medicine directed by the Asclepiad Democedes of Cnidus, and the homeland of numerous victorious athletes in the pan-Hellenic Games. In 510, following a *casus belli* in which Pythagoras himself was involved, Crotona crushed Sibaris, which never recovered.

Symposiarch. The person who was in charge of ordering the frequency and quantity of rounds of wine and how it was to be diluted. He was chosen before the second tables were brought in.

Symposium. A banquet. Although the fare at symposia included food, drink, and bright conversation, the etymology only accounts for the wine, for the term literally means "drinking together." The Roman term was *convivial*, which was a lot more poetic and along the lines of Hemingway's postulate that life involved working hard, making love, and eating and drinking with friends. Banquets were a normal part of the life of Hellenic aristocrats before the sixth century and were generally given in the men's chambers, amid all the weapons. They were the sites of impromptu poetic expressions and philosophizing, cup in hand, about life, destiny, changes of fortune, and all the nostalgia that Dionysus inspired. (One of the recognizable currents of archaic poetry cultivated by people like Alceus, Archilochus, Theognis, and Anacreon was the so-called "symposiac poetry," addressing how great it was to go to banquets.)

Synoecia (also Xynoecia). Synoikiai in Greek. The feasts of living together. They were held in honor of Theseus who had, on that very day, according to the myth, brought the people of Attica, until they dispersed, to live together. In later years, the anniversary was used to foster coexistence between the foreigners and the Citizens of Athens.

Syntaxis. Literally, in Greek, "in order." It referred to a combat formation. As with many terms of military origin, this one has come to mean something completely different.

Syria. In antiquity, this was a rather loose geographical concept. Herodotus (IV, 39) used the term to mean the strip that goes through Palestine from Phoenicia to Egypt, but commentators of Xenophon used it for the lands from Damascus to Niniveh. Strabo (Georg, 133) talked about a hollow Syria located between Lebanon and Anti-Lebanon. There was, furthermore, a nation of the same name to the north of Asia Minor, between Paphlagonia, Cappadocia, and Armenia.

Taenarus. A cape in Laconia containing a cave thought to be one of the most heavily traveled accesses to hell.

Talent. Six thousand drachmas.

Talthybius, the Herald. Cf. *Agamemnon.*

Tantalus. He is attributed a number of different fathers, wives, and kingdoms, but the versions currently in fashion make him out to be king of a region in Lydia, beside Mount Sipylus. Having been a great friend and guest of Zeus in Olympus, he betrayed his confidence with two abominations. First, he began to smuggle ambrosia to share with his mortal friends; then, he prepared a banquet for the Olympians and slyly included in the menu a stew made with the flesh of his own son, Pelops. For those two execrations, he was condemned to suffer eternal hunger and thirst. He hung over a swampy lake from the branch of a tree that bore juicy pears, shining apples, figs, olives, and pomegranates. When Tantalus would try to take one, the winds tore it out of his hands. The soft waves of the lake reached his midriff, sometimes even to his chin, but when he bent his neck to drink, the water receded; if he cupped some water with his hands, it escaped through his fingers and his parched lips received putrid mud, that only increased his thirst. Cf. *Pelops.*

Tartessus. According to Herodotus (I, 163), Phocian mariners were the first Greeks to visit Iberia. There they came into contact with Tartessus, a city founded by the Phoenicians on the ocean to the west of the Pillars of Hercules (Straits of Gibraltar). The king of the Tartessians was the victim of a deception by Hercules. Cf. *Geryon.*

Taureas. It was to this Palaestra that Socrates went as soon as he returned from Potidaea (Plato, *Charmides,* 154a).

Telephus. Son of Hercules. A king of the Mysians who was the inspiration for a number of tragedies, including one by Sophocles.

Tempestuous. An epithet of Zeus. Another of his epiphanies, as the deity who governed winter. He was popularly worshiped by farmers and sailors. During the month of Maimakterion, when Athena took her extended ritual vacations, the altars of Zeus Maimaktes (tempestuous) and Zeus Georgos (agricultural) were the only ones that received sacrifices.

Temple of . . . The temples are entered according to the proper name, i.e., a deity (Hephaestus), a person (Solon), or a geographical place (Dodona).

Tetralogy. Three tragedies and a satirical drama with which tragedians competed in the contests of the Greater Dionysia. The prize was for the set of four works.

Thales of Miletus. An Ionian philosopher and mathematician who flourished in the early sixth century. He introduced into Greece elements of Chaldean astronomy and Egyptian geometry. In the Classical tradition, he appeared as one of the Seven Wise Men of Greece. His name is linked to a number of theorems. During his travels he is reputed to have learned to estimate the height of the pyramids by measuring their shadows, as well as to calculate solar eclipses, so that on his return to his country he was able to predict the eclipses of 585. He is also credited with a theory on the flooding of the Nile. If any books were written by Thales, they must have been lost at a very early date. In his *Metaphysics* (I, 3; 983 b 20), Aristotle presented him as the creator of a Cosmogonic theory that sought to find in the multiplicity of things a unique substantial element, which for him was water. What may undoubtedly be inferred from several commentators of his work is that he helped liberate natural philosophy from its mythological entanglement. Contemporary critics unanimously consider him to be the first known representative of Greek philosophy and reserve for him the highest esteem as founder of western science. Cf. *Ionia*.

Thamimasadas. Poseidon, among the Scythians.

Thargelia of Miletus. An illustrated hetaera who was an agent of the Persian secret service in Greece. (Plutarch, *Pericles*, 24).

The Good and the Beautiful. This is the way the aristocracy of Athens referred to itself. One incredible writer has attempted to render the Greek idea of *kaloskagathia* as "The Beautiful People" without giving a thought to the wealth of meanings implicit in the ancient concept of "good and beautiful," which alludes to a rich fabric of ancient lineages, moral precepts, and military valor.

Themistocles. 525–450? A *homo novus* of thoroughly obscure origins whose genius, in the throes of the early democratic fervors, allowed him to momentarily break the balance between Philaeids and Alcmeonidae to assume some of the highest positions. He led the Greeks to victory in Salamis; his policies turned Athens into a great naval power; he persuaded his compatriots to build the Long Walls joining the City with the harbor within the greatest walled area in all of Hellas. Although he was not allowed to play any role in the founding of the Delian League, there can be no doubt that it was one more fruit of his naval policies. Ancient historians offer no reasons for his loss of public favor. Plutarch says quite literally, "The demos was fed up with Themistocles" (Cimon, 5). Ostracized around 471, he took asylum in Argos. His Athenian and Spartan enemies accused him of conspiring in favor of the Persians. After a long and spectacular getaway from Greece, he arrived at the court of Artaxerxes, where he attained great influence by offering his plans for another invasion of Greece. The Great King granted him the income from Magnesia, Myus, and Lampsacus. It was said that Magnesia alone provided him with fifty talents a year. His promises, however, were never fulfilled, and he died a very controversial death around the year 450.

Theodorus of Samos. Father of Pythagoras and famous in his own right in the sixth century as a cutter of precious stones.

Theognis of Megara. Elegiac poet who flourished toward the end of the sixth century. Born to an aristocratic Megaran family, he lived most of his life in exile. His works revealed the gentlemanly ideals of a landowner ruined by the advance of democracy. He praised hospitality and drinking wine at symposia among the good and the beautiful. He was capable of a great deal of tenderness and sensitivity. He was moved by the song of birds in the morning, but he was galled by the thought that others were enjoying his lands. Most of his poems were dedicated to Cyrnus, a shield bearer. He counseled the young man to stay away from the people, the vile masses whose contact could rot the soul. He did, however, admit that it was possible to improve the masses, as could be done with asses and deer. Cf. *Symposium*.

Theoi. "Gods" in Greek.

Theoroi. In general, but particularly in Plato, it refers to people who travel to see the world. In connection with the pan-Hellenic Games, they are "observers" sent officially by the cities to witness the competition.

Theseia. Also known as Synoecia or "feasts of living together." The feasts began on the sixteenth of Hecatombaion, the mythical date on which Theseus brought together the dispersed inhabitants of Attica. Cf. *Synoecia*.

Theseion. The Temple of Theseus. Its location in Athens is a matter of controversy. From a passage by Aristotle (*Const. of Athens*, 15), we suppose that it was close to the hill of the Acropolis.

Theseus. Aegeus, King of Athens, without issue. One day in Corinth, the witch Medea offered to give Aegeus a son through magical arts if he promised to give her safe haven in Athens. Aegeus accepted and continued his travels. In Troezene he stopped to see his old friend Pittheus who, under a spell cast by Medea, got him drunk and took him to the bed of his wife Aethra. When he awoke in her arms, he made her promise that if she bore a son she would not abandon him or send him off to foreign lands, but bring him up secretly in Troezene. Before leaving, Aegeus hid his sword and his sandals under a heavy rock. If some day the child were able to lift the rock and recover his father's things, Aethra was to send him to Athens. Aethra did bear a child, whom she named Theseus and who grew up beautiful, strong, and courageous. When he was sixteen, he lifted the rock without difficulty and left for Athens. It was a difficult trip. In Epidaurus he was ambushed by Periphetes the Gimp, who employed against Theseus the gigantic bronze mace he used to kill wayfarers. But Theseus wrestled it away from him and beat him to death with it. He fell in love with the weapon and kept it always near him. Later, when he was crossing the Isthmus of Corinth, he had to deal with Sinis the Pine-bender, a massive prankster and bastard son of Poseidon. One of Sinis's favorite jokes was to make pilgrims fly. When he noticed someone approaching, he would bend a pine tree until the tip touched the ground and would then feign difficulties in order to get the unsuspecting person to help him. As soon as the person gave him a hand, he would loose the tree and follow the flight of the victim with a smile on his lips. When Sinis heard the noise of the lethal crash, he would celebrate his prank with a bout of laughter that shook the trees. But when he met Theseus, the joke went sour. With his arms tied to a pair of bent pine trees, the two halves of Sinis went their own ways. In Cromion Theseus was able to hunt down and kill a monstrous boar that had killed so many of the locals that no one could till the fields without finding a corpse somewhere. Following the

589

coast of the isthmus, Theseus came to a narrow pass high on a cliff where the bandit Sciron had his lair. This one would await his victims sitting on a rock that blocked their path; when they approached, he would tell them to wash his feet. Anyone who refused would be kicked off the cliff into the sea where a giant turtle was waiting to devour them. But Theseus parried the kick, grabbed Sciron's leg, whirled him around, and flung him off the cliff without mercy. Closer to Athens he met with Coercion the Arcadian, another bully who forced passersby to wrestle with him. He would squeeze so hard that their bodies would explode in his arms. But Theseus applied a double waist hold, then took Coercion by the knees, lifted him into the air, and, much to the delight of Demeter, who was watching the encounter, nailed him head-first into the ground down to a depth of two palms. Already in Attica, arriving in the heights of Corydallus, Procrustus invited Theseus to spend the night in his home by the side of the road, where he had two beds: a small one for tall men and a long one for short men. But Procrustes could not abide excesses or shortfalls, so the short he would stretch until they fit the long bed, and for the tall he would saw off whatever did not fit. Of course, that night it was Procrustus who slept with perfect measurements. The story goes that Theseus trimmed him down both in length and in width. Upon crossing the Cephisus, Theseus carried out some purification ceremonies, and when he entered Athens, he was wearing a long white tunic and his hair was braided. This occurred precisely on the eighth of Hecatombaion, in midsummer. As he passed by the Temple of Apollo Delphinium, which was still under construction, some of the masons thought he was a girl and had the effrontery to ask how it was that she was out on her own. Theseus's only reply was to unyoke an ox from a cart and pitch the beast over the temple. Once he was in Athens, he almost succumbed to the intrigues of Medea, but once again he was victorious and had the witch banished. A short time later another term was up for the Athenians to send to King Minos of Crete a tribute of seven boys and seven virgins to be devoured by the Minotaur, a monster with the head of a bull, born of the union between the wife of Minos and a white bull. Reaching Crete among the young people of the tribute, Theseus evoked the love of the king's daughter, Ariadne, who gave him a magic ball of thread given to her by Daedalus. Theseus rolled the ball, which unwound of its own accord, leading him to the monster's lair. Scholars still have not come to an agreement on whether he killed the Minotaur with a sword, also given to him by Ariadne, if he did it with his bare hands, or if he used the famous bronze mace he had taken from Periphetes the Gimp. Whatever he used, the fact is that he killed the Minotaur and rewound the thread to emerge triumphant and escape from Crete, again aided by Ariadne, whom he later abandoned on an island. (There are several contradictory versions of the fate of the unfortunate young lady.) In previous deliveries of the youthful tribute, the ship returning from Crete flew black sails as a sign of mourning. On that occasion, King Aegeus added a white flag, which should have heralded the safe return of his son. But arriving on the coasts of Attica, Theseus forgot that detail, and Aegeus, seeing the black sails, threw himself into the sea, which from that day on carried his name. Theseus then became king of Athens. Cf. *Amazons, Amphitrite, Peribasia, Pirithous, Synoecia.*

Thesmophoria. Autumnal festivals in honor of Demeter in which only women participated. Originally they were ceremonies of thanksgiving at the end of the agricultural year and were held in the demos of Halimunte. By the fifth century, the festivities held in the City were already much more mystical and sectarian, as seen in Aristophanes's *Thesmorphoriazusae.* The name comes from *thesmophoros,* "legislator," one of the epithets of Demeter, who besides teaching mortals to cultivate the soil, instituted marriage and became the founder of civil society.

Thetes. According to the legislation introduced by Solon, this was the fourth and last class of Athenian citizens, those whose lands produced less than 150 medimni of grain. In the fifth century, they were practically all salaried workers, who served in the light infantry and made up most of the naval personnel.

Thiasos. The mob that celebrated sacrifices with dancing and chanting. The term was used particularly for the Dionysian fraternities, made up of exalted maenads who roamed the streets or the countryside in tumultuous processions.

Tholos. In Athens, it was a rotunda where the sacred fire of the City was kept. This is where the Prytanes dined with their distinguished pensioners.

Thrace. A very rough and mountainous region shared today by Greece, Turkey, and Bulgaria. On the west, it bordered on Chalcidice and Macedonia; on the south, with the Aegean; on the east, with the Pontus; and on the north, with Scythia.

Three-headed Goddess. Cf. *Hecate.*

Throne. Thronos, in Greek. A Greek chair with lateral supports for the arms.

Thucydides. 471–401. Herodotus had in this brilliant Athenian aristocrat a worthy follower who, with the strictest historical rigor known in antiquity, wrote an account of the Peloponnesian War. Two decades of exile gave him time enough to gather materials, visit the scenes of the main battles, and talk to the protagonists on both sides. His intention was to convey the facts, objectively proven, for the benefit of posterity. To this he devoted all his energies. He discarded all mythical elements and, convinced that eyewitnesses twist the facts, he worked intensively to get to the truth. He argued that the Trojan War had nothing to do with the abduction of Helen, but was rather the result of political necessity. He also stated that the alleged superiority of

591

the Greek race was lacking in anthropological foundations. He showed little reverence for the historians who preceded him, including Herodotus. He is a model of intellectual honesty and impartiality; his knowledge of people, places, and events make his narrative of the Peloponnesian War a work of incalculable scientific merit. Furthermore, his literary style was also outstanding, and he had an uncanny instinct for significant detail, for the sharp design of characters and situations, and for developing intrigue. Although he included speeches that he reconstructed from memory or composed in the oratorical style of the times, as an omniscient narrator he never resorted to the superficial embellishment of rhetoric. He stated that his own work "has been composed as a durable asset and not as a contest piece to win a prize and be read a single time." And in fact, he is the most authoritative source for the history of Hellas during the last third of the very important fifth century.

Thunderer. An epithet of Zeus.

Thurii. An Athenian colony in southern Italy. Its urban layout was designed by Hippodamus of Miletus in the year 443. The more benign biographers of Pericles see in the Thurii adventure the first act of "an honest piece of broadminded statesmanship"(*Cambridge Ancient History*, t. V, p. 169). In fact, it was the intention of Pericles to materialize the dream of his teacher, Anaxagoras of Clazomene, by erecting on the ruins of Sybaris a city governed by philosophers and artists, by the rule of a new justice in which truth would be the object of worship. Some of the most outstanding personalities of the time, including Herodotus and Protagoras of Abdera, firmly believed in that dream and went there to make their contributions. It would seem to be the first Utopia of the West.

Tiresias. A famous seer of Thebes. Homer tells us in *The Iliad* (X, 494) that Tiresias alone, after his death, received from Persephone intelligence and knowledge.

Tisias. Together with his teacher, Corax of Syracuse, Tisias wrote the first manual on rhetoric about which we have knowledge (Lesky, A., *Geschichte der Griechischen Literatur*, Bern, 1963, p. 392).

Tolmides. An Athenian general who lost the battle of Coronea in the year 447.

Tombs of the Heroes. Ancient Greece and Rome never closed off cemeteries. Tombs could be placed anywhere, although the preferred place was by the side of roadways. In Athens, the martyrs of the nation, those killed in combat, had a place reserved for them close to the Dipylon gate, where the Sacred Way began.

Toxaris. The tomb of this more or less mythical Scythian was located along the way to the Academy. Upon it was engraved his effigy with a book in his left hand and a bow in his right. The Athenians were thankful to him for having rid the City of a plague by prescribing that they wet down the streets with wine. He was revered as a hero, and under the name "Foreign Doctor," he was offered sacrifices. Cf. *Lucian of Samosata*.

Trapeza. "Table," in Greek. The diminutive, trapezion, was used particularly for the little tables installed by bankers in the agora.

Trapezites. Bankers. They carried out exchange operations with monetary specie, made mortgage loans, received capital in deposit, and paid the corresponding interest; they acted as agents for transfers of monies, issued letters of exchange, contracted maritime and agricultural insurance, etc. In Athens, they were generally foreigners who had to pay a license to practice their profession.

Trema. In Greek, a hole or opening.

Triassic Plains. On the eve of the naval battle that would determine the destiny of Greece resulting from the Persian invasion, a number of the local residents in the plains swore that they had seen a dusty whirlwind rising over the Eleusis. They watched in wonder as it moved on with the roar of a marching army. According to the testimony of freemen who took all the appropriate oaths, at the head of the whirlwind marched Athena, the Virgin Warrior, followed by Apollo himself. They were leading their hosts, who were discreetly cloaked for the occasion. They were coming to aid the Greeks, heading for the wave-kissed Salamis.

Tribade. A woman homosexual. The word stems from the verb root "trib," which means, "to rub." We have preferred this expression to the word "lesbian," which we have used for people from Lesbos. However, a short time later, Aristophanes was already using the verb "lesbiazo" for female homosexuality (*The Frogs*, 1308).

Tribunal of the Areopagus. Cf. *Areopagus*.

Tribunal of the King. Located in the Royal Portico that, according to Pausanias (1,3,1), was the first building one saw as he or she entered the agora from the Dipylon. Nothing certain is known about its design or size. Some speculate that the Royal Portico also contained the home of the Basileus or Archon King, who presided over the Tribunal. This court heard cases of different forms of impiety, but it should be understood that many of the violations considered today to be against society were then considered to be against religion. Thus the Tribunal of the King also heard cases of murder, arson, abortion, attempts to tyrannize the Athenian demos, etc.

Triton. A deity of the sea. Son of Poseidon and Amphitrite.

Trivium. The crossings of three roads where altars were erected to the three-headed Hecate.

Twelve Gods. Zeus, Athena, Dionysus, Demeter, Apollo, Artemis, Hera, Poseidon, Hecate, Ares, Hephaestus, and Aphrodite Urania.

Two Goddesses. Demeter and her daughter Persephone (Ceres and Proserpine in Roman mythology). Oaths by the Two Goddesses were usually reserved for women. Cf. *Demeter*.

Tyche. This Goddess (*Fortuna*, in Latin) received from her father, Zeus, the privilege of managing the destinies of mortals. To represent the ups and downs of fortune, she was depicted running and dribbling a ball. Anyone who saw her would try to catch her by the hair, which flowed in the air behind her as she ran. (And it is very probable that the ancients identified her with falling stars; they made their wishes to the stars at the very moment that their manes of light crossed the skies behind them.)

Tyrtaeus. Elegiac poet of the seventh century. It is said that he was of Athenian stock, but he wrote in Sparta, in the local Doric dialect. In its most ancient forms, the elegy was a song accompanied by the flute, an instrument used for military marches and feasts. From the latter use stemmed the elegy of symposia and the erotic elegy; from the former, the martial elegy, employed by Callinus of Ephesus and Tyrtaeus. Callinus sang that it was better to die gloriously in the heat of battle than to live a life of ignominy hidden away at home. It is said that the poetic harangues of Tyrtaeus helped placate the revolt of the Mesenians against Sparta. His verses exude a genuine indignation against cowards, and there is something pure and altruistic in his praise of a glorious death. The reader should be aware that citizens of a defeated polis could expect the humiliations of mendacity, exile, or slavery. Soldiers were to fight on to the end to save their children, women, and old people from the unspeakable consequences of defeat.

Unnamable. The God of war and the most important deity among the Scythians. Identified with the Hellenic Ares.

Urania. Cf. *Aphrodite*.

Virgin Warrior. One of the epithets of Athena.

Vulgar. Cf. *Pandemos*.

Xaire. In Greek, "enjoy," "be happy." It was a popular greeting.

Xanthippus. The name of Pericles's father and of his firstborn.

Xenophanes of Colophon, 565–470? Elegiac poet. Xenophanes was another great Ionian traveler who wound up settling in Italy. He was an iconoclast and a detractor of antiquated conceptions. He preached high monotheism and made fun of Homer and his anthropomorphic fornicating and thieving Gods. From studying seashells imbedded in rocks and the imprints of marine animals, he deduced that there must have been a time when the Earth was covered by the sea. The old history of philosophy made Xenophanes the teacher of Parmenides and, thus, the founder of the Eleatic school.

Xerxes. Son of Darius; king of Persia from 485 to 465; defeated by the Greeks at Salamis. Cf. *Darius, Marathon, Salamis*.

Xiphos. A pointed, double-edged sword. It was used to thrust and to slash. The more ancient models were made of several blades of bronze welded together. It was about eighty centimeters long and had a grip in the form of a spike. In Classical times, swords were usually shorter, made of iron, and had a blade that was narrower by the hilt. The xiphos was kept in a leather- or metal-covered wooden scabbard, and it was carried strapped across the back in such a way that the grip protruded below the left pectoral.

Xystron. A kind of currycomb with sharpened wooden edges used to scrape the anointed skin.

Zalmoxis. God of medicine of Thracian origin. Among other things, he taught how to immortalize (Plato, *Charmides,* 156c). Herodotus explained that he had first been a man, a slave and disciple of Pythagoras.

Zeus. Son of Cronus and Rhea. Brother to Hestia, Demeter, Hera, Poseidon, and Hades. Regarding his childhood and his rise to Olympic power, we have presented a very fragmentary and free version, based on an inspired summary by a British scholar who rounded up reports from some twenty chroniclers of myths of antiquity. When Cronus had already swallowed his five children, Rhea gave birth to Zeus. It was at the end of night, on Mount Lycaeus in Arcadia, where no creature cast a shadow. After bathing him in the river Neda, Rhea turned him over to Mother Earth, who took him to Crete to have him raised by the nymph Adrastea, with the help of her sister Io and the goat Amalthea. He was nourished with honey and the milk of Amalthea, which he shared with Pan, his foster brother. Zeus was grateful to the three nymphs for their kindness, and when he became lord of the universe, he placed the image of Amalthea among the stars that form the constellation Capricorn. He also borrowed one of her horns, which resembled a cow's horn, and gave it to Io and Adrastea, in whose hands it became a Cornucopia or "horn of plenty," which was always full of whatever its mistress desired. Around the golden crib of the child Zeus, which was always hanging from a tree so that Cronus could never find it in the heavens or on Earth or in the sea, the Curetes, also sons of Rhea, clanged their spears on their shields to drown out the crying of the infant so that his father could not hear him. When the time came for Rhea to give the child to Cronus, she fooled him and gave him a rock wrapped in the swaddling clothes of her last baby, which Cronus swallowed. Later, he began to suspect that he had been bamboozled and started to persecute Zeus, who turned himself into a serpent and his two nurses into bears. (Thence the constellations of the serpent and the two bears.) Zeus grew up among pastors and lived in a cave on Mount Ida. His first consort was the Titan Metis, who lived beside the ocean current. It was she who advised him to volunteer to be cupbearer for Cronus. To aid him in his mission of revenge, Rhea brought him salt and mustard that he mixed with honeyed wine. Cronus vomited up that emetic and with it came the rock and Zeus's three sisters and two older brothers. It was obvious that Cronus had acted with a stupidity that was unworthy of the lord of the universe. The Titans concluded that he was past his virile prime and decided to stage a coup d'état under the command of Atlas to begin the war against the

595

Olympians. Zeus and his brothers made short work of Cronus and, with the help of the Cyclops, defeated the Titans, who were banished to one of the British Isles in the extreme western reaches. Atlas was condemned to bear the weight of the world on his shoulders. But the female Titans were left free, thanks to the good offices of Metis and Rhea (Graves, Robert, *The Greek Myths*, chap. 7). As sovereign of Olympus, Zeus ruled with a heavy hand, cunning, and patience to get his unruly family into some kind of order. From his marriage with Hera were born Ares, Hephaestus, and Hebe, but by hook or by crook, with consent or without, he also had Metis (whom he later swallowed to be able to give birth to Athena); Dione (with whom he shared the oracle at Dodona); Themis (with whom he had the Horae and the Moirai); Eurynome, mother of the Graces; Mnemosyne, mother of the Muses; Demeter, mother of Persephone; Maia, mother of Hermes; Leto, mother of Apollo and Artemis; Semele, mother of Dionysus; Danae, mother of Perseus; as well as Io, Europa, and an endless list of Goddesses, Titanes, Nymphs, and mortals. He became a partridge to seduce Maia; a cuckoo to seduce Hera; a swan to lure Nemesis and Leda; a golden rain for Danae; flame and rock for Aegina; a white bull to attract Europa; a stud pony for Dia; a beautiful mortal to have Semele; eagle's feathers for Ganymede—just to mention the most famous of his escapades. Among his other outstanding accomplishments: having overthrown Cronus, he gave to his two brothers the kingdoms of the Sea and the Underworld (Cf. *Hades, Poseidon*); he gave birth to Athena through his head (Cf. *Athena*); he pitched Hephaestus from Olympus (Cf. *Hephaestus*); he countenanced the rape of Kore (Cf. *Demeter, Persephone*); he struck Lasius down (Cf. *Plutos*); he condemned Sisyphus the snitch, Ixion the ingrate, and Tantalus for killing his own son. And he turned his cupbearer Ganymede into the constellation of Aquarius. Zeus was venerated (or placated) with the most contradictory epithets and references, including: Bellicose, Benign, Fly-Chaser, Guider of the Moirai, Hospitable, Lupine, Of the Enclosure, Of the Guests, Of the Hatchet, Of the Heights, Of the Supplicants, Of the White Poplar, Olympic Protector, Savior, Soother, Tempestuous. Homeric epithets included: Arrogant; Best; Bounteous, Cheater; Cronid; Cruel, Fulminator; Gatherer of Clouds; Longsighted; Most Glorious; Most Terrible; Of the Bitter Winter; Pelasgian; Prudent, Supreme Arbiter; Thunderer, Who Looses the Lightning Bolts; Who Reigns in Dodona; Who Reigns in Ida; Who Resides in the Ether. Cf. *Bellicose, Herkeios, Hospitalis, Tempestuous.*